Deehalter laid his open sights in the middle of the thing's breastbone and squeezed off the shot.

The soft-nose spiked through the lower mandible and into the throat, exiting through the creature's back. The thing hurtled backwards and struck _____ thin limbs thrashed, shredding remnants _____ the strength of a grizzly. _____ _____ roat was small, but Deel_____ _____ ullet would have left a wo_____

The entrance wou_____ _____ling to its feet.

Deehalter screamed and shot it through the chest, an off-center impact that spun the creature again to the concrete. This time Deehalter could see the plastic flesh closing on the scale-dusted torso. The big man braced his rifle in front of him and leaped through the window to his right, then rolled and jumped to the ground. The jeep was only twenty feet away and he ran for it.

Deehalter flipped the power on and stabbed at the starter button under the clutch pedal. The engine ground but did not catch. There was a tearing noise behind him, and despite himself the big man turned to look. The creature was in the cow yard fence. The top strand was electrified. Blue sparks crackled about the thing's foreclaws. Then the hot wire snapped and the thing's legs cut the remaining strands like sickles through fog.

Deehalter fired one-handed and missed. He steadied the rifle, locking his left elbow on the tubular seat-frame and knocked the creature back into the cow yard with no top to its skull. Then the engine chugged and the big farmer threw the jeep into second gear at higher revs than the worn clutch was used to. Spewing gravel but without the power to sideslip, the vehicle churned forward.

He headed toward Sac Ridge and the mound from which the horror must have come. He had looked down the creature's gaping jaws and would rather anything than die between them.

—from "The Red Leer"

BAEN BOOKS BY DAVID DRAKE

The RCN Series
With the Lightnings
Lt. Leary, Commanding
The Far Side of the Stars
The Way to Glory
Some Golden Harbor
When the Tide Rises
In the Stormy Red Sky
What Distant Deeps
The Road of Danger
The Sea Without a Shore
(forthcoming)

Hammer's Slammers
The Tank Lords
Caught in the Crossfire
The Butcher's Bill
The Sharp End
*The Complete Hammer's
Slammers, Vol. 1* (omnibus)
*The Complete Hammer's
Slammers, Vol. 2* (omnibus)
*The Complete Hammer's
Slammers, Vol. 3* (omnibus)

**Independent Novels
and Collections**
All the Way to the Gallows
Cross the Stars
Foreign Legions,
ed. by David Drake
Grimmer Than Hell
Into the Hinterlands
(with John Lambshead)
Loose Cannon
Night & Demons
Northworld Trilogy
Patriots

Ranks of Bronze
The Reaches Trilogy
Redliners
Seas of Venus
Starliner

The General Series
Warlord with S.M. Stirling
(omnibus)
Conqueror with S.M. Stirling
(omnibus)
The Chosen
with S.M. Stirling
The Reformer
with S.M. Stirling
The Tyrant with Eric Flint
The Heretic
with Tony Daniel

**The Belisarius Series
with Eric Flint**
An Oblique Approach
In the Heart of Darkness
*Belisarius I: Thunder
Before Dawn* (omnibus)
Destiny's Shield
Fortune's Stroke
*Belisarius II: Storm at
Noontide* (omnibus)
The Tide of Victory
The Dance of Time
*Belisarius III: The Flames
of Sunset* (omnibus)

Edited by David Drake
*The World Turned
Upside Down*
(with Jim Baen & Eric Flint)

To purchase these and all other Baen Book titles in e-book format,
please go to www.baen.com.

NIGHT &
DEMONS

—✦—

DAVID DRAKE

NIGHT & DEMONS

A Baen Book

Baen Publishing Enterprises
P.O. Box 1403
Riverdale, NY 10471
www.baen.com

ISBN: 978-1-4767-3618-1

Cover art by Alan Pollack

First Baen mass market printing, December 2013

Distributed by Simon & Schuster
1230 Avenue of the Americas
New York, NY 10020

Library of Congress Cataloging-in-Publication Data: 201202957

Printed in the United States of America

10 9 8 7 6 5 4 3 2 1

⚜ CONTENTS ⚜

Acknowledgments

"Denkirch" © 1967 by David Drake; first published in *Travelers by Night*.

"Lord of the Depths" © 1971 by David Drake; first published in *Dark Things*.

"Arclight" © 1973 by David Drake; first published in *The Magazine of Fantasy and Science Fiction*, April 1973.

"The Song of the Bone" © 1973 by David Drake; first published in *Whispers*, December 1973.

"The Shortest Way" © 1974 by David Drake; first published in *Whispers*, March 1974.

"Something Had to Be Done" © 1975 by David Drake; first published in *The Magazine of Fantasy and Science Fiction*, February 1975.

"The Master of Demons" © 1975 by David Drake; first published in *Dark Horizons #11*, Winter/Spring 1975.

"The Barrow Troll" © 1975 by David Drake; first published in *Whispers*, December 1975.

"Awakening" © 1975 by David Drake; first published in *Nameless Places*.

"Black Iron" © 1975 by David Drake; first published in *Nameless Places*.

"Firefight" © 1976 by David Drake; first published in *Frights*.

"Blood Debt" © 1976 by David Drake; first published in *The 4th Mayflower Book of Black Magic Stories*.

"The Hunting Ground" © 1976 by David Drake; first published in *Superhorror*.

"Children of the Forest" © 1976 by David Drake; first published in *The Magazine of Fantasy and Science Fiction*, November 1976.

"Smokie Joe" © 1977 by David Drake; first published in *More Devil's Kisses*.

"Best of Luck" © 1978 by David Drake; first published in *The Year's Best Horror Stories: Series VI*.

"The Red Leer" © 1979 by David Drake; first published in *Whispers II*.

"Men Like Us" © 1980 by David Drake; first published in *Omni*, May 1980.

"Than Curse the Darkness" © 1980 by David Drake; first published in *New Tales of the Cthulhu Mythos*.

"The Automatic Rifleman" © 1980 by David Drake; first published in *Destinies v2, #4*, Fall 1980.

"The Dancer in the Flames" © 1982 by David Drake; first published in *Whispers*, August 1982.

"The False Prophet" © 1989 by David Drake; first published in *Vettius and Friends*.

"The Land Toward Sunset" © 1995 by David Drake; first published in *Cormac Mac Art*, by Robert E. Howard. Riverdale, NY: Baen.

"The Waiting Bullet" © 1997 by David Drake; first published in *Weirdbook 30 Combined* with *Whispers*, Spring, 1997.

"Dragon, the Book" © 1999 by David Drake; first published in *Catfantastic V*, A. Norton and M. H. Greenberg, eds. New York, NY: DAW.

"Codex" © 2003 by David Drake, first published by Sidecar Preservation Society.

"The Elf House" © 2004 by David Drake; first published in *Masters of Fantasy*.

"A Land of Romance" © 2005 by David Drake; first published in *The Enchanter Completed*.

NIGHT &
DEMONS

THE RED LEER

I was born in Dubuque, Iowa, and at age ten moved with my family to Clinton, fifty miles south along the Mississippi River. Outsiders tend to think of Iowa as flat. Much of the state is, but where I come from the bluffs rise straight up out of the river. Dubuque has an operating cable car (funicular railway) that a wealthy banker built to carry him from his office in the floodplain to his home on the bluffs 300 feet above. The view out over the river into Illinois is spectacular.

Others thought so too. All over the area are Amerind grave mounds looking down from the bluffs. One of them's on the farm that belonged to my father-in-law.

My dad was an electrician, but nobody in Iowa is very far from a farm. Family friends had farms when I was a boy; my wife's family were and are dairy farmers. I've spent enough time on and around some of the most productive family farms in the world to have a feeling for the life.

Which is very, very hard. The work has to be

1

done every day, no matter how you feel or what the weather's doing: you can't call in sick and tell the cows that they won't be milked this morning. The machinery is dangerous beyond the imagination of a modern factory worker; the organo-phosphate insecticides were invented just in time for World War II, where they provided the Nazis with the first nerve gases; and even city-dwellers know that if anybody gets rich from agriculture, it isn't the family farmer.

The characters in this story are modeled on real people but they're not my in-laws. The farm is one my in-laws owned, including details like the curio cabinet and the hunting rifle.

I frequently use a story that has greatly impressed me as a model for one of my own. This isn't quite so direct a case as some, but I want to mention the similarities to Theodore Sturgeon's "Killdozer." The title (which was the genesis of the story) comes from Robert Browning's "Childe Roland to the Dark Tower Came."

✢ ✢ ✢

As he swung the tractor for a final pass across Sac Ridge Field, Deehalter saw that dirt had been turned on the side of the Indian mound. The big man threw in the hand clutch of the Allis-Chalmers and throttled the diesel back to idle as he glared at the new trench through the barbed wire. "That goddam Kernes," he whispered. "If I've got to work with him much longer . . . ."

He revved the engine and slammed the tractor back in gear. The farmer's scowl was as black as the hair curling up his arms from the backs of his hands to the shirtsleeves rolled at his biceps.

At the south end of the field, Deehalter raised the cultivator and drove the Allis down the long, looping trail back to the farm buildings. There was a way of sorts straight west from the top of the ridge, but it was too steep for the tractor. The more gradual slope took Deehalter through half a dozen gates and eventually back to the buildings from the southwest. To the left loomed the barn and the three concrete silos peering over its roof at him. The milking parlor was a one-story addition to the barn's east side, facing the equipment shed and the gas pump. And at the pump was Tom Kernes with his ten-year old son, Deehalter's nephew, putting gas in the jeep.

Deehalter pulled up beside them and let the diesel clatter for a moment before he shut it off. Kernes, a short, ginger-headed man, looked up. His arms were not tan but a deep red, with brighter slashes where the straps of his undershirt had interrupted part of the sunlight. Kernes was thirty-five, five years younger than his brother-in-law, but his crinkly, sunburned face would have passed for any age. "Finish Sac Ridge already, Dee?" he asked in his pleasant, throaty voice. The tension in his muscles showed that he had correctly read Deehalter's anger.

"Kernes, what've you been doing with the Indian mound?" the bigger man demanded from the tractor seat. "You know to leave that the hell alone!" A pick and shovel lay in the back of the jeep. Deehalter noticed them and a black flush moved across his face.

Kernes's skin was too red to show the blood, but his voice rose to the challenge. "When Old John owned the farm, he could say what he pleased; but he's dead now. I'm damned if I'm not going to get an Indian skull like yours." Gesturing eastward at the ridge, the little man added, "I own half this goddam place and I'm going to get a skull."

The curio cabinet in Deehalter's parlor had been assembled by his grandfather before the first world war. Among its agates and arrowheads, sword-cane and ostrich plumes, was a brown human skull. The family had always assumed the skull came from a mound somewhere, but not even Old John had been sure. It fascinated Kernes, perhaps only because Deehalter had refused to give it to him. The main house and its furnishings, including the cabinet, had gone to Deehalter under his father's will— just as the new house in which his sister Alice lived with Kernes and their children had gone to her. The rest of the six-hundred-acre farm was willed to Deehalter and Alice jointly, with the provision that if either of them tried to partition the property, the whole of it went to the other. Deehalter had talked to a lawyer and he was sure Kernes had done the same. The worst news either of the men had heard in a long time was that the will would probably stand up in court.

"There's a law against digging up mounds," Deehalter muttered.

"There's a law against keeping an Indian skull on display," the shorter man blazed back. "You going to bring the law in here, Dee?"

"Well," Deehalter said lamely, "you don't get everything in the mound. You've no right to that."

Kernes stood, arms akimbo, sweat from the June sun

glittering on his face. "If I do all the goddam digging, I do," he said. "And anyhow, I get the skull out first."

Deehalter wiped his face with his huge, calloused palm. He didn't like to fool with the mound. Old John had whaled him within an inch of his life thirty years ago, when he had caught his son poking into the smooth slope with a posthole digger. But Deehalter remembered also the nightmare that had awakened him for months after that afternoon, and that dream was of nothing so common as a beating by his father. Still, to let Kernes take everything. "All right," Deehalter said, "I'll help you dig. But I get my pick of anything besides a skull. Wouldn't be surprised if there was gold in with a chief." Actually, Deehalter knew enough about mounds to doubt there would be anything that would interest a non-archeologist—often the mounds hadn't even been built over a body. But that wasn't anything the big farmer was going to say to his brother-in-law.

"Dad," said the Kernes boy unexpectedly." If Uncle Dee helps you, you don't need me, do you?"

Kernes looked at the child as though he wanted to hit him. "Go on, then," he snapped. "But I want that goddam toolshed painted when I get back. All of it!"

The boy took off running for the house. Wiener, the farm's part-collie, chased after him barking. "Kid's been listening to his mother," Kernes grumbled. "From the way Alice's been carrying on, you'd think Old John was going to come out of his grave if I dug up that mound. He must've knocked that into her head with a maul."

"He was strong on it," Deehalter agreed absently."I know when he was a boy, there was still a couple Sac

Indians on the farm. Maybe they talked to him. But he was strong about a lot of things."

"Well, you ready to go?" Kernes demanded. He had hung up the pump nozzle and now remembered to cap the jeep's tank.

Deehalter grimaced. "I'll put the cultivator in the shed," he said. "Then we'll go."

Kernes drove, taking the direct trail through the east pasture. There was a rivulet to ford and a pair of gullies that had to be skirted, but the hard going didn't start until they reached the foot of the ridge. They had bought the jeep ten years before from Army surplus, and the sharp grades of the ridge slope made the motor wheeze even in the granny gear. Cedars studded the slope, interspersed with bull thistles whose purple bracts were ready to burst open. There was a final switch-back just before the trail reached the summit. As Kernes hauled the wheel hard to the left, the motor spluttered and died. Deehalter swung out of the jeep and walked the last thirty yards while the smaller man cursed and trod on the starter.

The mound was built on the north end of the ridge. That part had never been opened as a field because the soil was too thinly spread above the bedrock. The mound was oval, about fifteen feet long on the east-west axis and three or four feet high. Though small, it was clearly artificial, a welt of earth on the smooth table of the ridge. Kernes' trench was in the center of the south side, halfway in and down to the level of the surrounding soil. Deehalter was examining the digging when the jeep heaved itself up behind him and was cut off again.

"We just kept hitting rocks," the smaller man explained. "We didn't get near as far as I'd figured before we started."

Deehalter squatted on his haunches and poked into the excavation with a finger like a corncob. "You didn't hit rocks," he said, "you hit a rock. One goddam slab. There's no way we're going to clear that dirt off it without a week of work or renting a bulldozer. And even if we cleared down *to* the rock, that slab's a foot thick and must weigh tons. We're just wasting our time here—or we would be if we didn't go on back right now."

Kernes swore. "We could hook a chain to the Allis—" he began.

Deehalter cut him off. "We'd have to get the dirt off the top first, and that'd take all goddam summer. This was a bad idea to start, and it got worse quick. Come on, let's go back." He straightened.

"What about dynamite?" blurted Kernes.

Deehalter stared at his brother-in-law. The smaller man would not meet his gaze but continued, "There's still a stick under the seat from when you blew up the beaver dam. We could use it."

"Kernes," Deehalter said, "you're so afraid of that dynamite that you'd rather leave it in the jeep than touch it to get it out. Besides, it'll blow the shit out of anything under that slab—if there is anything and the slab's not flat on bedrock all the way across. What're you trying to prove?"

Kernes' red face grew even brighter with embarrassment, oranger. "Look," he said, "I'm gonna get into this goddam thing if I got to hire a contractor. I said I would and I will. You don't want to help, that's your goddam business."

Deehalter eyed him a moment longer. "Oh, I'll do my part," he said. He gestured to the pick and added, "You see if you can cut a slot an inch deep and maybe eight inches long in the seam between the top slab and the bedrock. I'll get the dynamite ready." He grinned. "Unless you want to do that instead?"

Kernes' only response was to heft the tool with a choked grip and begin chopping at the stone.

Deehalter flipped the jeep's seat forward and lifted out the corrugated cardboard box beneath it. There was, as Kernes had said, still one stick of dynamite left along with a roll of wire and a smaller box of blasting caps. The explosive terrified Kernes in the way snakes or spiders do other men. Deehalter had deliberately refused to take the stick out of the jeep despite his brother-in-law's frequent requests. Finally Kernes had ceased to mention it—until now. Kernes was so stubbornly determined to have an Indian skull that he had overridden his fear of the explosive. It occurred to Deehalter that he was doing the same thing himself with his fear of the mound.

The big farmer leaned against the jeep as he dug a fuze pocket in the dynamite with a pencil stub. Kernes was chipping the soft rock effectively, even in the confined space. "Not too wide," Deehalter warned as he twisted the leads from the blasting cap onto the extension wire.

He didn't like what they were doing. Shapes from long-ago nightmares were hovering over his mind, unclear but no less unpleasant for that. He'd never heard of Indians using stone in their mounds, and that bothered him too.

Still, why not? The Mississippi Basin was rich in soft yellow limestone, already layered by its floodings and strandings in the shallow seas of its deposition. So it wasn't the stone or anything else rational which was eating at Deehalter; it was just that something felt cold and very wrong inside him.

"That enough, Dee?" Kernes asked, panting. His sleeveless undershirt was gray with sweat.

Deehalter leaned forward. "It'll do," he acknowledged. Kernes was shrinking back from the explosive in Deehalter's hand. "Run the jeep over the crest of the ridge and get the hood open. There's enough wire to reach to there."

While his brother-in-law scrambled to obey, Deehalter knelt in the trench and made his own preparations. First he set the blasting cap in the hole in the end of the dynamite. Then he carefully kneaded the explosive into the slot Kernes had cut in the rock. The heavy waxed paper and its fillings of sawdust, ammonium nitrate, and nitroglycerin were hot and deformed easily. A lot of people didn't know how to use dynamite; they wasted the force of the blast. Deehalter didn't want to blow the mound open, but he'd be damned if he wouldn't do it right if he did it at all.

When the dynamite had been molded into the rock, the big man shoveled dirt down on top of it and used his boots to firmly tamp the pile. The thin wire looped out of the earth like the shadow of a grass blade. Deehalter hung the coil on the pick handle, using it as a loose spindle from which to unwind the wire as he walked to the jeep.

"This far enough away?" Kernes asked, eying the mound apprehensively.

"Unless a really big chunk comes straight down,"

Deehalter said, silently pleased at the other man's nervousness. "Christ, it's just one stick, even if it is sixty-percent equivalent."

Kernes bent down behind the jeep. Deehalter squatted at the front, protected from the blast by the brow of the hill. He held the bare end of one wire to the negative post of the battery, then touched the other lead to the positive side. Nothing happened. "Goddammit," he said, prodding the wire to cut through the white corrosion on the post.

The dynamite exploded with a loud thump.

"Jesus!" Kernes shouted as he bounced to his feet. Deehalter, more experienced, hunched under his baseball cap while dirt and tiny rock fragments rained over him and the jeep. Then at last he stood and followed his brother-in-law. The smaller man was now cursing and trying to brush dirt from his head and shoulders with his left hand; in his right he carried a battery spotlight.

Acrid black smoke curled in the pit like a knot of snakes. The sod walls of the trench looked as they had before the explosion, but the earth compacted over the charge was gone and the exposed edge of the rock slab had shattered. Because the limestone could neither move nor compress, the shock had broken it as thoroughly as a twenty-foot fall could have.

Kernes bent down over the opening and grasped a chunk of stone to toss out of the way. The dynamite fumes looped a tendril over his face. Kernes coughed and quivered, and for an instant Deehalter thought the other man lost focus. Then Kernes was on his feet again, fanning the shovel blade to clear the smoke faster and crying, "By God, Dee, there's really something in there! By God!"

Deehalter waited, frowning, as Kernes shoveled at the rubble. A little prying with the blade was enough to crumble the edge of the slab into fist-sized pieces like a three-dimensional jigsaw puzzle. More dirt fell in, but that was easily scooped away. The actual opening stayed small because the only cavity in the bedrock was a shallow, water-cut basin. It sloped so gradually that even after a two-foot scallop had been nibbled from the overlying slab there was barely enough room to reach an arm into the hollow.

The fumes had dissipated. Kernes scattered a last shovelful of dirt and gravel, then tossed the tool aside as well. Kneeling down with his face as close to the opening as he could get it and still leave room for the spotlight, he began to search the cavity. "Goddamn," Kernes said suddenly. "God*damn!*" He tried to reach in left-handed, found there was too little room, and shoved the light back out of the way since he had already located the object in his head. The spotlight beam touched grass blades shaded from the sun, a color rather than an illumination.

"Look at this, Deehalter!" cried Kernes as he scrabbled backward. "By God!"

"I've seen skulls before," the black-haired man said sourly, eyeing the discolored bone which his brother-in-law held hooked through the eye sockets. The lower jaw was missing, but the explosion seemed to have done little damage. Unless the front teeth . . . .

"There's other stuff in there, too," Kernes bubbled.

"Then it's mine," said Deehalter sharply.

"Did I goddamn say it wasn't?" Kernes demanded. "And you can get it out for yourself, too," he added, looking down at his shirt, muddied by dirt and perspiration.

Deehalter said nothing further. He lay down carefully in the fresh earth and directed the spotlight past his head. He could see other bones in the shallow cavity. The explosion had shaken them, but their order was too precise for any large animals to have stripped away the flesh. Indeed, the bundles of skin and tendon still clinging to the thighs indicated that not even mice had entered the tomb. The stone-to-stone seal must have been surprisingly close.

Metal glittered beyond the bones. Deehalter marked its place and reached in, edging himself forward so that his shoulder pressed hard against the ragged lip of the slab. He expected to feel revulsion or the sudden fear of his childhood, but the cavity was dry and empty even of death. His wrist brushed over rib bones and he thought the object beyond them was too far; then his fingertips touched it, touched them, and he lifted them carefully out.

Kernes stopped studying the skull in the sunlight from different angles. "What the hell you got there, Dee?" he asked warily.

Deehalter wasn't sure himself, so he said nothing. He held the two halves of a hollow metal teardrop, six inches long. On the outside it was black and bubbled-looking; within, the spherical cavity was no larger than a hickory nut. The mating surfaces and the cavity itself were a rich silver color, untarnished and as smooth as the lenses of a camera.

"One of them's mine," said Kernes abruptly. "The skull and half the rest." He reached for one of the pieces.

"Like hell," said Deehalter, mildly because he was concentrating on the chunks of metal. His big shoulder blocked Kernes away without effort. "Besides, it's all one thing," he added, holding the sections so that the polished surfaces mated. Then, when he tried to part them, the halves did not reseparate.

"Aw," Kernes said in disbelief and again put a hand out for the object. This time Deehalter let him take it. Despite all the ginger-haired man's tugging and pushing, the teardrop held together. It was only after Kernes, sweating and angry, had handed back the object that Deehalter found the trick of it. You had to rotate the halves along the plane of the separation—which, since there was no visible line, was purely a matter of luck the first time it worked.

"Let's get on home," Deehalter said. He nodded westward toward the sun. Sunset was still an hour away, but it would take them a while to drive back. The ridge was already casting its broad shadow across the high ground to the east. "Besides," Deehalter added, almost under his breath, "I don't like the feeling I get up here sometimes."

But it was almost two weeks before Deehalter had any reason for his uneasiness . . . .

Despite the full moon low in the west and the light of the big mercury vapor lamp above the cow yard to the north of the barn, the plump blonde stumbled twice on the graveled path to the car. The second time she caught Deehalter's arm and clung there giggling. More to be shut of her than for chivalry, the farmer opened the passenger door of the Chrysler and handed her in. Naturally, she flopped across his lap when he got in on the driver's side. He pushed her upright in disgust.

It was 3 a.m. and there were no lights yet in Alice and her husband's house. Deehalter knew they had seen him bring Wendy home in the evening, knew also that Wiener would awaken them as he chased the car. Kernes had once complained to Deehalter, red-faced, about the example he set for his nephew and nieces by bringing whores home to their grandfather's house. Deehalter had told him that under the will it was his house, and that when Kernes and Alice quit fucking in *their* house, he'd consider quitting it in his. The smaller man hadn't quite taken a swing as Deehalter had hoped he might.

When the car began to scrunch down the drive past the new house, Wiener came loping toward them from the barn. He barked once every other time his forefeet touched the ground. The noise was more irritating than even a quick staccato would have been. The car windows were closed against the night's damp chill. Deehalter's finger was poised on the switch to roll the glass down and shout at the mongrel, when Wendy's scream snapped his head around.

The bank to the left sloped up from the drive, so the thing standing there was only in the edge of the lights. It was wire thin and tall—twice the height of a man at a fleeting glance, though a part of Deehalter knew that was the effect of the bank and the angle. A flat lizard-snout of teeth glittered sharply. Then the beast turned and the big car leaped forward down the drive as Deehalter floored the accelerator. Wendy was still screaming, her face buried in her hands, when the car banged over the slotted cattle-guard and fishtailed onto the gravel county road.

Deehalter kept his speedometer dangerously above sixty for the first three miles, until they reached the tavern and gas station at Five Points. There he braked to a stop and turned on the dome light. The girl whimpered. Deehalter's big hands gripped her shoulders and hauled her upright. "Shut up," he said tightly.

"W-what was it?" she blubbered.

"Shut up, for Christ's sake!" Deehalter shouted. "It wasn't a goddamned thing!" He brought his face close to Wendy's. The girl's eyes were as fearful as they had been minutes before at the sight of the creature. "You saw a cat in the headlights, that's all. You're *not* going to get everybody and his brother tramping over my farm shooting my milking herd. You're going to keep your goddamned mouth shut, do you hear?"

The blonde was nodding to the rhythm of Deehalter's words. Tears streamed from her eyes, and when she tried to wipe them she smeared the remains of her eye shadow across her cheeks.

Deehalter released her suddenly and put the car in gear. Neither of them spoke during the rest of the ride to town. When the big farmer stopped in front of the girl's apartment, she stumbled out and ran up the steps without bothering to close the car door. Deehalter locked it after he slammed it shut.

He drove back to the farm at a moderate pace that slowed appreciably as he came nearer. The night had only its usual motions and noises now. Deehalter was waiting in his locked car an hour later, alone with nothing but a memory to disturb him, when Kernes came out of his house to start milking.

After lunch—a full meal of fried steak and potatoes; Deehalter had cooked for himself and his father as well

before Old John died—the big man walked down the drive
and began searching the grassy bank to the left of it. Once
when he looked up, he saw his sister watching him intently
from the Kernes' kitchen window. He waved but she
ducked away. Toward three o'clock, Kernes himself came
back in the jeep from inspecting the fences around the
northwest pasture. Deehalter hailed him. After a moment's
hesitation, the ginger-haired man swung the vehicle up the
bank and stopped.

"Come look at this," Deehalter said. The turf was
marked fuzzily where he pointed. "Doesn't it look like
three claw prints?" he asked.

Kernes looked at him strangely. "Claw prints? What do
you mean, Dee?"

"It—oh, Christ, I don't know," said the big man,
straightening and lifting his cap to run his hand through his
hair. He looked glumly back past the barn to the long bulk
of Sac Ridge.

"Haven't seen Wiener today, have you?" Kernes asked
unexpectedly.

"Not since I took Wendy home this morning," replied
Deehalter, his own expression odd. "Barked at the car as
usual. You must've heard him."

"Learned to sleep through it, I guess," said Kernes, and
the words did not quite ring true . . . though that might
have been the blurred print on the ground and Deehalter's
blurred memory of what had made the print. Kernes got
into the jeep. "Usually he chases a rabbit, he gets back for
breakfast. Kids've about worried me to death about that
damn dog."

"I'll ride to the barn with you," Deehalter said. They

did not speak about the dog—or the print—for the rest of the afternoon.

In the evening, after Deehalter had finished his turn at milking, Alice came out to the barn to help wash down the equipment. Alice Kernes was ten years younger than her brother. Though they had never been close, there was a thread of mutual affection despite Deehalter's reciprocated hatred for his brother-in-law. Alice hummed as she polished the glass tubing and stainless steel; she was a short woman with her black hair tied back by a kerchief and a man's shirt flapping over the waistband of her gray skirt.

"Wiener been back yet?" Deehalter asked with feigned disinterest.

"No, have you seen him?" Alice said, pausing to catch the shake of Deehalter's head. "Susie's been crying all day. Tom went out to quiet the dog down this morning and I think he scared him off. But he'll be back tonight, I figure."

Deehalter flipped the switch that would drain the water now being cycled through the transfer piping. "Kernes got up to chase him?"

"Uh-huh. Did you get the big tank?"

"Yeah, we can call it a night," Deehalter said. Bloodstains are hard to identify in heavy grass, harder even than footprints in the sod beneath, so he made no mention of the splotches he had found thirty yards from the drive that afternoon. There had been no body, not even a swatch of dog fur torn off in a struggle.

But despite that, Deehalter guessed that the mongrel would not be coming home that night.

‡ ‡ ‡

A cow awakened Deehalter with a blat like a cut-off klaxon horn. His Remington .30-06 leaned against the window frame, bathed in moonlight. Deehalter stripped a shell into the autoloader's chamber from the full magazine before he pulled on his dungarees and boots. Shirtless, his baggy trousers weighted down by the rest of the box of ammunition, Deehalter unlocked the front door and began running across the yard.

There were one hundred and sixty cattle in the barn, and from the noise they had all gone wild. Over their bellows came clatters and splintering as the frantic tons of beef smashed the fittings of the barn. Normally in the summer, the cows were free to wander in and out of the yard and to the pasture beyond, but tonight Deehalter had penned them for safety. He was a hundred feet from the electric fence of the yard, cursing his mistake in having concentrated the herd and then left it unprotected, when one of the black-and-white Holsteins smashed from the barn into the cow yard through both halves of the Dutch door.

There was something behind it.

The thing's tongue and the blood on its jaws were black in the mercury floodlight. Erect against the side of the barn it was almost eight feet tall, though only the shadows gave mass to its spindly limbs. It saw Deehalter and skidded on the slippery concrete, its claws rasping through the slime. Deehalter threw his rifle to his shoulder. It was as if he were aiming at a skeleton made of coat hangers, the thing was so thin. Deehalter's hands shook. The creature bent forward, cocking its hips back for balance. It opened its jaws so wide that every needle tooth seemed pointed at the farmer. Then it screamed like a plunging shell as Deehalter fired. His bullet punched neatly through the side of the barn ten feet above the ground.

With a single stride, the creature disappeared back within the building. Deehalter slammed another shot through the empty doorway.

Panting, the big man knelt and fumbled out the box of ammunition without letting go of the rifle. His shoulder ached. The empty cases shone silver pale on the grass to his right. When Deehalter had reloaded, he shuffled forward again. He held his rifle out as if he were thrusting it through fluid. The yard was filled with milling cows. Deehalter moved past them to the low milking parlor and tried in vain to peer through the dusty windows. Then, holding the rifle awkwardly like a huge pistol, he unlatched the door and flipped on the light. There was nothing in the parlor, and its metal gates to the barn were still closed.

Deehalter turned on the lights in the main building. There was only a score of frightened cows still within. The half-loft eight feet above the bare floor had only a little straw in it. The loft door in the south wall hung askew. There were deep scratches around its broken latch. From the left, Deehalter grimly surveyed the barn. The interior walls were spattered with blood. A heifer was dead in her stall; long gouges reddened the hides of several others of the herd.

It was almost dawn. The black-haired farmer stood at the loft door, cursing and staring out into the red sunrise, which pulled the shadow of the ridge like a long curtain over the pasture.

The door to the milking parlor banged. Deehalter swung around and raised the muzzle of his rifle. It was Kernes barefooted and in torn pajamas with Alice, wide-eyed, behind him. Seeing the blood and the dead heifer, she shouted at her husband, "My God, Tom, have you and George been shooting cows?"

Kernes gaped. Deehalter couldn't understand why the question was directed at his brother-in-law. "No, it was a, a—" Deehalter began and stuttered to a halt, uncertain both of the truth and what he should say about it. To change the subject he said, "We got to phone Doc Jepson. Some of the cows've been—cut."

"Phone the vet?" blazed Alice—Kernes still had not spoken. She reached back into the parlor for the extension which hung on the wall higher than a cow carries its head. "We'll call the Sheriff, we'll call—"

"Put down that goddamn phone!" Deehalter said, not loudly but too loudly to be ignored by anyone who knew him well.

Alice was in a rage herself, but she stepped back from the phone and watched her brother descend carefully from the loft. "What did it, George?" she asked.

"I didn't get a good look."

"God *dammit*, George," Alice said, letting go of her anger now that Deehalter had cooled enough not to shoot her dead in a fury. "Why won't you let me get help?"

"Because we're in the milk business," the big man said, sagging against the ladder in mental exhaustion. Kernes wasn't really listening; Alice's face was blank. "Because if we go tell people there's an eight-foot lizard on our farm—"

Kernes swore. Deehalter shouted, "All right, I saw it,

what the hell's the difference? Something killed the cow, didn't it?" He glared at the others, then went on, "First they'll think we're crazy. And then when they learn it's true, they'll say, 'Strontium 90,' or 'What're they spraying their fields with to do that?' or 'There's something in their water.' And we'll never sell another pint of milk from here as long as we live. You *know* what the dairy business is like!"

Alice nodded sharply. "Then we'll just raise hogs," she said, "or corn—or we'll sell the farm and all get jobs with Purina, for God's sake. Spring Hill Dairies isn't the whole—"

"Alice!"

Kernes' eyes were flicking from one sibling to the other, a spectator rather than a referee. Alice glared at him, then said to her brother, "All right, George. But I'm taking the kids into town to stay with Iris until you come to your senses." Then, to her husband, she added, "Tom, are you coming, too?"

"If you leave here, Kernes," said Deehalter quietly, "you'll never come back. I don't give a shit what the law says."

The men stared at each other. "I'll stay," Kernes said. Alice banged through the gate and into the milking parlor without a look behind her. "I'd have stayed anyway, Alice!" the smaller man shouted.

"Call Doc Jepson," Deehalter repeated wearily. "We can tell him it was dogs or something—" the tooth marks were too high and broad for that to be other than a transparent lie—"and hope we can scotch this thing before worse happens."

Numbly, Kernes made the call. As the little man hung

up, they heard the rasping starter of the old station wagon. A moment later, gravel spattered as Alice rocketed down the drive. Almost as fast as he himself had driven the night before, Deehalter thought.

"It's because of what we took out of that mound," Kernes said in a small voice.

Deehalter shook his head in irritation. "This thing didn't come from a skull or a little bit of iron," he snapped. "It's big, big enough to kill a Holstein."

"It was there just the same," Kernes replied. "We've got to close that grave up with everything in it again. Then maybe we'll be okay."

"You're nuts," Deehalter said. But he remembered the thing's eyes and the gape of its jaws; and he knew that sometime that day he would help Kernes bury the objects again.

Deehalter walked to the mound and the parked jeep without speaking. In the field behind him, the crows settled noisily on the carrion again.

Kernes had lifted out a pair of shovels and the gunny sack holding the objects. "Well?" he asked.

"Yeah," said Deehalter with a shrug, "it was Wiener."

Kernes began to undo the knot which closed the sack's throat. Without looking up, he said, "I think it's the moon. That's why it didn't come out when we opened the mound. It needed the full moon to bring it out."

"Bullshit," said Deehalter." I *saw* the thing and it's not moonlight, it's as solid as you or me. Damn sight solider than old Wiener there," he added with a grim twist of his head. "Moonlight's just light, anyway."

"Fluorescent light's just light too," Kernes retorted, "but it makes plants grow like they don't with a regular light bulb. Christ, Dee, don't you *feel* the moon on you at night?"

Deehalter did, but he wasn't about to admit that weakness even in the noon sun. Kernes had paused after opening the bag, unwilling either to dump the contents back into the hole without ceremony or to touch them again barehanded. The big man hesitated also. Then he glanced at the guns in easy reach, between the front seats of the jeep, and lifted out the skull.

The bone felt warm. Because Deehalter had not really taken a look at it before, he did so now at this last opportunity. The teeth were damaged in a way that at first he could not explain. Then the farmer cursed, set the skull down on the ground, and stretched out in the open trench. The angle was too flat for Deehalter to have been able to see anything even if he had brought a flashlight this trip, but his fingertips found the shallow grooves he expected in the under-surface of the slab.

"Christ," he muttered, standing up again. "That poor sucker was alive when they covered him up in there. He didn't have a damned thing to dig with, so he tried to scrape through the stone with his teeth."

Kernes stared at the skull and looked a little sicker than he had before. His finger traced but did not touch the front teeth. All four of the incisors were worn across the flats as if by a file. They had been ground down well into the nerve canals. One of the front pair had cracked about halfway from the root. "Yeah, I'd seen that but I didn't think . . . " he said. "Jesus, what a way to go. He surely must've known he couldn't chew his way through a foot of rock."

"Maybe he didn't know there was a foot of it," Deehalter said. "Besides, he didn't have a lot of choice."

Carefully, the big man set the skull as far back into the mound as his arm would reach. The litter of bone and rock chips within scrunched under his shirtsleeve.

The rippled, iron teardrop was still closed. Deehalter looked at it for a moment, then twisted it to split the halves because they had been separate when he found them. The metal divided with a soft gasp like a cold jar being opened. Deehalter set the halves under the slab as carefully as he had the discolored skull.

Almost before he rolled out of the way, his brother-in-law was tossing a shovelful of earth into the hole. Kernes worked feverishly at the soil pile he and his son had thrown up in digging the pit. By the time Deehalter had brushed himself off and picked up a shovel, the blast-crumbled edge of the slab had been buried again.

They finished their work before noon, leaving on the mound's side a black scar that sealed off the greater blackness within.

The barn windows were green fiberglass which the western moonlight outlined sharply against the walls. The diffused illumination was weak and without distinct shadows. It made the loft floor an overlay of grays on grays which wobbled softly as Deehalter paced along it. The cattle penned below murmured, occasionally blatting loudly at their unfamiliar restraint. At each outburst, Deehalter would pause and lean over the loft rail with his rifle forward; but the bellowing was never for any reason that had to do with why two armed men were watching the barn tonight.

At the north end of the loft, Deehalter stopped and looked out the open loading door. The cow yard below was scraped and hosed off daily, but animal waste had stained the concrete an indelible brown which became purple in the mercury light.

To the left, within the fence of the cow yard and in the corner it formed with the barn, hunched Kernes with a shotgun loaded with deer slugs. From Deehalter's angle, the smaller man was foreshortened into a stump growing from the concrete. Nothing moved in the night, though the automatic feeder in the hog pens flapped several times. As Deehalter watched silently, Kernes looked up at the moon. Despite the coolness of the night and the breeze from the west, Kernes pulled out a handkerchief and wiped his forehead.

Deehalter turned and began pacing back to the south end of the barn. He had finished his thermos of coffee hours ago, and it was only by staying in motion that he was able to keep awake. He couldn't understand how Kernes could huddle in the same corner since ten o'clock and still be alert; but then, Kernes wasn't a person Deehalter *wanted* to understand.

Deehalter peered out the south door. Nothing, nothing, of course nothing. A fox barked in the invisible distance and the big man's grip tightened on his rifle stock. He caught himself before he threw a bullet out into the night in frustration; then he began to pace back.

But each time the creature had come, it was in the near dawn. As if it were striding to the farm from far away, or because it got a late start. The notch he and Kernes had blasted in the Indian mound faced southwest. Moonlight would not have entered it until nearly morning. But there was no living thing in that narrow rock basin, only a litter of bones and what was probably a meteorite.

Why had that Indian been sealed up alive?

Nothing but bones and iron in the mound. Briefly, Deehalter's mind turned over a memory of awakening to seize his rifle in the pattern of moonlight etched across his room by the Venetian blinds. Now he held the weapon close and bent forward to look at his brother-in-law.

Kernes had moved slightly, out along the electric fence. The yard light colored his shirt blue but could not throw a shadow forward into the glare of the full moon. Kernes was staring west at that mottled orb. His shotgun barrel traced nervous arcs, rising and slipping back to a high port. It was almost as if the smaller man were wishing he could fire at the moon, but catching himself a moment before he did anything that . . . crazy.

Kernes' body *slithered.*

"Kernes!" Deehalter screamed.

The man below turned and was a man again. The shotgun had fallen to the concrete. Kernes' clothing was awry from having something monstrously thin start to clamber out of it. Part of Deehalter's mind wondered what Kernes had thought in the mornings when he found himself naked in the pasture, his tangled pajamas outside his house.

Now the small farmer was looking up at Deehalter, his face as dead and horrified as that of the statue of Laocoon. Then he changed again, and the long jaws spread to hiss at the man above. Deehalter laid his open sights in the middle of the thing's breastbone and squeezed off the shot.

The bullet flew high because of the angle, but the big man was hunter enough to have allowed for that. The soft-nose spiked through the lower mandible and into the throat, exiting at last through the creature's back. The jacketed lead, partly expanded but with only a fraction of its energy gone, slapped the concrete beyond and splashed away in a shower of sparks and a riven howl.

The thing that had been Kernes hurtled backwards and slid until it struck the fence. Its stick-thin limbs thrashed, shredding remnants of its clothing with claws and the strength of a grizzly. Its jaws snapped. The hole in its throat was small, but Deehalter knew that the supersonic bullet would have left a wound cavity like a pie tin in the back.

The entrance wound had closed. The beast was scrabbling to its feet.

Deehalter screamed and shot it through the chest, an off-center impact that spun the creature again to the concrete. This time Deehalter could *see* the plastic flesh closing on the scale-dusted torso. He remembered Wiener and the gullied throat of the Holstein. With only that instant's hesitation, the big man braced his rifle in front of him and leaped through the window to his right. The fiberglass panel sprang out in a piece as the frame tore. Deehalter stumbled headlong onto the low roof of the milking parlor, rolled, and jumped to the ground. The jeep was only twenty feet away and he ran for it.

There was no ignition lock. Deehalter flipped the power on and stabbed at the starter button under the clutch pedal. The engine ground but did not catch. There was a tearing noise behind him, and despite himself the big man turned to look. The creature was in the cow yard fence. The top strand was electrified. Blue sparks crackled about the thing's foreclaws. Its shape was in a state of flux so swift as to be almost subliminal. It was as if superimposed holograms of Kernes and the creature he had become were being projected onto the fence. Then the hot wire snapped and the thing's legs cut the remaining strands like sickles through fog.

Deehalter fired one-handed and missed. He steadied the rifle, locking his left elbow on the tubular seat-frame, and knocked the creature back into the cow yard with no top to its skull. Then the engine chugged and the big farmer threw the jeep into second gear at higher revs than the worn clutch was used to. Spewing gravel but without the power to sideslip, the vehicle churned forward.

For choice, Deehalter would have run west for the county road as he had two nights before in his Chrysler. That would have meant turning and trying to race past the cow yard, where the creature was already on its feet again and striding toward him. Deehalter had small need of his imagination to picture that scene: the long-clawed arms hooking over the steering wheel and plucking him out like the meat from a walnut half, leaving the empty jeep to careen into a ditch. He was headed instead toward Sac Ridge and the mound from which the horror must have come.

Deehalter had the headlights on, but they were mounted too low to show up potholes in time even at moderate speed—and his present speed was anything but moderate. The jeep jounced so badly that only the big man's grip on the steering wheel kept him in the vehicle. The shovels in the back did spin out into the night. It occurred to Deehalter that the rifle which he had wedged butt-downward beneath the back seat might fire and end him permanently as it had been unable to do to the thing pursuing. He did not care. He only knew that he had looked down the creature's gaping jaws and would rather anything than die between them.

Despite his panic, Deehalter shifted into compound low to cross the stream, knowing that any attempt to mount the slippery bank in a higher gear would have meant sliding back into certain death. On the rutted pasture beyond, he revved and slam-shifted. He was proud of his skill only for the instant before the low moon flicked a leaping shadow across the corner of his eye. Fear washed away pride and everything else.

Despite the ruts the jeep made good time in the pasture, but as the old vehicle began to climb the side of the ridge Deehalter knew the creature must be gaining. There was no choice, nowhere else to run. If he turned either north or south, the thing's long shanks would cut it across the slant of his right angle.

Where had the creature come from originally? Perhaps the Indians had known; but even if the teardrop was the source, it could as easily have fallen a million years before and a thousand miles away, carried south on a glacier. Deehalter could picture a nervous band of Sacs dragging one of their number to the rock basin, bound or unconscious. Or would it have been a tribe from the pre-Columbian past? There was nothing in the mound to date it. Something had come from the cocoon of iron and been trapped again between layers of rock. Trapped until he and Kernes had freed it in a vapor which merged with the black tendrils of the dynamite.

As Deehalter neared the top of the ridge, he glanced sideways. The creature was a foot behind him and a foot to the left, its right leg poised to stride and its yard-long right arm poised to rip the farmer's throat open. Deehalter slammed on the brakes, acting by reflex. It was the proper reflex, even though the jeep stalled. The beast's claws swept where Deehalter's head should have been, and its body belled and rebounded from the unyielding fender. For a moment, the thing sprawled backwards on the hillside; then it twisted upright, lizard-quick, and lunged.

Deehalter touched the muzzle of his Remington to the scaly ribs and blew the creature a dozen yards down the hill. The cartridge case sailed away in a high arc, the mouth of it eroded by the excessive pressures from the blocked muzzle.

And though Deehalter still had the part box in his pocket, that had been the last round in the weapon.

In stalling, Deehalter had flooded the jeep's engine. He leaped out, winded already with fear, and topped the ridge with two long strides. The headlights were waning yellow behind him, where he could already hear the creature moving. The sky to the east was the color of blood. Deehalter ran for the mound as if its gentle contours could protect him. He tried to jump to its top, but his foot sank in the soft earth of the diggings. The big man windmilled forward onto his face in the grass beyond. His grip on the empty rifle had flayed his right knuckles against the ground. His twisted ankle gave a twinge; it might or might not bear his weight again.

Deehalter turned, trying to fumble another cartridge into the breech of the rifle. It was too late. Hissing like a cat in a lethal rage, the creature leaped delicately to the top of the mound.

It was even thinner than it had looked when flickering shadows had bulked its limbs. It had to be thin, of course, with only Kernes' hundred and thirty pounds to clothe its frame. The curve of the mound made the creature's height monstrous, even though its legs were poised to lunge and it carried its flat skull forward like that of a near-sighted mantis. The narrow lips drew apart in a momentary grin, gray-white and then crimson as the first rays of the sun touched the creature over the rim of the next hill.

For a moment the leer hung there. Deehalter, on his back, stared at it like a rabbit spitted by the gaze of a hunting serpent. Then the thing was gone and the fear was gone, and Deehalter's practiced fingers slid a live round into the chamber of the ought-six.

"Wh-what's the matter, Dee?" Kernes whimpered. He was pitiful in his nakedness, more pitiful in his stunned surprise at where he found himself. Kernes really hadn't known what was happening, Deehalter realized. Perhaps Alice had begun to guess where her husband had been going in the night. That may have been why she had been so quick to run, before suspicion could become certainty.

"Dee, why're you looking at me like that?" Kernes begged.

Deehalter stood. His ankle only throbbed. If his first bullet had killed the creature as it should have, he would have buried the body and claimed that something had dragged Kernes away. Perhaps he would have buried it here in the mound from which the creature had escaped to begin with. Alice and Dr. Jepson could testify to the cattle's previous injuries, whatever they might surmise had caused them.

The same story would be sufficient now.

"Goodbye, you son of a bitch," Deehalter said, and he raised his rifle. He fired point blank into the smaller man's chest.

Kernes *whuffed* backwards as if a giant had kicked him. There was a look of amazement on his face and nothing more; but momentarily, something hung in the air between the dead man and the living, something as impalpable as the muzzle blast that rocked the hillside—and as real.

Deehalter's flesh *gave* and for a startled second he/it knew why the Indians had buried their possessed brother alive, to trap the contagion with him in the rock instead of merely passing it on to raven and slay again. . . .

Then the sun was bright on Deehalter's back, casting his shadow across the body of the man he had murdered. He recalled nothing of the moment just past.

Except that when he remembered the creature's last red leer, he seemed to be seeing the image in a mirror.

A LAND OF
ROMANCE

L. Sprague de Camp had greater influence on me as an SF reader and writer than anyone else. After World War II, a number of fans became publishers, joining August Derleth of Arkham House in reprinting works from Golden Age and earlier pulps. The Clinton (Iowa) Public Library in 1957 had a large collection of these books. (The entrance of major publishers, particularly Doubleday, into the SF market in the early '50s crushed the niche companies with the exception of Arkham House itself.)

Two of the small presses, Fantasy Press and Fantasy Publishing Company, Inc. collected a good deal of Sprague's fiction from Astounding and Unknown (Worlds). Either his rigor, intelligence, and focus on plot formed my opinion of what SF and fantasy should be, or they perfectly matched the model lurking somewhere in my childish subconscious.

In later years I got to know Sprague on terms of friendship, though we weren't as close as I was with Manly Wade Wellman, his contemporary and friend from the '30s and '40s. I encouraged Jim Baen to reprint the stories of Sprague's which I most liked. I did introductions for the volumes and stories in the style of Sprague's work as part of that encouragement.

Harry Turtledove, who like me was greatly influenced by Sprague, proposed a de Camp Festschrift to Baen Books. I happily wrote "A Land of Romance" for it, trying to create a story that Sprague might've written for Unknown.

I'll add two minor notes about the story itself. The full name of the former Secretary of Defense is Robert Strange McNamara, and the greatest buffalo meat entrepreneur in the country is Ted Turner (at the time I wrote the story, Mr. Jane Fonda). Both of those facts have bearing on the text.

‡ ‡ ‡

T he marketing bullpen at Strangeco Headquarters held seventy-five desks. Howard Jones was the only person in the huge room when the phone began ringing. He ignored the sound and went on with what he was doing. It was a wrong number—it had to be. Nobody'd be calling seriously on a Sunday morning.

Dynamic twenty-five-year-old executive . . . . Howard sucked in his gut as he typed, not that there was much gut to worry about. Ready to take on adventurous new challenges . . . .

The phone continued to ring. It could be the manager

of one of the Middle Eastern outlets where they kept a Friday-Saturday weekend, with a problem that only a bold—a *swashbuckling*—marketing professional like Howard Jones could take on. Did Strangeco have a branch in the Casbah of Algiers?

The company slogan circled the ceiling in shimmering neon letters: IT'S NOT A SANDWICH—IT'S A STRANGEWICH! SLICES OF KANGAROO, CASSOWARY, AND ELK IN A SECRET DRESSING! STRANGEWICH—THE HEALTHY ALTERNATIVE!

The phone *still* rang. Howard's image staring from the resume on the screen had a stern look. Was he missing his big chance? The caller could be a headhunter who needed the hard-charging determination of a man willing to work all the hours on the clock.

Howard grabbed the phone and punched line one. "Strangeco Inc!" he said in what he hoped was a stalwart tone. "Howard Jones, Assistant Marketing Associate speaking. How may I help you?"

"Oh!" said the male voice on the other end of the line. "Oh, I'm very sorry, I didn't mean to disturb anybody important."

Sure, a wrong number. Well, Howard had known that there wouldn't really be a summons to a life of dizzying adventure when he—

"I'm at Mr. Strange's house," the voice continued, "and I was hoping somebody could come over to help me word an advertisement. I'm sorry to have—"

"Wait!" Howard said. He knew the call couldn't be what it sounded like, but it was sure the most interesting thing going this Sunday morning. It *sounded* like the most interesting thing of a lifetime for Howard Albing Jones.

"Ah, sir," he continued, hoping that the fellow wasn't offended that Howard had bellowed at him a moment ago. "You say you're calling from Mr. Strange's house. That would be, ah, which house?"

"Oh, dear, he probably does have a lot of them, doesn't he?" the voice said. "I mean the one right next door, though. Do you think that you could send somebody not too important over to help me, sir?"

Howard cleared his throat. "Well, as a matter of fact, I wouldn't mind visiting the Strange Mansion myself. But, ah, Strangeco staff isn't ordinarily allowed across the skyway, you know."

"Oh, that's all right," the voice said in obvious relief. "Mr. Strange said I could call on any of his people for whatever I wished. But I really don't like to disturb you, Mr. Jones."

"Quite all right, Mister . . ." Howard said. "Ah, I'm afraid I didn't catch your name?"

"Oh, I'm Wally Popple," the voice said. "Just come over whenever you're ready to, Mr. Jones. I'll tell the guards to send you down."

He hung up. Howard replaced his handset and stared at the resume photograph. That Howard Jones looked very professional in blue suit, blue shirt, and a tie with an insouciant slash of red. Whereas today—Sunday— Assistant Marketing Associate Jones wore jeans and a Fuqua School of Business sweatshirt.

Howard rose to his feet. Daring, swashbuckling Howard Jones was going to risk entering the Strange Mansion in casual clothes.

✥ ✥ ✥

A transparent tube arched between the third floors of the Strange Mansion and Strangeco Headquarters to connect the two sprawling buildings. When Strange occasionally called an executive to the mansion, the rest of the staff lined the windows to watch the chosen person shuffle through open air in fear of what waited on the other side.

Shortly thereafter, sometimes only minutes later, the summoned parties returned. A few of them moved at once to larger offices; most began to clean out their desks.

Only executives were known to use the skyway, though rumor had it that sometimes Robert Strange himself crossed over at midnight to pace the halls of his headquarters silently as a bat. Now it was Howard Jones who looked out over cornfields and woodland in one direction and the vast staff parking lot in the other.

The skyway was hot and musty. That made sense when Howard thought about it: a clear plastic tube was going to heat up in the bright sun, and the arch meant the hottest air would hang in the middle like the bubble in a level. Howard had never before considered physics when he daydreamed of receiving Robert Strange's summons.

The wrought-iron grill at the far end was delicate but still a real barrier, even without the two guards on the other side watching as Howard approached. They were alert, very big, and not in the least friendly.

Muscle-bound, Howard told himself. I could slice them into lunchmeat with my rapier!

He knew he was lying, and it didn't even make him feel better. Quite apart from big men *not* necessarily being slow, this pair held shotguns.

"Good morning!" Howard said, trying for "brightly" and hitting "brittle" instead. "I have an urgent summons from Mr. Popple!"

Christ on a crutch! What if this was some kid's practical joke? Let's see if we can scam some sucker into busting into the Strange Mansion! Maybe they'll shoot him right where we can watch!

Howard glanced down, which probably wasn't the smartest thing to do now that he wasn't protected by the excitement of the thing. At least he didn't see kids with a cell phone and gleeful expressions peering up expectantly.

One of the guards said, "Who're you?" His tone would have been a little too grim for a judge passing a death sentence.

Howard's mind went blank. All he could think of was the accusing glare of his resume picture—but wait! Beside the picture was a name!

"Howard Albing Jones!" he said triumphantly.

"Nothing here about 'Albing,'" said the other guard.

The first guard shrugged. "Look, it's Sunday," he said to his partner. Fixing Howard with a glare that could've set rivets, he said, "We're letting you in, buddy. But as Howard Jones, that's all. That's how you sign the book."

"All right," said Howard. "I'm willing to be flexible."

One guard unlocked the grating; the other nodded Howard toward a folio bound in some unfamiliar form of leather, waiting open on a stand in the doorway. The last name above Howard's was that of a regional manager who'd been sobbing as he trudged into the parking lot for the last time.

The first guard pinned a blank metal badge on

Howard's sweatshirt, right in the center of Fuqua. "Keep it on," he said. "See the yellow strip?"

He gestured with his shotgun, then returned the muzzle to point just under where the badge rested.

An amber track lighted up in the center of the hallway beyond. The glow was so faint that it illuminated only itself. Focusing his eyes on it meant that Howard didn't have to stare at the shotgun.

"Right," he said. "Right!"

"You follow it," said the guard. "It'll take you where you're supposed to go. And you *don't* step off it, you understand?"

"Right," said Howard, afraid that he sounded brittle again. "I certainly don't want you gentlemen coming after me."

The other guard laughed. "Oh, we wouldn't do that," he said. "Pete and me watch—" he nodded to the bank of TV monitors, blanked during Howard's presence "—but we ain't cleared to go wandering around the mansion. Believe me, buddy, we're not ready to die."

Howard walked down the hall with a fixed smile until the amber strip led him around a corner. He risked a glance backwards then and saw that the light was fading behind him. He supposed it'd reappear when it was time for him to leave.

He supposed so.

Howard hadn't had any idea of what the inside of the Strange Mansion would be like. There were a thousand rumors about the Wizard of Fast Food but almost no facts. Howard himself had envisioned cathedral-vaulted ceilings and swaying chandeliers from which a bold man could swing one-handed while the blade of his rapier parried the thrusts of a score of minions.

There might be chandeliers, stone ledges, and high balconies on the other side of the blank gray walls but that no longer seemed likely. The corridor surfaces were extruded from some dense plastic, and the doors fitted like airlocks with no external latches.

The amber strip led through branching corridors, occasionally going downward by ramps. The building sighed and murmured like a sleeping beast.

Howard tried to imagine the Thief of Baghdad dancing away from foes in this featureless warren, but he quickly gave it up as a bad job. It was like trying to imagine King Kong on the set of *2001*.

The strip of light stopped at a closed door. Howard eyed the blank panel, then tried knocking. It was like rapping his knuckles on a bank vault, soundless and rather painful.

"Hello?" he said diffidently. "Hello!"

The corridor stretched to right and left, empty and silent. The amber glow had melted into the surrounding gray, leaving only a vague memory of itself. What would Robin Hood have done?

"*Hello!*" Howard shouted. "*Mister Popple!*"

"Hello," said the pleasant voice of the girl who'd come up behind him.

Howard executed a leap and pirouette that would have done Robin—or for that matter, a Bolshoi prima ballerina—proud. "Wha?" he said.

The girl was of middle height with short black hair and a perky expression that implied her pale skin was hereditary rather than a look. "I'm afraid Wally gets distracted," she said with a smile. "Come around through my rooms and I'll let you in from the side. The laboratory started out as a garage, you know."

"Ah, I was told not to leave . . ." Howard said, tilting forward slightly without actually moving his feet from the point at which the guide strip had deposited him. After the guards' casual threats, he no longer believed that the worst thing that could happen to him in the Strange Mansion was that he'd lose his job.

"Oh, give me that," the girl said. She deftly unpinned the badge from Howard's sweatshirt and pressed her thumb in the middle of its blankness, then handed it back to him. "There, I've turned it off."

She walked toward the door she'd come out of, bringing Howard with her by her breezy nonchalance. He said, "Ah, you work here, miss?"

"Actually, the only people who work here are Wally and the cleaning crews," the girl said. "And my father, of course. I'm Genie Strange."

She led Howard into a room with low, Japanese-style furniture and translucent walls of pastel blue. It was like walking along the bottom of a shallow sea.

"Have you known Wally long?" Genie said, apparently unaware that she'd numbed Howard by telling him she was Robert Strange's daughter. "He's such a sweetheart, don't you think? Of course, I don't get to meet many people. Robert says that's for my safety, but . . ."

"I've enjoyed my contact with Mr. Popple so far," Howard said. He didn't see any reason to amplify the truthful comment. Well, the more or less truthful comment.

Genie opened another door at the end of the short hallway at the back of the suite. "Wally?" she called. "I brought your visitor."

The laboratory buzzed like a meadow full of bees. The lighting was that of an ordinary office; Howard's eyes had adapted to the corridors' muted illumination, so he sneezed. If the room had been a garage, then it was intended for people who drove semis.

Black silk hangings concealed the walls. Though benches full of equipment filled much of the interior, the floor was incongruously covered in Turkish rugs— runners a meter wide and four meters long—except for a patch of bare concrete around a floor drain in an outside corner.

"Oh, my goodness, Mr. Jones!" said the wispy little man who'd been bent over a circuit board when they entered. He bustled toward them, raising his glasses to his forehead. "I'd meant to leave the door open but I forgot completely. Oh, Iphigenia, you must think I'm the greatest fool on Earth!"

"What I think is that you're the sweetest person I know, Wally," the girl said, patting his bald head. He blushed crimson. "But just a little absentminded, perhaps."

"Mr. Jones is going to help me advertise for a volunteer," Wally said to the girl. "I don't see how we can get anybody, and we really *must* have someone, you know."

"Pleased to meet you, Mr. Jones," Genie said, offering her hand with mock formality.

"Ah, Howard, please," Howard said. "Ah, I have a position with Strangeco. A very lowly one at present."

"That's what my father likes in employees," Genie said in a half-joking tone. "Lowliness. My stepfather, I should say. Mother buried two husbands, but Robert buried her."

Howard shook her hand, aware that he was learning things about the Wizard of Fast Food that the tabloids would pay good money for. Remembering the uneasiness he'd felt while walking through the mansion, he also realized that the money he'd get for invading Strange's privacy couldn't possibly be good enough.

An area twenty feet square in the center of the lab was empty of equipment. Across it, beyond Wally as Howard faced him, was what looked like an irregular, razor-thin sheet of glass on which bright images flickered. If that was really the flat-plate computer display it looked like, it was more advanced than anything Howard had heard of on the market.

"Well, Mr. Popple . . ." Howard said. If the conversation continued in the direction Genie was taking it, Howard would learn things he didn't think he'd be safe knowing. "If you could tell me just what you need from me?"

"Oh, please call me Wally," the little man said, taking Howard's hand and leading him toward the thin display. "You see, this piece of mica is a, well, a window you could call it."

Wally glanced over his shoulder, then averted his eyes with another bright blush. As he'd obviously hoped, Genie was following them.

"I noticed that shadows seemed to move in it," Wally said, peering intently at what indeed was a piece of mica rather than a high-tech construction. Hair-fine wires from a buss at the back touched the sheet's ragged circumference at perhaps a hundred places. "That was six years ago. By modulating the current to each sheet separately—it's not one crystal, you know, it's a series of sheets like a stack of paper and there's a dielectric between each pair—I was able to sharpen the images to, well, what you see now."

Howard eyed the display. A group of brightly dressed people walked through a formal garden. The women wore dresses whose long trains were held by page boys, and the men were in tights and tunics with puffed sleeves. They carried swords as well, long-bladed rapiers with jeweled hilts.

"How do you generate the images, Wally?" Howard said. "This isn't fed from a broadcast signal, is it?"

"They aren't generated at all," Genie said. "They're real. Show Howard how you can move the point of view, Wally."

Obediently the little man stepped to the computer terminal on the bench beside the slab of mica. On the monitor was a graph with about thirty bars in each of two superimposed rows.

Wally touched keys, watching the mica. A bar shrank or increased at each stroke, and the picture shifted with the jerking clarity of a rotated kaleidoscope.

"Hey!" said Howard as what he thought was a lion turned and raised its feathered head. Its hooked beak opened and the long forked tongue vibrated in a cry which the mica didn't transmit. "That's a chimera!"

"I thought so at first," said Genie, "but they're supposed to be part goat, too."

"I don't think it's anything that has a name in our world," Wally said, making further small adjustments. "Of course the people seem to be, well, normal."

"Not normal where I come from!" Howard said. Except maybe in his dreams. "And what do you mean about *our* world? Where's that?"

He pointed. The image tumbled into a scene of vividly dressed gallants fencing while a semicircle of women and other men watched. The duelists were good, *damned* good, and they didn't have buttons on their swords.

"Robert thinks it's fairyland," Genie said. Her tone was neutral, but Howard heard emotion just beneath the surface of the words. "He thinks Wally's a wizard. Robert also thinks he's a wizard himself."

"Your father has been very generous in supporting my researches, Iphigenia," the little man said, glancing toward but not quite at Genie. "I wish I could convince him that these effects are ordinary science—"

He paused and added self-consciously, "Ordinary physics, at any rate. I'm afraid my researches have been too empirical to qualify as proper science. But the underlying laws are physical, not magic."

The mica showed the dim interior of a great hall, the sort of place that Howard had imagined the Strange Mansion might be. A troupe of acrobats capered on the rush-strewn flagstones, executing remarkable jumps while juggling lighted torches.

Splendid men and gorgeous women watched from tables around the margins of the hall, and over the balcony railings peered children and soberly dressed servants. At the center of the high table was a grave, bearded man wearing a crown. He held a crystal staff in which violet sparks danced.

Beside the king, occasionally rubbing its scaly head on the back of his carved throne, was a dragon the size of a rhinoceros. It didn't look exactly unfriendly, but its eyes had the trick of constantly scanning in every direction.

"I . . ." said Howard. "Wally, this is wonderful, just completely amazing, but I don't understand what you want me for. You've already succeeded!"

The image shifted again. Instead of answering, Wally gazed with rapt attention at the new scene. A spring shot from a wooded hillside to splash over rocks into a pool twenty feet below. Butterflies hovered in the flowery glade; in the surrounding forest were vine-woven bowers.

"Wally built the window on his own," Genie said in a low voice. "What Robert is interested in is opening a door into . . . that."

She nodded toward the mica. A couple, hand in hand, walked toward the pool. The man knelt, dipped a silver goblet into the limpid water, and offered it to the lovely woman at his side. She sipped, then returned the cup for him to drink in turn.

Wally shuddered as though he'd been dropped into the pool. He tapped his keyboard several times at random, blurring the image into a curtain of electronic snow.

He turned to Howard and said, speaking very quickly to focus his mind somewhere other than where it wanted to go, "Mr. Strange felt that if we could see the other place, we could enter it. A person could enter it. He's correct—I sent a rabbit through the portal last week—but I don't think anyone will be willing to go when they realize how dangerous it is. That's why I need you to help me write the advertisement for the volunteer, Mr. Jones."

This was going to work better if the little guy was relaxed . . . which probably wouldn't happen as long as Genie Strange was in the same room, *that* was obvious, but Howard at least had to try to calm him down.

"Howard, Wally," Howard said, patting Wally on the shoulder. "Please call me Howard. Now, what's dangerous about the trip? Do you wind up wearing a fly's head if things go wrong?"

"No, it wasn't that, Mister—ah, Howard," Wally said, pursing his lips. "The problem occurred later."

He adjusted the values on his display again, bringing the image of the royal entertainment back onto the mica. A young girl danced on the back of a horse which curveted slowly, its hooves striking occasional sparks from the flagstones. It was pretty ordinary-looking except for the straight horn in the center of its forehead.

Seeing that Wally wasn't going to say more, Howard raised an eyebrow to Genie. She shrugged and said, "I didn't see it myself—Robert won't let me in here while the tests are going on. But all that really happened is that the rabbit hopped out, perfectly all right, and a lizard ate it. The same thing could have happened anywhere."

"The lizard stared at the poor rabbit and drew it straight into its jaws, step by step," Wally said without looking at the others. "It knew it was doomed but it went anyway. I've never in my life seen anything so horrible."

Then you don't watch the TV news a lot, Howard thought. Aloud he said, "It was a basilisk, you mean? Not just a lizard?"

"It was a lizard," Wally insisted stubbornly. "But it wasn't a lizard from, well, this world. It was horrible, and there are any number of other horrible things over there. It's really too dangerous to send somebody into that world, but that's the only way we can get . . . things."

"Well, an assault rifle ought to take care of any basilisks that come by," Howard said reasonably. "Or dragons either, which is more to the point. Basilisks aren't supposed to be big enough to eat people."

He sighed. "I hate to say this, Wally, but science always seems to win out over romance. I *really* hate to say it."

"But that's just what I mean, Howard," Wally said despairingly. "I had a leash on the bunny so I could pull it back, but it didn't pass through the portal. The leash was still lying on the floor when the bunny disappeared. The volunteer won't be able to take a gun or even clothes, and I really don't believe he'll be able to bring the scepter back for Mr. Strange."

"Robert thinks that purple scepter gives the fairy king his power," Genie said, her hands clasped behind her back as if to underscore the restraint in her voice. "Robert wants someone to go through Wally's portal and steal the scepter."

With absolutely no feeling she added, "Robert sacrificed a black hen the night Wally sent the rabbit through. He did it over the drain there—"

She nodded toward the bare concrete.

"—but you can still smell the blood caught in the pipe. Can't you?"

"Now, Iphigenia," Wally said, blushing again. "Your father has his ways, but he's been very generous with me."

Howard's nose wrinkled. He'd noticed a faint musty odor, but the room was so ripe with the smells of electronics working—ozone, hot insulation, and flux—that he hadn't given any thought to it. He still wasn't sure that what he smelled was rotting blood rather than mildew or wet wool, but now that Genie'd spoken he wouldn't be able to get the other notion out of his mind.

"Wally, you're a genius!" the girl said so forcefully as to sound hostile. "You could go anywhere and find somebody to fund your work! I only wish you had."

Wally turned and looked her in the face for the first time. "Thank you for saying that, Iphigenia," he said, "but it isn't true. I went many places after I first saw what the mica could do, and they all sent me away. Your father thinks I'm a magician and he's wrong; but he doesn't call me crazy or a charlatan."

A door—the door that the light had led Howard to—opened. Robert Strange, identifiable from the rare photos that appeared in news features but much craggier and *harsher* in person, stepped through. He wore a long-sleeved black robe embroidered with symbols Howard didn't recognize, and through the sash at his waist he'd thrust a curved dagger of Arab style. Hilt and scabbard both were silver but decorated with runes filled with black niello.

"Who are you?" Strange demanded, his eyes fixed on Howard. His voice was like scales scraping on stone, and his black pupils had a reptilian glitter.

The news photographs hadn't shown the long scar down Strange's left cheekbone. There were many ways he could've been cut, but only one reason Howard could imagine that a man with Strange's money wouldn't have had the scar removed by plastic surgery: pride. It was a schlaeger scar, a vestige of the stylized duels with heavy sabers that still went on secretly at the old German universities. The purpose of a schlaeger bout wasn't to defeat one's foe but rather to get the scar as proof of courage and disregard for the laws which banned the practice.

Mind you, Howard was pretty sure that Strange's opponent had left his share of blood on the hall's floor as well.

"He's a—" said Genie before either Howard or Wally could speak.

"Iphigenia, go to your quarters at once," Strange said in the same rustling tone as before. He didn't speak loudly, but his voice cut through the buzz of electronics as surely as a mower would the flowery meadow that Howard thought of when entering the room. "You disturb Master Popple. I've warned you about this."

"But there's nobody else to *talk* to!" Genie said. Though she complained, she walked quickly toward the door of her suite.

Strange returned his attention to Howard. "I said," he repeated, "who are you?"

"Mr. Strange, I asked M—that is, Howard to help me—" Wally said.

"I'm the volunteer you requested for your experiment, sir," Howard said without the least suggestion of a quaver in his voice. "Wally here—Mr. Popple—noted that the agent won't be able to carry a gun into the other realm, so my skill with a rapier is crucial."

"You know how to use a sword?" Strange snapped.

"Yes, sir," Howard said, standing very straight and keeping his eyes on the tycoon's, hoping that would make him look open and honest. Even though Howard was telling the truth about the fencing, Strange's whole tone and manner made it seem that everything he was being told was a lie.

Besides considering that Strange might have him shot as a spy, there was the possibility that the Wizard of Fast Food would demand Howard duel him to prove his skill. Beating Strange would be dangerous—rich men were self-willed and explosive if they didn't get what they wanted. Losing to Strange might be even worse, especially since Howard didn't imagine he'd have buttons on his swords any more than the folk on the other side of the mica window did.

"Since I'm an employee of Strangeco," Howard continued, visualizing the Thief of Baghdad dancing over palace walls while monsters snarled beneath, "my devotion to you is already assured."

"You work for me?" Strange said. Then, as if he could remember each of the thirty thousand Strangeco employees worldwide, he said, "What's your name?"

The door swung *almost* shut behind Genie. "Howard Albing Jones, sir," Howard said.

"Assistant Marketing Associate in the home office," Strange said. *My God, maybe he did know all thirty thousand!* "Devoted, are you? Pull the other leg, boy! But that doesn't matter if you've got the guts for the job."

"Yes, sir, I do," Howard said. He cleared his throat and went on, "I think I could honestly say I've been training all my life for this opportunity."

"You practice the Art also, Jones?" Strange demanded, the hectoring doubt back in his voice. "The Black Arts, I mean. That's what they call it, the pigmies who adepts like me crush under our heels!"

"Ah, I can't claim to be an adept, sir," Howard said. He couldn't *honestly* claim to be anything but a guy who occasionally watched horror movies. As far as that went, he knew more about being a vampire than being a magician.

"No?" said Strange. "Well, I am, Jones. That's how I built Strangeco from a corner hot dog stand into what it is now. And by His Infernal Majesty! that's how I'll rule the world when I have the staff of power for myself. Nothing will stop me, Jones. Nothing!"

"Mr. Strange, I'm your man!" Howard said. He spoke enthusiastically despite his concern that Strange might reply something along the lines of, "Fine, I'll take your kidneys now to feed my pet ferrets."

"If you serve me well, you won't regret it," Strange said. Unspoken but much louder in Howard's mind was the corollary: *But if you fail, I won't leave enough of you to bury!*

"Master Popple, can you be ready to proceed in two hours?" Strange asked. When he talked to Wally, there was a respect in his tone that certainly hadn't been present when he spoke to Howard or Genie.

"Well, I suppose . . ." Wally said. He frowned in concentration, then shrugged and said, "I don't see why not, if Howard is willing. I suppose we could start right now, Mr. Strange."

"It'll take me the two hours to make my own

preparations," Strange said with a curt shake of his head. "I respect your art, Master Popple, but I won't depend on it alone."

As he strode toward the door, Strange added without turning his head, "I'll have a black ewe sent over. And if that's not enough—we'll see!"

"Now hold your arms out from your shoulders, please, Howard," Wally said as he changed values on his display. Howard obeyed the way he would if a barber told him to tilt his head.

Waiting as the little man made adjustments gave Howard enough time to look over the room. Much of the racked equipment meant nothing to him, but his eyes kept coming back to a black cabinet that looked like a refrigerator-sized tube mating with a round sofa.

"Wally?" he said, his arms still out. "What's that in the northeast corner? Is it an air conditioner?"

"Oh, that's the computer that does the modulations," Wally said. "You can put your arms down now if you like. I used a Sun workstation to control the window, but the portal requires greatly more capacity. I'd thought we'd just couple a network of calculation servers to the workstation, but Mr. Strange provided a Cray instead to simplify the setup for the corrections."

"Oh," said Howard, wondering what a supercomputer cost. Pocket change to the Wizard of Fast Food, he supposed.

"Now if you'll turn counterclockwise, please . . ." Wally said. "About fifteen degrees."

Howard wore a cotton caftan that came from Genie's

suite. She'd brought it in when Howard protested at standing buck naked in the middle of the floor with security cameras watching. Howard was willing to accept that the clothes wouldn't go through the portal with him, but waiting while Pete and his partner chuckled about his masculine endowments was a different matter.

Not that there was anything wrong with his masculine endowments.

Genie didn't stay, but Howard knew she was keeping abreast of what went on through the part-open door. He wasn't sure whether he was glad of that or not.

The mica window looked onto the glade where Howard would enter the other world if everything went right. Occasionally a small animal appeared briefly—once Howard saw what looked very much like a pink bass swimming through the air—but Wally had chosen the site because it was isolated. There was only so much you could get from leaves quivering, even if they did seem to be solid gold.

The carpets, layered like roof shingles over the concrete, weren't the neutrally exotic designs you normally saw on Oriental rugs. Some of these had stylized camels and birds, sure; but one had tanks, jets, and bright explosions, while peacock-winged devils capered as they tortured people against the black background of the newer-looking rugs.

Around where Howard stood was a six-pointed star drawn in lime like the markings of a football field. Howard would've expected a pentacle, but he didn't doubt Strange knew what he was doing.

All Howard himself was sure of was that he was taking a chance at adventure when it appeared. If that was a bad idea, then he hoped he wouldn't have long to regret his decision.

It might be a very bad idea.

"There," said Wally. "There's nothing more I can do until we actually begin building the charge. Then I may have to—"

Robert Strange entered through a pedestrian door set in one of the six vehicle doors along the outside wall. The black sheep he led looked puzzled, a feeling which Howard himself echoed.

"You're ready, Master Popple?" he asked.

"*Ey-eh-he-e*," said the sheep. Strange jerked the leash viciously. The cord looked like silver, but it was functional enough to choke the sheep to silence when Strange lifted his arm.

"Yes, Mr. Strange," Wally said. "I'm a little worried about Howard's mass, though. Eighty-seven kilos may be too much."

"Too much?" snapped Strange. "If you needed more transformers, you should have said so!"

"Too much for the fabric of the universe, Mr. Strange," said Wally, as mild as ever but completely undaunted at the anger of a man who scared the living crap out of Howard Jones. "I really don't want to go to more than thirty kilowatts."

Strange sniffed. "The subject's ready?" he said. "You, Jones; you're ready?"

"*Ey-eh-he?*" the sheep repeated, rolling its eyes. Her eyes, Howard assumed, since Strange said he was fetching an ewe. The tycoon's dagger hilt winked in the bright laboratory lighting.

"Yes, sir!" Howard said.

Strange grimaced, then bent and tied the leash around

a ring set in the drain. He turned his head to Howard and said, "You know what you're going to do?"

"Sir, I'm going to enter the other land," Howard said. "I'll take the scepter from the king of that land and return here to you with it."

As a statement of intent it was concise and accurate. As a plan of action it lacked detail, but there wasn't enough information on this side of the portal to form a real plan. Howard was uneasily aware that his foray, even if he wound up in a dragon's gullet, would provide information so that the next agent could do better.

"All right," Strange said. "Give me a moment and then proceed."

There were drapes bunched among the wall hangings. As Strange spoke, he drew them along a track in the ceiling to separate his corner of the room from Howard and Wally. The ewe bleated again.

"You may begin, Master Popple," Strange called, his voice muffled by the thick fabric. He broke into a musical chant. The sounds from his throat weren't words, or at least words in English.

"You're ready, Howard?" Wally said.

Howard nodded. His throat was dry and he didn't want to embarrass himself by having his voice crack in the middle of a simple word like, "Yes."

Wally rotated a switch, cutting the ceiling lights to red beads among the dimming ghosts of the fluorescent fixtures. The sheet of mica, bright with the daylight of another world, shone like a lantern beside the little man as he typed commands.

There was a reptilian viciousness to Strange's voice,

and the sheep was managing to whimper like a frightened baby. The hair on Howard's arms and the back of his neck began to rise. For a moment he thought that was his reaction to the sounds coming from beyond the drapes, but as the fluorescents cooled to absolute black Howard saw a faint violet aura clinging to three racks of equipment.

Wally was generating very high frequency current at a considerable voltage. Howard decided he didn't want to think about *how* high the voltage was.

Wally muttered as he worked. Though Howard could see his lips move, the words weren't audible over the hum of five transformers along the outside wall. The opening between Genie's door and the jamb was faintly visible.

The air spluttered. Howard felt a directionless pull, unpleasant without being really painful. Violet light flickered through the mica, a momentary pulse from the world across the barrier.

Strange shouted a final word. The sheep bleated on a rising note ending in so awful a gurgle that Howard pressed his hands to his ears before he remembered that moving might affect Wally's calculations. The ewe's hooves rattled on the concrete; the curtain billowed as the animal thrashed.

Howard would've covered his ears even if he had thought about Wally. The sound was *horrible*.

Wally typed, his eyes on the computer display. He'd sucked his lower lip between his teeth to chew as he concentrated. The transformers hummed louder but didn't change tone.

Howard felt the indescribable pull again. In the other world the violet haze formed again, this time in the shape of a human being.

A blue flash and a *BANG!* like a cannon shot engulfed the lab, stunning Howard into a wordless shout. He clapped his hands, a reflex to prove that he was still alive.

The air stank of burning tar. Dirty red flames licked from one of the transformers on the outside wall. Howard drew in a deep breath of relief. He immediately regretted it when acrid smoke brought on a fit of coughing.

Strange snatched open the curtains, his face a mask of cold fury. The ewe lay over the drain, her legs splayed like those of a squashed insect. Her eyes still had a puzzled look, but they were already beginning to glaze.

Wally changed values at his keyboard with a resigned expression. Howard looked for a fire extinguisher. He didn't see one, but he walked past Wally and turned the main lights back on. The transformer was smoldering itself out, though an occasional sizzle made Howard thankful that the floor was covered with non-conductive wool.

"What went wrong?" Strange said. "I know that the transformer failed; *why* did it fail?"

"The load was too great," Wally said simply. "We very nearly succeeded. If we replace the transformer—"

"We'll double the capacity," Strange said. "We'll make another attempt tonight, at midnight this time. I never thought you were careful enough with your timing, Master Popple."

"Sir, I don't think it would be safe to increase output beyond—" Wally said.

"We'll double it!" Strange said, his tone a rasp like steel grating on rib bones. "If we don't need the extra wattage, then we won't use it, but we'll use as much as it requires!"

He looked disgustedly at the dagger in his hand, then

wiped the blade on the curtain and sheathed the weapon. He strode past Howard and Wally to the hall door; Howard watched him with a fixed smile, uncomfortably aware that instinct tensed him to run in case Strange leaped for his throat.

The Thief of Baghdad might've had a better idea. On the other hand, Howard didn't remember the Thief of Baghdad facing anything quite like Robert Strange.

Strange thumped the hall door closed; it was too heavy to bang. At the sound, Genie's door opened a little wider and the slim girl returned. She grimaced when she saw the ewe. It'd voided its bowels when it died, so that odor mingled with the fresh blood and burned insulation.

"Are you all right, Wally?" she asked. "And you, Howard. I'm not used to there being anybody but Wally here."

"I'm sorry you had to see that, Iphigenia," Wally said with a perturbed glance toward the ewe. "You really shouldn't have come in until the crew has cleaned things up."

"Wally, I've lived with Robert for fifteen years," Genie said bluntly. "There've been worse things than the occasional dead animal. I was worried about you and Howard."

"It just tickled a little," Howard said. If he let himself think about events in the right way, he was pretty sure he could make the last ten minutes or so sound more heroic than they'd seemed while they were happening.

"There wasn't any risk, Iphigenia," Wally said. At first he didn't look directly at her, but then he raised his eyes with an effort of will. "Ah—I really appreciate your concern, but right now I have something important to discuss with Mr.—with Howard, that is. Can you, I mean would you . . . ?"

"All right, Wally," the girl said, sounding puzzled and a little hurt. She nodded to Howard and walked to her room with swift, clean strides. This time the door shut firmly.

One of the vehicular doors in the outside wall started up with a rumble of heavy gears. A team of swarthy men, beardless but heavily mustached, stood beside a flatbed truck. They entered, paying no attention to Howard and Wally. One lifted the sheep over his shoulder and walked back to the truck with it; his three fellows started disconnecting the wrecked transformer. They talked among themselves in guttural singsongs.

"Will you come here please, Howard?" Wally said, showing no more interest in the workmen than they did in him. He adjusted the mica screen to show the spring again. "I, ah, have a favor to ask you."

A couple—not the same ones as before—sat on the pool's mossy coping, interlacing the fingers of one hand as they passed a cup back and forth with the other. Wally tightened the focus so that their mutually loving expressions were unmistakable.

"Yes, Wally?" Howard prodded.

"The water of this spring appears to have certain properties," Wally said. He looked fixedly at Howard to avoid watching the couple who'd begun to fondle one another. The statuesque blonde lay back on the sward and tugged her partner over her without bothering to walk to the privacy of the nearby bowers. "You'll have noticed that."

"I sure notice something," Howard said. He wasn't sure how he felt about the show: it was real people, not actors. Well, actors were real people too but they knew they were going to be watched.

The workmen hoisted the transformer by hand instead of bringing in a derrick for the job. It must weigh close to half a ton. They walked out and slid it onto the truck bed, forcing a squeal from the springs.

Wally grimaced and blurred the image to bright sparkles within the mica sheet. "If I succeed in opening the portal to the other world, Howard," he said, "you'll have a very difficult job to gain the king's scepter. I don't believe in magic, not here or there either one, but the animal guarding the king appears formidable."

"The dragon," Howard said. "Yeah, it does."

If Howard let himself consider the details of how he was going to get the scepter, it'd scare the spit out of him. By limiting his thoughts to vague swoops across the hall on a handy rope, followed by a mighty leap from a balcony-level window, he was managing to keep his aplomb.

"And of course we're not sure it'll be possible to bring inanimate objects through the portal in this direction, since we can't do it while going the other way," Wally continued with a solemn nod. He started to refocus on the spring, then snatched his hand back from the keyboard with a blush.

"I understand all the difficulties and dangers you'll face, Howard," Wally said. He stared in the direction of Genie's closed door; he looked as if he was about to cry. "Regardless, I'd like you to do me a favor if you can. I'd like you to bring me a phial of water from the spring we just looked at. I . . . I'd be very grateful."

You poor little guy! Howard thought. Aloud he said, "Ah, Wally? I'll do what I can—"

Which might not be a heck of a lot. *If* Howard arrived, he'd be bare-assed naked and in the middle of a bunch of guys with swords they knew how to use. Not to mention the occasional dragon.

"—but you know, it isn't that hard to, ah, meet girls." He paused to choose the next words carefully. "Lots of times just being around one for a while is enough to, you know, bring the two of you together. If you play your cards right."

The truck drove off with a snort of diesel exhaust as the garage door began to rumble down. The corpses of the sheep and transformer lay together in the bed of the vehicle.

"I've never played cards at all, Howard," the little man said with a sad smile. "I guess this is hard for a handsome young man like you to understand, but . . ."

He turned his head away and wiped his eyes fiercely.

"Hey, that's all right, Wally," Howard said, patting him on the back. "Sure, I'll take care of that if there's, you know, any way to do it. No problem."

Compared to the rest of the assignment, that was the gospel truth.

"Thank you, Howard," Wally said through a racking snuffle. "I'm, well, I'm lucky to have met a real hero like you in my time of need."

Only faintly audible through the heavy doors, another big truck was pulling up outside. A relay clicked and the machinery began to rumble again.

"I feel sure we're going to succeed," Wally added. "If

we have to double the field strength, well, that's just what we're going to do. No matter what!"

Wally sounded a lot more cheerful when he made that promise than Howard was to hear it.

With the six new transformers in place, the line almost filled the outside wall. On that side only the curtained-off corner—they were already drawn—didn't have machinery squatting on it. Howard could still smell burned insulation. He'd never thought he'd be thankful for a stink like that, but it covered other possible reminders of the afternoon's experiment.

Wally looked at Howard and tried to force a grin. His expression would've been more appropriate for somebody being raped by a Christmas tree.

"Hey, buck up, buddy," Howard said. "We're going to be fine!"

Funny, but telling the lie made Howard feel that the words might possibly be true. Logically he knew a lot better.

The door hidden behind the curtain opened. Howard heard a *clink* over the hum of machinery as something hard brushed against the raised lintel. He wondered what animal Strange was bringing in to sacrifice this time. Howard had expected a heifer or maybe an elephant, but Strange would've had to raise the vehicular door to bring in animals that big.

Strange stuck his head out between two curtain panels. "Are you ready to proceed, Master Popple?" he asked. He held the curtains together so that all Howard could see was the throat of his garments. He seemed to be wearing the same silver-marked black satin as in the afternoon.

"I believe—" Wally said. He caught Howard's terse nod and continued, "Yes, we're ready, Mr. Strange. It'll take ninety seconds from whenever we start to build the field."

"Start now, then," Strange said curtly. He drew the curtains tight behind him and began to chant. His words had considerable musical power despite being complete gibberish. That was also true of opera, of course, so far as Howard was concerned.

Wally tried to smile again, then busied himself with his keyboard. The mica window looked onto the glade, empty save for trees and the flitting passage of a bird whose plumage was as purely blue as the summer sky. Howard watched the scientist, and he watched images on the mica; but more compelling than those, he listened through the curtains at his back to the sound of Robert Strange's voice chanting.

Howard felt the hairs lift from his body. Where those of his chest touched the loose caftan they tickled like the feeling at the back of a dry throat that you can't seem to swallow away. Violet haze blurred the air beyond the mica.

Genie Strange screamed.

Howard turned. The door to Genie's room was closed—closed and latched. The drapes around Strange and his activities bulged outward.

Genie hopped through and fell, dragging a section of the velvet down. The scarf used to gag her had slipped out of her mouth; it was the only garment she was wearing. Her wrists and ankles were tied together behind her back, but she'd managed to undo the cord that'd bound her to the drain.

Robert Strange, his face as hard and contorted as that

of a marble demon, stepped out behind her. He grabbed a handful of Genie's black hair with his free hand.

"Hey!" Howard said. There was a bank of equipment between him and the Stranges. As gracefully as if he'd been practicing all his life, Howard took two running steps, planted his right palm on the rack, and leaped over with his legs swung off to his left side. Even the Thief of Baghdad would be impressed—

Until the caftan's billowing hem caught the chassis full of plug-in circuits on top of the rack. As Howard's legs straightened, the tightening cloth spilled him like a lassoed steer. Strange looked at him without expression.

Howard sprang up. The torn caftan, bunched now around his ankles, tripped him again.

Strange lifted Genie's head, avoiding her attempts to bite him. He poised the curved dagger in his right hand over her throat. Howard grabbed the sides of the rug on which he'd fallen and jerked with all his strength, snatching Strange's feet out from under him.

"You . . . !" shouted Strange as he toppled backward. Genie'd tossed her short hair free of his grip, but he didn't lose the dagger in his other hand. It was underneath when the Wizard of Fast Food hit the concrete.

The chassis that Howard'd dragged to the floor with him was popping and spluttering, but he wasn't prepared for the flash of violet light that filled the interior of the lab. It was so intense that Howard only vaguely noticed the accompanying thunderclap. He heard Wally cry out and turned.

Wally wasn't there. His clothing, from brown shoes to the pair of reading glasses he wore tilted up on his forehead, lay in the middle of the hexagram. The hundred and twenty-three pounds of Wally Popple had vanished.

Except for an image in the mica window.

Howard lifted Genie before he remembered that her stepfather and the dagger might be of more immediate concern. He looked back.

He'd been right the first time. Strange's face was turned toward Howard. He looked absolutely furious. He'd managed to thrash into a prone position while dying, but the silver hilt projecting from the middle of his back showed that dying was certainly what he'd done.

The transformer on the far left of the line shorted out. The one next to it went a heartbeat later, and when the third failed it showered the room with blobs of flaming tar. One of them slapped the mica window, and shattered it like a bomb.

"Can you please untie me, Howard?" asked the girl in his arms. "Though the way things are starting to happen in here, maybe that could wait till we're outside."

"Right!" said Howard. "Right!"

He paused to shrug off what was left of the caftan; it had started to burn as well. Somehow he couldn't get concerned about what the guards thought of him now.

Because he and Genie were going to be gone for at least three weeks and a fourth besides if the Chinese authorities agreed to open Tibet to Strangeco—which they would; Howard Jones wasn't called the Swashbuckler of Fast Food for nothing—Howard stopped by the mansion's former garage for a moment. He liked to, well, keep an eye on how things were going.

He'd had the big room cleaned and nearly emptied immediately after the wedding, but he still smelled the bitterness of burned insulation. He supposed it was mostly in his mind by now.

Genie'd wanted to tear the garage down completely since it held nothing but bad memories for her, but she'd agreed to let Howard keep the room so long as he'd had the door into her old suite welded shut. She wasn't the sort of girl to object to the whim of the man who'd saved her life; besides, she loved her husband.

Howard went to the skeletal apparatus on the one rack remaining in the room. Three hair-fine filaments were still attached to the top edge of a piece of mica no bigger than a quarter.

Howard bent to peer into it. If you looked carefully at the right times, you could see images in the mica.

The focus wandered. Howard hadn't tried to adjust the apparatus himself or let anybody else take a look at it. Mostly all there was to see was snow, but this time he was in luck.

The peephole looked out at the spring where couples used to cavort. Wally was there with his entourage, checking the generating turbine he'd built to power the first electric lights in his new home. If Howard understood the preparations he'd seen going on in the royal palace last week, telephones were about to follow.

When Wally turned with a satisfied expression, Howard waved. He knew the little fellow couldn't see him, but it made Howard feel he was sort of keeping in touch. Wally walked out of the image area surrounded by courtiers.

Howard checked his watch and sighed; he needed to get moving. He'd promised the company fencing team that he and Genie would at least drop in on their match with Princeton. After Howard instituted morning unity-building fencing exercises throughout Strangeco, a number of the employees had become fencing enthusiasts.

Howard took a last look at the pool in the other world. He'd never seen Wally take a sip of the water, and it didn't seem likely that he ever would.

After all, a powerful wizard like Master Popple had to beat off beautiful women with a stick.

SMOKIE JOE

I've recently begun writing big-budget fantasy novels. The first question interviewers ask me is almost invariably, "Why did you switch from military SF to fantasy?"

The truth—as this volume proves—is that I started out writing fantasy. After I got back from Southeast Asia in 1971 I had first-hand knowledge of war and the military. I used that background in science fiction stories which eventually (and I mean eventually) got me a name for writing military SF; but I love fantasy, and I've never stopped writing it.

A British writer and editor, Michel Parry, edited a number of interesting original (or partly original) horror and fantasy anthologies in the 1970s. These didn't pay a lot—I believe everything I sold Michel was at a penny a word—but they were sales (and to real publishers like Mayflower and Star) at a time when there were very few outlets in the US for fantasy. (More places in the US would buy SF. For the most part I got rejections from them, but there were at least magazines to which I could send my stories.)

One of Michel's odder endeavors was to edit
Devil's Kisses and More Devil's Kisses, *anthologies
of erotic horror stories, under the name Linda
Lovecraft—the trademark of a chain of British sex
shops. My understanding is that Linda Lovecraft,
like Juan Valdez, was the figment of a marketing
weasel's imagination; I recall Michel saying that
he'd wondered if he was going to have to appear in
court in drag and a blond wig after the raid.*

We'll get to the raid later.

*Michel asked me to submit to the second volume;
I wrote "Smokie Joe." (The idiosyncratic spelling
"smokie" seemed right for the character. I don't
know why.) There's sex in it, but I don't want to
meet the person who gets an erotic thrill from this
one.*

*"Smokie Joe" is a deal-with-the-Devil story (set
in Joliet, Illinois, though the setting isn't crucial to
the plot). My problem with most of the genre is that
the Devil doesn't come through as really evil. My
Devil is evil; and I don't trivialize evil, especially
since I came back from Viet Nam.*

Michel sent me a copy of More Devil's Kisses
*hot off the presses. That was a good thing, because
no sooner had the book hit the newsstands than the
police impounded all copies on an obscenity
complaint and briefly locked up the in-house editor.
The charges were dropped when the publisher
(Corgi) pulped the whole edition.*

*Because the matter didn't go to trial, there's no
certainty as to which precise matters were the*

subject of the complaint. The best bet is that the
Chris Miller piece had caused the problem, but that
was a reprint from a magazine which had been sold
in Britain without objection. The only other
evidence is that when the book was brought out in
Germany, two stories were dropped; Miller's and
"Smokie Joe."

   I've not only been banned in Britain, I've been
banned in Germany, too.

✢ ✢ ✢

It was Saturday night but Tom Mullens' numbers parlor
was as still as the morgue Big Tom expected to grace
the next day. He was sweating. He pretended not to,
thinking that it would be read as fear by the three sets of
eyes trained on him across the counting table; but the
drops runneled out of his still-dark curls and down his
beefy face. He had always bragged that his two knobbly
fists made him a match for any cheap gunman. Tullio's boys
didn't work cheap, and Big Tom's throat had clogged with
the old boast when he saw the cratered offal their Uzis had
left of seven of his runners.

   Lod Mahoney couldn't have cared less about Mullens'
sweat: his eyes were blind and staring with his own fear.
Lod was a paunchy, balding fifty-five, the armpits and long
sleeves of his white shirt moist but his bow tie still a neat
dark band of respectability. He had stayed this final,
terrible week with Big Tom not out of loyalty but because
he was only the bookkeeper he appeared to be. Criminal in
his associations, not his instincts, Lod did not know how to
run.

   If Big Tom looked a boar at bay, his son Danny had the

sulky nervousness of a well-whipped dog. His eyes darted back and forth among the others in the room, excited to be where he had never before been allowed, but pettish to know that it was only because his father did not trust him loose. Danny's adolescent face was an armature for the conflicting emotions his mind threw on it. On Monday gunshots had called him to a window. Memory of what he had seen in the street now dolloped occasional terror onto his expression.

Across from Big Tom, his hands delicate but almost as dark as the scarred maple on which they lay, smiled Smokie Joe. His goatee bobbled in a humor that no one with him in the room could see. "I can find a couple hard boys," he said in a honey-golden voice, "who can get you out of this yet, Big Tom."

"What?" Mullens snarled, clenching a fist to wipe away the smirk he was sure underlay the words. But Smokie Joe's calm belied a joke. The black eyes were placid, the perfect features composed beneath the slick black hair. "Iceman," Big Tom muttered, but aloud he demanded, "All right, what's the hitch? What does anybody out of a funny farm want to get mixed up with me now?"

"Oh, well," his slim lieutenant said with the same suave ease that had taken him to the top of Mullens' organization in the brief months since he had appeared. He spread his palms upward. "They'll want a piece of the action, sure. Half of anything they generate after things get straightened around."

"That's nothing!" Big Tom said, astounded.

"Tom, they'll be Syndicate—" blurted Mahoney, a new fear stamping itself across his face.

"Do you think I care?" Mullens shouted. He stood, his eyes flicking to the blinds drawn across windows in which bullet-proof Lexan had replaced the glass. He rolled his arms as if lifting a huge weight to his chest. "I won't look at where help comes from now if it'll take out Tullio," he said. "My grandmother always said she was a witch, you know? When I saw this coming six months ago I opened her spellbook and prayed to the Devil he should help me. And I meant it, by God."

"Thought it was that simple?" smiled Smokie Joe as he, too, rose to his feet. "One thing, though," he added, leaning forward a little so that his knuckles rested on the table. "You've got a choice, Big Tom. But after you choose, there's no going back . . . Do you understand?"

"I won't go back on my word," Mullens said. He took a deep breath because Smokie Joe seemed to have grown, to bulk huge in the artificial light. "I swear on my mother's grave."

"On your soul, Tom Mullens," demanded the honeyed voice.

"I swear on my soul."

"What the Hell do you think—" Danny Mullens began, but Smokie Joe's contempt froze him at his father's side.

"Hold your tongue when men talk, boy," Joe sneered. Then, to the entranceway door that should have been guarded by slack-faced Rudy Luscher, he called, "Come on in, boys."

The door opened. Both the figures standing there were tall and dressed with the greasy casualness of backyard mechanics. One was thin and pale, the other a squat giant whose stumpy legs gave him the build of a dwarf twice magnified. "Nick, Angelo; meet Big Tom Mullens, your new employer," said Joe, his hand indicating the newcomers with the grace of an emcee bringing on the star turn.

"Where the fuck is Rudy?" Big Tom asked. "Drunk, asleep . . ." the giant shrugged.

"If your people were any good, you wouldn't need us." His voice was incongruously as sweet as a chapel bell. "You want us to take out Tullio, Mr. Mullens?"

"Goddamned right," Mullens agreed with an angry nod. "Any way you can."

"And we're part of your organization afterwards," the corpse-pale newcomer added. Neither of them had any expression in their eyes. "We get half of anything we bring in, and you give us a free hand."

"I already said so!" Big Tom blazed." Now, do you stand here all night waiting for Tullio to set up one last hit?"

Smokie Joe broke in with a laugh that chilled the room. "Oh, don't worry about Tullio. Not after tomorrow morning." He was still laughing when Nick and Angelo turned and left the room. They closed the door very gently behind them.

The black Cadillac got a final dab before Tullio's chauffeur folded the chamois and stepped back. Every Sunday morning he parked squarely in front of St. Irenaeus to let out two bodyguards and his employer: Tullio had not missed mass or made confession in thirty-seven years. By now people knew not to take Tullio's place at the curb. People knew—or they learned, like the owner of the red VW was going to learn. The chauffeur spat a gobbet that dribbled down the suitcase lashed like a dorsal fin to the Volkswagen's roof.

The small bomb behind the altar of St. Irenaeus rattled the Sunday quiet and shivered the rose window on the street side. The chauffeur's jaw trembled. He dropped the cloth and jumped in to crank the big, silent engine of the Cadillac. The church doors slammed back, the bodyguards fanning to right and left with pistols in their hands. Tullio stumbled out behind them, his thin face yellow except where spatters of the priest's blood had marked it. The trio scuttled down the steps, their eyes darting about the street like lizards' tongues. Ruthless elbows and gun butts had ripped the gangsters through shocked churchgoers, but now the doors spilled out net-veiled women and men in dark suits.

The directional mine on the Volkswagen's roof sawed them down with over a thousand steel pellets.

Tullio's chauffeur hammered at his door, wedged by the force of the explosion. The four-inch glass of the windshield was fogged with shatter marks. The church facade was a haze of powdered stone; fresh splinters raised a hundred rosettes against the dark wood of the doors.

The steps of the church were an abattoir. In the middle of it sat Enrico Tullio, screaming like one of the damned. Much of the blood splashing him now was his own.

"Seventeen fucking bodies," screamed Big Tom Mullens, "and you didn't get Tullio! He'll use an H-bomb on us now if he has to!"

"Tullio won't use anything," Nick said unconcernedly. He opened his black eyes and stared full at Mullens. The heavy gang-boss felt the impact. His stomach sucked in and he used the back of his right fist to wipe spittle from his mouth.

"Tullio lost his guts through the holes that Claymore put in him," amplified Smokie Joe from the chair he had leaned back against the wall. "Sure, he'll live. He'll set up somewhere else, maybe go back to Chi and crawl to the boys who backed him for the takeover here. But *you've* seen the last of him, Big Tom. Every time he hears your name he'll remember the blast and the blood pouring down the stone beside him. When you play for keeps, you play the man; and Tullio knows now he can't play as hard as you."

The phone rang, loud and terrible in the silent room. Danny Mullens bit blood from his lower lip and backed against the wall. Big Tom stared at the phone as if it were a cobra clamped on his leg.

"Go ahead, Big Tom," rolled Smokie Joe's smooth voice. "It can't be worse than you're already thinking, can it?"

Mullens shot him a glance full of violence. He had no one to back a play, though, beyond a terrified sixteen-year-old and a bookkeeper shock-stoned to immobility. He turned his anger on the caller instead, snarling, "Hello!" into the receiver. His red Irish face changed as he listened, moving through neutral blankness to beaming, incredulous triumph. "Sure," he boomed, "but you got one hour. If you can't get through the hospital bullshit by then, then God have mercy on you, Tullio—because I sure as Hell won't."

Whooping, Big Tom slammed down the receiver and swung over the table as if it were a vaulting horse. His arms embraced the two torpedoes. In his bubbling happiness he did not notice that they were still as coldly aloof as when he thought he had been tongue-lashing them for failure.

"Time to talk about payment, isn't it, Big Tom?" suggested Smokie Joe easily.

"Pay? Oh, Christ, yeah," Mullens said with startled generosity. "Look, what do you guys really want for what you done?"

"What you promised," said bone-pale Angelo. "Half the take my girls pull in."

"And half of what I turn from skag," Nick added. "That'll be plenty when a few kids get strung out and start pushing it to their friends."

"Huh?" Big Tom said. "Jesus, nobody could get hooked on the shit that gets out here. It's already been cut fifteen to one."

"I've got contacts in Asia," Nick grinned. "What I move'll be pure as Ivory Soap."

His words jogged a scrap of newsreel in Big Tom's memory. "You were in Viet Nam, weren't you?" he asked. "That's where you learned to use one bomb to set up the real one out in front."

"We were in Nam," Angelo agreed with a smile that would have made a shark flinch. "We were sort of instructing there."

Lod Mahoney stepped to Mullens' side and caught him by the wrist. "Tom," he pleaded, "for the love of God, you don't mean to go into heroin? There's money, there's all the money we need in numbers. You know the people you got to deal with in drugs and whores."

"Money?" sneered Smokie Joe from the other side.

"Peanuts! If you stick with that, you'll be a set-up for somebody else like Tullio who knows what can be done by a guy who's willing to. And if you welsh on us now, Big Tom, you won't have our help the next time it happens. What'll it be?"

Mullens tongued both corners of his lips, looking from Mahoney to the expectant violence of the two torpedoes. "I gave my word," he said at last. "I'll back anything you need to set up."

Their smiles dreadful reflections of one another, Nick and Angelo stepped to either side of the whimpering bookkeeper. "Smart cookie," said Smokie Joe. Nick's fist smashed Lod beneath the breastbone. As Mahoney doubled over, Angelo punched him in the back with enough power to pop a rib audibly. The plump man writhed on the floor like a crushed dog.

"He ain't dead," Nick said."He ain't even unconscious. But his spleen's busted and he'll bleed out in ten, twenty minutes."

Danny Mullens turned his face to the wall and vomited.

"Get rid of the meat, boys," Smokie Joe ordered. "Never trust somebody who gets religion," he added earnestly to Big Tom as Nick and Angelo carried Mahoney out the door. "They're worse than the ones who've been goody-goody all the time. They think they've got something to make up for, and they don't mind putting your ass in the hot seat if they decide it's the 'right' thing to do."

The forelegs of Joe's chair thumped the floor as he stood. He tapped Big Tom playfully on the shoulder. "Come on, give us a smile. We're going places." Big Tom shook himself, a great bull of a man tearing loose the jaws of an emotion that troubled him. He forced a bloodless smile. "Yeah, up."

"In a manner of speaking," said Smokie Joe.

"I can't believe this," said Big Tom Mullens, shoving the account book across the scarred table.

"You think I'm cheating you?" asked Smokie Joe without rancor. "I'm not. And Nick and Angelo will keep their part of the bargain."

"It's not that I think you're dragging me down," Mullens admitted, frowning perplexedly at the slim figure. Smokie Joe had proven as perfect an accountant as he had been an operations man before Lod's—death. "It's—well, Hell, Joe; I don't see how Nick could bring in this *much*, starting from scratch with no street organization. And Angelo running a cat-house in a college town—Christ, he could sell ice to Eskimos."

Joe laughed in a satisfied way, a father preparing to explain to his son how he has gotten the stalled lawnmower to work. "There's no secret about Nick," he said. "Sure, people push skag for money; but the best pushers are the ones who've just been turned on to it themselves. They're riding the crest, they're happy, and they want all their friends to be up there with them. God's a white powder to them, and they've got just as much enthusiasm as Paul the Apostle did."

Smokie Joe's laughter as he stood was suddenly a terrible thing. He faced the window for a rippling but unshaded view through the Lexan panels. "And these kids, they're so smart. They 'know' they can't get hooked if they only snort the stuff, it doesn't put enough in their bloodstream. Only they don't know that what we sell is 97% pure heroin—not until it's too late for them to care."

Big Tom pressed his temples. The wealth that had trickled, then poured in over the past months had not improved his appearance. His suits were tailored silk, but his belly had begun to slop over his belt and sweat quickly marked whatever he wore. Perhaps his hair had not really thinned and it was only the heightened ruddiness of his face that made it seem so. "What about Angelo, then?" he asked.

Smokie Joe turned. "You sell a customer what no one will give him," he said quietly. "I think a tour will do better than any words I could use to explain. Come on, let's take a ride down to Third Street."

"At three in the afternoon?"

Joe cocked a thin line of eyebrow. "At ten in the morning, Big Tom. Even bankers have started staying open the hours customers want—and we're selling what they can't get free, remember?"

The drive was short and without further discussion. Big Tom's headquarters were in the old industrial section, near the railroad station and the car shops. Angelo had set up in a huge frame house, a Victorian leftover on the outskirts of the business district. The previous owner had once refused to sell, Mullens remembered, preferring to hold the property against future rezoning to commercial or apartment use. Until now, Big Tom had not wondered why the old fellow had decided to sell to Angelo.

Smokie Joe swung the car through the alley entrance to the fenced courtyard behind the house. There were already three cars within: a Buick, a Chrysler, and a rusted gray Nash. "The staff doesn't park here," Joe said. "Of course the girls don't leave at all."

The door opened before either of the visitors rang. Angelo gave Smokie Joe a brief nod that could have been either recognition or obeisance. "Good you could come, Mr. Mullens," he said."I think you'll be impressed by our operation—your operation, that is."

Within, the house appeared to have been little modified from its original design. Down the rear stairs came a pair of laughing men, a huge black with boots, a loincloth, and a whip; and a middle-aged white man who used the brim of his hat to shield his face when he saw Big Tom. Mullens had already recognized Judge Firbairn.

Firbairn scurried out the door. The black nodded to Angelo, eyed Joe and Mullens with mild interest before he swaggered down the front hall and into a room to the side. Something had dripped from his quirt onto Big Tom's wrist. It seemed to be blood.

"That's Prince Rupert," Angelo volunteered. "Some of our customers prefer watching to doing. Rupert does real nice for them. And we use him for other things, too, of course."

"Why does he pad his crotch that way?" Big Tom asked, disgusted but unwilling to admit it.

"It's not padded," Smokie Joe cut in, heading his employer down the high-ceilinged hall. "He has lymphogranuloma, and the scarring in his case has led to elephantiasis."

"Jesus God!" Mullens grunted. "I don't know how you could pay a woman enough for that."

"We couldn't," agreed Angelo with a smile. He unlocked the first doorway to the left. "Not money, at least. All the girls are strung out. So long as they get their four jolts a day, they don't care—they don't even *know*—who does what to them."

He threw open the door. Big Tom gagged as he took in the bed, the extensive props, and the mewling woman who lay in the midst of them. He pulled the door closed himself. "She's only eighteen!" he said.

Angelo spread his palms. "They age quicker than you'd think," he replied. "Then we got to sell them south or to Asia."

"They come to us, Big Tom," said Smokie Joe. His eyes were as intense as diamond needles. "Remember that. Everyone of them asks, uses the words, for everything that's done to her. If they change their minds later, that's too bad."

Mullens shook nausea from his mind. "How in Hell are you running this? No fix on earth would cover up a deal like—" He waved his hands to save words he did not want to speak.

"Think Judge Firbairn would sign a search warrant for this place?" Smokie Joe gibed.

"There's other judges in the district. They haven't all been here."

"You'd be surprised," said Angelo. "And even some who don't . . ."

His voice trailed off but Smokie Joe had already opened the door of a converted broom closet and unlocked a drawer of the filing cabinet within. "Suppose you were about to launch a push against—well, you'd call them 'the forces of crime and decay' when you held your press conferences, I suppose. Then your daughter got drunk enough to take a dare from some girlfriends—girls she'd grown up with, though maybe if you'd paid more attention you wouldn't have cared for some of the company they'd been keeping recently. Took a dare and got in a little deeper than she expected.

"So the next morning," Smokie Joe continued, snaking out a packet of photographs, "a messenger brings you a roll of Super-8 movie film. What do you do then, Mayor Lawrence?"

Big Tom Mullens riffed through the photographs. "Jesus Christ, you *did* get Betty Jane Lawrence! Jesus Christ! She goes to school with my son, he's *dated* her!"

"Still think Prince Rupert wears padding?" Angelo asked.

"That's—God, I want to puke," Big Tom groaned, handing the stills back to his smiling lieutenant. "His cock, it looks like it's *rotting.*"

"Well, LGV is an incurable disease, you know," Smokie Joe agreed. "Not so very bad for a while, if you have the personality Prince Rupert does. And if you have an employer who gives you some fringe benefits.

"Want to see more?" he asked, waving at the scores of file folders. When Big Tom shook his head sickly, Joe slammed the drawer and continued, "Between payoffs and this kind of pressure, Angelo here isn't in any danger. Nick's operation is a little different, though, since the heat on him is mostly state and we don't have the same kind of locks on that."

"What's the matter?" Big Tom asked, turning toward

the outside door as if it were the gate of his prison. "Couldn't you get a picture of the whole Drug Enforcement Division having a circle jerk?"

"Oh, anything is possible," Smokie Joe said agreeably, following the big racketeer down the hall. "We'll have better luck if we give the state boys something to go after besides us, though. Shall Nick arrange a little diversion for them, Big Tom?"

"Arrange whatever you want," Mullens said. "I'm not sure I give a goddamn about anything. Except that I don't want to see you any more today, and I don't want to see Angelo *ever.*"

He slammed the door behind him, within inches of Smokie Joe's smile. From the front of the house came a scream, then another and another in rhythmic pulses. The smile grew broader.

Big Tom Mullens slapped folded newspaper down in front of Smokie Joe who waited for him with a stack of account books. "I'm getting goddam sick and tired of people playing goddamn games with me," he snarled. "I get a call from Shiloh Academy saying Danny hasn't showed up for classes in a month and a half. I get here and Nick hands me this paper, asking how I like the job he did for me. *What* job?"

Joe calmly unfolded the paper. "It's not unusual for boys your son's age to drop out of school, you know," he said.

"I'm not spending eight fucking grand a year for that kid to drop out!" Big Tom said. "He's getting chances I never had to really make it by going straight, mixing with all the kids whose folks had money without having to scramble for it. If Danny thinks he's going to throw that away, I'll blow his fucking head off!"

"The money doesn't matter, Big Tom," said Smokie Joe. "You've got more money now than you could have dreamed of a year ago." He smoothed the front page and rotated it back to Mullens. "Nick probably means the headline," he said.

Big Tom mimed the words with his lips, then read aloud, " 'LSD Poisons Bloomington Reservoir; Hippie Terror-Plot Slays Scores; City Paralyzed.' What the Hell?"

"It's the diversion you told us to make," Smokie Joe explained with a smile. "Acid goes through the treatment plant without being filtered out. We backed it up with a letter to the *Daily News* saying that unless marijuana was legalized and the army was disbanded in three days, we'd do the same to every other city in the country. So now the drug boys—and just about everybody else—are not only in Bloomington and out of our hair, they've just about dropped hard drugs statewide to hassle hippies about pot. Slick, isn't it?"

Big Tom's mouth was open but no sounds were coming from it. His palms were flat on the table to support his weight, but his forearms were trembling.

The door opened. Big Tom spun around. "Danny!" he cried. Then, "Hey, what in Hell happened to you?"

The boy wore a greasy sport coat and a pair of coordinated slacks from which most of the right cuff had been torn. While his father had gone to flesh in the past year, Danny was now almost as cadaverous as Angelo. He looked down at himself in mild surprise. "Hadn't paid much attention to how I look," he said. "Not since I went to the doctor." His hand clenched a sheet of slick paper which he thrust at his father. "Does this mean anything to you?" he demanded.

Big Tom scowled at the sheet, a page torn from a medical text. "I can't even read this crap," he said. "No, it don't mean anything."

"Then maybe this does." The tone would have snapped Big Tom's head around even if the movement of Danny's hand from beneath his coat had not. Smokie Joe was watching the boy with an expression of bored resignation, that remained unchanged at the sight of a .45 automatic wavering in the thin fist.

"The men have business to take care of, boy," Smokie Joe drawled. His fingers drummed absently among the account books. "Why don't you take your little play toy out and close the door behind you?"

"You *bastard,*" the boy said, swinging the pistol full on the slim, seated figure. "You're the real cause, aren't you? I ought to use this on you."

"Sure, kid," Smokie Joe agreed, tilting his chair back a little, "but you don't have the guts. You probably don't even have the guts to use it on yourself."

"Don't I?" Danny asked. He looked at the baffled rage in his father's eyes, then back to Smokie Joe's cold scorn. The pistol seemed to socket itself in his right ear of its own volition.

"Wait, Danny!" Big Tom cried. He threw his hands out as the gun blasted. The windows shuddered. Danny's eyeballs bulged and the ruin of his head squished sideways with the shot before his body slumped to the floor.

Big Tom more stumbled than knelt beside his son. Smokie Joe scooped up the torn page from where it had fallen. "Sure," he said, "he probably tried curing it himself with what his roommate had leftover from a dose of clap last year. When the doctor told him what he had and what his chances were of getting rid of it now, Danny wouldn't want to believe him—who would?—and picked up a book to check it out. '*Lymphogranuloma venereum* is a disease of viral origin, usually transmitted by sexual intercourse.' Well, the only important thing about LGV is that it's like freckles—it won't kill you, but you'll carry it till you die."

Mullens was squeezing his son's flaccid hands. "Normally just blacks get it," Smokie Joe went on. He squatted beside the wax-faced racketeer. "That isn't . . . shall we say, a law of God? Give her a chance and a white girl can catch it. And given a chance, she can pass it on to . . . ." Joe's hand reached past Mullens to unhook Danny's belt. "Funny thing—you wouldn't have expected Betty Jane to have been interested in a man for a *long* time after Prince Rupert was done with her. Maybe she was too stoned to care, or maybe Danny-boy used a pretty— direct—approach. There's no real harm done by screwing a girl, is there?" He jerked down Danny's slacks.

The boy wore no underpants. His penis was distorted by three knotted sores slimed with yellow pus.

Big Tom choked and staggered upright. His right hand had wrapped itself around the butt of the automatic. Smokie Joe raised an eyebrow at it. "That's a mistake, Big Tom. Don't you hear that siren? When the police arrive, they're going to think you shot your own son. Better let me take care of it—just tell me to and I'll fix it so you won't be bothered. You don't care *how* I take care of it, do you?" He stretched out his hand toward the pistol.

"I'll see you in Hell first!" Big Tom grated.

"Sure, Big Tom," said Smokie Joe. "If that's how you want it."

Big Tom crashed out the six shots still in the pistol's magazine. Amid the muzzle blasts rolled the peals of Smokie Joe's Satanic laughter.

AWAKENING
⊰⊱

Many of the SF writers of the 1930s and '40s were fascinated by Charles Fort's collections of unexplained phenomena. My friend Manly Wade Wellman told me that F. Orlin Tremaine, the editor of Astounding *from 1933 till John W. Campbell took over at the end of 1938, had bought the rights to Fort's collection* Lo! *to mine for story ideas. I'm not sure that's true, but Tremaine certainly did serialize the book. I didn't see a pulp magazine until one of my high school teachers loaned me a couple issues of* Weird Tales, *but as a teenager I read lots of SF from the period in anthologies.*

Fort's technique was to go through scientific journals and note oddities which he then retailed in four volumes beginning with The Book of the Damned. *He threw out a number of speculations on what caused the data he reported: "I think we're property," or "Perhaps somebody is collecting Ambroses," which are familiar even to people who don't have the faintest notion of where the phrases come from. Personally, I'm convinced that Fort was joking—that is, that he believed the items were as true as anything else you'd find reported in, say,* Nature, *but that he understood the causes of the phenomena he reported were unknowable on the available data.*

Then again, maybe he was a humorless wacko who believed in wild conspiracies. Goodness knows, a lot of the people who've followed in his footsteps fit that category.

SF stories led me to Charles Fort, but then I read him for his own sake. As for what I myself believe: I believe that the world is a very strange place, certainly stranger than I can explain.

I haven't used much Fortean material in my fiction because I find attempting to explain the phenomena leads to very silly results. This is as true of fiction like Donald Wandrei's "Something from Above" as it is of Philip Klass' "scientific" explanations of all UFOs as plasma effects (a notion that plasma physicists find ludicrous). Once in a while I tried, though. "Awakening" is an example.

I'm not sure that I'd bother to include this little mood piece in Balefires *were it not for one thing: this is the only story I sold while I was in Viet Nam. I wrote it in longhand and typed up a second draft on the orderly room typewriter one Sunday morning in Di An. While I sat typing the story, there was a bang behind me. I looked back over my shoulder and watched the ammo dump destroy itself in a series of increasingly loud explosions. Never a dull moment . . . .*

I sent my typescript to my wife Jo, at home in Chapel Hill. She retyped it and mailed it to Mr. August Derleth, the proprietor of Arkham House, who'd bought two previous stories from me. He took "Awakening" for $25. That's one of the few good things that happened to me in Southeast Asia.

✣ ✣ ✣

They remained some time in silence in the shadowed parlor, alternately sipping their tea and staring idly at the dim trees to be seen beyond the gauze curtains. At last Mab cleared her throat, a little coughing sound. The man looked up. "Mab?"

"Frank, I think it's time we try. We'll never see Missy's equal, you know."

Frank set down his cup and saucer on the old walnut table. He ran his left hand through the mane of iron-gray hair he cultivated, almost all that was left of the splendid man he had looked in his youth. "I suppose you're right," he finally admitted. "My . . . aspirations aren't what they were, I suppose. And Mab, I'm very much afraid the girl isn't ready yet. She still doesn't think of herself as one of us."

"Missy has had a year in this house, Frank."

"She had twelve in the alley and the orphanage, learning that witches are hags that live in dark corners, learning to laugh when one is pushed into the oven. Her first reaction . . . well, Missy isn't a subtle child."

Mab, matronly in a print of pastel roses, clucked disapproval. "Nor is she stupid. The time Missy spent here was more than enough for her to realize what she is, and what we are. It's our duty as her elders to keep her from wasting herself."

Frank bit absently on the setting of his ring. "She can't be forced—no, I don't mean physical force, of course not. But we can't make her believe what she doesn't want to believe; what she's been conditioned not to believe. It won't help even to prove to her that she has the Power. That would only mean to her that she herself is evil, and she'd hate you for it. At best she'd not join us; at worst, with her Power . . ."

Mab smiled. "Now Frank, it's the girl's strength that worries you. But it's time and past time that I stepped down. I was never a very good Maid—now I know what you want to say, I was very well trained. You taught me everything that could be taught; you were wonderfully patient. But I never had the Power; that can't be learned."

"Yet she can't even read Latin," said Frank, sadly shaking his head.

"No," agreed Mab in a firm tone, "and perhaps she never will. Our Missy isn't a scholar. But she has an understanding of things that you and I can hardly imagine."

She reached over to the table and rang a sharp ping from the bell.

"Madam?"

The girl in the doorway wore a maid's uniform with a cap and apron. Dark hair and large eyes accented her triangular face.

"Madam?" she repeated.

"Missy, Mr. Birney and I—"

"Oh, Mab," cut in Frank, lifting his corpulence from the overstuffed chair, "perhaps I'll leave you and Missy to discuss matters by yourselves."

"Frank, you'll wait, won't you?"

"In the hallway." Frank nodded to the two women and closed the hall door behind him.

"Well, Missy," Mab continued, "I—but do sit down, Dearest; this isn't business."

She waved to the seat Frank had vacated, but the girl took a slat-back chair farther from her mistress.

"You've been with me some time now, and you have gotten to know myself and the group of friends that meet here. We'd like you to join us tonight."

The girl fluttered her hands. "Ma'am, that wouldn't be right, not me. I'm not your sort."

"But you are our sort," Mab insisted calmly. "The mirror in your room, for instance—"

Panic flashed across Missy's face and Mab quickly added, "Oh, don't worry, Dearest, that's why we put it there. It was an old glass and rather difficult to find, but we knew it was meant for you."

"I'll not do wrong things," the girl insisted sullenly.

There was a light squalling outside the kitchen door, a scratch of claws and a dark-tipped Siamese cat slipped into the parlor. It curled silently under the girl's chair but kept its eyes on Mab.

"We wouldn't have you do wrong," Mab continued with a toss of her gray hair, "but everything proves that it's right for you to join us. Even the way animals treat you—it isn't only Kaimah, is it, Dearest?"

The girl said nothing, only squirmed a little on her seat.

"They aren't like that with me," Mab said, "but I don't really have the Power. But you do, Missy. To an amazing degree."

"No, Ma'am," Missy whispered. "I haven't nothing. I shan't have it."

Mab appeared not to have heard. "Frank was disappointed when you ignored the books we left about, but I understand. Perhaps you'll want them after you've been with us awhile."

"Ma'am, Ma'am," breathed the girl, twisting her apron between narrow hands, "I don't want to be with you, I want to go . . ."

"Because we're witches?" Mab questioned gently. "There's nothing wrong in being a witch, Darling."

"I don't want to be a witch," cried Missy, slipping from her chair and moving behind it as if the wooden back were a shield. The cat retreated between her legs, not hissing, but stiff-legged and its backbone edged with a high comb of fur.

"But Dearest," pressed Mab inexorably, "you're already a witch—"

"Oh, no!"

"—the most powerful witch I have ever met."

"NO!" the girl screamed, and a gabbling cry burst from the older woman as the first blast of searing heat struck her. Mab half-rose from her chair, cocooned in white flame that melted flesh and shrank her very bones in its hissing roar.

"Mab! Mab!" Frank shouted, bursting into the room.

There was no answer. The room was empty save for a shrunken mummy fallen back on the scorched upholstery of the chair. That, and the thick layer of soot that covered everything.

The open door to the kitchen quivered in the draft.

DENKIRCH

This is where I started. Everybody has to start somewhere, but I've got to admit that a lot of writers have done so more auspiciously.

In 1961 I borrowed a few issues of Weird Tales from my high school teacher. One had a box ad for Skull-Face and Others by Robert E. Howard, who'd written the Conan stories. I'd read Conan the Conqueror as half of an Ace Double and loved it. Even though the ad was over ten years old, I took a chance and wrote the publisher, Arkham House, to see if the book was still available.

Mr. August Derleth wrote back, saying Skull-Face was out of print but enclosed a catalog of available titles. I began buying Arkham House books, getting an introduction to pulp fantasy and horror as Mr. Derleth selected it. (Incidentally, a few years later he sold me a copy of Skull-Face, which wasn't quite as out of print to a good customer as it had been to a stranger.)

In the summer of 1965 my fiancée Jo (since 1967 my wife Jo) and I drove from Dubuque to Sauk City *to see Arkham House. We met Mr. Derleth and his children, saw Arkham House Publishers (which he was running out of his house), and bought books.*

One of those books had just come in: The Inhabitant of the Lake, *a collection of horror stories by a young Briton, J. Ramsey Campbell. There was a flap photo of the author. Young was right— Ramsey looked no more than fifteen and in fact was only eighteen. He'd sold Mr. Derleth his first story two years earlier for an Arkham House anthology.*

I was nineteen. The teacher who'd loaned me the Weird Tales, *Mr. Eugene Olson, had sold fiction himself; indeed, the year after I graduated, he became a full-time writer under what's now his legal name, Brad Steiger. Because of Mr. Olson I knew it was possible to write professionally, and I'd told myself for a number of years that when I got old enough I was going to sell a story.*

"Old enough" was obviously sixteen. I was well past that already.

I went home (with the pile of books I'd bought) and sent Mr. Derleth a letter asking whether he might be willing to buy a story if I wrote one good enough to publish. He grudgingly said yes.

I wrote what I thought was a story and sent it to him. It was 1,600 words long and titled "Post Mortem." (I was a Latin major and thought a Latin pun was a great idea for a title. Really.) Mr. Derleth sent the story back with the note that it was a good outline, now I should expand it into a story; and by the way, the title was terrible. I went busily to work and emerged with a piece about 4,000 words long and titled (as I best I can remember) "The Stars Are Hell."

Mr. Derleth sent it back again, saying that I was close. I just needed to take out the purple passages. I didn't know what a purple passage was, but I did my best. Since I was modeling the writing style on that of Mr. Derleth's own worst copies of bad H.P. Lovecraft prose, there was a lot of florid writing in the story. I sent it off again.

This time I got back a check for $35 and a note from Mr. Derleth saying that the story still wasn't right. He'd edit it himself; I should compare the published version with my carbon (this was in the days before copy machines were everywhere) to learn how not to write a story the next time.

I hadn't even known I was supposed to keep a carbon.

I don't think the edit was very extensive, but Mr. Derleth changed the title to the name of the central character. I don't like that style of title (which Mr. Derleth used frequently in his own work), but it was better than any of mine.

I recently reread "Denkirch" for the first time in forty years and realized it was a good pastiche of minor Weird Tales stories from about 1938. That's a positive comment on my craftsmanship, but it was a very silly thing to do in 1966.

So that was my first sale. You could call it a remarkable success story: I sold the first story I submitted to the first editor I sent it to. But—

I've heard of would-be writers being crushed by rejection letters. I was so devastated by my first acceptance that it was six months before I even tried to write another story.

✢ ✢ ✢

N ow I sleep only by day or when the sky is cloudy, and when the stars gleam bright in the heavens I walk little back streets, avoiding other people, for I do not care to be reminded of my humanity and my inevitable fate. My acquaintances think me odd, but they would not understand if I told them that on clear nights the stars speak to me, and that if I did not walk I would go mad. So I walk the lonely streets, and the echoing cadence of my stride helps to muffle the rhythmic whispers, but still my mind is forced back to Denkirch, who proved Man's unique place in the universe.

I met Denkirch at college when, at the end of our first semester, each of our roommates requested transfers and we found ourselves shifted together. Although he was a physics and electronics engineering major, and I was prelaw in history, we found we had a surprising amount in common. Our general outlooks were very similar, both of us vaunting pure knowledge and refusing to accept anything sacred or profane, as being beyond the grasp of human intelligence.

I was as bored by Denkirch's majors as he was contemptuous (albeit silently) of mine, but I had a tremendous respect for the work he was doing. Not only did he take staggering course loads by special permission so that he could complete both majors in four years, but he taught himself a vast assortment of foreign languages as well. These included Oriental and Oceanic dialects in addition to the normal European and classical languages, there were a few tongues of which I had never heard before. Once in particular I remember seeing an aged, oddly unpleasant-looking book bound in faded snakeskin lying on Denkirch's desk. When I asked him what it was, he had answered, "A treatise on certain antiquities, in R'lyehan."

I am a reasonably intelligent man, but Denkirch was beyond a doubt one of the most brilliant men of this or any age. He had a superb, balanced intellect—far less common than genius—and it was this that gave him the drive and the ability to turn our idle discussions into something very tangible.

Mostly we argued about the place of the individual man in the Universe, both from interest and because it was equally outside our dissimilar majors. We were both romantics, believing the universe was purposeful, but I argued that each man was only a steppingstone to that purpose, while Denkirch insisted that the individual was immortal. I based my argument on the extreme rarity of even possible spiritual manifestations and Denkirch took the other tack, pointing out the exceptions for which no other explanation was satisfactory. It was an inexhaustible topic since neither of us had concrete proof, but the question caught Denkirch's fancy and even in college he began to go deeper into the subject than I could follow.

After graduation I entered a Chicago law firm while Denkirch had no trouble getting an excellent teaching position at Cal Tech. We kept in touch, and in the mounting excitement of my friend's letters I saw that the material he was uncovering on his fancy was rapidly turning it into an obsession. After a few years he left Cal Tech for MIT, simply because it would bring him nearer to the great eastern libraries he wanted to consult and, when he stopped mentioning his project a little later, I realized that it was a result of success, not failure. He was on the brink of a great discovery but feared, like all scholars, to blurt out his suspicions until he was absolutely sure. Then one day he resigned his teaching post and moved to southern Illinois, and even without his letter I would have known that he was searching for privacy to put his theories into practice.

For six months I heard no more from Denkirch. Then a short letter came, asking me to join him and giving directions on how to reach him. I noticed that he was not actually living in any town but was several miles outside the nearest one, a tiny place called Merriam, of only three hundred souls.

It was foolish for me to leave then. I was a junior partner with great things ahead of me if I were successful in a major case to be tried within the month, but despite this I had no thought of refusal. Denkirch was my friend and to us who have few that is no little thing, but even more convincing was the sense of overwhelming importance which clung to even that prosaic letter. It was not just that I knew the answer to a great philosophical question might be close at hand, it was more; and if I had known how much more, I would have hidden myself in a place so remote that I never again would have heard of Denkirch or he of me.

In the late afternoon of the next day I reached Merriam, which was just a straggle of houses on the highway, and then turned left on to a narrow, rutted gravel road marked by a big country-type mailbox with "Samuel Denkirch" stenciled on it. On the right side of the lane the ground was cut away in a high bank to a level above the top of the car and crowned with a wobbling barbed wire fence silhouetted against the low sun. The pasture to the left looked rocky and unpromising, an occasional clump of wild sumac standing out among the tall thistles and rank grass as a deep red blotch in the waning light and giving a frightful, blood-spattered appearance to an otherwise merely ugly landscape. The road was in as uncared-for a condition as the pasture and fences but had obviously been used much more recently. Heavy trucks seemed to have driven over it shortly after a rain, and the resultant ruts were nearly six inches deep except in places where a slab of rock underlay the sprinkling of gravel and jarred my teeth, even though I was proceeding in second gear.

Due to my slow progress the road seemed much longer than it probably was, and I began to wonder whether I had made the correct turn after all, despite the mailbox. It would have been quite impractical to try to turn around since the road itself was far too narrow and was hemmed in by the high bank and, on the left, a drainage ditch, but the feeling of portentousness that had been with me ever since I had received Denkirch's invitation was growing steadily and beginning to take on a distinctly sinister cast. The car's jouncings and scrapings were an almost welcome diversion from the formless depression that was settling over my mind, a depression not wholly to be explained by my worry that I had taken the wrong turn or even by the funereal scenery. However, just as I had decided to return to the highway even if I had to back out to avoid being lost at night amid a maze of unfamiliar country roads, I came to the top of a gently rising hill and saw what had to be Denkirch's house only a half-mile beyond.

That it had to be my friend's house was quite clear from the forest of antennas sprouting from and around it. The area around the house had probably been thickly wooded before Denkirch had bought the farm; now almost a score of thick stumps ringed the worn but otherwise normal looking two-story house, the boles having been dragged into a great pile in a nearby field where, presumably, they could no longer interfere with the antennas which had usurped the grounds. Indeed, the antennas were all that kept the house from seeming as deserted as the pastures around it. The roof of the house sagged and the white paint had cracked and blistered in those places in which it had not peeled off completely. The barn and sheds had been pulled down or had simply collapsed by themselves, and the grass on the lawn was high and weed-choked.

The antennas, seeming to have a life of their own, presided over this slowly decaying ruin: a horizontal grid on the roof, a ten-foot dish just west of the house, and at least a score of poles and beams and coils mounted on stumps, chimney, roof, and sidewalls—some static and some in constant jerky motion, spinning or nodding like crows on a fence. But the lowering ruler of the scene was a great, copper-mesh cone whose wide mouth opened to the sky more than twenty feet above the ground. As I watched, it caught a last ray from the setting sun and, its color deepened like that of the sumac, loomed over the house like a monster cobra. For a moment I felt a twinge of inexplicable panic which, although it quickly passed, still further heightened my feeling of black foreboding.

I stopped in front of the house where, in fact, the road ended. It was a warm August evening, just at that time when normally everything seems to be at its most serene; but tonight there was a sinister difference. Perhaps it was the low hum of the antenna rotors, so out of place among the cicadas and lonely bird calls. Even the stars seemed evil, although they were unusually splendid against the dark blue evening sky. They glared back as I glanced at them, and I quickly looked down again to see Denkirch just opening the screen door of the porch.

"I was afraid you'd broken down on this miserable road," he said as we shook hands, and I too had been worried by the thought. But somehow the weeds and rocks were at least natural, while the antennas, especially the cone, had a very strange aura about them that increased my nervousness even more.

Denkirch apologized for the appearance of the house and the unburnt pile of trees. "I've been meaning to get someone in to really clean up the place, but I just haven't gotten around to it," he said. "Besides, I have trouble getting any kind of help out here. I even have to pick up my own groceries in Merriam."

"Is the place supposed to be haunted?" I asked, gazing through the screen at the dark-muffled ruins of the farmyard.

"No, nothing like that. The farm just ran down as its last owner grew older, and by the time he died the buildings were even more worthless than the land, which never had been good. No," he repeated, "the problem is me and my gear. The townsfolk seem to be afraid of it. I suppose some ignorant fool has been spreading the story that I have everything here from an atomic pile to a death ray. But let's not stand here talking—come in and see the shop."

I watched Denkirch himself with as much interest as I did the tremendous mass of instrumentation and printed material which he showed me. He had changed a great deal since I had last seen him. He had been thin and active; now he was cadaverous and jumpy. Worse and yet more subtle was the change in his attitude toward his project, his deep interest having become a burning fanaticism that would carry through at any cost. All these things could be easily explained as normal results of overwork which would pass with the completion of the experiment, but deep within me I knew that Denkirch, too, felt the shadowy terror that slowly approached.

The conversion of the ramshackle farm into a modern experimental station must have been a tremendous job in itself. More fascinating to me than the instruments was the room filled with thousands of books, mostly technical handbooks and circuit diagrams, but a surprising number of very ancient manuscripts or facsimiles of manuscripts in languages I could not identify, much less read. These were the pre-scientific works dealing with spiritual escape from the temporal shell which Denkirch had considered most accurate and informative.

"There's a tendency among moderns who use the ancient texts at all," he said, "to abide by them strictly, muttering the precise gibberish and using all manner of abominations in the ritual, usually something pertaining to a corpse. Now this is both foolish, since the true spells were a form of self-hypnosis, most unlikely to work identically on two different people, and dangerous as well—or at least liable to be disconcerting—because it just might work. These works tell of a great number of seers who went into trances but instead of awakening with wonderful stories of far-distant places, just didn't awaken at all. Still, their mishaps gave me the clue I needed and now I can proceed with electronic help where a direct attempt was so often final."

The other rooms were filled with equipment which, although impressive to me, did not hold the marvels that it doubtless would have had for another engineer. Quite a lot of the instrumentation was search radar, fairly basic and only unusual in its almost completely automatic functioning. It not only ran itself but could even check itself in case of failure, making an operator necessary only to replace the faulty parts. Denkirch had found that iron tended to distort some of his instruments, and the radar was to give warning if a plane were close overhead (the house was not far from the Chicago-St. Louis air route) so that he would not attempt to return then. At the time I did not understand just what Denkirch meant, but, as with other things, I soon learned.

Even with a similar high degree of automation, the remaining instruments—everything from a radio-telescope to devices for registering the precise rotational speed of the Earth at any given instant—seemed to be more than one man could reasonably handle, and I asked Denkirch why he did not have at least a lab assistant.

"I did," he said with a frown, "two of them, as a matter of fact. They had been students of mine at MIT and should have been perfect for the job, but I guess neither one of them liked the country. Two weeks after they had helped me to set up here they said that they couldn't take the atmosphere any longer and left." Then he shivered slightly, and when he spoke again his eyes shone with something of the fear that he must have been feeling for the last six months, perhaps even longer. "You know, Johnnie," he said, "I can't really blame them. I suppose it's the isolation of this godforsaken place. Do you feel it too?"

I admitted I did feel somewhat uneasy, but as I spoke the blackness I had pushed to the back of my mind flooded over me again, an inky coldness of fear that was all the worse for being unreasonable. How even Denkirch's rigid will had kept him from insanity for all the time he must have been subjected to the same thing, I do not know.

Finally, having toured the whole of the upper floors, Denkirch led me down a steep flight of steps to what had been the cellar and was now, he said, the heart of his project. At the bottom he flipped a bank of light switches and I saw that a large diesel generator stood near the stairs, while the rest of the cellar was separated by a recent-looking partition with a curtained doorway towards which Denkirch motioned me. When I entered, shoving aside the curtains, a terribly familiar sheen of copper met me. Another cone, a duplicate of the one outside, hung from its apex within.

Taking a closer look as Denkirch entered behind me, I saw the considerable amount of labor that had been expended to mount the great antenna. Both upper floors had been pierced on account of its height and the well closed in, explaining why I had seen no indication of it upstairs. The delicate copper cobwebbing was streaked with the shadows of the aluminum framework by which it was supported, and at the point at which it was attached some twenty feet above my head a large crystal glittered in the fluorescent light. It was truly awe-inspiring, yet still a sense of active malignity hung over it.

Another disquieting object intruded on my awareness when I glanced down from the cone, for directly beneath it and completely covered by its wide opening was a normal single bed and mattress, but one equipped with wide canvas straps and with its legs bolted to the floor. On three sides of the bed and underneath it were instrument racks, and on one of them rested a large helmet to which were attached dozens of leads.

Denkirch then gave me my first real knowledge of what he intended to do and how he would accomplish it as he explained the various pieces of apparatus. He began by plugging a set of earphones into the panel at the head of the bed and telling me to put them on. As I did so, he seated himself at an instrument console along one wall and set several switches on it. The lights dimmed slightly as the surrounding machinery began to hum, and then a faint crackling began to come through the earphones. After a minute or so individual words stood out from the buzz in the background, and then a sudden, constant stream of names and occupations poured out, one after another without pause or stop. Some were in languages that I knew and some I could not even guess at, but all were delivered in the same flat, expressionless monotone of a congregation

reading a unison prayer. "Maria Varrones, dependiente . . .
Daniel Mulvihill, solicitor . . . Hauptmann Gerhard Kleppe,
Leibstandarte Adolph Hitler . . ."

"What is this?" I gasped as I took off the earphones.
"They sound like talking corpses."

"The minds of the dead," Denkirch corrected me, "not
their bodies. And they're not even dead in the usual sense,
of course. I always told you that the human mind was too
wonderful an instrument to be thrown away after one
using, Johnnie. There's my proof, out among the stars."

Then he went on to tell me the whole story, the story
of the masterpiece of the most talented man of our
generation. First he read everything he could on earlier
attempts to penetrate the afterlife; the Elijahs and Bridey
Murphies, the Cagliostros and Buddhas, and many
explorers more ancient and terrible than they, hinted at on
little-known parchments and inscriptions which must in
themselves have raised a dark shadow over Denkirch's
mind. This prodigious labor was followed by yet a greater
one, the correlation of this data and the elimination of the
less promising areas of endeavor.

In the end Denkirch had come to startling yet well-
buttressed conclusions regarding human minds and bodies.
As he had believed from the start, the mind did have an
eternal existence apart from that of any one body, but it
became clear that at no time could the mind be totally free;
in other words, if it left one body it would be forced to
instantly enter another.

I did not then understand why my palms began to
sweat at those words; now it is only too clear what my

subconscious mind realized and my conscious did not, but I merely wiped my hands on my thighs as I listened.

The obvious inference to be drawn from the situation Denkirch had just explained was that minds were transferred from the dead to the newborn—reincarnation or transmigration of souls. This was seductively simple but could not be applied to the human race alone since births and deaths would almost never balance precisely. An excess of minds might possibly be accommodated by housing two or more in one body, and this was the probable explanation of the trance visions of some of the greater wizards. They had simply suppressed the original mind of another body and looked through its eyes for a time, and the body's normal owner shortly drove the intruder back. Still, the large surplus of births over deaths meant that at least some minds had to be created afresh with their bodies, and the great rarity of provable cases of reincarnation—in human bodies, at least—indicated that this was true in all but a handful of cases. Where then did the minds of most dead men go? To the stars, Denkirch decided, and set about to prove it.

His first attempts were based on radio-telescopes and were complete failures. Then he began to work from the opposite end, modifying an encephalograph, and with this relatively crude instrument he caught the first hints of those terrible whispers from the stars, and that night he held all the knowledge of this primal mystery that he later only reinforced. All, that is, but its underlying meaning.

Later improvements had followed, far simpler than that final result that hung above the bed on which I sat, but just as effective for listening to the minds of our ancestors.

Denkirch had earlier noted that different historical periods were grouped in recognizable parts of the sky, although there was considerable overlapping. Meaningful names were rare, of course, but many occupations gave keys to determine their dating. For instance, an auto mechanic had to be fairly recent, and a private of the Iron Brigade was just as useful as Abraham Lincoln. In general the most recent names were clustered on or in the direction of Deneb in Orion, while those of the period around World War I could be expected to be heard when the antenna was directed toward the Pleiades, and so on. It seemed probable that with the death of each occupied body, the human mind marched one more step in a slow, majestic procession around the universe.

This knowledge, this proof of his contentions, was soon not enough for Denkirch. He had a list of names, but what he now wanted was first-hand knowledge of the universe.

I can still remember how Denkirch looked that night as he talked, unconsciously pacing the room and waving his arms, the glitter in his eyes far brighter than that the soft fluorescents could give them. "Johnnie, you used to tell me that death would be oblivion. Now I can prove to you that it's not oblivion, it's the universe in all its wonder and glory! Think of it, Johnnie—thundering nitrogen cataracts under a pale green sun. Night in the dazzling center of a globular cluster! What have you ever wanted to see? You will—just wait for it. And now with this"—he waved toward the great cone waiting silently above me—"we won't even have to wait."

With that last sentence—his declaration of triumph— my spirits, which had been caught up despite themselves by his wild enthusiasm, sagged again into blind despair. I knew there was something wrong. Not in the theories, for they had been confirmed by the instruments; not in the instruments, for Denkirch was far too logical even in his fanaticism to accept his results without duplicating them in numerous cross-checks; still, somewhere. . . .

"Do you mean the cones are matter transmitters?" I asked as the full significance of Denkirch's words sank in.

"Well, not transmitters, at least," he answered, "and I only designed them to receive minds, but I dare say they'd work quite well for matter, too, if it could somehow be sent to them. Basically, though, they're designed to do a job similar to that of my earlier passive receivers and they will do everything the earlier ones would, as you heard. They go just one step farther. Not throwing a body across the universe, but pulling a mind back, and that's all that's necessary."

As Denkirch went on to explain his masterpiece I felt the same awe at its magnitude of conception as I had when he recounted the steps leading up to it, but under the soft cushion of marvel lay the same rending claws of fear, and my stomach knotted as I listened.

The difference between the cones and their forerunners lay in their ability to actively snatch a mind back from wherever it had gone when it left its original body. Lack of this feature, Denkirch thought, had prematurely exiled many ancient mystics to far worlds. If they, by sheer force of will, directed their spirits to another already occupied body, they would quickly be forced back into their own again. If instead they freed their minds without giving them any basic direction, as was probably the more common occurrence, they would be pulled irresistibly to Deneb just as though their bodies had died, unable to return without the same spiritual discipline by means of which they had come and which the alien environment might well make impossible until after their terran bodies had slipped into a mindless death.

The cones, keyed to Denkirch's mind when it was released from his body (also an electronic process, since Denkirch was a scientist rather than a mystic), would pull it back from Deneb when they were activated. Between the time his mind was severed from his brain by what he described as an interference field and the time I turned on the cones, Denkirch would have as much freedom on some strange planet as his newborn body would give him; freedom to run or burrow or fly or perhaps just to sit and absorb the newness of his surroundings.

At this point he stopped pacing and returned to the control console, motioning me to join him. Most of its eight-foot length was covered with dials, but to one end a helmet much like the one on the bed was connected. There were only two other things built into the three feet of the console nearest the helmet, a large three-position switch and a small red indicator light similar to the generator lights of most new cars.

"You'll wear this helmet," Denkirch said. "With it on you'll be in perfect contact with all my senses as long as the switch is in the second position. That is, as long as I'm on Deneb everything I experience in any way will be as clear to you as if it were you who were undergoing it. The only difference is that you won't be able to control the new body, as I will. In ten minutes or so—you'll be able to use your own eyes when they're open, though things may look like a double exposure—make sure the red light isn't on and pull the switch to the third position to turn on the cones. The light is connected to the radar, and if it's on, a plane is nearly overhead. Just wait till it blinks out before pulling the switch."

Then, always a scientist, his mind picked up the puzzling thread it had brushed and he asked a simple, musing question that caused me to break out into a sweat again, "I wonder why I can only pick up the identities of the dead? You'd think that either all the surface thoughts would come through, or none at all. Surely members of other races don't spend all their time repeating their human names, do they?"

But this seemed only a minor matter, soon to be clarified along with much greater mysteries, and Denkirch returned to the business at hand.

"All you have to do," he repeated, "is put your helmet on, move the switch to the second jog to free my mind, and then to the third in ten minutes to bring me back."

I waited a moment, locking my hands across my knees to keep them from shaking, and asked the question whose answer I already feared: "When do you plan to try it out?"

"When?" he echoed, surprised. "Why tonight, of course. The sky is clear, the static level is low—what more could we ask?"

For the next forty-five minutes I waited in silent resignation as Denkirch gave his equipment a final check, until at last he stepped back, and regarded it for a moment, arms akimbo, and said, "Well, I guess all that remains is to turn it on and let it warm up."

He touched a switch on the far end of the console and the room shook as the nearby generator picked up speed. The shaking died away again to a low purr after a few minutes and Denkirch explained, "That was just the capacitors charging. The cones will soak up a lot of power when they kick in. There's a light switch above the console that you ought to flip before you turn on the apparatus. It turns off everything but the necessary instruments, to keep the load down when you turn on the cones. The dial lights will be enough for you to see by when your eyes adjust, and besides, most of what you'll see will be through my eyes."

With that Denkirch sat down on the bed, slipped on the helmet there, and lay down full length with his arms at his sides. "Would you strap me in, Johnnie?" he said with his words somewhat muffled by the chinstrap of the helmet. "I doubt that it makes much difference, but there is a slim chance that my body might move a little after my mind is disconnected, and I wouldn't want to damage my helmet and keep you from seeing what is going on, you know."

The clasp clicked shut and I walked from the bed to the console trying to think of words to explain to Denkirch what I feared. But it wasn't a fear that could be explained; it was too basic for that.

The helmet leads were too short for me to reach the light switch with the helmet on, so I turned out the lights and then sat down to wait until I could see again before attempting to put the cumbersome thing on . . . perhaps more, and in a way that minute was the most horrible thing I underwent that night. It was as if I had awakened an instant before my alarm went off in the morning, still comfortably composed in bed but knowing the strident clamor would burst out at any moment. This and more, for it was the ultimate blissful dream that was about to be shattered, and my subconscious knew it though it could not speak.

Denkirch called out from the darkness behind me, "Are you ready?"

The hours of fear I had been feeling finally broke through my dignity and I cried, "Denny, this is wrong! For God's sake forget about this and just publish the rest of your findings. Those alone are enough to make you as rich and famous as you could want."

"No," he answered, "I already am as rich and famous as I want to be. I just want truth. I'm not taking a wild risk, but even if I were it would be worth it for the chance of advancing human understanding as much as this will. Pull the switch, Johnnie."

Just as he finished, the red aircraft-warning light winked on in front of me.

"There's a plane overhead," I said eagerly, certain now of at least a short delay. If we had delayed. . . . But it might have made no difference.

"That doesn't matter for the first stage and it will be gone before I come back. Pull the switch."

And, God help me, I did. But there is no god, is there? No god, no heaven, only the hells that glitter down on us every clear night. It was obvious as soon as I closed the switch that Denkirch had been perfectly correct. What neither of us had realized until then was how completely powerless the terran ego would be in the new body. I had not even begun to move my hand before it yanked down the switch almost of its own accord and I sat, quivering in the darkness with my own and Denkirch's screams still echoing through my mind.

Can you imagine—can you begin to imagine!—what it is to be totally alien? Your body, your world, even your mind except for that tiny, impotent speck of ego that screams, "This is not I," and screams the louder for knowing that it is and it will be forever, body after body, eon after eon, until space and time are no more! And that is why I no longer sleep on cloudless nights, for the stars in their myriads greet me in my dreams whispering, "Soon you will be with us, every one of us," and a high, thin scream from the Pleiades tells me where Denkirch is now.

An unlikely story, I know, and I myself might have thought it a dream had I not turned and seen in the green witchlight of the glowing dials the last earthly remains of Samuel Denkirch. Then I hurled my helmet into the console and fled from the cellar that blazed behind me as sputtering arcs from the shattered instruments ignited the frame walls; nor do I remember anything afterwards but my own screams until a highway patrol car stopped me in Indiana. Perhaps the return itself had been fatal, but I rather think it was the atmosphere; for Denkirch had returned to Earth as the tentacled abomination he had become on Deneb. . . .

DRAGON, THE BOOK

In the summer of 1987 I went to Iceland with my wife and son. The trip wasn't my idea—travel rarely is, as my PTSD made airports very uncomfortable environments even before 9/11—but I gained a great deal from it.

Partly I saw a lot of really neat things. Some of these were obvious: glaciers and volcanoes and geysers (including Geyser itself) and waterfalls and similar sorts of things that are featured in tourist brochures. Others were a lot less obvious. For example, once the driver carrying us to a glacier stopped, rushed out of the van, and came back cradling between his hands the plover that he'd seen hiding in the tundra. (Yes, he put the plover back.)

Besides the things I saw, however, I got books and pamphlets which took me deeper into Iceland's unique physical and cultural environment. These weren't all unique to the country: probably the most valuable single book I brought back was Hollander's translation of The Poetic Edda, published by the University of Texas Press. But I also bought many small volumes on Icelandic history and culture, as well as translations of lesser known sagas; books that I wouldn't have found back home.

Iceland is one thread of this story's background. The other thread is Andre Norton, who may have been the SF writer who most influenced me and the other writers of my generation.

The first SF book I bought (for 35 cents) was Andre's The Stars Are Ours. Through the ad pages in the back of that volume I ordered more of her books. In addition to being exciting stories, Andre's work made me think. My Ranks of Bronze grew directly out of Star Guard, and The Last Planet provided a glimpse of a recognizable human future in which my present was a myth lost in shadow. As well as being marvelously entertaining to a 14-year-old, her works were subtly educational.

In 1998 one of my friends was in correspondence with Andre, who commented that she was putting together a new volume in her Catfantastic anthology series. Did my friend suppose that Mr. Drake might be interested in doing a story for her? (She separately commented that she loved her fans, but that the book could use a greater leavening of professionals and of males.)

I became a writer by doing short stories, and I continued writing stories for a quite while after I learned to write novels. (A process which took twelve years after my first story sale.) After the

*length of my novels increased in the '90s, however,
I simply didn't have time for stories except in
exceptional circumstances.*

*A request from Andre Norton was as exceptional
as circumstances come.*

*A notion had been kicking around in the back
of my mind for the decade since I read the collection
of Icelandic folklore. I reread the folktale and
checked a few other references for visuals. (I like to
have a picture of the setting in front of me when I'm
describing a scene). With that background, I wrote
the story and sent it to Andre, who told me in a
handwritten note how much she liked it.*

The boy who bought The Stars Are Ours *still
lives inside the much older, much more cynical
Nam vet who became a professional writer. I
continue to glow because Andre Norton liked my
story*

✣ ✣ ✣

Through the forest's bare branches glittered stars as
cold as shattered hope; there was no moon. Hardin
the Wizard shouted the final word of his spell and threw
down the book bound in pale cockatrice skin. Lightning
flashed from the empty sky and rent the great oak.

Hardin flinched from the power he had summoned,
but the cat, his familiar, arched her back and spat at the
hissing ruin. The air was dense with the dry odor of seared
wood and the biting, sulfurous stench of the thunderbolt.

The oak swayed, then with a long groan of despair
toppled away from Hardin and his familiar. Branch and
bark and heartwood that was old when men first came to

the island crashed through the lesser vegetation and hammered a trench deep in the soil. The ground continued to vibrate long after the impact.

Hardin muttered a word and snapped his fingers. Witchfire lighted above him, casting its sickly glow over the scene. He stepped cautiously into the crater the oak's roots had stirred when they ripped out of the earth. The cat hopped to a stone turned up by a twisted rootlet, then gathered herself and made another graceful bound to where an iron-bound box rested at the bottom of the pit.

Hardin pointed to the latch of the box; he spoke a word to no effect. Scowling, he uttered a second word. Pins clattered, but the lock held, and the cat turned her face up to Hardin and laughed.

Hardin shouted a final word of power. A white flash tore from his fingertip, splitting the lock and twisting the straps back.

Throwing open the lid, Hardin drew out the ancient book within. On the front board the leather binding showed dimples from which great feathers had been plucked, and on the back were the lesser pits of a mammal's fur; but all the cover was from a single hide.

Hardin raised the book *Gryphon* and opened it. "There is no wizard more powerful than I!" he shouted to the starlit sky.

"Bishop Holar is a greater wizard yet, Hardin," said the cat with a cat's grin.

Hardin looked down at his familiar. "Bishop Holar has been in his tomb this hundred years past!" he said.

"Aye, Hardin," said the cat. "And still Bishop Holar is a greater wizard than you."

Hardin closed *Gryphon*. There was a sound like distant thunder. "We will go home, now," said the wizard.

Hardin stood in a corner of his loft, turning the pages of *Gryphon* on the lectern before him. The shutters at his shoulder were thrown back. Through them came the light of sunset and the odor of blooming honeysuckle. The cat slept beside the layer of ash which insulated the coals smoldering on the open hearth in the center of the room.

Glaring at the cat, Hardin said, "*Gryphon* will make me greater than Bishop Holar ever was!"

The cat grinned and stretched, but she did not turn toward the wizard. A pole sturdy enough to be the forepost of a warship jutted from the wall, holding a pot over the coals. The oak shaft was carved with the likenesses of a cockatrice; and a gryphon swallowing the cockatrice; and a dragon engulfing the lesser pair.

"Bishop Holar was buried with the book *Dragon* in his arms, Hardin," the cat said. "You will never be as great as he while he holds *Dragon* and you do not."

Hardin strode angrily around the lectern. "I will open the wall of Holar's tomb so that you may bring the book to me," he said.

The cat twisted onto her other side and looked at the wizard. "You sent my mate to fetch fire from the cell of the Younger Kalias, Hardin," she said. "The—"

"He lost the path!" Hardin said. "Had he followed my instructions—"

"The rock closed over him," the cat continued. As she spoke, she showed her claws and sheathed them again. "For three days I heard him wailing; then he died."

Hardin grimaced and touched the lectern. "That was before I had the book *Gryphon*," he said. "With *Gryphon* I could have protected him, as I can protect you."

The cat rolled from the hearth and walked past Hardin. Her tail was high. First lifting her forepaws, she hopped to the window ledge with a surge of her hindquarters. The sun had sunk to a pool of bloody light on the horizon.

"Bishop Holar has *Dragon*," said the cat. She turned to face the wizard. "I owe you service, but I do not owe you my life. You will not send *me* to fetch *Dragon*, Hardin."

Hardin's right hand clenched in a fist. With an oath he struck the cabinet on the north wall, making the pewter plates jangle within.

The cat grinned at him.

The moon was at zenith. Cold light flooded through the open southern windows, by its angle twisting into knowing leers the faces carved on the casement. At the lectern, Hardin read *Gryphon* by a glow like foxfire which hovered over the pages of the book.

The cat entered by the window and leaped down, her pads thumping on the pine floor as she landed. The wizard stared at her with brooding eyes.

The cat licked herself, eyeing Hardin over her shoulder. At last she paused and said, "You're up late, Hardin. Are matters well with you?"

"I am well," said the wizard, hiding his anger as best he might. "I have all the power of *Gryphon* in my tongue now, cat. I will draw Bishop Holar from his tomb, and he will give me the book *Dragon*."

The cat laughed, a throaty rasping with more of mockery than humor in it. "You are not strong enough, Hardin," she said. "If you try, you will burn, and all the world will burn with you."

"I will force Bishop Holar to my bidding!" Hardin said. "You are my servant and must stand by me. When I signal, you will quench the flames so that the world remains for me to rule!"

"I will save the world and your body from the flames, Hardin," the cat said. "But Bishop Holar will have your soul as his toy for all eternity, for he is a greater wizard than you."

Hardin closed *Gryphon* with a sound like mountains splitting. He lifted the book from the lectern.

"Come!" he said. "This night I will make you human so that you have hands to do my will."

Hardin took the brazier from its cabinet and the crystals he kept in an ivory casket. With them in his hands and his familiar following, the wizard strode from his house and into the neighboring grove.

The leaves of the oaks whispered like the wings of demons.

Moonlight through the leaves cut shadows as sharp as appliques of black cloth. Hardin set his brazier in the center of the grove and arranged the crystals in its bed. He laid no fuel of the ordinary sort for his fire.

The cat lay at her full length as she watched him. She was silent, but her tail twitched away her tension in sudden strokes.

Hardin whispered and touched the array. Pale flames,

yellow and blue and the green of burning copper, sprang from the brazier. Hardin took up the book *Gryphon* and began to chant.

The words echoed softly, as though from the walls of a cavern. The cat rose to her feet and paced about the brazier with a mincing step unlike her usual stride.

Hardin turned the page, continuing to call out the spell. The fire burned brighter. Its flames had the weight of stained glass, hinting at scenes of another world.

The cat danced, pirouetting on all fours. Her throat pulsed with her cries, but no sound could be heard over the booming thunder of the spell.

The cat rose to her hind legs. The flames were a bright, throbbing crimson like that of blood ripped from a rabbit's lungs. The oaks twisted their limbs away from the power in their midst.

Hardin shouted the final word of his incantation. The flames vanished with the suddenness of spiderweb burning, and the wizard slumped to the ground.

The cat continued to dance, spinning and rising onto her toes. Moonlight was white on her skin, and the flood of her long hair was as black as the night between the stars.

Hardin watched her, his face sallow with exhaustion. The cat laughed, at the wizard and at the moon.

The bishop's seat had been moved to Witsted after Holar died, and the parish of Vann had withered like wheat slain by a black frost. The sea breeze that rose up the cliffs covered the ruined churchyard in an eternal fog. Gravestones had toppled, yews had grown to mounds of shaggy gloom, and rust had frozen the gates open.

Hardin led, carrying the brazier and crystals as well as the book *Gryphon*. The cat had refused that burden or any. She wore a cape for the sake of modesty, and even that with bad grace. Her legs, as bare as the wind, scissored beneath the fur-trimmed hem.

The churchyard's back wall was in a swale, and the ground near the three tombs there was wetter even than the rest of the enclosure. Tree branches dripped into pools of standing water. The cat hissed in irritation as she followed the wizard.

They were alone in the churchyard. The cat unpinned the cape and swept it from her shoulders. It dropped, partly on a fallen marker and partly in the water pooling over a sunken grave.

Hardin arranged his crystals within the brazier: quartz and tourmaline; chrysoprase and chalcedony; and in the center, a jagged piece of bloodstone whose red streaks ran like arteries through a green matrix. He spoke a word to light his witchfire, and the flames sprang up red.

The cat looked at the fire, then looked at Hardin. Her lips drew back in what could have been either a smile or a sneer.

"Are you ready?" Hardin asked. *Gryphon* was open in his hands and his face was tense.

"I will serve you as I must, Hardin," said the cat. "But if you proceed as you intend, you will regret it for all eternity, for Holar is greater than you."

"Enough!" said the wizard. "You will do my will, and I will do all else that is needful."

Words stood out in letters of cold fire from the pages of the book *Gryphon*. Hardin began to intone them; the night trembled to the rhythms of his voice. The flames brightened, and the cat shook her long hair loose in the night breeze.

The three bishops' tombs had walls of flint nodules set in mortar and their roofs were of local slate, but the doors had been fashioned from imported marble. Crosses were carved on the first door and the second; but if there had ever been a cross on the door of Holar's tomb, it had rotted from the stone. The marble was black with damp, and the firelight hinted at faces in the stains.

Hardin chanted. Distant thunder echoed his words, and the gulls on the cliffside below called nervously. Heat from the brazier cleared the air around it, but the atmosphere of the churchyard took on a brooding weight more oppressive than the fog.

The flames climbed. Gray light oozed through the door of the tomb on the left. It coalesced as Hardin spoke, as though the words of his incantation were hammerblows that forged formlessness into the wraith of a stern old man.

The cat postured before the figure, arching and twisting her nude body. The wraith looked at her in fury. He would have raised his hand for a blow, but chains of fire gripped him. To Hardin, the wraith said, "Stop while you can, you fool!"

Hardin paused, panting with the effort past and awareness of the labor yet to come. "I dare not stop," the wizard said. His face was bleak and set. "And I shall not stop!"

Hardin resumed chanting. The cat laughed as she danced, but her throaty gurgle was lost in the sound of syllables thundering like waves driven onshore by a winter gale.

The flames blazed yellow. At each syllable they leaped higher than the top of the ancient cypress whose roots had crumbled a corner of the wall before squirming through a dozen graves. Hardin's voice rose in pitch but did not falter. The pages of *Gryphon* turned at the bare touch of his fingers.

Another blob of light formed on the door of the center tomb, the way water beads as it soaks through canvas. Hardin spoke and the light congealed, becoming the figure of a man with a thin, ascetic face. This wraith nodded to his predecessor, still locked in fiery constraint, then gazed sadly at Hardin.

The cat grinned and offered herself, thrusting her pelvis toward the second figure. He would have signed the cross before him, but bonds of fire shackled his limbs as they had his predecessor's.

"Young man," said the saintly figure to Hardin, "cease now; for the sake of your soul and for the world of men."

"My soul is lost unless I gain *Dragon*," said the wizard. His voice rasped like stone on stone, and his eyes were puzzled to be gazing again on things of this world rather than what they glimpsed in the pages of *Gryphon*. "I will not cease!"

Hardin chanted, and the brazier glared white as the light of the desert sun. The wraiths stood watching. The first scowled, but the lips of the second moved in prayer.

The earth groaned a low, dismal note like the call of an ox dying. The door of the third tomb split with a whipcrack. Through the opening stepped a dapper man in bishop's robes, holding a book whose red leather binding still showed the pattern of great scales.

Bishop Holar looked at the wraiths drawn from the other tombs. The first figure glared at him, but the second continued to pray with the same sad expression as when he viewed Hardin the Wizard.

Bishop Holar chuckled and turned to Hardin. "Well done, boy," he said in a silver voice, "far better than I had expected of you. But you may as well give over now and leave me to my—"

Holar smiled.

"To my rest, shall I say?"

The cat smiled back at Holar. Her expression was a mirror of the bishop's own, each as cruel as a hook-bladed knife.

"I will have the book *Dragon*," said Hardin in nearly a falsetto.

"Your familiar has used your pride to dig a pit for you, boy," said Bishop Holar with a nod of respect toward the cat. "She has mocked you till you tried this thing, knowing that if you did it, I would break you or between us we would break the world. Leave off now, while you can!"

"I cannot leave off," said Hardin in a despairing whisper.

Bishop Holar sniffed; his right hand, as white and delicate as a woman's, stroked the cover of the book *Dragon*. "So I see," he said. "Well, it will be as it must be, then."

Hardin resumed his chant. All the world was silent except his voice.

The fire was a stake of white light through the heart of the sky. Through the shaft of flame could be seen the shapes of rocks and plants and figures; but not such as are seen in the world of men.

The cat paced, her face twisting with hope and eagerness; and with not a little fear as well. Hardin continued the incantation. His visage was set like a skull and his voice was a child's piping, but still he spoke the words.

No longer did the wizard's hands turn the pages of *Gryphon*. The parchment leaves turned of themselves, and as they turned, the light of the fiery letters on them hung in the air like the afterimage of a lightning stroke.

Bishop Holar sneered, but he, too, showed the tension. Holar took a step forward, unwilling to advance but doing so nonetheless.

Hardin's lips moved, but no longer was the chant audible as words from his tongue. Pulses too deep to be sound throbbed through the cosmos, making the sky and ground tremble together.

The fire was a sword cleaving the heavens. The fronds of a nearby willow curled back; the trunk split with a despairing hiss.

Bishop Holar's arm began to straighten, extending the book *Dragon*. His movement was slow, as slow as the face of a glacier grinding down the notch of a valley.

The fire was a pressure as palpable as stone, and it roared like an angry god. The fronds of the great cypress shriveled and burst into flame.

"Hardin!" said the cat. "Your fire will swallow you and the world with you unless I smother it now. Is it your will that I save you, Hardin, or do you choose to go to hell in a bath of flame?"

Hardin's mouth formed the words of power; his tongue had no more volition than a boulder has, careening down a hillside. His right hand moved in a desperate gesture toward the fire he had lighted but could not quench.

The cat bent with a supple motion to grip one of the tripod's three clawed feet. She straightened, lifting the brazier of chiseled iron with an ease that belied the slender delicacy of her arms. Grinning at Hardin, she overturned it and thrust the basin into the pool over a sunken grave. Steam from the stagnant water flooded the churchyard in a hot cloud.

A thunderclap threw Hardin backward, drowning Bishop Holar's cry of triumph. The book *Gryphon* fell to the ground. It erupted into ruddy flames which blazed until they had consumed leaves and binding utterly. The soil where the tome had lain was baked to glass without even a dusting of ash upon its heat-crazed surface.

The two wraiths had vanished. Bishop Holar remained. He bowed low to the cat, then walked back into his tomb carrying *Dragon* in the crook of his arm. His step was unsteady, for the strain had been great for even such as he.

Hardin's body lay where he had fallen. His chest moved, but his eyes were empty. From Hardin's still form separated a wraith of gray light in the wizard's semblance.

The wraith looked at the familiar, then looked for a last time at the world it was leaving. With the jerky motion of a marionette, Hardin's soul followed Bishop Holar within the tomb. The edges of the cracked marble flowed together as though they had never ruptured.

From Bishop Holar's tomb came a yowl like the agony of a starving cat, diminishing slowly into silence. On the blackened stone of the tomb door was an additional face, tortured and despairing.

Dawn was breaking. The cat laughed to the sky as she danced about the slack-jawed form of the one who had slain her mate.

THE FALSE PROPHET
※ 片 ※

Latin has been my soul's anchor ever since my second semester of college. I don't know why that should be, but I can tell you how it happened.

I took two years of Latin in high school because it was that or Spanish. Neither option appealed to me, but I had to take some foreign language. My grades were adequate but nobody was going to mistake me for a Latin scholar, and I don't recall getting any particular pleasure from the classes.

My plan in college (the University of Iowa) was to major in chemistry, go to law school, and become a patent attorney. Chemistry required German, so I started German with the expectation that I'd never read another line of Latin.

I pretty quickly realized that I wasn't cut out to be a chem major (or, I suspected, a patent attorney), so I switched to history. I continued with German (which I didn't actively dislike), because I didn't believe that I could ever get back into Latin after a year away from the language.

That's when things get kind of odd. College was

a complete disruption of my life. Everything had changed. I don't mean everything was bad—Iowa's huge library in particular was a wonderful resource for somebody like me who can get interested in a wide range of subjects—but everything was different. I found myself thinking of Latin as the one part I might reclaim of the, well, youth which I'd surrendered when I left home.

I borrowed an old copy of the Latin book I'd used in high school and studied it on my own. Studied it for the first time, really: in high school I'd shown a flair for sight translations but I hadn't bothered much about grammar. I started regular course work in my third semester and took about all the Latin courses offered at Iowa before I graduated. (I wound up with thirty semester hours and asked if I could call Latin a double major with my history. The administration agreed.)

I entered Duke Law School in 1967. That was stressful, too; I took Latin courses in the main university to settle me. (They'd never had anybody do that before, but there were no rules against it.)

When I was drafted out of law school I couldn't take courses, but I carried my Oxford Classical Text of Horace through basic training and as much of Southeast Asia as I saw. I continue to read Latin for pleasure. I also read extensively on classical subjects, because they interest me and I've got a good formal grounding from my undergraduate days.

Naturally I've used a lot of classical backgrounds

in my fiction, SF as well as fantasy and horror. I wrote "The False Prophet" to fill out a collection of previously written stories in a classical milieu.

Something I've come to realize is that many readers think they know things about ancient Rome. When they read a contrary statement in a story of mine, some assume I've made a stupid mistake. Well, I do make stupid mistakes (for example, the time I nearly severed a tendon while sharpening a knife), but when the subject is Roman history or culture, the smart money is going to bet on me.

A universal case is that educated people don't want to believe that Roman shields were made of plywood. I had a stranger call me from California to tell me that plywood hadn't been invented until the nineteenth century. Roman shields were made of three plies of (generally) birch, glued together. The grain on the front and back layers ran crosswise, but it was vertical on the central ply. Archeologists call the material plywood (what on Earth else would they call it?); the educated man in the street finds that truth ridiculous.

I once complained that I should feel lucky that I don't get similar objections when I mention that most Roman buildings were concrete. The next day I got a query from an editor who wanted to know whether my mention of "Roman concrete" was a mistake.

A similar problem involves readers who believe that colloquial Latin should be translated into something closer to William Morris than to normal

*English. There's a place for high style, but it doesn't
get much use among soldiers or ordinary people in
general, now or two thousand years ago. My
dialogue (like that of Martial, Catullus, Petronius,
and a very long list of other Latin writers) tends to
be colloquial in form.*

*A lot of reading and research went into these
stories; but my heart went into them, too.*

✢ ✢ ✢

The big young man, grinning at Dama through the
doorway of the City Prefect's private office, had the
look of a killer. Dama knew the fellow's name, Lucius
Vettius—and knew that he was an officer in the imperial
guard, though at the moment he wore a civilian toga. Dama
smiled back. "The virtuous Marcus Licinius Dama!"
bellowed the nomenclator in a strong Syrian accent. Why
couldn't Gaius Rutilius Rutilianus—who was, by Mithra,
City Prefect of Rome—buy servants who at least
pronounced Latin properly?

"He didn't mention that you're only a merchant!"
Menelaus whispered to Dama in amazement. "No, he
didn't," Dama agreed without amplifying his response. The
nomenclator was wearing a new tunic. So was the
doorkeeper who'd let Dama and his older companion into
Rutilianus's reception room with a crowd of over a hundred
other favor-seekers. The tunics were best-quality Egyptian
linen and represented a hefty outlay—

Even to Dama, who imported them along with the silks
which were his primary stock in trade. "His companion,"
cried the nomenclator, "the learned Faustus Pompeius
Menelaus!" The nomenclator paused. "Known as The

Wise." Menelaus suddenly looked ten years younger. He straightened to his full height and fluffed his long gray beard.

Though Dama said nothing as the pair of them stepped into Rutilianus's private office, the nomenclator had earned himself a bonus by the degree to which his ad-libbed comment had brightened the old man's face.

Menelaus and Dama's father had remained friends throughout the latter's life. Dama stopped visiting his parent when disease and pain so wracked the older man that every conversation became a litany of insult and complaint; but Menelaus continued to come, to read aloud and to bear bitter insults because to do so was a philosopher's duty—and a friend's.

"Well, he sure looks the part, doesn't he?" quipped Caelius, one of the four civilians standing around the Prefect's couch. "Got any owls nesting in that beard, old man?"

"Looking the part's easy enough," countered Vulco. "If you want a philosopher of *real* learning, though, you'll hire Pactolides."

"I think it's unchristian to be hiring *any* sort of pagan philosopher," said Macer. "Severiana won't like it a bit."

"My wife doesn't make the decisions in *this* house," the Prefect said so forcefully that everyone listening knew that Rutilianus was as much voicing a wish as stating a fact.

The Prefect shifted his heavy body on the couch and scratched himself. Though the morning air was comfortable by most standards, Rutilianus was sweating despite having dispensed with the formality of his toga while handling this private interview.

The men were the Prefect's friends, advisors, and employees—and wore all those separate masks at the same time. Except for Vettius (who was about Dama's age), they'd accompanied Rutilianus during his governorships in Spain and North Africa. They carried out important commissions, gave confidential advice—and picked up the bits and scraps which form the perquisites of those having the ear of high office.

"Anyway," offered Sosius, "I don't think that there's anything sinful about hearing advice on living a good life, even if it does come from a pagan."

For what Dama had paid Sosius, he'd expected more enthusiastic support. Pactolides was getting much better value for his bribe to Vulco.

"Well, let's hear what he says for himself," the Prefect said, still peevish at the mention of his wife. He nodded toward Menelaus. "You *can* speak, can't you?" he demanded. "Not much use in having a personal philosopher who can't, is there?"

"Pactolides can speak like an angel," muttered Vulco. "Voice like a choirboy, that man has . . . ."

Dama prompted his friend with a tap on the shoulder. Menelaus stepped forward and bowed. "If ever there was a man who was rightly afraid when called to speak in your presence, noble Rutilianus," the old philosopher boomed, "it is I; and I sense—" he made a light, sweeping bow to the Prefect's companions "—that those who participate in your counsels are well able to see my distress."

Menelaus was a different man as soon as he began his set oration—confident, commanding; his tones and volume pitched to blast through the chatter filling a rain-crowded basilica when he addressed his students in one corner. Dama had worried that the old man's desperate need for a job would cause him to freeze up when the opportunity was offered. He should have known better.

"—for my heart is filled with the awareness of the way you, armed like Mars himself, preserved the liberty of this Republic; and now, wearing the toga, increase its civil glory. For—"

The soldier, Vettius, crooked a finger toward Dama and nodded in the direction of the garden behind the office.

Rutilianus's other councilors looked bored—Vulco was yawning ostentatiously—but the Prefect himself listened to the panegyric with pleasure. He nodded with unconscious agreement while Menelaus continued, "—while all those who have borne the burden of your exalted prefecture are to be praised, to you especially is honor due."

Vettius, waiting at the door into the garden, crooked his finger again. Dama pursed his lips and followed, walking with small steps to disturb the gathering as little as possible—though Menelaus in full cry couldn't have been put off his stride by someone shouting *Fire!* and the Prefect was rapt at the mellifluous description of his virtues.

The garden behind Rutilianus's house had a covered walk on three sides, providing shade at all times of the day. The open area was large enough to hold a dozen fruit trees as well as a small grape arbor and a variety of roses, exotic peonies, and other flowers.

Military equipment was stacked beside the door: a bronze helmet and body armor modeled with idealized muscles over which a pair of naiads cavorted; a swordbelt supporting the sheathed dagger and long, straight-bladed spatha of a cavalryman; and a large, circular shield in its canvas cover.

Vettius followed Dama's eyes toward the gear and volunteered, "I'm army—seconded to the City Prefect for the time being."

There were two ways for Dama to handle his response. He made the snap decision that concealing his knowledge from this big, hard-eyed soldier couldn't bring any dividends equal to getting the man's respect from the start.

"Yes," he said. "A decurion in the squadron of Domestic Horse."

Vettius was surprised enough to glance sideways to make sure that canvas still covered the gilt spikes and hearts against the blue background of his shieldface. "Right, that's me," he agreed mildly. "The Prefect's bodyguard, more or less. The name's Lucius Vettius—as I suppose you knew."

There was no question in the final clause, but Dama nodded his agreement anyway. He'd done his homework— as he always did his homework before a major sale.

This business, because it was personal and not merely a matter of money, was the most major sale of his life . . . .

"Let me hope," rolled Menelaus's voice through the open door and window of the office, "that my words today can be touched by a fraction of the felicity with which all Rome greeted the news that you had been appointed her helmsman."

"I was wondering," Vettius said, "just how much you'd paid Sosius?"

Dama prodded the inside of his cheek with his tongue.

"The reason I'm wondering," the soldier continued, "is that he's taking money from Pactolides, too." He laughed. "Vulco's an unusually virtuous councilor, you know."

Dama grimaced bitterly. "Yeah," he agreed. "Vulco stays bought."

"My words are driven out under the compulsion of the virtue and benignity which I see before me . . ." Menelaus continued in an orotund voice.

"I hadn't thought," continued Dama, choosing his words carefully, "that a decurion was worth bribing. Until now that I've met you."

"I'd have taken your money," Vettius said with the same cold smile as before. "But it wouldn't've gained you anything. What I'd really like from you, Citizen Dama . . ."

Dama nodded his head upward in agreement. "Go ahead," he said.

If not money, then a woman? A *particular* woman to whom a silk merchant might have access . . . ?

". . . is information." The flat certainty with which the words came out of Vettius's mouth emphasized the size and strength of the man speaking. He had black hair and spoke with a slight tang of the Illyrian frontier.

"Go ahead," Dama repeated with outward calm.

From the office came ". . . though I fear that by mentioning any particular excellence first, I will seem to devalue . . . ."

"I can see why the old man wants to be Rutilianus's tame philosopher," Vettius said. "It's getting harder and harder to scrape up enough pupils freelance to keep him in bread, onions, and a sop of wine . . . ."

Dama nodded.

"Thing is, I'm not quite clear what *your* part in the business might be, Citizen."

This time the soldier's smile made Dama measure in his mind the distance between him and the hilt of the sword resting against the wall. Too far, almost certainly.

And unnecessary. Almost certainly.

"Menelaus was a friend of my father's," Dama said. "A good friend. Toward the last, my father's only friend. Menelaus is too proud to take charity from me directly— but he was glad to have me stand beside him while he sought this position in the Prefect's household."

Vettius chuckled. "Stand beside him," he repeated ironically. "With a purse full of silver you hand out to anybody who might ease your buddy's road."

". . . speak of the River Tagus, red with the blood of the bandits you as Governor slaughtered there?"

"He doesn't know that," snapped Dama.

"But you do, merchant," the soldier said. "You take your family duties pretty seriously, don't you?"

"Yeah, I do," agreed Dama as simply as if he didn't know he was being mocked . . . and perhaps he was not being mocked. "Menelaus is my friend as well as my duty, but—I take all my duties seriously."

The big man smiled; this time, for a change, it gave his face a pleasant cast. "Yeah," he said. "So do I."

"I can see that," Dama agreed, feeling his body relax for the first time since his interview with this big, deadly man began. "And it's your duty to guard Rutilianus."

"More a matter of keeping things from hitting the Prefect from somewhere he's not looking," Vettius said with a shrug. "So I like to know the people who're getting close to him."

He grinned. "Usually I don't much like what I learn. Usually."

Dama nodded toward the office, where Menelaus's measured periods had broken up into the general babble of all those in the room. "I think we'd better get back," he said. "I'm glad to have met you, Lucius Vettius."

And meant it.

The Prefect called, "Ah, Vettius," craning his neck to see over his shoulder as Dama and the soldier reentered the room. "We rather like Menelaus here, don't we, gentlemen?"

Yes yes/Well-spoken indeed/Seems solid for a pagan—

"Well, being able to spout a set speech doesn't make him learned, sir," crabbed Vulco.

He fixed Menelaus with a glare meant to be steely. Vulco's head was offset so that only one eye bore, making him look rather like an angry crow.

"Tell me, sirrah," he demanded, "who was it that Thersites fed his sons to? Quick, now—no running around to sort through your books."

The philosopher blinked in confusion. Dama thought for a moment that his friend had been caught out, but Menelaus said, "Good sir, Atreus it was who murdered the sons of his brother Thyestes and cooked them for their father."

Dama suppressed a laugh. Menelaus had paused in order to find a way to answer the question without making his questioner look *too* much of a fool.

Vulco blinked. "Well, that seems all right," he

muttered, fixing his eyes on his hands and seeming to examine his manicure.

"Yes, well," Rutilianus agreed. "But you, Lucius Vettius. What information do *you* have for us?"

Everyone else in the room looked at the tall soldier: Menelaus in surprise, the Prefect and his companions with a partially concealed avidity for scandal; Dama with a professionally blank expression, waiting to hear what was said before he decided how to deal with anything that needed to be countered.

Vettius glanced at Dama. "I'd suggested to His Excellency," he said, "that he let me see what I could learn about the learned Menelaus."

"Of course," Rutilianus agreed, raising his eyebrows. "After all, we need to be sure of the man who's going to be responsible for the moral training of my children."

His companions bobbed and muttered approval.

Vettius took a bi-fold notebook of waxed boards from the wallet in the bosom of his toga, but he didn't bother to open the document before he said, "Menelaus comes from Caesarea in Cappadocia where his father was one of the city councilors."

Like Dama's father.

"Was schooled in Gaza, then Athens. Returned home and taught there for most of his life. Moved to Rome about five years ago. Gives lessons in oratory and philosophy—"

"Epicurean philosophy," the subject of the discussion broke in, before Dama could shush him.

"Epicurean philosophy," Vettius continued, giving Dama—rather than Menelaus—a grin that was not entirely friendly. "In the Forum of Trajan; to about a dozen pupils at any one time. Doesn't get along particularly well with the other teachers who've set up in the same area. For the past three months, he's been attacking one Pyrrhus the Prophet in his lectures, but the two haven't met face to face."

Dama was ready this time. His finger tapped Menelaus's shoulder firmly, even as the older man opened his mouth to violently—and needlessly—state his opinion of Pyrrhus.

"Well, we *know* he's a philosopher!" Caelius said. "What about his personal life?"

"He doesn't have much personal life," Vettius said. He betrayed his annoyance with a thinning of tone so slight that only Dama, of those in the office, heard and understood it. "When he's a little ahead, he buys used books. When he's behind—"

Menelaus winced and examined the floor.

"—which is usually, and now, he pawns them. Stays out of wineshops. Every few months or so he visits a whore named Drome who works the alleys behind the Beef Market."

"These aren't," Vettius added dryly, "expensive transactions."

Dama looked at the philosopher in amazement. Menelaus met his gaze sidelong and muttered, "Ah, Dama, I—thought that when I grew older, some impediments to a calm mind would cease to intrude on my life. But I'm not as old as that yet. I'm ashamed to admit."

Macer opened his mouth as if about to say something. Lucius Vettius turned toward the man and—tapped his notebook, Dama thought, with the index finger of his left hand.

Dama thought the soldier's gesture might be only an idle tic; but Macer understood something by it. The councilor's eyes bulged, and his mouth shut with an audible clop.

"Last year," Vettius continued calmly, "Menelaus moved out of his garret apartment at night, stiffing his landlord for the eight days' rent."

"Sir!" the philosopher blurted in outrage despite Dama's restraining hand. "When I moved there in the spring, I was told the roof tiles would be replaced in a few days. Nothing had been done by winter—and my books were drenched by the first heavy rains!"

"The pair of Moors sharing the room now—" said Vettius.

"If you want to believe—" Vulco began.

"—say the landlord told them when they moved in that the roof tiles would be replaced in a few days," Vettius continued, slicing across the interruption like a sword cutting rope. "That was three months ago."

He turned to the philosopher and said coldly, "Do you have anything to add to *that*, Faustus Menelaus?"

Menelaus blinked.

Dama bowed low to the soldier and said, "My companion and I beg your pardon, sir. He did not realize that the life of an exceptionally decent and honorable man might contain, on close examination . . . incidents which look regrettable out of context."

"Well, still . . ." Rutilianus said, frowning as he shifted on his couch. "What do you fellows think?"

All four of his civilian companions opened their mouths to speak. Macer was fractionally ahead of the others, blurting, "Well, Severiana certainly won't be pleased if an opponent of Pyrrhus the Prophet enters your household!"

"Didn't I tell you to leave my wife out of this?" Rutilianus snarled.

Macer quailed as though he'd been slapped. The other civilians froze, unwilling to offer what might not be the words the aroused Prefect wanted to hear.

Vettius looked at them with cool amusement, then back to Rutilianus. "If I may speak, sir?" he said.

"Of course, of course, Lucius," Rutilianus said, wiping his forehead with a napkin. "What do you think I should do?"

Dama squeezed Menelaus's shoulder very firmly, lest the old philosopher interrupt again—which Dama was quite sure would mean disaster. The soldier wasn't the sort of man whose warnings, voiced or implied, were to be ignored without cost.

"I can't speak to the fellow's philosophy," Vettius said. He paused a half-beat, to see if Menelaus would break in on him; and smiled when the philosopher held his peace. "But for his life—Citizen Dama stated the situation correctly. The learned Menelaus is an exceptionally decent and honorable man, fit to enter your household, sir—"

Vulco started to say something. Before the words came out, the soldier had turned and added, in a voice utterly without emotion, "—or your council. From a moral standpoint."

Vulco blanched into silence.

Dama expressionlessly watched the—almost—

exchange. This Vettius could go far in the imperial bureaucracy, with his ability to gather information and his ruthless willingness to use what he had. But the way the soldier moved, his timing—thrusting before his target was expecting it, ending a controversy before it became two-sided—those were a swordsman's virtues, not a bureaucrat's.

Dama's right palm tingled, remembering the feel of a swordhilt. In five years, he'd turned his father's modest legacy into real wealth by a willingness to go where the profits were as high as the risks. He knew swordsmen, knew killers. . . .

"Even with the . . . ?" the Prefect was saying. His eyes looked inward for a moment. "But yes, I can see that anyone's life examined closely might look—"

Rutilianus broke off abruptly as if in fear that his musings were about to enter territory he didn't care to explore.

"Well, anyway, Menelaus," he resumed, "I think we'll give you—"

"Gaius, dearie," called a silk-clad youth past the scowling nomenclator, "there's somebody here you just *have* to see."

Rutilianus looked up with a frown that softened when he saw the youth—the boy, really—who was speaking. "I'm busy, now, Ganymede. Can't it wait . . . ?"

"Not an eentsy minute," Ganymede said firmly, lifting his pert nose so that he looked down at the Prefect past chubby cheeks.

"Oh, send him in, then," Rutilianus agreed with a sigh.

The nomenclator, his voice pitched a half-step up with

scandal and outrage, announced, "The honorable Gnaeus Aelius Acer . . ." he paused ". . . emissary of Pyrrhus the Prophet."

"*That* charlatan!" Menelaus snapped.

"It ill behooves a pagan to criticize a Christian, you!" Macer retorted.

"Pyrrhus is no Christian!" said Menelaus. "That's as much a sham as his claim to know the future and—"

Dama laid a finger across his friend's lips.

A young man whose dress and bearing marked his good family was being ushered in by the nomenclator.

Rutilianus glanced from the newcomer to Menelaus and remarked in a distant tone, "A word of advice, good philosopher: my wife believes Pyrrhus to be a Christian. A belief in which I choose to concur."

He turned to the newcomer and said, "Greetings, Gnaeus Acer. It's been too long since you or your father have graced us with your company."

Instead of responding with a moment of small talk, Acer said, "Pyrrhus to Gaius Rutilianus, greetings. There is—"

There was a glaze over the young man's eyes and his voice seemed leaden. He did not look at the Prefect as his tongue broke into singsong to continue:

"—one before you

"With whose beard he cloaks for boys his lust.

"Cast him from you hastily

"And spurn him in the dust."

Pyrrhus's messenger fell silent. "I think there's a mistake—" Dama began while his mind raced, searching for a diplomatic way to deny the absurd accusation.

Menelaus was neither interested in nor capable of diplomacy. "That's doggerel," he said, speaking directly to the Prefect. "And it's twaddle. I've never touched a boy carnally in my life."

After a pause just too short for anyone else to interject a comment, the philosopher added, "I can't claim that as a virtue. Because frankly, I've never been tempted in that direction."

"Vettius?" the Prefect asked, his eyes narrowing with supposition.

The soldier shrugged. "I can't prove an absence," he said—his tone denying the possibility implicit in the words. "But if the learned Menelaus had tastes in that direction, *some* neighbor or slave would surely have mentioned it."

"In his wallet—" Acer broke in unexpectedly.

"—the debaucher keeps

"A letter to the boy with whom he sleeps."

"That," shouted Menelaus, "is a lie as false and black as the heart of the charlatan whose words this poor deluded lad is speaking!"

Vettius reached toward the bosom of the philosopher's toga.

Menelaus raised a hand to fend off what he saw as an assault on his sense of propriety. Dama caught the philosopher's arm and said, "Let him search you now. That will demonstrate the lie to all these gentlemen."

Vettius removed a cracked leather purse whose corners had been restitched so often that its capacity was reduced by a third. He thumbed up the flap—the tie-strings had rotted off a decade before—and emptied it, item by item, into his left palm.

A stylus. A pair of onions.

"I, ah," Menelaus muttered, "keep my lunch. . . ."

Dama patted him to silence.

A half-crust of bread, chewed rather than torn from a larger piece. The lips of Rutilianus and his companions curled.

A tablet, closed so that the two boards protected the writing on their waxed inner sides. All eyes turned to the philosopher.

All eyes save those of Gnaeus Acer, who stood as quietly as a resting sheep.

"My notebook," explained Menelaus. "I jot down ideas for my lectures. And sometimes appointments."

Vettius dumped back the remainder of the wallet's contents and opened the tablet.

"It's in Greek," he commented. He shifted so that light from the garden door threw shadows across the marks scored into the wax and made them legible.

"Yes, I take my notes—" the philosopher began.

"'Menelaus to his beloved Kurnos,'" Vettius said, translating the lines rather than reading them in their original. "'Kurnos, don't drive me under the yoke against my will—don't goad my love too much.'"

"What!" said Dama.

"*Oh* . . . !" murmured several of the others in the room.

"'I won't invite you to the party,'" the soldier continued, raising his voice to a level sufficient to bark commands across the battlefield, "'nor forbid you. When you're present, I'm distressed—but when you go away, I still love you.'"

"Why, that's not my notebook!" Menelaus cried. "Nor

my words. Why, it's just a quotation from the ancient poet Theognis!"

Dama started to extend a hand to the notebook. He caught himself before he thought the gesture was visible, but the soldier had seen and understood. Vettius handed the tablet to Dama open.

Pyrrhus's messenger should have been smiling—should have shown *some* expression. Gnaeus Acer's face remained as soft and bland as butter. He turned to leave the office as emotionlessly as he'd arrived.

Menelaus reached for Acer's arm. Dama blocked the older man with his body. "Control yourself!" he snarled under his breath.

The message on the tablet couldn't have been written by the old philosopher . . . but the forgery was very good.

Too good for Dama to see any difference between Menelaus's hand and that of the forger.

"Lies don't change the truth!" Menelaus shouted to the back of Gnaeus Acer. "Tell your master! The truth will find him yet!"

"Citizen Menelaus," the Prefect said through pursed lips, "you'd better—" his mind flashed him a series of pictures: Menelaus brawling with Pyrrhus's messenger in the waiting room "—step into the garden for a moment while we discuss matters. And your friend—"

"Sir," Vettius interjected, "I think it might be desirable to have Citizen Dama present to hear the discussions."

"We don't owe an explanation to some itinerant pederast, surely?" said Caelius.

Rutilianus looked at him. "No," he said. "I don't owe anyone an explanation, Caelius. But my friend Lucius is correct that sometimes giving an explanation can save later awkwardness—even in matters as trivial as these."

For the first time, Dama could see that Rutilianus had reached high office for better reason than the fact that he had the right ancestors.

A momentary tremor shook Menelaus's body. The philosopher straightened, calm but looking older than Dama had ever seen him before.

He bowed to the Prefect and said, "Noble Rutilianus, your graciousness will overlook my outburst; but I assure you I will never forgive my own conduct, which was so unworthy of a philosopher and a guest in your house."

Menelaus strode out the door to the garden, holding his head high as though he were unaware of Caelius's giggles and the smug certainty in the eyes of Vulco.

"Citizen Dama, do you have anything to add?" the Prefect said—a judge now, rather than the head of a wealthy household.

"There is no possibility that the accusation is true," Dama said, choosing his words and knowing that there were no words in any language that would achieve his aim. "I say that as a man who has known Menelaus since I was old enough to have memory."

"And the letter he'd written?" Macer demanded. "I suppose *that's* innocent?"

Dama looked at his accuser. "I can't explain the letter," he said. "Except to point out that Pyrrhus knew about it, even though Menelaus himself obviously had no idea what was written on the tablet."

Caelius snickered again.

"Lucius Vettius, what do you say?" Rutilianus asked

from his couch. He wiped his face with a napkin, dabbing precisely instead of sweeping the cloth promiscuously over his skin.

"In my opinion," the soldier said, "the old man didn't know what was on the tablet. And he isn't interested in boys. In my opinion."

"So you would recommend that I employ the learned Menelaus to teach my sons proper morality?" Rutilianus said.

For a moment, Dama thought—hoped—prayed—

The big soldier looked at Dama, not the Prefect, and said, "No, I can't recommend that. There're scores of philosophers in Rome who'd be glad of the position. There's no reason at all for you to take a needless risk."

And of course, Vettius was quite right. A merchant like Dama could well appreciate the balance of risk against return.

Pyrrhus the Prophet understood the principles also.

"Yes, too bad," Rutilianus said. "Well-spoken old fellow, too. But—" his eyes traced past the nomenclator as if hoping for another glimpse of the boy Ganymede "—some of those perverts are just too good at concealing it. Can't take the risk, can we?"

He looked around the room as his smiling civilian advisors chorused agreement. Vettius watched Dama with an expression of regret, but he had no reason to be ashamed of what he'd said. Even Dama agreed with the assessment.

The wheezing gasp from the garden was loud enough for everyone in the office to hear, but only Vettius and Dama understood what it meant.

Sosius was between Vettius and the garden door for an instant. The soldier stiff-armed him into a wall, because that was faster than words and there wasn't a lot of time when—

Vettius and Dama crashed into the garden together. The merchant had picked up a half-step by not having to clear his own path.

—men were dying.

It looked for a moment as though the old philosopher was trying to lean his forehead against the wall of the house. He'd rested the pommel of Vettius's sword at an angle against the stucco and was thrusting his body against it. The gasp had come when—

Menelaus vomited blood and toppled sideways before Dama could catch him.

—the swordpoint broke the resisting skin beneath Menelaus's breastbone and slid swiftly upward through the old man's lungs, stomach, and heart.

Vettius grabbed Menelaus's limp wrist to prevent the man from flopping on his back. The swordpoint stuck a finger's breadth out from between Menelaus's shoulder blades. It would grate on the stone if he were allowed to lie naturally.

Dama reached beneath the old man's neck and took the weight of his torso. Vettius glanced across at him, then eased back—putting his own big form between the scene and the excited civilians spilling from the office to gape at it.

"You didn't have to do that, old friend," Dama whispered. "There were other households . . ."

But no households who wouldn't have heard the story

of what had happened here—or a similar story, similarly told by an emissary of Pyrrhus the Prophet. Menelaus had known that . . . and Menelaus hadn't been willing to accept open charity from his friend.

The old man did not speak. A trail of sluggish blood dribbled from the corner of his mouth. His eyes blinked once in the sunlight, twice—

Then they stayed open and began to glaze.

Dama gripped the spatha's hilt. One edge of the blade was embedded in Menelaus's vertebrae. He levered the weapon, hearing bone crack as the steel came free.

"Get back!" the merchant snarled to whoever it was whose motion blurred closer through the film of tears. He drew the blade out, feeling his friend's body spasm beneath his supporting arm.

He smelled the wastes that the corpse voided after mind and soul were gone. Menelaus wore a new toga. Dama'd provided it "as a loan for the interview with Rutilianus."

Dama stood up. He caught a fold of his own garment in his left hand and scrubbed the steel with it, trusting the thickness of the wool to protect his flesh from the edge that had just killed the man he had known and respected as long as he had memory.

Known and respected and loved.

And when the blade was clean, he handed the sword, pommel-first, to Lucius Vettius.

There were seats and tables in the sideroom of the tavern, but Vettius found the merchant hunched over the masonry bar in the front. The bartender, ladling soup from one of the kettles cemented into the counter, watched hopefully when the soldier surveyed the room from the doorway, then strode over to Dama.

The little fella had been there for a couple hours. Not making trouble. Not even drinking *that* heavy . . .

But there was a look in his eyes that the bartender had seen in other quiet men at the start of a real bad night.

"I thought you might've gone home," Vettius said as he leaned his broad left palm on the bar between his torso and Dama's.

"I didn't," the merchant said. "Go away."

He swigged down the last of his wine and thrust the bronze cup, chained to the counter, toward the bartender. "Another."

The tavern was named *At the Sign of Venus*. While he waited for the bartender to fill the cup—and while he pointedly ignored Dama's curt demand to *him*—Vettius examined the statue on the street-end of the counter.

The two-foot-high terracotta piece had given the place its name. It showed Venus tying her sandal, while her free hand rested on the head of Priapus's cock to balance her. Priapus's body had been left the natural russet color of the coarse pottery, but Venus was painted white, with blue for her jewelry and the string bra and briefs she wore. The color was worn off her right breast, the one nearer the street.

Dama took a drink from the refilled cup. "Menelaus had been staying with me the past few days," he said into the wine. "So I didn't go back to my apartment."

The bartender was keeping down at the other end of the counter, which was just as it should be. "One for me,"

Vettius called. The man nodded and ladled wine into another cup, then mixed it with twice the volume of heated water before handing it to the soldier.

"Sorry about your friend," Vettius said in what could have been mistaken for a light tone.

"Sorry about your sword," Dama muttered, then took a long drink from his cup.

The soldier shrugged. "It's had blood on it before," he said. After a moment, he added, "Any ideas about how Pyrrhus switched the notebook in your friend's purse?"

Like everyone else in the tavern, the two men wore only tunics and sandals. For centuries, togas had been relegated to formal wear: for court appearances, say; or for dancing attendance on a wealthy patron like Gaius Rutilius Rutilianus.

Dama must have sent his toga home with the slaves who'd accompanied him and Menelaus to the interview. The garment would have to be washed before it could be worn again, of course . . .

"It wouldn't have been hard," the merchant said, putting his cup down and meeting Vettius's eyes for the first time since walking behind his friend's corpse past the gawping servants and favor-seekers in the reception hall. "In the street, easily enough. Or perhaps a servant."

He looked down at the wine, then drank again. "A servant of mine, that would probably make it."

Vettius drank also. "You know," he said, as if idly, "I don't much like being made a fool of with the Prefect."

"*You're* still alive," Dama snapped.

Vettius looked at the smaller man without expression. The bartender, who'd seen *that* sort of look before also, signaled urgently toward a pair of husky waiters; but the soldier said only, "Yeah. We are alive, aren't we?"

Dama met the soldier's eyes. "Sorry," he said. "That was out of line."

"Been a rough day for a lot of people," said Vettius with a dismissive shrug. "For . . . just about everybody except Pyrrhus, I'd say. Know anything about that gentleman?"

The merchant chuckled. "I know what I've heard from Menelaus," he said. "Mostly that Pyrrhus isn't a gentleman. He's a priest from somewhere in the East—I've heard Edessa, but I've heard other places. Came here to Rome, found an old temple that was falling down and made it his church."

Dama sipped wine and rolled it around his mouth as if trying to clear away the taste of something. Maybe he was. He'd felt no twinge at mentioning Menelaus's name, even though his friend's body was still in the process of being laid out.

Menelaus had always wanted to be cremated. He said that the newer fashion of inhumation came from—he'd glance around, to make sure he wasn't being overheard by those who might take violent offense—mystical nonsense about resurrection of the body.

Vettius looked past Dama toward the bartender. "You there," he called, fishing silver from his wallet. "Sausage rolls for me and my friend."

To the merchant he added, as blandly as though they *were* old friends, "There's something about a snake?"

"Yes . . ." Dama said, marshalling his recollections. "He claims to have one of the bronze serpents that Christ set up in the wilderness to drive away a plague. Something like that. He claims it talks, gives prophecies."

"Does it?"

Dama snorted. "I can make a snake talk—to fools—if there's enough money in it. And there's money in this one, believe me."

He bit into a steaming sausage roll. It was juicy; good materials well-prepared, and the wine was better than decent as well. It was a nice tavern, a reasonable place to stop.

Besides being the place nearest to the Prefect's doorway where Dama could get a drink.

He poured a little wine onto the terrazzo floor. The drops felt cool when they splashed his sandaled feet. Vettius cocked an eyebrow at him.

"An offering to a friend," Dama said curtly.

"One kind of offering," the soldier answered. "Not necessarily the kind that does the most good."

Dama had been thinking the same thing. That was why he didn't mind talking about his friend after all . . . .

For a moment, the two men eyed one another coldly. Then Vettius went on, "Happen to know where this temple Pyrrhus lives in might be?"

Dama hadn't mentioned that Pyrrhus lived *in* his church. It didn't surprise him that the soldier already knew, nor that Lucius Vettius probably knew other things about the Prophet.

"As it happens," the merchant said aloud, "I do. It's in the Ninth District, pretty near the Portico of Pompey. And—"

He popped the remainder of his sausage roll into his

mouth and chewed it slowly while Vettius waited for the conclusion of the sentence.

An open investigation of Pyrrhus would guarantee the soldier an immediate posting to whichever frontier looked most miserable on the day Rutilianus's wife learned what he was doing to her darling.

You know, I don't much like being made a fool of with the Prefect.

Vettius wasn't going to get support through his normal channels; but it might be that he could find someone useful who took a personal interest in the matter . . . .

Dama washed down the roll with the last of his wine. "And since it's a Sunday," he resumed, "they'll be having an open ceremony." He squinted past Venus and the smirking Priapus to observe the sun's angle. "We'll have plenty of time to get there, I should think."

He brought a silver coin from his purse, checked the weight of it with his finger, and added a bronze piece before slapping the money onto the counter. "To cover the wine," Dama called to the bartender. "Mine and my friend's both."

The two men shouldered their way into the crowded street, moving together as though they were a practiced team.

They heard the drum even before they turned the corner and saw the edges of a crowd which Vettius's trained eye estimated to contain over a thousand souls. Dusk would linger for another half-hour, but torches were already flaring in the hands of attendants on the raised base of a small temple flanked by three-story apartment buildings.

"Are we late?" the soldier asked.

Dama dipped his chin in negation. "They want places near the front, and a lot of them can't afford to buy their way up."

His eyes narrowed as he surveyed the expensively dyed cloaks and the jewelry winking in ears and coiffures of matrons waiting close to the temple—the church—steps. "On the other hand," he added, "a lot of them *can* afford to pay."

The crowd completely blocked the street, but that didn't appear to concern either the civic authorities or the local inhabitants. Vettius followed the merchant's eyes and muttered, "Pyrrhus himself owns the building across the street. He uses it to house his staff and put up wealthy pilgrims."

A flutist, playing a counterpoint on the double tubes of his instrument, joined the drummer and torch-bearers on the porch. Two of the attendants at the back of the crowd, identifiable by their bleached tunics and batons of tough rootwood, moved purposefully toward Vettius and Dama.

The merchant had two silver denarii folded in his palm. "We've come to worship with the holy Pyrrhus," he explained, moving his hand over that of one of the attendants. The exchange was expert, a maneuver both parties had practiced often in the past.

"Yes," said the attendant. "If you have a request for guidance from the holy Pyrrhus, give it on a sealed tablet to the servants at the front."

Dama nodded and reached for another coin. "Not now," said the attendant. "You will be granted an opportunity to make a gift directly to the divinity."

"Ah . . ." said Vettius. "I don't have a tablet of my own. Could—"

The other attendant, the silent one, was already handing Vettius an ordinary tablet of waxed boards. He carried a dozen similar ones in a large scrip.

"Come," said—ordered—the first attendant. His baton, a dangerous weapon as well as a staff of office, thrust through the crowd like the bronze ram of a warship cleaving choppy waves.

There were loud complaints from earlier—and poorer—worshippers, but no one attempted physical opposition to the Prophet's servant. Vettius gripped Dama's shoulder from behind as they followed, lest the pressure of the crowd separate them beyond any cure short of open violence.

"Pyrrhus's boys aren't very talkative," Vettius whispered in the smaller man's ear. "Drugs, perhaps?"

Dama shrugged. Though the attendant before them had a cultured accent, he was as devoid of small talk and emotion as the messenger who brought deadly lies about Menelaus to the Prefect. Drugs were a possible cause; but the merchant already knew a number of men—and a greater number of women—for whom religious ecstasy of one sort or another had utterly displaced all other passions.

Pyrrhus's converted temple was unimposing. A building, twenty feet wide and possibly thirty feet high to the roof-peak, stood on a stepped base of coarse volcanic rock. Two pillars, and pilasters formed by extensions of the sidewalls, supported the pediment. That triangular area was ornamented with a painting on boards showing a human-faced serpent twined around a tau cross.

The temple had originally been dedicated to Asklepios, the healing god who'd lived part of his life as a snake. The current decoration was quite in keeping with the building's pagan use.

There were six attendants on the temple porch now. The newcomers—one of them was Gnaeus Acer—clashed bronze rattles at a consistent rhythm; not the same rhythm for both men, nor in either case quite the rhythm that the staring-eyed drummer stroked from his own instrument.

The guide slid Vettius and Dama to within a row of the front of the crowd. Most of the worshipers still ahead of them were wealthy matrons, but a few were country folk. Vettius thought he also saw the flash of a toga carrying a senator's broad russet stripe. More attendants, some of them carrying horn-lensed lanterns rather than batons, formed a line at the base of the steps.

Dama had paid silver for a second-rank location. The first rank almost certainly went for gold.

The merchant had opened a blank notebook and was hunching to write within the strait confines of the crowd. The tablet Vettius had been given looked normal enough at a glance: a pair of four-by-five-inch boards hinged so that they could cover one another. One of the boards was waxed within a raised margin of wood that, when the tablet was closed, protected words written on the soft surface. A cord attached to the back could be tied or sealed to the front board to hold the tablet shut.

Dama finished what he was doing, grinned, and took the tablet from Vettius. "Shield me," he whispered.

Vettius obediently shifted his body, though the two of

them were probably the only members of the crowd who weren't focused entirely on their own affairs.

Dama had been scribbling with a bone stylus. Now, using the stylus tip, he pressed on what seemed to be a tiny knot through the wooden edge of the tablet supplied to Vettius. The knot slipped out into his waiting palm. A quick tug started the waxed wooden back sliding away from the margin of what had seemed a solid piece.

"Pyrrhus the Prophet has strange powers indeed," Vettius said as he fitted the tablet back together again. "Let me borrow your stylus."

He wrote quickly, cutting the wax with large, square letters; not a calligrapher's hand, but one which could write battlefield orders that were perfectly clear.

"What are you asking?" Dama whispered.

"Whether Amasius will die so that I get promoted to Legate of the Domestic Horse," the soldier replied. He slapped that tablet closed. "I suppose the attendants seal these for us?"

"Ah . . ." said Dama with a worried expression. "That might not be a tactful question to have asked . . . ah, if the information gets into the wrong hands, you know."

"Sure wouldn't be," Vettius agreed, "if I'd signed 'Decurion Vettius' instead of 'Section Leader Lycorides.'"

He chuckled. "You know," he added, "Lycorides is about dumb enough not to figure how a question like that opens you up to blackmail."

He grinned at the pediment of the church and said, "Pyrrhus would figure it out, though. Wouldn't he?"

Dama watched a heavy-set woman in the front rank wave her ivory tablet at an attendant. She wore a heavy cross on a gold chain, and the silk band which bound her hair was embroidered with the Chi-Rho symbol. Menelaus may not have thought Pyrrhus was a Christian; but, as the Prefect had retorted, there were Christians who felt otherwise.

"Hercules!" Vettius swore under his breath. "That's Severiana—the Prefect's wife!"

He snorted. "And Ganymede. That boy gets around."

"Want to duck back now and let me cover?" the merchant offered.

Vettius grimaced. "They won't recognize me," he said in the tone of one praying as well as assessing the situation.

An attendant leaned toward Dama, past the veiled matron and her daughter in the front rank who were reciting prayers aloud in Massiliot Greek.

"If you have petitions for advice from the Prophet," the man said, "hand them in now."

As the attendant spoke, he rolled a lump of wax between his thumb and forefinger, holding it over the peak of the lantern he carried in his other hand. Prayers chirped to a halt as the women edged back from the lantern's hissing metal frame.

Dama held out his closed notebook with the cord looped over the front board. The attendant covered the loop with wax, into which Dama then firmly pressed his carnelian seal ring. The process of sealing Vettius's tablet was identical, except that the soldier wore a signet of gilt bronze.

"What're you asking?" Vettius whispered under cover of the music from the porch and the prayers which the women resumed as soon as the attendant made his way into the church with the tablets.

"I'm asking about the health of my wife and three children back in Gades."

"You're not from Spain, are you?" the soldier asked—reflexively checking the file of data in his mind.

"Never been there," Dama agreed. "Never married, either."

The door of the church opened to pass an attendant with small cymbals. He raised them but didn't move until the door shut behind him.

The music stopped. The crowd's murmuring stilled to a collective intake of breath.

The cymbals crashed together. A tall, lean man stood on the porch in front of the attendants.

"Mithra!" the merchant blurted—too quietly to be overheard, but still a stupid thing to say here.

Dama understood about talking snakes and ways to read sealed tablets; but he didn't have the faintest notion of how Pyrrhus had appeared out of thin air that way.

"I welcome you," Pyrrhus cried in a voice that pierced without seeming especially loud, "in the name of Christ and of Glaukon, the Servant of God."

Vettius narrowed his eyes.

Dama, though he was uncertain whether the soldier's ignorance was real or just pretense, leaned even closer than the press demanded and whispered, "That's the name of his snake. The bronze one."

"Welcome Pyrrhus!" the crowd boomed. "Prophet of God!"

A double *crack!* startled both men but disturbed few if

any of the other worshipers. The torch-bearing attendants had uncoiled short whips with poppers. They lashed the air to put an emphatic period to the sequence of statement and response.

Pyrrhus spread his arms as though thrusting open a double door. "May all enemies of God and his servants be far from these proceedings," he cried.

"May all enemies of Pyrrhus and Glaukon be far from these proceedings!" responded the crowd.

Crack crack!

"God bless the Emperors and their servants on Earth," Pyrrhus said. Pyrrhus *ordered,* it seemed to Vettius; though the object of the order was a deity.

"Not taking any chances with a treason trial, is he?" the soldier muttered.

"God bless Pyrrhus and Glaukon, his servants!" responded the crowd joyously.

The merchant nodded. Those around them were too lost in the quivering ambiance of the event to notice the carping. "What I want to know," he whispered back, "is how long does this go on?"

"Pyrrhus! Liar!" a man screamed from near the front of the gathering. The crowd recoiled as though the cry were a stone flung in their midst.

"Two months ago, you told me my brother'd been drowned in a shipwreck!" the man shouted into the pause his accusation blew in the proceedings.

The accuser was short and already balding, despite being within a few years of Vettius's twenty-five; but his features were probably handsome enough at times when rage didn't distort them.

"Blasphemer!" somebody cried; but most of the crowd poised, waiting for Pyrrhus to respond. The attendants were as motionless as statues.

"His ship was driven ashore in Malta, but he's fine!" the man continued desperately. "He's home again, and I've married his *widow!* What am I supposed to do, you lying bastard!"

Pyrrhus brought his hands together. Dama expected a clap of sound, but there was none, only the Prophet's piercing voice crying, "Evil are they who evil speak of God! Cast them from your midst with stone and rod!"

What—

"You've ruined my—" the man began.

—*doggerel,* Dama thought, and then a portly matron next to the accuser slashed a line of blood across his forehead with the pin of the gold-and-garnet clasp fastening her cloak. The victim screamed and stumbled back, into the clumsy punch of a frail-looking man twice his age.

The crowd gave a collective snarl like that of dogs ringing a boar, then surged forward together.

The paving stones were solidly set in concrete, but several of the infuriated worshipers found chunks of building material of a size to swing and hurl. Those crude weapons were more danger to the rest of the crowd than to the intended victim—knocked onto all fours and crawling past embroidered sandals, cleated boots, and bare soles, all kicking at him with murderous intent.

Vettius started to move toward the core of violence with a purposeful look in his eye. The merchant, to whom public order was a benefit rather than a duty, gripped the bigger man's arm. Vettius jerked his arm loose.

Tried to jerk his arm loose. Dama's small frame belied his strength; but much more surprising was his willingness to oppose the soldier whom he knew was still much stronger—as well as being on the edge of a killing rage.

The shock brought Vettius back to present awareness. The accuser would probably survive the inept battering; and one man—even a man as strong and determined as Lucius Vettius—could do little to change the present odds.

The mob jostled them as if they were rocks in a surf of anger. "Two months ago," Dama said, with his lips close to the soldier's ear, "he'd have been one of those kicking. That's not why we're here."

The victim reached the back of the crowd and staggered to his feet again. A few eager fanatics followed some way into the darkness; but Pyrrhus spread his arms on the porch of the church, calming the crowd the way a teacher can appear and quiet a schoolroom.

Whips cracked the worshipers to attention.

"Brothers and sisters in God," the Prophet called, clearly audible despite the panting and foot-shuffling that filled the street even after the murderous cries had abated. "Pray now for the Republic and the Emperors. May they seek proper guidance in the time of testing that is on them!"

"What's that mean?" Dama whispered.

The soldier shrugged. "There's nothing special *I* know about," he muttered. "Of course, it's the sort of thing you could say anytime in the past couple centuries and be more right than wrong."

Pyrrhus's long prayer gave no more information as to

the nature of the "testing" than had been offered at the start, but the sentences rambled through shadowy threats and prophetic thickets barbed with words in unknown languages. On occasion—random occasions, it seemed to Vettius—the Prophet lowered his arms and the crowd shouted, "Amen!" After the first time, the soldier and merchant joined in with feigned enthusiasm.

Despite his intention to listen carefully—and his absolute need to stay awake if he were to survive the night—Vettius was startled out of a fog when Pyrrhus cried, "Depart now, in the love of God and his servants Pyrrhus and Glaukon!"

"God bless Pyrrhus, the servant of God!" boomed the crowd, as though the meaningless, meandering prayer had brought the worshipers to some sort of joyous epiphany.

Whips cracked. The musicians behind Pyrrhus clashed out a concentus like that with which they had heralded the Prophet's appearance—

Pyrrhus was gone, as suddenly and inexplicably as he'd appeared.

The crowd shook itself around the blinking amazement of Vettius and Dama. "I don't see . . ." the merchant muttered. The torches trailed sparks and pitchy smoke up past the pediment, but there was no fog or haze sufficient to hide a man vanishing from a few feet away.

"Is this all—" Vettius began.

"Patience," said Dama.

The attendants—who hadn't moved during the near riot—formed a double line up the stepped base of the building to where the drummer opened the door. Worshipers from the front of the crowd, those who'd paid for their places and could afford to pay more for a personal prophecy, advanced between the guiding lines.

Vettius's face twisted in a moue as he and Dama joined the line. *He* shouldn't have to be counseled in patience by a silk merchant . . . .

The private worshipers passed one by one through the door, watched by the attendants. A man a couple places in front of Vettius wore an expensive brocade cloak, but his cheeks were scarred and one ear had been chewed down to a nub. As he stepped forward, one of the attendants put out a hand in bar and said, "No weapons. You have a—"

"Hey!" the man snarled. "You leave me—"

The attendant on the other side reached under the cloak and plucked out a dagger with a wicked point and a long, double-edged blade.

The pair of women nearest the incident squealed in horror, while Vettius poised to react if necessary. The man grabbed the hand of the attendant holding his dagger and said, "Hey! That's for personal reasons, see?"

The first attendant clubbed the loaded butt of his whip across the back of the man's neck. The fellow slumped like an empty wineskin. Two of the musicians laid down their instruments and dragged him toward the side of the building. Twittering, the women stepped past where he'd fallen.

Vettius glanced at Dama.

"I'm clean," the merchant murmured past the ghost of a humorless smile. He knew, as Vettius did, that the man being dragged away was as likely dead as merely unconscious.

That, along with what happened to the fellow who'd

married his brother's wife, provided the night's second demonstration of how Pyrrhus kept himself safe. The Prophet might sound like a dimwitted charlatan, and his attendants might look as though they were sleepwalking most of the time; but he and they were ruthlessly competent where it counted.

As he passed inside the church, Dama glanced at the door leaves. He hoped to see some sign—a false panel; a sheet of mirror-polished metal; *something*—to suggest the illusion by which Pyrrhus came and left the porch. The outer surface of the wooden leaves had been covered with vermillion leather, but the inside showed the cracks and warping of age.

These were the same doors that had been in place when the building was an abandoned temple. There were no tricks in them.

A crosswall divided the interior of the church into two square rooms. The broad doorway between them was open, but the select group of worshipers halted in the first, the anteroom.

Crosswise in the center of the inner room, Pyrrhus the Prophet lay on a stone dais as though he were a corpse prepared for burial. His head rested on a raised portion of the stone, crudely carved to the shape of an open-jawed snake.

Behind the Prophet, against the back wall where the cult statue of Asklepios once stood, was a tau cross around which twined a metal-scaled serpent. The creature's humanoid head draped artistically over the crossbar.

Pairs of triple-wick lamps rested on stands in both rooms, but their light was muted to shadow by the high, black beams supporting the roof. A row of louvered clerestory windows had been added just beneath the eaves when the building was refurbished, but even during daylight they would have affected ventilation more than lighting.

Vettius estimated that forty or fifty people were allowed to enter before attendants closed the doors again and barred them. The anteroom was comfortably large enough to hold that number, but the worshipers—he and Dama as surely as the rest—all crowded toward the center where they could look through the doorway into the sanctum.

Bronze scales jingled a soft susurrus as the serpent lifted its head from the bar. "God bless Pyrrhus his servant!" rasped the creature in a voice like a wind-swung gate.

Vettius grabbed for the sword he wasn't carrying tonight. He noticed with surprise that Dama's arm had curved in a similar motion. Not the sort of reflex he'd have expected in a merchant . . . but Vettius had already decided that the little Cappadocian wasn't the sort of merchant one usually met.

"God bless Glaukon and Pyrrhus, his servants," responded the crowd, the words muzzed by a harshly echoing space intended for visual rather than acoustic worship.

"Mithra!" Dama said silently, a hand covering his lips as they mimed the pagan syllables.

He knew the serpent was moved by threads invisible in the gloom. He knew one of Pyrrhus's confederates spoke the greeting through a hole in the back wall which the bronze simulacrum covered.

But the serpent's creaking, rasping voice frightened him like nothing had since—

Like nothing ever had before.

Goods of various types were disposed around the walls of the anteroom. Sealed amphoras—sharp-ended jars that might contain anything from wine to pickled fish—leaned in clusters against three of the four corners. From wooden racks along the sidewalk hung bunches of leeks, turnips, radishes—and a pair of dead chickens. In the fourth corner was a stack of figured drinking bowls (high-quality ware still packed in scrap papyrus to protect the designs from chipping during transit) and a wicker basket of new linen tunics.

For a moment, Vettius couldn't imagine why the church was used for storage of this sort. Then he noticed that each item was tagged: they were worshipers' gifts in kind, being consecrated by the Prophet's presence before they were distributed. Given the number of attendants Pyrrhus employed in his operation, such gifts would be immediately useful.

Pyrrhus sat up slowly on the couch, deliberately emphasizing his resemblance to a corpse rising from its bier. His features had a waxy stillness, and the only color on his skin was the yellow tinge cast by the lamp flames.

"Greetings, brothers and sisters in God," he said. His quiet, piercing voice seemed not to be reflected by the stone.

"Greetings, Pyrrhus, Prophet of God," the crowd and echoes yammered.

A pile of tablets stood beside the couch, skewed and colorful with the wax that sealed each one. Pyrrhus took the notebook on top and held it for a moment in both hands. His fingers were thin and exceptionally long, at variance with his slightly pudgy face.

"Klea, daughter of Menandros," he said. The elder of the two praying women who'd stood in front of Vettius during the open service gasped with delight. She stepped through the doorway, knelt, and took the tablet from the Prophet's hands. "Remarriage," Pyrrhus said in the singsong with which he delivered his Verses, "is not for you but faith. You may take the veil for me in death."

"Oh, Prophet," the woman mumbled as she got to her feet. For a moment it looked as though she were going to attempt to kiss Pyrrhus.

"God has looked with favor on you, daughter," the Prophet said in a distant, cutting voice that brought the suppliant back to a sense of propriety. "He will accept your sacrifice."

From the bosom of the stola she wore, Klea took a purse and thrust it deep within the maw of the stone serpent-head which had served Pyrrhus as a pillow. The coins clinked—gold, Dama thought; certainly not mere bronze—beneath the floor. The bench served as a lid for Pyrrhus's treasury, probably a design feature left from the days the building was a temple.

"Oh, Master," the woman said as she walked back to her place in the anteroom.

Tears ran down her cheeks, but even Vettius's experience at sizing up women's emotions didn't permit him to be sure of the reason. Perhaps Klea cried because she'd been denied remarriage during life . . . but it was equally likely that she'd been overcome with joy at the prospect of joining Pyrrhus after death.

The Prophet took another from the stack of tablets. "Hestiaia, daughter of Mimnermos," he called, and the younger of the pair of women stepped forward to receive her prophecy.

Pyrrhus worked through the series of requests tablet by tablet. A few of the responses were in absolute gibberish—which appeared to awe and impress the recipients—and even when the doggerel could be understood, it was generally susceptible to a variety of meanings. Dama began to suspect that the man who'd been stoned and kicked from the gathering outside had chosen the interpretation he himself desired to an ambiguous answer about his brother's fate.

A man was told that his wife was unfaithful. No one but the woman herself could know with certainty if the oracle were false.

A woman was told that the thief who took her necklace was the slave she trusted absolutely. She would go through her household with scourge and thumbscrew . . . and if she found nothing, then wasn't her suspicion of this one or that proof her trust hadn't been complete after all?

"Severiana, daughter of Marcus Severianus," the Prophet called. Vettius stiffened as the Prefect's simpering wife joined Pyrrhus in the sanctum.

"Daughter," said Pyrrhus in his clanging verse, "blessed of God art thee. Thy rank and power increased shall be. Thy husband's works grow anyhow. And morrow night I'll dine with thou."

Dama thought: Pyrrhus's accent was flawless, unlike that of the Prefect's nomenclator; but in his verse he butchered Latin worse than ever an Irish beggar did. . . .

Vettius thought: Castor and Pollux! Bad enough that the Prefect's wife was involved with this vicious phony. But if Pyrrhus got close to Rutilianus himself, he could do real harm to the whole Republic . . . .

"Oh beloved Prophet!" Severiana gurgled as she fed the stone serpent a purse that hit with a heavier *clank!* than most of the previous offerings. "Oh, we'll be so honored by your presence!"

"Section Leader Lycorides!" Pyrrhus called. Vettius stepped forward, hunching slightly and averting his face as he passed Severiana. The timing was terrible—but the Prefect's wife was so lost in joy at the news that she wouldn't have recognized her husband, much less one of his flunkies. Though Pyrrhus's thin figure towered over the previous suppliants who faced him one-on-one, Vettius was used to being the biggest man in any room. It hadn't occurred to him that he too would have to tilt his head up to meet the Prophet's eyes.

Pyrrhus's irises were a black so deep they could scarcely be distinguished from his pupils; the weight of their stare gouged at Vettius like cleated boots.

For a moment the soldier froze. He *knew* that what he faced was no charlatan, no mere trickster preying on the religiously gullible. The power of Pyrrhus's eyes, the inhuman perfection of his bearded, patriarchal face—

Pyrrhus was not merely a prophet; he was a *god.*

Pyrrhus opened his mouth and said, "Evil done requited is to men. Each and every bao nhieu tien."

The illusion vanished in the bath of nonsense syllables. Vettius faced a tall charlatan who had designs on the official whom it was Vettius's duty to protect.

Rutilianus would be protected. Never fear.

"God has looked with favor on you, son," Pyrrhus prodded. "He will accept your sacrifice."

Vettius shrugged himself to full alertness and felt within his purse. He hadn't thought to bundle a few coins in a twist of papyrus beforehand, so now he had to figure desperately as he leaned toward the opening to the treasury. He didn't see any way that Pyrrhus could tell if he flung in a couple bits of bronze instead of real payment, but . . . .

Vettius dropped three denarii and a Trapezuntine obol, all silver, into the stone maw. He couldn't take the chance that Pyrrhus or a confederate *would* know what he had done—and at best expose him in front of Severiana.

He stepped back into place.

"Marcus Dama!" the Prophet called, to the surprise of Vettius who'd expected Dama to use a false name. Diffidently lowering his eyes, the little man took the notebook Pyrrhus returned to him.

"God grants us troubling things to learn," the Prophet singsonged. "Sorrows both and joys wait your return."

A safe enough answer—if the petitioner told you he'd left his wife and three minor children behind in Spain months before. Dama kept his eyes low as he paid his offering and pattered back to Vettius's side.

There were half a dozen further responses before Pyrrhus raised his arms as he had before making an utterance from the porch. "The blessings of God upon you!" he cried.

A single tablet remained on the floor beside the stone bench. Vettius remembered the well-dressed thug who'd tried to carry in a dagger . . . .

"God's blessings on his servants Pyrrhus and Glaukon!" responded that majority of the crowd which knew the liturgy.

"Depart in peace . . ." rasped the bronze serpent from its cross, drawing out the Latin sibilants and chilling Dama's bones again.

The doors creaked open and the worshipers began to leave. Most of them appeared to be in a state of somnolent ecstasy. A pair of attendants collected the tablets which had been supplied to petitioners who didn't bring their own; with enough leisure, even the most devout believer might have noticed the way the waxed surface could be slid from beneath the sealed cover panel.

The air outside was thick with dust and the odors of slum tenements. Dama had never smelled anything so refreshing as the first breath that filled his lungs beyond the walls of Pyrrhus's church.

Almost all of those who'd attended the private service left in sedan chairs.

Vettius and Dama instead walked a block in silence to a set of bollards protecting an entrance to the Julian Mall. They paused, each lost for a moment in a landscape of memories. No one lurked nearby in the moonlight, and the rumble of goods wagons and construction vehicles—banned from the streets by day—kept their words from being overheard at any distance.

"A slick operation," Vettius said.

The merchant lifted his chin in agreement but then added, "His clientele makes it easy, though. They come wanting to be fooled."

"I'm not sure how . . ." Vettius said.

For a moment, his tongue paused over concluding the question the way he'd started it: *I'm not sure how Pyrrhus managed to appear and disappear that way.* But though he knew that was just a trick, the way some sort of trick inspired awe when Pyrrhus stared into the soldier's eyes . . . neither of those were things that Vettius wanted to discuss just now.

". . . he knew what your question was," Vettius's tongue concluded. "Is the tablet still sealed?"

"Sealed again, I should guess," Dama said mildly as he held the document up to the full moon. "They could've copied my seal impression in quick-drying plaster, but I suspect—yes, there."

His fingertip traced a slight irregularity in the seal's edge. "They used a hot needle to cut the wax and then reseal it after they'd read the message."

He looked at his companion with an expression the bigger man couldn't read. "Pyrrhus has an exceptional memory," he said, "to keep the tablets and responses in proper order. He doesn't give himself much time to study."

Vettius gestured absently in agreement. The soldier's mind considered various ways, more or less dangerous, to broach the next subject.

Three wagons carrying column bases crashed and rumbled past, drawn by teams of mules with cursing drivers. The loads might be headed toward a construction site within the city—but more likely they were going to the harbor and a ship that would carry them to Constantinople or Milan.

Rome was no longer a primary capital of the empire. It

was easier to transport art than to create it, so Rome's new imperial offspring were devouring the city which gave them birth. All things die, even cities.

Even empires . . . but Lucius Vettius didn't permit himself to think about *that*.

"It doesn't appear that he's doing anything illegal," the soldier said carefully. "There's no law against lying to people, even if they decide to give you money for nothing."

"Or lying about people," Dama said—"agreed" would imply there was some emotion in his voice, and there was none. "Lying about philosophers who tell people you're a charlatan, for instance."

"I thought he might skirt treason," Vettius went on, looking out over the street beyond. "It's easy to say the wrong thing, you know. . . . But if Pyrrhus told any lies—" with the next words, Vettius would come dangerously close to treason himself; but perhaps his risk would draw the response he wanted from the merchant "—it was in the way he praised everything to do with the government."

"There was the—riot, I suppose you could call it," Dama suggested as his fingers played idly with the seal of his tablet.

"Incited by the victim," the soldier said flatly. "And some of those taking part were—very influential folk, I'd estimate. There won't be a prosecution on that basis."

"Yeah," the merchant agreed. "That's the way I see it too. So I suppose we'd better go home."

Vettius nodded upward in agreement.

He'd have to go the next step alone. Too bad, but the civilian had already involved himself more than could have been expected. Dama would go back and make still more money, while Lucius Vettius carried out what he saw as a duty—

Knowing that he faced court martial and execution if his superiors learned of it.

"Good to have met you, Marcus Dama," he muttered as he strode away through a break in traffic.

There was a crackle of sound behind him. He glanced over his shoulder. Dama was walking toward his apartment in the opposite direction.

But at the base of the stone bollard lay the splintered fragments of the tablet the merchant had been holding.

The crews of two sedan chairs were dicing noisily— and illegally—beside the bench on which Vettius waited, watching the entrance to Pyrrhus's church through slitted eyes. Business in the small neighborhood bath house was slack enough this evening that the doorkeeper left his kiosk and seated himself beside the soldier.

"Haven't seen you around here before," the doorkeeper opened.

Vettius opened his eyes wide enough to frown at the man. "You likely won't see me again," he said. "Which is too bad for you, given what I've paid you to mind your own business."

Unabashed, the doorkeeper chewed one bulb from the bunch of shallots he was holding, then offered the bunch to the soldier. His teeth were yellow and irregular, but they looked as strong as a mule's.

"Venus!" cried one of the chairmen as his dice came up all sixes. "How's *that*, you Moorish fuzzbrain?"

"No thanks," said Vettius, turning his gaze back down the street.

The well-dressed, heavily veiled woman who'd arrived at the church about an hour before was leaving again. She was the second person to be admitted for a private consultation, but a dozen other—obviously less wealthy—suppliants had been turned away during the time the soldier had been watching.

He'd been watching, from one location or another in the neighborhood, since dawn.

"I like to keep track of what's going on around here," the doorkeeper continued. He ate another shallot and belched. "Maybe I could help you with what you're looking for?"

Vettius clenched his great, calloused hands, only partly as a conscious attempt on his part to warn this nuisance away. "Right now," he said in a husky voice, "I'm looking for a little peace and—"

"Hey there!" one of the chairmen shouted in Greek as the players sprang apart. One reached for the stakes, another kicked him, and a third slipped a short, single-edged knife from its hiding place in the sash that bound his tunic.

Vettius and the doorkeeper both leaped to their feet. The soldier didn't want to get involved, but if a brawl broke out, it was likely to explode into him.

At the very best, that would disclose the fact that he was hiding his long cavalryman's sword beneath his cloak.

The pair of plump shopowners who'd hired the sedan chairs came out the door, rosy from the steam room and their massages. The chairmen sorted themselves at once into groups beside the poles of their vehicles. The foreman of one chair glanced at the other, nodded, and scooped up the stakes for division later.

Vettius settled back on the bench. Down the street, a quartet of porters were carrying a heavy chest up the steps of the church. Attendants opened the doors for the men.

Early in the morning, the goods Vettius had seen in the building's anteroom had been dispersed, mostly across the street to the apartment house which Pyrrhus owned. Since then, there had been a constant stream of offerings. All except the brace of live sheep were taken inside.

Pyrrhus had not come out all day.

"A bad lot, those chairmen," the doorkeeper resumed, dusting his hands together as though he'd settled the squabble himself. The hollow stems of his shallots flopped like an uncouth decoration from the bosom of his tunic. "I'm always worried that—"

Vettius took the collar of the man's garment between the thumb and forefinger of his left hand. He lifted the cloth slightly. "If you do not leave me alone," he said in a low voice, "you will have something to worry about. For a short time."

Half a dozen men, householders and slaves, left the bath caroling an obscene round. One of them was trying to bounce a hard leather ball as he walked, but it caromed wildly across the street.

The doorkeeper scurried back to his kiosk as soon as Vettius released him.

Three attendants, the full number of those who'd been in the church with Pyrrhus, came out and stood on the porch. Vettius held very still. It was nearly dusk—time and past time that the Prophet go to dinner.

If he was going.

Pyrrhus could lie and bilk and slander for the next fifty years until he died on a pinnacle of wealth and sin, and that'd still be fine with Lucius Vettius. There were too many crooked bastards in the world for Vettius to worry about one more or less of 'em. . . .

Or so he'd learned to tell himself, when anger threatened to build into a murderous rage that was safe to release only on a battlefield.

Vettius wasn't just a soldier anymore: he was an agent of the civil government whose duties required him to protect and advise the City Prefect. If Pyrrhus kept clear of Rutilianus, then Pyrrhus had nothing to fear from Lucius Vettius.

But if Pyrrhus chose to make Rutilianus his business, then . . .

A sedan chair carried by four of Pyrrhus's attendants trotted to the church steps from the apartment across the street. A dozen more of the Prophet's men in gleaming tunics accompanied the vehicle. Several of them carried lanterns for the walk back, though the tallow candles within were unlighted at the moment.

Pyrrhus strode from the church and entered the sedan chair. He looked inhumanly tall and thin, even wrapped in the formal bulk of a toga. It was a conjuring trick itself to watch the Prophet fold his length and fit it within the sedan, then disappear behind black curtains embroidered with a serpent on a cross.

Three attendants remained on the porch. The

remainder accompanied the sedan chair as it headed northeast, in the direction of the Prefect's dwelling. The attendants' batons guaranteed the vehicle clear passage, no matter how congested the streets nearer the city center became.

Vettius sighed. Well, he had his excuse, now. But the next—hours, days, years; he didn't know how long it'd take him to find something on this "Prophet" that'd stick. . . .

The remainder of the soldier's life might be simpler if he didn't start at all. But he was going to start, by burglarizing Pyrrhus's church and private dwelling while the Prophet was at dinner. And if that didn't turn up evidence of a crime against the State, there were other things to try . . . .

A hunter learns to wait. It would be dead-dark soon, when the sun set and the moon was still two hours beneath the horizon. Time then to move to the back of the church which he'd reconnoitered by the first light of dawn.

Men left the bath house, laughing and chatting as they headed for their dinners. Vettius watched the three attendants, as motionless as statues on the church porch; as motionless as he was himself.

And he waited.

When Vettius was halfway up the back wall of the church, a patrol of the Watch sauntered by in the street fronting the building.

Watch patrols were primarily fire wardens, but the State equipped them with helmets and spears to deal with any other troubles they might come across. This group was dragging the ferules of its spears along the pavement with a tremendous racket, making sure it *didn't* come across such troubles . . . but Vettius still paused and waited for the clatter to trail off in the direction of the Theater of Balbus.

Back here, nobody'd bothered to cover the building's brick fabric with marble, and the mortar between courses probably hadn't been renewed in the centuries since the structure was raised as a temple. The warehouse whose blind sidewall adjoined the back of the church two feet away was also brick. It provided a similarly easy grip for the cleats of Vettius's tight-laced boots.

Step by step, steadying himself with his fingertips, the soldier mounted to the clerestory windows beneath the transom of the church. Each was about three feet long but only eight inches high, and their wooden sashes were only lightly pinned to the bricks.

Vettius loosened a window with the point of his sword, then twisted the sash outward so that the brickwork continued to grip one end. If matters went well, he'd be able to hide all signs of his entry when he left.

He hung his cloak over the end of the window he'd swung clear. He'd need the garment to conceal his sword on the way back.

The long spatha was a terrible tool for the present use. He'd brought it rather than a sturdy dagger or simply a prybar because—

Because he was still afraid of whatever he thought he'd seen in Pyrrhus's eyes the night before. The sword couldn't help that, but it made Vettius *feel* more comfortable.

There was a faint glow from within the building; one

lamp wick had been left burning to light the Prophet's return home.

Vettius uncoiled his silken line. He'd thought he might need the small grapnel on one end to climb to the window, but the condition of the adjoining walls made the hooks as unnecessary as the dark lantern he'd carried in case the church was unlighted. Looping the cord around an end-frame of the window next to the one he'd removed, he dropped both ends so that they dangled to the floor of Pyrrhus's sanctum.

He had no real choice but to slide head-first through the tight opening. He gripped the doubled cord in both hands to keep from plunging thirty feet to the stone floor.

His right hand continued to hold the hilt of his naked sword as well. Scabbarded, the weapon might've slipped out when he twisted through the window; or so he told himself.

Pyrrhus's bronze serpent gaped only a few feet from Vettius as he descended the cord, hand over hand. The damned thing was larger than it had looked from below, eighteen—no, probably twenty feet long when you considered the way its coils wrapped the cross. Shadows from the lamplight below drew the creature's flaring nostrils into demonic horns.

At close view, the bronze head looked much less human than it had from the anteroom. There were six vertical tubes in each eye. They lighted red and green in alternation.

Vettius's hobnails sparked as he dropped the last yard to the floor. The impact felt good.

Except for Pyrrhus's absence, the sanctum looked just

as it had when the soldier saw it the night before. He went first to the couch that covered the Prophet's strongbox. It was solid marble, attached to the floor by bronze pivots. Vettius expected a lock of some sort, but only weight prevented the stone from being lifted. So . . . .

He sheathed his sword and gripped the edge of the couch with both hands. Raising the stone would require the strength of three or four normal men, but—

The marble pivoted upward, growling like a sleeping dog.

The cavity beneath was empty.

Vettius vented his breath explosively. He almost let the lid crash back in disgust, but the stone might have broken and the noise would probably alert the attendants.

Grunting—angry and without the hope of immediate triumph to drive him—Vettius lowered by main strength the weight that enthusiasm had lifted.

He breathed heavily and massaged his palms against his thigh muscles for a minute thereafter. Score one for the Prophet.

Vettius didn't know precisely what he'd expected to find in the crypt, but there *had* to be some dark secret within this building or Pyrrhus wouldn't have lived in it alone. Something so secret that Pyrrhus didn't dare trust it even to his attendants . . . .

Perhaps there was a list of high government personnel who were clients of Pyrrhus—or who supplied him with secret information. The emperors were—rightly—terrified of conspiracies. A list like that, brought to the attention of the right parties, would guarantee mass arrests and condemnations.

With, very probably, a promotion for the decurion who uncovered the plot.

If necessary, Vettius could create such a document himself; but he'd rather find the real one, since something of the sort *must* exist.

The bronze lamp had been manufactured especially for Pyrrhus. Counterweighting the spouts holding the three wicks was a handle shaped like a cross. A human-headed serpent coiled about it.

Vettius grimaced at the feel of the object as he took it from its stand. He prowled the sanctum, holding the light close to the walls.

If there was a hiding place concealed within the bricks, Vettius certainly couldn't find it. The room was large and clean, but it was as barren as a prison cell.

There was a faint odor that the soldier didn't much like, now that he'd settled down enough to notice it.

He looked up at the serpent, Glaukon. Lamplight broke the creature's coils into bronze highlights that swept from pools of shadow like great fish surfacing. Pyrrhus might have hidden a papyrus scroll in the creature's hollow interior, but—

Vettius walked through the internal doorway, stepping carefully so that the click of his hobnails wouldn't alarm the attendants outside. He'd check the other room before dealing with Glaukon.

He didn't much like snakes.

The anteroom had a more comfortable feel than the sanctum, perhaps because the goods stored around the walls gave it the look of a large household's pantry. Vettius swept the lamp close to the top of each amphora, checking the tags scratched on the clay seals. Thasian wine from the shipowner Glirius. Lucanian wine from the Lady Antonilla. Dates from—Vettius chuckled grimly: my, a Senator. Gaius Cornelius Metellus Libo.

A brace of rabbits; a wicker basket of thrushes sent live, warbling hopefully when Vettius brought the lamp close.

In the corner where the stacks of figured bowls had been, Vettius found the large chest he'd watched the porters stagger in with that evening. The label read: *A gift of P. Severius Auctus, purveyor of fine woolens.*

A small pot of dormice preserved in honey. Bunches and baskets of fresh vegetables.

The same sort of goods as had been here the night before. No strongbox, no sign of a cubbyhole hidden in the walls.

Which left Vettius with no better choice than to try that damned bronze serpent after—

Outside the front doors, the pins of a key scraped the lock's faceplate.

Bloody buggering Zeus! Pyrrhus should've been gone for hours yet!

Vettius set down the lamp with reflexive care and ran for the sanctum. Behind him, the key squealed as it levered the iron dead-bolts from their sockets in both doorframes.

He'd be able to get out of the building safely enough, though a few of the attendants would probably fling their cudgels at him while he squirmed through the window. The narrow alley would be suicide, though. They'd've blocked both ends by the time he got to the ground, and there wasn't room enough to swing his spatha. He'd go up instead, over the triple-vaulted roof of the warehouse and down—

The door opened. "Wait here," called the penetrating, echoless voice of Pyrrhus to his attendants.

Vettius's silken rope lay on the floor in a tangle of loose coils. It couldn't have slipped from the window by itself, but. . . .

The door closed; the bolts screeched home again.

Vettius spun, drawing his sword.

"Beware, Pyrrhus!" cried the bronze serpent. "Intruder! Intruder!"

Vettius shifted his weight like a dancer. Faint lamplight shimmered on the blade of his spatha arcing upward. Glaukon squirmed higher on the cross. Its somewhat-human face waved at the tip of the bar, inches from where the rope had hung. The creature's teeth glittered in wicked glee.

A chip of wood flew from the cross as Vettius's sword bit as high as he could reach; a hand's breadth beneath Glaukon's quivering tail.

"Come to me, Decurion Lucius Vettius," Pyrrhus commanded from the anteroom.

He couldn't know.

The flickering lamplight in the other room was scarcely enough to illuminate the Prophet's toga and the soft sheen of his beard. Vettius was a figure in shadow, only a dim threat with a sword even when he spun again to confront Pyrrhus.

Pyrrhus couldn't know. But he knew.

"Put your sword down, Lucius Vettius," the Prophet said. For a moment, neither man moved; then Pyrrhus stepped forward—

No, that wasn't what happened. Pyrrhus stepped *away* from himself, one Pyrrhus walking and the other standing rigid at the door. There was something wrong about the motionless figure; but the light was dim, the closer form hid the further . . .

And Vettius couldn't focus on anything but the eyes of the man walking toward him. They were red, glowing brighter with every step, and they were drawing Vettius's soul from his trembling body.

"You are the perfect catch, Lucius Vettius," Pyrrhus said. His lips didn't move. "Better than you can imagine. In ten years, in twenty . . . there will be no one in this empire whom you will not know if you wish to, whom you cannot sway if you wish to. On behalf of Pyrrhus the Prophet. Or whatever I call myself then.

"Put your sword down, Lucius Vettius."

The hilt of Vettius's sword was hot, as hot and glowing as the eyes of the approaching Pyrrhus. He couldn't hold the blade steady; light trembled along its sharp double edges like raindrops on a willow leaf.

But it didn't fall from his hand.

Pyrrhus stepped through the doorway between the rooms. His shoulder brushed the jamb, brushed through it—form and stuccoed brickwork merging, separating; the figure stepping onward.

"I will have this empire," Pyrrhus said. "And I will have this world."

Vettius stared down a black tunnel. At the end of the tunnel glared Pyrrhus's eyes, orange-hot and the size of the universe. They came nearer yet.

"And when I return to those who drove me out, when

I return to those who would have *slain* me, Lucius Vettius," said the voice that echoed within the soldier's skull, "they will bow! For mine will be the power of a whole world forged to my design . . . .

"Put down your sword!"

Vettius screamed and swung his blade in a jerky, autonomic motion with nothing of his skill or years of practice to guide it. Steel cut the glowing eyes like lightning blasting the white heart of a sword-smith's forge—

The eyes gripped Vettius's eyes again. The Prophet's laughter hissed and bubbled through the soldier's mind.

"You are mine, Lucius Vettius," the voice said caressingly. "You have been mine since you met my gaze last night. Did you think you could hide your heart from me?"

Vettius's legs took a wooden, stumbling step forward; another step, following the eyes as they retreated toward the figure standing by the outer door. The figure of Pyrrhus *also,* or perhaps the only figure that was really Pyrrhus. The soldier now understood how the Prophet had appeared and vanished on the church porch the night before, but that no longer mattered.

Nothing mattered but the eyes.

"I brought you here tonight," said the voice.

"No . . ." Vettius whispered, but he wasn't sure either that he spoke the word or that it was true. He had no power over his thoughts or his movements.

"You will be my emperor," the voice said. "In time. In no time at all, for me. With my knowledge, and with the weapons I teach you to build, you will conquer your world for me."

The glowing eyes shrank to normal size in the sockets of the thing that called itself Pyrrhus. The bearded phantasm moved backward one step more and merged with the figure that had not moved since entering the church.

"And then . . ." said the figure as all semblance of Pyrrhus drained away like frost in the sunshine, ". . . I will return home."

The toga was gone; the beard, the pudgy human cheeks. What remained was naked, bone-thin, and scaly. Membranes flickered across the slit-pupiled eyes, cleaning their surfaces; then the reptilian eyes began to carve their path into Vettius's mind with surgical precision.

He heard the creak of hinges, a lid rising, but the sound was as faint and meaningless as a seagull's cry against the thunder of surf.

"Pyrrhus!" shrieked the bronze serpent. "Intruder! Guards! Guards! *Guards!*"

Vettius awakened, gasping and shaking himself. He felt as though he'd been buried in sand, a weight that burned and crushed every fiber of his body.

But it hadn't been his body that was being squeezed out of existence.

The chest—*A gift of P. Severius Auctus, purveyor of fine woolens*—was open. Dama was climbing out of it, as stiff as was to be expected when even a small man closed himself in so strait a compass. He'd shrugged aside the bolt of cloth that covered him within the chest, and he held the scabbard of an infantry sword in his left hand.

His right drew the short, heavy blade with a musical *sring!*

"Guards!" Glaukon shouted again.

The serpent had left its perch. It was slithering in long curves toward Dama.

Pyrrhus reached for the doorlatch with one reptilian hand; Vettius swung at him off-balance. He missed, but the spatha's tip struck just above the lock plate and splintered its way deep into the age-cracked wood.

Pyrrhus hissed like tallow on a grill. He leaped toward the center of the room as the soldier tugged his weapon free and turned to finish the matter.

Glaukon struck like a cobra at Dama. The merchant, moving with a reflexive skill that would have impressed Vettius if he'd had time to think, blocked the bronze fangs with the scabbard in his left hand. Instead of a clack as the teeth met, light crackled like miniature lightning.

Dama swore in Greek and thrust with his sword at the creature's head. Glaukon recoiled in a smooth curve. The serpent's teeth had burned deep gouges into the scabbard's iron chape.

Vettius pivoted on the ball of his left foot, bringing his blade around in a whistling arc that would—

Pyrrhus's eyes blazed into the soldier's. "Put down your sword, Lucius Vettius," rang the voice in his mind. Vettius held as rigid as a gnat in amber.

There were shouts from outside. Someone knocked, then hammered the butt of his baton on the weakened panel. Splinters of gray wood began to crack off the inside.

Glaukon was twenty feet of shimmering coils, with death in its humanoid jaws. Dama feinted. Glaukon quivered, then struck in earnest as the merchant shifted in the direction of Pyrrhus who was poising in the center of the anteroom as his eyes gripped Vettius.

Dama jumped back, almost stumbling over the chest in which he'd hidden. He was safe, but the hem of his tunic smoldered where the teeth had caught it.

Put—

Several batons were pounding together on the door. The upper half of a board flew into the room. An attendant reached through the leather facing and fumbled with the lock mechanism.

—down your sword, Lucius Vettius.

Dama's sword dipped, snagged the bolt of cloth that had covered him, and flipped it over the head of the bronze serpent. Wool screamed and humped as Glaukon tried to withdraw from it.

Dama smiled with cold assurance and stabbed where the cloth peaked, extending his whole body in line with the blow. The sharp wedge of steel sheared cloth, bronze, and whatever filled the space within Glaukon's metal skull.

The door burst inward. Pyrrhus sprang toward the opening like a chariot when the bars come down at the Circus. Vettius, freed by the eyes and all deadly instinct, slashed the splay-limbed figure as it leaped past.

The spatha sliced *in* above the chin, shattering pointed, reptilian teeth. *Down* through the sinuous neck. *Out,* breaking the collar bone on the way.

The blood that sprayed from the screaming monster was green in the lamplight.

Attendants hurled themselves out of the doorway with bawls of fear as the creature that had ruled them bolted through. Pyrrhus's domination drained with every spurt from his/its severed arteries. Men—men once more, not the Prophet's automatons—hurled away their cudgels and lanterns in their haste to flee. Some of the running forms were stripping off splattered tunics.

The point of Dama's sword was warped and blackened. The merchant flung his ruined weapon away as he and Vettius slipped past the splintered remnants of the door. Behind them, in the center of a mat of charred wool, the serpent Glaukon vomited green flames and gobbets of bronze.

Pyrrhus lay sprawled in a green pool at the bottom of the steps. The thin, scaly limbs twitched until Vettius, running past, drove his spatha through the base of the creature's domed skull.

The soldier was panting, more from relief than exertion. "Where did he come from?" he muttered.

"Doesn't matter." Dama was panting also. "*He* didn't expect more of his kind to show up."

"I thought he was a phony. The tablets—"

They swung past the bollards where they'd talked the previous evening. Dama slowed to a walk, since they were clear of the immediate incident. "He was a charlatan where it was easier to be a charlatan. That's all."

Vettius put his hand on the smaller man's shoulder and guided him to the shadow of a shuttered booth. "Why didn't you tell me you were coming back tonight?" the soldier demanded.

Dama looked at him. "It was personal," he said. Their faces were expressionless blurs. "I didn't think somebody in the Prefect's office ought to be involved."

Vettius sheathed his blade and slid the scabbard

parallel to his left leg. If the gods were good, the weapon might pass unnoticed on his way home in the cloud-swept moonlight. "I was already involved," he said.

The merchant turned and met Vettius's eyes. "Menelaus was my friend," he replied, almost too softly to be heard. "Lucius Vettius, I didn't come here with a sword tonight to *talk* to my friend's killer."

In the near distance, the night rang with cries of horror. The Watch had discovered the corpse of Pyrrhus the Prophet.

BLACK IRON

Ammianus Marcellinus was the last great Latin historian and in fact the only great Latin historian to follow Tacitus, his predecessor by some three hundred years. (There were major historians of the second and third centuries AD—and after—but they wrote in Greek.) He had an enormous impact on me, and one small aspect of his influence is "Black Iron."

Ammianus was an officer in the imperial bodyguard during the middle of the fourth century AD, the period covered by the surviving books of his history. Emperors used their bodyguards as couriers and for other special missions. Ammianus was not only in a position to talk to virtually anyone in the empire, he was personally present at some of the most important events of his time. Though Ammianus isn't as good a writer as Tacitus (who's one of the finest prose stylists in Latin or any other language), he paints a vivid picture of his world.

That world was sliding into blood and chaos. It would not emerge from darkness for centuries.

The timing may be important here. I read Ammianus while I was in Vietnamese language school and during interrogation training afterwards. The future I saw before me was one of blood, chaos, and darkness, so I could identify— indeed had to identify—with the ancient soldier and historian as I read his work.

I came back to the World, reentered law school, and resumed writing fiction. "Black Iron" is the first story I wrote after my return. It's also the first story I wrote after getting to know two Chapel Hill fantasy writers, Manly Wade Wellman and Karl Edward Wagner.

Karl had just dropped out of UNC medical school to write full time (he later completed his schooling and got his MD). Manly was a giant of SF and fantasy; he'd been making virtually his whole living from freelance writing since the late '30s. Neither Karl nor I was ever a student of Manly's, but we were his junior colleagues and friends. We got together regularly for family meals and to read to one another the fiction we were working on.

This was the first thing I read to Manly and Karl. There would be many other stories over the years.

Ammianus was in Amida when the Persians besieged and captured that city. It wasn't a critically important event in the millennia-long struggle between Mesopotamia and the Mediterranean Basin, but Ammianus produced a bleak, brilliant piece of first-hand reporting. When I visited Turkey many years later, I stood on the enormous walls of

*Amida (modern Diyarbakir) and thought of
Ammianus.*

*One further thing about "Black Iron" is worth
mentioning. I sent the story to Mr. Derleth, who'd
bought three previous stories from me. He wrote me
a letter of acceptance in June 1971, and followed it
with an Arkham House check dated July 3.*

*The next morning Mr. Derleth died of a heart
attack. This was not only the last story I was to sell
him, it was the last story he bought from anyone.*

☩ ☩ ☩

Vettius' markers were of green tourmaline that glinted
cruelly in the lamplight. The pieces had been carven
by a Persian. Though as smoothly finished as anything
Dama had seen in the West, the heads had a rudeness, a
fierceness of line that he disliked. Living near the frontier
had shaken him, he thought with a sigh.

The soldier moved, taking one of Dama's pieces. The
slim Cappadocian countered with a neat double capture.

"God rot your eyes!" Vettius exploded, banging his big
hand down on the game board. "I should know better than
to play robbers with a merchant. By the Bull's blood, you're
all thieves anyway. Doris, bring us some cups!"

The little slave pattered in with a pair of chalices. As
she left the room Vettius slapped her on the flank and said,
"Don't come back till you're called for."

The girl smiled without turning around.

"Little slut," the soldier said affectionately. Then, to
Dama, "How do you want your wine?"

"One to three, as always," the blond merchant replied.

"I thought maybe your balls had come down since I

saw you last," Vettius said, shaking his head. "Well, here's your wine; water it yourself."

He filled his own cup with the resin-thickened wine and slurped half of it. "You know," he said reflectively, "when I was on Naxos three years ago I made a special trip to a vineyard to get a drink of this before they added the pitch to preserve it in transport."

Vettius paused. "Well," Dama pressed him, "how was it?"

"Thin," the soldier admitted. "I'd rather drink Egyptian beer."

He began to laugh and Dama joined him half-heartedly. At last Vettius wiped the tears from his eyes and gulped the rest of his wine. When he had refilled his cup he rocked back on his stool and gazed shrewdly at his friend. "You brought a bolt of cloth with you tonight," he said.

"That's right," Dama agreed with a thin smile. "It's a piece of silk brocade, much heavier than what we usually see here."

Vettius smiled back at him, showing his teeth like a bear snarling. "So I'm a silk fancier now?" he asked. "Come on, nobody will come until I call them. What do you have under the silk that you didn't want my servants to see?"

Dama unrolled the silk without answering. The lustrous cloth had been wound around a sword whose hilt gleamed richly above a pair of laths bound over the blade. He tugged at the hilt and the laths fell away to reveal a slim blade, longer than that of a military sword. The gray steel was marked like wind-rippled water.

"Do you believe that metal can be enchanted?" Dama asked.

"Stick to your silk, merchant," the soldier replied with a chuckle, and took the sword from Dama. He whipped the blade twice through the air.

"Oh, yes," he went on, "it's been a long time since I saw one of these."

Setting the point against the wall, the big soldier leaned his weight against it. The blade bowed almost double. The point shifted very slightly and the steel sprang straight, skidding along the stone. The sword blurred, humming a low note that made both men's bowels quiver.

"Thought the way it bends was magical, hey?"

Dama nodded. "I thought it might be."

"Well, that's reasonable," Vettius said. "It doesn't act much like a piece of steel, does it? Just the way it's tempered, though. You know about that?"

"I think I know how this blade was tempered," the merchant answered.

"Yeah, run it through a plump slave's butt a few times to quench it," Vettius said off-handedly. His fierce smile returned. "Not very . . . civilized, shall we say? But not magic."

"Not magic?" Dama repeated with an odd inflexion. "Then let me tell you the rest of the story."

Vettius raised his cup in silent consent.

"I was in Amida . . ." the merchant began, and his mind drifted back to the fear and mud-brick houses overlooking the Tigris.

"We knew that Shapur was coming, of course; that spring, next spring—soon at least. He'd made peace with the Chionitae and they'd joined him as allies against Rome. Still, I had a caravan due any day and I didn't trust anyone else to bring it home to Antioch. It was a gamble and at the time it seemed worth it."

Dama snorted to himself, "Well, I guess it could have been worse."

"Aside from waiting to see whether my people would arrive before the Persians did, there was nothing to do in Amida but bake in the dust. It had never been a big place and now, with the shanties outside the wall abandoned and the whole countryside squeezed in on top of the garrison, there wasn't room to spit."

The merchant took a deep draught of his wine as he remembered. Vettius poured him more straight from the jar. "Mithra! There were two regiments of Gaulish foot there, half-dead with the heat and crazy from being cooped up. That was later, though, after the gates were shut.

"Wealth has its advantages and I'd gotten a whole house for my crew. I put animals on the ground floor and the men on the second; that left me the roof to myself. There was a breeze up there sometimes.

"The place next door was owned by a smith named Khusraw and I could see over his wall into the courtyard where his forge was set up. He claimed to be Armenian but there was talk of him really being a Persian himself. It didn't matter, not while he was turning weapons out and we needed them so bad."

"He made this?" Vettius asked, tapping the sword with his fingernail. The steel moaned softly.

Dama nodded absently, his eyes fixed on a scene in the past. "I watched him while he worked at night; the hammer ringing would have kept me awake anyway. At night he sang. He'd stand there singing with the hearth glaring off him, tall and stringy and as old as the world. He had a little slave to help him, pumping on the bellows. You've seen a charcoal hearth glow under a bellows?"

Vettius nodded. "Like a drop of sun."

Dama raised his eyebrows. "Perhaps," he said, sipping at his thick wine, "but I don't find it a clean light. It made everything look so strange, so flat, that it was hours before I realized that the plate Khusraw was forging must have weighed as much as I did."

"Siege armor?" the soldier suggested.

"Not siege armor," Dama replied. "There were other plates too, some of them that he welded into tubes, singing all the time."

The blond Cappadocian paused to finish his wine. He held out the cup to his host with a wan smile. "You may as well fill it again. I'm sweating it out faster than I drink it."

He wiped his brow with a napkin and continued. "It was a funny household in other ways. Khusraw, his wife, and his son—a boy about eight or ten. You can't really say with Persians. Those three and one slave boy I never heard to speak. No other servants in the house even though the woman looked like she was about to drop quints.

"I saw her close one day, trying to buy a sword for my foreman, seeing the way things were tending. Her belly looked wrong. It didn't shift like it ought to when she moved and she didn't seem to be carrying as much weight as if she were really pregnant. Padded or not, there was something strange about her.

"As for my own problem, that was decided the morning the Persians appeared. Oh, I know, you've fought them; but Lucius, you can't imagine what they looked like stretched all across the horizon with the sun dazzling on their spearpoints and armor. Mithra! Even so, it didn't seem too bad at first. The walls were strong and we were sure we could hold out until Ursicinius relieved us."

Vettius made a guttural sound and stared at the table. Dama laid his hand on the big soldier's forearm and said, "Lucius, you know I meant nothing against you or the army."

Vettius looked up with a ghost of his old smile, "Yeah, I know you didn't. No reason for me to be sensitive, anyhow. I didn't give the orders.

"Or refuse to give them," he added bitterly after a moment's reflection. "Have some more wine and go on with your story."

Dama drank and set his cup down empty. "Until things got really serious I spent most nights on my roof. Khusraw was working on a sword, now, and I forgot about the other stuff he had been forging. But everytime he had the metal beaten out into a flat blade he folded it back in on itself and started over."

The soldier nodded in understanding, running his finger along the watermarked blade. The merchant shrugged.

"Very late one night I awakened. Khusraw stood beside the forge and that evil white light flared over the courtyard every time the bellows pulsed. Tied to the anvil was a half-filled grain sack. The only noise, though, was the thump of the bellows and perhaps a whisper of the words Khusraw was chanting, and I couldn't figure out what had awakened me. Then another moan came from the house. That sound I knew—Khusraw's wife was in labor and I thought I'd been wrong about her belly being padded.

"Out in the courtyard the smith laid one hand on the grain sack. With the other, all wrapped in hides, he took the blade out of the hearth. The slave let the bellows stop and for an instant I could see both pairs of eyes reflecting the orange steel of the sword. Then Khusraw stabbed it through the sack. There was a terrible scream—"

"I'll bet there was!" Vettius interjected, his eyes glittering like citrines.

"—and inside the house the woman screamed too. Khusraw drew the blade out, half-quenched and barely visible, then plunged it back in. There was no scream but his wife's, this time. The slave had fallen to his knees and was making gabbling noises. When the smith drove the sword into the sack a third time, the woman bawled in the last agony of birthing and there was a crash of metal so loud I thought a Persian catapult had hit Khusraw's house. He ran inside shouting, 'My son! My son!' leaving the sword to lie crossways through that sack."

Dama paused. Vettius tossed him a fresh napkin and poured out more wine. "His own son," the soldier mused. "Strange. Maybe Romulus really did sacrifice his brother to make his city great the way the old legends say."

The merchant gave him a strange smile and continued. "That was the last night I spent in the house. Our garrison was too worn down to hold out any longer and every able man in the city had to help on the walls.

"Seventy-three days," Dama said, shaking his head. "It doesn't sound like much to hold out, does it? Not in so strong a city. But there were so many Persians . . .

"No matter. The end came when a section of wall collapsed. The Persians didn't bring it down, we did ourselves—built it too high and it toppled. We tried to mass in the breach as the Persians poured through."

Dama paused with a wry grin. "Oh, you would have liked that, Lucius; the dust was sticky with blood. The armory had been buried when the wall fell and because the Persians were pushing us back, whenever a man lost his weapon he was out of the fight. I dodged out of the melee when my sword shattered on a shield boss. Then, when I had caught my breath I ran to Khusraw's shop, thinking he might still have some weapons I could carry back to the fighting.

"The front of the shop was empty, so I burst into the back. The smith was alone, holding a slender box open on his lap. When he saw me he slammed the lid shut, but I'd already caught the glint of steel inside. 'Give me the sword!' I said. 'No!' he cried, 'it's for my son to carry to King Shapur.' I grabbed the box, then, and knocked him down with my free hand. There was no time to talk and gods! but I was afraid.

"I tore the box open and drew this sword while Khusraw shouted something I didn't understand. Something clanged in the inner room. I turned to see the door swing open, and then I knew what the smith had made of his forgings.

"It was about a man's height, but from the way the ground shook there must have been twenty manloads of iron in it. I took a step back and the thing followed me. Even with the weight I might have thought it was a man in armor, but the eyes! They were little balls of cloudy orange. No one could have seen out through them, but they swiveled as I moved.

"I cut at the head of the . . . the iron man. The sword bounced off. As sharp as the blade was, it only scratched the thing. Khusraw was backed against the wall to my left. He began to cackle, but I couldn't take my eyes off his creation long enough to deal with him.

"I thrust at the thing's throat. The point caught where the neck joined that black iron skull, but I didn't have enough strength to ram it home. Before I could recover, the iron man closed its hand over the blade. I yanked back and the sword shrieked out of its grip, slicing the metal fingers as neatly as it would have flesh."

Dama laughed grimly and tossed down his wine. "I've mentioned how Khusraw was giggling at me? Well, he stopped then. He shouted, 'Son!' and jumped at me, just as his toy tried to smash me with its fist. I ducked and the steel hand caught Khusraw on the temple and slammed him into the wall. I tried to dodge through the door then, but my boot slipped in the blood. I scrambled clear of the thing's foot, but it had me backed against the wall.

"I thrust again, at the face this time. The tip skidded into an eye socket without penetrating, and the weight of the iron drove the hilt against the wall behind me. The blade bent but the very weight on it held the hilt firm. Then, as the thing reached for my head, the swordpoint shifted and the blade sprang straight, driving itself through the skull. The remaining eye went black and the thing crashed to the floor.

"There wasn't time to think then. I tugged the sword free and ran into the street to find the Persians had . . . well, the rest doesn't matter, I suppose. I was one of the lucky ones who slipped out of the city that night."

The soldier sighted down the length of the blade. "So your smith put his own son's soul in the sword and it wrecked his machine for him," he said at last.

The slender merchant ran a hand through his blond hair, the tension gone from him now that he had finished his story. "No, I don't think so," he said quietly. "You're forgetting Khusraw's wife."

"Her pregnancy?" the soldier asked in bewilderment.

"She wasn't pregnant," Dama explained, "she was just a vehicle. The smith had his materials, a soul and a body. Somehow his wife's pretence of labor allowed him to join them. The thing was alive, an automaton."

Vettius shook his head. "What you're calling an automaton—there must have been a dwarf inside with some very clever machinery."

Dama smiled gently. "There was no man inside. Lucius, when I pulled that sword free it was as clean as you see it now; no blood, no brains sticking to it."

The soldier looked from his friend to the sword. The blade had a faint green cast to it now as it caught the reflection of the gaming pieces so finely carven by some Persian craftsman.

THE SHORTEST WAY

❦❦

Before I sent off my first story, I told myself that someday a story of mine would be published. After that first sale, I decided I'd like to sell another so that I wouldn't be a one-shot author.

Let me tell you, selling stories is an addiction. The need just gets worse.

I did well enough in law school that I was offered a place on the Duke Law Journal at the beginning of my second year. The upperclassman describing the journal told me that if I was really lucky, in my third year I might be able to publish a one-paragraph Note under my own name. "It's a real thrill to see your name in print!" he said.

And I thought, "You twit. People pay to put my name in print!"

But that wasn't true: August Derleth had paid to put my name in print, and he was dead. I was going to have to find another market if I hoped ever to sell again.

Two professional magazines in 1971 published some fantasy. I sent Fantastic a story which vanished utterly, an event perhaps concerned with the problems that later got the editor a felony conviction for drug dealing. After that experience, Fantastic *was no longer a potential market for me.*

And there was The Magazine of Fantasy and Science Fiction, *an excellent periodical which at about that time published a heroic fantasy novella by a writer with a high literary reputation. (It wasn't a very good story per se, which should have warned me.)*

I wrote "The Shortest Way" and submitted it to F&SF with a covering letter that said, "I know you don't publish much heroic fantasy . . ." It came back with a nice personal rejection from the editor, Mr. Ferman, agreeing that they didn't publish much heroic fantasy though this was a good story.

Close only counts in horseshoes and hand grenades. And indeed, my friend Karl had an even closer brush: one of his heroic fantasies ("The Dark Muse") came back from F&SF already copyedited. Mr. Ferman had decided very late in the game not to publish.

"The Shortest Way" is based on the Sawney Beane legend. I'd heard of Sawney Beane many years before, but I first got the details when I read The Complete Newgate Calendar *in the Duke Law School library. (I didn't like law school, but there were compensations.) The road itself is a real one in Dalmatia, torn up in the third century BC for reasons archeology can't determine. And I used the*

same two characters for the story as I had in "Black Iron": I'd started writing a series.

Stu Schiff—Stuart David Schiff, DDS—started Whispers *magazine in 1972 with the stated intention of replacing* The Arkham Collector *(which had died with Mr. Derleth) as a home for new fantasy-themed fiction, poetry, and articles. (Stu would've used the title* Whispers from Arkham *if Arkham House had agreed. They didn't.) He bought the story and published it in the third issue of the magazine, with a wonderful Lee Brown Coye coverillo.*

At the time I wrote "The Shortest Way," I wasn't sure "Black Iron" would ever be printed. (It finally came out in 1975 as part of an anthology Gerry Page put together for Arkham House, using all the material Mr. Derleth had acquired before his death, filled out by the considerable amount Gerry himself bought for the volume.) The stories don't have to be read in any particular order; they're just part of the same world.

Even so, the decision to write these stories in series probably had something to do with me a little later writing a second story about a group of future mercenaries called Hammer's Slammers. That was the choice that got me started on a real career writing, though I didn't know it at the time.

✣ ✣ ✣

The dingy relay station squatted beside the road. It had a cast-off, abandoned look about it though light seeped through chinks in the stone where mortar had crumbled. Broken roof slates showed dark in the moonlight like missing teeth. To the rear bulked the stables where relays for the post riders stamped and nickered in their filthy stalls, and the odor of horse droppings thickened the muggy night.

The three riders slowed as they approached.

"Hold up," Vettius ordered. "We'll get a meal here and ask directions."

Harpago cantered a little further before halting. He was aristocrat enough to argue with a superior officer and young enough to think it worthwhile. "If we don't keep moving, sir, we'll never get to Aurelia before daybreak."

"We'll never get there at all if we keep wandering in these damned Dalmatian hills," Vettius retorted as he dismounted. His side hurt. Perhaps he had gotten too old for this business. At sunup he had strapped his round shield tightly to his back to keep it from slamming during the long ride. All day it had rubbed against his cuirass, and by now it had left a sore the size of his hand.

The shield itself galled him less than what it represented. A sunburst whose rays divided ten hearts spaced around the rim had been nielloed onto the thin bronze facing: the arms of the Household Cavalry. Leading a troop of the emperor's bodyguard should have climaxed Vettius's career, but he had quickly discovered his job was really that of special staff with little opportunity for fighting. He was sent to gather information for the emperor where the stakes were high and the secret police untrustworthy. There was danger in probing the ulcers of a dying empire, but Vettius found no excitement in it; only disgust.

Dama chuckled with relief to be out of his saddle again.

He used his tunic to fan the sweat from his legs, looking inconsequential beside the two powerful soldiers. Though he was a civilian, a sword slapped against his thigh. In the back country, weapons were the mark of caution rather than belligerence. He nodded toward the still-silent building, his blond hair gleaming as bright in the moonlight as the bronze helmets of his two companions. "If it weren't for the light, I'd say the place was empty."

The door of the station creaked open, making answer needless. The man who stood on the threshold was as old and gnarled as the pines that straggled up the slopes of the valley. He faced them with wordless hostility. The last regular courier had passed, and he had been dozing off when this new party arrived. Like many petty officeholders, the stationmaster reveled in his authority—but did not care to be reminded of the duties that went with his position.

Vettius strode forward holding out a scroll of parchment. "Food for us," he directed, "and you can give our horses some grain while we eat."

"All right for you and the other," the stationmaster rasped. "The civilian finds his own meal."

"Government service," Harpago muttered. He spat.

Vettius began kneading one wrist with his other hand. The little merchant touched his friend's elbow, but Vettius shook him away. "I'll take care of it my own way," he said. His temper had worn thin on the grueling ride, and the stationmaster's sneering slovenliness gouged at his nerves.

"Old man," he continued in a restrained voice, "my authority is for food and accommodations for me and my staff. The civilian is with me as part of my staff. Do you dispute the emperor's authority?"

The stationmaster reared back his head to look the soldier in the eyes. "Even the emperor can't afford to feed every starving thief who comes along," he began.

Vettius slapped him to the ground. "Will you call my friend a thief again?" he grated.

The old man's eyes narrowed in hatred as he sullenly dabbed at his bleeding lip, but he shook his head, cowering before the soldier. "I didn't mean it that way."

"Then take care of those horses—and be thankful I don't have you rub them down with your tongue." Vettius stamped angrily into the station, Harpago and Dama behind him.

"Food!" Vettius snapped. A dumpy peasant woman scurried to open a cupboard.

"I could have paid something, Lucius," the merchant suggested as they seated themselves at the trestle table. "After all, I came because I thought I could set up some business of my own here."

"And I brought you because I need your contacts," his friend replied. "The traders here won't tell me if they think the governor really is trying to raise money for a rebellion."

He paused, massaging the inside of his thighs where they ached from holding him into his stirrupless saddle since early dawn. "Besides," he added quietly, "it's been a long day—too long to be put upon by of some lazy bureaucrat."

Dama sighed as the serving woman set down barley bread and cheese. "Not much of a meal anyway, is it?" he said. "I thought the empire fed its post couriers better than this, even in the back country."

"And I thought we were going to get directions here,"

Harpago complained. "If we don't get to Aurelia before the fair ends we'll find all the merchants scattered—and then how are we going to learn anything?"

"We'll find a way," Vettius assured him sourly. He took a gulp of the wine the woman had poured him, then slammed the wooden cup back on the table. "Gods! That's bad."

"Local vintage," Dama agreed. "Maybe I should try to sell some decent wine here instead of silk."

The older soldier swigged some more wine and grimaced wryly. "Old man!" he shouted. After a moment the stationmaster came to the door. He limped slightly and his swollen lip was a blotch of color against his tight face.

The soldier ignored the anger in the old man's eyes."How far is it to Aurelia?" he demanded.

"By which road?" the other growled.

Vettius touched the pommel of his spatha so that the long straight blade rattled against the bench. "By the shortest way," he said testily.

"You have to . . ." the stationmaster began, then paused. He seemed to consider the matter carefully before he started again. "The shortest way, you say. Well, there's a road just past the station. If you turn north on it, it's only about twenty miles. But you'll have to look well, because nobody's been over that road for fifty years and the beginning is all grown over with trees."

The serving woman suddenly chattered something in her own language. The man snarled back at her and she fell silent.

"Could you catch any of that?" Vettius asked Dama under his breath.

The little Cappadocian shrugged. "She said something about bandits. He told her to be quiet. But I don't really know the language, you know."

"Bandits we can take care of," Harpago muttered, one finger tracing a dent in the helmet he had rested on the table.

"How else can we get to Aurelia?" Vettius questioned, half-squinting as if to measure the stationmaster for a cross.

"You can keep on into Pasini, then turn back west on the Salvium road," the other replied without meeting the officer's eyes. "It's several times as long."

"Then we go by the straight route?" Vettius said, looking at his companions questioningly.

Harpago rose and reslung his shield.

"Why not?" Dama agreed.

The stationmaster watched them mount and ride off. His gnarled face writhed in terrible glee.

"What did they do, tear the whole road up?" Harpago asked. Even with the stationmaster's warning they had almost ridden past the junction. The surfacing flags and concrete certainly had been taken up. Seeds had lodged in the road metal beneath. They had grown to sizable trees by now, so that the only sign of the narrow road was a relative absence of undergrowth.

"The locals must have torn up this branch because it wasn't used much and they were tired of the labor taxes to repair it," Vettius surmised. "They probably used the stone to fill holes on one of the main roads."

"But if this leads to the district market town, it should have gotten quite a lot of use," Dama argued.

"At least it'll guide us to where we're going," Harpago put in, plunging into the trees.

The pines grew close together and their branches frequently interlocked; riding through them was difficult. Vettius began to wonder if they should stop and turn back, but after a hundred yards or so the torn up section gave way to regular road.

Dama paused, looking back in puzzlement as his fingers combed pine straw out of his hair. "You know," he said, "I think they planted those trees on the roadbed when they tore up the surface."

"Why should they do that?" Vettius snorted.

"Well, look around," his friend pointed out. "The road is cracked here, too, but there aren't any trees growing in it. Besides, the trees don't grow as thickly anywhere else around here as they do on that patch of road. Somebody planted them to block it off completely."

The soldier snorted again, but he turned in his saddle. Dama had a point, he realized. In fact, the pines might even be growing in crude rows. "Odd," he admitted at last.

"Sir!" called Harpago, who had ridden far ahead. "Are you coming?"

Vettius raised an eyebrow. Dama laughed and slapped his horse's flank. "He's young; he'll learn."

"Sorry if I seem to push," the adjutant apologized as they trotted onward, "but I don't like wasting time on this stretch of road. It's too dark for me."

"Dark?" Vettius echoed in amazement. For the first time he took more than cursory notice of their surroundings. The swampy gully to the left of the road had once been a drainage ditch. Long abandonment had left it choked with reeds, while occasional willows sprouted languidly from its edge. On the right, ragged forest climbed the slope of the valley. Scrub pine struggled through densely interwoven underbrush to form a stark, desolate landscape.

But dark? The moonlight washed the broken pavement into a metal serpent twisting through the forest. The trees were too stunted to overshadow the road, and the paving stones gleamed against the contrast of frequent cracks and potholes. Even the scabbed boles of the pines showed silver scales where the moon touched them.

"I wouldn't call it dark," Vettius concluded aloud, "though you could hide a regiment in those thickets."

"No, he's right," Dama disagreed unexpectedly. "It does seem dark, and I can't figure out why."

"Don't tell me both of you are getting nervous of shadows," jeered Vettius.

"I just wonder why they blocked off this road," the merchant replied vaguely. "From the look of the job it must have taken most of the district. Wonder what that stationmaster sent us into. . . ."

Miles clattered gloomily by under their horses' hooves. It was fell, wasteland, a wretched paradigm for much of the empire in these latter days. This twisting valley could never have been much different, though. The humid bottoms had never been tilled; perhaps a few hunters had taken deer among its drooping pines. For the others who had come this way—lone travelers, donkey caravans, troops in glittering armor—the valley was only an incident of passage.

Now even the road was crumbling. Although only a short distance had been systematically destroyed, nature and time had taken a hand with the remainder. The flags had humped and split as water seepage froze in the winter, and one great section had fallen into the gully whose spring torrents had undercut it. They led their horses over the rubble while the pines drank their curses.

The usual nightbirds were hushed or absent.

Even Vettius began to feel uneasy. The moonlight weighed on his shoulders like a palpable force, crushing him down in his saddle. The moon was straight overhead now. Occasional streaks of light pierced the groping branches to paint the dark trunks with swordblades.

It *was* dark now. No white face would gleam from the forest edge to warn of the bandit arrow to follow in an instant. Was it fear of bandits that made him so tense? In twenty years' service he had ridden point in tighter places!

Letting his horse pick its own way over the broken road, Vettius scanned the forest. He took off his helmet and the tight leather cap that cushioned it. The air felt good, a prickly coolness that persisted even after he put the helmet back on, but there was no relief from the ominous tension. Grunting, he tried to hike his shield a little higher on his back.

Dama chuckled in vindication. "Nervous, Lucius?" he asked.

Vettius shrugged. "The woman at the station said there were bandits."

"On an abandoned piece of road like this?" Dama laughed bitterly. "I wish she were here now. I'd find out for sure what she did say. Do you suppose she knew any Greek besides 'food' and 'wine'?"

"No, she was too ugly for other refreshment," Vettius said. His forced laughter bellowed through the trees.

After a short silence, Harpago said, "Well, at least we should be almost to Aurelia by now."

"Look where the moon is, boy," Vettius scoffed. "We've only been riding for two hours or so."

"Oh, surely it's been longer than that," the younger man insisted, looking at the sky in amazement.

"Well, it hasn't," his commander stated flatly.

"Shall we rest the horses for a moment?" Dama suggested. "That pool seems to be spring fed, and I'm a little thirsty."

"Good idea," Vettius agreed. "I'd like to wash that foul wine out of my mouth too."

"Look," Harpago put in, "Aurelia must be just around the next bend. Why don't we ride on a little further and see—"

"Ride yourself if you want to be a damned fool," snapped Vettius. He didn't like to be pushed, especially when he was right.

Harpago flushed. He saluted formally. When Vettius ignored him, he wheeled and rode off.

Vettius unstrapped his shield and looked around while the Cappadocian slurped water from his cupped hand. The adjutant was out of sight now, but the swift clinking of his horse's hooves reached them clearly.

"If that young jackass doesn't learn manners, somebody's going to break his neck before he gets much older," Vettius grumbled. "Might even be me."

Dama dried his face on his sleeve and began filling the water bottles. "It's something in the air here," he explained. "We're all tight."

The soldier began scuffing at a stump fixed beside the roadway. Decayed wood flaked away under his hobnails and the wasted remnants of a bronze nail clinked on the pavement. "They crucified somebody here," he said.

"Umm?"

"These posts along the road," Vettius explained. "There were several others back a ways. They're what's left of crosses when the top rots away."

Around the bend the hoofbeats faltered and a horse neighed in terror. Vettius swore and slipped his left arm through the straps of his shield. Metal crashed on stone.

Someone screamed horribly.

The big soldier vaulted into his saddle. With one swift jerk Dama loosed the cloak tied to his pommel, snapped it swiftly through the air to wrap protection around his left arm. He scrambled astride his horse.

"Wait!" Vettius said. "You aren't dressed for trouble. Ride back and get help."

"I don't think I will," the merchant remarked, drawing the short infantry sword that was belted over his tunic. "Ready?"

"Yes," Vettius said. His spatha shimmered in his hand.

They rounded the bend at a gallop. Wind caught at their garments. The Cappadocian's tunic bulked out into a squat troll shape while Vettius's short red officer's cape flew straight back from his shoulders. When a man looked up at their approach, the soldier let out the terrible banshee howl he had learned from his first command, a squadron of Irish mercenaries, as they slaughtered pirates on the Saxon Shore.

One of the men in the road howled back.

Harpago's horse pitched wildly as two filthy, skin-clad men sawed at its reins. Startled by Vettius's howl, a dozen similar shapes in the middle of the road parted to disclose the adjutant himself. He lay on his back with his eyes wide open to the moon. One of the slayers was still lapping at the blood draining from Harpago's torn throat.

The bandits surged to meet them. A youngster with matted hair and a wool tunic too dirty to show its original color swung a club at Vettius. It boomed dully on his shield, and the bandit snarled in fury. Vettius struck back with practiced grace, felling the club wielder with an overarm chop, then stabbing another opponent over his own back as he recovered his blade. Dropping the reins, he smashed his shield down into the face of a third who was hacking at his thigh below his studded leather apron. Her rough cloak fell away from her torso as she pitched backwards.

Dama had ridden down one of the bandits. He was trading furious strokes with a second, a purple-garbed patriarch with a sword, when a third man crawled under his horse's belly and stabbed upward with a fire-hardened spear. The beast screamed in agony and threw the Cappadocian into the gully. He struggled upright barely in time to block the blow of a human thighbone used as a bludgeon, then thrust his assailant through the neck.

"Get Harpago's horse!" Vettius shouted as he cut through the melee to relieve his friend.

Dama caught at the beast's reins. A bandit, his mouth

smeared with gore, clubbed him across the shoulders and he dropped them again. Stunned, he staggered into the horse. Before his opponent could raise his weapon for another blow, Vettius had slashed through his spine. Drops of blood sailed off the tip of the soldier's sword as each blow arced home.

Dama threw himself onto the saddle. As he struggled to swing a leg astride, the purple-clad swordsman who had engaged him earlier slipped behind Vettius's horse and cut at the blond merchant's face. Vettius wheeled expertly and lopped off the bandit's right arm.

The handful of surviving bandits fell back in mewling horror. Then a baby bawled from the darkness as his mother tore him from her breast and dropped him to the ground. The woodline crackled with frantic movement. Savage forms rushed from the black pines—children scarcely able to walk and feral women. In the hush their bare feet scratched on the stone. Their men, braced by their numbers, moved forward purposefully.

All looked bestially alike.

Vettius took the reeling bandit chief by the hair and thrust his blade against his bony throat. The ghoulish horde moaned in baffled rage, but hesitated.

Then one of the women snarled deep in her throat and rushed at the riders alone. Dama, reeling in his saddle, slashed at her. She ducked under his sword and raked the merchant's leg with teeth and horny nails. Dama hacked awkwardly at her back. The woman cried shrilly each time the heavy blade struck her, but only at the fourth blow did she sag to the pavement.

"Let's get out of here!" Dama cried, gesturing at the

clot of savage forms. He could face their crude weapons, but the bloodlust in their eyes was terrifying.

Vettius was chopping at the bandit's neck with short strokes. At last the spine parted and the soldier howled again, flaunting his trophy as he kicked his horse into a gallop.

As they rounded the next bend, Dama glanced over his shoulder. Harpago's body was again covered by writhing men. Or things shaped like men.

A mile down the road they halted for a moment, looking to their wounds and gulping air. The merchant hung his head low to clear it. His face was still pale when he straightened.

Vettius had dropped his trophy into a saddlebag, so that he could grip the reins again with his left hand. He continued to rest the spatha on his saddlebow instead of sheathing it.

"We'd better be going," he said curtly.

The eastern sky was perceptibly brighter when their foam-spattered horses staggered into another stretch of dismantled roadway. The riders' skin crawled as they forced their way between the files of trees, but the passage was without incident. Beyond lay Aurelia, a huddle of mean houses surrounded by the tents of the merchants come for the fair.

Light bobbed as a watchman raised his lantern toward them. "You!" he called, "Where did you come from?"

"South of here," Vettius replied bleakly.

"Gods," the watchman began, "nobody's come that way

in—" The riders had come within the circle of lantern light and his startled eyes took in their torn clothes and bloody weapons. "Gods!" he blurted again, "Then the story *is* true."

"What story?" Dama croaked, his gaze fixed on the watchman. Absently, he wiped his sword on his ruined tunic.

"There was a family of bandits—cannibals, really—living on that stretch—"

"You knew of that and did nothing?" Vettius roared, his face reddening with fury. "By the blood of the Bull, I'll have another head for this!"

"No!" the watchman squealed, cringing from the upraised sword. "I tell you it's been fifty years! For a long time they killed everybody they attacked, so it went on for years and years without anyone knowing what was happening. But when somebody got away, the governor brought in a squadron of cavalry. He crucified them all up and down the road and left them hanging there to rot."

Vettius shook his head in frustration. "But they're still there!" he insisted.

The watchman gulped. "That's what my grandfather said. That's why they had to close that road fifty years ago. Because they were still there—even though all of them were dead."

"Lucius," the merchant said softly. He had opened his friend's saddlebag. A moment later the severed head thumped to the ground.

Rosy light reflected from eyes that were suddenly vacant sockets. Skin blackened, sloughed, and disappeared. The skull remained, grinning at some secret jest the dead might understand.

LORD OF THE DEPTHS

"Lord of the Depths" is a more or less conscious copy of "Queen of the Black Coast," one of the best of Robert E. Howard's Conan stories. The details of my story grew out of classical models, however.

I have a Latin edition of Pliny's Natural History, and during my honeymoon I read chunks of it. One interesting bit was that Alexander the Great sent a squadron under Nearchos from the Indus to Babylon by sea while Alexander himself marched back overland with his army. Pliny noted that en route the sailors found very large, aggressive squid. I assumed that Nearchos had been on an exploring voyage with a few ships.

The other classical influence was Juvenal's 14th satire. In it he rails against the mad lust for wealth that causes ships' captains to load their vessels to the gunwales, risking death for a fraction more profit.

Juvenal is a brilliant and evocative writer. Critics always talk about his bitterness and invective, but I find far more interesting his *remarkable ability to draw character with a line or two. I hope I've been able to learn something from his craftsmanship in general, but the scene just mentioned certainly shaped the present story.*

I didn't specifically reference Alexander in "Lord of the Depths," and I deliberately didn't learn any more about Nearchos's voyage than what I'd found in Pliny's passing mention in a discussion of squids. I didn't want to sully my fiction with reality. (If this seems very silly to you, it seems even sillier to me now. I can't imagine why I felt that way, but I know that I did.)

In fact Nearchos was in command of a fleet of thousands of ships which were intended to supply Alexander and the army on the march. They failed to do so because the Greeks didn't learn about the South Asian monsoon until some two centuries later. I could have turned the real event into a story; but it would've been very different.

I wrote "Lord of the Depths" during my first year in law school and sent it to Mr. Derleth. He requested that I cut a scene which he said didn't fit: the viewpoint characters are chased by a giant lizard which is killed by an arrow from the catapult on the deck of one of the vessels. (Mr. Derleth wasn't exactly wrong—the scene was unnecessary. I don't think it hurt the story, though. He liked to fiddle with things.) When I made that change, he bought the story for $50, the most he ever paid me.

This was my second sale. Those of you who've already read "Denkirch" will note that I made an

*entirely different set of mistakes in this one. I like
to think of that as the story of my life: an unending
quest to find new fashions in which to screw up.*

✣ ✣ ✣

There were five of the ships. I, deck watch on the
leader, the kerkouros *Flyer,* turned from the
invariance of sea and moonlit jungle to glance back along
our wake. Behind us stretched our sisters *Foresight* and
Crane, dragged like us over a thousand leagues of plain and
desert to reach their element at last in the Great River and
thence to the sea. For all their mishandling, the light craft
were far more seaworthy than the trieres *Service* or the
Dominator, a great fiver wallowing far astern. Built on the
River, the larger ships had suffered for lack of
knowledgeable craftsmen and seasoned wood. Both had
leaked from the start and the *Dominator* had warped to the
point that a dozen crewmen choked in the bilges to keep
the level down.

We were running by night, for the heat of the days was
too great to live, much less row, on the glancing oven of
the water. At dawn we would beach our craft, cook what
had been caught during the night or foraged on the shore,
and pray to find fresh water—all but a handful of our casks
had been of green wood also. Then we would seek shade
and rest, cursing all the while the madness of our leader to
order the voyage, and our own to obey him.

The breeze was gentle and we scudded before it, easily
distancing the heavier vessels though their sides crawled
with oars. Their captains had formed the crews into shifts
to work some of the oars at all times in a vain effort to keep
abreast of their nimbler kinsmen, but only in rough seas

where weight told and we needs must reduce sail did they succeed. The larger ships had been a mistake. Whereas we had crews of only eighteen and the beaks stripped off for ease on the long portage, the decked ships had been sent off in full fighting trim. The *Dominator* bore three hundred men, artillery fore and aft, and a bronze ram of ten talents, cast from our leader's spoils and fit only to warp the seams worse on such a voyage as ours.

Far back from the silvery darkness came the triple soughing of the *Dominator*'s command horn: Close up! It meant, as always, reef sails and await the sluggards. I sighed in vexation, for we were many months from home as was and with the penteres leaking like the pails of the Belides the situation could only get worse. A flash from starboard and shore recalled my attention as I leaned over to roust Hipporion, our bosun; the moon was glinting from something smooth in the jungle, metal or polished marble.

"Lay your dream-wench aside, Hylas," I said, for with such a nickname we mocked the grizzled old bosun. "There's something to be seen."

He only grunted as he awoke, but his eye followed my gesture right enough.

"I suppose we're to bugger ourselves while the *Fornicator* closes up again?" he growled, and at my nod roared, "Off and on, ladies, it's time to pretend we're sailors again. Begging your pardon, sir."

This last to Antiopas, a brave man and our captain, but a better horseman than sailor. He snapped awake, pawing for the long cavalry sword now stowed below as too awkward even for dignity. "What's the matter, Hylas?" he complained. "What couldn't a detail handle that we all must be up for?"

"Xenias has found something of interest, sir," the bosun answered and pointed toward the shore. More was visible now, stonework and what seemed the remains of a pier jutting from the jungle.

"Would it be a difficult landfall?" Antiopas questioned.

"With a pier for hope and a leadsman for certainty, I don't see any problem," the bosun decided, and I took the lead while he shouted orders to the rest of the crew. The *Foresight,* following or perhaps anticipating our action, trailed us in while the *Crane*'s less adventurous captain held position offshore.

I swore as I retrieved the third cast and we stood but a bow-shot from the shore.

"What bottom?" Hylas queried.

"None at all," I answered, well aware of the fool I sounded. The bosun, surprised, took the line without comment and cast it himself. The twenty fathoms shot through his hands butter smooth. "Horns of Tanit, there *is* no bottom!" he snarled. "Take it gentle," he warned the four men on sweeps. "We've a strange coast here and I've no desire to learn of further oddities the hard way."

I continued to sound as we crawled toward the shore. Finally, within a ship's length of the pier, I found bottom at sixty feet. There was no rise to speak of after that, even when the crumbling stone was alongside.

The climate had long since devoured the bollards, but an ornamental stone bench at the end of the pier and parallel to the shore was still sturdy enough to hold us by a couple turns of hawser. The pier was almost the only bare stone visible. The buildings, not bathed in salt, were completely overgrown save where a massive pediment had been pried loose by questing tendrils recently enough to leave the substructure bare. Without that there would have been little to catch my eye, for the pier was low among the waves.

"I'm going to take out a party," the captain remarked to Hylas. "You'd better be ready to get us out of here fast if we must."

Antiopas took five others with him, carrying javelins and staying within sight of the ship for the most part. The *Foresight* docked across from us but her captain kept all on board to wait for Antiopas to report. The arms chests had been opened and that, more than the ruins themselves, made us uneasy. Just as the *Dominator* signaled again one of the men on shore picked something from the ground and called to his mates. The six of them gathered but distance and the uncertain light hid the object they were discussing. Then they began to jog back in evident excitement. "Sir," called Hylas as the captain approached, "the flagship is signaling."

"Call 'em in!" Antiopas shouted back. "We're not leaving here till we've done a mite more searching."

He raised his hands and the heavy torque he carried shone softly in the moonlight. Colors were washed out, but the perfect lack of corrosion left no doubt of what the ornament was made. If a single piece of jewelry contained several pounds of gold, a further search was indeed worthwhile.

For the night we dragged the lesser ships including the

Service ashore stern first. There was a sand beach and it appeared that the bottom sloped rather gently in most places. A channel of some sort, far too great not to be natural, led straight seaward from the pier. The fiver, too massive for us to beach it, was lashed to the pier with some difficulty as it seemed that there never had been any bollards or other provision for docking ships. Between the bench and anchors the *Dominator* was adequately held, but it seemed a queer thing to some.

A few men spent the night searching, but for my own part I felt that sunshine and a clear head were better comrades than enthusiasm and stretched out on the beach. Events proved me right for dawn and the third hour had come before more gold was found.

When the discovery came it made up for the delay by its sheer magnitude. While I led a party through a ruin on the west of the city, which was laid out as a semicircle with streets raying out from the pier, someone in the far quadrant tugged on a bronze ring and raised a shout that soon had almost everyone milling around him.

When I finally got close enough to see what had been found—it wasn't until crewmen had begun to empty it—I saw a huge underground room, bare but for the tons of gold jewelry scattered over its floor. It was circular and reached by eight staircases around the rim, the only integral marring of its emptiness. A man writhed in mosaic at the bottom of the stairs at which I stood. The design was continued in a widening wavy line leading toward the center. It was too far and too dark to see what lay there or at the other entrances, and I did not care to remain in the room. Perhaps it was a theatre of some sort, though there seemed no provision for ventilation; certainly the jewelry had not been stored there. Yet why would thousands of people have packed the great room, then closed the doors and died so many years ago that not even bones remained? For thus it must have happened. I am not a philosopher; say only that we met stranger sights before we were clear of the port.

During the day three more chambers were found; it was easier when we knew what to look for. There was gold aplenty; in fact, there was more than perhaps the ships could safely hold. The sailing master of the *Dominator* held several angry conclaves with high officers but to no avail: gold continued to stream into the fiver's hold.

We had the *Flyer* loaded before the evening meal. This was poor enough, dried fish and bitter fruit, but the gold gave it the savor of ambrosia. We had not been able to fish as normally and the hunting parties found nothing but a few birds that graced the Admiral's table. Perhaps they had spent more time looking for gold than for food; still, the jungle appeared more barren than expected.

Work continued for most of the next day; the Admiral seemed bound to leave no scrap of value behind him though it meant he must follow it to the sea bottom. Antiopas was a sensible man for all his lubberliness, and when the bosun pronounced us loaded to the limits of safety he refused to have more aboard us. There was no small sparking of tempers at his announcement, but because Antiopas had high connections indeed, no one cared to overrule him on a point bearing on his own command's safety. Not, at least, when he was so obviously correct.

As a result, we of the *Flyer*'s crew were free while others hauled metal aboard. I proposed a genuine exploring jaunt—not just a search for more gold. The captain gave permission to any who cared to go though he was of two minds himself, fearing the ship might be overloaded in his absence. In the end he decided that he could easily enough dump such excess over the side if it came to that and joined us.

We were six altogether, Antiopas and the bosun, and four of us crewmen, more adventurous or more bored. We followed the central street, heading with unspoken agreement for the huge domed structure on the edge of the jungle. Clearly it was a temple or palace, more likely the former, and when a people dies as this one had, one wonders what gods it had worshipped. The jungle had recovered everything and the state of the road made me wish I had brought along a chopper. In some spots saplings had displaced paving blocks and had grown into trees, and vines covered practically everything.

The distance was greater than expected as well as being fatiguing; the enormous size of the dome had made it seem deceptively close. When at last we reached the treble base of the structure we all were spent and rested a while in the shade of the dome.

Without any particular intent I rubbed a patch of stone clear of vegetation. The result was disquieting: a round, slit-pupiled eye glared at me from the center of a nest of carven swirls. A cat, I mused, but didn't care to look at the decoration again. To avoid it I started climbing the steps to the yawning portal and the others followed.

There was little left of the bronze doors, but the

building itself, which was black and not of marble, had been very well preserved. The jungle had made few inroads on the interior, perhaps because relatively little light came through the top of the dome which was open save for a flat ellipse that spanned it. It could have been for structural reasons—I know little of domes, barbaric, inward straining things that they are—but the effect was unpleasantly similar to the carven eye outside. We could see well enough when our eyes adjusted, however. Much of the floor had been cut away in a pattern of swirls like that surrounding the eye graven on the plinth. The central portion, directly under the dome's center, had a small platform raised like an altar but the floor around it was sunken also.

"A sunburst, do you suppose?" the captain asked.

"I saw a carving outside," I replied. "It looked like some kind of eye."

"If this isn't the damnedest thing," Hylas said. "How do you get to the altar?"

I walked a few steps around the hall to get a different view. It was just as the bosun said: the altar was completely separated from the walkway around the edge of the building by a sunken area some ten feet deep. Then a sailor jumped down and made another discovery.

"Look, a drain," he called. "This whole thing must'a been a pool."

We all looked where he stood beside a stone grating in the sunken part.

"Maybe for sacrifices?" someone suggested, thinking of the Orphic rites in which the communicants knelt beneath a grate while the victims were slaughtered above them.

"Zeus, no," the discoverer disagreed, peering through the grate. "I can't even see bottom."

"Say, there's something on the altar," somebody called.

A shaft of sunlight was splashing from a green gem of some sort on the altar. None of us could see just what it was because of the dazzle but we all had hopes of a huge emerald.

"Did anybody bring a rope?" I asked, and blank looks answered me. "Well, who'll give me a boost, then?"

Leon, a brawny fellow and just the man for the job, was willing and we jumped down into the empty pool with the others following us. The central orb was surfaced and drained just as the tapered, recurved arms had been; neither gave any clue to its purpose.

The altar was on a floor-height pedestal, round and about four feet in diameter. Since the altar itself was rectangular there would be no trouble standing if I could mount to begin with. After a moment's discussion Leon braced himself against the pedestal with one hip jutting. I took a short run and jumped from his hip to shoulder, then swung myself up in front of the altar. There was an awkward piece of balancing for a moment since the ledge was only a foot and a half wide at most, but there was no need of a second attempt.

My first feelings on seeing the stone were merely of disappointment. It was a delicate piece of carving about the size of my fist, but the material was only some sort of glass. A second glance changed my disappointment to horror; I finally recognized the temple's motif. Dropping the little figurine into my tunic I leaped down beside Leon again.

"What's it worth?" he questioned eagerly.

"Damn little," I said. "Let's get out of here."

We padded across the smooth floor to the others who had managed to pry up a grating with their spears.

"Well, let's see it," Antiopas demanded. I dropped the little stone in his palm.

"By Castor!" he swore. "A glass octopus."

"Hell of a thing for a temple," somebody muttered. "Do you s'pose it belongs here?"

"Take another look at the pool," I said, "or these eye designs all over. Eight arms and a cat slitted eye; that's what they worshipped, all right."

"And that explains what this pool was for," the captain added.

Leon blinked and looked shocked. He'd been a Highlander raised and I don't think he much cared to be in an octopus pool, even after the beasts were long gone. Well, I wasn't too happy about it, either.

"Captain!" one of the men called. "There's noises down here."

We all gathered around the drain, uneasily aware that we had to climb a ten-foot wall to leave.

"Just water sloshing down there," Hylas said. "It's what you'd expect under a drain."

"A long way down," Antiopas said thoughtfully.

There was a flicker of yellow in the depths.

"Zeus Father and Savior!" cried Antiopas, leaping back as we all did.

Then, while the rest of us stood in trembling panic, his face cleared and he began to laugh, pointing at the top of the dome.

"The reflection," I gasped in sudden understanding. "It wasn't an eye, it was just a reflection of the skylight in the water."

No one was quite sure what happened then because we all were looking up when Hylas screamed and pitched through the opening. There was a splash, or perhaps that had come before; when I instinctively peered over the edge there was nothing below but a roil of bubbles.

We lifted each other out in tense silence, all but Leon, that is, who babbled to himself of what he had seen at the corner of his eye. He screamed during the night and my own dreams were bloody and mare-wracked until a gray dawn awoke me.

The captain was waiting when I opened my eyes. "Sleep well?" he asked.

I winced. "And yourself?"

He turned his palms up. "It was bad enough when I only dreamed of drowning. Though it looks as if that too may come today."

I glanced at the sky. It marched solidly with black cumuli though the wind was still for the nonce.

"We'll not set out today," I said.

"Really? You're bosun now, you know, and I'll take your word for it—but the *Dominator* seems to be making ready."

I nodded. "The Admiral wants some sea room," I guessed. "Remember, we've no proper harbor here and the fiver can't be beached. He'll try to keep her bow to the storm with the oars and take no chance of her being pounded to pieces against the shore. Though for my own part, I'd worry more that the wallowing slut's keel would split and spill me in the middle of it."

A messenger bore out my prediction within the hour and the *Dominator* put out alone. The storm refused to break, however, and she rode a half-mile out on a smooth sea while the sultry heat grew more and more oppressive. The water was so calm that Antiopas and I, sitting in the bows of the *Flyer,* could see the channel in the sea bottom as a straight dark streak in the green.

"Where do you suppose it leads?" he asked.

"Where does a mountain lead?" I replied with a shrug.

Antiopas persisted. "This end leads to the pier," he said. "At least that far; the other end . . . ."

He was voicing thoughts that had occurred to me also. "The drains," I said. "I suppose they have to lead somewhere."

Neither of us spoke for a while. When I did, I deliberately avoided what both of us were thinking of.

"Pity the baggars below decks on her," I said, thumbing toward the penteres.

"Pity the all of us, damned to this voyage," Antiopas replied and fumbled in his pouch. "Do you suppose there is any value to this?" he continued, bringing out the octopus figure.

I took a closer look at the little idol, hefting it in my hand. "Just glass," I answered. "Not very pretty, the gods know. Besides, I don't much like the idea of carrying other people's gods around. Why don't we just drop it over the side and be done?"

"Images of gods," Antiopas corrected me. "A stone is not the god but the symbol of the god."

Then why go to temples if the gods aren't there? I thought but said nothing and watched the play of light within the figurine. The glass was so smooth that it slipped in my grasp and a tiny drop of blood formed where one of the arms pricked me.

"Castor!" Antiopas swore, "The *Dominator*'s moving; she's heading in. Now what under heaven for?"

I looked up from the idol. The surface had been roiled by the fiver's oars and there was another patch of foam far beyond her, almost on the horizon from where we sat though much nearer the penteres. I rose and pointed to it without speaking.

Antiopas stood, too, and his face had gone white. One part of my mind remembered the little brown men telling us how these seas could rise in minutes, horizon to horizon, and sweep everything beneath them. Still I felt no fear, neither of that nor of what I knew in truth was approaching. The idol burned in my palm.

All along the shore men were staring in confusion at the *Dominator*, whose battlegong was clanging. As we watched, the sea darkened in front of the penteres and there was another splash of foam.

"That's no wave—" Antiopas began and broke off in horror to stare at the figurine in my hand. "Herakles who purged the world," he whispered, "be with us now."

Some started to run then but I think only the two of us realized what was coming. The crew of the *Service* was readying the catapult on her forecastle. Although the Admiral must have realized by then that the *Dominator* was not the quarry, the great fiver continued to cut through the sea pursuing now instead of fleeing.

The third time it arose it was half the distance between the shore and the swiftly approaching *Dominator*. The sacklike body squirmed—gods, it was huge!—to bring one slit-pupiled eye around to glare at us. Then it dived with another spurt of foam.

Someone had fired the *Service*'s catapult before joining the rout. The bolt glanced off the waves, probably useless even if better aimed. Men were streaming away from the shore, their shouts drowning the thunder of the penteres's drummer hammering out the strokes as the bronze prow boiled through the glassy sea. There were only two men on her deck now, the helmsman and the Admiral himself. Even as I watched the helmsman dived overboard and the Admiral took the wheel. Probably the crew had no idea of what was happening; their only view was through the oarslots and ventilator gratings.

"Run, you fool!" someone shouted in my ear and it was Antiopas, my captain. But I could not move for it was not yet time, though the god was as fire in my hand.

"The bench," I whispered, "I should be on the bench."

"Run!"

An arm snaked over the side and wrapped about the rail. The *Flyer* shuddered as she slid off the beach and continued to slant into the water toward the great weight that was dragging her down. I stared into the water as the ship lurched again and two more arms rippled up, two arms and a chalk-white beak larger than I was.

Antiopas screamed and slashed with his sword, not at the tentacle that curled toward him but the god in my hand. Then our bow heaved up and disintegrated, hurling us shoreward, as the *Dominator*'s oak and gold and great bronze ram smashed through the *Flyer* and ground what was beneath her into the mud of the bottom forever.

We buried our dead—and there were many, for the penteres had crumpled to the mast step—beneath an honest mound with none of the decaying marble to defile them. The gold we gave to the sea, may it lie there forever. Yet still there is that which rots unburied in my mind, and my dreams are ill dreams for a sailor.

THE LAND
TOWARD SUNSET

Jim Baen and I were friends for the last thirty-odd years of his life. When he realized he was dying, he called and asked me to write his obituary; his ashes are scatterered in the grove beside my house.

During our friendship, Jim—as editor and then as publisher—published the lion's share of my fiction. There is a causal relationship between the two facts, but it's not the simple one that some people have assumed.

At Karl Wagner's birthday party in December 1980, one of the writers present announced to the gathering, "David Drake sells books and I don't just because he's a friend of Jim Baen!" The fellow made the statement aloud because he was drunk, but I'm sure the Jack Daniels had merely loosened his tongue rather than putting the idea in his head.

Jim as editor at Ace had bought my first book, the collection Hammer's Slammers, when other houses had turned it down. That edition sold over

300 thousand copies, and the stories have never been out of print in book form since.

I was grateful to Jim for taking a chance on me. He was pleased at the sales (which were good enough that editors whom I'd never met took notice of me). That business success brought Jim and me into greater friendly contact from which a very close friendship grew.

If I'd simply gone for the money, I probably would have earned more during the '80s than I did by sticking with people whom I liked and trusted— mostly Jim and his Ace publisher, Tom Doherty. I'm pretty sure that my career would be in worse shape now, though; and my life would certainly be and have been less good.

As far as our business relations went, Jim turned to me when he had a screwy notion (when he needed a rewrite man on Newt Gingrich's first book, Window of Opportunity, *for example), and in turn he indulged my whims. One of those whims became the Robert E. Howard Library, which Jim handed me to edit after he had bought the rights to Howard's non-Conan fantasies.*

Jim didn't like either heroic fantasy or Robert E. Howard's writing, but he knew I loved both. He bought the rights as a playhouse for me without saying a word ahead of time. We were friends.

My deal with Jim was that I would edit up to eight volumes (I did seven; there wasn't another volume of material that I wanted to preserve) and that I would write a pastiche novelette to fill out the

Cormac Mac Art volume. I would be paid a thousand dollars for the novelette, and Jim gave me my choice of a two percent royalty on Cormac or one percent on all the volumes.

I took the one perecent, which was a good plan. The Robert E. Howard Library became a nice little profit center for me and Baen Books both over the next few years. Doing business with friends doesn't necessarily mean you're a bad businessman.

Cormac Mac Art was a 6th century Irish reiver whom Howard created in an attempt to sell to the adventure magazines. None of the stories he wrote about the character sold during Howard's lifetime, but they were dusted off and published during the Conan/sword and sorcery boom of the '70s.

I bought the small-press Cormac collection (Tigers of the Sea) when it appeared in 1974, but the character didn't enter my writing life until 1977. Then Andy Offutt, who was writing a series of Cormac pastiches for Zebra Books, asked me to provide him with a Cormac plot outline. When Andy rejected the result, I changed the character's name and developed the plot into my first novel: The Dragon Lord.

"The Land Toward Sunset" is the story I wrote for the collection. I did not try to copy Howard's style: this is a David Drake story, using Howard's themes and character. And the character isn't really Cormac but Turlogh O'Brian, a fantasy version of Cormac whom Howard created for Weird Tales.

Putting together a collection, let alone a series of

collections, is like doing a jigsaw puzzle. I could have added the two Turlogh stories to the Cormac volume of the REH Library, but then I would have needed to write a Bran Mak Morn story to fill out that volume. For a lot of reasons, I preferred to write about Cormac.

I'm pleased with the novelette on rereading, but I'm also amused at the little bits which I threw in because they fascinated me at the time (and often now as well). A close reading will show that at the time I wrote the story, I thought the myrrhine of the Romans was agate. I now believe the term referred to Blue John (banded fluorite), but my error is enshrined here.

I'll close with one final anecdote about the project, though it involves not this novelette but the conclusion which I wrote for an unfinished Cormac story (Tigers of the Sea). The leader of a Pictish warband is wearing a headdress of feathers plucked from the tail of the black sea eagle: the erne (or ern). I had never seen the word appear outside a crossword puzzle. Thanks to Cormac Mac Art and the Robert E. Howard Library, the bird got to take a bow in a real sentence.

❖ ❖ ❖

"Stroke!" bellowed Cormac Mac Art from the starboard bow oar. Stormwinds shredded his voice—even *his* voice—before the words carried down the thirty pairs of Viking rowers.

On the quarterdeck the captain, Wulfhere Skullsplitter, leaned vainly with all his bearlike might against the steering oar. The corposant glowed on the peak of Wulfhere's helmet, on the tips of the powerful Danish bow he slung even at this venture across his chest, and on the hairs of his red beard blowing like a bonfire in the storm.

"Stroke!" Cormac cried. The wind clawed the command and braided it into the mindless shriek of a seabird, another sport of the storm. He should have saved his effort for the oar, nineteen feet of straight-grained pine, salt-crusted and fighting the Gaelic reiver's strength as if it too were viciously alive.

They'd gambled against the weather, hoping to strike Saxon steadings in a season when no raiders were expected. The weather had thrown the higher dice, blasting out of the northeast with a laughing fury.

That storm was natural. It had tossed and buffeted the pirates, flinging them along a course the windgods chose, but the ship was well-found and well-manned. They would have ridden it out in time, then made their way back to England and plundered with violence redoubled for their oar-strained muscles.

Now winds and currents gripped to drag the vessel straight to Hell. Doom's glowing portal gaped to starboard, closer every heartbeat despite anything the tired oarsmen could do.

"Stroke!" Cormac pulled, his feet braced against a strake and his buttocks rising from the sea chest which supported him on the recovery stroke. The bow oar, longer and therefore heavier than those of the lower-riding stern, flexed dangerously against its deer-antler thole.

Where nothing but storm should be, a purple-green,

unnatural hoop of light a hundred feet in diameter drew the vessel. The rising arc towered unmoved despite the gale; the lower half glowed through the white-capped sea. Wind and water roared toward the hoop's hazy throat, bearing the raiders with them.

The Danes were stark Vikings who had faced death a hundred times in the dance of swords and axes. Cormac had thought no disaster could cow them, but this Hell-sent apparition had crushed many of the men to apathy. They sat on their sea chests, watching with dull eyes as their doom approached.

Even so, at least a score of the pirates were rowing, men nearly as strong as Cormac himself. Their oars would have driven the supple longship through calm seas faster than a man on shore could walk. For all their efforts, the vessel continued to slip sideways toward the glowing circle.

Wulfhere leaned outward to fight the counterthrust on his steering oar, a ten-foot slab carved from the heartwood of a mighty oak. The oar's deep bite from the roiling sea was not enough to overcome the uncanny pull of the current. Wulfhere's mouth was open, bellowing defiance to whatever god or demon gripped his ship and crew. The quavering corposant that now clung to all the vessel's peaks and edges was itself stained by the hoop's purple-green light.

"Stro—"

But before the vain command was flung to the wind's mockery, Cormac saw Wulfhere—his oathbrother, his companion of a score of bloody battles in which they two stood back to back and defied the world, his *friend*—lurch over the rail of the longship. It was not the oak which had given way before the Dane's desperate might, but rather the knot of tough spruce root which bound the oarshaft to the wort in the vessel's side.

Still clutching the tiller, his face bearing a look of surprise, Wulfhere pitched head first into the waves. For all the Dane had been born at the water's edge and had sailed the pirate seas since before he was twelve, he could no more swim than he could fly.

Vikings shouted in muffled consternation at this new disaster on the brink of a still-greater one. Cormac dropped his oar and mounted the rail. Like his friend, he was fully armed. This blind storm could have swept them together with another ship, and all ships were foes in these Viking seas. The survivors would have been the crew which had prepared for instantaneous slaughter.

Now Cormac's sword, his steel cap, and the coat of fine ring mail which had protected a Roman officer in the days before the empire's ruin were only so much weight and hindrance to his movements. No matter.

The Gael went into the sea in a clean dive, his eyes fixed on his sinking friend. The Dane still gripped the steering oar, but his armored weight was too great for the oak to buoy to the surface.

Cormac reached Wulfhere in three powerful strokes. He grasped the collar of the Dane's iron-scaled corselet. The current was as fierce as a millrace.

For a moment the circle of light was a glowing bar above and beneath the struggling pair. Then the apparition closed behind them and Cormac felt an instant of vertigo. He fell toward nothing at all.

✢ ✢ ✢

The transition from nowhere to *somewhere* was as abrupt as thought. There was no impact, only the shock of cold stone flooring beneath Cormac and awareness that purple-green light streamed through the pillared side-aisles and clerestory windows of a vast building.

Cormac scrambled to his feet. Wulfhere rose simultaneously, iron-shod boots clashing on the floor. Without discussion or even consideration, the long-time companions placed themselves back to back, a sword's length apart, as they surveyed their new surroundings.

The Dane moved with a catlike grace that belied his bulk. He slipped from his belt the bearded axe he favored; Cormac drew his longsword.

"Where *is* this place?" Wulfhere demanded peevishly.

Above them arched a dome three hundred feet in diameter, gold or gold-plated unless the eerie light tricked Cormac's eyes. The dome rested on sixteen massive pillars, arranged in pairs. The shafts were of red-veined yellow marble with sharp-edged fluting of the Doric order, but the bases and capitals were ornate and apparently solid silver.

The dome was at one end of a rectangular building six hundred feet long. The remainder of the structure formed a pillared courtyard, an anteroom to the domed sanctum of what was clearly a temple. Nothing moved but the whispering breeze.

Cormac glanced again at the floor set with stone hexagons three feet across their parallel flats. The veined yellow marble formed roseate patterns with slabs of black and with pure white slabs, though the bilious light stained the latter to its own hue. The blocks were bedded into place with strips of metal—not lead, but rather gold so pure that it was as soft and pliable as lead.

The huge structure had an aura of age as uncanny as the evil light which bathed it.

"What is this place?" Wulfhere shouted. His voice woke echoes from the pillars and then, a half-second delayed, from the dome above them.

A crowd of men and women poured in through the temple's front entrance, chittering to one another. The folk had brown complexions and were so short that Cormac's first thought was of a tribe of monkeys playing in ancient ruins.

There were nearly a hundred of them. They wore clothing so dull and shapeless that it required a moment's consideration to be certain it was of woven fabric rather than the pelts of beasts.

Cormac's shield, a small buckler, was strapped to his back. He tugged it free, settling the paired handles into his left fist. The iron boss and rim themselves were useful weapons, though none of this crowd appeared to be armed.

"Keep away!" Wulfhere shouted over his left shoulder to the little strangers.

The Dane was poised with his axe lifted in both hands. The blade's hooked lower edge could drag a horseman from his mount or pull an opponent's shield clear for a quick upward thrust to finish a battle. As a threat against these brown strangers, the weapon looked as out of place as it would have been in a sheepfold.

The little folk spilled around Cormac and Wulfhere. Their voices were as constant and meaningless as the buzz of bees. The tallest of the folk barely rose to the height of

Cormac's armpit. They fingered the reivers' clothing and accoutrements, pressing close in wonder but never making eye contact.

Wulfhere shouted a great curse. He raised his foot and thrust out, not so much kicking as pushing off the most insistent of the folk who tugged at his dagger sheath. The little man—or perhaps a woman—skidded across the floor, squealing in terror. The whole crowd darted back with the suddenness of a flock of pigeons changing course.

A door at the back of the building opened. Cormac had missed the hinged panel in the coffering which ornamented all the walls. Through the doorway stepped a man in a purple robe with gold lace at the throat and hem. He was black-haired and of normal height, though nowhere near the size of the armored warriors.

The newcomer raised his hand and called to the stunted folk in a liquid version of what was obviously the language that they chirped among themselves. The crowd bobbed to the floor in abasement, then dispersed through the front door and pillared side aisles. A dozen or so remained beneath the dome, waiting for further direction.

"Peace be on you, strangers," the man called in rough-hewn but intelligible Gaelic. "I am Creon, the—king, I suppose you would say, of this accursed isle. And this—"

Creon didn't look around, but through the doorway behind him stepped another figure: a woman, younger and dressed in white with gold trim. Her features, like her pale complexion and black hair, were similar to those of the man; but whereas Creon was merely handsome, the woman was startlingly beautiful.

"—is my daughter Antheia," Creon finished, smiling

slightly to notice the reivers staring with interest and appraisal toward the woman.

"What *is* this place?" Cormac called, echoing Wulfhere's demand of moments before.

"This place . . ." said Antheia. Her voice had a bell-like clarity, and the Gaelic rolled from her tongue without Creon's stilted choppiness. ". . . is all that remains of fabled Atlantis."

"You speak Gaelic," Wulfhere said accusingly. He lowered his axe only to high port, slanted across his chest; one hand on the end of the helve, the other gripping just beneath the broad blade. Cormac knew that his friend could lop Creon and his daughter into halves with a single stroke; and he knew also that Wulfhere was extremely dangerous when, as now, he was confused.

"Yes," Antheia said in German so distorted that it was a moment before the words fell into Cormac's mental template. "And we learned the speech of Saxon castaways also. Though not—" she added with a smile when she saw the reivers' puzzled expressions "—very well, I gather."

A bustle at the temple's distant entrance spun Wulfhere. He lifted his axe for a blow that could crush through an elephant's armor. Some of the stunted folk were back now, bringing wicker trays covered with fruits, nuts and berries.

The Dane lowered his axe in embarrassment, then thrust the helve back under his belt. Cormac smiled faintly and sheathed his sword. He'd want to dry the scabbard, wipe and oil the blade . . . but in good time, not just now.

"You are Atlanteans, then?" he asked.

Creon smiled without humor. "*They* are Atlanteans," he said, gesturing toward the brown servants bringing in the trays of viands. "My daughter and I are the last descendants of the Athenians who conquered the island in the moments before its collapse into the sea."

Creon crossed his arms and swept his grim gaze around the temple and the folk within it. "We Greeks decayed in numbers," he said. "*They* decayed in stature and intelligence—in the arts and in everything that raises humanity from the beasts. The end must be very soon for the Atlanteans and us, their masters, alike."

"Where *are* we?" Wulfhere demanded in a snarl of frustration. He strode toward the pillared side-aisle, moving with a speed and grace that belied the notion that a man the Dane's size must be clumsy.

A brown-skinned woman offered Wulfhere ripe pears. He danced around her. There was no contact, but the Atlantean dropped her tray in terror and hid her face in her hands.

Cormac slid by instinct to Wulfhere's left side as he left the nave, ready to cover the Dane if an axe-stroke drew the bigger man off-balance. They had survived, the two of them, because they fought as a team rather than as two individuals. A hundred times each had blocked the side-thrust spear from his friend's armpit or the sword swung at the back of the other's helmet.

At the moment, no armed foe threatened Cormac and Wulfhere in this place, this Atlantis; but the Gael had known evil enough in his wanderings to feel its presence here.

They stepped out onto the edge of the slab which

leveled the temple's foundations. A paved court had once surrounded the building, but grass and even mighty trees now shouldered aside the blocks of hexagonal marble.

A rectangular building clad in tin or tarnished silver faced the temple. The expanse of courtyard between the buildings had been kept clear of vegetation. The silver structure was two stories high and of considerable size, though it was by no means comparable to the domed temple. Atlantean servants with trays scuttled from there to the temple. They halted nervously when they noticed Cormac and Wulfhere watching them.

Antheia came out beside the reivers. Cormac couldn't read the hint of a smile she gave him. He noticed for the first time that Antheia's robe was clasped at the left shoulder by a brilliant ruby. That stone and the similar jewel which her father wore were the only objects in this *place* which seemed unaffected by the sickly light.

The thought drew Cormac's gaze upward. He squinted, holding the back of his left hand across his eyes so that the fingers formed slitted protection.

He'd expected the sun, however distorted or cruelly filtered its beams might be. Instead, a ball of purple-green light hung only a moderate distance—miles or at most tens of miles—above the temple's dome. The ball had a measurable diameter rather than being a dazzling point like the true sun.

Swirls of sickly color paraded across the sphere's displayed surface. Its glow provided the sole illumination of the world below.

Cormac lowered his eyes, shivering despite himself. Until he saw *that*, he hadn't truly believed that something had snatched him from his former reality. Wherever Atlantis was, it was not in a place or time that Cormac's world knew.

"How did we get here, girl?" Wulfhere asked in a soft voice. Only someone who knew the Dane as well as Cormac did would have realized that Wulfhere was on the edge of berserk fury.

"Sometimes the bubble in which we all are trapped draws things from outside itself," Antheia replied. She spoke calmly, but a tic in the corner of her eye suggested she read Wulfhere's mood better than the Gael had feared she would. "Driftwood, seabirds . . . Men, not often, but often enough in the millennia since the bulk of the island sank."

"In my day and that of my daughter," said Creon, who joined them from between two of the close-set columns, "there have been Christian monks from Ireland and pirates who call themselves Saxons and Jutes. And yourselves, good sirs."

He nodded with sad finality.

An animal hooted in pain or triumph from the near distance. The sound was the first sign that anything existed beyond the ruins fringing the overgrown courtyard.

"How do we get out of here, then?" Cormac demanded. His voice didn't rise after the second syllable, but that was only because he consciously suppressed the spike of terror. "How do we return to the world we came from?"

Though that world was a storm-tossed sea ready to swallow the reivers within minutes or less . . .

"No one has left Atlantis in ten millennia," Creon said.

"None of my ancestors succeeded, none of the later castaways. We are all trapped."

"Though there are worse worlds to be trapped in," his daughter added with a speculative look at Cormac. "Especially now."

The Gael was in no mood for a woman, even a woman as lovely as Antheia. He eyed the pillar behind him.

The temple's outer columns were massive constructions in their own right, though they were nowhere near the size of the eight pairs which directly supported the dome. The shafts were about four feet in diameter, wider than a man could encircle with his arms.

The columns had been assembled from stone barrels as thick as they were wide. The cylinders were rolled onto the site with relative ease, then fluted and polished when transport was complete.

When the columns were first erected, the joints between the barrels may have been so close as to be invisible from all but the most careful examination. However, even if the atmosphere of Atlantis were always as still as this silent, muggy present, it decayed the stone to a degree.

Over the ten thousand years Creon claimed—and surely it could not have been *so* long? But over however many years, cracks that originally wouldn't pass a knifeblade were etched away into ledges for Cormac's fingers and toeholds for his boots. He began to climb as he had often climbed the friable rock of a seacliff, preparing to take a coast watcher unaware.

Below him, Cormac heard the Dane say, "These others, then—where are they? I don't care about your monks, but if there are Saxons, they are no friends to me."

"The last monk died a year ago," Antheia responded. "Cearbhall, his name was. He was an old man, and never well since the storm which carried him to us, to here."

She didn't speak loudly, but her voice carried over the skritch of Cormac's boots as he mounted from handhold to foothold. The Gael took no risks: three of his limbs were always anchored when he raised the fourth to its new position.

The surroundings of the temple opened out into a verdant jungle. Greenery was occasionally punctuated by a gleaming metal roof or, more often, by a lonely wall which was all that survived of a building.

"The Saxons were men of action, as you gentlemen are," Creon said. "Though I hope their example will prevent you from seeking the same doom. The ground on which we stand is an island. It's surrounded by a belt of water—a moat, you could almost say. Before the collapse, the island was joined to a pair of encircling ring islands and to the mainland beyond by bridges, but those were thrown down by earthquakes when most of the continent sank."

A fig tree grew out of the side of the column forty feet in the air. Seven thumb-thick stems sprouted from where a bird had picked apart the fruit and left pulp containing a seed.

The roots were anchored deep within the column, wedging thousands of tons of stone apart by hydrostatic pressure. Fig wood wasn't especially strong, but the green stems would at worst give warning before they started to crack. Cormac let the plant take enough of his weight that he could survey the horizon.

"Only the innermost of the ring islands was preserved

with the temple when the continent sank," Antheia said. "All that remains of Atlantis—all that there is of this world—ends on that island. But Aslief and his Saxons wouldn't believe that, and they died trying to reach what would have been an impenetrable barrier anyway."

Cormac could see a broad belt of water half a mile from where the temple rose. A fish jumped in it. There was nothing unusual about its mackerel-like shape or silvery scales; but unless the angle was deceptive, the fish was ten or a dozen feet in length.

The water belt's unnaturally smooth margins were perfectly circular except where a stand of willows broke the marble coping. The land across the water was similar to that of the central island, though there were fewer visible signs of ruined buildings. Either the earthquake's destruction had been more extensive toward the boundaries of the preserved portion of the continent, or the structures had been less gigantic to begin with.

The further edge of the ring island blurred into purple-green haze, as though the light of the false sun above had been compressed into a membrane. The transition didn't look impenetrable, but there was little to be told from miles' distance in any event.

He and Wulfhere would build a raft—or a true boat, if the Greeks could provide better tools than Cormac's sword and the Dane's war axe. With that and oars or a pole, they would cross to the ring island.

A quick tramp through the undergrowth would bring them to the boundary; and one way or another they would find a way through, though it were a wall of solid steel that they faced when they got there . . .

"The Saxons built a raft," Creon said. "We warned them of monsters in the water, but they would go anyway. Aslief said they feared not men nor devils, so long as they had their swords in their hands."

"This Aslief," Wulfhere asked. "Was he a man of my height or lacking little of it? The fellow I'm thinking of has blond hair and a silver-mounted spear with a blade broad as a shovel's."

"You've described him to the life," said Antheia. "Aslief Gorm's Bane, he called himself when first he appeared with his men. Was he a friend of yours, sir?"

"No," said Wulfhere without inflection. "But Gorm was my sister's son. I little thought to meet his slayer here."

"Nor shall you," Creon objected. "Aslief and his men built a raft, as I said, and the monsters had their way with them."

Three gigantic fish leaped in unison as close as that of veterans forming the shield wall. Cormac wondered what the creatures lived on. Though the belt of water was half a mile broad and several miles in length . . . if it was as deep as it looked, the volume could support an enormous and varied culture.

"Do you take me for a fool or a townsman?" Wulfhere demanded harshly. "What sort of monster threatens a shipload of Vikings?"

"A monster that rises beneath a raft," Antheia said. Her thin voice suggested her nostrils had tightened with anger at being called by implication a liar. "A monster that plucks the limbs from men as they try to swim to safety. A monster which leaves the bodies of those who sink for the squids with armored shells, which would be danger enough."

Where the giant fish had leaped a moment before, a fifty-foot shadow rose to the surface. The head made Cormac think of a smooth-skinned crocodile, but crocs were neckless. This creature had a neck half the enormous length of its head.

The body was barrel-shaped and powerful. Instead of legs it had flippers which, as the Gael watched, rotated like a seabird's wings for another stroke. The creature drove forward at speed remarkable in something so large. Its hide was black and shiny; conical teeth to cut as well as pierce filled the long jaws.

Another age would call the creature a Kronosaur. Cormac had no word for it, but *sea monster* was both accurate and evocative.

The Kronosaur submerged with no more commotion than an arrow makes slicing the water. No sign of the creature remained on the surface, though waves of its swift underwater passage buffeted the margins of the land.

As the monster dived, Cormac caught a glimpse of movement on the shore of the ring island. It could have been a goat rising on hind legs to nibble leaves, or even a trick of light and breeze which fluttered the pale undersurface of foliage into the semblance of a human figure. The distance was too far for certainty.

Cormac was certain nonetheless: there were men across the haunted water. He started down, moving with the same easy caution as he had mounted to the vantage point.

The view had given him information, but that opened more questions than it answered. The only thing of which

Cormac Mac Art was certain was that he had to get out of this place—though escape meant drowning in the clean salt seas of his own world.

Perhaps the color of the light here made him uneasy. There was nothing else to justify the loathing he felt.

"Who did this, then?" Wulfhere demanded. "Who cut this place off and left it as a trap for decent seamen?"

The Dane's great fingers played with his axe, lifting it a few inches and then slapping it down against the supporting belt. If his agitation continued to build, he was likely to slide the weapon free and begin making passes that were the last prelude to berserk rage.

If frustration drove Wulfhere berserk without an obvious enemy, well . . . the Dane would find an enemy.

"The continent of Atlantis had been raised from the sea by the might of its wizards," Creon said. "The land was always unstable. The Atlanteans turned their wizardry against us—against our Athenian ancestors when our fleet approached. When we broke through their defenses, the whole system began to collapse. Only enough of the power remained to save the very citadel—this island, and the first of the rings surrounding it."

Cormac dropped to the stone beside the Greeks and Wulfhere. Brown-skinned servants watched from the interior of the temple, but none of them came out to join their rulers.

"There's men across the water!" Cormac said cheerfully, clasping his friend enthusiastically by the shoulders. He had to deflect Wulfhere from the path his mind was treading or they'd none of them be safe. "People, at any rate—women as well as men, I suppose."

He fixed Creon with hard eyes. "That's correct, isn't it? There *are* people on the outer island?"

"Yes, certainly," Creon agreed without hesitation. "Some scores, perhaps hundreds of Atlanteans. They're taller and straighter than their relatives here—"

He gestured dismissively toward the servants waiting within the aisle of the temple.

"—but they've sunk even deeper into savagery. They live like beasts."

Cormac gave Wulfhere a friendly shake and released him. The Dane would be all right now. The trouble with Wulfhere was that in a doubtful situation, he always turned to his axe for succor. In the bloody age left by Rome's collapse, Wulfhere's instinct for slaughter had proved a major survival trait, but here it could cause problems.

"We're fortunate that the water provides a barrier," Antheia added coolly. "Otherwise they would have slaughtered us long since. And probably have killed their own kin, too. Mere animals."

Cormac looked at the woman. "If the Atlanteans were such great magicians . . ." he said, his tones rasped like steel on a whetstone, "how is it you could crush them to their present state?"

"Because," Antheia responded with a smile as shimmering and hard as a sword edge, "we were greater magicians yet. And before you ask—I have no Atlantean blood myself. Some of the greatest Athenian wizards were women, and one of them reached the citadel before the collapse."

Wulfhere shook himself like a bear drying its fur in the

shelter of a cave. His eyes were bright, but they had lost the glaze of madness which had begun to shutter them.

"I want food," he said in a deep rumble. "And I don't mean muck like what those midgets were offering us. I want meat!"

Creon smiled. "Yes," he said. "I asked the servants to begin boiling a goat as soon as you arrived. We'll go to the palace now."

Antheia laughed and laid the tips of her slim fingers on Cormac's armored shoulder. "And if one goat isn't enough," she said, leading the Gael toward the front door of the temple as though her touch was a leash, "then we will cook more until you're satisfied. After that we can consider your other appetites, not so?" Her laughter was birdsong in shadowed jungle.

The palace was the metal-clad building facing the temple. Antheia led the way there with her hand resting lightly on Cormac's arm. She talked not of the present but of the Atlantis that once had been, of the time when the island on which they stood was only the governmental complex controlling a continent. The city proper was built on the mainland beyond the ring island—lost for thousands of years beneath the storm-tossed seas.

The Gael looked over his shoulder when they were midway between palace and temple. The latter actually looked larger from the outside than it had when he was within. A pediment bright with statues of unblemished gold glared down, supported on four sweeping pillars. Though the peak was only half as high as the curve of the dome, it gave the impression of looming upward.

The temple's interior closed in on itself. Creon and Antheia had come from the vaults under the nave to greet the reivers. Cormac wondered what lay there.

The palace looked increasingly run-down as they drew closer. The silver had been applied in finger-thick slabs rather than mere foil over the stone, but many plates hung skewed from their rivets or had fallen away completely. Though the surfaces were black with oxide, they still reflected the sickly light of the false sun.

"Doesn't that thing ever set?" Cormac demanded harshly. The shock of anger he felt as he spoke warned him that his nerves were nearly as close to the edge as Wulfhere's.

"It will burn so long as this world remains," Antheia said. "The highest wizards of Atlantis created this place to be their final refuge, the den in which they could survive though all the continent else were conquered by an enemy."

She showed Cormac a smile as bitter as that of a victim for her executioner. "They didn't expect that we would penetrate their sanctum so swiftly and displace them," she said. "But on the other hand, we—my ancestors—didn't expect to be trapped here forevermore."

She hugged herself close to the Gael, as though she were unaware of his salt-crusted armor and his lack of response. "We have lamps within the palace," she said. "We'll shutter the windows while we eat. And afterwards—"

Antheia gave a throaty chuckle. "Afterwards, there's no need for light at all, unless you want one."

✛ ✛ ✛

Under other circumstances, Wulfhere might have complained that the goat wasn't well enough done—and in all truth, it was scarcely cooked at all. The longship had been tossed for a day and a half, giving the crew no opportunity to eat more than mouthfuls of hard bread washed down with ale heavily salted by the spray.

Hunger conquered the Dane's normal insistence on meat boiled till it fell off the bones. He wolfed down chunks of the dark, grainy goat, tearing it away with his strong teeth. The servants provided wine and, when the Dane asked for it, mead with a musty, powerful kick that he drank with still greater gusto.

Wulfhere was relaxing, though he still wore his iron corselet. He hung his axe from the top of the table beside him without consideration for the scar its hook put in the ivory inlays. Creon and Antheia didn't appear to notice.

The four of them sat on backless stools of bronze cast in a filigree. The furniture was draped with wool dyed muddy purple. The fabric was obviously of more recent manufacture than the metalwork.

Cormac looked around. A thought had frozen his jaws midway through a morsel of shoulder muscle more red than pink. Atlantis was a display of human progress, from the magnificent past to a present of near-bestial savagery. And wasn't this a description of the outer world as well, where Rome's collapse had loosed on the seas creatures like—

Creatures like Cormac Mac Art.

Cormac gave a choking snarl of a laugh. *He* hadn't made the world. If Mankind's natural state was barbarism—so be it. And so much the worse for soft folk who lacked Cormac's strength, his speed, and his absolute willingness to die so long as he was able to kill . . .

The two Greeks stared at him. He'd drawn their eyes when he laughed, though they might not have realized the sound *was* laughter. Wulfhere slammed down an agate cup for the servant with the sack of mead to refill— again. He fished a gobbet of meat from the pot with his dagger.

"Just thinking about how we were going to get out of here," Cormac lied to the Greeks.

"You bet we are," the Dane muttered. If he'd waited for an Atlantean to serve him, the meat would have been sliced into at least a dozen bites before it was transferred to Wulfhere's plate. "But first we're going to have a little something to eat . . ."

The walls of the dining room were covered in brass with low reliefs depicting planting and harvest. Reed torches, their pith soaked in oil, burned in free-standing sconces of delicate bronze. The wavering rushlights emphasized the artistry of the ancient furnishings.

The ceiling had painted decorations within the coffers, but these were by now no more than shadows. The soot of millennia caked them. That brought home to Cormac the age of this place better than did the deteriorated stone of the temple.

Cormac reached for his wine cup, a broad goblet of silver-mounted rock crystal. Only lees remained in it. Before a servant could act, Antheia took the footed bowl herself and filled the cup with unmixed wine. The local vintage was raw, but its alcohol content was higher than that of any wine which Cormac had drunk before.

Perhaps something about the light affected the vines, or it might be that the fermenting culture was an ancient one.

"Are you becoming—satisfied?" Antheia asked coquettishly, apparently oblivious of her father across the round table. She had doffed her outer robe for dinner. The inner tunic was white also and diaphanous. Antheia wore a girdle and bandeau of metal network, confining but not in the least concealing her breasts and hips.

The ruby brooch, pinned now to the shoulder of the tunic, glowed with an internal fire which owed nothing to the quivering torches. The bezel was of untarnished electrum, cast in the shape of a serpent swallowing its own tail. Cormac looked at the stone, wondering how much of the ancient wizards' magic remained under the control of their descendants.

Antheia's breasts were small but full enough to sag slightly within the mesh bandeau. She deliberately brushed her bosom across Cormac's eyes as he stared at the ruby. The fabric of her tunic was slick as glass, and her nipples were erect.

"So you're only interested in my jewelry?" she gibed, straightening away from the Gael. "And I took you for a man!"

Wulfhere flung a rack of rib bones under the table, then slurped his mead bowl empty. The floor was of stone hexagons like those of the temple, though these were all of the yellow marble. The masons had set them so that the red veins matched from slab to slab, with only the metal edging to break the pattern.

There were no hounds under the table to devour the

Dane's leavings. Cormac supposed the servants would clean up after the guests left the room. Creon, nibbling on fruit throughout the meal, smiled indulgently at the Dane. If he noticed his daughter's interest in Cormac—and he could scarcely not have noticed—then he was complaisant regarding her behavior.

Not that the slim Greek could stop the reivers from doing anything they pleased . . .

Cormac looked at Antheia. She smiled and tossed her head. A golden net gathered the hair at the base of her skull, but beneath that the black strands fell free to her supple waist.

He was fed and rested and out of the sickly glare of the false sun. Antheia did please him. She would have pleased a monk vowed to celibacy.

Cormac lurched to his feet. The wine had even more of a bite than he'd realized, but he'd never in his life drunk so much that he couldn't prove himself a man in whatever terms the arena required.

Antheia slipped a rushlight from its sconce. Her smile was enchantment itself. "Come," she said. "There are some remains of the old magic in my apartment that will amuse you."

Wulfhere set down his empty goblet. The servant bent to it. The Dane gave a rumbling belch that startled the little Atlantean away with a squeal.

"Be well, my daughter," Creon said. "I'll endeavor to entertain our other guest while you're gone."

Cormac followed the woman into a hallway which once had been paneled with ivory and rare woods. The organic materials had rotted to dust, leaving only the frames of precious metals clinging to the stone core. Servants peered nervously from alcoves.

Twenty yards down the corridor, Antheia opened a door and motioned Cormac inside before shutting it behind them. There was a latch but no lock. The panel was leather-covered wood. Curlicues of brass nails studded it in an attempt at decoration. The Gael could have punched his fist through the door.

Antheia thrust her torch into a sconce shaped like an open-mouthed dragon. The room's other furnishings consisted of a bronze bench and number of metalwork chests against the walls. A circular bed was visible through the open doorway to an inner room.

Cormac reached for the woman. She eeled through his arms, caught his right hand and pressed it to her breast, and was out of reach again before he could turn the touch into a grip.

"Take that nasty armor off," Antheia commanded lightly as she opened one of the chests. The container was almost as tall as she was, but it was no more than a foot through or across.

"It won't get in the way," Cormac rumbled thickly. "The first time, at any rate."

He started for the woman. She giggled. Trails of blue light, wavering like threads being spun into a skein, lifted from the top of the device as she fingered it.

"See?" Antheia said. "Ancient magic, as I told you. Touch it—it feels good."

The light wobbled slowly from the chest and began to extend vaguely in the direction of Cormac and the door.

"Turn that off," Cormac said.

He was rapidly becoming sober again. His shoulders hit stone, startling him to the edge of white rage before he realized that he'd backed against the wall. He hadn't thought he'd moved so far away . . .

Silvery horns a few inches long rotated on the top of the chest, emitting blue light the way a spider's spinnerets ooze silk. Antheia's fingers danced on a metal pad behind the horns. Her eyes were on Cormac rather than the controls she manipulated. The skein of blue continued to expand, but it no longer snuffled toward the Gael.

"Silly, it's harmless," the woman laughed. "Watch me."

There was commotion down the hall, metal banging on stone. A bench had overturned.

"Wulfhere?" Cormac called. His right hand hovered near the pommel of his sword. Embarrassment prevented him from drawing the weapon. He didn't have a good reason for being so afraid.

Antheia, one slim hand still on the controls of the device, stepped fully into the blue light. The pattern flowed past and around her like water pouring over a glass statue. The jewel on her shoulder blazed with redoubled fury, taking no color from the skein through which it glared.

A sheen, vaguely purple and as thin as isinglass, lay on the woman's skin and garments. The hue tinged both the portion within the blue light, and her legs from the thighs down which were below the skein.

"See?" Antheia said. "Harmless."

Her voice bubbled as though she were speaking from underwater. She held her free hand out to Cormac enticingly. The blue threads lurched in his direction again.

"Stop—" Cormac shouted. His sword sang from its scabbard. "—that, or—"

The suite's flimsy door burst inward. A brown-skinned man with the muscular body of an athlete lunged through the opening. He wore a beaded breechclout, a headband, and a torque of copper strips. His stone-headed axe was already swinging down in a mighty cast as the door flew out of his way.

Cormac stabbed the warrior sideways through the rib cage. The fellow didn't realize the Gael was present until the sword sliced his lungs and took the two lower chambers off his heart. The savage tried to cry out, but his surprise drowned in a spray of blood from his mouth and nostrils.

There were ten or a dozen warriors in the corridor behind the first victim, pressing forward and carrying the corpse with them as Cormac tried to clear his sword. Steel shrieked against bone as he dragged the blade back.

The skein of blue light enveloped Antheia wholly. Her visage was harsh and desperate. The first savage's axe hung at the edge of the blue cocoon. The weapon sank slowly toward the floor, as if it had fallen into a vat of cold treacle.

Cormac fumbled with his left hand, trying to find the buckler which ought to hang behind his hip. The shield was in the dining room where he'd left it.

A spear slammed Cormac full in the chest. His mail was of double-wound links riveted for strength. It held, but the blow rocked him bruisingly. His attackers might be the same race as the Atlantean servants, but there was nothing physically degenerate about them.

Cormac jumped back, finally freeing his weapon. He swung clumsily but with desperate speed to block the blade of a savage slashing at his face. The other sword was bronze, cast in the attractive curves of a poplar leaf. Cormac's steel—a long Roman cavalry weapon, forged in Bilbao—sheared tile bronze where it narrowed near the grip, then clopped into the savage's unprotected skull.

The man went down like a toppling statue. His headband fluttered behind him. Its severed ends were bloody.

The spearman thrust for Cormac again. This time the Gael was ready for him. The spearshaft was wrist-thick cornelwood, too sturdy to sever confidently with a swordblade. Cormac instead used the shaft itself as a chopping block to lop off the savage's leading hand. The spearpoint wavered aside without the left hand to guide it. Cormac back-slashed through the savage's throat, choking his scream into a gurgle.

Cormac drew the dagger from his belt and waded into his opponents at close quarters. These Atlantean savages were sturdy men, but they were naked and none of them was near the Gael's size.

The blade of the Spanish dagger was five fingers broad at the hilt. Cormac ripped the edge up through cartilage where ribs joined the breastbone. He used the dying victim as a shield while his sword struck right and left above the limp shoulders. Two more savages fell, hacked so fiercely that Cormac's steel split their collarbones and severed the great blood vessels rising from the heart.

A bronze warhammer smashed into Cormac's side. The Atlantean was squat and powerful. He'd swung the weapon with both arms and the full strength of his body. Despite the mail and its quilted leather backing, the impact shot dazzling pain through Cormac's ribs. It numbed his side for an instant.

The savage had been pulled off balance by his own blow. He stumbled forward as he tried to follow up the shocking impact. Before he could recover, the Gael's dagger took him at the base of the jaw, thrusting upward like a gaff through the gills of a struggling trout. The body went into spastic convulsions as Cormac flung it aside.

The surviving savages broke and ran. Metal clanged as they tripped on fallen equipment. Some of them flung weapons away to speed their flight.

Cormac staggered after them. He ignored Antheia; she remained in her wrap of clinging light. The stone axe had finally reached the floor. A spear, caught in the same ambiance, was sinking slowly after the axe.

There was a stitch in Cormac's side from the hammerblow, and pain blurred his vision every time his right heel hit the floor. The tip of the Gael's sword ripped red sparks along the stones at eye height; weakness from the injury had caused him to drift closer to the wall than he had understood. He cursed and brought his mind back in focus by an effort of will.

If the tip of a broken rib had pierced his lung, he would know it by now from the bloody froth he'd be exhaling. *That* hadn't happened, and anything else was mere pain.

Pain was nothing at all when Wulfhere was at risk and there were enemies to kill.

The servants had disappeared. The last of the attacking savages darted into the dining room. The Gael followed, thrusting the fleeing man through the small of the back.

The dining room was chaos. Two rushlights remained,

but most of the illumination now came from a skein of glowing threads like those which had wavered toward Cormac in the moments before the savages attacked.

Creon stood within a ball of blue light emanating from another vertical chest. Instead of manipulating the control panel, the Greek gestured. Pseudopods of fibrous light extended in the directions he stretched his arms. The threads gripped the throats of two savages, lifting their bodies off the floor as it throttled them.

More than a score of other savages crowded the room, stabbing and hacking at the envelope of light. A number of the attackers were women. An age-frail man held out a wand that could, in the doubtful illumination, have been either crystal or metal. Instead of a cloth headband, he wore a cap of spiral mesh formed from wires of gold, silver, and their alloy electrum.

A hexagonal block had been displaced from the flooring. As Cormac entered the room, he saw Wulfhere's bound legs disappearing into the hole beneath where the slab had been.

Cormac hit the savages as a scythe does a wheatfield. There was no time for finesse: numbers would bear him down if his foes had an instant to organize against the fresh danger. The Roman sword whirled in wide arcs. When a savage ducked close, Cormac disemboweled him with a hooking cut of the dagger.

A sword's point is the trained killer's tool. The edge is spectacular but far less lethal in its effects. Cormac knew that well, but at this juncture he slashed nonetheless instead of thrusting deep for each opponent's life.

A well-placed thrust lets a man's life out in a minute or

so when his heart has pumped the blood vessels empty. During that minute, the victim is as deadly an opponent as before he got his death wound.

What Cormac required to survive this maelstrom was terror and disablement. An eight-inch gouge along a rib cage spread like the jaws of Hell when tensioning muscles drew the edges of the skin apart. The wound wasn't as dangerous as a heart thrust, but the shock of it stunned the victim and terrified his friends.

A hand severed at the wrist could no longer hold an axe. A head wound need not penetrate the skull to bludgeon the victim into dazed helplessness.

The chieftain with the wand shouted an order. Surviving savages scrambled down the hole in the flooring. Cormac's attack had been so sudden and overwhelming that there was no real attempt to withstand him. Warriors, some of them women, flung up weapons for self-protection, but in the dim-lit chaos they didn't realize their assailant was alone and therefore vulnerable.

Cormac was in a killing rage. He didn't care if his foes ran or stood. The Gael sheared the spine of a fleeing savage, then swung at the chieftain who raised the wand against him.

The tip of the wand spun tendrils of blue fire like those emanating from the Greeks' devices. Light caught the blade, slowed it, and finally froze the sword in mid-air.

"May the pigs eat your flesh!" Cormac screamed as he pressed close and stabbed upward with his dagger.

The chieftain dodged back. More tendrils whirled from the wand tip and wrapped the Gael's left wrist. Their touch was cold as a drowned corpse.

Behind the chieftain, the last of his whole-bodied followers dived into the hole. The savage tugged on the hexagon he and his fellows had displaced to launch their attack. The stone toppled into the hole sideways and stuck, wedged by its great weight against the sides of the cavity.

Crippled victims of the Gael's attack screamed and groped on the floor, blind from head wounds and fear. Creon continued to hold the pair his device had captured. The Greek's face looked as strained as that of a man being crucified.

Cormac forced his body toward the chieftain. His sword and left hand were held as firmly as if gyved to the living rock. A separate tendril flicked down to wrap his right wrist lest he drop the sword and strike his opponent with his clenched fist.

Antheia entered the room, carrying a sword from one of the savages. A handful of the stunted servants followed her.

"Father!" she cried. She had aged decades since Cormac last saw her.

The Atlantean chieftain spun away. Blue fibers released Cormac from their grip. The chieftain hurled his wand toward the hole. It struck the skewed block and clattered down to the savages below.

The chieftain was toppling forward. Cormac's sword tore deeply through his back and spine, but the Roman steel was slicing a man already dead.

The volume of light encircling Creon sucked inward with the abruptness of a bubble bursting. The Greek staggered, scarcely able to keep his feet when the strain of his activity was released.

"They got through the tunnels," he gasped to his daughter. "Despite the Guardian. They had a wand of power."

Creon looked . . . old, *ancient*. Cormac was reminded of the withered features of the chieftain as the two of them struggled breast to breast.

The Gael stripped the breechclout from a corpse. The garment was made of leather, sliced thin and sueded. Clamshells individually smaller than a fingernail were stitched hollow-side out in a pattern, alternating blue nacre with yellow.

Cormac wiped his sword, then his dagger, with the breechclout. He inhaled in racking gasps. He had to bring his quivering muscles and his breathing under control before he attempted the next stage of what was necessary.

The room's walls and ceiling were splotched with traceries of blood slung from the Gael's swordpoint. Most of a man's wadded scalp stuck over the lintel. The floor looked flat, but thousands of years of footsteps had worn troughs in the stone. Blood pooled there, as much as an inch deep.

"A wand of power?" Antheia repeated. "After so long? That's impossible!"

"No, but the drain is terrible," Creon replied. "Look, this is the one who was using it."

He touched the corpse of the chieftain with the toe of his sandal. The forearm of the corpse crumbled. The flesh was as dry and flaky as if it had baked for a year in desert sunlight.

"Where," said Cormac, "is Wulfhere?"

His chest still pumped vast amounts of air through his

open mouth, but his breathing had settled into a regular pattern instead of the desperation of a man saved from drowning. Cormac didn't have his full strength back, but the spasms that had followed his adrenaline-fueled exertions had passed.

He wasn't in perfect condition; but life wasn't perfect, and the present situation was *far* less than perfect. His body would serve.

The Greeks stared at him.

"The Atlanteans took your friend with them," Creon said. "Tribesmen from the ring, attacking through the tunnels beneath the moat. I can't imagine what they wanted with him. They can't have known anyone was present but Antheia and I."

The Greek looked at his daughter and added, "I captured two of them. Did you . . . ?"

She shook her head sharply. "No," she said, "no. Are any of these suitable for use?"

She glanced around the carnage the Gael had left of the raiding party. Lopped limbs, coils of intestines tangling the feet of a victim who had tried to run despite his wound; a woman who lay limp in a roundel of blood, her glassy eyes staring upward . . .

"No," Antheia said. "I see."

"Where did they take him?" Cormac repeated in a voice so loud that the words battered the walls like fists.

"How—" Antheia said and froze, seeing her death at the end of the hot reply. She had aged horribly. The price of the power she and her father wielded was nearly as high as that of the wand Cormac watched kill its user.

"I suppose they would have taken him to wherever

they live on the ring island," Creon said. "If the Guardian doesn't get them all, despite the wand. I wouldn't believe they could make it past him, had they not done so."

Creon backed and sagged against the chest from which the light sprang. Cormac poised, but the Greek was only reaching for support. He looked like a scarecrow instead of the vibrant man of middle age who had greeted the castaways.

Cormac had sheathed his dagger after he cleaned it. Now he shot the long sword back in its scabbard and stepped to the hole in the floor. He could glimpse light of sorts past the skewed block, a pale glow too even to come from a lamp.

"You can't go down there!" Antheia protested. "The Guardian is—"

"Unless the savages killed it?" Creon suggested in sudden fear.

Antheia turned on him. "With a single wand?" she snarled. "Don't be a fool. You and I together couldn't manage it, and that was when it was smaller!"

Cormac touched the block of stone, not gripping it but judging the texture and finding places at which he *could* grip.

"You can't go down there," Creon said in shocked anger. "It's—you'd be throwing yourself away, merely feeding the Guardian."

Cormac looked back over his shoulder. The savages whom Creon had choked comatose were on the floor where the device dropped them. Servants bound the captives' wrists and legs with ribbons of raw silk, no less strong for its lustrous beauty.

Bandages of the same material wrapped Wulfhere's ankles as the savages dragged the Dane away.

Cormac straightened in a smooth motion that proved his muscles were under his full control. He raised one of the bronze stools by a leg and shook the draping fabric from it. Creon started back; servants ran squealing in wide-eyed terror.

Antheia's left hand closed on her ruby brooch. Her face was cool and emotionless.

Cormac swung the stool overhead as he would have used a flail. He released the metal an instant before it crashed into the chest from which Creon spun blue light. The Gael didn't want to touch the device, and he didn't want to touch *anything* that touched the device in the moment of its destruction.

Bronze chest and bronze stool melded in a ringing crash. The metal glowed, not blue but a hot yellow-orange like the core of a charcoal kiln. Molten bronze spattered in all directions with the smell of something foul burning.

The servants had fled. A dying savage moaned softly. The Greeks stood transfixed.

"So you'd treat us as you were doing these folk?" the Gael shouted, gesturing left-handed toward the bound savages. "Choke us, tie us—and then what, I wonder?"

His voice had a musical lilt, as playful as a cat's paw. He spat on Creon's sandaled foot. "Get out of here before I deal with you as I did your evil toy!"

The Greeks swept from the room, silent and blank-faced. A spot on Creon's robe smoldered from a spark thrown out by his melting device.

Cormac squatted and gripped the block of stone. The iron chape of his scabbard skittered on the floor.

Wulfhere's bow and quiver stood in a corner, but the bearded axe had vanished with the Dane. Hope had no more to do with Cormac's actions than fear did, but—

If Wulfhere believed in anything, he believed not in a god or gods but rather in that axe which had cut through every foe he faced. So long as the Dane and his axe were together, woe to their enemies.

Cormac squeezed and lifted. The stone block was twice a man's weight and awkward, with no proper handholds. Gravity and friction on the sides of the hole fought the Gael's strength. Human muscles won the struggle, raising the block with a grating snarl.

Spinning as his knees straightened, letting the stone's inertia carry the weight past him, Cormac rose from the hole. He released his burden at a calculated moment. The great hexagon smashed down on the welded mass of what had been Creon's device of power, crushing the ruin flat with a few additional sputters.

Cormac snatched up his shield, drew his sword, and dropped feet first into the tunnel beneath.

The ground—the pavement—was a full eight feet below the tunnel's brick ceiling. The savages were folk of moderate height, even though they weren't stunted like their kin who served the Greeks. Cormac wondered how they'd been able to lift a massive slab so high above their heads—then remembered the wand. The price for its power was a high one, but that power was real.

The tunnel was a drain, choked at its inner end by silt

and rubble swept down on storm waters. The lower end, leading to a greater cavern beyond, had been cleared in the immediate past sufficiently to pass a line of hastening warriors. The dirt was freshly turned, and a copper-headed mattock stuck in the wall. Its shaft had broken when the user tried to lever out a stone which was actually part of the masonry.

Cormac followed his swordpoint from the tunnel.

The light he had seen came from the coat of fungus which slimed the floor and stone columns of the vast world that opened before him. The roof, forty—fifty—sixty feet above the sloping floor, was covered in metal which repelled the fungus.

Ripples across the ceiling indicated that the metal had been twisted fiercely at some time in the past; some of the support pillars had a shaken look. Pumps sighed like mighty lungs in the unguessed distance.

This underworld had been a vast dockyard in the time before the fall of Atlantis. Ramps, now dry save for the fungus, slanted upward from channels to central quays. The sloping surfaces were meant to hold vessels drawn out of the water. A fleet that could have required docks of such extent was—

Was beyond present conception, even for a reiver who had travelled as widely as Cormac Mac Art.

There was no sign of the ships. If they had been docked here at the moment of collapse, then millennia had finished the business of destruction. Fungus lay smooth on the ramps, without so much as a mound to indicate where vessels had been berthed in the dim past.

The channels were twenty feet deep, sufficient for

ships of greater draft than any which coursed the seas of Cormac's age. The water had vanished, drained or pumped away when magic ripped the citadel from its proper time and space. Cormac wondered at the power which circulated air and water in this trap that held him; but, like the false sun lighting the surface above, it was a matter beyond his immediate interest.

First he would find and free Wulfhere. Then they would escape. Nothing else mattered.

The savages' trail was easy to follow in the disturbed fungus. They'd crossed a channel, then turned outward along the axis of a quay. Weapons and equipment were scattered at the bottom of the channel. The surface was trampled in a broad circle as though there had been a battle.

Cormac thought there were no bodies, until he noticed that a human forearm lay where fungus had been kicked up in a wave. The bones were crushed at both wrist and elbow ends.

The illumination was deceptive. Because the glow was weak and shadowless, Cormac found it hard to judge distances. He thought he saw movement to his right side. He poised with his buckler advanced, but it was only a vertical slash across a pillar's coating. The slanting mark seemed to move when the Gael caught it in the corner of his eye.

Half of a woman's body lay a hundred yards from the mouth of the drainage tunnel. Her torso had been chewed away, but the legs were still joined to the pelvis. The head had fallen twenty yards further along the track.

The woman's features were shrunken with age; milky

cataracts closed both eyes. She'd already been dead or next breath from dead when some creature devoured her body.

Cormac jogged on, planting his boots squarely to keep from slipping on the glowing slime. Echoes passed strangely among the channels and pillared aisles. The pump's sighing was overlaid by a quavering note that might have been either a harmonic or a completely unconnected sound. Occasionally he felt a rumble so deep that it seemed bowel-loosening vibration rather than noise.

As the Gael strode forward, he kept an eye out for signs of whatever had eaten the savage's body. "The Guardian" Creon and his daughter spoke of, no doubt; but they had given no description. There were no tracks in the fungus coating. Was the creature winged?

Cormac glanced up—and saw, reflected in the smooth metal ceiling, the pattern that had eluded him at ground level. Curving ripples marked the fungus, each a yard long and nested together into a fuzzy line. He'd assumed they were caused by stress markings in the quay.

A similar track paralleled the first, five yards farther from the path the savages had worn. The nests of arcs faced one another, concave sides to concavities. Something many-legged and fifteen feet wide had followed the raiders as they returned through the tunnels.

A human leg lay on the stone where it had dribbled from jaws that bolted the remainder of the corpse. The muscles were shrunken with age and more than age, like those of the chieftain who struggled with Cormac in the palace. The savages were using the wand to fend off their pursuer—and the wand was using them up.

Farther along the track were fragments of another

body, too shredded to determine even the species had not Cormac known it must be human. Corpses the wand of power had drained would provide little further sustenance.

As he neared the rim of this bubble world, Cormac found increasing evidence of the damage done when Atlantis submerged. Pillars were twisted on their axes. Some remained staggeringly upright only because of the weight of the ceiling sagging upon them. The metal sheathing was buckled in ridges as much as a foot deep, tracing the curve of ancient Shockwaves.

Purple-green light swelled in the near distance. A column had collapsed, dragging with it a section of the surface above. Dirt and rubble lay in a broad ramp toward the world above, though its top lay thirty feet below the hole in the ceiling.

The bones of large animals lay in and near the mound of debris. Half-buried and half-crumbling was the skull of an elephant with a curving tusk longer than that of its kin in Cormac's day. The other tusk was broken off short. Beasts from the ring island had stumbled into the pit and been killed by the fall, just as happened regularly in sinkholes in the world beyond Atlantis.

A purple-green blur tinging the pillars far to Cormac's right suggested there were other, similar tears in the cavern's fabric. He couldn't guess at the total, two or three or possibly scores.

But whatever the number of such pitfalls, they provided sufficient food to keep *something* alive for a very long time.

Cormac started up the tumbled ramp, though he didn't know how he would deal with the thirty-foot gap between the top of it and the surface. He didn't have materials for a grapnel. Perhaps he could improvise something with strips of clothing and his dagger . . .

Clicks, rapid and increasingly loud, came from the glowing vagueness. Echoes hid the direction of approach. Cormac pivoted on his left heel, keeping his buckler close to his body and his swordarm cocked at his side to slash or stab.

A centipede the size of a nightmare curled like a tidal wave over the ramp toward him.

Cormac shouted, thrust out his shield, and whipped his longsword around in an overarm cut. He might as well have slashed at a landslide.

The creature had one feathery antenna and a stump where the other should have been. Its mouth parts were multiple, side-hinged, and hideous. Mandibles dripping a corrosive poison stabbed out, the right glancing along the steel boss of Cormac's buckler as the other thrust toward his chest.

Cormac's sword rang against the centipede's headshield and rebounded, though the edge left a scar on the chitinous armor. There were other scars, some of them fresh. The blow did nothing to prevent the mandible from striking.

Cormac's mail held, but the ribs beneath were those bruised or cracked during the fight in Antheia's suite. Pain was a white blur that shifted the universe out of focus. Cormac's sword swung again unaffected.

The centipede's eyes were in clumps of six to either side of its armored head. The Gael's steel edge crushed through the lenses of three of the left-hand cluster, splashing clear ichor. The creature's weight rammed Cormac backward off the ramp.

The centipede was a jointed tube, six feet in diameter and longer than the Gael could guess under the circumstances. The legs, one pair to each body segment, splayed out to either side. Their joints sprouted hairs as coarse as tiger whiskers.

Each leg was tipped by a pair of pincers the size of blacksmith's shears. The creature lifted the front of its body so that the first trio of leg pairs remained free to grip its prey.

Cormac fell on his back. He screamed and chopped sideways with the edge of his shield, clearing two of the pincers fumbling at his mail. The creature's mandibles drew back for another attempt. Behind them plates of chitin clashed and spread, their margins jagged to serve as teeth.

Cormac thrust upward into the mouth. The jaw plates closed on his sword, gripping it firmly. Steel shrieked as the Gael drove the point further by main force.

The centipede tossed its head and flung Cormac thirty feet in the air. He bounced off the creature's curving back, then crashed down onto the heap of rubble. His helmet flew into the cavern. He still held his sword and, for a wonder, his buckler.

Cormac got to his feet as the centipede circled like a river of gleaming bone. Sticky juices streaked his blade, but he knew he hadn't stabbed deep enough to do serious damage. The centipede's body was so thick that he wasn't sure he *could* reach a vital spot.

The monster wasn't used to steel weapons, nor to a

swordarm as strong as that of Cormac Mac Art. The creature would, nonetheless, crush and devour the man just as surely as the sun rose and set in the world beyond this hellpit wrenched out of time . . .

The centipede started toward him. Cormac poised.

"Cormac!" bellowed a familiar voice.

Cormac's sword rang against the centipede's headshield, rupturing another of the bulging eyes. Powerful hands gripped beneath his armpits and lifted him bodily.

The centipede's head and forequarters rose effortlessly, fluidly. The mandibles spread like the jaws of a spring trap. Drops of pale venom winked on the hollow tips. The remaining antenna, longer than the Gael's body, nodded forward.

Cormac brought his Roman blade around in a sideways stroke that didn't endanger the man who held him from behind. His edge sang on the feathery chitin, severing the antenna near its midpoint and sending the fragment out into the trampled slime.

The centipede flowed forward unaffected. Cormac shouted and drew his knees up against his chest. The creature's mandibles clacked together like the lock of a catapult releasing.

Cormac slashed down between his feet. The blow swiped only air. He and the man holding him swayed abruptly upward, pulled by numbers of folk on the surface above the hole in the ceiling.

The centipede quivered over the mound of soil and bones, returning in the direction from which it had appeared. The beast had either given up once its prey rose above the height to which it could comfortably reach, or its damaged vision had lost Cormac in the relatively bright light streaming through the roof of the cavern.

Fresh body segments slid past all the time that Cormac dangled from the hole. The claws, scissoring forward in perfect rhythm, sounded like skeletons tumbling down a scree of other bones.

The Gael's head rose at last above the surface of the ring island. A large fish slapped nearby, in the belt of water. The foliage was rich and full, though the light of the false sun gave it a cast Cormac found unpleasant. After the guardian who prowled the tunnels below, however . . .

A pair of brown-skinned children stared at the Gael wide-eyed. The adults were all tugging on the rope which had raised Wulfhere and Cormac to safety.

Wulfhere released Cormac, who stepped thankfully to solid ground. The Gael's knees wobbled with reaction to the stress just ended. The pain in his rib cage was cold fire.

The Dane stood arms akimbo, grinning. "I figured you'd be coming," he said. "Matter of fact, I was going down to look for you. The folks here who saved me from that Greek wizard—"

Wulfhere gestured with his big thumb toward the dozen savages behind him. They were rubbing their palms where the rope had rubbed the skin into incipient blisters. One of them, a very young woman, wore an ornately beaded vest and carried the wand of power thrust beneath the tie of her breechclout. She stepped up beside the Dane.

"—didn't think it was a good idea; but I thought it was a better idea than having you down there alone with our leggy friend."

Cormac took a deep breath. He shot his sword home in its sheath.

"You were both right," he said.

"I am Loughra," said the girl with the wand of power. "I am Queen of Atlantis, now that my brother is dead."

Thus far, her voice was animated by a sense of cold pride. She looked around her domain—fleshy vegetation, two children, and a double handful of adults. In a sudden break, which reminded Cormac of how young she really was, Loughra added, "We're all dead, now or shortly. Kanin and the others wouldn't let me take the wand when we fled. It was my right."

She glared at her fellows. Most of them were her seniors. Several were in their seventies or even older, though their features lacked the preternatural ancientness with which the wand branded those who used it.

"It was my right!" Loughra shouted.

The other Atlanteans stared at their hands or the far distance. They had the look of survivors of a beaten army . . . as indeed they were. Between those slaughtered when they attacked the palace and the numbers the Guardian or wand had devoured in the cavern, most of the tribe had died this day.

Cormac eyed the savages. Now that he was among rescuers rather than trading blows in blood-spattered chaos, he was struck by their high foreheads and the craftsmanship displayed in their dress and equipment.

One of the band held a steel-headed spear whose seven-foot shaft was reinforced with metal strips for half its length. The broad blade was inlaid with runes of silver.

Ichor from the centipede dulled the runes carved into the steel. The Atlantean wiped at it with a wad of bark cloth.

Wulfhere followed Cormac's eyes. "Yes, Aslief's," the Dane agreed. "We'll meet in Valhalla, it seems, but not before. Gorm was honored to fall to such a foe."

Cormac looked at his friend in surprise.

"Aslief the Saxon came to us just before Hotin and Balla were born," Loughra explained, nodding toward the pair of children. Two-year-olds, Cormac guessed. It would be difficult to tell time in a place without day, night or seasons.

"He and his men fought their way past the wizards who would have drained them as they do all their captives. The Saxons built a raft, but the water monsters tipped it and took all but Aslief himself. We healed his wounds, and at the end he led us against the wizards."

"The oily bastard Creon who choked me silly with his blue light?" Wulfhere said. "He's not the descendant of the wizards who came here all that time ago. He and his daughter *are* those wizards. They drink the blood of everyone they catch to keep themselves young."

The Dane's finger unconsciously traced the hammer rune on the flat of his axe.

"Not the blood, but the life," Loughra corrected. "Though it comes to the same thing. Aslief led us through the tunnels. He fought the Guardian while the rest of us opened the way into the palace."

"A good job, that," Wulfhere said softly as his finger moved. "I hadn't really seen the leggy one—"

To avoid omen, the Dane didn't say "the Guardian," though that was merely a title rather than a name.

"—until I went down after you. Handling him for however long with a spear was man's work.

"Poseidon has forsaken us," Loughra said miserably. "He caused the monsters—"

Creon and Antheia, not the beasts in the water and cavern; and from what Cormac now believed, the term was well-applied.

"—to be prepared with their magic when we arrived. Otherwise we would have ended their reign forever!"

It wasn't just the Greeks' magic that turned the attack into a catastrophe, Cormac realized uneasily. A moment before he had thought the eyes of the Atlantean survivors were dull, torpid. Now his mind put a sinister cast on their expressions.

"I have no friends on the other side of a battle line!" Cormac said harshly. He eased his right foot backward, to brace him if he needed to clear his sword in the next instant. "Whatever he may have been before or become since."

Wulfhere stepped close to the Gael and hugged him, pinning his arms. "The folk here kept me tied while they carried me through the runnels," the Dane rumbled. "Otherwise I would have killed them all before they could explain they were rescuing me . . . and the one with legs would have eaten me as he did Aslief, like as not."

Wulfhere released his friend.

"It was Poseidon's will," said Loughra. "You were no more than his instrument."

"A big fellow, Aslief," Wulfhere said with a grimly reflective expression on his face. His eyes were focused well beyond the artificial horizon. "His flesh delayed the leggy one for some time, even after it had gotten past his spear."

Cormac stretched his powerful arms up and back, working the weight of his armor loose from the grooves it dug in his muscles as he stood motionless. Something large shrieked half a mile away. He remembered the elephant skull in the cavern beneath.

"The folk here say there's no way out," Wulfhere said without emotional loading. "That much of the Greeks' story was true. They say we can stay here with them on the island."

"There are no children born here anymore," Loughra said. "Hotin and Balla were the last, and before them, none for—half my lifetime. Poseidon has forsaken us."

The elephant trumpeted again. Cormac looked at the Atlantean queen, but his mind considered all the threads of the net that knotted about him.

The ring of water was broad and deep enough to be a world in itself. The creatures there would live and breed for so long as the bubble that was Atlantis remained. There was no realistic chance that men could live to cross it. That Aslief had done so was a comment on the number of Saxons whom he'd led: more meat than there were hungry maws to devour it.

The cavern was another matter. Hard-shelled creatures could live indefinitely without food. Cormac had once found a spider beneath a helmet which had been rusting for at least three years. The helmet rim, stamped into the wet soil during a massacre, blocked any potential prey—but the spider, silent and patient, waited nonetheless alive in its ragged web.

Creon and Anthea spoke of "the Guardian" as if the centipede were as old as they were; but also as if it were alone. A single creature could be killed, but not, Cormac judged from his own experience, by weapons in the hands of two pirates and the surviving Atlanteans.

Something had to be done. The Greeks, like bad husbandmen, had cropped the fittest of their herd of servants for millennia so that now only stunted rejects remained. Forced by circumstances of their own creation, Creon and his daughter had turned their powers beyond the boundaries of the world in which they were trapped, snatching folk out of the sea.

Irishmen, Saxons, the leaders of a band of Danish pirates.

"Speaking for myself . . ." Wulfhere said, watching the Gael sidelong, waiting for cues on a visage which for the moment was as quiet as cast bronze, ". . . I just want to get out of this place."

"That was all I wanted before," Cormac whispered. "Now—I still want to leave. But first we'll put an end to the folk who brought us here, not so, my friend?"

He looked at Wulfhere and smiled. It was a terrible expression.

The Dane shrugged his mighty shoulders and smiled back. "If you want it so much, why not?" he said. "I've killed people for less." Wulfhere laughed, the audible equivalent of the Gael's visage. "I've killed people to test the edge of a new sword!"

The reivers clasped their right arms; hand to elbow, wrist to wrist. They both laughed. In a moment, the distant elephant trumpeted again in frightened surmise.

✣ ✣ ✣

"This is madness!" Loughra cried in sudden fury as she watched the reivers' preparations. "You'll die for no reason!"

Her words echoed unconsciously those of Creon when he realized Cormac was determined to follow the Dane's captors into the tunnels. The humor of the thought was no more than the quiver of butterfly wings around the grim monolith of Cormac's concentration, but it was present to that extent.

Wulfhere checked the balance of the spear which had been Aslief's. Spears weren't the Dane's weapon of choice, but neither was the centipede a normal opponent.

"A man can die but once," he said without concern. "And besides, Othinn loves brave men."

"We won't help you with this!" Loughra said. "If you stayed here with us—perhaps the monster's spell against children won't work on you and, and . . ."

"No one asked you for help," Cormac said. He ignored the remainder of the girl's—the woman's—statement. The first female he'd gotten involved with on Atlantis had nearly brought his death. He wasn't sure that Loughra was a safer bet than Antheia had been; and anyway, he had other business.

The Gael braced his heels against the ground and tugged with all his strength at the cords of bull sinew which anchored the rope ladder to three separate trees. Aslief had constructed the ladder to accept his weight and that of the entire Atlantean raiding party climbing down behind him, but Cormac believed in being doubly sure when that was possible.

"It would make a fine saga, would it not?" Wulfhere commented. "How the two of us went into the dragon's cave and fought him?"

Wulfhere eyed his axe critically. He buffed the steel on his trouser leg. He'd worked on the edge with an oilstone for an hour, though he hadn't used the weapon since a raid in the Orkneys nearly a month earlier. Creon's snare of blue light had caught the Dane with no target for his steel and fury.

"Of course," he added, "it isn't really a dragon. And there won't be anyone left to write the saga. But it would be a fine one."

"We aren't going to fight anything if we're lucky," Cormac muttered. "Down and back, that's all."

He looked at the ladder and their equipment, then to his hulking friend. "The gear's ready. Are you?"

"To *not* fight?" Wulfhere said. "But whatever you say, little man. You understand more of this business than I do."

Cormac kicked the ladder into the opening. Bamboo battens stiffened the rungs, though cross-ropes would provide support even if a rung cracked under the reivers' weight. The hollow wood clattered now.

Cormac dropped hand over hand into the glowing cavern.

Cormac's boots hit the pile of rubble. The vast cavity was filled as before by an echoing sigh. It would fade to the impression of silence in a few moments, deadening the way the sound of surf on a rocky strand did. That was dangerous, because the background the mind taught itself to discount was still loud enough to conceal the approach of an enemy.

Conceal the approach of the Guardian.

Cormac pivoted his head as he jumped clear. Wulfhere crashed to the ground with an angry grunt. The Dane's axe was jagged lightning in a battle, but climbing wasn't a skill on which the big man prided himself.

"What now?" he demanded, checking around him as the Gael had done. "You're not planning to fight, but the one with the legs may have his own ideas."

"This way," Cormac said, loping off the ramp and along the quay. "We're going to pull one of the pillars farther down the tunnel."

"With ourselves beneath it?" Wulfhere muttered. There was a touch of perverse pride in his voice. "Well, I said I'd follow."

There was no sign of the centipede. The creature had a huge area to patrol. They could do their work and be out before it found them.

"What's wrong with this one?" Wulfhere asked peevishly as Cormac led him past a pillar. The Dane didn't like to run any more than he liked climbing.

"Not far enough," Cormac said, though it was a pity. The top half of the pillar was skewed at a 30-degree angle, and a vertical crack ran from there to the ground. It would be easy to complete the job earth tremors had started; but that wouldn't do any good.

"Why didn't you tell the folk above what you planned?" Wulfhere said. "Why make a secret of it?"

"They wouldn't have helped," the Gael said. The truth was that his paranoid need for secrecy was deeper than his rationalizations of it, though there was truth in the rationalizations too. "They might have tried to hinder. Our reasons aren't theirs."

The next pillar was 50 yards farther on. Cormac hoped it would do. Each echoing clack of his hobnails flashed an image of the centipede into his mind.

"This one!" he said. He thrust his prybar between two tilted courses of the pillar's masonry.

The savages made their tools and weapons from the cladding of ruined buildings—bronze, tin, copper, and brass so pale it might almost pass for gold. They had no iron or steel, but this bar was of sturdy bronze stiffened by cruciform ridges.

Perhaps the centipede wouldn't be able to sense the reivers because its antennae were injured.

Perhaps a Druid would appear, make a pass with his golden sickle, and snatch Cormac and the Dane back into the world where they belonged.

Wulfhere eyed the situation, then thrust the point of Aslief's spear beside the prybar. He twisted and, without seeming effort, levered onto the floor an ashlar that outweighed him.

The block hit with a crash, skipped on one corner, and finally lay flat. Cormac inserted his bar vertically between stones of the next course up. He pried, easing his weight onto the tool until the full tigerish strength of his muscles was deployed. The bronze bent, though he'd inserted the bar deep enough that the fulcrum was on the fat part.

Wulfhere thrust, leaned into his spear, and grunted. The block sprang free. The stone beside it sagged loose and followed. A quick jerk from Cormac's tool wrenched a block from the lower course.

The masonry was set without mortar. The pillar's core was concrete and aggregate, shattered ages past by the torquing as Atlantis sank. All the reivers had to do was to strip a course from the ashlar sheathing and the ceiling's weight would—

The centipede, a darkness spattering glowing dollops of fungus from its claws, swept down on them.

"Finish the job!" Cormac shouted. He dropped the prybar, drew his sword, and reached behind his left hip for the slung buckler. The command and the complex of movements came from his subconscious. "I'll hold him!"

"No!" boomed Wulfhere, dragging the spear free of the crevice into which he'd inserted it for the next stage of the demolition work.

"Our only chance is to bring the roof down, you boneheaded Dane!" Cormac screamed. Waving his shield high above him, he took three accelerating steps to meet the centipede.

The creature paused, lifting its head and three foremost body segments against the shield's perceived threat. Cormac ducked low. Mandibles clashed above his head.

He was in a forest of legs, hair-tufted and jagged with chitinous edges. The Gael cut to the right and backhanded left. His bright steel bit through the flexible membrane covering a joint.

Ichor, transparent and of no color but that of the fungus glow, dripped from the rent. The lower leg dangled limp.

The centipede curled back on itself like a wave

rebounding. The mandibles were cocked for another stroke. Jawplates clashed and reopened behind the poison-dripping points. As soon as the creature attacked, its limited brain function put in motion all the apparatus of eating.

Cormac dived, shouldering aside the injured limb. He rolled to his feet again just clear of the centipede's flowing form. Its head slid beneath body segments in a chitinous knot. The centipede's damaged eyes and antennae—the olfactory receptors—prevented it from spotting its prey again for a moment.

Masonry crashed in a miniature avalanche, a dozen blocks or more in rapid succession. Wulfhere worked with spear and prybar simultaneously. The Dane was attacking the pillar with the same precision and casual strength that he would have displayed while demolishing a hostile shield wall.

If he was aware of Cormac and the centipede, he gave no sign of the fact.

Cormac breathed in shuddering gulps. The centipede located him and came on again. The stumps of its antennae waved.

The Gael stepped toward the creature. His stride wasn't as firm as he'd expected. His right boot slid on the fungus coating.

The centipede's head whipped around in a quick arc, slamming its mandibles into Cormac from the left side. The shield held, but the arm holding it went numb. The blow flung him down, skidding and spinning across the stones.

The centipede came on. Its claws clicked like blades of the mechanical harvesters of Northern Gaul. Cormac kicked, trying to swing so that his armored torso protected his bare legs from the yard-long mandibles.

Wulfhere grabbed the Gael by the shoulder and dragged him clear with neither hesitation nor delicacy. The centipede's tons of rippling mass hit the pillar with the violence of a ship being launched.

The wobbling masonry collapsed, showering down in chunks that would crush any man, armored or no. The centipede's legs continued to row the creature forward, unaffected by the blocks and massive fragments which glanced from its chitinous back.

Cormac scrambled away on all fours—his boots, his shield, and the knuckles of his sword hand. The buckler rang like a gong each time it hit the floor, but not even Cormac could hear it over the continuing destruction of ancient Atlantis.

The metal ceiling sagged after the crumbling pillar, then tore. Water sprayed down, increasing to a torrent. The reivers had succeeded: the caverns here lay beneath the moat, not solid ground.

It remained to be seen whether the two of them would escape to savor their victory.

The Dane was kneeling nearby, gripping to his belly a block with one concave side. It had been part of the pillar's flaring capital.

For an instant, Cormac couldn't imagine what his friend was doing. Then he realized that the massive stone had taken a hop toward Wulfhere and that the Dane had trapped it between his torso and the ground instead of letting it smash over and past him. The shock knocked the breath from his body.

Cormac lifted his friend, though he didn't dare sheathe his sword or drop the buckler. He thrust his blade and right hand beneath the Dane's arm and dragged him up, off the block that had nearly killed him.

"Come on, you lazy scut!" Cormac shouted. "How am I supposed to get out of here without you to carry me?"

Mud, reeds, and something that flapped in and out of the fallen water like a tossed coin cascaded with the torrent through the ceiling. The spread of the influx was easily measured by the degree to which darkness displaced the fungus glow. Faint phosphorescence glimmered through the first touch of water, but any quantity of the muddy fluid choked and poisoned the light.

Wulfhere staggered forward, though he was bent over and breathed in short gasps. He'd lost Aslief's spear. His left hand lay on Cormac's hip so that the Gael could guide their paired flight. Wulfhere's mind and body had both been stunned by the blow. He could follow a friend's lead, and at need he could fight.

The axe was in the Dane's right hand. Wulfhere Skullsplitter could always fight.

Water raced ankle deep over the cavern's floor. The surface was even more treacherous than the slime of fungus had made it before. Sharp tearing sounds punctuated the roar of water. The torrent was expanding the hole through which it drained, gouging out the ring's underpinning fabric once its integrity had been breached.

A blaze of purple-green light marked their goal. The illumination was almost painfully bright to eyes adapted for the soft omnipresence of the fungus. The rope ladder swayed gently in a breeze driven by the rush of water displacing air from the cavern.

Wulfhere took his hand from Cormac's side and turned with his axe lifting. Cormac felt his friend's motion and rotated with him reflexively, as the two of them had done on a hundred battlefields before.

The centipede rushed toward them in a spray thrown by its pulsing legs.

Cormac shouted and waved his shield in the creature's face. The centipede reared as it had done before. The bundles of ganglia that served it as a brain were able to react in only one fashion to a stimulus, no matter how frequently that stimulus was repeated. Wulfhere, swinging with both hands and stepping into the stroke, sheared off the right-side leg of the fourth body segment.

The centipede came down on the Gael, ignoring the sword slash aimed between head and body. Cormac's blade nicked the chitin of the headshield, but the joint was too well-protected to be damaged by a sword.

Legs pinned Cormac on his back in slopping water. The mandibles scissored together. His buckler's plywood core shattered under the repeated contact. The right mandible pierced it, tearing along Cormac's wrist. The Gael snouted and stabbed upward, blinded by his buckler jerking in front of his eyes on the poison fang.

Wulfhere chopped, drew clear, and chopped again. Each blow left a leg dangling by a few shreds of chitinous armor. The Dane was withdrawing his axe for a fourth stroke, as methodical as a woodcutter, when the centipede whipped to escape an attack that even its mass was forced to recognize.

The Dane helped Cormac up with his left hand. He held the axe raised in his right and never took his eyes off the centipede. The creature circled the two men and the pile of rubble. Its long body had a brownish cast in the light falling through the hole in the cavern roof.

"You all right?" Wulfhere asked. Back to back, the companions began to climb the ramp. The centipede rippled past, its legs pulsing hypnotically. At any moment it would come on again.

"I'll do," Cormac said. He flexed his left hand. The mandible had bruised him when it smashed through his shield, but the skin was unbroken. He was limping slightly. Foreleg pincers had torn the muscles of both thighs.

The pair reached the top of the rubble pile. As soon as one of the men started to climb the ladder, the centipede would be over the other like surf on sand.

"You get up that ladder," Cormac ordered harshly. "I'll be right behind you."

"Your mother's a whore," said the Dane. "You were first down, you'll be first up. Get moving!"

The water was knee deep across all visible parts of the cavern. Its rushing flow ate at the edges of the ramp. A further section of roof followed the fallen pillar into the cataract.

The centipede drove up the ramp on scores of uninjured legs, its mandibles wide. The reivers shifted apart, giving each room to use his weapon unimpeded. Wulfhere lifted his axe two-handed over his right shoulder.

Cormac braced his right foot behind him, prepared this time to thrust with the full weight of his body behind the swordpoint. He didn't know whether his steel would

turn or break or drive straight through the headshield, and
he was sure that even with what passed for a brain removed
the centipede would live long enough to kill and eat the
both of them. A man must fight, even when he knows he
cannot win.

A small figure dropped from the rope ladder and
darted between the men: Loughra, the wand in her right
hand. Its blue glare lighted her body as it wrapped the
oncoming centipede in threads that not even the monster's
armored strength could break. The girl aged as swiftly as
salt melts in a puddle.

Cormac started toward her. Wulfhere grabbed the
Gael's arm with his left hand.

Cormac turned. "Let me go!" he shouted.

Wulfhere dragged him back toward the ladder. "Come
on!" he said. "It's too late for her."

Cormac tried to club the Dane with the pommel of his
sword. Wulfhere blocked the blow with his axe helve.
"Come on!" he repeated.

Wulfhere was right. Loughra, a 17-year-old girl when
she jumped from the ladder, now crouched as a toothless
crone in the blaze of her wand. The centipede's legs
thrashed furiously, unable to break the grip of the blue web
clinging to its head and forward body segments. The power
required to freeze the tons of rapacious carnivore was
enormous—

As was the cost of that power. A surge of water driven
by a further collapse of the ceiling tugged at Loughra's
waist and almost dragged her down with it.

Cormac sheathed his sword and leaped for the ladder.
The rungs were set a foot-and-a-half apart. Cormac took

them two at a time, hurling himself up onto the surface like wax blown from a jar of beer stoppered too early. The battens flexed but did not break under his step.

An ongoing geyser of muddy water spewed from the belt of water, high enough that Cormac could see it above the vegetation surrounding the sinkhole. He drew his sword. None of Loughra's tribe was present.

Wulfhere clambered up to the surface beside him, panting like a blown horse. The Dane's legs were wet to the knees.

The ground shook. An enormous jet of water shot twice as high as the previous norm, then sank back out of sight. The bottom must have dropped from acres of the ring lake. Water surged nearly to the sinkhole's lip.

"Now's the time to cross on the dry bottom," the Gael said. He bent and braced his hands on his knees to make it easier to draw in the breaths for which his lungs burned. "Before they're expecting us. Creon and Antheia."

A four-horned deer sprinted through the undergrowth, thrown into blind panic by destruction on a geological scale. Cormac didn't know what draining the lake into the cavern would do to Atlantis in the long term, nor did he care. In the short term, it would permit Cormac to get within the length of his sword of the Greek who brought him here.

The centipede, swirling in the currents raging below, gripped the lip of the sinkhole with a foreleg. It had managed to shed Cormac's shield from its mandible. Its jawplates worked furiously on the remnants of Atlantis's last queen.

Cormac's sword slashed the joint articulating the

pincered foot. Wulfhere reversed his axe and drove the back of it as a hammer into the creature's headshield. The chitin around the right-hand cluster of eyes, damaged by the Gael's sword in the cavern below, shattered like a terra cotta pot.

Another leg reached up to replace the first. The Dane had in the cavern severed the forelimbs on the other side.

Cormac sliced this leg off at the last joint also. Wulfhere brought his blade around in a figure eight, cutting the edge deep into the pulpy mass where he had crushed the armor.

The centipede slid away from the opening, rolling onto its back as it disappeared. The jaws still masticated their prey, but Loughra had defeated the monster before she died.

"Yes," said Wulfhere through his gasping inhalations. "Let's go kill Greeks. Would there were more than two."

The bed of the ring lake was knee deep in soupy mud. Eventually the sediment might dry out or slurp after the water into the caverns, but Cormac hadn't had the time to waste. Cursing and holding his sword high to keep it clean, he tramped toward the central citadel with Wulfhere beside him.

A fish five yards long flopped wildly nearby. Its jaws could easily swallow a man. A bad hop might bring the fish down on top of the reivers, but its mind was no longer on food. The false sun threw a sickly hue across the creature's silvery scales.

The carrion feeders would feast tonight.

They were hallway across the ring. The march was

exhausting and had already taken far longer than Cormac had allowed for. Creon and Antheia would have time to prepare for the reivers' return, though the Gael could hope that other aspects of the disaster would absorb the Greeks' attention.

It didn't matter. The way Cormac felt now, he would have charged a shield wall, naked and barehanded.

"That wand is well-lost where it can't kill more folk the way it's done so many," he snarled suddenly. "She didn't have to do that!"

"Nor did we," the Dane said. "Who knows why a man does a thing? Even a *man.*"

Wulfhere's boots squelched up and down in a steady beat. Cormac rushed forward in bursts of twenty yards or so, then waited panting to recruit his strength before sprinting another stretch.

The marble coping which surrounded the central island had stood a foot-and-a-half above the previous water level. Now the men could see that in addition there was twice that height of stone discolored by algae, and the glistening depth of muck besides. The whole combined in a sheer height greater than Cormac wanted to clamber after struggling in armor through the gooey bottom.

A hundred yards to the right of the reivers' intended approach stood a half-ruined marble gazebo, above a staircase down into what had been the water. The Gael changed his angle to intersect the structure. Beyond it loomed the back of a silver-clad building which he supposed was the palace.

A shelled and tentacled creature lay half-submerged in the mud nearby. More than a score of ten-foot arms lay flaccid on the surface. Cormac thought for a moment that the creature was dead, but he noticed that the pupil of its lidless eye was tracking him. He made sure that their path was beyond the arms' radius.

Wulfhere nodded toward the creature. "I suppose I'd rather tramp through mud," the Dane said, "than swim with things like that."

A scaly head appeared over the curve of the land. One eye caught the wading men. The head swiveled on a neck holding it ten feet in the air; both eyes focused on the potential prey.

The Kronosaur hooted angrily and came slithering across the mud toward them.

"Or swim with that one," muttered Wulfhere. "Though walking with it may not be much better."

"Run!" Cormac shouted.

The men were a hundred yards from dry land where the advantage would be theirs. The Kronosaur was at least five times as far from them, but the fifty-foot monster's paddle feet propelled it with reasonable efficiency through the mud. The beast couldn't survive the draining of the lake indefinitely, but it was alive now and furious as well as hungry.

Maybe if he and Wulfhere stood still where they were?

But the Kronosaur had already marked its prey. Besides, their dragging footprints trailed through the mud behind them like a frozen wake.

The men shambled across the muck in slow motion. There was nothing heroic about being drowned in a slough or disappearing down a gullet sized for vastly larger fish.

"If we—" Wulfhere called.

"—reach the steps—" he went on. Words spurted out in clumps each time the Dane's right boot slopped down.

"—can you hold—"

"—the thing alone?"

"Yes!" Cormac snarled.

His world was fire, not mud. The muscles of his legs burned, his pumping arms burned, and the flames from his blazing chest curled up and threw a blood-red filter across his eyes.

The Gael didn't know what Wulfhere intended, nor did he care. He was completely focused on reaching the protection of the gazebo before the Kronosaur gulped him down. He was also completely certain that he wouldn't succeed, that he would die in a lizard's gut and worse, that he would *fail*—

Cormac's hobnails clashed on the marble stairs. Up two, up two more. Well out of the mud, firm footing for a battle.

Cormac spun. The Dane clumped past him, splashing mud on the steps as his boots slammed down. The Kronosaur, heaving a ten-foot bow wave through the greasy muck, darted its head toward the men. The tongue shot out. It was forked and black-veined against spongy magenta flesh.

Cormac's sword described a perfect arc that flicked off one lobe of the tongue. Blood sprayed.

The Kronosaur jerked back its head and clopped its long jaws shut over the damaged organ. Its chest throbbed, expelling waste air in twin funnels of vapor from the nostrils above its eye sockets. The flaps that closed the air passages during dives pulsed open and shut within each breath cycle.

Cormac backed two steps upward, then two more. The monster came on again. Its back was covered in black scales with a green undercoat. Rosette patterns glowed in the light of the false sun.

The tip of Cormac's blade ripped across the gums of the Kronosaur's upper jaw. It wasn't a dangerous wound, but nothing the Gael could achieve with a sword could endanger a something the size of this creature.

Pain snatched the huge head back with a high-pitched bellow. Unlike the centipede, the reptile had enough brain cells to react to being hurt. Sword pricks, however expertly placed, wouldn't stop the Kronosaur forever, but they encouraged the beast to caution.

Cormac backed, placing each foot precisely. If he slipped, it would be over in an eye blink. He reached the top of the staircase. The gazebo's domed roof had collapsed, but most of the columns still stood. They offered protection against the creature's darting thrusts.

The Kronosaur hunched, then advanced like a land slip. It propelled itself by matched rearward strokes of its front paddles. The smaller hind paddles provided little besides rudder effect. The great body crashed into the staircase, shattering and displacing the ancient marble. The head lanced down like that of a starling taking a grub.

Cormac jumped forward beneath the attack and thrust up into the Kronosaur's throat. The beast's powerful neck muscles were iron-hard. The Gael's point bit but turned a hand's breadth deep, gouging a broad bloody track instead of cutting a vein or the windpipe.

The creature shrieked in fury and tossed its head. The jaws had found a pillar when they missed their intended prey. The Kronosaur's teeth were squat cones with rounded tips, very thick at the base. They were optimized for crushing the shells of armored cuttlefish like the creature the reivers had skirted near the shore.

The teeth ground marble with the same relentless power that was intended for calcite shells. Stone flaked and crumbled. The shaft was constructed of separate cylinders connected internally by lead cramps. The Kronosaur shook its head, flinging the stone barrels wildly as the metal tore.

The beast humped its body for a further advance. The Kronosaur was clumsy on dry land, but it was by no means inert. The paddles swept forward, throwing the Gael twenty feet up the slope when one chanced to swipe him as he tried to thrust again.

The Kronosaur's eyes and instincts tracked Cormac as a motion. The head swung in, jaws open. The teeth would make as little account of chain mail as they did of powdering a stone pillar.

An arrow pinned the forked tongue to the lower palate.

The Kronosaur screamed and raised its head to locate the new enemy. Wulfhere stood on a walkway of overgrown marble slabs, halfway down from the palace. His bow was in his hands. As Cormac scrambled to his feet, the Dane loosed another arrow into the reptile's open mouth.

The Kronosaur bellowed and heaved itself through the ruined gazebo, smashing the still-standing eight-inch columns in its haste to reach its tormentor. It hurt the beast to shift its weight on dry ground with paddles, but the creature moved with clumsy speed nonetheless.

Cormac stabbed behind the ribs as the creature

wallowed past. Because he thrust against the grain of the scales, his blade sank nearly the length of his forearm into the reptile's flesh. The wound had no evident effect.

Wulfhere held his ground as coolly as he would in the face of a charge by armored cavalry. The long Danish bow snapped an arrow deep in the ridge of bone above the Kronosaur's right eye socket, then another into the eye itself.

The beast twisted its head and slewed right. Its primeval brain was unable to compensate swiftly for the loss of binocular vision.

Wulfhere, regular as the drips of a waterclock, shot into the creature's throat. Arrows sank to their fletching when they struck the creases which permitted the neck to flex.

Cormac set his right boot against the Kronosaur's side for the leverage he needed to withdraw his sword. He succeeded, but it was like pulling the blade from living rock.

The beast turned toward him with the massive abruptness of a landslide. The Gael made an instant decision. He hurled himself toward and under the huge body. Belly plates scraped his boot as he rolled clear. The Kronosaur's bulk slammed down on the spot Cormac had been standing a moment before.

It hadn't been attacking him: it was trying to get away. Wulfhere's arrows had the effect of hornet stings on a human; and, like hornets, they were as potentially lethal in sufficient number.

The Dane paused. He had an arrow nocked, but he wasn't tensing the bowstring of human hair. The Kronosaur hurled itself back onto the lakebed with a vast outspewing of cushioning mud.

"Good work with that—" Cormac began.

Wulfhere lifted and drew the bow with a smooth motion, his arms working together. He loosed the shaft at the moment of maximum tension. The arrow's flight was almost too swift for human eyes to mark. A tuft of goose-quill fletching sprang from the back of the Kronosaur's head, where the foramen magnum opened to pass the spinal cord into the skull.

The beast continued to flop forward across the lake bottom. Its muscles were controlled only by the autonomic nervous system, the way a headless chicken runs.

Wulfhere cast down his bow. That had been his last arrow.

Cormac massaged his right wrist with his left hand. Stabbing so deeply through tough muscle had put enormous strain on those muscles and small bones. "It was already running away," he said.

"Yes," the Dane said. "Now we know that it won't come back."

Cormac shrugged, then stripped a handful of leaves with which to clean reptile blood from his blade. "Let's go find some Greeks," he said.

Earthshocks made foliage tremble as the reivers approached the rear of the palace. A thick silver plate shook from its mounting rivets and clanged to the walkway ahead of them.

Wulfhere chuckled. "They think we're come to collect a debt owed," he said.

"And so we are," Cormac said. His voice was as thin as the light dancing along the edge of his sword.

The door was a recent replacement panel of wood and leather. It hung open as the Dane had left it when he rushed through to retrieve his bow and quiver. He hadn't had time to worry then about what was waiting within. The reivers entered now with tense caution, weapons ready and bodies tautly prepared to spring into lethal action.

No one was in the service suite just inside the door. The next chamber was the dining room. The bodies of savages killed during the raid had vanished, but blood and the wrecked furniture remained. Heavy rubbish—broken marble statues and the base of a large column—had been piled over the hole in the flooring.

A pair of stunted servants stood looking out through the far door, whispering to one another. They squealed and tried to run when the reivers appeared behind them. Cormac made a tigerish leap and caught the female before she could escape.

Wulfhere bent toward the captive. "Where are your masters?" he shouted. The Atlantean covered her face with both hands and keened in a high-pitched voice.

"I'll handle it," Cormac said. Though they didn't have a language in common . . .

He lifted the servant to her feet. She weighed no more than a normal child. For that matter, she might *be* a child. All her folk had wizened features, reminding Cormac of the toll exacted by the wizardry used here.

"Creon?" he said, trying not to snarl in a threatening fashion. "Antheia? Listen to me, child."

He tried to keep tone soothing though the words

themselves could not be. She ought to recognize the names, at least.

"Where are Creon and Antheia?"

The captive continued to cry. The male servant unexpectedly poked his head around the doorjamb and chittered. He pumped his small arm, pointing behind him with his index and middle fingers extended together.

Cormac released the female servant. The reivers glided together through the door. Their Atlantean guide scampered ahead, giving the bigger men looks of obvious terror over his shoulder. He ran out the front door of the palace and pointed again, this time toward the temple beyond.

"Right, let's go," the Dane muttered. He broke into a heavy-footed jog, the best speed of which he was capable. Cormac matched him in an easy lope. The Gael bent his right arm so that the swordblade swayed gently in front of his body.

The servant guide cowered beside the entrance as the reivers passed. When Cormac looked back to check possible pursuit, he saw the Atlantean couple hugging one another in the doorway.

The earth chuckled to itself. Blocks of the courtyard's paving chipped their edges together and hopped a hand's breadth in the air.

Cormac extended his stride to enter the temple just ahead of his companion. There was no one present in the nave, though legions could have concealed themselves in the pillared aisles.

The dome was a thunderous echo chamber, but the source of the vast booming was in the vaults underneath.

The door from which the Greeks had initially appeared was at the far end of the building. It hung open again.

"This way," called Cormac. He realized that he couldn't hear his own voice, though that didn't matter: Wulfhere had seen the doorway on his own.

The men paused to right and left of the portal, bringing their breathing under control before they went to the next stage. A spiral staircase led down. The metal was lustrously silver in color but untarnished through the ages since it was built. The backless treads and slender balustrades vibrated like hummingbirds' wings in the noise surrounding them. The reivers couldn't see the floor from the angle at which they stood.

Cormac slipped through the doorway an instant before Wulfhere committed himself. The helical staircase was only wide enough for one man at a time.

The treads augered down for hundreds of feet to a surface of water lifted into standing waves by thunderous vibration. Purple-green lights like miniatures of the false sun depended from nodes on the walls. They were shaking also.

Huge silvery spheres spun in the hollow volume without any material support. The water had risen to bathe their lower sides, making the rotation noticeably erratic. Froth whipped by the globes' touch flew as high as the doorway.

Cormac would have missed Creon and Antheia in the chaotic hugeness were it not for the spiteful blue light that drew his eyes. The Greeks' tiny figures and their undamaged power device were near one side of the circular chamber.

The walls had begun to buckle under the thrust of water filling the dockyard caverns beyond. Water shifted blocks inward and spewed between the interstices. Antheia was attempting to push the heavy stones back into place with threads of blue fire.

The scale of the catastrophe was beyond the capacity of the Greeks' remaining tool. For so long as someone's life force energized it, the device could withstand the pressure; but the water was patient and omnipresent. If one path was blocked, it would find another . . .

A form that must be Creon's bobbed on the surface beside the device. The tool had stripped him to a husk that floated like pith.

Antheia, as shrunken as a fly drained in a spider's web, stood at the controls. She turned her face toward the doorway above. She tried to lift an arm, but she lacked the strength.

Cormac thought of Loughra in the jaws of the centipede. He did not smile, but there was no pity in his heart.

The blue glare vanished. A hundred feet of wall burst inward before a rush of water. Balls spun into one another, disintegrating in vivid violet light.

Wulfhere tugged the Gael's arm insistently. The reivers retreated into the nave.

Cormac slammed the door closed, but the rumbling sound was the whole world. A pillar fell from somewhere in the clerestory. It shattered on the floor like a bomb. The reivers ran by mutual instinct toward an aisle. That was the shortest distance out of the huge structure, though there was no certain safety outside either.

The floor beneath the dome buckled upward in a rolling motion, like that of a hound shaking its loose skin. Massive hexagonal paving blocks flipped and fell. The pillars began to sway.

Cormac sprinted across the thirty-foot aisle. The parallel lines of columns nodded their tops together, then away. The nave imploded as trusses cracked. Chunks of the coffered dome cascaded down like snowflakes in a blizzard. The flat roof above the aisle ripped along its axis.

The outer line of columns shook a few of its ornate capitals onto the courtyard beyond, then rocked inward again and collapsed toward the ruin of the nave. Stone barrels weighing a half-ton each bounced and danced in the rubble, dwarfed by the scale of destruction around them.

Cormac, his long Roman blade quivering in his right hand, leaped off the temple slab in a flat dive. It was ten feet down from the slab to the courtyard when he leaped, six feet as the ground heaved up to meet him when he was halfway through the maneuver, ten feet again when he tucked and rolled. The slabs shook themselves and lifted the Gael to his feet as though he and the dying world were a pair of practiced acrobats.

The dome and its support columns had plunged into the vaults beneath the temple. Now a gout of high-pressure steam lifted thousands of tons of shattered stone back from the pit. Tunnel ceilings ruptured in a web of fog and destruction, displacing foliage and buildings already ruined by time.

"Wulfhere!" Cormac shouted vainly. The sound was a cataclysmic pressure that drove the very breath from his lungs. The Gael stumbled forward. Slabs slid one by one into the expanding crater which had already engulfed the temple.

The false sun grew dim—shaded by the gush of steam, Cormac thought; but more than that as well. The light's hue had changed from purple-green to saffron as pale as the flames above ill-vented coal.

"Wulfhere!"

The Dane's huge hand groped his. They clutched each other, left to left, because each had his weapon out in his right fist. There was nothing to fight here, but a man clings to what matters to him in the hour he knows to be his last.

An axe, a sword, and a friend as the world ends.

The false sun faded until it gave no more light than the moon does in daytime. A distant roar penetrated from all directions, riding over the crackling destruction of the last of Atlantis.

The surface ruptured again at the edge of the courtyard. A pine hundreds of feet high toppled over and smashed to the ground a few yards from where the men stood. They didn't run. The tree was only a hint of motion in the non-light and besides, there was no place to run.

The sky shattered like a giant eggshell. The light of a normal sun, filtered by the mists of the northern seas of Earth, dissolved the tumbling shards. A foam-toothed wave surged from all margins of what remained of Atlantis, swallowing the land down inexorably.

Atlantis was sinking forever.

Cormac sheathed his sword with a clang of guard against the iron lip of its scabbard. They had a moment before the ground crumbled beneath them.

"Come on!" he cried to Wulfhere, tugging the Dane with him toward the tree which had nearly crushed them a moment ago. There was light now to move by.

The reivers threw themselves into the branches of the pine. Cormac thought of binding himself in with his sword belt, but he couldn't tell the attitude at which the tree would float. Besides, there wasn't enough time.

There was no time at all. A salt wave surged over them, pounding and washing the reivers clean of the taint of a world that should have died millennia before.

The tree surged, twisted, and started to roll. Cormac bellowed as the trunk rotated down. Saltwater drowned what he expected to be his final shout of defiance. The massive trunk didn't crush him against the marble pavement after all. The ground had already vanished into the depths of the present sea.

The tree shuddered in decreasing arcs around its axis until it stabilized, bobbing slightly in the choppy waves. Cormac crawled to the upper side. The tree weighed scores of tons, and the branches acted as natural outriggers. The weight of a man, even a big man in iron armor, wasn't enough to significantly affect its balance.

He had been looking for Wulfhere ever since the wave struck. A hand reached out of the sea and clutched a branch ten feet down the trunk.

Cormac hopped to his feet, balancing on the log as he had often done on a ship's rail. Before he could reach out to help, Wulfhere's other hand, then his head and shoulders shot up from the sea. The Dane took a higher grip and threw himself astride the tree the way he mounted a horse when required to: accomplishing the task by main strength and awkwardness, but accomplishing it nonetheless.

"I was beginning to think you'd deserted me," Cormac said.

Wulfhere took the axe from under his belt and sank the blade deep in the soft wood between them. The helve gave the men something to grip with their hands besides the coarse bark.

"What do you mean, *me* desert?" he said. "I'm the captain, remember?"

Something raised itself from the nearby waves and dived again. Possibly a fish—really only a flash of movement in the corner of Cormac's eyes. But very likely a Kronosaur or two had survived the collapse of the bubble world also.

He began to laugh. To survive *that,* and still to be swallowed whole by a lizard!

"It wasn't *that* funny," the Dane grumbled. "I don't suppose you've got anything to eat in that wallet of yours?"

"I don't—" the Gael began, but the words choked as motion again glimmered in his peripheral vision. He jumped to his feet.

Wulfhere braced Cormac's stance with a hand on his knee. "If you go over," the Dane warned, "you're on your own."

"*I* don't have anything to eat," Cormac said, "but I'll bet *they* do. It's our ship, and a lubberly lot they look, too, with half the oars shipped and no sail set though the weather's turned fair."

He drew his sword and waved it overhead in a glittering steel arc. "Hey! You farmers. Hey!"

Wulfhere rose, stretched, and bellowed, "Ahoy the ship! Hakon, you lazy scut! Get a proper stroke going!"

The wallowing longship was a quarter-mile away and the breeze was at best neutral. Despite the conditions, someone aboard the vessel heard their captain's shout. Crewmen waved. More of the oars hit the water.

Cormac and Wulfhere sat down again, waiting for the rescue neither of them had dared imagine. "Glad you decided to come along," the Dane said without looking at his companion. "Thanks."

Cormac gave a harsh, mocking laugh. "I wouldn't have missed it for the world," he said.

And he could almost believe the words as he spoke them, except that a vision of little Loughra veiled his sight of the returning longship.

CHILDREN OF THE FOREST
✦ ⋈ ✦

Many years ago I mentioned that I was a Fortean to a careful reporter who was taping the interview. My several psychiatrist friends were hugely amused when the printed version stated that I was a Freudian. Since then I've been careful to give an explanation of what I mean by the word.

Charles Fort collected reports of anomalous events from periodicals (largely from scientific journals) and published them in four volumes from 1919 to 1932. These include reports of things which are now accepted as true (for instance, giant squid and ball lightning) but which orthodox science at the time rejected as observer errors; matters which are unexplained but aren't especially controversial (for instance, unconfirmed sightings of astronomical bodies by respectable observers); and utterly bizarre things like a rain of frogs in England or a *rain of shaved meat in Kentucky. Fort didn't write about UFOs, but they're part of modern Fortean interests.*

Now—the fact that I'm interested in such things doesn't mean I believe in all of them. There are people who do, just as there are people who believe that disproving a report of spontaneous human combustion disproves all such reports. I consider both groups delusional (and I consider people who think you get real science or real history from a TV show to be deeply ignorant, but that's a slightly different matter).

One of the most entertaining writers on Forteana (and on natural history generally) was Ivan T. Sanderson. He was capable of modifying his data to improve a story, but he was a fine writer and a man of great culture and intelligence.

One of Sanderson's essays was on wudewasas, woodhouses (yes, that's what the name of the humorist P.G. Wodehouse comes from): the drawings of wild men found in the margins of medieval manuscripts. He speculated that there'd been a European version of the Sasquatch, but that it was man-sized rather than a giant like the wild man of the Northwest United States.

The likelihood that this is true (or for that matter, the likelihood that Bigfoot is running around Northern California) didn't matter for my purposes. I thought the notion would work for a story, so I wrote "Children of the Forest."

The form goes back to the fairy tales which I

*loved even before I could read. It's become
fashionable to give fairy tales a modern slant or to
twist them. I wasn't trying to be clever, but I did
try to treat the realities of medieval life and its class
structure with the same sort of realism that I'd
bring to a story set in Viet Nam.*

*When "Children . . ." was first published in
F&SF, it brought me two angry letters. (Only one
other story of mine from the '70s aroused any
comment at all.) I'm not sure what that means, as
the letter writers were incensed about completely
different aspects of the story (and both were
wrong). It may simply indicate that when I'm on,
my fiction arouses an emotional reaction in readers.*

If so, well, that's what I'm trying to do.

✤ ✤ ✤

When Teller came in from the field, gnarled as his
hoe-handle and looking twice his forty years, his
wife said, "The cow has gone dry, man." Teller scowled.
She had slapped out her words like bolts from a crossbow.
He understood them, understood also why she was
whetting the black iron blade of their only knife. From his
wife, warped and time-blackened by the same years that
had destroyed him, Teller turned to his daughter Lena.

And Lena was a dazzle of sunlight in the darkened
hut.

She was six, though neither of her parents could have
told a stranger that without an interval of mumbling and
dabbing fingers to cracked lips. But there were no
strangers. In the dozen years since the Black Death had
swept southern Germany, the track that once led to the

high road and thence to Stuttgart had merged back into the Forest. The hut was all of civilization, a beehive with two openings in its thatch. Teller now stooped in the doorway; above him was the roof hole that served as chimney for the open fire in the center of the room. By that fire sat Lena, easing another baulk of wood under the porridge pot before looking at her father. Her smile was timid, but the joy underlying it was as real as the blond of her sooty hair. She dared not show Teller the welts beneath her shift, but she knew that her mother would not beat her in his presence.

"I said, the cow has gone dry," the woman repeated.

The rasp of iron on stone echoed her words. "You know we can't go on until the harvest with three mouths and no milk."

"Woman, I'll butcher—"

"You will not." She slid to the floor and faced him, bandy-legged and shorter on her own legs than when sitting on the stool. "The meat will rot in a month, we have no salt. Three mouths will not last the summer on the cow's meat, man.

"Three mouths will not last the summer."

She was an iron woman, black-faced and black-hearted. She did not look at Lena, who cowered as her mother stepped forward and held out the wood-hafted knife to Teller. He took it, his eyes as blank as the pit of his mouth opening and closing in his beard. "Perhaps . . . I can hunt more . . . ?"

"Hoo, coward!" mocked the woman. "You're afraid to leave the clearing now for the woods devils, afraid to go out the door to piss in the night!" The reek of the wall across from the pine-straw bedding proved her statement. "You'll not go hunting, man."

"But—"

"Kill her. *Kill her!*" she shrieked, and Lena's clear voice wailed hopelessly as a background to the raucous cries. Teller stared at the weapon as though it were a viper which had crawled into his hand in the night. He flung it from him in a fury of despair, not hearing it clack against the whetstone or the *ping!* of the blade as it parted.

The woman's brief silence was as complete as if the knife had pierced her heart instead of shattering. She picked up the longest shard, a hand's breadth of iron whose edge still oozed light, and cradled it in her palms. Her voice crooned without meaning, while Teller watched and Lena burrowed her face into the pine needles.

"We can't all three eat and live to the harvest, man," the woman said calmly. And Teller knew that she was right.

"Lena," he said, not looking at the girl but instead at his cloak crumpled on the earthen floor. It was steerhide, worn patchily hairless during the years since he had bartered eggs for it from a passing peddler. That one had been the last of the peddlers, nor were there chickens anymore since the woods demons had become bolder.

"Child," he said again, a little louder but with only kindness in his voice. He lifted the cloak with his left hand, stroked his daughter between the shoulder blades with his right. "Come, we must go for a little journey, you and I."

The woman backed against the hut wall again. Her eyes and the knife edge had the same hard glitter.

Lena raised her face to her father's knee; his arm, strong for all its stringiness, lifted her against his chest. The cloak enveloped her and she thrashed her head free. "I'm hot, Papa."

"No, we'll play a game," Teller said. He hawked and spat cracklingly on the fire before he could continue. "You won't look at the way we go, you'll hide your head. All right, little one?"

"Yes, Papa." Her curls, smooth as gold smeared with river mud, bobbled as she obediently faced his chest and let him draw the leather about her again.

"The bow, woman," Teller said. Silently she turned and handed it to him: a short, springy product of his own craftsmanship. With it were the three remaining arrows, straight-shafted with iron heads, but with only tufts remaining of the fletching. His jaw muscles began to work in fury. He thrust the bow back to her, knots of anger dimpling the surface of his bare left arm. "String it! String it, you bitch, or—"

She stepped away from his rage and quickly obeyed him, tensing the cord without difficulty. The wood was too supple to make a good bow, but a stiffer bowshaft would have snapped the bark string. Teller strode from the hut, not deigning to speak again to his wife.

There was no guide but the sun, and that was a poor, feeble twinkling through the ranked pines and spruces. It was old growth, save in slashes where age or lightning had brought down a giant and given opportunity to lesser growth. Man had not made serious inroads on this portion of the Forest even before the Plague had stripped away a third of the continent's population. Fear had driven Teller and his wife to flee with their first child, leaving their village for a lonely clearing free from contamination. But there were other fears than that of the Black Death, things only hinted at in a bustling hamlet. In the Forest they became a deeper blackness in the shadows and a heavy padding on moonless nights.

They were near him now.

Teller lengthened his stride, refusing to look to the sides or behind him. He was not an intelligent man, but he knew instinctively that if he acknowledged what he felt, he would be lost. He would be unable to move at all, would remain hunched against a tree trunk until either starvation or the demons came for him.

Lena began humming a little tune. Though off-key, it was recognizable as a lullaby. Teller's wife had never bothered to rock Lena to sleep, but their elder daughter, born before the panicked flight into the wilderness, had absorbed enough of the memories of her babyhood to pass them on to her sister. It was not the Plague that had taken the girl, nor yet the demons. Rather, there had been a general malaise, a wasting fed by seven years in an environment that supported life but did nothing to make life supportable. In the end she had died, perhaps saving Teller the earlier agony of a journey like the one he made now.

Far enough, he decided. A spruce sapling thrust up from among three adult trees. Though its bole was only a hand's breadth in diameter, the first branches were a full ten feet in the air. It formed a post firmer than that on which Sebastian was martyred.

"Now, Lena," Teller said as he put the girl down, "you'll wait here by this tree for a while."

She opened her eyes for the first time since she had

left the house with her father. The conifers around her were spearpoints thrust through the earth. Black-green branches shuddered in a breath of wind. The girl screamed, paused, and screamed again.

Teller panicked at the sound and the open terror of her bright blue gaze. He stopped fumbling at the cord knotted about his waist and struck open-handed, his palm smudging the soot on her cheek. Lena bounced back against the spruce trunk, stunned mentally rather than physically by the blow. She closed her mouth unblinking, then spun to her feet and ran. Teller gulped fear and remorse as he snatched up his bow to follow.

Lena ran like a startled fawn. She should not have been able to escape a grown man, but the fearsome shadows came to her aid. When Lena dodged around the scaly bole of a hemlock, Teller, following, was knocked sprawling by a branch. He picked himself up, picked up also the arrows he had scattered as he fell. He nocked the one with the most fletching, though he could not have explained to a questioner what he meant to do with it. "Lena?" he called. The trees drank his voice.

A rustle and a stutter of light caught his attention, but it was a squirrel's flag tail jerking on a spruce tip. Teller eased the tension on his bowstring.

There was another sound behind him, and he turned very quickly.

Lena, trembling in the crease of a giant that had fallen so long ago that the trees growing around it were of nearly equal girth, heard her father blundering nearby. Her frightened whimper was almost a silence itself, no more than the burr of a millipede's feet through the leaf mould in front of her nose. She heard Teller call, then a ghastly double cry that merged with the twang of a bow. No more voices, then, but a grunt and the *chock!* of something hollow crushing against a tree trunk.

For a moment, then, there was real silence.

"Coo-o?" trilled a voice too deep to be birdlike. "Coo-o-o?" it repeated, closer now to Lena though unaccompanied by the crackling brush that had heralded her father's progress. "Coo?" and it was directly above her. Almost more afraid to look up than not to, Lena slowly turned her head.

It was leaning over the log to peer down at her, a broad face set with sharp black eyes and a pug nose. The grinning lips were black, the skin pink where it could be glimpsed beneath the fine, russet fur. Lena's hands swung to her mouth and she bit down hard on her knuckles. The creature vaulted soundlessly over the log. It was about the height of Lena's father, but was much deeper in the chest. Palms and soles were bare of the fur that clothed the rest of it. Its right hand reached out and plucked away the arrow that flopped from its left shoulder. A jewel of blood marked the fur at that point, but the creature's torso and long arms were already sticky with blood not its own.

The hands reached down for Lena. She would have screamed again, but her mind was folding up within her as a white blur.

"Coo-ree?" questioned a liquid voice in Lena's ear, and she blinked awake. A girl with a shy grin was watching her, a child so innocent that Lena forgot to be afraid. Even though the child was as furry as the adult who must have brought Lena to the grassy hollow in which she now lay. A smile that bared square, yellowed teeth split the fur and the little—shorter even than Lena though more compactly built—creature held out a double handful of hemlock nodules, painstakingly knocked clean of dirt. The skin of her hands was a rich onyx black in contrast to the broken, copper-colored fingernails.

As shyly as her benefactress, Lena took the roots and crunched one between her teeth. The nodule had a rich, almost meaty, flavor and a texture pleasant to her gums. She smiled back. A twittering at the crest of the hollow caused her to spin about and gape at the broad-chested male creature she had met in the woods, now with a smaller companion to either side. On the right was a four-dugged female, slimmer than the male and slightly hunched. The remaining woods man—but Lena's mind still shrieked demon, troll—was another child, obviously male and of lighter coloration than his parents. His cublike roundness had not yet given way to ropy adult musculature, and his nervous smile was a reflection of his sister's.

Lena stood. Her body had gone cold and the bright sunlight seemed suddenly to glance away as from a block of ice. The adult male had washed since she first saw him: his pelt was smooth and clean save for the smudged left shoulder. Another drop of blood oozed to the surface and the female, seeing it, cooed in vexation and nuzzled the wound. Her teeth chopped as she cleaned it. The male pushed her gently away, his eyes locked with Lena's. Trembling with courage she had not known was hers, Lena bit off another hemlock nodule, then extended the remainder of the bunch toward the watching woods folk.

The three before her began to caper with joy, and a warm, furry arm encircled Lena's waist from behind.

They were foragers and therefore by necessity wanderers, the family of which Lena was now a part. After a month in the bowl which chance or ancient vulcanism had pocked into the Jura Mountains, they spent a pair of weeks combing a stream with a different sleeping place every night. Food was plentiful in that spring and the summer it wore into: roots and berries, spruce tips and the tender shoots of other vegetation; birds' eggs while they lasted, but never the birds themselves. Lena was almost too young to remember the last of her parents' hens. Still, learning that they had succumbed to nest raiding, not slaughter, calmed a remaining bristle of unease.

She tried not to think of Teller at all.

Kort was the father of the family, even-tempered but awesomely strong. Rather than climb a hardwood to pick nuts before the squirrels had combed them, he would find a boulder or the largest fallen limb in the neighborhood and smash it against the tree trunk, showering himself and the ground with the ripe offerings. It was Kort, too, who trudged off on day-long journeys to the cave in which the family wintered, carrying in a bark-cloth basket the dried excess of their gleaning. The winter stores were kept beneath a stone too tight-fitting for a mouse to slide around and too massive for a bear's awkward limbs to thrust aside.

But if Kort's strength was the shaft which supported the family's existence, it was the quick mind of Kue-meh, his mate, which provided directing force. Her fingers wove the strips of cambium into fabric as smooth and as supple as the wool and linen of the villages beyond the Forest. The woods folk used the cloth for carrying bulky goods, not as clothing, though Lena once ineptly wove a crossbelt for herself when her shift disintegrated. Kue-meh guided the foraging, judging its progress and determining when and where the family would move. She could tell at a glance which hickory nut was sound and sweet, which had been emptied in its shell by a worm.

At first the children were never wholly alone, for there were dangers in the Forest. Not the bears, so much, for their strength and ugly tempers were outweighed by clumsiness and their preference for other food. Even Lena was soon able to scramble up a tree before a peevish grunt gave way to a charge. Lynxes were more of a potential threat, for they were swift and had the blood-lust common to all cats. Still Chi, the female woods child and smallest of the three, weighed forty founds by now and was too strong and active to be a comfortable victim.

The wolves, though, the wolves . . . .

They feared nothing very greatly, those lean gray killers. Fire, perhaps; but the woods folk feared it more and Lena learned to avoid the flames after being cuffed fiercely away from a lightning-slashed tree. From spring through fall the wolves padded through the Forest alone and in pairs, tracking a plump doe or a healthy fawn to rip down and devour. Like most powerful carnivores, the wolves chose their prey not for its weakness but for its taste—and after years of chaos and the Plague, some of them had found a taste for men.

Lena's long legs, and the new sense of freedom brought by roaming the Forest with folk who thought it home, not exile, took her and Faal, the young male, almost into long-toothed jaws. They were digging root nodules, using sharpened stakes and cloth bags while Kue-meh wove. Faal went around one side of a huge hemlock, Lena the other—the far side. The empty woods, a chorus of blacks and greens and browns, spoke to her suddenly. Dropping her equipment with a silent giggle, Lena darted off among the aisles of trees.

Faal heard the pad of her feet—months in the wild had trained Lena's step, but not beyond notice of ears that had been born there. He followed her without calling or even thinking. Faal was swiftly gaining his father's deep chest, but he showed signs of being in Kort's mental image as well. The two children were gone a minute or longer before Kue-meh looked up from her own work and Chi to notice that her other charges were gone. She hooted in anger, but Faal was already beyond earshot and Lena was ahead of him.

She was a shuttle racing over a loom of needles and spruce twigs. Faal was stronger and his lungs might have brought him abreast of her in time, but Lena's legs would have been the envy of a doe. Faal on his stumpy limbs could not outsprint the girl. But the two wolves which converged on Lena in a grove of beeches were quicker yet.

Lena stopped, too startled at first to be frightened. Faal had aimed a playful tackle at her before he saw the reason for her halt. He flopped to the leaf mould instead and skidded. The nearer of the red-tongued wolves lowered its tail and hunched.

Lena stepped without thought between Faal and the gray killer. The wolf drew back. It was more than the scent of a true man, the reivers with iron and fire, where only woods folk had been expected. There was something within Lena herself that allowed her, a slim six-year-old, to face down a pair of wolves. They stood for an instant, each of them half again the girl's size; then they bolted. Only their fresh spoor was visible a moment later when Kue-meh raced into the glade, Chi under her left arm and a six-foot pine knot in her right hand. Lena and Faal were pummeled heavily for the run, but Kue-meh spent the rest of the afternoon in thought. Afterwards she let all three children stray, so long as her own two kept close to Lena.

Early hunger and a vegetarian diet should have stunted Lena's growth. Instead she gained willowy inches to quickly overtop Faal and Chi. The woods folk were a cleanly people and the grime that had disfigured Lena's first six years disappeared in the ice-fed stream nearest the hollow in which she joined the family. It never returned. Her skin was clear and did not, even bare to the sun and the wind, take on the swarthy cast of her parents'. In the summer she was a warm brown, traced with the thin scabs of bramble cuts; in the winter her complexion counterfeited the creamy yellowness of old ivory polished by loving hands.

For all the beauty of her body and skin, Lena's hair was her crown. It had never been cut, a result of her mother's apathy rather than any interest in the girl's adornment. Washed out and laboriously carded with twigs by all four of the woods folk, it flowed down her back like liquid gold. Loose, it was a bright flood behind her as she ran—but then it snagged and caught and diminished. Faal began to plait it in the evening imitating Kue-meh's bark weavings. Simple at first, the patterns grew increasingly complex and changed nightly. The hair was Faal's delight. During the long winter evenings he spent hours braiding and reopening her tresses, then braiding them again. Lena bore the attention, but her mind strayed beyond the boy's gentle fingers.

There was another predator in the Forest, though Lena was twelve before she encountered it. She was miles from the high crag the family then occupied, following Kort to the winter cave, when a horn wound in the near distance. Kort's reaction was to panic. He danced in a little circle of indecision, then began scrambling up a princely fir tree. The bag of stores jerked with every hunch of his back, scattering bunches of hemlock nodules. Kort's feet and long right arm—his left held the bag and, in any case, would not lift above shoulder height since the arrow wound had healed—had shot him halfway up the trunk before he realized that Lena's progress was much slower than his own. There was more than a difference in strength. Though the woods folk did not have opposed big toes either, their control of their foot muscles was much greater than that of Lena's subspecies.

Kort scrabbled down again, chattering haste in an angry voice. Lena, terrified by the uncertain situation, tried to obey and lost her grip, slipping ten feet to the ground. Kort's nervous rage burst out in a clatter of syllables. Finally the stocky male threw himself up the bole in leaps that would have been impressive even if horizontal. He caught the bag of provisions in the crotch of a huge limb eighty feet in the air, then dropped back to Lena's level in four incredible stages. Slinging the girl with as little ceremony as he had the bag, he remounted the tree with equal speed. Shuddering with fear, pressed between the bole and Kort's great gasping breaths, Lena stared at the ground so far below that it trembled in the breeze. The horn blew again, very nearby.

A stag wobbled out of a clump of firs, its tongue grayish and drooling from the corner of its jaw. Twenty yards from the tree in which Kort and Lena sheltered, the deer fell under the whipsaw impact of a pair of mastiffs. Each dog looked as large as the victim. The stag cartwheeled. One of the great brindled dogs clamped on the deer's throat, the other caught the right foreleg. There was a flurry of humus. The stag's spine snapped like the first crack that follows the lightning.

There were a dozen dogs swirling on the forest floor now, hounds trained to back off after guiding the killer mastiffs to their prey. They belled and leaped for gobbets of the deer still thrashing in its death throes. The riders were on them then, two green-garbed huntsmen with full beards and long whips with which they cut at the milling pack . . . and a third man, a youth whose hair gleamed almost white in a stray beam of sun. He rocked back in the saddle of his great gray stallion and laughed to the sky. Lena froze to see his face lifting, but he was not searching the treetops, he was only bubbling over with the joy of the kill.

He was splendid, perfect in her eyes.

There were more riders, scores of men on foot including dog handlers as shaggy and grim as the beasts they dragged off the mangled stag. A huntsman's broad knife flashed and he raised the deer's ears and tail to the laughing youth. An unexpected warmth had driven the fear from Lena's mind. She watched, empty even of wonder at the scene beneath her—more men by ten times than she had ever before seen—while her eyes drank in every motion, every nuance of the young rider in red and gold.

Quick knives unlaced the deer, spilling the entrails to the reward of the hounds. The mastiffs sat aloof on their haunches, nearly the height of the footmen who skirted them with nervous eyes. Those killers were fed once daily and scorned to show interest in the game they brought down. Only their tongues . . . they flashed and rolled, infinitely flexible as they wiped clean the bloody jowls.

The babble thinned as did the crowd below. The hounds were tired and sated. They whined when the handlers chained them in pairs, but they allowed the men to lead them back the way they had come. Two brawny retainers slung the gutted deer on a pole and trotted off behind the youth on horseback. Riders drifted after them, talking and laughing as they passed out of earshot. Nothing remained but a ragged circle trampled black on the leaf mould. The horn was playing a caracol that seemed to hang in the air even after it was actually inaudible.

"The Ritter Karl," Lena was whispering to herself. She slurred into the heavy Swabish of her parents the name purred by the retainers. "Karl von Arnheim. . . ."

Kort, already reslinging the load of food, paid her no attention. But Lena continued to roll the syllables under her tongue.

✢ ✢ ✢

Months passed. Occasionally there were true men in the Forest: a pair of nervous travelers with packs and staves, whistling into the shadows; a vagabond whose rags were streaked with pus from the ulcers they covered; once a dozen men together, armed and as lean as the wolves . . . these wore mismated finery and as many as a dozen rings on each hand.

The von Arnheim hunt did not pass close enough for Lena to hear and run to it.

The woods folk travelled, but they did not roam. Lena's wanderings, at first for hours and then for days, were a cause of great concern to the family. Kue-meh pleaded with her, but the soft, cooing language of the folk had no words for the emotions that were driving the girl. The pleading stopped in time, for none of the family could catch Lena now if she ran. A foraging people learn not to waste effort. Some useful knowledge came from the trips: food sources that the family could exploit now or in the future, caves that opened into spacious chambers from throats too narrow for a bear to enter. But more and more, Lena's travels were to the edge of the fields of men; and this she did not explain to the woods folk, knowing instinctively that if she had, nothing would have kept Kue-meh from ordering an immediate move scores of miles deeper into the Forest.

And already the trips were considerable endeavors. Settlements had shrunk back from the trees, save for scattered households as Teller's had been. There were more of those than Lena would have guessed in the days when the Forest was a prison wall, but rarely did the inhabitants attempt to farm the thin soil as had her parents. Most were charcoal burners, blackened men or couples too bent to display sexual distinctions, hiking ever further to find the hardwoods that stoked their greedy kilns. Their huts were ragged shambles, sometimes lean-tos sprawled against some Forest giant; but the kilns were anchors, too slow and demanding of construction to be abandoned for new sites nearer the fuel. The increasing journeys to find an oak in the evergreen forest, then to fell it and laboriously drag back lengths with a shoulder harness, left no time for the necessary leisure of building another kiln.

Spread by the Plague, the lonely farmers were men who had tried to escape Death by running and had delayed his approach by a score of miserable years. The charcoal burners were caught between the upper and nether millstones of shrunken markets and scarcer raw materials, the farmers between declining fertility and impoverishment of tools. The third group, the meat hunters, had shrunk also though they might have been expected to increase. Game had returned to the fringe lands when men had melted away in the black ooze of the Plague, but the Forest had grown darker. Even those who had made their living in it for decades began to edge out into the sunlight.

The demons that haunted the minds of humans in the Forest were not the woods folk. In all her ramblings, Lena found no sign of hairy men other than Kort and his family.

She searched farther, into the lands where farms still sprawled in the open and men plowed behind animals, instead of prodding the soil with a stick. In the dusk she eeled along hedgerows so silently that the hens nesting in them did not stir. Where there were dogs, they rose and stalked stiff-legged over to Lena. After they sniffed at her, they whined and walked away. Occasionally a persistent brute would nuzzle the girl until her fingers stroked a rumbling purr from its rib cage. None of the beasts barked or attacked her.

The domestic animals were new to her, but she paid them little attention. Lena had come to the lands of men to find a man.

The farmers' huts were windowless, occasionally stone or proper wood but more often wattle and daub. The girl's eyes found chinks when the buildings were lighted, raked the faces of sleepy residents when they stumbled out to relieve themselves on the ground. But the man she sought would not be found in a hovel. It was long months before she came to understand that, however, since her upbringing had been silent about the Herren, the Masters.

As the seasons passed, as a month of searching became twelve, Lena's life was still almost wholly within the Forest. The trips beyond were windows of excitement that sparkled to set off well-loved panels of wood. The tall child had become a tall girl, muscled like a deer but with the same lithe slimness she had borne from the first. The woods folk did most things with grace, but they could not run. Faal watched Lena's sudden fits of exuberance, her flashing spurts across a clearing or through a briar thicket without misstep. His eyes glowed with the wonder and delight of a prophet to whom an angel was descending.

At night his copper nails glinted as they plaited her hair in wondrous fashion.

In a human world with little romance, the golden wraith became a legend before she was truly a rumor. Cottagers nodded and swilled thin beer as one of their number embellished an instant's vision. Sometimes Lena became a messenger from God or a Hell-sprite, searching for an infant's soul to steal. More often the stories were rooted deeper in the soul-earth of the peasants than Christ would ever be, and lowered voices spoke of Forest shadows and spirits of the Earth.

Marvel in most listeners became professional curiosity in gray Rausch the huntsman. His belt knife, honed to a wire edge on a stream-tumbled egg of granite, had silver mountings and the rampant wyvern crest of the von Arnheims. The late Ritter, Karl's father Otto, had presented it to Rausch twenty-one years before to replace the knife his junior huntsman had broken on a boar's scapula. Barehanded, ignoring the blood-slick tusks, Rausch had wrestled the beast to the dirt at the feet of the Ritter's pregnant wife. From that day he rode at Otto's right stirrup and that of Karl after him. He would not have exchanged that blade for the Emperor's sceptre.

Save for when von Arnheim hunted, Rausch's time was his own. If he chose to examine a hedgerow on his knees, snuffling like a gray-jowled hound, who was there to gainsay him? So Rausch listened and he watched, while as carefully as a cathedral mason his mind was constructing the hunt that would crown him and his master.

When the first hound belled, Lena ignored it. She knew now from long experience that the dogs were not her enemies. She had been away from the family the past three days, spending the daylit hours in the Forest fringe and the nights deeper into the open lands than she had ever gone before. The castle sitting gray on a detached plateau had drawn her eyes months earlier, but anticipation itself had delayed her approach to it. Now at last she had slipped to the very edge of its straggling curtain walls, let her fingers caress the rough stone. It could easily be climbed, but its hidden interior made the act not a moment's but a thing for long pondering in the Forest depths. That in her mind, Lena had started back, her course across the fields more hasty than deliberate since she had let the dawn stride too nearby as she studied the wall.

The second joyous bugling would have been a surface impression as well, except for the prompt echo of the hunting horn.

Lena was already among the trees. Her first reaction was that of her foster father, to choose the highest and secrete herself in the upper branches. A premonition that this hunt was no chance crossing of her path drove her instead to headlong flight. Panic rode her, a brutal jockey whose violence spewed out the strength that might otherwise have carried her free.

For a mile she sprinted, leaping obstacles and dreading at every instant that the hounds would give tongue again. They did not. She half-turned, then, her nerves begging for the object of their fear, and her right shoulder brushed an oak sapling. It was no more than a glancing blow, but it sufficed to break her stride and allow reaction to her masterless effort throw her to the ground.

And as she lay sobbing on the needle-strewn earth, the hounds and the horn sounded again. She had gained on her pursuers; but they knew, dogs and men, that a hunt was decided in its last moments, not the first. They suited their pace to that certainty. With proper governance, Lena could have run all day. In the darkness, when the men were blind and the dogs nervously unwilling to range ahead, she would have disappeared. A night of sleepless excitement and the disastrous sprint had gutted her. Fear drove Lena back to her feet, but she had lost the ability to force the pace.

With leisure to choose the course, Lena might have led the hunt into empty stretches of the Forest where only squirrels would have been disturbed by its passage. Terror eliminated all chance of such forethought and she plunged straight as a plumb line for the distant cedar copse in which she had last huddled with the woods folk. Perhaps she would have done the same in any event: Lena had never before been hunted, and she lacked the instincts of the wild-born.

The sun was well up before a bright goosequill signaled the nearest of the hunters to Lena's backward glance. The feather bobbed, visible when the green hat and man and charger beneath it were not. She turned as if unfeeling, her face an ivory cameo, her legs scissors of bronze. She did not pump her arms as she ran, avoiding a practice that could stitch a runner's torso with cramps while the great veins of his legs still balanced oxygen and poisons in the working muscles.

The hounds were close behind her. The men may not have known how close, for except in that instant's flash down an aisle of trees they had been beyond sight. Rausch left little to chance, and two of the riders were horse handlers leading picked remudas. But time was lost changing from foundered mounts to fresh ones, and the strings could not follow with the ease of the unhindered riders through brush that clutched at leadropes. The dogs, loping with their muzzles high and quivering with the fresh scent, yelped madly but did not attempt to close the twenty yards separating them from their quarry. They were the fingers of Death, but not his jaws.

In a noon-bright clearing deep in the Forest, Lena stumbled a second time. She rolled smoothly to her feet and collapsed, her reflexes whole but her body without the strength to effect them. The hounds were in a yapping, yelping circle around her. When she tried to rise again the foam-smeared breast of a great stallion slammed her down.

Lena's lungs were balls of yellow fire. Above her bellowed the green-suited hunter, a little man who had unslung his cocked arbalest to wave it as a signal of triumph.

The knobbed end of a ten-foot tree limb dashed his brains out with the effectiveness of a trebuchet.

Kue-meh, bandy-legged and slight, had darted through the pack. If her strength was inferior to that of Kort, it was still beyond the standards of true men—and the female had the cold will to overcome panic and act in the face of catastrophe. The hounds gave back, snarling. The riderless horse lurched away from the dragging weight still caught in the reins. Two more men, Karl in red silk and cloth-of-gold and Rausch beside him, his grim face a fortress in the midst of chaos, burst into the clearing in which their victim lay: Kue-meh hissed at them and waggled her brain-spattered club.

Rausch reined up and his left hand caught his master's bridle as well, preventing the youth from thrusting into the deadly circle of the club. Then he whistled and from behind his horse, stark as Furies, loped a pair of mastiffs.

There was neither choice nor hope. Kue-meh strode forward as boldly as if her death were not certain. She swung at the nearer of the mastiffs, missing her aim as it reared back. Kort bellowed from the edge of the clearing, but his rage was too late. The second mastiff 's leap ended with its fangs grinding on the bones of Kue-meh's right shoulder. She cried out despairingly as the first dog's jaws closed on her head.

Her neck popped loudly.

The smack of a hunting crossbow was simultaneous.

Halfway between the brush and the killer dogs, Kort's body jerked backwards. The fourth hunter had ridden into the clearing, having paused first to lay a square-headed quarrel in the launching groove of his weapon. The great iron bolt lifted Kort, carrying part of his breastbone with it through the back of his ribs.

The mastiffs stalked away as the pack began to scuffle for its trophies. The archer slung his arbalest from the saddle of his blowing horse and dismounted to whip the dogs away from Kort. Rausch, too, slipped to the ground, a purposeful thumb on the edge of his blade as he walked toward Kue-meh.

"No, these—creatures—are unclean," the Ritter said, triumph vibrant through the weariness of his voice. "We won't carry those back. Let the dogs eat." He lifted himself out of the saddle. His eyes remained fixed on Lena's, holding her firm as a snake would a rabbit. His breeches and tunic were shot with gold no brighter than his unbound hair. Froth from the succession of horses he had ridden to death blackened his calves and thighs, and his tunic was dark with his own sweat. Still his broad shoulders did not droop and there was laughter on his tongue after he splashed it with wine from the skin Rausch offered. "So . .

. she gave us a run, did she not, my Rauschkin? But I think she was worth a few horses, no . . . ? And even poor Hermann, he rode well, but it was his own fault if he let a troll brain him."

In a more businesslike voice he added to Rausch, "Be ready to hold her arms."

Lena's eyes were open, staring. But even if the fact registered on her mind, she would not at first have understood why von Arnheim was unlacing his breeches.

Eventually, awareness returned. They had tied her for the ride back to the castle, her wrists to the saddlehorn and her ankles lashed to one another beneath the horse's belly. That pain she had escaped as during the grim, slow jogging she lay slumped over the corpse of Hermann who hung crosswise in front of her. Her blond hair was matted over a pair of transverse welts. Rausch had finally used the loaded end of his whip to quiet the girl for his master.

Her thighs were sticky with blood, some of it from the brambles.

She was in a tiny room when she awakened. Outside, a mastiff growled. It had a low rumble, penetrating without being loud, that could terrify in a way that the frenzied barking of lesser beasts could not. The hour was long past sundown, but odor alone told Lena that she had been thrust into an empty kennel with the mastiffs on guard at the opening. Unlike Karl's human retainers, the great dogs could be depended on to keep all others away from what was, for now, the Ritter's property alone.

Lena squirmed to the doorway. A horse-huge mastiff lay across it. The beast's head was raised and one of the dog handlers, well aware of the brute's capabilities, was scuttling away across the muddy courtyard. Only the casks of strong ale, broached for the Ritter's triumph, had given the man courage to approach as closely as he had.

Awakened by the intruder, the brindled dog turned to lick its own flanks. Lena froze, but moonlight on her hair drew the broad muzzle into the opening. The eyes were calm and dark-pupiled, larger than a man's. The mastiff's tongue flapped against Lena's temple like a soft rag, sponging at the blood caked there.

Fearfully—no present kindness would erase memory of Kue-meh's last moment of life—Lena brushed her fingers across the dog's forehead, then caressed the upthrust ears. Power burred again in the dog's thorax, but it now was rich with delight. The head gave back, directed by the girl's proddings where it could not have been forced, and let her worm out into the open.

The courtyard was empty of all but the two dogs and a squalor which even the gentle moon limned clearly. The second, fawn-colored, mastiff whined and nuzzled Lena wetly. There was a faint murmuring from the other kennels, wattled domes little different in design from the huts of the peasants. No man or other dog appeared to try the wrath of the killer who now supported the girl on either side.

Her hands absorbing strength from the skin folded over the dogs' withers, Lena made her way to the wall. Behind her, the tower of the keep climbed seventy feet from the ground. No lights gleamed through its arrow-slits. The drink that had enspirited one man had crumpled all his fellows. Even perfect success could only briefly have counteracted the exertion required to gain it, and the Ritter's ale-sodden feast had done for the stay-at-homes as well. Three crossbowmen snored away their guard on the tower, and the occasional sounds from beyond the low wall to the inner court came from the fowl arid pigs of the humans quartered there. The snorts of the horses sharing the outer courtyard with Lena and the dogs were muted. Seven had been ridden to death during the morning or had been swallowed in the Forest beyond later recall by the exhausted hunters.

Lena touched the stones of the curtain wall, massive gray blocks more of nature than of man. She was beyond strength or weakness now, as inanimate as the limestone in which her hands found natural holds. The larger, brindled mastiff raised itself to its full height on the wall and licked the sole of her foot. Then she was over, sliding down the face of the wall and beginning to run the instant she touched the rocky soil below. This time there was no pursuit.

She followed the trail broken by the day's long hunt, knowing the confused scents would hinder the dogs if they were loosed on her. As she passed them, her hands plucked off berries and the pale, tender shoots of budding spruce. Once, in splashing across a rill, she paused for three quick gulps and a mouthful that she absorbed over the next minutes rather than swallowing. Her pace was not particularly swift, but it was as regular as a machine's.

The forest floor paid little mind to dawn or darkness, but the needles of sunlight piercing to the loam were nearly vertical when Lena reached the scene of death and capture. Kort lay huddled, flies black on the raw wounds which crows had already enlarged. Three of the birds croaked angrily from the limb to which Lena's intrusion had sent them, pacing from side to side and hunching their pinions.

Kue-meh's face, undisturbed by the fangs of the pack, bore a look of peculiar kindliness and peace. It was the face with which she had greeted Lena seven years before, less resigned than willing to accept. Lena looked away. It was not that for which she had returned.

"Coo-ee?" she called softly.

The Forest grew very silent. Even the crows left off their grumblings.

"Coo-ee?" the girl repeated. The bushes parted as she knew they must, and Chi, then Faal, stood timidly before her. Gurgling sounds that were partly tears and partly words of a language even older than that of the woods folk, Lena threw herself into their arms. She hugged their smooth, furred bodies like the shades of her lost innocence. At last she thrust them back to arm's length. Wiping her face free of the mingled tears, she said, "We must go now, very quickly. There are places in the Forest so far away from here that the Others will never come. They will never find us again."

She spoke and led the way into the Forest without a glance behind her. Chi followed at once. Faal, a picture of his father now in all but the gray that had tinged Kort's fur, hesitated. As yet he lacked the consciousness of strength that would let him unconcernedly follow into the unknown. But in a moment he ran to catch the females and, as he shambled on at Lena's side, his fingers began caressing the tawny gold of her hair.

THE BARROW TROLL

When I was very young my family was given a run of a 1938 children's magazine called Jack and Jill. The last feature in each issue was a serial, and one of those serials was an adaptation of "Beowulf."

I have no idea who did that version (I'm not even sure that I was able to read myself at the time; it may have been something my parents read to me), but it was really excellent. I didn't appreciate how good it was until much later. In the adaptation there's reference to the warriors' shields of yellow linden, a vividly realistic detail that I've remembered all my life since.

Twenty-odd years ago while I was plotting what became my first novel, I did a close reading of "Beowulf" in a literal translation. The shields of yellow linden weren't there. They must have been added by the adaptor to anchor the story in physical reality—which doesn't mean familiar reality, but rather something concrete that the reader can put his mental hands around even if he *doesn't precisely understand its purpose. That was an important lesson for me.*

And for those of you who wonder (as I did), "linden" is the common continental name for trees Americans call basswood. They're generally called lime trees in Britain.

Besides "Beowulf" I read and reread The Age of Fable, *Bulfinch's retelling of Norse myth in a series of connected stories. (I had no idea how hard it would be to do that until I tried the same thing many years later in the Northworld trilogy.) Then I read translations of the "Eddas," the Icelandic originals from which Bulfinch had worked—*

And finally I came to the Icelandic sagas themselves. I found their style and outlook very similar to my own. The narration is terse. Although the tales are fiction or at least fictionalized, there's a real attempt to keep the action realistic: even supernatural events are described in a realistic fashion.

Also the sagas contain a great deal of humor, but it's understated and frequently black beyond modern imagination. (For example, the posse hunting Gunnar arrives at his house. One of their number goes to the door to scout the situation. Gunnar stabs him with a spear. The scout walks back to his fellows who ask, "Is Gunnar home?" "I don't know," the scout replies, "but his spear is." And drops dead.)

Incidentally, my taste for that sort of joke is one of the reasons folks often think there's no humor at all in my fiction. They're wrong, but they're probably happier people for not understanding.

"The Barrow Troll" was an attempt to turn the elements I found in saga narration into a modern fantasy short story. Michel Parry bought it for a British collection titled Savage Heroes, *but Stu Schiff brought the story out in* Whispers *magazine before its British publication.*

I think "The Barrow Troll" succeeds at what it attempts about as well as anything that I've written.

✣ ✣ ✣

Playfully, Ulf Womanslayer twitched the cord bound to his saddlehorn. "Awake, priest? Soon you can get to work."

"My work is saving souls, not being dragged into the wilderness by madmen," Johann muttered under his breath. The other end of the cord was around his neck, not that of his horse. A trickle of blood oozed into his cassock from the reopened scab, but he was afraid to loosen the knot. Ulf might look back. Johann had already seen his captor go into a berserk rage. Over the Northerner's right shoulder rode his axe, a heavy hooked blade on a four-foot shaft. Ulf had swung it like a willow-wand when three Christian traders in Schleswig had seen the priest and tried to free him. The memory of the last man in three pieces as head and sword arm sprang from his spouting torso was still enough to roil Johann's stomach.

"We'll have a clear night with a moon, priest; a good night for our business." Ulf stretched and laughed aloud, setting a raven on a fir knot to squawking back at him. The berserker was following a ridge line that divided wooded slopes with a spine too thin-soiled to bear trees. The flanking forests still loomed above the riders. In three days, now, Johann had seen no man but his captor, nor even a tendril of smoke from a lone cabin. Even the route they were taking to Parmavale was no mantrack but an accident of nature.

"So lonely," the priest said aloud.

Ulf hunched hugely in his bearskin and replied, "You soft folk in the south, you live too close anyway. Is it your Christ-god, do you think?"

"Hedeby's a city," the German priest protested, his fingers toying with his torn robe, "and my brother trades to Uppsala . . . . But why bring me to this manless waste?"

"Oh, there were men once, so the tale goes," Ulf said. Here in the empty forest he was more willing for conversation than he had been the first few days of their ride north. "Few enough, and long enough ago. But there were farms in Parmavale, and a lordling of sorts who went a-viking against the Irish. But then the troll came and the men went, and there was nothing left to draw others. So they thought."

"You Northerners believe in trolls, so my brother tells me," said the priest.

"Aye, long before the gold I'd heard of the Parma troll," the berserker agreed. "Ox broad and stronger than ten men, shaggy as a denned bear."

"Like you," Johann said, in a voice more normal than caution would have dictated.

Blood fury glared in Ulf's eyes and he gave a savage jerk on the cord. "You'll think me a troll, priestling, if you don't do just as I say. I'll drink your blood hot if you cross me."

Johann, gagging, could not speak nor wished to.

With the miles the sky became a darker blue, the trees a blacker green. Ulf again broke the hoof-pummeled silence, saying, "No, I knew nothing of the gold until Thora told me."

The priest coughed to clear his throat. "Thora is your wife?" he asked.

"Wife? Ho!" Ulf brayed, his raucous laughter ringing like a demon's. "Wife? She was Hallstein's wife, and I killed her with all her house about her! But before that, she told me of the troll's hoard, indeed she did. Would you hear that story?"

Johann nodded, his smile fixed. He was learning to recognize death as it bantered under the axehead.

"So," the huge Northerner began. "There was a bonder, Hallstein Kari's son, who followed the king to war but left his wife, that was Thora, behind to manage the stead. The first day I came by and took a sheep from the herdsman. I told him if he misliked it to send his master to me."

"Why did you do that?" the fat priest asked in surprise.

"Why? Because I'm Ulf, because I wanted the sheep. A woman acting a man's part, it's unnatural anyway.

"The next day I went back to Hallstein's stead, and the flocks had already been driven in. I went into the garth around the buildings and called for the master to come out and fetch me a sheep." The berserker's teeth ground audibly as he remembered. Johann saw his knuckles whiten on the axe helve and stiffened in terror.

"Ho!" Ulf shouted, bringing his left hand down on the shield slung at his horse's flank. The copper boss rang like thunder in the clouds. "She came out," Ulf grated, "and her hair was red. 'All our sheep are penned,' says she, 'but you're in good time for the butchering.' And from out the hall came her three brothers and the men of the stead, ten in all. They were in full armor and their swords were in their hands. And they would have slain me, Ulf Otgeir's son, *me*, at a woman's word. Forced me to run from a woman!"

The berserker was snarling his words to the forest. Johann knew he watched a scene that had been played a score of times with only the trees to witness. The rage of disgrace burned in Ulf like pitch in a pine faggot, and his mind was lost to everything except the past.

"But I came back," he continued, "in the darkness, when all feasted within the hall and drank their ale to victory. Behind the hall burned a log fire to roast a sheep. I killed the two there, and I thrust one of the logs half-burnt up under the eaves. Then at the door I waited until those within noticed the heat and Thora looked outside.

"'Greetings, Thora,' I said. 'You would not give me mutton, so I must roast men tonight.' She asked me for speech. I knew she was fey, so I listened to her. And she told me of the Parma lord and the treasure he brought back from Ireland, gold and gems. And she said it was cursed that a troll should guard it, and that I must needs have a mass priest, for the troll could not cross a Christian's fire and I should slay him then."

"Didn't you spare her for that?" Johann quavered, more fearful of silence than he was of misspeaking.

"Spare her? No, nor any of her house," Ulf thundered

back. "She might better have asked the flames for mercy, as she knew. The fire was at her hair. I struck her, and never was woman better made for an axe to bite—she cleft like a waxen doll, and I threw the pieces back. Her brothers came then, but one and one and one through the doorway, and I killed each in his turn. No more came. When the roof fell, I left them with the ash for a headstone and went my way to find a mass priest—to find you, priestling." Ulf, restored to good humor by the climax of his own tale, tweaked the lead cord again.

Johann choked onto his horse's neck, nauseated as much by the story as by the noose. At last he said, thick-voiced, "Why do you trust her tale if she knew you would kill her with it or not?"

"She was fey," Ulf chuckled, as if that explained everything. "Who knows what a man will do when his death is upon him? Or a woman," he added more thoughtfully.

They rode on in growing darkness. With no breath of wind to stir them, the trees stood as dead as the rocks underfoot.

"Will you know the place?" the German asked suddenly. "Shouldn't we camp now and go on in the morning?"

"I'll know it," Ulf grunted. "We're not far now—we're going downhill, can't you feel?" He tossed his bare haystack of hair, silvered into a false sheen of age by the moon. He continued, "The Parma lord sacked a dozen churches, so they say, and then one more with more of gold than the twelve besides, but also the curse. And he brought it back with him to Parma, and there it rests in his barrow, the troll guarding it. That I have on Thora's word."

"But she hated you!"

"She was fey."

They were into the trees, and looking to either side Johann could see hill slopes rising away from them. They were in a valley, Parma or another. Scraps of wattle and daub, the remains of a house or a garth fence, thrust up to the right. The firs that had grown through it were generations old. Johann's stubbled tonsure crawled in the night air.

"She said there was a clearing," the berserker muttered, more to himself than his companion. Johann's horse stumbled. The priest clutched the cord reflexively as it tightened. When he looked up at his captor, he saw the huge Northerner fumbling at his shield's fastenings. For the first time that evening, a breeze stirred. It stank of death.

"Others have been here before us," said Ulf needlessly.

A row of skulls, at least a score of them, stared blank-eyed from atop stakes rammed through their spinal openings. To one, dried sinew still held the lower jaw in a ghastly rictus; the others had fallen away into the general scatter of bones whitening the ground. All of them were human or could have been. They were mixed with occasional glimmers of buttons and rust smears. The freshest of the grisly trophies was very old, perhaps decades old. Too old to explain the reek of decay.

Ulf wrapped his left fist around the twin handles of his shield. It was a heavy circle of linden wood, faced with leather. Its rim and central boss were of copper, and rivets of bronze and copper decorated the face in a serpent pattern.

"Good that the moon is full," Ulf said, glancing at the bright orb still tangled in the fir branches. "I fight best in the moonlight. We'll let her rise the rest of the way, I think."

Johann was trembling. He joined his hands about his saddle horn to keep from falling off the horse. He knew Ulf might let him jerk and strangle there, even after dragging him across half the northlands. The humor of the idea might strike him. Johann's rosary, his crucifix—everything he had brought from Germany or purchased in Schleswig save his robe—had been left behind in Hedeby when the berserker awakened him in his bed. Ulf had jerked a noose to near-lethal tautness and whispered that he needed a priest, that this one would do, but that there were others should this one prefer to feed crows. The disinterested bloodlust in Ulf's tone had been more terrifying than the threat itself. Johann had followed in silence to the waiting horses. In despair, he wondered again if a quick death would not have been better than this lingering one that had ridden for weeks a mood away from him.

"It looks like a palisade for a house," the priest said aloud in what he pretended was a normal voice.

"That's right," Ulf replied, giving his axe an exploratory heft that sent shivers of moonlight across the blade. "There was a hall here, a big one. Did it burn, do you think?" His knees sent his roan gelding forward in a shambling walk past the line of skulls. Johann followed of necessity.

"No, rotted away," the berserker said, bending over to study the post holes.

"You said it was deserted a long time," the priest

commented. His eyes were fixed straight forward. One of the skulls was level with his waist and close enough to bite him, could it turn on its stake.

"There was time for the house to fall in, the ground is damp," Ulf agreed. "But the stakes, then, have been replaced. Our troll keeps his front fence new, priestling."

Johann swallowed, said nothing.

Ulf gestured briefly. "Come on, you have to get your fire ready. I want it really holy."

"But we don't sacrifice with fires. I don't know how—"

"Then learn!" the berserker snarled with a vicious yank that drew blood and a gasp from the German. "I've seen how you Christ-shouters love to bless things. You'll bless me a fire, that's all. And if anything goes wrong and the troll spares you—I won't, priestling. I'll rive you apart if I have to come off a stake to do it!"

The horses walked slowly forward through brush and soggy rubble that had been a hall. The odor of decay grew stronger. The priest himself tried to ignore it, but his horse began to balk. The second time he was too slow with a heel to its ribs, and the cord nearly decapitated him. "Wait!" he wheezed. "Let me get down."

Ulf looked back at him, flat-eyed. At last he gave a brief crow-peck nod and swung himself out of the saddle. He looped both sets of reins on a small fir. Then, while Johann dismounted clumsily, he loosed the cord from his saddle and took it in his axe hand. The men walked forward without speaking.

"There . . ." Ulf breathed.

The barrow was only a black-mouthed swell in the

ground, its size belied by its lack of features. Such trees as had tried to grow on it had been broken off short over a period of years. Some of the stumps had wasted into crumbling depressions, while from others the wood fibers still twisted raggedly. Only when Johann matched the trees on the other side of the tomb to those beside him did he realize the scale on which the barrow was built: its entrance tunnel would pass a man walking upright, even a man Ulf's height.

"Lay your fire at the tunnel mouth," the berserker said, his voice subdued. "He'll be inside."

"You'll have to let me go—"

"I'll have to nothing!" Ulf was breathing hard. "We'll go closer, you and I, and you'll make a fire of the dead trees from the ground. Yes . . . ."

The Northerner slid forward in a pace that was cat-soft and never left the ground a finger's breadth. Strewn about them as if flung idly from the barrow mouth were scraps and gobbets of animals, the source of the fetid reek that filled the clearing. As his captor paused for a moment, Johann toed one of the bits over with his sandal. It was the hide and paws of something chisel-toothed, whether rabbit or other was impossible to say in the moonlight and state of decay. The skin was in tendrils, and the skull had been opened to empty the brains. Most of the other bits seemed of the same sort, little beasts, although a rank blotch on the mound's slope could have been a wolf hide. Whatever killed and feasted here was not fastidious.

"He stays close to hunt," Ulf rumbled. Then he added, "The long bones by the fence; they were cracked."

"Umm?"

"For marrow."

Quivering, the priest began gathering broken-off trees, none of them over a few feet high. They had been twisted off near the ground, save for a few whose roots lay bare in wizened fists. The crisp scales cut Johann's hands. He did not mind the pain. Under his breath he was praying that God would punish him, would torture him, but at least would save him free of this horrid demon that had snatched him away.

"Pile it there," Ulf directed, his axehead nodding toward the stone lip of the barrow. The entrance was corbelled out of heavy stones, then covered over with dirt and sods. Like the beast fragments around it, the opening was dead and stinking. Biting his tongue, Johann dumped his pile of brush and scurried back.

"There's light back down there," he whispered.

"Fire?"

"No, look—it's pale, it's moonlight. There's a hole in the roof of the tomb."

"Light for me to kill by," Ulf said with a stark grin. He looked over the low fireset, then knelt. His steel sparked into a nest of dry moss. When the tinder was properly alight, he touched a pitchy faggot to it. He dropped his end of the cord. The torchlight glinted from his face, white and coarse-pored where the tangles of hair and beard did not cover it. "Bless the fire, mass-priest," the berserker ordered in a quiet, terrible voice.

Stiff-featured and unblinking, Johann crossed the brushwood and said, "In nomine Patris, et Filii, et Spiritus Sancti, Amen."

"Don't light it yet," Ulf said. He handed Johann the

torch. "It may be," the berserker added, "that you think to run if you get the chance. There is no Hell so deep that I will not come for you from it."

The priest nodded, white-lipped.

Ulf shrugged his shoulders to loosen his muscles and the bear hide that clothed them. Axe and shield rose and dipped like ships in a high sea.

"Ho! Troll! Barrow fouler! Corpse licker! Come and fight me, troll!"

There was no sound from the tomb.

Ulf's eyes began to glaze. He slashed his axe twice across the empty air and shouted again, "Troll! I'll spit on your corpse, I'll lay with your dog mother. Come and fight me, troll, or I'll wall you up like a rat with your filth!"

Johann stood frozen, oblivious even of the drop of pitch that sizzled on the web of his hand. The berserker bellowed again, wordlessly, gnashing at the rim of his shield so that the sound bubbled and boomed in the night.

And the tomb roared back to the challenge, a thunderous *BAR BAR BAR* even deeper than Ulf's.

Berserk, the Northerner leaped the brush pile and ran down the tunnel, his axe thrust out in front of him to clear the stone arches.

The tunnel sloped for a dozen paces into a timber-vaulted chamber too broad to leap across. Moonlight spilled through a circular opening onto flags slimy with damp and liquescence. Ulf, maddened, chopped high at the light. The axe burred inanely beneath the timbers.

Swinging a pair of swords, the troll leapt at Ulf. It was the size of a bear, grizzled in the moonlight. Its eyes burned red.

"Hi!" shouted Ulf and blocked the first sword in a shower of sparks on his axehead. The second blade bit into the shield rim, shaving a hand's length of copper and a curl of yellow linden from beneath it. Ulf thrust straight-armed, a blow that would have smashed like a battering ram had the troll not darted back. Both the combatants were shouting; their voices were dreadful in the circular chamber.

The troll jumped backward again. Ulf sprang toward him and only the song of the blades scissoring from either side warned him. The berserker threw himself down. The troll had leaped onto a rotting chest along the wall of the tomb and cut unexpectedly from above Ulf's shield. The big man's boots flew out from under him and he struck the floor on his back. His shield still covered his body.

The troll hurtled down splay-legged with a cry of triumph. Both bare feet slammed on Ulf's shield. The troll was even heavier than Ulf. Shrieking, the berserker pistoned his shield arm upward. The monster flew off, smashing against the timbered ceiling and caroming down into another of the chests. The rotted wood exploded under the weight in a flash of shimmering gold. The berserker rolled to his feet and struck overarm in the same motion. His lunge carried the axehead too far, into the rock wall in a flower of blue sparks.

The troll was up. The two killers eyed each other, edging sideways in the dimness. Ulf's right arm was numb to the shoulder. He did not realize it. The shaggy monster leaped with another double flashing and the axe moved too slowly to counter. Both edges spat chunks of linden as they withdrew. Ulf frowned, backed a step. His boot trod on a ewer that spun away from him. As he cried out, the troll grinned and hacked again like Death the Reaper. The shield-orb flattened as the top third of it split away. Ulf snarled and chopped at the troll's knees. It leaped above the steel and cut left-handed, its blade nocking the shaft an inch from Ulf's hand.

The berserker flung the useless remainder of his shield in the troll's face and ran. Johann's torch was an orange pulse in the triangular opening. Behind Ulf, a swordedge went *sring!* as it danced on the corbels. Ulf jumped the brush and whirled. "Now!" he cried to the priest, and Johann hurled his torch into the resin-jeweled wood.

The needles crackled up in the troll's face like a net of orange silk. The flames bellied out at the creature's rush but licked back caressingly over its mats of hair. The troll's swords cut at the fire. A shower of coals spit and crackled and made the beast howl.

"Burn, dog-spew!" Ulf shouted. "Burn, fish-guts!"

The troll's blades rang together, once and again. For a moment it stood, a hillock of stained gray, as broad as the tunnel arches. Then it strode forward into the white heart of the blaze. The fire bloomed up, its roar leaping over the troll's shriek of agony. Ulf stepped forward. He held his axe with both hands. The flames sucked down from the motionless troll, and as they did the shimmering arc of the axehead chopped into the beast's collarbone. One sword dropped and the left arm slumped loose.

The berserker's axe was buried to the helve in the troll's shoulder. The faggots were scattered, but the troll's hair was burning all over its body. Ulf pulled at his axe. The troll staggered, moaning. Its remaining sword pointed down at the ground. Ulf yanked again at his weapon and it slurped free. A thick velvet curtain of blood followed it. Ulf raised his dripping axe for another blow, but the troll tilted toward the withdrawn weapon, leaning forward, a smoldering rock. The body hit the ground, then flopped so that it lay on its back. The right arm was flung out at an angle.

"It was a man," Johann was whispering. He caught up a brand and held it close to the troll's face. "Look, look!" he demanded excitedly. "It's just an old man in bearskin. Just a man."

Ulf sagged over his axe as if it were a stake impaling him. His frame shuddered as he dragged air into it. Neither of the troll's swords had touched him, but reaction had left him weak as one death-wounded. "Go in," he wheezed. "Get a torch and lead me in."

"But . . . why—" the priest said in sudden fear. His eyes met the berserker's and he swallowed back the rest of his protest. The torch threw highlights on the walls and flags as he trotted down the tunnel. Ulf's boots were ominous behind him.

The central chamber was austerely simple and furnished only with the six chests lining the back of it. There was no corpse, nor even a slab for one. The floor was gelatinous with decades' accumulation of foulness. The skidding tracks left by the recent combat marked paving long undisturbed. Only from the entrance to the chests was a path, black against the slime of decay, worn. It was toward the broken container and the objects which had spilled from it that the priest's eyes arrowed.

"Gold," he murmured. Then, "Gold! There must—the

others—in God's name, there are five more and perhaps all of them—"

"Gold," Ulf grated terribly.

Johann ran to the nearest chest and opened it one-handed. The lid sagged wetly, but frequent use had kept it from swelling tight to the side panels. "Look at this crucifix!" the priest marveled. "And the torque, it must weigh pounds. And Lord in heaven, this—"

"Gold," the berserker repeated.

Johann saw the axe as it started to swing. He was turning with a chalice ornamented in enamel and pink gold. It hung in the air as he darted for safety. His scream and the dull belling of the cup as the axe divided it were simultaneous, but the priest was clear and Ulf was off balance. The berserker backhanded with force enough to drive the peen of his axehead through a sapling. His strength was too great for his footing. His feet skidded, and this time his head rang on the wall of the tomb.

Groggy, the huge berserker staggered upright. The priest was a scurrying blur against the tunnel entrance. "Priest!" Ulf shouted at the suddenly empty moonlight. He thudded up the flags of the tunnel. "Priest!" he shouted again.

The clearing was empty except for the corpse. Nearby, Ulf heard his roan whicker. He started for it, then paused. The priest—he could still be hiding in the darkness. While Ulf searched for him, he could be rifling the barrow, carrying off the gold behind his back. "Gold," Ulf said again. No one must take his gold. No one ever must find it unguarded.

"I'll kill you!" he screamed into the night. "I'll kill you all!"

He turned back to his barrow. At the entrance, still smoking, waited the body of what had been the troll.

THAN CURSE THE DARKNESS
⊰ ⊱

I'm an HPL fan and started my career writing for Arkham House, the publisher founded to preserve Lovecraft's stories in book form, but "Than Curse the Darkness" is my only Cthulhu Mythos story. ("Denkirch" is Lovecraftian, but its model was HPL'S early—pre-Mythos—story "Polaris.") Ramsey Campbell, the unwitting spur to me writing my first story for publication, commissioned this one for an anthology he was editing for Arkham House, "New Tales of the Cthulhu Mythos."

Something that'd always puzzled me about the Mythos is why the Great Old Ones had human minions, since it was explicitly stated that if the Great Old Ones returned to Earth they would blast away all present life. Why would humans serve something that in human terms was absolute evil?

Writing a story is a very good way to focus logically on a question. I found an answer that satisfied me in human history. I set my story in the Congo Free State while it was still the personal possession of King Leopold II, but I could have picked any number of times or places. (Knowledge of history isn't an altogether cheerful accomplishment.) Things got a little better in the Congo after Leopold defaulted on a loan and the Belgian government took over the running of the colony, but only a little better.

At about the time this story was set, my friend Manly Wade Wellman was born in Portuguese West Africa (now Angola), just south of the Congo. (His parents were medical missionaries.) Manly retained a deep interest in Africa all his life, and his library contained many volumes about the continent.

Histories looking back at a period can explain what happened at a time and place, but contemporary works do something even more valuable (at least for a fiction writer): they explain what people at the time thought was happening. For the story's background I used books from Manly's library like Actual Africa—The Coming Continent, *as well the works of missionaries protesting Belgian atrocities and modern overviews of the "development" of the Congo Basin.*

Does that sound like a lot of research for a fantasy story? Well, maybe, but it's a habit I've kept throughout my career. I think it's stood me in good stead.

One writing difficulty I had with the story was in deciding on the viewpoint character. I wrote about half the piece, stopped, and threw out the whole business to start again with a female scholar instead of a male adventurer as my main protagonist. Things fell into place then.

The title, by the way, is from the motto of *The Christophers*, a religious society: *It is better to light one candle than to curse the darkness.*

What with the research, the rewriting, and the fact that I was working a full-time job as Assistant Town Attorney for Chapel Hill at the time, "Than Curse the Darkness" took me five months to complete. This had an unexpected but very beneficial side-effect.

One night shortly after I'd sent the story to Ramsey, the phone rang. By "night," I mean my wife and I were asleep. The caller introduced himself as Roger Elwood (whom I knew of as an indefatigable SF/fantasy/horror anthologist but had never met or dealt with). He told me that he was now editing a line of novels, and he'd been given my name. Would I like to write novels?

I was absolutely dumbfounded. At the time I'd only sold about ten stories and not all those had appeared in print. I blurted that I appreciated his call, but I couldn't possibly write a novel: I'd just taken five months to write a novelette. Mr. Elwood said he regretted that, because he was prepared to offer me a two-book contract right now on the phone, if I could turn the first one in six months. I repeated my refusal, and he went elsewhere.

That's how I avoided the Laser Books debacle, which blighted (and in some cases destroyed) the careers of so many of those who took similar offers.

I think I'd have refused the offer under any circumstances, but my recent struggle to do a good job on "Than Curse the Darkness" armored me against the thought of "easy money." Writing isn't easy if you care about the result. Laser Books taught a lot of people not to care about their work. If there's a worse lesson to learn early in your career, I don't know what it is.

I had to wait several more years to sell a novel. I don't regret that delay.

✢ ✢ ✢

"What of unknown Africa?" —H. P. Lovecraft

The trees of the rain forest lowered huge and black above the village, dwarfing it and the group of men in its center. The man being tied to the whipping post there was gray-skinned and underfed, panting with his struggles but no match for the pair of burly Forest Guards who held him. Ten more Guards, Baenga cannibals from far to the west near the mouth of the Congo, stood by with spears or Albini rifles. They joked and chattered and watched the huts hoping the villagers would burst out to try to free their fellow. Then killing would be all right . . . .

There was little chance of that. All the men healthy enough to work were in the forest, searching for more trees to slash in a parody of rubber gathering. The Law said that each adult male would bring four kilograms of latex a week to the agents of King Leopold; the Law did not say that the agents would teach the natives how to drain the sap without killing the trees it came from. When the trees died, the villagers would miss their quotas and die themselves, because that too was the Law—though an unwritten one.

There were still many untouched villages further up the river.

"If you cannot learn to be out in the forest working," said a Baenga who finished knotting the victim to the post with a jerk that itself cut flesh, "we can teach you not to lie down for many weeks."

The Forest Guards wore no uniforms, but in the Congo Basin their good health and sneering pride marked them more surely than clothing could have. The pair who had tied the victim stepped back, nodding to their companion with the chicotte. That one grinned, twitching the wooden handle to unfurl the ten-foot lash of square-cut hippopotamus hide. He had already measured the distance.

A naked seven-year-old slipped from the nearest hut. The askaris were turned to catch the expression on the victim's face at the first bite of the chicotte, so they did not see the boy. His father jerked upright at the whipping post and screamed, "Samba!" just as the feathery *hiss-crack!* of the whip opened an eight-inch cut beneath his shoulder blades.

Samba screamed also. He was small even for a forest child, spindly and monkey-faced. He was monkey quick, too, darting among the Guards as they spun. Before anyone could grab him he had wrapped himself around the waist of the man with the whip.

"Wau!" shouted the Guard in surprise and chopped down with the teak whip handle. The angle was awkward. One of his companions helped with a roundhouse swing of his Albini. The steel butt-plate thudded like a mallet on a tent stake, ripping off the boy's left ear and deforming the whole side of his skull. It did not tear him loose from the man he held. Two Forest Guards edged closer, holding their spears near the heads so as not to hit their fellow when they thrust.

The whipped man grunted. One of the chuckling riflemen turned in time to see him break away from the post. The rough cord had cut his wrists before it parted. Blood spattered as he took two steps and clubbed his hands against the whip-wielder's neck.

The rifleman shot him through the body.

The Albini bullet was big and slow and had the punch of a medicine ball. The father spun backward and knocked one of the Baengas down with him. Despite the wound he stood again and staggered forward toward Samba. A pink coil of intestine was wagging behind him from the bullet's exit hole. Both the remaining rifles went off. This time, when the shots had sledged him down, five of the spearmen ran to the body and began stabbing.

The Baenga with the whip got up, leaving Samba on the ground. The boy's eyes were open and utterly empty. Lt. Trouville stepped over him to shout, "Cease, you idiots!" at the bellowing knot of spearmen. They parted immediately. Trouville wore a waxed moustache and a white linen suit that looked crisp save for the sweat stains under his arms, but the revolver at his belt was not for show. He had once pistoled a Guard who, drunk with arrogance and palm wine, had started to burn a village which was still producing rubber.

Now the slim Belgian stared at the corpse and

grimaced. "Idiots," he repeated to the shame-faced Baengas. "Three bullets to account for, when there was no need at all to fire. Does the Quartermaster charge us for spear-thrusts as well as bullets?"

The askaris looked at the ground, pretending to be solely concerned with the silent huts or with scratching their insect bites. The man with the chicotte coiled it and knelt with his dagger to cut off the dead man's right ear. A thong around his neck carried a dozen others already, brown and crinkled. They would be turned in at Boma to justify the tally of expended cartridges.

"Take the boy's too," Trouville snapped. "He started it, after all. And we'll still be one short."

The patrol marched off, subdued in the face of their lieutenant's wrath. Trouville was muttering, "Like children. No sense at all."After they were gone, a woman stole from the nearest hut and cradled her son. Both of them moaned softly.

Time passed, and in the forest a drum began to beat.

In London, Dame Alice Kilrea bent over a desk in her library and opened the book a messenger had just brought her from Vienna. Her hair was gathered in a mousy bun from which middle age had stripped all but a hint of auburn. She tugged abstractedly at an escaped lock of it as she turned pages, squinting down her prominent nose.

In the middle of the volume she paused. The German heading gave instructions, stating that the formula there given was a means of separating death from the semblance of life. The remainder of the page and the three that followed it were in phonetic transliteration from a language few scholars would have recognized. Dame Alice did not mouth any of those phrases. A premonition of great trees and a thing greater than the trees shadowed her consciousness as she read silently down the page.

It would be eighteen years before she spoke any part of the formula aloud.

Sergeant Osterman drank palm wine in the shade of a baobab as usual while Baloko oversaw the weighing of the village's rubber. This time the Baenga had ordered M'fini, the chief, to wait for all the other males to be taken first. There was an ominous silence among the villagers as the wiry old man came forward to the table at which Baloko sat, flanked by his fellow Forest Guards.

"Ho, M'fini," Baloko said jovially, "what do you bring us?"

Without speaking, the chief handed over his gray-white sheets of latex. They were layered with plantain leaves. Baloko set the rubber on one pan of his scales, watched it easily overbalance the four-kilogram weight in the other pan. Instead of setting the rubber on the pile gathered by the other villagers and paying M'fini in brass wire, Baloko smiled. "Do you remember, M'fini," the Baenga asked, "what I told you last week when you said to me that your third wife T'sini would never sleep with another man while you lived?"

The chief was trembling. Baloko stood and with his forefinger flicked M'fini's latex out of the weighing pan to the ground. "Bad rubber," he said, and grinned. "Stones, trash hidden in it to bring it to the weight. An old man like you, M'fini, must spend too much time trying to satisfy your wives when you should be finding rubber for the King."

"I swear, I swear by the god Iwa who is death," cried M'fini, on his knees and clutching the flapping bulk of rubber as though it were his firstborn, "it is good rubber, all smooth and clean as milk itself!"

Two of the askaris seized M'fini by the elbows and drew him upright. Baloko stepped around the weighing table, drawing his iron-bladed knife as he did so. "I will help you, M'fini, so that you will have more time to find good rubber for King Leopold."

Sergeant Osterman ignored the first of the screams, but when they went on and on he swigged down the last of his calabash and sauntered over to the group around the scales. He was a big man, swarthy and scarred across the forehead by a Tuareg lance while serving with the French in Algeria.

Baloko anticipated the question by grinning and pointing to M'fini. The chief writhed on the ground, his eyes screwed shut and both hands clutched to his groin. Blood welling from between his fingers streaked black the dust he thrashed over. "Him big man, bring no-good rubber," Baloko said. Osterman knew little Bantu, so communication between him and the Guards was generally in pidgin. "Me make him no-good man, bring big rubber now."

The burly Fleming laughed. Baloko moved closer, nudged him in the ribs. "Him wife T'sini, him no need more," the Baenga said. "You, me, all along Guards—we make T'sini happy wife, yes?"

Osterman scanned the encircling villagers whom curiosity had forced to watch and fear now kept from dispersing. In the line, a girl staggered and her neighbors edged away quickly as if her touch might be lethal. Her hair was wound high with brass wire in the fashion of a dignitary's wife, and her body had the slim delight of a willow shoot. Even in the lush heat of the equator, twelve-year-olds look to be girls rather than women.

Osterman, still chuckling, moved toward T'sini. Baloko was at his side.

Time passed. From deep in the forest came rumblings that were neither of man or of Earth.

In a London study, the bay window was curtained against frost and the gray slush quivering over the streets. The coal fire hissed as Dame Alice Kilrea, fingers tented, dictated to her male amanuensis. Her dress was of good linen but two buttons were missing, unnoticed, from the placket, and the lace front showed signs of lunch bolted in the library . . . . "and, thanks to your intervention, the curator of the Special Reading Room allowed me to handle Alhazred myself instead of having a steward turn the pages at my request. I opened the volume three times at random and read the passage on which my index finger fell.

"Before, I had been concerned; now I am certain and terrified. All the lots were congruent, referring to aspects of the Messenger." She looked down at the amanuensis and said, "Capital on 'Messenger', John." He nodded.

"Your support has been of untold help; now my need for it is doubled. Somewhere in the jungles of that dark continent the crawling chaos grows and gathers strength. I am armed against it with the formulas that Spiedel found in the library of Kloster-Neuburg just before his death; but that will do us no good unless they can be applied in time.

You know, as I do, that only the most exalted influence will pass me into the zone of disruption at the crucial time. That time may yet be years to come, but they are years of the utmost significance to Mankind. Thus I beg your unstinting support not in my name or that of our kinship, but on behalf of life itself.

"Paragraph, John. As for the rest, I am ready to act as others have acted in the past. Personal risk has ever been the coin paid for knowledge of the truth."

The amanuensis wrote with quick, firm strokes. He was angry both with himself and with Dame Alice. Her letter had driven out of his mind thoughts of the boy whom he intended to seduce that evening in Kettners. He had known for some time that he would have to find another situation. The problem was not that Dame Alice was mad. All women were mad, after all. But her madness had such an insidious plausibility that he was starting to believe it himself.

As presumably her present correspondent did. And the letter to him would be addressed to "His Royal Highness . . . ."

In most places the trees grew down to the water edge, denser for being able to take sunlight from the side as well as from above. The margins of the shallow backwaters spread after each rain into sheets thick with vegetable richness and as black as the skins of those who lived along them. In drier hours there were sand banks and easy expanses on which to trade with the forest folk.

Gomes's dugout had already slid back into the slough, leaving in the sand the straight gouge of its keel centered in the blur of bare footprints. A score of natives still clustered around Kaminski's similar craft, fondling his bolts of bright-patterned cloth or chatting with his paddlers. Then the steamship swung into sight around the wooded headland.

The trees had acted as a perfect muffler for the chuffing engine. With a haste little short of panic, the forest dwellers melted back into concealment. The swarthy Portuguese gave an angry order and his crew shipped their paddles. Emptied of its cargo, the dugout drew only a few inches of water and could, had there been enough warning, have slid up among the tree roots where the two-decked steamer could never have followed.

Throttled down to the point its stern wheel made only an occasional slapping, the government craft edged closer to Gomes. On the Upper Kasai it was a battleship, although its beamy twenty-four meters would have aroused little interest in a more civilized part of the world. Awnings protected the hundreds of askaris overburdening the side rails. The captain was European, a blond, soft-looking man in a Belgian army uniform. The only other white man visible was the noncom behind the Hotchkiss swivel-mounted at the bow.

"Messieurs Gomes and Kaminski, perhaps?" called the officer as the steamship swung to, a dozen yards from the canoe. He was smiling, using his fingertips to balance his weight on the starboard bridge rail.

"You know who we are, de Vriny—damn you," Gomes shot back. "We have our patent to trade and we pay our portion to your *Societe Cosmopolite*. Now leave us!"

"Pay your portion, yes," deVriny purred. "Gold dust

and gold nuggets. Where do you get such gold, my fine mongrel friends?"

"Carlos, it's all right," called Kaminski, standing in his grounded boat. "Don't become angry—the gentleman is doing his duty to protect trade, that is all." Beneath the sombrero which he had learned to wear in the American Southwest, sweat was boiling off Kaminski. He knew his friend's volcanic temper, knew also the reputation of the blond man who was goading them. Not now! Not on the brink of the success that would gain them entree to any society in the world!

"Trade?" Gomes was shouting. "What do they know about trade?" He shook his fist at de Vriny and made the canoe rock nervously, so that the plump Angolan woman he had married a dozen years before put a calming hand on his leg. "You hold a rifle to the head of some poor black, pay him a ha'penny for rubber you sell in Paris for a shilling fourpence. Trade? There would be no gold coming out of this forest if the tribes didn't trust us and get a fair value for the dust they bring!"

"Well, we'll have to explore that," grinned the Belgian. "You see, your patent to trade was issued in error—it seems it was meant for some Gomez who spelled his name with a 'z'—and I have orders to escort you both back to Boma until the matter can be resolved."

Gomes's broad face went saffron. He began to slump like a snow figure on a sunny day. "They couldn't take away our patent because of a spelling mistake their own clerks made?" he whined, but his words were more of a sick apostrophe than a real question.

The Belgian answered it anyway. "You think not? Don't

you know who appoints the judges of our Congo oh-so-Free State? Not Jews or nigger-wenching Portu-gees, I assure you."

Gomes was probably bracing his sagging bulk against the thwart, though he could indeed have been reaching for the Mauser lying across the pack in front of him. Presumably that was what the Baenga thought when he fired the first shot and blew Gomes into the water. Every Forest Guard with a rifle followed in a ragged volley that turned the canoe into a chip dancing on an ornamental fountain. Jets of wood and water and blood spouted upward.

"Christ's blood, you fools!" de Vriny cried. Then, "Well, get the rest of them, too!"

Kaminski screamed and tried to follow his paddlers in a race for the tree line, but he was a corpulent man whose boots punched ankle-deep into the soft sand. The natives had no chance either. The Hotchkiss stuttered, knocking down a pair of them as the gunner checked his range. Then, spewing empty cases that hissed as they bounced into the water, the machine gun hosed bullets across the other running men. Kaminski half-turned as the black in front of him pitched forward hemorrhaging bright blood from mouth and nose. That desire to see his death coming preserved the trader from it: the bullet that would otherwise have exited through his forehead instead drilled through both upper maxillary bones. Kaminski's eyes popped out as neatly as oysters into a gourmet's silver spoon. His body slapped hard enough to ripple the sand in which it came to rest face up.

The firing stopped. Capsized and sinking, Gomes's shattered dugout was drifting past the bow of the steamer.

"I want their packs raised," deVriny ordered. "Even if you have to dive for them all day. The same with the packs on shore—then burn the canoes."

"And the bodies, master?" asked his Baenga headman.

"Faugh," spat the Belgian. "Why else did the good Lord put crocodiles in this river?"

They did not take Kaminski's ear because it was white and that would attract comment. Even in Boma.

Time passed. Deep in the forest the ground spurted upward like a grapefruit hit by a rifle bullet. Something thicker than a tree bole surged, caught at a nearby human and flung the body, no longer distinguishable as to sex or race, a quarter mile through the canopy of trees. The earth subsided then, but in places the surface continued to bubble as if made of heated tar.

Five thousand miles away, Dame Alice Kilrea stepped briskly out of her solicitors's office, having executed her will, and ordered her driver on to the Nord Deutscher-Lloyd Dock. Travelling with her in the carriage was a valise containing one ancient book and a bundle of documents thick with wax, ribbons, and gold foil—those trappings and the royal signatures beneath. On the seat across from her was the American servant she had engaged only the week before as she closed her London house and discharged the remainder of her establishment. The servant, Sparrow, was a weasely man with tanned skin and eyes the frosty color of lead cast in too hot a mold. He said little but glanced around frequently; and his fingers writhed as if with separate life.

✢ ✢ ✢

Occasionally chance would merge the rhythm of mauls and axes splitting wood in a dozen parts of the forest. Then the *thunk-thunk-THUNK* would boom out like a beast approaching from the darkness. Around their fire the officers would pause. The Baengas would chuckle at the joke of it and let the pounding die away. Little by little it would reappear at each separate group of woodsmen, finally to repeat its crescendo.

"Like children," Colonel Trouville said to Dame Alice. The engineer and two sergeants were still aboard the *Archiduchesse Stephanie*, dining apart from the other whites. Color was not the only measure of class, even in the Congo Basin. "They'll be cutting wood—and drinking their malafou, wretched stuff, to call it palm wine is to insult the word 'wine'—they'll be at it almost till dawn. After a time you'll get used to it. There's nothing, really, to be done, since we can only carry a day's supply of fuel on the steamer. While they of course *could* find and cut enough dry wood by a reasonable hour each night, when one is dealing with the native 'mind'. . . ."

De Vriny and Osterman joined in their Colonel's deprecating laughter. Dame Alice managed only a preoccupied smile. During the day, steaming upriver from the Stanley Pool, she had stared at the terrain in which her battle would be joined: heavy forest, here mostly a narrow belt fringing the watercourse but later to become a sprawling, barely penetrable expanse. The trees climbed to the edge of the water and mushroomed over the banks. Dame Alice could imagine that where the stream was less than the Congo's present mile breadth the branches would meet above in laced blackness.

Now at night, blackness was complete even on the lower river. It chilled her soul. The equatorial sunset was not a curtain of ever-thickening gauze but a knifeblade that separated the hemispheres. On this side was death, and neither the laughter of the Baenga askaris nor the goblets of Portuguese wine being drunk around Trouville's campfire could change that.

Captain de Vriny swigged and eyed the circle. He was a man of middle height with the roundedness of a bear, a seeming softness which tended to mask the cruelty beneath. Across from him, Sparrow dragged on the cigarette he had rolled and lit his face orange. The captain smiled. Only because his mistress, the mad noblewoman, had demanded it, did Sparrow sit with the officers. He wore a cheap blue-cotton shirt, buttoned at the cuffs, and denim trousers held up by suspenders. Short and narrow-chested, Sparrow would have looked foolish even without the waist belt and the pair of huge double-action revolvers hanging from it.

Dame Alice was unarmed by contrast. Like the men she wore trousers, hers tucked into low-heeled boots. De Vriny looked at her and, shaping his mocking smile into an expression of friendly interest, said, "It surprises me, Dame Alice, that a woman as well-born and, I am sure, delicate as yourself would want to accompany an expedition against some of the most vicious sub-men on the globe."

Dame Alice lifted the faintly bulbous tip of her nose and said, "It's no matter of wanting, Captain." She eyed deVriny with mild distaste. "I don't suppose you want to come yourself—unless you like to shoot niggers for lack of better sport? One does unpleasant things because someone must. One has a duty."

"What the Captain is suggesting," put in Trouville, "is that there are no lines of battle fixed in this jungle. A spearman may step from around the next tree and snick, end all your plans—learned though we are sure they must be."

"Quite," agreed Dame Alice, "and so I brought Sparrow here—" she nodded to her servant—"instead of trusting to chance."

All heads turned again toward the little American.

In French, though the conversation had previously been in English to include Sparrow, deVriny said, "I hope he never falls overboard. The load of iron-mongery he carries will sink him twenty meters through the bottom muck before anyone knows he's gone."

Again the Belgians laughed. In a voice as flat and hard as the bottom of a skillet Sparrow said, "Captain, I'd surely appreciate a look at your nice pistol there."

De Vriny blinked, uncertain whether the question was chance or if the American had understood the joke of which he had been made the butt. Deliberately, his composure never more than dented, the Belgian unhooked the flap of his patent-leather holster and handed over the Browning pistol. It was small and oblong, its blued finish gleaming like wet sealskin in the firelight.

Sparrow rotated the weapon, giving its exterior a brief scrutiny. He thumbed the catch in the grip and stripped out the magazine, holding it so that the light fell on the uppermost of its stack of small brass cartridges.

"You are familiar with automatic pistols, then?" asked Trouville in some surprise at the American's quick understanding of a weapon rarely encountered on his native continent.

"Naw," Sparrow said, slipping the magazine back home. His fingers moved like those of a pianist doing scales. "It's a gun, though. I can generally figure how a gun works."

"You should get one like it," de Vriny said, smiling as he took the weapon back from Sparrow. "You would find it far more comfortable to carry than those—yours."

"Carry a toy like that?" the gunman asked. His voice parodied amazement. "Not me, Captain. When I shoot a man, I want him dead. I want a gun what'll do the job if I do mine, and these .45s do me jist fine, every time I use'um." Sparrow grinned then, for the first time. De Vriny felt his own hands fumble as they tried to reholster the Browning. Suddenly he knew why the askaris gave Sparrow so wide a berth.

Dame Alice coughed. The sound shattered the ice that had been settling over the men. Without moving, Sparrow faded into the background to become an insignificant man with narrow shoulders and pistols too heavy for his frame.

"Tell me what you know about the rebellion," the Irishwoman asked quietly in a liquid, attractive voice. Her features led one to expect a nasal whinny. Across the fire came snores from Osterman, a lieutenant by courtesy but in no other respect an officer. He had ignored the wine for the natives' own malafou. The third calabash had slipped from his numb fingers, dribbling only a stain onto the ground as the bearded Fleming lolled back in his camp chair.

Trouville exchanged glances with de Vriny, then shrugged and said, "What is there ever to know about a native rebellion? Every once in a while a few of them shoot at our steamers, perhaps chop a concessionaire or two when he comes to collect the rubber and ivory. Then we get the call"—the Colonel's gesture embraced the invisible *Archiduchesse Stephanie* and the dozen Baenga canoes drawn up on the bank beside her. "We surround the village, shoot the niggers we catch, and burn the huts. End of rebellion."

"And what about their gods?" Dame Alice pressed, bobbing her head like a long-necked diving bird.

The Colonel laughed. De Vriny patted his holster and said, "*We* are God in the Maranga Concession."

They laughed again and Dame Alice shivered. Osterman snorted awake, blew his nose loudly on the blue sleeve of his uniform coat. "There's a new god back in the bush, yes," the Fleming muttered.

The others stared at him as if he were a frog declaiming Shakespeare. "How would *you* know?" de Vriny demanded in irritation. "The only Bantu words you know are 'drink' and 'woman.'"

"I can talk to B'loko, can't I?" the lieutenant retorted in a voice that managed to be offended despite its slurring. "Good ol' Baloko, we been together long time, long time. Better fella than some white bastards I could name . . . ."

Dame Alice leaned forward, the firelight bright in her eyes. "Tell me about the new god," she demanded. "Tell me its name."

"Don' remember the name," Osterman muttered, shaking his head. He was waking up now, surprised and a little concerned to find himself center of the attention not only of his superiors but also of the foreigner who had come to them in Boma as they readied their troops. Trouville had tried to shrug Dame Alice aside, but the Irishwoman had displayed a patent signed by King Leopold himself . . . . "Baloko said it but I forget," he continued, "and he was drunk, too, or I don' think he would have said. He's afraid of that one."

"What's that?" Trouville interrupted. He was a practical man, willing to accept and use the apparent fact that Osterman's piggish habits had made him a confidant of the askaris. "One of our Baenga headmen is afraid of a Bakongo god?"

Osterman shook his graying head again. Increasingly embarrassed but determined to explain, he said, "Not their god, not like that. The Bakongos, they live along the river, they got their fetishes just like any niggers. But back in the bush, there's another village. Not a tribe; a few men from here, a few women from there. Been getting together one at a time, a couple a year, for Christ . . . maybe twenty years. They got the new god, they're the ones who started the trouble.

"They say you don' have to pay your rubber to the white men, you don' have to pray to any fetish. Their god gonna come along and eat up everything. Any day now."

Osterman rubbed his eyes blearily, then shouted, "Boy! Malafou!"

A Krooman in breeches and swallow-tailed coat scurried over with another calabash. Osterman slurped down the sweet, brain-stunning fluid in three great gulps. He began humming something meaningless to himself. The empty container fell, and after a time the Fleming began to snore again.

The other men looked at one another. "Do you suppose he's right?" the Captain asked Trouville.

"He could be," the slim Colonel admitted with a shrug. "They might well have told him all that. He's not much better than a nigger himself despite the color of his skin."

"He's right," said Dame Alice, looking at the fire and not at her companions. Ash crumbled in its heart and a knot of sparks clawed toward the forest canopy. "Except for one thing. Their god isn't new, it isn't new at all. Back when the world was fresh and steaming and the reptiles flew above the swamps, it wasn't new either. The Bakongo name for it is Ahtu. Alhazred called it Nyarlathotep when he wrote twelve hundred years ago." She paused, staring down at her hands tented above the thin yellow wine left in her goblet.

"Oh, then you *are* a missionary," de Vriny exclaimed, glad to find a category for the puzzling woman. Her disgusted glance was her reply. "Or a student of religions?" de Vriny tried again.

"I study religions only as a doctor studies diseases," Dame Alice said. She looked at her companions. Their eyes were uncomprehending. "I . . ." she began, but how did she explain her life to men who had no conception of devotion to an ideal? Her childhood had been turned inward to dreams and the books lining the cold library of the Grange. Inward, because her outward body was that of an ugly duckling whom everyone knew had no chance of becoming a swan. And from her dreams and a few of the very oldest books had come hints of what it is that nibbles at the minds of all men in the darkness. Her father could not answer or even understand her questions, nor could the Vicar. She had grown from a persistent child into an iron-willed woman who lavished on her fancy energies which her relatives felt would have been better spent on the Church . . . or, perhaps, on breeding spaniels.

And as she had grown, she had met others who felt and *knew* what she did.

She looked around again. "Captain," she said simply, "I have been studying certain—myths—for most of my life. I've come to believe that some of them contain truths or hints of truths. There are powers in the universe. When you know the truth of those powers, you have the choice of joining them and working to bring about their coming— for they are unstoppable—or you can fight, knowing there is no ultimate hope for your cause and going ahead anyway. Mine was the second choice." Drawing herself even more rigidly straight, she added, "Someone has always been willing to stand between mankind and Chaos. As long as there have been men."

De Vriny snickered audibly. Trouville gave him a dreadful scowl and said to Dame Alice, "And you are searching for the god these rebels pray to?"

"Yes. The one they call Ahtu."

From the score of firelit glades around them came the *thunk-thunk-THUNK* of axe and wedge, then the booming native laughter.

"Osterman and de Vriny should have their men in position by now," said the Colonel, pattering his fingertips on the bridge rail as he scanned the wooded shore line. "It's about time for me to land, too."

"Us to land," Dame Alice said. She squinted, straining

forward to see the village the Belgian force was preparing to assault. "Where are the huts?"she finally asked.

"Oh, they're set back from the shore some hundreds of meters," Trouville explained offhandedly. "The trees hide them, but the fish weirs—" he pointed out the lines of upright sticks rippling foam tracks down the current— "are a good enough guide. We've stayed anchored here in the stream so that the villagers would be watching us while the forces from the canoes downriver surrounded them."

Muffled but unmistakable, a shot thudded in the forest. A volley followed, drawing with it faint screams.

"Bring us in," ordered the Colonel, tugging at the left half of his moustache in his only sign of nervousness.

The *Archiduchesse* grated as her bow nuzzled into the trees, but there was no time now for delicacy. Forest Guards streamed past the Hotchkiss and down the gangplank into the jungle. The gunner was crouched behind the metal shield that protected him only from the front. Tree boles and their shadows now encircled him on three sides.

"I suppose it will be safe enough on the shore," said Trouville, adjusting his harness as if for parade instead of battle. "You can accompany me if you wish—and if you stay close by."

"All right," said Dame Alice as if she would not have come without his permission. Her hand clutched not a pistol but an old black-bound book. "If we're where you think, though, you'll need me very badly before you're through here. Especially if it takes till sunset." She swung down the companionway behind Trouville. Last of all from the bridge came Sparrow, grimy and small and deadly as a shark.

The track that wound among the trunks was a narrow line hammered into the loam by horny feet. It differed from a game trail only in that shoulders had cleared the foliage to greater height. The Baengas strode it with some discomfort—they were a Lower Congo tribe, never quite at home in the upriver jungles. Trouville's step was deliberately nonchalant, while Dame Alice tramped gracelessly and gave an accurate impression of disinterest in her physical surroundings. Sparrow's eyes twitched around him as they always did. He carried his hands waist-high and over his belted revolvers.

The clearing was an anticlimax. The score of huts in the center had been protected by a palisade of sorts, but the first rush of the encircling Baengas had smashed great gaps in it. Three bodies, all of them women, lay spilled in the millet fields outside. Within the palisade were more bodies, one of them an askari with a long iron spearhead crosswise through his rib cage. About a hundred villagers, quavering but alive, had been forced together in the compound in front of the chief's beehive hut by the time the force from the steamer arrived. Several huts were already burning, sending up shuddering columns of black smoke.

Trouville stared at the mass of prisoners, solidified by fear into the terrible, stinking apathy of sheep in the slaughtering chute. "Yes . . ." he murmured appreciatively. His eyes had already taken in the fact that the fetishes which normally stood to the right or left of a well-to-do family's doorway were absent in this village. "Now," he asked, "who will tell me about the new god you worship?"

As black against a darkness, so the new fear rippling

across faces already terrified. Near the Belgian stood an old man, face knobbed by a pattern of ritual scarring. He was certainly a priest, though without a priest's usual trappings of feathers and cowrie shells. Haltingly he said, "Lord, l-lord, we have no new gods."

"You lie!" cried Trouville. His gloved fingertip sprang out like a fang. "You worship Ahtu, you lower-than-the-apes, and he is a poor weak god whom our medicine will break like a stick!"

The crowd moaned and surged backwards from the Colonel. The old priest made no sound at all, only began to tremble violently. Trouville looked at the sky. "Lieutenant Osterman," he called to his burly subordinate, "we have an hour or so till sunset. I trust you can get this carrion—" he pointed to the priest— "to talk by then. He seems to know something. As for the rest . . . de Vriny, take charge of getting the irons on them. We'll decide what to do with them later."

The grinning Fleming slapped Baloko on the back. Each seized one of the priest's arms and began to drag him toward the shade of a baobab tree. Osterman started to detail the items he needed from the steamer and Baloko, enthusiastic as a child helping his father to fix a machine, rattled the list off in translation to a nearby askari.

The evening breeze brought a hint of relief from the heat and the odors, the oily scent of fear and the others more easily identified. Osterman had set an overturned bucket over the plate of burning sulphur to smother it out when it was no longer needed. Reminded by Trouville, he had also covered the brush of twigs he had been using to spread the gluey flames over the priest's genitals. Then, his work done, he and Baloko had strolled away to add a bowl of malafou to the chill. "Thank you, Lieutenant," which was all the praise Trouville had offered for their success.

The subject of their ministrations—eyes closed, wrists and ankles staked to the ground—was talking. "They come, we let them," he said, so softly and quickly that Trouville had to strain to mutter out a crude translation for Dame Alice. "They live in forest, they not bother our fish. Forest here evil, we think. We feel god there, we not understand, not know him. All right that anybody want, wants to live in forest."

The native paused, turning his head to hawk phlegm into the vomit already pooled beside him. Dame Alice squatted on the ground and riffled the pages of her book unconsciously. She had refused to use the down-turned bucket for a stool. Sparrow paid only scant attention to the prisoner. His eyes kept picking across the clearing, thick and raucous now with Baengas and their leg-shackled prisoners; the men and the trees beyond them. Sparrow's face shone with the frustrated intensity of a man certain of an ambush but unable to forestall it. Shadows were beginning to turn the dust the color of the noses of his bullets.

The priest continued. The rhythms of his own language were rich and firm, reminding Dame Alice that behind Trouville's choppy French were the words of a man of dignity and power—before they had brought him down. "All of them are cut men. First come boy, no have ears. His head look me, like melon that is dropped. Him, he hear god Ahtu calling do what god tell him.

"One man, he not have, uh, manhood. God orders, boy tells him . . . he, uh, he quickens the ground where Ahtu sleeps.

"One man, he only half face, no eyes . . . him sees, he sees Ahtu, he tells what becoming, uh, is coming. He—"

The priest's voice rose into a shrill tirade that drowned out the translation. Trouville dispassionately slapped him to silence, then used a rag of bark cloth in his gloved hand to wipe blood and spittle from the fellow's mouth. "There are only three rebels in the forest?" he asked. If he realized that the priest had claimed the third man was white, he was ignoring it completely.

"No, no . . . many men, a ten of tens, maybe more. Before we not see, not see cut men only now and now, uh, again, in the forest. Now god is ripe and, uh, his messengers. . . ."

Only a knife edge of sun could have lain across the horizon, for the whole clearing was darkening to burnt umber where it had color at all. The ground shuddered. The native pegged to it began to scream.

"Earthquake?" Trouville blurted in surprise and concern. Rain forest trees have no deep tap roots to keep them upright, so a strong wind or an earth tremor will scatter giants like straw in the threshing yard.

Dame Alice's face showed concern not far from panic, but she wholly ignored the baobab tottering above them. Her book was open and she was rolling out syllables from it. She paused, turned so that the pages opened to the fading sun; but her voice stumbled again, and the earth pitched. It was sucking in under the priest whose fear so gripped him that, having screamed out his breath, he was unable to draw another one.

"Light!" Dame Alice cried. "For Jesus's sake, light!"

If Trouville heard the demand against the litany of fear rising from the blacks, guards and prisoners alike, he did not understand. Sparrow, his face a bone mask, dipped into his shirt pocket and came out with a match which he struck alight with the thumb of the hand that held it. The blue flame pulsed above the page, steady as the ground's motion would let the gunman keep it. Its light painted Dame Alice's tight bun as she began again to cry words of no meaning to any of her human audience.

The ground gathered itself into a tentacle that spewed up from beneath the prisoner and hurled him skyward in its embrace. One hand and wrist, still tied to a deep stake, remained behind.

Two hundred feet above the heads of the others, the tentacle stopped and exploded as if it had struck a plate of lightning. Dame Alice had fallen backward when the ground surged, but though the book dropped from her hands she had been able to shout out the last words of what was necessary. The blast that struck the limb of earth shattered also the baobab. Sparrow, the only man able to stand on the bucking earth, was knocked off his feet by the shock wave. He hit and rolled, still gripping the two handguns he had leveled at the afterimage of the light-shot tentacle.

Afterwards they decided that the burned-meat odor must have been the priest, because no one else was injured or missing. Nothing but a track of sandy loam remained of the tentacle, spilled about the rope of green glass formed of it by the false lightning's heat.

Colonel Trouville rose, coughing at the stench of ozone as sharp as that of the sulphur it had displaced. "De Vriny!" he called. "Get us one of these devil-bred swine who can guide us to the rebel settlement!"

"And who'll you be finding to guide you, having seen this?" demanded the Irishwoman, kneeling now and brushing dirt from the fallen volume as if more than life depended on her care.

"Seen?" repeated Trouville. "And what have they seen?" The fury in his voice briefly stilled the nightbirds. "They will not guide us because one of them was crushed, pulled apart, burned? And have I not done as much myself a hundred times? If we need to feed twenty of them their own livers, *faugh!* the twenty-first will lead us—or the one after him will. This rebellion must end!"

"So it must," whispered Dame Alice, rising like a champion who has won a skirmish but knows the real test is close at hand. She no longer appeared frail. "So it must, if there's to be men on this earth in a month's time."

The ground shuddered a little.

Nothing moved in the forest but the shadows flung by the dancers around the fire. The flames spread them capering across the leaves and tree trunks, distorted and misshapen by the flickering.

They were no more misshapen than the dancers themselves as the light displayed them.

From a high, quivering scaffold of njogicane, three men overlooked the dance. They were naked so that their varied mutilations were utterly apparent. De Vriny started at the sight of the one whose pale body gleamed red and orange in the firelight; but he was a faceless thing, unrecognizable. Besides, he was much thinner than the plump trader the Belgian had once known.

The clearing was a quarter-mile depression in the jungle. Huts, mere shanties of withe-framed leaves rather than the beehives of a normal village, huddled against one edge of it. If all had gone well, Trouville's askaris were deployed beyond the hut with Osterman's group closing the third segment of the ring. All should be ready to charge at the signal. There would not even be a fence to delay the spearmen.

Nor were there crops of any kind. The floor of the clearing was smooth and hard, trampled into that consistency by thousands of ritual patterns like the one now being woven around the fire. In, out, and around—crop-limbed men and women who hobbled if they had but one foot; who staggered, hunched and twisted from the whippings that had left bones glaring out of knots of scar tissue; who followed by touch the motions of the dancers ahead of them if their own eye-sockets were blank holes.

There was no music, but the voices of those who had tongues drummed in a ceaseless chant: "Ahtu! Ahtu!"

"The scum of the earth," whispered deVriny. "Low foreheads, thick jaws, skin the color of a monkey's under its hair. Your Mr. Darwin was right about Man's descent from the apes, Dame Alice—if these brutes are, in fact, kin to Man."

"Not *my* Mr. Darwin," the Irishwoman replied.

The Krooman steward, in loincloth now instead of tailcoat, was behind the three whites with a hissing bull's-eye lantern. Dame Alice feared to raise its shutter yet, though, and instead ran her fingers nervously along the margins of her open book. Three other blacks, armed only with knives, stood by de Vriny as couriers in case the whistle signals were not enough. The rest of the Captain's force was invisible, spread to either side of him along the margin of the trees.

"Don't like this," Sparrow said, shifting his revolvers a millimeter in their holsters to make sure they were free in the leather. "Too many niggers around. Some of 'em are apt to be part of the mob down there, coming back late from a hunt or something. Any nigger comes running up in the dark and I'm gonna let 'im hold one."

"You'll shoot no one without my order," deVriny snapped. "The Colonel may be sending orders, Osterman may need help—this business is going to be dangerous enough without some fool killing our own messengers. Do you hear me?"

"I hear you talking." A stray glimmer of firelight caught the throbbing vein in Sparrow's temple.

Rather than retort, the Belgian turned back to the clearing. After a moment he said, "I don't see this god you're looking for."

Dame Alice's mouth quirked. "You mean you don't see a fetish," she said. "You won't. Ahtu isn't a fetish."

"Well, what kind of damned god is he then?" de Vriny asked in irritation.

The Irishwoman considered the question seriously, then said, "Maybe they aren't gods at all, him and the others . . . it and the others Alhazred wrote of. Call them cancers, spewed down on Earth ages ago. Not life, surely, not even *things*—but able to shape, to misshape things into a semblance of life and to grow and to grow and to grow."

"But grow into *what,* madame?" de Vriny pressed.

"Into what?" Dame Alice echoed sharply. Her eyes flashed with the sudden arrogance of her bandit ancestors, sure of themselves if of nothing else in the world. "Into this earth, this very planet, if unchecked. And we here will know tonight whether they can be checked yet again."

"Then you seriously believe," de Vriny began, sucking at his florid moustache to find a less offensive phrasing. "You believe that the Bakongos are worshipping a creature which would, will, begin to rule the world if you don't stop it?"

Dame Alice looked at him. "Not 'rule' the world," she corrected. "Rather *become* the world. This thing, this seed awakened in the jungle by the actions of men more depraved and foolish than I can easily believe . . . this existence, unchecked, would permeate our world like mold through a loaf of bread, until the very planet became a ball of viscid slime hurtling around the sun and stretching tentacles toward Mars. Yes, I believe that, Captain. Didn't you see what was happening last night in the village?"

The Belgian only scowled in perplexity.

A silver note sang from across the broad clearing. De Vriny grunted, then put his long bosun's pipe to his lips and sounded his reply even as Osterman's signal joined it.

The dance broke apart as the once-solid earth began to dimple beneath men's weight.

The Forest Guards burst out of the tree line with cries punctuated by the boom of Albini rifles. "Light!" ordered Dame Alice in a crackling alto, and the lantern threw its bright fan across the book she held. The scaffolding moved, seemed to sink straight into ground turned fluid as water. At the last instant the three figures on it linked hands and shouted, "Ahtu!" in triumph. Then they were gone.

In waves as complex as the sutures of a skull, motion began to extend through the soil of the clearing. A shrieking Baenga, spear raised to thrust into the nearest dancer, ran across one of the quivering lines. It rose across his body like the breaking surf and he shrieked again in a different tone. For a moment his black-headed spear bobbled on the surface. Then it, too, was engulfed with a faint plop that left behind only a slick of blood.

Dame Alice started chanting in a singsong, molding a tongue meant for liquid Irish to a language not meant for tongues at all. A tremor in the earth drove toward her and those about her. It had the hideous certainty of a torpedo track. Sparrow's hands flexed. De Vriny stood stupefied, the whistle still at his lips and his pistol drawn but forgotten.

The three couriers looked at the oncoming movement, looked at each other . . . disappeared among the trees. Eyeballs white, the Krooman dropped his lantern and followed them. Quicker even than Sparrow, Dame Alice knelt and righted the lantern with her foot. She acted without missing a syllable of the formula stamped into her memory by long repetition.

Three meters away, a saw-blade of white fire ripped across the death advancing through the soil. The weaving trail blasted back toward the center of the clearing like an ant run blown by carbon disulphide.

De Vriny turned in amazement to the woman

crouched so that the lantern glow would fall across the black-lettered pages of her book. "You did it!" he cried. "You stopped the thing!"

The middle of the clearing raised itself toward the night sky, raining down fragments of the bonfire that crowned it. Humans screamed—some at the touch of the fire, others as tendrils extruding from the towering center wrapped about them.

Dame Alice continued to chant.

The undergrowth whispered. "Behind you, Captain," Sparrow said. His face had a thin smile. De Vriny turned, calling a challenge. The brush parted and a few feet in front of him were seven armed natives. The nearest walked on one foot and a stump. His left hand gripped the stock of a Winchester carbine; its barrel was supported by his right wrist since there was a knob of ancient scar tissue where the hand should have been attached.

De Vriny raised his Browning and slapped three shots into the native's chest. Bloodspots sprang out against the dark skin like additional nipples. The black coughed and jerked the trigger of his own weapon. The carbine was so close to the Belgian's chest that its muzzle flash ignited the linen of his shirt as it blew him backwards.

Sparrow giggled and shot the native through the bridge of his nose, snapping his head around as if a horse had kicked him in the face. The other blacks moved. Sparrow killed them all in a ripple of fire that would have done justice to a Gatling gun. The big revolvers slammed alternately, Sparrow using each orange muzzle flash to light a target for his other hand. He stopped shooting only when there was nothing left before his guns; nothing save a writhing tangle of bodies too freshly dead to be still. The air was thick with white smoke and the fecal stench of death. Behind the laughing gunman, Dame Alice Kilrea continued to chant.

Pulsing, rising, higher already than the giants of the forest ringing it, the fifty-foot-thick column of what had been earth dominated the night. A spear of false lightning jabbed and glanced off, freezing the chaos below for the eyes of any watchers. From the base of the main neck had sprouted a ring of tendrils, ruddy and golden and glittering over all with inclusions of quartz. They snaked among the combatants as flexible as silk; when they closed, they ground together like millstones and spattered blood a dozen yards up the sides of the central column. The tendrils made no distinction between Forest Guards and the others who had danced for Ahtu.

Dame Alice stopped. The column surged and bent against the sky, its peak questing like the muzzle of a hunting dinosaur. Sparrow hissed, "For the love of *God*, bitch!" and raised a revolver he knew would be useless.

Dame Alice spoke five more words and flung her book down. The ground exploded in gouts of cauterizing flame.

It was not a hasty thing. Sparks roared and blazed as if the clearing were a cauldron into which gods poured furnaces of molten steel. The black column that was Ahtu twisted hugely, a cobra pinned to a bonfire. There was no heat, but the light itself seared the eyes and made bare flesh crawl.

With the suddenness of a torn puffball, Ahtu sucked inward. The earth sagged as though in losing its ability to move it had also lost all rigidity. At first the clearing had been slightly depressed. Now the center of it gaped like a drained boil, a twisted cylinder fed by the collapsing veins it had earlier shot through the earth.

When the blast came it was the more stunning for having followed a relative silence. There was a rending crash as something deep in the ground gave way; then a thousand tons of rock and soil blew skyward with volcanic power behind them. Where the earth had trembled with counterfeit life, filaments jerked along after the main mass. In some places they ripped the surface as much as a mile into the forest. After a time, dust and gravel began to sprinkle down on the trees, the lighter particles marking the canopy with a long flume downwind while larger rocks pattered through layer after layer of the hindering leaves. But it was only dirt, no different than the soil for hundreds of miles around into which trees thrust their roots and drew life from what was lifeless.

"Goddamn if you didn't kill it," Sparrow whispered, gazing in wonderment at the new crater. There was no longer any light but that of the hooked moon to silver the carnage and the surprising number of Forest Guards straggling back from the jungle to which they had fled. Some were beginning to joke as they picked among the bodies of their comrades and the dancers.

"I didn't kill anything," Dame Alice said. Her voice was hoarse, muffled besides by the fact that she was cradling her head on her knees. "Surgeons don't kill cancers. They cut out what they can find, knowing that there's always a little left to grow and spread again . . . ."

She raised her head. From across the clearing, Colonel Trouville was stepping toward them. He was as dapper and cool as always, skirting the gouge in the center, skirting also the group of Baengas with a two-year-old they must have found in one of the huts. One was holding the child by the ankles to drain all the blood through its slit throat while his companions gathered firewood.

"But without the ones who worshipped it," Dame Alice went on, "without the ones who drew the kernel up to a growth that would have been . . . the end of Man, the end of Life here in any sense you or I—or those out there— would have recognized it. . . . It'll be more than our lifetimes before Ahtu returns. I wonder why those ones gave themselves so wholly to an evil that would have destroyed them first?"

Sparrow giggled again. Dame Alice turned from the approaching Belgian to see if the source of the humor showed on the gunman's face.

"It's like this," Sparrow said. "If they was evil, I guess that makes us good. I'd never thought of that before, is all."

He continued to giggle. The laughter of the Baengas echoed him from the clearing as they thrust the child down on a rough spit. Their teeth had been filed to points which the moonlight turned to jewels.

THE SONG OF
THE BONE
⊰⊱

I read a two-volume translation of the Finnish epic
Kalevala in Viet Nam. "The Song of the Bone" is set
in Norway in Viking times, but a wedding feast
from the *Kalevala* is the genesis of this story.

I didn't write "The Song of the Bone" till after
I'd gotten back to the World. I didn't have a
potential market. Because I was pretty depressed
about the piece when I finished it I didn't try to
send it anywhere. (I was pretty depressed about
most things at the time, frankly. It was some years
before I was able to look straight at Nam, and a very
long time before that didn't make life even more
depressing. I'm not sure I'm out of that stage quite
yet.)

Stuart David Schiff, an army dentist who'd just
been assigned to Ft. Bragg in Fayetteville, came to
a Sunday afternoon get-together at the home of the
Murray brothers, collectors extraordinaire, in
Durham. Stu was planning to start a small-press

fantasy/horror magazine to replace The Arkham
Collector. *Part of his reason for doing so was that
he'd been art editor on Meade Frierson's huge 1971
fanzine HPL and didn't feel that he'd gotten proper
recognition for his work. By doing the production
himself, he'd keep that from happening again.*

*Stu wanted fiction, but he didn't plan to pay for
it. I gave him "The Song of the Bone," but I told him
I thought he was making a mistake: free fiction was
generally going to be worth what he paid. I thought
my story was valueless, which was the only reason
I was giving it to him.*

*Stu took the piece, but much more important he
took my advice: after the second issue of* Whispers
*he began paying a penny a word for stories. We're
both convinced that the decision to pay for fiction is
the reason that* Whispers *was there to keep alive the
fantasy/horror short-story genre during the 1970s.*

*The difference between low pay (and a penny a
word was as good as some professional SF
magazines were paying at the time) and no pay was
the difference between being a professional and
being a dilettante. That was important to some of
us, me included, even though it was nearly a decade
before I even dreamed of making a living from
writing fiction.*

*On the next issue I became Stu's assistant editor.
Throughout* Whispers's *run, I read all the fiction
that came to the magazine, sending on the ones I
thought were publishable to Stu. It was a
frustrating job, but I'm glad I did it. Mr. Derleth*

had spent more time on me than I was worth. I
couldn't repay him, but I could pass the effort on.

⁜ ⁜ ⁜

Olaf was king in Drontheim and prayed to the White Christ, but there were other gods still in the upcountry and it was to them that Hedinn and his wife sacrificed in the evening. Finished, they waited a moment to watch the clouds that piled up high over the tops of the firs. Hedinn smiled as the first of his cows walked across the clearing toward the cattle shed, the rest following in a silent procession. On the left side pattered a black mongrel which snapped at the nose of a cow that began to stray, and at the end of the line shambled Gage the herdsman, almost lost in the gloom of the forest behind him.

"He doesn't have a staff," Gudrun said to her husband. "How does he keep them in line like that?"

Hedinn shrugged. "He seems to whistle at them. He's got forest blood in him, you know, and they can do things with animals. Mostly the dog does the work anyway."

The herdsman turned toward the couple and, though darkness and distance hid his features, Gudrun shuddered. "Ugh," she said, "I wish we didn't have to look at him. Why don't you sell him to a trader?"

"Now, Sweetning," Hedinn said, stroking his wife's fine hair with affection, "he's a good herdsman despite his looks. And we'd never get a worn kettle for him, you know."

The dog had waited for his master at the shed door. They entered together, Gage closing the door behind them.

"He sleeps with the cows, then?" Gudrun asked in surprise.

"In a corner of the cowshed," her husband agreed. "He and his dog together. And he eats any scraps the cook cares to give him. He's really no trouble for the work he does," Hedinn concluded complacently, "if you can learn to stand his face, Darling."

Gudrun laughed and patted her husband's arm. "Other men don't matter at all, Sweetning, no other men."

"Ooh, Gudrun, how do I look?" Inga asked, pirouetting in a blue embroidered dress that showed her buxom charms to the full above a belt of copper disks. Gudrun leaned back against the wall and stared critically at her sister-in-law. The girl's thick braid was hanging loose, not gathered about her head, and it shone in the lamplight. A few strands had become tangled in Inga's necklaces of facetted tin beads.

"Here now," said Gudrun, freeing the hairs, "you mustn't throw yourself around like that or you'll not be fit to meet Bjorn. You must not dishonor the house or your brother."

"Oh, tush," the younger girl complained, "they'd never notice, they'll be so drunk by now. Why couldn't Bjorn have seen me while he was still able to see?"

"The brideprice had yet to be discussed," Gudrun chided. "It wouldn't have been proper. And no matter who can appreciate it, you must look your best for your husband."

"Oh, I do want to be pretty," Inga answered petulantly, "but I don't think Bjorn wants a wife who's just a stick doll and sits in the corner doing nothing. You know," the girl added with a speculative grin, "they say he really is a bear, just like his name. All rough and strong. . . ."

Gudrun nodded sternly to silence the girl. "You're as ready as you can be," she said, "and the men are waiting."

The two women stepped out into the warm May darkness where the sliver moon hid in the overcast. The summer kitchen blazed with light and servants trotted between it and the main hall. Two empty tuns of mead stood outside the open main door already. It was difficult to believe that the roisterers could possibly have put away that much liquor and still down the quantities of venison being carried in.

"Oh!" gasped Inga as she saw the squatting shape lighted by the glare through the hall doorway. "But it's just Gage."

The herdsman turned and stared at the women. At his feet lay his black mongrel, gnawing on a deer haunch. Gage looked more human with his stubby legs folded under him, but his limbs were almost as shaggy as his dog and his sloping forehead was scarcely human.

As the women started to edge around him, Gage swept the bone from his dog's mouth and flourished it to Inga, who squealed and shied back.

With a silly mocking grin, the herdsman set the bone between his molars and crunched the end to splinters.

He was still grinning as Gudrun propelled the younger girl into the hall with a firm hand on her waist.

Fish oil lamps in wall niches lit the hall, but the best quality oil was already gone and a film of soot had begun to settle over the room. No one seemed to notice it; some were already too drunk to stand and one had vomited—a fox skin had been tossed over the ejecta but a sour odor permeated the room. Only one had actually collapsed, though, and most were in full voice.

The women paused uncertainly at the doorway. After a moment Hedinn looked up from his argument with the hulking young man beside him and saw them. He stood and shouted something unintelligible and unnoticed in the general din. Angry, he picked up his bronze drinking cup, reconsidered, and drew the sword that he wore at his belt like everyone else. He slammed the hilt twice on the table, jouncing it on the trestles and rocking the sleeper onto the floor. Slowly the room quieted.

There were about twenty men packed into the hall, Hedinn's relatives and retainers and those of the prospective bridegroom. Negotiations for the bride-price and dower had been sharper than either of the two prosperous farmers had expected, so that the temper of the hall was harsh despite the drink. As a result Hedinn glared at Bjorn and his voice rang louder than needful, "My sister!"

Bjorn rose a little unsteady, and squinted across the table. "Haw!" he cried, flushing, "she'll do for a milch cow if not for a wife. But we'll turn her trinkets to real silver and gold when I wed her."

Hedinn turned white but it was Gudrun who spoke. "Husband, must we hear each beardless beggar prate as we feed him?"

Inga screamed as Bjorn snatched at his sword, but his own uncle Skeggi pinned the youth in a hammerlock and wrestled him back from his host. The table crashed over on its side and those not too befuddled drew. Skeggi roared, "Get him clear! No blood! No blood!"

Two or three of the others of Bjorn's party aided Skeggi in forcing him outside. Hedinn and his own people crowded back away from the door, unable to help and barely unwilling to hinder.

Never had Bjorn looked more the bear his name meant. Even with four big men clinging to him he had managed to draw his broadsword but had not quite come to the point of using it on his own kinsmen. With a convulsive effort they rushed him through the door, but he shook free outside it.

Gage scrambled away but his dog yelped in fear of being trampled. In sheer berserk fury Bjorn whirled and lopped the black mongrel in two. His overhand blow finished in shattering the sword-blade against a cobblestone, leaving the dog's corpse in a great splash of blood. The right forepaw twitched, making dark ripples in the lamplight.

Skeggi held back a man prepared to seize Bjorn again. The farmer turned slowly, his anger washed away by the shock that had numbed his whole side.

"Quick, a horse," Skeggi commanded. One of the servants dropped his platter and ran to the shed. Aided in tense silence by two of Bjorn's men he saddled the nearest horse, a big roan, and led it to Skeggi who was holding his nephew by the arm. Skeggi grunted and lifted Bjorn into the saddle where he sagged, almost too stupefied to put his feet in the stirrups.

"Now lead him out of here before he wakes up," Skeggi snapped to one of the men. "We'll follow. This night has gone on long enough."

Because she had stepped to the door, leaving Inga to weep inside the hall, Gudrun was the only one to see Gage put two fingers to his mouth and give a short whistle.

The horse whickered softly, then whinnied and tore the reins free. Before any of the half-drunken men could stop it, the roan had galloped blindly into the forest.

"Not on foot, you frog-spawn!" Skeggi bellowed to the men stumbling after Bjorn. "Saddle horses!"

Inga cried herself to sleep, but Gudrun was standing in the kitchen doorway when Hedinn and his men rode back in the pre-dawn.

"Where is Bjorn?" she asked quietly as her husband approached.

"Dead," Hedinn answered in a flat, expressionless voice. "The horse must have dragged him a mile. We never did find his leg."

"There's hot water inside," Gudrun said.

She stood beside Hedinn as he plunged his face into the water. When he straightened she began massaging her husband's neck, loosening the tense muscles. At last Gudrun turned Hedinn around to face her.

"Did you see Gage kill him?" she asked.

"Don't talk about Gage now, Sweetning," Hedinn ordered wearily.

"Gage killed Bjorn, Hedinn; he whistled and the horse—"

"Stop it!" her husband snapped. "It's more important than whether you like a herdsman, now. There's a man dead after being insulted in my house; a man's dead!"

Gudrun stared at him without expression, then ran her hand down the curve of his biceps. "It's been a long night, Sweetning; let's go to bed."

✢ ✢ ✢

Gudrun was alone in the hall when she heard the cows returning that evening. An unfamiliar sound, a high trill, drew her to the door to watch. Gage was blowing a pipe of some sort. A shadow wavered near the head of the file and a cow jerked back into line.

Gudrun began to walk toward the herd. Her belly started to tremble and she ran, hair loosening to stream out behind her splendid body. The herdsman glanced up and paused as she approached.

The woman stopped a body-length from him, breathing in tight, controlled pants. In his hand Gage held a bone flute crudely drilled with finger holes. It was a small thigh bone, and Gudrun remembered the dog's mangled body as Gage raised the flute to his lips. The sound whispered between them, surprisingly musical to come from such a brutish minstrel.

A small black shadow danced on the grass, so real that Gudrun saw its pink tongue loll. Gage began to play louder . . . .

Gudrun screamed and snatched the flute away, crushing the fresh bone between her fingers.

"Witch!" she shouted. "Killer witch!"

The herdsman made a guttural sound. Somewhere behind her Gudrun heard her husband call and whirled to run.

"Hedinn! He tried to rape me! Kill him, KILL HIM!"

But before Hedinn could reach her, Gage had disappeared into the forest and the cattle were already beginning to stray.

In the night she heard the whistling as she lay on the

low couch with her husband. For a moment she pretended that it wasn't real, was only a dream, but another trill from the darkness froze her. Still she waited, bone cold, until the sound rippled around her a third time. It seemed to be nearer.

"Hedinn," she whispered, shaking her sleeping husband, "Hedinn."

"Uh . . . ?" grunted Hedinn. "Sweetning?"

"Shh. Listen."

After a moment Hedinn padded over to a window and loosed its leather flap to peer out. He swore and began to pull on his boots.

"Is it him?" Gudrun whispered.

"It's him, yes," Hedinn answered, groping for his sword.

"Then call the men out," Gudrun hissed.

"I don't need help to teach that dog vomit a lesson," Hedinn said, throwing open the door. Gudrun followed him barefoot.

The herdsman faced them fifty paces away, his expression shaded by his thick shock of hair. He carried a bone, large enough to make a dangerous club. Not a club though, Gudrun knew, for she could see the shadows of finger holes as on the smaller flute.

This had been a man's thigh, a large man's.

Hedinn stalked toward his slave, his sword held low across his body.

"Wait!" Gudrun screamed, running after her husband as Gage raised the flute to his lips. There was no whisper of sound this time, no keening, but a full-throated skirling that turned Gudrun's sweat acid.

A bear loomed up beside Gage, swinging its right paw with terrible precision. Hedinn's ribs caved in and his body hurtled back against his wife.

Gudrun screamed again as the bear waddled hugely toward her, and the laughter of the thigh bone rang behind it.

THE MASTER
OF DEMONS

I was in correspondence with Ramsey Campbell for much of the 1970s. When he became president of the British Fantasy Society, I joined the organization (the original anthologies in which most of my fantasy and horror appeared were all British anyway). At Ramsey's request I then wrote "The Master of Demons" for the club's fantasy magazine, Dark Horizons.

Dark Horizons didn't pay for its material. My warning to Stuart about the value of gift stories might be recalled here. Having said that, I felt free to experiment on this story. I'm not dissatisfied with the result, though this stylistic form isn't one I've ever tried when I expected to be paid for my work.

The core of the story is the fact that William the Conqueror swore, "By the face of Lucca!" Lucca is a shrine of the Virgin in Northern Italy, but the source I used stated that the meaning of the oath was unknown. William's career and the fact that his father was called Robert the Devil gave me the basic notion.

The story's set in Late Medieval Europe, when there was a unique climate for learning. Classical science and literature were returning to the intellectual mainstream, but much was being discovered for the first time as well. Scholars all spoke Latin, so a Catalan and a Bohemian might meet in Bologna, for example, to discuss Arab researches into optics.

The division between what we now consider science and what we call mysticism were less obvious some hundreds of years ago also. (It's useful to remember that Newton developed calculus to simplify astrological computations.)

I wish I could have gotten more of the wonder of the period into this story; but I hope at least some of it comes through.

☩ ☩ ☩

There is a hierarchy in Hell and this Hermann of Prague knew; but the way of it he failed to grasp, so this is the story of his pride and his ignorance and what came of them. Perhaps he had been born in Prague, but at the end he lived alone in a room cut from the rock of a sea-pounded crag on the western edge of the continent.

His tower of glass was the key, the tall helix squirming into the air from a bulb of purple fluid. Without that the parchment of Andromedes would have been worthless, mere words in the darkness.

And even possession of the memoirs of the bitter Greek stemmed from the dreaming glass. There had been

rumors, hints; but only that until Hermann lit an oil lamp
beneath the base of the helix. Then, nude, he smeared his
body with an ointment of fats and belladonna before
reclining on a couch to watch the purple liquid stir and
bubble, lighted by the one lamp alone. As the sluggish
blobs of color mounted in the closed tube and the drug
took hold it seemed as if the helix lengthened immensely,
and Hermann's mind followed the bubbles into a height of
discord and whispers. In time the lamp burned out and the
fluid dripped back into its reservoir, but when Hermann
awoke he knew where the manuscript was hidden and how
it might be had.

Even so it was three years before Hermann had the
parchment to hand, but to argue with necessity is time ill
spent and there had been no other way. It was a short
chronicle of knowledge and failure, of wisdom made
useless by the inadequacy of its goals. In the midst of the
Greek a single line in Latin stood out, not a gloss for it too
was written in Andromedes's own crabbed hand:
QUICVNQVE+DAEMONEM+LVCCAE+DOMINVM+
CLAMARE+FECERIT+CONSPICABITVR+POTESTA
TEM+INFINITAM. Whosoever shall cause the spirit
Luccae to cry "Master!!" shall glimpse unbounded power.

This line drew Hermann's eyes as the Great Bear does
a mariner's and as he read and reread it he began to
tremble at its implications. No longer did he dream of the
Earth, its castles and fertile vales, but of power that stalked
among the aeons and diced with suns.

In the end he turned again to the ointment and the
purple whispers that never questioned, never advised, only

answered the questions put to them with a hard, icy truth. He was afraid, now; for though Hermann had no conception of the fullness of the forces he dealt with, he knew of Luccae and dreaded it. But to stop was to die in his own time, and the pride was on Hermann to take what fate offered. And so the tower, and so the dreams; in the morning his fear was greater for knowing more of his task, but he began his preparations.

And this, too, was a slow business, for it demanded much of the true mercury with which to lay out the pentacle. If Luccae was to be caught there must be no chance for it to escape later. First the hydragyrum, then the two spells to commit to memory. The first to send him into the place, the time where Luccae danced and waited for the sun to explode; the second to return him and it, at the split-second that would leave Luccae within the pentacle and Hermann outside it: else the magician could crouch in lone safety while all the world besides melted into unholy alchemy.

So Hermann waited until the pentacle was ready and the stars had united in such a way to make the unthinkable possible. Then he spoke three words that stilled the mutter of the city around him, three words and a fourth that was drowned in the thunderclap which tore a hole in the universe and hurled him through it.

The great sun hung right overhead, a gorgon that licked at the sky with long serpents of fire. Across the barren rocks writhed the shadows of the three dancers: the first, washed purple by the deep red light, pounded his splay feet in time to the sound that howled through his nose, as long as he was tall. The second pranced, goat-footing it over rocks that sparked beneath him. His mouth was twisted into a rictus of delight and never a sound came from it.

The third was perched on a low pedestal: it was Luccae and only its face danced. One eye, as moribund as the sun, burned in the center of a thousand shifting patterns; every one of them a dead damned soul, each of them Hermann himself.

But Hermann stood and whispered the syllables of return without a pause or stumbling. The wailing and click of hooves continued but only Luccae remained, only its face warping and growing and weaving a net for Hermann's soul. But he was drunk with dreams of power and could not be bound; the words rippled off his tongue heedless of the shape that expanded before his eyes until it filled the whole world. As the final word rang out in the sudden silence Hermann stepped back without looking and the sound of sea crashed around him.

He was safe, and Luccae glared within a prison as ceaselessly changing as its own face.

And then to the mastering. For the first time the magician's dream spiral failed him and he woke from his stupor with nothing but the memory of fruitless chittering. Hermann was numb with terror by then, but he could not stop; Luccae squatted in his mind though he had curtained off the pentagram. Sooner or later he would make a mistake, would break the line. Unless . . .

Hermann's lore was as great as his recklessness in using it to do what his dream had told him could not be done: to crush Luccae to the point it must admit his dominance and lordship. And here Hermann misunderstood as he had been intended; but it was too late by then and his fate was closing on him.

He took a great smoky garnet and strung it on a silver wire to the ceiling. From his cabinets he took a tiny box of orange crystals and a phial of deep blue liquid. The box he opened and set beneath the stone. Then, though he need not have done so, Hermann ripped away the hangings between him and Luccae. The red eye glared at him and the garnet blazed back. Hermann unstoppered the phial and began chanting the words of congruity. On the twenty-first syllable he tilted the liquid into the box and stepped back as a serpent of smoke shot up to seize the garnet.

For all the power of Luccae it was trapped beyond self-preservation, for the stone was dead and the smoke that hissed about it was horribly alive. The psychic leverage on the garnet washed Luccae's face to a frozen gray, glazed the fire of the single eye, and held the flicker of souls to a muddy trembling. A minute, another minute—

—and Luccae spoke.

It was a sound without earthly counterpart, but Hermann heard it and understood in the final instant his mistake. Then the sea and rock boiled together as Luccae's Master came to free His liege.

THE DANCER
IN THE FLAMES

I spent most of 1970 as an interrogator with the 11th Armored Cavalry Regiment. The experience changed my life in many ways, some of them good.

Most of the changes were not good. When I hear people quote Nietzsche, "What does not kill us makes us stronger," I always think "Yeah, but stronger what?" Not stronger human beings, of that I'm sure.

I don't think it ever occurred to me to send "The Dancer in the Flames" anywhere but to Stu Schiff. F&SF would've taken six months or more to reply, and I assumed the reply would be a rejection.

Now I'm not quite so sure. It surprises me that a number of people with backgrounds in literature praise this story as a study in alienation, when I thought it was just a fantasy about Viet Nam.

To me, Viet Nam was alienation. I wish it had been a fantasy.

The viewpoint character is an officer. I was not.

The setting, incidents, and attitudes depicted are all real. If you ask Nam vets what the most popular song In Country was, they'll all tell you, "We Gotta Get Out of This Place."

This isn't a story which I like very much. One of the reasons is that I don't much like the person who lived the background I'm writing about here. We've been stuck with each other since 1970, though.

✦ ✦ ✦

The flames writhing out of the ashtray were an eyeball-licking orange. For an instant Lt. Schaydin was sure that the image dancing in them was that of the girl he had burned alive in Cambodia, six months before. But no, not quite; though the other's face had been of Gallic cast too.

The two enlisted men had turned at the sound of the officer brushing back the poncho curtain which divided his tent from the rear compartment of the command track. Radios were built into the right wall of the vehicle above a narrow counter. On that counter rested the CQ's clipboard and a cheap glass ashtray, full of flame. The men within—Skip Sloane, who drove the command track and was now Charge of Quarters, and the medic Evens—had been watching the fire when Schaydin looked in. It was to that ten-inch flame which the lieutenant's eyes were drawn as well.

He stared at her calves and up the swell of the hips which tucked in at a waist that thrust toward him. She looked straight at Schaydin then and her mouth pursed to call. Above the image hung the black ripples of smoke which were her hair. Abruptly the flame shrank to a wavering needle and blinked out. The compartment was lighted only by the instrument dials, pitch-dark after the orange glare. The air was sharp with the residue of the flame; but more than that caused Schaydin's chest to constrict. He remembered he had called out some joke as he touched the flamethrower's trigger and sent a loop of napalm through the window of the hooch they were supposed to destroy. The Cambodian girl must have been hiding in the thatch or among the bags of rice. She had been all ablaze as she leaped into the open, shrieking and twisting like a dervish until she died. But this tiny image had not screamed, it had really spoken. It/She had said—

"How did you do that?" Schaydin gasped.

The enlisted men glanced at each other, but their commander did not seem angry, only—strange. Sloane held up a twenty-ounce block of C4, plastic explosive. Sweat rolled down the driver's chest and beer gut. He wore no shirt since the radios heated the command vehicle even in the relative coolness of the Vietnamese night. "You take a bit of C4, sir," Sloane said. His hairy thumb and forefinger gouged out an acorn-sized chunk of the white explosive. Another piece had already been removed. "It takes a shock to make it blow up. If you just touch a match to it in the open, it burns. Like that."

Sloane handed the pellet to Schaydin, who stood with a dazed look on his face. The C4 had the consistency of nougat, but it was much denser. "We ought'a air the place out, though," the driver continued. "The fumes don't do anybody much good."

"But how did you get it to look like a woman? "Schaydin demanded. "I could see her right there, her face, her eyes . . . and she was saying. . . ."

Evens reached past the lieutenant and flapped the poncho curtain to stir the dissipating tendrils of smoke. "C4 makes a pretty flame," the stocky medic said, "but you don't want to get the stuff in your system. We used to have a mascot, a little puppy. She ate part of a block and went pure-ass crazy. Seeing things. She'd back into a corner and snap and bark like a bear was after her. . . . Middle of that afternoon she went haring out over the berm, yapping to beat Hell. We never did see her again."

The medic looked away from his CO, then added, "Don't think you ought to breathe the fumes, either. Hard to tell what it might make you see. Don't think I want to burn any more C4, even if it does make the damnedest shadows I ever hope to see."

The lieutenant opened his mouth to protest, to insist that he had seen the image the instant he pushed the curtain aside; but he caught his men's expressions. His mind seemed to be working normally again. "You guys just saw a—fire?"

"That's all there was to see," said Evens. "Look, it's late, I better go rack out." Sloane nodded, tossing him the part block of explosive. The medic edged past Schaydin, into the tent and the still night beyond.

"Time for a guard check," Sloane said awkwardly and reseated himself before the microphone. One by one the heavy-set man began calling the vehicles sited around the circular berm. The tracks replied with the quiet negative reports that showed someone was awake in each turret. The CQ did not look up at his commander, but when Schaydin stepped back from the compartment and turned away, he heard a rustle. Sloane had pulled the poncho closed.

Schaydin sat down on the edge of his bunk, staring at the morsel of explosive. He saw instead the girl he had glimpsed in the flame. She had danced with her body, writhing sinuously like a belly dancer as her breasts heaved against the fire's translucence. Schaydin couldn't have been mistaken, the girl had been as real as—the Cambodian girl he had burned. And this girl's expression was so alive, her fire-bright eyes glinting with arrogant demand. *What had the Cambodian girl been crying? But her eyes were dulled by the clinging napalm. . . .*

The pellet of C-4 came into focus as Schaydin's fingers rotated it. All right, there was a simple way to see whether his mind had been playing tricks on him.

Schaydin set the ball of explosive on top of a minican, the sealed steel ammunition box prized as luggage by men in armored units. C4 burned at over 1,000 degrees, the lieutenant remembered, but it would burn briefly enough that only the paint would scorch. The flame of Schaydin's cigarette lighter wavered away from the white pellet and heated the case in his hand. Then a tiny spark and a flicker of orange winked through the yellow naphtha flare. Schaydin jerked his lighter away and shut it. Fire loomed up from the *plastique.* Its hissing filled the tent just as the roar of an incoming rocket does an encampment.

And the dancer was there again.

The engineer platoon ran a generator which powered lights all over the firebase through makeshift lines of commo wire. Left-handed and without looking at it, Schaydin jerked away the wire to his tent's light bulb. The sputtering fire brightened in the darkness, and in it the girl's features were as sharp as a cameo carven in ruddy stone. But the mouth moved and the dancer called to Schaydin over the fire-noise, "Viens ici! Viens a Marie!" Schaydin had studied French as an undergraduate in divinity school, enough to recognize that the tones were not quite those of modern French; but it was clear that the dancer was calling him to her. His body tensed with the impossible desire to obey. Sweat rimmed all the stark lines of his muscles.

Then the flame and the girl were gone together, though afterimages of both danced across Schaydin's eyes. The lieutenant sat in the dark for some time, oblivious of the half-movement he might have glimpsed through a chink in the poncho. The CQ turned back to his microphone, frowning at what he had watched.

Schaydin was more withdrawn than usual in the morning, but if any of his fellow officers noticed it, they put it down to the lieutenant's natural anxiety about his position. The next days would determine whether Schaydin would be promoted to captain and take on for the rest of his tour the slot he now held in place of the wounded Capt. Fuller. Otherwise, Schaydin would have to give up the company to another officer and return to Third Platoon. Schaydin had thought of little else during his previous week of command, but today it barely occurred to him. His mind had been drifting in the unreality of Southeast Asia; now it had found an anchorage somewhere else in time and space.

The thin lieutenant spent most of the day in his tent, with the orange sidewalls rolled up to make its roof an awning. The first sergeant was stationed permanently in the Regiment's base camp at Di An, running an establishment with almost as many troops as there were in the field. In Viet Nam, even in a combat unit, a majority of the troops were noncombatants. Bellew, the Field First, was on R&R in Taiwan, so an unusual amount of the company's day-to-day affairs should have fallen on the commander himself.

Today Schaydin sloughed them, answering the most pressing questions distractedly and without particular interest. His eyes strayed often to his minican, where the paint had bubbled and cracked away in a circle the size of a fifty-cent piece.

She had seemed short, though he could not be sure since the image had been less than a foot tall when the flames leapt their highest. Not plump, exactly, for that implied fat and the dancer had been all rippling muscularity; but she had been a stocky girl, an athlete rather than a houri. And yet Schaydin had never before seen a woman so seductively passionate, so radiant with desire. Every time Schaydin thought of the dancer's eyes, his groin tightened; and he thought of her eyes almost constantly.

Come to me . . . . Come to Marie . . . .

The activities of the firebase went on as usual, ignoring Schaydin just as he did them. Second Platoon and some vehicles from Headquarters Company bellowed off on a Medcap to a village ten kilometers down Route 13. There the medics would dispense antibiotics and bandages to the mildly ill. The troops would also goggle at ravaged figures whom not even Johns Hopkins could have aided: a child whose legs had been amputated three years past by a directional mine; a thirty-year-old man with elephantiasis of the scrotum, walking bowlegged because of the bulk of his cantaloupe-sized testicles. . . .

Chinook helicopters brought in fuel and ammunition resupply in cargo nets swinging beneath their bellies. Schaydin did not notice their howling approach; the syncopated chop of their twin rotors as they hovered; the bustle of men and vehicles heading toward the steel-plank pad to pick up the goods. The lieutenant sat impassively in his tent even when the howitzer battery fired, though the hogs were lofting some of their shells to maximum range. The muzzle blasts raised doughnuts of dust that enveloped the whole base. Schaydin's mind's eye was on a dancing girl, not men in baggy green fatigues; the roar he heard was that of a crowd far away, watching the dancer . . . and even the dust in Schaydin's nostrils did not smell like the pulverized laterite of Tay Ninh Province.

"Time for the officers' meeting, sir," Sloane murmured.

Schaydin continued to sit like a thin, nervous Buddha in a lawn chair.

"Sir," the driver repeated loudly, "they just buzzed from the TOC. It's already 1500 hours."

"Oh, right," muttered the lieutenant dizzily. He shook his head and stood, then ran his fingertips abstractedly over the blackened minican. "Right."

The Tactical Operations Center was merely a trio of command vehicles around a large tent in the middle of the firebase. Schaydin had forgotten to carry his lawn chair with him. He pulled up a box which had held mortar shells and sat facing the acetate-covered map with its crayoned unit symbols. The afternoon rain started, plunging sheets of water that made the canvas jounce like a drumhead. It sounded like an angry crowd.

The Civil Affairs Officer and the lieutenant from the military intelligence detachment shared a presentation on the results of the Medcap. They proved that zero could be divided in half to fill twenty minutes. Then the Operations Officer described F Troop's morning sweep. It had turned up two old bunkers and some cartridge cases, but no signs of recent occupation. The sector was quiet.

The balding S-3 switched to discussing the operation planned in two days. When he directed a question to Schaydin, the lieutenant continued to rock silently on his box, his eyes open but fixed on nothing in the tent.

"Schaydin!" the squadron commander snarled. "Stop sitting there with your finger up your butt and pay attention!"

"Yes, sir!" Schaydin's face flushed hot and his whole body tingled, as if he had just been roused from a dead faint. "Would you please repeat the question, sir?"

The meeting lasted another ten minutes, until the rain stopped. Schaydin absorbed every pointless detail with febrile acuteness. His flesh still tingled.

After Col. Brookings dismissed his officers into the clearing skies, Schaydin wandered toward the far side of the defensive berm instead of going directly to his tent. He followed the path behind one of the self-propelled howitzers, avoiding the pile of white cloth bags stuffed with propellant powder. The charges were packed in segments. For short range shelling, some of the segments were torn off and thrown away as these had been. Soon the powder would be carried outside the perimeter and burned.

Burned. A roaring, sparking column of orange flame, and in it—

Schaydin cursed. He was sweating again.

Three ringing explosions sounded near at hand. The noise had been a facet of the background before the rain as well, Schaydin remembered. He walked toward the source of the sounds, one of First Platoon's tanks. It had been backed carefully away from the berm, shedding its right tread onto the ground, straight as a tow line between the vehicle and the earthen wall. Four men hunched behind a trailer some yards from the tank. One of them, naked to the waist, held a detonator in his hand. The trooper saw Schaydin approaching and called, "Stand back, sir. We're blowing out torsion bars."

The lieutenant stopped, watching. The trooper nodded and slapped closed the scissors handle of the detonator. Smoke and another clanging explosion sprang from among the tank's road wheels. The enlisted men straightened. "That's got it," one of them murmured. Schaydin walked to them, trying to remember the name of the tall man with the detonator, the tank commander of this vehicle.

"What's going on, Emmett?" Schaydin asked.

None of the enlisted men saluted. "Emery, sir," the TC corrected. "Our tank had six torsion bars broke, so she steered and rode like a truck with square wheels. Back in the World they've got machines to drift out torsion bars, but here we're just using a couple ounces of C4 to crack each one loose." The tall noncom pointed at the block of explosive dropped on the ground beside him. Its green sandwich backing had been peeled away from both sides, and half the doughy white *plastique* had been pinched off. Several copper blasting caps lay on the ground beside the C4.

Emery ignored the lieutenant's sudden pallor. He stopped paying attention to Schaydin entirely since it was obvious that the officer was not about to help with the job. "Come on, snakes," Emery said, "we got a lot to do before sundown."

The crewmen scrambled to their fifty-ton mount, hulking and rusted and more temperamentally fragile than any but the men responsible for such monsters will ever know. Schaydin's staring eyes followed them as he himself bent at the knees and touched the block of C4. Its smooth outer wrapper was cool to his fingers. Without looking at the explosive, Schaydin slid it into a side pocket of his fatigue trousers. He walked swiftly back to his tent.

Tropic sunset is as swift as it is brilliant. It crams all the reds and ochres and magentas of the temperate zones into a few minutes which the night then swallows. But the darkness, though it would be sudden, was hours away; and Schaydin's pulsing memory would not let him wait hours.

Sloane was radio watch this afternoon. The driver sat on the tailgate of the command vehicle with his feet on the frame of his cot. He was talking to the staff sergeant who would take over as CQ at 2000 hours. They fell silent when Schaydin appeared.

"Go ahead, Skip, get yourself some supper," the lieutenant said stiffly. "I'll take the radio for a while."

"S'okay, sir, Walsh here spelled me," Sloane said. He

pointed at the paper plate with remnants of beef and creamed potatoes, sitting on his footlocker. "Go ahead and eat yourself."

"I said I'd take the radio!" Schaydin snapped. He was trembling, though he did not realize it. Sloane glanced very quickly at his commander, then to the startled sergeant. The driver lowered his feet from the cot and squeezed back so that Schaydin could enter the track. The two enlisted men were whispering together at the open end of the tent when their lieutenant drew the poncho shut, closing off the rest of the world.

It was dim in the solid-walled vehicle, dimmer yet when Schaydin unplugged the desk lamp. Radio dials gleamed and reflected from the formica counter, chinks of light seeped in past the curtain. But it would serve, would serve . . . .

The texture of the C4 steadied Schaydin's fingers as he molded it. The high sides of the ashtray made it difficult to ignite the pellet. The hot steel of the lighter seared his fingers and he cursed in teary frustration; but just before Schaydin would have had to pull away winked the spark and the orange flare—and in it, the girl dancing.

Her head was flung back, the black, rippling, smoky hair flying out behind her. Schaydin heard the words again, "A Marie! Ici! Viens ici!"

The radio was babbling, too, on the command frequency; but whatever it demanded was lost in the roar of the crowd. Passion, as fiercely hot as the explosive that gave it form, flashed from the girl's eyes. "Come to me!"

The flame sputtered out. Schaydin was blind to all but its afterimage.

The compartment was hot and reeking. Sweat beaded at Schaydin's hairline and on his short, black moustache. He stripped the backing away from the rest of the explosive and began to knead the whole chunk, half a pound, into a single ball.

"Battle Six to Battle One-Six," the radio repeated angrily in Col. Brookings's voice. "Goddammit, Schaydin, report!"

The ashtray had shattered in the heat. Schaydin swept the fragments nervously to the floor, then set the lump of explosive on the blood-marked formica. A shard of clear glass winked unnoticed in the heel of his hand. He snapped his lighter to flame and it mounted, and she mounted—

—and she called. Her hands could not reach out for him but her soul did and her Hell-bright eyes. "Viens ici! Viens!"

The dancer's smooth flesh writhed with no cloak but the flame. Higher, the radio dials melting, the lizard-tongue forks of the blaze beading the aluminum roof—Schaydin stood, his ankles close together like hers. He did not reach for her, not because of the heat but because the motion would be—wrong. Instead he put his hands behind his back and crossed his wrists. Outside the curtain, voices snarled but the dragon-hiss of the C4 would have drowned even a sane man's senses. She twisted, her eyes beckoning, her mouth opening to speak. Schaydin arched, bending his body just so and—

"Come!"

—and he went.

The poncho tore from Col. Brookings's fingers and a

girl plunged out of the fiery radio compartment. She was swarthy but not Vietnamese, naked except for smoldering scraps of a woolen shift. Neither Brookings nor the enlisted men could understand the French she was babbling; but her joy, despite severe burns on her feet and legs, was unmistakable.

No one else was in the vehicle.

On October 14, 1429, the assembled villagers of Briancon, Province of Dauphiné, Kingdom of France, roared in wonderment. The witch Marie dé la Barthe, being burned alive at the stake, suddenly took the form of a demon with baggy green skin. The change did not aid the witch, however, for the bonds still held. Despite its writhing and unintelligible cries, the demon-shape burned as well in the fire as a girl would have.

CODEX

I wrote "Codex" in December, 1967 (I finished it on December 14), a few months after I had begun law school at Duke University. Coursework doesn't frighten me, but change does. Moving to the South and entering law school were big changes, and the question of what I was going to do after I graduated was a huge cloud over the future.

I didn't worry about Viet Nam. This was before Robert S. McNamara, in one of his last gifts to the American people, cancelled the graduate student draft deferment and emptied grad schools to feed his meat-grinder in Southeast Asia.

Libraries have always been refuges for me. Duke had a number of very good libraries, and I browsed their contents contentedly. Because of mentions in secondary sources, I looked for and found the Periplus Maris Erythraei. *This wasn't a history book, it's a book that was history.*

The Periplus *told me about the sailing and trading conditions up and down the shores of the Indian Ocean in the first century AD: what products could be found in each port and what the locals wanted in exchange for their produce. The writer—presumably a trading captain himself—didn't care who ruled a village (except as a consumer of luxuries) or what gods the locals worshipped. All that mattered to him was what they had to sell and how much you had to pay them.*

This view of the ancient world as ordinary people doing ordinary things was completely different from the one I'd held until that time. It was also a view of ordinary people in contact with aliens, both literally (the Latin word alienus *means a foreigner) and figuratively: to an Alexandrine Greek, a native of Zanzibar or Sri Lanka might as well be from Venus.*

Recently I had learned that writing could help me to deal with fear. I had sold a story, "Denkirch," in my last year as an undergraduate at Iowa, so I tried again to lose myself in fiction. "Denkirch" was a Lovecraftian pastiche; this time I wrote a contemporary SF story about the arrival of aliens (the interplanetary kind) in a college town.

I set "Codex" in Iowa City, where I'd lived for four years, rather than in Durham to which I'd just moved. My story gives a capsule of college life in approved student housing just before the culture changed completely under the impact of birth control pills.

The book collection I describe did exist, though the characters themselves are fictional. Many years later I learned that the householder (who worked at the U of I library) had been stealing books by the carload before they were catalogued. (Truth may not have aliens in it, but it can be extremely strange.)

I finished the rough draft of "Codex," but I never submitted it. I don't remember precisely why, but there weren't many short-fiction markets at the time and the story had problems even I could see. It wasn't published until 2003, when the Nameless Presences of the Side-Car Preservation Society asked me if I had something they could bring out as a chapbook.

There are certainly things wrong with "Codex," but it has more merit than simply giving a glimpse of a now-vanished past. I had a lot to learn about how to pace and structure a story; but when I did, the obvious ability to research proved to be of great value to me as a writer.

I guess the other reason I'm including "Codex" here is that it's an example of the direction I might have gone if I hadn't been drafted into the Viet Nam War. I would like to be the person I thought then that I was going to become: a guy who was afraid of the future instead of one who is bleakly despairing about the past.

✤ ✤ ✤

Bob McElroy had the finest personal collection of books that Carter knew of; it made it all the more unfortunate that the man was an ass about books.

Carter's realization of that fact had come shortly after

meeting McElroy at a friend's rooming house. There was a bull session going on, several of the fellows from the house and a few other outsiders. Carter had stayed for an hour or so, drinking coffee and arguing Viet Nam—more pro than con, but not very pleased about matters.

When he got up off the arm of the chair where he'd been sitting, he mentioned that he had a real bitch of an assignment in Latin Survey that he'd better get cracking on. One of the outsiders (start bombing the hell out of Hanoi and they'll listen to reason) looked up.

"Have you read any medieval Latin?" he asked.

Carter had, he admitted, but not a lot. Some of Bishop Gregory's history, a mite of Iordanes.

The other fellow got up also. He looked a little older than Carter's twenty-one, smallish with dark, short hair.

"You might be interested in some of the things I've got, then. Manuscripts."

"I'd like to see them," Carter agreed. "Do you have them in town?"

"Come on over now," the other offered, "they're back at the house with the rest of my collection."

So, the two of them had shrugged into their coats and left behind an argument that was centering on MacArthur's recall. Carter learned that his new acquaintance was Bob McElroy, that he was a grad student in history, and that his father-in-law had bought them a rooming house only five blocks from campus when he'd married Jeanette. It was approved housing, meaning the eight girls who lived upstairs had to sign in at night, but the entrance hall looked less like a dormitory lobby than a professor's study. A wealthy professor.

The furniture was a big desk, a floor lamp, and three cushioned chairs. The bookcases were built into the walls, which they covered save where the doors and the staircase prohibited. McElroy unlocked the center drawer of the desk and pulled it open. Carefully, he laid the top sheet on the desk and unfolded the tissue paper covering it.

"Fourteenth century," he announced proudly. Some monk had done a striking job on the initial letter; as a result, it was impossible to say what it was for the writhing vines that surrounded it. *"Que videlicet albanus paganus adhuc sum perfidorum mandata adversum Christianos saevirent."*

Carter read with difficulty, unused to the shapes of the letters and the lack of punctuation. "It's the devil to make out the words, isn't it?"

McElroy laughed and said there was worse than that. He took out another of the sheets—there were nearly a dozen of them in the drawer—and unwrapped it beside the other. It wasn't pretty, the parchment itself being an irregular width and dirty yellow as well. The writing was a faded brown and only the vertical strokes were easily visible. Carter could make neither head nor tail of it.

"My god," he said, "how do you read this?"

McElroy smiled. "I can't read any of it. I only had one year of Latin, in high school."

Carter looked at him sharply. "I thought . . . ." he began, running his eyes along the shelves . . . . "Yes, here it is. I saw it when we came in."

The book Carter had found and pulled out was one of a fine, leather-bound set. He opened it to the title page:

Epistulae Erasmi

✢ ✢ ✢

"If you can read this, you can read a good deal."

McElroy took the book, running his hand down the age-mottled page. "Erasmus, isn't it?" he said. "I picked up quite a bit of stuff in Paris two years ago. There's more here, too," waving at the shelves in general. "I really ought to study it some more. How long do you think it would take me to get to where I could read things?"

Carter was stunned at the hundreds of dollars—lord, more—that had been wasted in filling the shelves. McElroy wasn't just a snob who wanted atmosphere; he was a collector, a real bibliomaniac. He hadn't read most of his books, couldn't read many of them—but he loved them for themselves. So far as Carter was concerned, McElroy was an ass; not because of the money he spent on books— Carter would have done the same if able—but because he didn't read what he bought.

They saw each other fairly frequently after that. On occasion Carter would take a girl to McElroy's for the evening and the four of them would play bridge as McElroy's charges came in. More often Carter just stopped in during the afternoon and the two men would talk books, leafing through some of McElroy's newer acquisitions. Carter could translate the Latin tags found in 17th century materials McElroy was using for his thesis, sometimes giving help on the lessons with which he was trying to review his Latin outside of class. In return Carter listened with wonder at stories of browsing in London and Paris and borrowed magnificent volumes to read.

He noticed the *de Mercibus et Gentibus Ordinaris Solis* purely by chance. It was bound in leather with a metal spine and corner pieces, not particularly striking where it stood between a bound volume of Restoration religious propaganda and a black-letter edition of Ovid's *Amores*.

McElroy chanced to be out that afternoon, discussing his thesis with a professor. Jeanette—small, blond, and prone to curl up in armchairs, looking very nice indeed—was writing something at the desk. Carter, frowning as he looked at the title page, said, "Say Jeanette . . ."

"Mm?" She looked up, tossing her head a little to clear a lock of hair from her eyes.

"Got any notion where Bob picked this up?" Carter continued, handing the book to her, open.

Jeanette glanced at the title page, then the spine, and handed the book back to Carter. "I don't recall it particularly. Bob can tell you. Why? What does it say?"

"Regarding the commerce and peoples of the order of the sun," Carter translated. "Or maybe 'products and peoples.' I'd have to check a dictionary. But what bugs me is the last part. It really sounds like they're talking about the solar system, doesn't it?"

Jeanette pushed her letter aside, frowning herself. "Let me see it again," she said, taking the book from Carter. She flipped a few pages with practiced competence. "It's printed, all right," she said, "but the ink has faded enough it must be pretty old. Older than I'd expect to find mention of the solar system—in those words, I mean."

Carter nodded in agreement. "It looked older than Copernicus to me, too. When was he for sure, 1500?"

"Umm," the girl mumbled, closing her eyes to concentrate. "The book was published in 1543. Is there a date on this one?"

There wasn't. Beneath the title were the words:

Ezra beu Judah edidit
Barcinoni
decem annis post reditum eius

"Great," said Carter, scowling. "Ezra, son of Judah, published this at Barcino ten years after his return. Where the hell was Barcino?"

"That's it!" cried Jeanette, hopping to her feet and reaching for a massive 18th century atlas on one of the top shelves. She could only get her fingertips on it, so Carter handed it down to her. She got the map she wanted on the first try, Spain, and pointed gleefully to Carter, "All the names are in Latin; see there?"

She was pointing to a dot on the southeast coast, labeled, just as she had hoped, Barcino.

"Very good," said Carter with approval. "Barcelona. Now at least we know where it was printed."

"More than that!" the girl said, bursting with delight at her successful deduction. "Ferdinand and Isabella threw the Jews out of Spain in 1480."

"Well, I'll be damned," said Carter in amazement. "Sure, and Alexander VI let them into Rome and there was hell to pay over that. But where did you pick it up?"

Jeanette smiled. "Well, I graduated with a 3.88 in Spanish, you know. And you can't learn a language without learning something about the country. Don't you find that with Latin?"

Still smiling, now as much at Carter's surprise as at her success, she stretched to put the book away. Again Carter reached over her to take the book; this time their thighs brushed lightly.

The door opened and he stepped back, embarrassed, without any particular reason to be. It was McElroy, shaking his briefcase to clear the snow from it. "God," he said, "have you got any bright ideas about what the Council of State intended to do about the Scotch Presbyterians, Al?"

"Damn fools deserve whatever thesis topics they pick," Carter answered with a laugh. "Bryant didn't give you any help?"

"Nobody gave me any help," McElroy replied, shaking his head. "What's for dinner, Honey?"

Jeanette shrugged. "What would you like? I could take some fish out of the freezer."

"Damn it all," McElroy groaned, half-serious, "that's your job. Yes, that's why you're home, remember? So you can take care of the house. What did you do all afternoon?"

Carter, embarrassed again, stepped into the pause before Jeanette could say anything. "Don't knock her— you've got a very smart wife. She's just figured out where and when this book was published." He tapped the volume in his left hand.

"This one?" McElroy asked, taking the book when Carter handed it to him. "I got this . . . let me see: Paris, summer of '63. From the estate of Dr. Francois Geyer, along with a batch of other stuff. Turned out to be mostly novels he'd picked up as a boy when I got around to sorting it. There were some old medical books— Heidelburg, 1658 one of them. I kept them and this too, I guess. Most of the lot I resold. What did you say the date on this was?"

"Your wife figured it out. Somewhere between the invention of the printing press and 1480, at Barcelona."

"Not a chance," McElroy answered absently. "There wasn't any printing press at Barcelona until—oh, hell, a long time after 1480. Unless . . ."

His voice trailed off as he made careful comparisons between two pages. He turned another page, then whistled through his teeth. Reaching over to the desk he picked up a 6-inch rule, transparent except for the divisions. "Look here," he said, pointing out a capital "H" to Carter. "See the height of it? And this one?"

There were six capital "H"s scattered over the three pages. All of them differed from the rest in height, width, or some other peculiarity of design. "This son of a bitch was block printed or I'm King Tut," McElroy said as he pointed out the sixth "H." "Every plate separately carved, and it was a neat job, too."

"What's it worth?" Carter asked, suddenly impressed by the fact that the book through which he had been leafing nonchalantly was probably five hundred years old.

McElroy shook his head. "Can't say; it's out of my class. I'll get Hebard in Library Science to take a look at it."

He turned to Jeanette who was still standing near the atlas, looking as surprised as Carter was sure he too must. "Honey," McElroy asked, "have we got three steaks left? Al, you feel like dinner here? I think I owe it to you."

"Well, I was thinking of going out tonight—"

"Dilly? Just tell her to come on down. We'll get another steak if we don't have enough."

"No, no, just a girl from my chem lab," Carter, put off his train of thought by McElroy's assumption. Dilly was one of the girls upstairs; Carter had gotten serious enough about her earlier in the year that he had asked McElroy if there was any chance that a girl might not come in one night and not get reported to the Dean of Women. McElroy knew damned well what he meant and he hadn't made a bureaucratic fuss about it. He had told Jeanette, though, and it made Carter feel a little funny. It was actually worse because nothing came of it after all.

"Anyhow," Carter went on, when he remembered where he had been thinking, "I'd like to read that book tonight anyway, and I don't suppose you'd want it to leave the house. And I'm always ready for steak."

While Jeanette broiled the steaks, the two men hunted through the books McElroy kept stored in the attic, among which he was sure there was a Latin dictionary. Sure enough, Carter turned up a thick copy of Andrew's Freund. It wasn't the best to be hoped for—it was an 1850 edition—but it was better than anything Carter had in his room and saved a trip as well. Rather than start reading only to be interrupted by dinner, Carter set both books aside and talked to McElroy about Dungeness until Jeanette opened the kitchen door and called them to eat.

It was a pleasant meal, relaxed and comfortable to Carter who was used to sharing the kitchen with seven other men and bolting his food to get out of the way. The steaks were done to his taste although they hadn't been thawed before broiling. Even better, there were little side dishes of morels fried in butter. Carter remembered that McElroy had said something about having gone mushroom hunting last spring.

And it was nice to eat with a girl with as much going for her as Jeanette had. Without a wife, Carter reminded himself; your big trouble is that you're horny and likely to stay that way. He wasn't particularly shocked at the thought of adultery, but McElroy was about as much friend as Carter had, whatever Jeanette thought of the idea.

After dinner the men went back into the hall. Some of the girls were going out on study dates—it was Tuesday— but the door closing the entrance alcove and the central heating kept the room comfortable. The occasional snatches of conversation passed over Carter as he began to concentrate on his reading not bothering to write down the translation. McElroy had a pole lamp in one corner rigged with a 120-watt cone of light, isolated from the rest of the dimly lit room. He read more easily as he became used to the odd cursive letters.

After doing the dishes Jeanette came out and sat at the desk, across from her husband. They exchanged a few words; then she continued her letter and no one spoke for several hours.

Carter read, and the words began to crawl through his mind of their own accord. At first it was just another translation exercise, complicated by the print and the unclassical diction. Then, slowly, Carter began to realize what he was reading; that it wasn't Ovid writing of myths or Pliny of some Never-Never Land of travelers' imaginations. Carter felt less of wonder or horror than of shock at the writer's stunning nonchalance. He rarely used the dictionary and when he did, the word sought was frequently not in it. Occasionally one of the girls still upstairs said something loud enough to be heard. These voices, the wind, the scrape of Jeanette's pen—all were lost in the sibilant rustle of the ancient vellum.

It was past ten o'clock when Carter set the books aside and rubbed his head to clear it. The McElroys both looked up, half-startled as if by a broken spell.

"Done or giving up?" McElroy asked.

"Done, I think!' Carter answered, snapping the light off. "It isn't very long, you know. The pages are thick."

The alcove door rattled, then banged shut as the inner door opened. Marcia Byrd had come back from the library; close behind her was a couple, neither of whom Carter knew very well though he had seen them.

"Bob," the girl asked. "Is anybody in the lounge?"

"Don't think so," he answered, looking at Jeanette who shook her head.

The couple disappeared through the door beside the stairs leading to a comfortable room with a fireplace, the only place in the house the girls could entertain their dates. It was pretty much a first-come, first-served proposition since, although there was room for several couples, it was tacitly held to one at a time.

Marcia stayed downstairs and the four of them talked a while; McElroy got out a deck of cards and they played a few series of hearts, since Marcia didn't know how to play bridge and it didn't seem worthwhile to teach her then. A few more couples drifted in, kibitzed, and broke up again.

At a quarter of twelve Jeanette put everyone over with her second skunk hand in a row. Marcia went upstairs and McElroy tapped on the lounge door. Someone was liable to walk in without thinking at any time, but the possibility wasn't a certain deterrent when the weather got too cold for riverbanking.

The boy opened the door almost immediately. He already had his coat on. The girl went as far as the alcove with him where she kissed her goodbye. She came back in a moment, shivering, and called, "Goodnight all" as she ran up the stairs.

"God, that's all I needed," Carter muttered as she disappeared.

"What's that, Al?" McElroy asked with a curious frown.

"Didn't you notice? Her sweater was inside out."

McElroy roared and Jeanette giggled, but the laughter (though he joined it) made Carter all the more conscious of what he lacked.

"What do you think of the book," McElroy finally asked.

"It scares the Hell out of me," Carter answered frankly.

"Is it . . . . ?" Jeanette began. "I mean, what it sounded like?"

Carter nodded. Noticing McElroy's lack of understanding he picked up the book and opened it at random. "Here, Bob, this is what we mean:

"'On the western coast of the second continent, from the Tropic of Capricorn southward,'—literally, south of the southern solstial circle—'the inhabitants catch great squid; the beaks are of first quality. These may be had for shining balls'—*spheris nitentibus,* damned if I know what it means—'usually at one per eighty-four beaks, variations for quality. Care must be taken lest more than ten balls be dispensed in a locality and one of the chiefmen injure himself by excess. There are no beacons.'"

Jeanette was biting her lower lip gently; McElroy

himself had a look of outright puzzlement. "But, what does it mean?" he asked.

Carter smiled grimly. "That's what the next part tells:

"'The Pathioni, whose ships call yearly at Rakka, import vast quantities of squid beaks for use in the cradles'—I'm not sure the literal meaning is quite what he meant—'of their young. The vanes are of lesser suitability and can not be profitably transported at this date. Without constant changes of the crushed material their young are liable to a disease likely to blind them; the population is too great for the native supply to suffice.

"'This area is far to the Southeast of Spain.'

"Now do you understand?" Carter finished.

"Who wrote this?" gasped McElroy, half-rising from his chair.

Jeanette was strangely calm. "It wasn't one person, was it, Al?" she said quietly. "Is it all like that, two voices?"

Carter nodded in approval. "You noticed that right off? I had to read half a dozen chapters before I did. Yes, the notes, so to speak, were probably written by our friend Ezra, don't you think. I've got a feeling I could guess where he returned from, now."

"But then who wrote the rest?" McElroy demanded angrily, not so much disbelieving as refusing to believe.

Jeanette stood, unconsciously holding her hands out to Carter, where he slumped in a chair beside the desk. "Al, this is wonderful! Don't you see, not only peace, but trade—we aren't alone any more."

"Not alone, not alone," Carter repeated with grim humor, keeping his eyes fixed on the book. "Want to hear some more?

"'Beacon 42 marks a source of first grade adipocere, 100 talents per year, plus varying quantities of lesser grades. Competition must be strictly controlled at risk of disaster from excess demands. Merchants desiring a billet must enroll with Setcor Coordination or face capital charges.

"'The inhabitants of Harmozia bury alive 100 women or 200 young children every year in pits dug for the purpose. Within the space of the year the bodies are converted to pure adipocere by the action of the ground water which is of special virture in that locale. In return, the Rakkadim supply the princes of the city with pleasures of wonderful sort.

"'It is said that in past ages when Shapur the Magnificent would have had the town razed, his troops were overwhelmed by the sands. It is likewise handed down that when the reigning prince became boastful at his immunity from Persia and would have taken a triple toll of his subjects to minister to his delight, the people called on their god whom they call Clutus. The earth swallowed much of the town, scattering the worshippers before the completion of the ceremony, but thereafter the levy have been fixed.'"

"Oh, dear God," Jeanette whispered, and the words were a prayer. "200 children."

"What the Hell is adipocere?" McElroy asked. "Is it a jewel?"

"Corpse-wax, bog butter, you know. What you get when you bury a body in warm, wet ground." Carter rubbed his forehead with his palms, then continued. "I doubt it mattered whether the bodies went into the ground living or dead, so long as they had a nice layer of fat to start the reaction. The Harmozians didn't know that, though, and I guess the Rakkadrim never got around to telling them. God!"

"But Al," Jeanette faltered, "what do they do with it? Surely they don't make candles of it like the Satanists."

Carter grimaced. "That was in an earlier note. They eat it. Apparently it's quite a delicacy."

Jeanette went so pale that the only color in her cheeks was the yellow of the lamplight. McElroy's Adam's apple was working convulsively.

"Are there more like that?" Jeanette asked, her knuckles tight against her cheekbones.

"Some. I don't intend to read them to you. There is one that interests me, though, if you wouldn't mind listening?"

They nodded assent. Carter leafed back through the book and began to read, "'Carven snail shells are of great value among the Garuli stars, but the trade in them must be actively discouraged since the Garuli claim a monopoly on the commodity and enforce it with their wonted savagery.

"'The Garuli are unable to handle snail shells without mutual destruction. Therefore, work of distinguished artistry in this (to them) impossible medium commanded higher price. They offered fine gems in exchange for average work, and for especially striking pieces they could be induced to give the fabled anthrax, the stone of power.

"'All trade was within the Epirotes, the Ligures and a people far west of Spain, dwelling between two continents. Some say that Semele was a queen of the Epirotes, not

Thebes, and that following her death, her people massacred the next company of merchants. Since that time, far past, the Factors believe the trade has lapsed.

"'Some claim that even today one who lets candlelight shine through a ruby in the moon's sight, and who calls the Rakkadrim to haggle will be answered—but that race has a short way with fraud.'"

Carter shut the book and looked up. "Do you see why it interested me, Bob?"

McElroy rubbed his chin with his left hand, then turned to his wife and asked, "Honey, don't we have a shell like that?"

Jeanette said nothing, only squeezed her hands together in her lap. McElroy took little notice, for he was glancing up at the little knick-knack shelf above the kitchen door, one of the few places not usurped by bookshelves. "Sure, there it is," he said as he rose. Stepping to the shelf he took down the greybrown shell at one end of it and hefted it in his hand before setting it on the desk.

It was perhaps four inches through at the thickest point, just above the base, and rose to a spiral peak in about the same distance. The concentrated light of the reading lamp threw the delicate reliefs into sharp contrast. The artist had created a continuous strip picture following the bands of the snail's growth, all the way to the peak where time had blurred them.

"I thought that's what it was," Carter mused. "I don't remember seeing one anywhere else; you didn't happen to pick it up in Milan, did you?"

McElroy shook his head. "No, I didn't get it. Where did it come from, Jean?"

Instead of answering, Jeanette asked, "What are you going to do, Bob?"

"Dammit, I don't know!" McElroy snapped back. "Where did it come from?"

"From Mexico," Jeanette said; raising her eyes but not looking at either the shell or her husband beyond it. "From a little village called Iguala, south of Mexico City. I was going to bring it back for Mom—three years ago, you remember? The summer before we were married? But she died in the accident and I kept it."

She began to cry, quietly, with her hands covering her face. After a moment she got up and strode swiftly into the lounge, closing the door behind her.

Both the men were uncomfortable. "She was pretty shook up about her mother," McElroy said. Carter nodded but privately questioned the explanation.

"What do you think?" McElroy went on, trying to break the awkwardness.

"I can't say," Carter answered, rubbing his left arm. "It's a funny thing, though; I remember Barnes telling us in geology that one of the reasons you don't find many fossil snails is that their shell is different from most animals: oysters, say. Aragonite, not calcite? It's all calcium carbonate, but the crystals are different—harder but not as stable. I don't know what it proves, except . . ."

"Except?" McElroy pressed.

"There's no way in the world somebody in the fifteenth century could have found that out unless it was told to him."

McElroy picked up the shell again, turning it in the light. "I wonder what it's supposed to be?" he remarked. Then, looking straight at Carter, "What do you think?"

The lounger door opened and Jeanette stepped into the room. Calmly, without an attempt to smile, she said, "I'm sorry; I'm a little funny tonight, I guess."

She sat down, looking at Carter rather than McElroy. "Shall I say what you're thinking instead? You're wondering what difference it could make, thousands of years later, even if this isn't some horrible joke? And you don't know."

Carter shrugged, then gave a nod of assent. Jeanette was perfectly right, he didn't know; and he wasn't sure he wanted to learn any more than she did.

McElroy licked his lips before speaking again. Then he asked very carefully, "Well, why don't we find out?"

No one answered him.

"Well, do you want to come?" McElroy persisted. "There's a moon tonight, a full moon. We can get out on the roof through the upstairs kitchen so we're above the trees. Why not?"

Carter said, "Jeanette," half-question in his voice.

Jeanette spread her hands, palm up, and smiled at him. "Well, we started it, didn't we? We might as well see it through. I'll get my pendant."

She got up and walked through the kitchen door, her skirts brushing Carter's chair as she rounded the desk.

When Jeanette had disappeared toward the bedroom, McElroy asked, "What's the matter, Al? You don't really want to go through with it, do you?"

Carter got up and began running his fingertips over the spines of the books just to be moving. "It might be dangerous," he finally said. "Ezra didn't give a very glowing account of the Garuli, you know. If they exist. And if they answer."

McElroy only grinned. "No sweat there; we've got the goods, remember?"

He touched the shell, adding, "Why do you suppose they didn't get it long ago? If it was made for them and that seems likely enough, doesn't it?"

Carter bent down for a close look. "Maybe they packed up instantly when Epirotes got restless; afraid of more of the same elsewhere," he suggested. "Or, it could have been fairly recently carven for all we know. The technique needn't have been lost simply because the market dried up. If there ever was one."

The door between kitchen and bedroom squeaked and McElroy said, "Damn. I forgot to tell her to look for candles."

"I got them," said Jeanette, holding up a long taper and a box of farmer's matches as she came through the door. "That's what took so long."

She had put on her coat as well, a thigh-length suede affair that hugged her close. A looser fit would probably have been warmer, but she looked painfully beautiful as she was.

"You have a ruby?" Carter asked as McElroy went out to the hall closet to get their coats.

"Oh yes; hadn't you seen it?" Jeanette replied. Reaching into a side pocket she brought out a thin silver loop to which had been fastened a ruby teardrop set in filagree. It was a good-sized stone, several carats at Carter's uneducated guess.

"It was my grandmother's," Jeanette explained. Shyly she added. "She gave it to me when we were married. I'm supposed to wear it after my first baby."

Carter smiled. Sometimes it was nice to have someone that could talk to you freely, as much as having someone to talk to.

McElroy tossed Carter his ski parka and put on his own topcoat. Carter slipped on his gloves and then took the candle and matches from Jeanette who tied a scarf under her chin. McElroy picked up the shell carefully in one gloved hand, a little awkwardly because of the difficulty in judging pressure with gloves on. Finally he cupped his left hand under the shell and took the book in his right.

"Wait," he said, pausing as the thought struck him. "What am I going to say to them?"

Carter shrugged. "Garuli, I have a fine snail shell to trade," he suggested. "If this works at all, it can't be much more complicated. Damned if I can see how it could work but . . . ."

He trailed off into another shrug.

"Well, let's go," McElroy said and led the way up the stairs. They walked as quietly as they could, but the shuffling brought one of the girls to peep out through her door, probably wondering who had come in late. No one said anything to her, nor did she ask.

Carter closed the door of the upstairs kitchen behind them so that the draft when they opened the window would not be noticed by the girls. The fire escape platform, an ugly wooden framework outside the west window, served as a porch in fine weather; it would make an adequate, if crowded, place from which to signal.

"Shall we light the candle inside?" Jeanette asked.

"Good idea," agreed Carter, handing her the candle so that he could strike a match. It was a new candle but lit quickly when Jeanette tilted it at an angle over the match-flame, allowing wax to run down the unsaturated wick.

"You better get the window, too," McElroy said. "My hands are full."

Carter nodded and tugged. When the window refused to move he checked the lock, then struck the sash a sharp blow with the heel of his hand and tried again. This time the window went up with hardly a squeal.

"After you," Carter said to McElroy with a sardonic flourish. When he turned to take the candle from Jeanette she shook her head.

"Go on," she said. "It'll be easier if I hand it to you."

The flame sputtered blue and went out anyway, as soon as the wind caught it outside. It was the vicious cold of an Iowa winter outside, well below zero with the biting wind that makes even Iowans wonder why they hadn't gone somewhere else to school. The wind had scoured clean the boards of the 6 x 3-foot platform but made the lack of a railing seem unusually dangerous. It howled at Carter as he gave Jeanette a hand as she ducked through the window.

It took three tries to relight the candle when the air calmed for a moment. Carter immediately cupped his hands around the flame to shield it from the next gust. When that steadied Carter took the candle in his left hand and said, "Quick Jeanette, before it goes out."

Jeanette fumbled in her pocket with clumsy fingers, then pulled off her right glove and found the pendant. A puff of wind blew out the flame before she could raise the ruby.

McElroy cursed out of irritation or nervousness. This

time one match was enough to relight the candle as Jeanette held it in her left hand. Carter quickly took it from her and held it below and behind the pendant, sighting across them at the glaring full moon.

McElroy didn't have to be told. "Garuli!" he shouted as though he expected his voice to carry unaided to them. "I have a shell to trade!"

The candle went out again. Jeanette tilted it up with a questioning glance at Carter. He shook his head. "We've done what we were supposed to. At least this damned wind has cleared the overcast away."

"What's that?" asked McElroy.

"The clouds are gone," Carter repeated.

McElroy took little notice. "Look," he said, "do you suppose I should repeat it in Latin?"

"I doubt it," Carter began. "If this gets through to them at all it won't—"

"There! There!"

Startled, both men followed Jeanette's pointing arm. It was about five hundred feet up when they saw it, a dull sphere standing dark against the moonlit sky. Whether it had been falling all the time or had somehow appeared just before Jeanette saw it, none of them could say. It grew as they watched, plunging toward them in utter silence. Jeanette gave a little cry and held herself tight against Carter's chest, but McElroy was too intent on the globe to notice.

Light shimmered over the sphere's undersurfaces and it slowed visibly, then drifted over to the platform as if blown by the wind. When it came to rest it was not quite touching the guttering, a twenty foot ball of no particular color, just out of reach. Then a six-foot-square flashed white and lay down forming a bridge to the platform for what might have been a man.

He was short and slender, the creature that stepped toward them, but he took no notice of the searing wind that blew his thin garments against him. His face looked grey though that might have been the light; his eyes were dull as stone; and the jewel at his throat burned like the red heart of Betelgeuse.

McElroy held out the shell, saying nothing. The Other stepped back with a flash of anger or fear. He snapped a glove from his belt and drew it carefully over his left hand, clearly displaying his six fingers. Then he took the shell, turned it to all sides, and finally looked up with a nod.

"No," said McElroy as the Other moved his hand toward a belt pouch. "No," he repeated, "not those. I want the big one, the Anthrax."

The Other obviously knew what McElroy was saying. He raised his bare hand to his throat, tapping the gem absently with his forefinger. At each touch the fires bellied around his hand, silhouetting it and dazzling the three watchers. Without further reflection he plucked the stone from its setting and dropped it in the cup of McElroy's gloved hand. Then he turned and stepped back into his ship, the hatch flowing shut behind him.

The globe began to rise and steadily increasing speed. Several hundred feet above the city, it flashed from red through violet and—disappeared.

The three of them stared at the lambent crystal in McElroy's hand. It still glowed but seemingly feebly, perhaps in comparison to its glory to the touch of the Other.

McElroy gripped the book between his upper arm and chest so that he could tap the stone with his right hand.

Still nothing happened.

"Oh, thank God," Jeanette whispered, the first words any of them had spoken since the globe appeared.

"Wait, I know," said McElroy and tugged off his right glove with his teeth.

"Bob! Don't!" Carter shouted and lunged for his friend across the narrow platform.

Startled, perhaps frightened, McElroy instantly seized the jewel with his bare hand. His body disintegrated in a soundless blast of light so sudden he had no time even to scream. The shattered corpse toppled into the electric lead-in and an intermittent arc sputtered like a grease fire. When it stopped, the street light had gone out.

Carter seized Jeanette by the shoulders, staring into her face washed white by horror. "Jeanette! Oh God, I'm so sorry. Semele had to see Zeus in his glory and it destroyed her—and I knew."

He groaned and tried to pull her close. She broke loose and shouted, "Kiss me! Why don't you kiss me right here! That's why you did it, isn't it? You knew as well as I did what would happen. Didn't you?"

With a groan of agony she stepped back to him, burying her tears in his coat.

"Allen, Allen, what have we done?" she moaned.

There were other questioning faces now, staring out of neighboring windows, but Carter had no answers for anyone.

Not anyone at all.

12-14-67

FIREFIGHT

⊱⊰

One of the best of many good things that's happened in the course of my writing career is that I got Kirby McCauley for an agent. (And incidentally, if these intros don't make it clear that I've been amazingly lucky all my life, then they're distorting a truth that I feel all the way to my bones.)

After Mr. Derleth died, I had to look for new markets. I managed to sell a story to F&SF but a lot of short fiction was being published in one-shot anthologies that I wasn't even going to hear about before they closed. I thought about agents, but I didn't really know how to go about getting one and I felt (rightly) that anybody who took me at that stage of my career was a pretty doubtful prospect himself.

A pulp dealer friend, Richard Minter, mentioned that a correspondent from Minneapolis, Kirby McCauley, had started representing fantasy writers. He was agent for a number of Weird Tales pros (Carl Jacobi, for example), but he also had new

Arkham House writers like Ramsey Campbell and Brian Lumley in his stable.

Would he represent me? Did I really want an agent? And perhaps most important, how painful would it be to be turned down? Pretty painful, I suspected, but I could delay the event by not writing McCauley.

Two things happened. F&SF published a Cthulhu Mythos novelette by Brian Lumley. Since the 1950s, the only Lovecraftian stories in the magazine had been parodies—it was far too sophisticated for "pneumatic prose" to quote one editor's comment about Lovecraft's own style. Yet here was an unabashed pastiche. I could only assume that Mr. Lumley's agent was an incredible salesman. (Oddly enough, that was precisely the correct assumption to draw from the event.)

Second, Marvel Comics brought out a digest-sized fantasy magazine, The Haunt of Horror. Much of it was written in-house by comics scripters, but there was also a new story by Ramsey Campbell. Mr. Campbell's agent was obviously on top of things.

Furthermore, I learned that The Haunt of Horror was being killed after the second issue (which was already at the printers). I'd missed my chance at a sale because I didn't have an agent like Kirby McCauley.

I didn't think I could simply write Kirby (well, Mr. McCauley) and tell him I wanted an agent. I'd just finished a story ("Contact!") that I intended to send to Analog. I sent it to Kirby with my query letter instead.

He wrote back with great enthusiasm (Kirby does everything with great enthusiasm; you can question his judgment sometimes, but never his gusto), saying that he was already aware of my writing and had intended to approach me shortly. He thought the story was great (he sent it on to Analog and got an acceptance by return mail, the fastest I've ever had in my life) and looked forward to a long and profitable association.

We've had that, though it was a lot of years before I made enough money to justify Kirby and his sister Kay keeping me on as a client. Kirby went from success to success, ratcheting clients up by orders of magnitude whether they started from nothing (like Karl Wagner) or from something already impressive (like Stephen King, who became Kirby's client after his early six-figure book deals).

In the course of his other activities, Kirby edited original anthologies. I wrote "Firefight" for the first of them, "Frights." The incident of a kid in the flame track breaking up an attack was quite real, though of course the enemy was an NVA battalion rather than anything supernatural.

As a matter of fact, the whole background is real. I look back at that time and realize that it was a completely different world.

But at the time it was the real world, and the only world I had.

✢ ✢ ✢

"Christ," Ginelli said, staring at the dusty wilderness, "if this is a sample, the next move'll be to Hell. And a firebase there'd be cooler."

Herrold lit a cigarette and poked the pack toward his subordinate. "Have one," he suggested.

"Not unless it's grass," the heavy newbie muttered. He flapped the sleeveless flak jacket away from his flesh, feeling streaks of momentary chill as sweat started from beneath the quilted nylon. "Christ, how d'you stand it?"

Herrold, rangy and big-jointed, leaned back in the dome seat and cocked one leg over the flamethrower's muzzle. Ginelli envied the track commander's build every time he looked at the taller man. His own basic training only four months before had been a ghastly round of extra physical training to sweat off pounds of his mother's pasta.

"Better get used to it," Herrold warned lazily. "This zippo always winds up at the back of the column, so we always wait to set up in the new laagers. Think about them—pretend you're a tree."

Ginelli followed his TC's finger toward the eight giant trees in the stone enclosure. It didn't help. Their tops reached a hundred feet into the air above the desolate plain, standing aloof from the activity that raised a pall of dust beside them. The shadows pooling beneath could not cool Ginelli as he squatted sun-dazzled on the deck of the flame track.

At least Colonel Boyle was just as hot where he stood directing placements from the sandbagged deck of his vehicle. Hieu stood beside him as usual. You could always recognize the interpreter at a distance because of the tiger fatigues he wore, darkly streaked with black and green. Below the two, radiomen were stringing the last of the tarpaulin passageways that joined the three command vehicles into a Tactical Operations Center. Now you could move between the blacked-out tracks in the dark; but the cool of the night seemed far away.

On the roof, Boyle pointed and said something to Hieu. The dark-skinned interpreter's nod was emphatic; the colonel spoke into his neck-slung microphone and the two vehicles ahead of the flame track grunted into motion. Herrold straightened suddenly as his radio helmet burped at him. "Seven-zero, roger," he replied.

"We movin'?" Ginelli asked, leaning closer to the TC to hear him better. Herrold flipped the switch by his left ear forward to intercom and said, "OK, Murray, they want us on the west side against that stone wall. There'll be a ground guide, so take it easy."

Murray edged the zippo forward, driving it clockwise around the circuit other tracks had clawed in the barren earth. Except for the grove within the roomy laterite enclosure, there was nothing growing closer than the rubber plantation whose rigid files marched green and silver a mile to the east. Low dikes, mostly fallen into the crumbling soil, ordered the wasteland. Dust plumed in the far distance as a motorbike pulled out of the rubber and turned toward the firebase. Coke girls already, Ginelli thought. Even in this desert.

Whatever the region's problem was it couldn't have been with the soil itself; not if trees like the monsters behind the low wall could grow in it. Every one of the eight the massive stonework girdled was forty feet around at the base. The wrinkled bole of the central titan could have been half that again.

The zippo halted while a bridge tank roared, churning the yielding dirt as it maneuvered its frontal slope up to the coarse laterite. The ground guide, a bare-chested tanker with a beaded sweat band, dropped his arms to signal the bridge to shut down, then motioned the flame track in beside the greater bulk. Murray cut his engine and hoisted himself out of the driver's hatch.

Common sense and the colonel's orders required that everyone on a track be wearing helmet and flak jacket. Men like Murray, however, who extended their tours to four years, tended to ignore death and their officers when comfort was at stake. The driver was naked to the waist; bleached golden hairs stood out wirelike against his deep tan. "Dig out some beers, turtle," he said to Ginelli with easy arrogance. "We got time to down 'em before they start puttin' a detail together." Road dust had coated the stocky, powerful driver down to the throat, the height he projected from his hatch with the seat raised and the cover swiveled back. Years of Vietnamese sunlight had washed all color from his once-blue eyes.

An ACAV pulled up to the flame track's right, its TC nonchalant in his cupola behind the cal fifty. To Ginelli's amazement, the motorbike he had seen leaving the rubber plantation was the next vehicle in line. It was a tiny green Sachs rather than one of the omnipresent Honda 50s, and its driver was Caucasian. Murray grinned and jumped to his feet. "Crozier! Jacques!" he shouted delightedly. "What the hell are you doin' here?"

The white-shirted civilian turned his bike neatly and

tucked it in on the shady side of the zippo. If any of the brass had noticed him, they made no sign. Dismounted, Crozier tilted his face up and swept his baseball cap away from a head of thinning hair. "Yes, I thought I might find you, Joe," he said. His English was slightly burred. "But anyway, I would have come just to talk again to Whites. It is grand to see you."

Herrold unlashed the shelter tarp from the load and let it thump over the side. "Let's get some shade up," he ordered.

"Jack was running a plantation for Michelin up north when we were in the A-Shau Valley," Murray explained. "He's a good dude. But why you down here, man?"

"Oh, well," the Frenchman said with a deprecating shrug. "Your defoliation, you know? A few months after your squadron pulls out, the planes come over. Poof! Plantation Seven is dead and I must be transferred. They grow peanuts there now."

Herrold laughed. "That's the nice thing about a job in this country," he said. "Always somethin' new tomorrow."

"Yeah, not so many VC here as up there," Murray agreed.

Crozier grimaced. "The VC I am able to live with. Like them? No. But I understand them, understand their, their aims. But these people around here, these Mengs—they will not work, they will not talk, only glare at you and plant enough rice for themselves. Michelin must bring in Viets to work the rubber, and even those, they do not stay because they do not like Mengs so near."

"But they're all Vietnamese, aren't they?" Ginelli asked in puzzlement. "I mean, what else could they be?"

The Frenchman chuckled, hooking his thumbs in his trouser tops. "They live in Viet Nam so they are Vietnamese, no? But you Americans have your Indians. Here are the Montagnards—we call them the Mountaineers, you know? But the Vietnamese name for them means 'the dirty animals.' Not the same folk, no no. They were here long before the Viets came down from the North. And the Meng who live here and a few other places, they are not the same either; not as the Viets or even the Montagnards. And maybe they are older yet, so they say."

The group waited a moment in silence. Herrold opened the Mermite can that served as a cooler and began handing out beer. "Got a church key?" he asked no one in particular. Murray, the only man on the track with a knife, drew his huge Bowie and chopped ragged triangles in the tops. Tepid beer gurgled as the four men drank. Ginelli set his can down.

"Umm," he said to his TC, "how about the co-ax?"

Herrold sighed. "Yeah, we don't want the son of a bitch to jam." Joints popped as he stood and stretched his long frame.

Crozier gulped the swig of beer still in his mouth. "Indeed not," he agreed. "Not here, especially. The area has a very bad reputation."

"That a fact?" Herrold asked in mild surprise. "At the troop meetin' last night the ole man said around here it'd be pretty quiet. Not much activity on the intelligence maps."

"Activity?" the Frenchman repeated with raised eyebrows. "Who can say? The VC come through the laborers' hootches now and again, not so much here as near

A-Shau, that is true. But when *I* first was transferred here three years ago, there were five, maybe six hundred in the village—the Mengs, you know, not the plantation lines."

"That little place back where we left the hardball?" Ginelli wondered aloud. "Jeez, there's not a dozen hootches there."

"Quite so," Crozier agreed with a grave nod of his head. "Because a battalion of Communists surrounded it one night and killed every Meng they found. Maybe twenty survived."

"Christ," Ginelli breathed in horror, but Herrold's greater experience caused his eyes to narrow in curiosity.

"Why the hell?" the tall track commander asked. "I mean, I know they've got hit squads out to gun down village cops and headmen and all. But why the whole place? Were they that strong for the government?"

"The government?" the civilian echoed; he laughed. "They spat at the District Governor when he came through. But a week before the Communists came, there was firing near this very place. Communist, there is no doubt. I saw the tracers myself and they were green.

"The rest—and this is rumor only, what my foremen told me at the time before they stopped talking about it— a company, thirty men, were ambushed. Wiped out, every one of them and mutilated, ah . . . badly. How they decided that the Mengs were responsible, I do not know; but that could have been the reason they wiped out the village later."

"Umm," Herrold grunted. He crumpled his beer can and looked for a litter barrel. "Lemme get on the horn and we'll see just how the co-ax is screwing up. "The can clattered into the barrel as the TC swung up on the back deck of the zippo again. The others could hear his voice as he spoke into the microphone: "Battle five-six, track seven-zero. Request clearance to test fire our Mike seven-four."

An unintelligible crackle replied from the headset a moment later. "No sir," Herrold denied, "not if we want it working tonight." He nodded at the answer. "Roger, roger." He waved. "OK," he said to his crew as he set down the radio helmet, "let's see what it's doin.'"

Ginelli climbed up beside Herrold, slithering his pudgy body over the edge of the track with difficulty. Murray continued to lounge against the side of the track. "Hell," he said, "I never much liked guns anyway; you guys do your thing."

Crozier stood beside his friend, interested but holding back a little from the delicacy of an uninvited guest. The machine gun had once been co-axial to the flamethrower. Now it was on a swivel welded to the top of the TC's dome. Herrold rotated it, aiming at the huge tree in the center of the grove. A ten-foot scar streaked the light trunk vertically to the ground, so he set the buckhorn sight just above it. Other troopers, warned by radio what to expect, were watching curiously.

The gun stuttered off a short burst and jammed. Empty brass tinkled off the right side of the track. Herrold swore and clicked open the receiver cover. His screwdriver pried at the stuck case until it sprang free. Slamming the cover shut, he jacked another round into the chamber.

BAM BAM BAM BAM BAM!

"God*damn* it," Herrold said. "Looks like we gotta take the whole thing down."

"Or throw rocks," Ginelli suggested.

Herrold cocked a rusty eyebrow. Unlike the thick-set newbie, he had been in country long enough to have a feel for real danger. After a moment he grinned back. "Oh, we don't have to throw rocks," he said. He unslung his old submachine gun from the side of the dome. Twenty years of service had worn most of the finish off its crudely stamped metal but it still looked squat and deadly.

Herrold set the wire stock to his shoulder; the burst, when he squeezed off, was ear-shattering. A line of fiercely red tracers stabbed from the muzzle and ripped an ascending curve of splintered wood up the side of the center tree.

"Naw, we're OK while the ole greasegun works," Herrold said. He laughed. "But," he added, "we better tear down the co-ax anyhow."

"Perhaps I should leave now," Crozier suggested. "It grows late and I must return to my duties."

"Hell," Murray protested, "stick around for chow at least. Your dinks'll do without babysittin' for that long."

The Frenchman pursed his lips. "He'll have to clear with the colonel," Herrold warned.

"No sweat," the driver insisted. "We'll snow him about all the local intelligence Jacques can give us. Come on, man; we'll brace him now." Crozier followed in Murray's forceful wake, an apprehensive frown still on his face.

"Say, where'd you get these?" Ginelli inquired, picking up a fat, red-nosed cartridge like those Herrold had just thumbed into his greasegun.

"The tracers?" the TC replied absently. "Oh, I found a case back in Di An. Pretty at night and, what the hell, they hit just as hard. But let's get crackin' on the co-ax."

Ginelli jumped to the ground. Herrold handed him a footlocker to serve as a table—the back deck of the zippo was too cluttered to strip the gun there—and the co-ax itself. In a few minutes they had reduced the weapon to components and begun cleaning them.

A shadow eased across the footlocker. Ginelli looked up, still holding the receiver he was brushing with a solvent-laden toothbrush. The interpreter, Hieu, had walked over from the TOC and was facing the grove. He seemed oblivious of the troopers beside him.

"Hey Hieu," the TC called. "Why the hell'd the colonel stick us here, d'ya know? We get in a firefight and these damn trees'll hide a division of VC."

Hieu looked around slowly. His features had neither the fragility of the pure Vietnamese nor the moon-like fullness of those with Chinese blood. His was a blocky face, set as ever in hard lines, mahogany in color. Hieu stepped up to the wall before answering, letting his hands run over the rough stone like two dried oak leaves.

"No time to make berm," he said at last, pointing to the bellowing Caterpillar climbing out of a trench near the TOC. The D-7A was digging in sleeping trailers for the brass rather than starting to throw up an earthen wall around the perimeter. "The wall here make us need ti-ti berm, I show colonel."

Herrold nodded. The stone enclosure was square, about a hundred yards to a side. Though only four feet high, the ancient wall was nearly as thick and would stop anything short of an eight-inch shell. But even with the work the wall would save the engineers on the west side, those trees sure played hell with the zones of fire. Seven of them looked to Herrold to be Philippine mahoganies; God knew what the monster in the middle was; a banyan, maybe, from the creviced trunk, but the bark didn't look like the banyans he'd seen before.

"Never saw trees that big before," the TC said aloud.

Hieu looked at him again, this time with a hint of expression on his face. "Yes," he stated. "Ti-ti left when French come, now only one." His fingers toyed with the faded duck of the ammo pouch clipped to his belt. Both soldiers thought the dark man was through speaking, but Hieu's tongue flicked between his thin lips again and he continued, "Maybe three, maybe two years only, there was other. Now only this. "The interpreter's voice became a hiss. "But beaucoup years before, everywhere was tree, everywhere was Meng!"

Boots scuffled in powdery dirt; Murray and the Frenchman were coming back from the TOC. Hieu lost interest in Herrold and vaulted the laterite wall gracefully. The driver and Crozier watched him stepping purposefully toward the center of the widely spaced grove as they halted beside the others.

"But who is that?" Crozier questioned sharply.

"Uh? That's Hieu, he's our interpreter," Murray grunted in surprise. "How come?"

The Frenchman frowned . . . "But he is Meng, surely? I did not know that any served in the army, even that the government tried to induct them anymore."

"Hell, I always heard he was from Saigon," Herrold answered. "He'd'a said if he was from here, wouldn't he?"

"What the hell's Hieu up to, anyhow?" Ginelli asked. He pointed toward the grove where the interpreter stood, facing the scarred trunk of the central tree. He couldn't see Hieu's hands from that angle, but the interpreter twitched in ritual motion beneath the fluid stripes of his fatigues.

Nobody spoke. Ginelli set one foot on the tread and lifted himself onto the flame track. Red and yellow smoke grenades hung by their safety rings inside the dome. Still lower swung a dusty pair of binoculars. Ginelli blew on the lenses before setting the glasses to his eyes and rotating the separate focus knobs. Hieu had knelt on the ground, but the trooper still could not tell what he was doing. Something else caught his eye.

"God damn," the plump newbie blurted. He leaned over the side of the track and thrust the glasses toward Herrold, busy putting the machine gun back together. "Hey Red, take a look at the tree trunk."

Murray, Crozier, and Ginelli himself waited expectantly while the TC refocused the binoculars. Magnified, the tree increased geometrically in hideousness. Its bark was pinkish and paper thin, smoother than that of a birch over most of the bole's surface. The gouged, wrinkled appearance of the trunk was due to the underlying wood, not any irregularity in the bark that covered it.

The tall catface in front of Hieu was the trunk's only true blemish. Where the tear had puckered together in a creased, blackened seam, ragged edges of bark fluttered in the breeze. The flaps were an unhealthy color, like skin peeling away from a bad burn. Hieu's squat body hid only a third of the scar; the upper portion towered gloomily above him.

"Well, it's not much to look at," Herrold said at last. "What's the deal?"

"Where's the bullet holes?" Ginelli demanded in triumph. "You put twenty, thirty shots in it, right? Where'd they go to?"

"Son of a bitch," the TC agreed, taking another look. The co-ax should have left a tight pattern of shattered wood above the ancient scar. Except for some brownish dimples in the bark, the tree was unmarked.

"I saw splinters fly," Murray remarked.

"Goddam wood must'a swelled right over 'em," Herrold suggested. "That's where I hit, all right."

"That is a very strange tree," Crozier said, speaking for the first time since his return. "There was another like it near Plantation Seven. It had almond trees around it too, though there was no wall. They call them god trees—the Viets do. The Mengs have their own word, but I do not know its meaning."

A Chinook swept over the firebase from the south, momentarily stifling conversation with the syncopated whopping of its twin rotors. It hovered just beyond the perimeter, then slowly settled in a circular dust cloud while its turbines whined enormously. Men ran to unload it.

"Chow pretty quick," Murray commented. It was nearing four o'clock. Ginelli looked away from the bird. "Don't seem right," he said. The other men looked blank. He tried to explain, "I mean, the Shithook there, jet engines and all, and that tree there being so old."

The driver snorted. "Hell, that's not old. Now back in California where they make those things"—his broad thumb indicated the banana-shaped helicopter—"they got redwoods that're really old. You don't think anything funny about that, do you?"

Ginelli gestured helplessly with his hands. Surprisingly it was Crozier, half-seated on the laterite wall, who came to his aid. "What makes you think this god tree is less old than a redwood, Joe?" he asked mildly.

Murray blinked. "Hell, redwoods're the oldest things there are. Alive, I mean."

The Frenchman laughed and repeated his deprecating shrug. "But trees are my business, you know? Now there is a pine tree in Arizona older than your California sequoias; but nobody knew it for a long time because there are not many of them and . . . nobody noticed. And here is a tree, an old one—but who knows? Maybe there are only two in the whole world left—and the other one, the one in the north, that perhaps is dead with my plantation."

"You never counted the rings or anything?" Herrold asked curiously. He had locked the barrel into the co-ax while the others were talking.

"No . . ." Crozier admitted. His tongue touched his lips as he glanced up at the god tree, wondering how much he should say. "No," he repeated, "but I only saw the tree once while I was at Plantation Seven. It stood in the jungle, more than a mile from the rubber, and the laborers did not care that anyone should go near it. There were Mengs there, too, I was told; but only a few and they hid in the woods. Bad blood between them and my laborers, no doubt."

"Well, hell, Jacques," Murray prompted. "When *did* you see it?" Crozier still hesitated. Suddenly realizing what the problem might be, the driver said, "Hell, don't worry about *our* stomachs, fer god's sake. Unless you're squeamish, turtle?" Ginelli blushed and shook his head. Laughing, Murray went on, "Anyhow, you grow up pretty quick after you get in the field—those that live to. Tell the story, Jacques."

Crozier sighed. The glade behind him was empty. Hieu had disappeared somewhere without being noticed. "Well," he began, "it has no importance, I am sure—all this happened a hundred miles away, as you know. But . . . .

"It was not long after Michelin sent me to Indochina, in 1953 that would be. I was told of the god tree as soon as I arrived at Plantation Seven, but that was all. One of my foremen had warned me not to wander that way and I assumed, because of the Viet Minh.

"Near midnight—this was before Dien Bien Phu, you will remember—there was heavy firing not far from the plantation. I called the district garrison since for a marvel the radio was working. But of course, no one came until it was light."

Herrold and Murray nodded together in agreement. Charging into a night ambush was no way to help your buddies, not in this country. Crozier cleared his throat and went on, "It was two companies of colonial paras that came, and the colonel from the fort himself. Nothing would help but that I should guide them to where the shooting had been. A platoon had set up an ambush, so they said, but it did not call in—even for fire support. When I radioed they assumed . . . ." He shrugged expressively.

"And that is what we found. All the men, all of them dead—unforgettably. They were in the grove of that god tree, on both sides of the trail to it. Perhaps the lieutenant had thought the Viets were rallying there. The paras were well-armed and did much shooting from the shells we found. But of enemies, there was no sign; and the paras had not been shot. They were torn, you know? Mutilated beyond what I could believe. But none had been shot, and their weapons lay with the bodies."

"That's crazy," Ginelli said, voicing everyone's thought. "Dinks would'a taken the guns."

Crozier shrugged. "The colonel said at last his men had been killed by some wild tribe, so savage they did not understand guns or would not use them. The Mengs, he meant. They were . . . wilder, perhaps, than the ones here but still. . . . I would not have thought there were enough of them to wipe out the platoon, waiting as it must have been."

"How *were* the men killed?" Herrold asked at last.

"Knives I think," the Frenchman replied, "short ones. Teeth I might have said; but there were really no signs that anything had fed on the bodies. Not the killers, that is. One man—"

He paused to swallow, continued, "One man I thought wore a long shirt of black. When I came closer, the flies left him. The skin was gone from his arms and chest. God alone knows what had killed him; but his face was the worst to see, and that was unmarked."

No one spoke for some time after that. Finally Murray said, "They oughta have chow on. Coming?"

Crozier spread his hands. "You are sure it is all right? I have no utensils."

"No sweat, there's paper plates. Rest'a you guys?"

"I'll be along," Herrold said. "Lemme remount the co-ax first."

"I'll do that," Ginelli offered. His face was saffron, bloodless beneath his tan. "Don't feel hungry tonight anyhow."

The track commander smiled. "You can give me a hand."

When the gun was bolted solidly back on its mount, Herrold laid a belt of ammunition on the loading tray and clicked the cover shut on it. "Ah," Ginelli mumbled, "ah, Red, don't you think it'd be a good idea to keep pressure up in the napalm tanks? I mean, there's a lotta Mengs around here and what Murray's buddy says . . . ."

"We'll make do with the co-ax," the TC replied, grinning. "You know how the couplings leak napalm with the pumps on."

"But if there's an attack?" Ginelli pleaded.

"Look, turtle," Herrold explained more sharply than before, "we're sitting on two hundred gallons of napalm. One spark in this track with the pressure up and we won't need no attack. OK?" Ginelli shrugged. "Well, come on to chow then," the TC suggested.

"Guess I'll stay."

"S'OK." Herrold slipped off the track and began walking toward the mess tent. He was singing softly, "We gotta get outa this place. . . ."

Crozier left just before the storm broke. The rain that had held off most of the day sheeted down at dusk. Lightning when it flared jumped from cloud-top to invisible cloud-top. It backlighted the sky.

The crewmen huddled under the inadequate tarpaulin, listening to the ragged static that was all Murray's transistor radio could pick up. Eventually he shut it off. Ginelli swore miserably. Slanting rain had started a worm of water at the head of his cot. It had finally squirmed all the way to the other end where he sat hunched against the chill wind. "Shouldn't somebody be on the track?"he asked. Regular guard shifts started at ten o'clock, but usually everybody was more or less alert until then.

"Go ahead, turtle, it's your bright idea," Murray said. Herrold frowned more seriously. "Yeah, if you're worried you might as well . . . Look, you get up in the dome now and Murray'll trade his first shift for your second. Right?"

"Sure," the driver agreed. "Maybe this damn rain'll stop by then."

Wearing his poncho over his flak jacket, Ginelli clambered up the bow slope of the zippo. The metal sides were too slimy with rain to mount that way. Except during lightning strokes, the darkness was opaque. When it flashed, the trees stabbed into the sudden bright skies and made Ginelli think about the napalm beneath from a different aspect. Christ, those trees were the tallest things for miles, and God knew the track wasn't very far away if lightning did hit one. God, they were tall.

And they were old. Ginelli recognized the feeling he'd had ever since the flame track had nosed up to the wall to face the grove: an aura of age. The same thing he'd sensed when he was a kid and saw the Grand Canyon. There was something so old it didn't give a damn about man or anything else.

Christ! No tree was as old as that; it must be their size that made him so jumpy. Dark as it was, the dinks could be crawling closer between lightning flashes too. At least the rain was slowing down.

The hatch cover was folded back into a clamshell seat

for the man on the dome. There was a fiber pillow to put over the steel, but it was soaked and Ginelli had set it on the back deck. For the first time he could remember, the thickness of his flak jacket felt good because the air was so cold. Water that slicked off the poncho or dripped from the useless flat muzzle of the flamethrower joined the drops spattering directly onto the zippo's deck. It pooled and flowed sluggishly toward the lowest point, the open driver's hatch.

The sky was starting to clear. An occasional spray fell, but the storm was over and a quarter moon shone when the broken clouds allowed it. Herrold stuck his head out from under the tarp. "How's it going, man?"

Ginelli stretched some of the stiffness out of his back and began stripping off the poncho. "OK, I guess. I could use some coffee."

"Yeah. Well, hang in there till midnight and get Murray up. We're gonna rack out now."

Shadows from the treetops pooled massively about the boles. Although there was enough breeze to make the branches tremble, the trunks themselves were solid as cliffs, as solid as Time. The scar at the base of the god tree was perversely moonlit. The whole grove looked sinister in the darkness, but the scar itself was something more.

Only the half-hour routine of perimeter check kept Ginelli awake. Voices crackled around Headquarters Troop's sector until Ginelli could repeat, "Seven zero, report negative," for the last time and thankfully take off the commo helmet. His boots squelched as he dropped beside the cot where Murray snored softly, wrapped in the mottled green-brown nylon of his poncho liner. Ginelli shook him.

"Uh!" the driver grunted as he snapped awake. "Oh, right; lemme get my boots on."

One of the few clouds remaining drifted over the moon. As Murray stood upright, Ginelli thought movement flickered on the dark stone of the wall. "Hey!" the driver whispered. "What's Hieu doing out there?"

Ginelli peered into the grove without being able to see anything but the trees. "That was him goin' over the wall," Murray insisted. He held his M16 with the bolt back, ready to chamber a round if the receiver was jarred. "Look, I'm gonna check where he's going."

"Jeez, somebody'll see you and cut loose," Ginelli protested. "You can't go out there!"

Murray shook his head decisively. "Naw, it'll be OK," he said as he slipped over the wall.

"Crazy," Ginelli muttered. And it suddenly struck him that a man who volunteered for three extra years of combat probably *wasn't* quite normal in the back-home sense. Licking his lips, he waited tensely in the darkness. The air had grown warmer since the rain stopped, but the plump newbie found himself shivering.

A bird fluttered among the branches of the nearest mahogany. You didn't seem to see many birds in country, not like you did back in the World. Ginelli craned his neck to get a better view, but the irregular moonlight passed only the impression of wings a drab color.

Nothing else moved within the grove. Ginelli swore miserably and shook Herrold awake. The track commander slept with his flak jacket for a pillow and, despite his attitude of nonchalance, the clumsy greasegun lay beside him on the cot. His fingers curled around its pistolgrip as he awakened.

"Oh, for god's sake," he muttered when Ginelli blurted out the story. Herrold had kept his boots on, only the tops unlaced, and he quickly whipped the ties tight around his shins. "Christ, ten minutes ago?"

"Well, should I call in?" Ginelli suggested uncertainly.

"Hell," Herrold muttered, "no, I better go tell the ole man. You get back in the dome and wait for me." He hefted his submachine gun by the receiver.

Ginelli started to climb onto the track. Turning, he said, "Hey, man." Herrold paused. "Don't be too long, huh?"

"Yeah." The track commander trudged off toward the unlighted HQ tent. A bird, maybe a large bat from its erratic flight, passed over Ginelli's head at treetop level. He raised the loading cover of the co-ax to recheck the position of the linked belt of ammunition.

There was a light in the grove.

It was neither manmade nor the moon's reflection, and at first it was almost too faint to have a source at all. Ginelli gaped frozen at the huge god tree. The glow resolved into a viridescent line down the center of the scar, a strip of brightness that widened perceptibly as the edges of the cicatrix drew back. The interior of the tree seemed hollow, lined with self-shining greenness to which forms clung. As Ginelli watched, a handful of the creatures lurched from the inner wall and fluttered out through the dilated scar.

Someone screamed within the laager. Ginelli whirled around. The tactical operations center was green and two-dimensional where the chill glare licked it. A man tore through the canvas passage linking the vehicles, howling and clutching at the back of his neck until he fell. A dark shape flapped away from him. The remaining blotches clinging to the green of the tree flickered outward and the scar began to close.

The cal fifty in the assault vehicle to the right suddenly began blasting tracers point blank into the shrinking green blaze. Heavy bullets that could smash through half an inch of steel ripped across the tree. It was like stabbing a sponge with ice picks. Something dropped into the ACAV's cupola from above. The shots stopped and the gunner began to bellow hoarsely.

Ginelli swiveled his co-ax onto the tree and clamped down on its underslung trigger. Nothing happened; in his panic he had forgotten to charge the gun. Sparkling muzzle flashes were erupting all across the laager. Near the TOC a man fired his M16 at a crazy angle, trying to drop one of the flying shapes. Another spiraled down behind him of its own deadly accord. His rifle continued to fire as he collapsed on top of it. It sent a last random bullet to spall a flake of aluminum from the flame track's side, a foot beneath Ginelli's exposed head.

A soldier in silhouette against the green light lunged toward the god tree's slitted portal and emptied his rifle point blank. The knife in his hand glowed green as he chopped it up and down into the edge of the scar, trying to widen the gap. "Murray!" Ginelli called. He jerked back his machine-gun's operating rod but did not shoot. He could hear Murray screaming obscenities made staccato by choppy bursts of automatic fire from behind him.

Ginelli turned his head without conscious warning. He had only enough time to drop down into the compartment as the thing swooped. Its vans, stretched batlike between arm and leg, had already slammed it upright in braking for the kill. The green glare threw its features in perfect relief against the chaos of the firebase: a body twenty inches long, deep-torsoed like a mummified pigmy; weasel teeth, slender cones perfectly formed for slaughter; a face that could have been human save for its size and the streaks of black blood that disfigured it. Tree light flashed a shadow across the hatch as the chittering creature flapped toward other prey for the moment.

Ginelli straightened slowly, peered out of the dome. There was a coldness in his spine; his whole lower body felt as though it belonged to someone else. He knew it wasn't any use, even for himself, to slam the dome hatch over his head and hope to wait the nightmare out. The driver's compartment was open; there was plenty of room between the seat and the engine firewall beside it for the killers to crawl through.

Taking a deep breath, Ginelli leaped out of the hatch. He ignored the co-ax. A shuffling step forward in a low crouch and he slid feet first through the driver's hatch. Throttle forward, both clutch levers at neutral. The starter motor whined for an instant; then the six-cylinder diesel caught, staggered, and boomed into life. An imbalance somewhere in the engine made the whole vehicle tremble.

Murray was still gouging at the base of the scar, face twisted in maniacal savagery. Chips flew every time the blade struck, letting more of the interior glare spill out. Ginelli throttled back, nerving himself to move.

"Murray!" he shouted again over the lessened throb of the diesel. "Get away—dammit, get away!"

A figure oozed out of the shadows and gripped Murray by the shoulder. Perhaps the driver screamed before he recognized Hieu; if so, Ginelli's own cry masked the sound. The Meng spoke, his face distorted with triumph. As the incredulous driver stared, Hieu shouted a few syllables at the god tree in a throaty language far different from the nasal trills of Vietnamese.

The tree opened again. The edges of the scar crumpled sideways, exposing fully the green-lit interior and what stood in it now. Murray whipped around, his blade raised to slash. An arm gripped his, held the knife motionless. The thing was as tall as the opening it stood in, bipedal but utterly inhuman.

Its face was a mirror image of Hieu's own.

Murray flung himself back, but another pallid, boneless arm encircled him and drew him into the tree. His scream was momentary, cut off when the green opening squeezed almost shut behind him and what Hieu had summoned.

The hooked moon was out again. Hieu turned and began striding toward the shattered laager. His single ammo pouch flopped open; the crude necklace around his neck was of human fingertips, dried and strung on a twist of cambium. Behind him a score of other human-appearing figures slunk out of the grove, every face identical.

Ginelli gathered his feet under him on the seat, then sprang back on top of the track. One of the winged shapes had been waiting for him, called by the mutter of the engine. It darted in from the front, banking easily around Ginelli's out-thrust arm. Ginelli tripped on the flamethrower's broad tube, fell forward bruisingly. Clawed fingers drew four bloody tracks across his forehead as the flyer missed its aim. It swept back purposefully.

Ginelli jumped into the dome hatch and snatched at the clamshell cover to close it. As the steel lid swung to, the winged man's full weight bounced it back on its hinges ringingly. Jagged teeth raked the soldier's bare right arm, making him scream in frenzy. He yanked at the hatch cover with mad strength. There was no clang as the hatch shut, but something crackled between the edges of armor plate. The brief cry of agony was higher pitched than a man's. Outside, the scar began to dilate again.

Ginelli gripped the valve and hissed with pain. Shock had numbed his right arm only momentarily. Left-handed he opened the feeds. His fingers found a switch, flicked it up, and the pump began throbbing behind him. His whole body shuddered as he swung the dome through a short arc so that the tree's blazing scar was centered in the periscope. The universal joint of the fat napalm hose creaked in protest at being moved and a drop of thickened gasoline spattered stickily on Ginelli's flak jacket.

With a cry of horrified understanding, Hieu leaped onto the stone wall between Ginelli and the tree. "You must—" was all the Meng could say before the jet of napalm caught him squarely in the chest and flung him back into the enclosure. There was no flame. The igniter had not fired.

Mumbling half-remembered fragments of a Latin prayer, Ginelli triggered the weapon again. Napalm spurted against the tree in an unobstructed black arch. The igniter banged in mid-shot and the darkness boomed into a hellish red glare. The tree keened as the flame rod's giant fist smashed against it. Its outer bark shriveled and the deep, bloody surge of napalm smothered every other color. Ginelli's fiery scythe roared as he slashed it up and down the trunk. Wood began to crackle like gunfire, exploding and hurling back geysers of sparks. A puff of dry heat roiled toward the laager in the turbulent air. It was heavy with the stench of burning flesh.

A series of swift thuds warned Ginelli of flyers landing on the zippo's deck; teeth clicked on armor. Something rustled from the driver's compartment. The trooper used his stiffening right hand to switch on the interior lights. The yellow bulbs glinted from close-set eyes peering over the driver's seat. Ginelli kicked. Instead of crunching under his boot, the face gave with a terrible resiliency and the winged man continued to squirm into the TC's compartment. A sparkling chain of eyes flashed behind the first pair. The whole swarm of killers was crowding into the track.

Ginelli's only weapon was the flame itself. Instinctively he swung the nozzle to the left and depressed it, trying to hose fire into the forward hatch of his own vehicle. Instead, the frozen coupling parted. Napalm gouted from the line. The flame died with a serpentine lurch, leaving the god tree alone as a lance of fire. The track was flooding with the gummy fluid; it clung to Ginelli's chest and flak jacket before rolling off in sluggish gobbets.

Bloody faces washed black with smears of napalm, the winged men struggled toward Ginelli implacably. His mind barely functional, the soldier threw open the hatch and staggered onto the zippo's deck. Unseen, one flyer still hung in the air. It struck him in the middle of the back and catapulted him off the vehicle. Ginelli somersaulted across the dusty, flame-lit cauldron. The napalm's gluey tenacity fixed the creature firmly against Ginelli's flak jacket; its hooked claws locked into the fabric while its teeth tore his scalp.

The huge torch of the god tree crashed inward toward the laager. A flaming branch snapped with the impact and bounded high in the air before plunging down on the napalm-filled flame track. Ginelli staggered to his feet, tried to run. The zippo exploded with a hollow boom and a mushroom of flame, knocking him down again without dislodging the vengeful horror on his back.

With the last of his strength, Ginelli ripped off the unfastened flak jacket and hurled it into the air. For one glistening instant he thought the napalm-soaked nylon would land short of the pool of fire surrounding the flame track. His uncoordinated throw was high and the winged killer had time to pull one van loose as it pinwheeled. It struck the ground that way, mired by the incendiary that bloomed to consume it.

Ginelli lay on his back, no longer able to move. A shadow humped over the top of the wall: Hieu, moving very stiffly. His right hand held a cane spear. The Meng was withered like a violet whose roots had been chopped away, but he was not dead.

"You kill all, you . . . animals," he said. His voice was thick and half-choked by the napalm that had hosed him. He balanced on the wall, black against the burning wreckage of the god tree. "All . . ." he repeated, raising the spear. "Cut . . . poison . . . burn. But you—"

Herrold's greasegun slammed beside Ginelli, its

muzzle blast deafening even against the background roar of the flames. A solid bar of tracers stitched redly across the Meng's chest and slapped him off the wall as a screaming ball of fire.

It was still four hours to dawn, Ginelli thought as he drifted into unconsciousness; but until then the flames would give enough light.

BEST OF LUCK

As I mentioned in discussing "Firefight," in 1973 Marvel Comics started a digest fantasy/horror magazine titled The Haunt of Horror. When they killed Haunt as a digest, they bruited the possibility of reviving it as a B&W horror comic with two pages of prose fiction. (I believe the purpose of the prose was to meet mailing criteria for a reduced postage rate.)

Two comic pages amounted to 1600 to 1800 words. I sat down to write a story which would fit that length. The result was "Best of Luck," another standard horror story using Viet Nam for its setting (as I'd done with "Arclight" and "Contact!").

The length was a problem. My first version of the story came to 2,000 words, short even for me but too long for the space. Even at the start of my career I understood something many writers fail to grasp: if there's a fixed amount of room available, turning in a story that is the fixed amount plus more is a sure route to rejection. I therefore cut out 200 words that really shouldn't have gone. I was never *satisfied with the story after that final edit.*

And Haunt *wasn't revived in any format, so it'd all been wasted effort anyway. The story dropped completely out of my mind.*

In 1977 Gerry Page, editor of The Year's Best Horror Stories *for DAW Books, changed the previous reprint-only format (to which Karl Wagner reverted when he took over from Gerry in a few years). He asked me if I had a new story to submit; I told him I didn't.*

Whereupon Kirby sold Gerry "Best of Luck." As I said, I'd forgotten about it.

Frankly, I wasn't thrilled to sell a story which I felt I'd crippled in the editing, but shortly afterward I got another surprise: NBC developed a horror anthology show, whose producers optioned "Best of Luck." Not only that, they later renewed the option. For quite a long time, "Best of Luck" was my most profitable story in total terms, let alone on a per-word basis.

I still wish I hadn't taken out that last 200 words.

✢ ✢ ✢

A Russian-designed .51 caliber machine gun fires bullets the size of a woman's thumb. When a man catches a pair of those in his chest and throat the way Capt. Warden's radioman did, his luck has run out. A gout of blood sprayed back over Curtis, next man in the column. He glimpsed open air through the RTO's middle: the hole plowed through the flailing body would have held his fist.

But there was no time to worry about the dead, no time to do anything but dive out of the line of fire. Capt. Warden's feral leap had carried him in the opposite direction, out of Curtis's sight into the gloom of the rubber. Muzzle flashes flickered over the silver tree-trunks as the bunkered machine guns tore up Dog Company.

Curtis's lucky piece bit him through the shirt fabric as he slammed into the smooth earth. The only cover in the ordered plantation came from the trees themselves, and their precise arrangement left three aisles open to any hiding place. The heavy guns ripped through the darkness in short bursts from several locations; there was no way to be safe, nor even to tell from where death would strike.

Curtis had jerked back the cocking piece of his M16, but he had no target. Blind firing would only call down the attentions of the Communist gunners. He felt as naked as the lead in a Juarez floor show, terribly aware of what the big bullets would do if they hit him. He had picked up the lucky Maria Theresa dollar in Taiwan, half as a joke, half in unstated remembrance of men who had been saved when a coin or a Bible turned an enemy slug. But no coin was going to deflect a .51 cal from the straight line it would blast through him.

Red-orange light bloomed a hundred yards to Curtiss' left as a gun opened up, stuttering a sheaf of lead through the trees. Curtis marked the spot. Stomach tight with fear, he swung his clumsy rifle toward the target and squeezed off a burst.

The return fire was instantaneous and from a gun to the right, unnoticed until that moment. The tree Curtis crouched beside exploded into splinters across the base, stunning impacts that the soldier felt rather than heard. He dug his fingers into the dirt, trying to drag himself still lower and screaming mentally at the pressure of the coin which kept him that much closer to the crashing bullets. The rubber tree was sagging, its twelve-inch bole sawn through by the fire, but nothing mattered to Curtis except the raving death a bullet's width above his head.

The firing stopped. Curtis clenched his fists, raised his head a fraction from the ground. A single, spiteful round banged from the first bunker. The bullet ticked the rim of Curtis's helmet, missing his flesh but snapping his head back with the force of a thrown anvil. He was out cold when the tree toppled slowly across his boots.

There were whispers in the darkness, but all he could see were blue and amber streaks on the inside of his mind. He tried to move, then gasped in agony as the pinioning mass shifted against his twisted ankles.

There were whispers in the darkness, and Curtis could guess what they were. Dog Company had pulled back. Now the VC were slipping through the trees, stripping the dead of their weapons and cutting the throats of the wounded. Wherever Curtis's rifle had been flung, it was beyond reach of his desperate fingers.

Something slurped richly near Curtis on his right. He turned his face toward the sound, but its origin lurked in the palpable blackness. There was a slushy, ripping noise from the same direction, settling immediately into a rhythmic gulping. Curtis squinted uselessly. The moon was full, but the clouds were as solid as steel curtains.

Two Vietnamese were approaching from his left side.

The scuff of their tire-soled sandals paused momentarily in a liquid trill of speech, then resumed. A flashlight played over the ground, its narrow beam passing just short of Curtis's left hand. The gulping noise stopped.

"Ong vo?" whispered one of the VC, and the light flashed again. There was a snarl and a scream and the instant red burst of an AK-47 blazing like a flare. The radioman's body had been torn open. Gobbets of lung and entrails, dropped by the feasting thing, were scattered about the corpse. But Curtis's real terror was at what the muzzle flash caught in midleap—teeth glinting white against bloody crimson, the mask of a yellow-eyed beast more savage than a nightmare and utterly undeterred by the bullets punching across it. And the torso beneath the face was dressed in American jungle fatigues.

"Glad to have you back, Curtis," Capt. Warden said. "We're way under strength, and replacements haven't been coming in fast enough. Better get your gear together now, because at 1900 hours the company's heading out on a night patrol and I want every man along."

Curtis shifted uneasily, transfixed by the saffron sclera of the captain's eyes. The driver who had picked him up at the chopper pad had filled Curtis in on what had gone on during his eight weeks in the hospital. Seventeen men had died in the first ambush. The condition of the radioman's body was blamed on the VC, of course; but that itself had contributed to rotted morale, men screaming in their sleep or squirting nervous shots off into the shadows. A month later, Warden had led another sweep. The lithe, athletic captain should have been a popular officer for his obvious willingness to share the dangers of his command; but when his second major operation ended in another disaster of bunkers and spider holes, the only emotion Dog Company could find for him was hatred. Everybody knew this area of operations was thick with VC and that it was Dog Company's business to find them. But however successful the operations were from the division commander's standpoint—the follow-ups had netted tons of equipment and abandoned munitions—Warden's men knew that they had taken it on the chin twice in a row.

It hadn't helped that the body of Lt. Schaden, killed at the captain's side in the first exchange of fire, had been recovered the next day in eerily mutilated condition. It looked, the driver whispered, as though it had been gnawed on by something.

They moved out in the brief dusk, nervous squads shrunk to the size of fire teams under the poundings they had taken. The remainder of the battalion watched Dog's departure in murmuring cliques. Curtis knew they were making bets on how many of the patrol wouldn't walk back this time. Well, a lot of people in Dog itself were wondering the same.

The company squirmed away from the base, avoiding known trails. Capt. Warden had a destination, though; Curtis, again marching just behind the command group, could see the captain using a penlight to check compass and map at each of their frequent halts. The light was scarcely necessary. The mid-afternoon downpour had washed clean the sky for the full moon to blaze in. It made for easier movement through the tangles of trees and vines, but it would light up the GIs like ducks in a shooting gallery if they blundered into another VC bunker complex.

The trade dollar in Curtis's pocket flopped painfully against him. The bruise it had given him during the ambush still throbbed. It was starting to hurt more than his ankles did, but nothing would have convinced him to leave it in his locker now. He'd gotten back the last time, hadn't he? Despite the murderous crossfire, the tree, and the . . . other. Curtis gripped his sweaty M16 tighter. Maybe it hadn't been Maria Theresa's chop-scarred face that got him through, but he wasn't missing any bets.

Because every step he took into the jungle deepened his gut-wrenching certainty that Dog Company was about to catch it again.

The captain grunted a brief order into the phone flexed to his RTO. The jungle whispered "halt" from each of the platoon leaders. Warden's face was in a patch of moonlight. His left hand cradled the compass, but he paid it no attention. Instead his lean, dominant nose lifted and visibly snuffled the still air. With a nod and a secret smile that Curtis shivered to see, the captain spoke again into the radio to move the company out.

Three minutes later, the first blast of shots raked through them.

The bullet hit the breech of Curtis's rifle instead of simply disemboweling him. The dented barrel cracked down across both of his thighs with sledge-hammer force. His left thumb was dislocated, though his right hand, out of the path in which the .51 cal had snatched the rifle, only tingled. Curtis lay on his back amazed, listening to the *thump-crack* of gunfire and bullets passing overhead. He was not even screaming: the pain was yet to come.

An American machine gun ripped a long red streak to within six inches of Curtis's head, no less potentially deadly for not being aimed at him. The wounded soldier fumbled open his breast pocket and clutched at the lucky piece. It was the only action to which he could force his punished body. The moon glared grimly down.

Something moved near Curtis. Capt. Warden, bareheaded, was snaking across the jungle floor toward him. Warden grinned. His face slumped suddenly like lead in a mold, shaping itself into a ghastly new form that Curtis had seen once before. The Warden-thing's fangs shone as it poised, then leaped—straight into a stream of Communist fire.

A two-ounce bullet meat-axed through the thing's chest back to front, slapping it against a tree. Curtis giggled in relief before he realized that the creature was rising to its knees. Fluid shock had blasted a great crater in the flesh over its breastbone, and the lower half of its face was coated with blood gulped out of its own lungs. The eyes were bright yellow and horribly alive, and as Curtis stared in fascination, the gaping wound began to close. The thing took a step toward the helpless soldier, a triumphant grimace sweeping over its distorted features.

Without conscious direction, Curtis's thumb spun the silver dollar toward the advancing creature. The half-healed wound-lips in the thing's chest seemed to suck the coin in. The scream that followed was that of an animal spindled on white-hot wire, but it ended quickly in a gurgle as dissolution set in.

✣ ✣ ✣

The stretcher team brought Curtis out in the morning. His right hand had been dipped into the pool of foulness soaking the ground near him, and the doctors could not unclench the fist from the object it was frozen on until after the morphine had taken hold.

ARCLIGHT

My unit was the 11th Cav—the Blackhorse Regiment. We had six-man intelligence teams in the field at battalion level (a uniquely low level for US forces in Nam). After a couple weeks at the regimental base in Di An, I requested transfer to one of the field units. I was assigned to Second Squadron, which'd just captured Snuol, Cambodia.

My first night in Cambodia coincided with an Arclight, a code-named operation which I now know should be written Arc Light. We didn't know how to write it at the time, not down where I was. In an Arc Light, B-52 bombers modified to carry the maximum number of conventional weapons (there's nothing like them in the Air Force inventory today, a matter which commanders noted with regret during the Gulf War) flew three abreast, raining 750-pound bombs on the jungle below. Depending on the number of planes in line behind the leaders, the swathe of utter destruction continued for miles or even many miles.

I've never seen anything like it in my life. (OK,

there are a number of other Viet Nam experiences I could say that about; but it's no less true.) The bombs were landing ten miles south of us, but you couldn't talk over the sound of the continuous explosions. The ground quivered, the whole horizon lit white, and it just kept going on and on and on.

I got back to the World and resumed writing. I wanted to do sword and sorcery, but as I've mentioned there wasn't a market for the genre in the professional magazines. My friends Manly and Karl suggested during one of our family get-togethers that I try using my Viet Nam experiences in a story instead of setting everything in the distant past.

Does that seem a pretty obvious notion? It certainly does to me—now. At the time . . . I dunno. I immediately followed my friends' suggestion, but I was aware even then that there was a lot of stuff from which I was trying to distance myself.

In fact, writing about Nam as fiction is the best therapy I could've found for the things that ailed me. Having said that, it was along the lines of a live-culture inoculation: the result can be expected to be very good, but the possibility of a disastrous outbreak as a direct result of the process was a real one.

I wrote "Arclight" and sent it to F&SF. Mr. Ferman, who'd rejected my sword and sorcery stories in a friendly fashion, bought this one for a little under two cents per word.

An acquaintance commented that the next story

*I wrote with a Southeast Asian setting ("Contact!")
read as though I thought everybody had been to
Nam. The objection is equally valid for "Arclight."
There's a lot of inadequately explained jargon and a
lot of hardware that's unfamiliar to somebody who
hadn't been immersed in it.*

*The problem is more basic than a failure of craft
(though it's certainly bad craftsmanship on my
part): it was symptomatic of a failure to grasp the
boundaries of civilian life. Most readers were
profoundly ignorant of matters that had been of
constant, life or death, concern to me; and I simply
didn't understand that.*

*This was my first sale to (and later became my
first appearance in) a professional SF magazine.*

✤ ✤ ✤

Grunting and snarling, the nineteen tracked vehicles
of G Troop struggled into a night defensive position.
From the road watched a family of impassive Cambodians.
The track commander of the nearest vehicle, three-six,
waved at them as his ACAV shuddered through a thirty-
degree arc and prepared to back into its position in the
laager. Red paint marked the track's flat aluminum sides
with the name "Horny Horse" and a graphic parody of the
regiment's stallion insignia. None of the stolid, flat-faced
onlookers gave any sign of interest, even when the ACAV
lurched sideways and began to tilt. The TC leaned out of
his cupola in the middle, vainly trying to see what was the
matter. Jones, the left gunner, looked out over the hole
opening under the tread and waved frantically, trying to
shout over the engine noise. The TC nodded and snapped

to the driver through his intercom, "Whip 'er right and gun 'er, Jody, we're falling into a goddamn bunker!"

The diesel bellowed as Jody let the left clutch full out and tramped on the foot feed. The ACAV slewed level again with the left tread spitting mangled vegetation behind it. "Cut the engine," the TC ordered, and in the sudden silence he shouted to the command track in the center of the rough circle of vehicles, "Captain Fuller! We're on a bunker complex!"

The shirtless, sweating officer dropped the can of beer he was starting to open and grabbed his dirty M16. No matter what you did, clean your rifle daily and keep it in a case, the choking dust kicked up by the tracks inevitably crept into it at the end of a day's move. And if they really were on a bunker complex, the move wasn't over yet. Everybody knew what had happened to E Troop last November when they laagered on an unsuspected complex and a dozen sappers had crept out inside the NDP that night.

The hole, an irregular oval perhaps a foot along the greater axis, looked uncompromisingly black against the red laterite of the bare ground. Worse, the tilted edge of a slab showed clearly at the back, proving the cavity below was artificial. Everybody knew the dinks had been building bunkers here in the Parrot's Beak for twenty years and more, but the captain had never seen a stone one before.

"Want me to frag it?" someone said. It was the redheaded TC of the track that turned the bunker up, Fuller saw. Casely, his name was. He held his unauthorized .45 in one hand, cocked, and a pair of smooth-hulled fragmentation grenades in the other.

"Gimme one of them," growled Sergeant Peacock, reaching his huge black arm toward the younger soldier. Casely handed one of the grenades to the field first and watched him expertly mold a pound and a quarter-stick of plastic explosive around it. The white explosive encased all the metal except the handle and the safety pin in a lumpy cocoon. "We'll try a bunker buster first to see if anybody's home," the sergeant said with satisfaction. "Better clear back." He pulled the pin.

All around the laager, men were watching what was going on beside three-six. Nobody was keeping a lookout into the jungle; but, then, the dinks didn't hit armored units in the daytime. Besides, the dozen Cambodians were still squatting in the road. Intelligence might be wrong, but the locals always knew when there was going to be trouble.

Peacock sidled closer to the hole, hunching down a little at the thought that a flat brown face might pop up out of it at the last instant, eyes glaring at him behind the sights of an AK. He gagged and blinked, then tossed the bomb the last yard with a convulsive gesture and darted back away.

"Jesus H. Christ!" he wheezed. "Jesus H. Christ! That stinks down there like nothing on earth!"

"How's that?" Fuller snapped, nervous about anything unusual. The bunker buster went off, a hollow boom like a cherry bomb in a garbage can, only a thousand times as loud. Dirt and whizzing fragments of stone mushroomed upward, drifting mostly toward three-six and showering it for thirty seconds. The crew covered their eyes and hunched their steel pots close to their shoulders.

Captain Fuller, kneeling beside the track under the

unexpected rain of dirt, suddenly choked and jumped to his feet swearing. "My God," he roared, "which way's the wind blowing?" The charnel reek that oozed out of the newly opened bunker was strong and indescribably foul. The troop had found NVA buried in the jungle for months in the damp warmth, found them and dug them up to search for papers; that stench had been nothing to this one.

"Must'a been a hospital," Sergeant Peacock suggested as he edged upwind of the pit. He was covering his nose with an olive-drab handkerchief. "Jesus," he repeated, "I never smelled anything like that."

Three-six's diesel ripped back into life and brought the track upwind of the hole in a wide circle. Ten yards away, its nose pointing out toward the road beside the next vehicle over, it halted and Casely descended again. He still held his pistol. "God, look at that," he said.

When the bunker buster had blown, it lifted the roof off a narrow crypt some ten feet long and half that wide. It could not have been more than inches below the surface of the soil at any point. Relatively little of the rubble kicked up by the explosion had fallen back into the cavity, leaving it open to the eyes of the men on its edge. Most of the litter on the floor of the crypt was of bones. All were dry, and many had been smashed to powder by the blast. One skull, whole by some mischance, goggled toward the north wall.

The idol glared back at it. It was about six feet high, cut out of streaky soapstone instead of the omnipresent laterite whose pocked roughness forms the walls and ornamentation of most Cambodian temples, even those of Angkor Wat. Though it stood on two legs, there was nothing manlike about the creature. A fanged jaw twisted into a vicious grimace, leering out over the beast's potbelly. One clawed arm rested on the paunch; the other, apparently the only casualty of the explosion, had been broken off at the shoulder and lay half-covered by the gravel on the floor. The gray-on-black marking of the stone blended to give the image a lifelikeness it should not have had; Fuller blinked, half-expecting blood to spurt from the severed arm. Over all lay the miasma of decay, slowly diffusing on the hot breeze.

Fuller hesitated a moment, peering over the edge. "Anybody see a door to this place?" he asked. None of the group slowly gathering on the edge of the crypt answered. The whole room had been faced with thin slabs of the same stone that formed the idol. Line after line of squiggly, decorative Cambodian writing covered their surface unintelligibly. Fragments from the roof of the crypt showed similar markings.

"That ain't no hospital," Sergeant Peacock asserted needlessly, wiping his palms on the seat of his fatigues. The light-green material darkened with sweat.

Jody Bredt, the undersized Private first Class who drove three-six, sauntered over with his gas mask in his hand. He took the war a little more seriously than most of the rest of the troop and kept his mask in the hatch with him instead of being buried in the bottom of his duffle bag. "Want me to take a look down there, Captain Fuller?" he asked importantly.

"Why don't you just put in for official tunnel rat?" his TC gibed, but the officer nodded appreciatively. "Yeah, go ahead. Be careful, for God's sake, but I think this may just have been an old temple."

Jody slipped his mask on, virtually blinding himself even in the bright sunlight. The lenses were dusty and scratched from knocking around in the track for months. A preliminary sniff had convinced him that the stench had almost dissipated, but he couldn't take the mask off now that he'd made such a production of it. Gingerly, he lowered himself over the edge. Sergeant Peacock knelt down to hold his wrist in case he slipped; there might be a mine under any of the delicately carven slabs. The gooks were clever about that sort of thing. Still, any mines down there should have gone off when the bunker buster did. He let his feet touch the ground with a little more confidence and ran his hand over the wall. "I don't see any swinging doors or anything," he reported. "Maybe they got in through the roof, huh?"

"Hell, we'll never know that now," Casely snorted. "Hey, Captain, I think the smell is pretty well gone. Let me go down there."

"Why?" Fuller grunted. "Want to take that statue back with you on R&R?"

The TC grinned. The captain knew his men pretty well. "Naw, too big. I did think one of them skulls would make kind of a nice souvenir if they don't check my hold baggage too close, though."

Fuller swore and laughed. "OK," he said, squatting down preparatory to jumping in himself, "go ahead, you found the place. But I want the rest of you guys back on your tracks. We're going to be leaving here in five, as soon as I get a look around myself."

"Hey, Red, throw me something," one of the bystanders begged Casely, but the captain waved him away peremptorily. "Go on, goddammit, I don't want all of you hanging around here in case the dinks are out there." He hopped down into the cavity, joining Casely and the driver whose mask hung from his hand again. The air was thick but had lost the earlier noisomeness.

Casely picked up the skull he wanted for a trophy with a finger through each of the eye-sockets. When he had lifted it waist high, the bone crumbled to powder. What was left of the skull shattered unrecognizably when it hit the floor. "Goddamn," the TC swore, kicking angrily at the heap of dust, "why didn't it do that when the frag went off if it had to do it at all? Now I got my hopes up and look what happens!"

Peacock, squatting like a black Buddha on the rim of the crypt, chuckled deep in his chest. "Why, the next dink we get, you just cut his head off and dry it out. How that be, Red? Get you a nice fresh head to take back to your wife."

Casely swore again. The captain was handling another of the bones. This one was a femur, sheared off some inches short of the knee joint. If the frag hadn't done it, the damage dated from the unguessable past. The bone was almost as dry and fragile as the skull that had powdered in Casely's hands. He tossed it up to the field first, shaking his head in puzzlement. "How old do you guess that is, Sarge?" he asked. "I don't think I ever saw anything that used up before."

"This old guy is still in fine shape," Jody put in, rapping the brutal idol on the nose with his gas mask. "Frag didn't hurt him hardly at all, did it?" He kicked at the broken limb lying near the statue. The others, more or less consciously, had been avoiding the idol with their eyes. If you looked too closely, the crude swirls on the thing that were supposed to represent hair seemed to move by themselves. Probably the grain of the stone.

"Goddamn," Fuller said. It was not entirely blasphemous the way he said it. "Will you look at that."

The driver's foot had shaken the broken arm, paw, whatever, out of the pile of rubble in which it lay. Previously unseen was the figure of the man—it was clearly a man—held in the monster's clawed grip. The man had been sculpted only a fraction of the size of the thing holding him, some thirty inches or so from foot to where the head would have been if it hadn't been broken off by the blast. Fuller looked more closely. No, the figure had been carved that way originally, limp and headless in the idol's claws. The beast-god's leering mouth seemed to take a further, even more unpleasant dimension. Fuller stretched his arm up to Sergeant Peacock. "Sarge, give me a hand. Come on, you two, we're getting out of here."

"Think the gooks been using this as a hospital?" Jody asked, scrambling up to the surface with a boost from Casely. Jody always missed the last word and didn't have quite the intelligence to supply it himself.

"I don't know what they're doing," Fuller grunted. "If there's one bunker around here, there could be a hundred though, and I'm not sitting around to find out. I think I'll ask for a B-52 strike here. God knows, they're flattening enough empty jungle they ought to be willing to hit a spot like this."

Casely picked up a bit of the crypt's roof and tossed it in his hand. "Hey," he said, "maybe some of those locals speak English. I'd like to know what these squiggles are saying."

"You're going to have to find them to ask," Peacock said with a shrug. "They must'a took off when the bunker buster went off."

"Umm," the redhead grunted. "Well, it makes a souvenir anyway." Around the circle of vehicles engines were starting up. One of the gunners signaled Casely with the radio helmet in his hand. "Come on, Red," he shouted, "we're moving out." Casely nodded and began jogging toward the track. He wasn't sorry to be leaving this place either. Not sorry at all.

Three-six had a full crew of four men, and so they split the guard into two-hour shifts from 2200 to 0600. The new location was a dead ringer for the one they'd just left, low jungle approaching the graveled length of Highway 13, but at least there didn't seem to be any bunkers. Or idols. Casely had last guard, a concession to his rank that meant he could get six hours sleep uninterrupted, but he couldn't seem to drop off soundly. The air was cool and misty, cloaking the tracks so closely that the Sheridan to the left in the laager was almost invisible. A good night for sappers. Casely could almost feel them creeping closer.

He glanced at his watch. Three o'clock, Jody's shift. The TC was stretched out on the closed cargo hatch of the ACAV while the two gunners slept inside on mattresses laid over the ranked ammo boxes. He should have been able to see Jody sitting in the cupola, staring out into the jungle. At first glance the driver wasn't there, and Casely sat up to make sure the little guy hadn't gone and done something unusually stupid. At the first sound of movement from behind him Jody gasped and straightened up from where he was hunched over the cupola's fifty-caliber machine gun. "Jeez, Red, it's you. Jeez, you gave me a shock there!" he whispered nervously.

Casely swung himself around to lean his left side on the sloping steel of the cupola and peer out in to the night. "Couldn't sleep," he muttered. The rustle of static escaping from the driver's radio helmet was comforting, mechanical.

"I think there's somebody out there," Jody blurted suddenly, waving his arm toward the mist. "I keep hearing something moving, kind of."

Something like thunder began in the far distance. It didn't seem loud until you tried to whisper over it. Unlike thunder, it didn't stop. The rustling, rumbling sound went on and on, and to the west the sky brightened intermittently with white flashes.

Jody tensed. "What the hell's that?" he stammered, his right hand already snaking for the cal fifty's charging handle. His TC chuckled and stopped him. "Christ, you are new," Casely said without malice. "This the first time you heard an Arclight?"

Jody's blank expression was evident even in the gloom. "Arclight," the TC repeated. "You know, a B-52 strike. Hell, that must be ten klicks away at least."

"Ten kilometers?" the driver said in surprise. "It scared me there for a minute."

"If there's any dinks under it, it'll scare them worse," Casely stated positively. "Wait till we go through one of the bombed areas, and you'll see. They just flatten whole swaths of the jungle, a quarter-mile wide and as long as there's planes in the strike. Don't leave a thing higher than the grass, either."

He glanced at his watch again and swore. "Look, I got to get some sleep. Wake me up in half an hour, huh?"

"You don't think there's something out there, Red?"

"Hell, I don't know," the TC grunted. "Keep your eyes open and wake me up in half an hour."

There was something pressing down on them from the dark, but it might have been the mist alone. Casely drew his poncho liner closer about him and fell back into a fitful sleep. He dreamed, aimlessly at first but then of the writing-covered crypt he had stood in that afternoon. He was there again, but the roof had been replaced and the walls were miles high. The idol was waiting for him. Its soapstone jaws grinned, and its remaining arm began to reach out. The stench rolled almost tangibly from its maw.

"Jesus God!" the TC blurted. His head rang with the blow he had given it, lurching uncontrollably against the cupola to get away from his dream. Even awake, the charnel fetor lay heavily in his nostrils. "Jesus," he repeated more softly. If he'd known the sort of nightmare he was due for, he'd have spelled Jody right then at 3:15 and let the driver dream it for him.

It was still pitch-dark; dawn and sunset are sudden things in the tropics. The illuminated hands of his big wristwatch were clear at five after four, though, twenty minutes after Jody should have waked him up. "Hey, turtle," he whispered, "I told you to get me up at a quarter of. You like guard so much you want to pull my shift too?"

No answer. Alarmed, Casely peered into the cupola. The light fabric of the driver's shirt showed faintly where his torso covered the receiver of the cal fifty. Despite all his talk about hearing something in the jungle, Jody had fallen asleep.

In the guts of the ACAV, the radio hissed softly. "Come on, Jody," Casely prodded. He put his hand on the driver's shoulder. Jody's body slipped fluidly off the seat, falling through the cupola into the vehicle's interior. One of the gunners snapped awake with a startled curse and turned on his flashlight.

On the back deck of the ACAV, Casely stared at the dark wetness on his hand. For a moment he was too transfixed even to look down into the track, to look down at Jody's torso sprawling in headless obscenity.

Captain Fuller yawned, then shook his head to clear it. "Sure hope we don't have another sapper tonight," he muttered. "Christ, I'm tired."

Sergeant Peacock methodically checked the tent flap, making sure it was sealed and not leaking light from the small yellow bulbs inside. The command track's engine was on, rumbling to power the lights and the two radio sets in the track itself behind the tent. It was midnight and voices crackled as the radio operator called the roll of the vehicles around the NDP.

"Tell the truth," Fuller went on with a grin of furtive embarrassment, "I wasn't sleeping too well last night even before Casely started shouting. Had one hell of a nightmare. Christ, what a thing that was."

"I knew the gooks to do it in Korea," Peacock said, his great brown eyes guarded. "Cut a fella's head off and leave his buddy sleeping right beside him. I guess they figured the story that got around did more good than if they just killed both of 'em."

The officer shrugged impatiently, lost in his own thoughts. "The dream, I meant. You don't expect your own dreams to go back on you over here. Christ, it's not as though we don't have enough trouble with the dinks."

"We moved ten klicks today," the black said mildly, shifting his bulk on his cot. "You were probably right, figuring there was a bunker system off in the jungle where we laagered last night. They'll just be glad we moved outa their hair; they won't chase us."

Captain Fuller wasn't listening. His face was peculiarly tense, and he seemed to be straining to catch a sound from outside the tent. "Who's moving around out there, Peacock?" he said at last.

The field first blinked. "Sir?" he said. The big man stood up, thrust his head through the tent flap, holding the edges of the material close to his neck to block off the light inside. There was nothing, nothing but an evil reek that seemed to permeate the whole area. He pulled back into the tent. "Everything seems all right, sir; they got a radio going in one of the tracks, maybe that's what you heard."

"No, no," the officer denied peevishly, "it was somebody moving around. I suppose it was just somebody taking a piss. Christ, I'm too jumpy to sleep and too tired to think straight when I stay awake. Goddamn it, I wish July was here so I could take my R&R and forget this damn place."

"Don't let dreams bother you," Sergeant Peacock counseled quietly. "I know about dreams; I had bad dreams when I was a baby, but my momma would wake me up and tell me it was all right, that it didn't mean anything. And that's so, once you wake up. Even that one last night—"

"Look, Peacock," the captain snarled, "what I don't need is a lecture from you on how childish I'm being. Besides, what do you know what I was dreaming last night?"

"Sorry, sir," the sergeant said with impassive dignity, "I'm sure I don't know what you were dreaming about. I meant my own dream about the idol—you know, the one back at yesterday's first NDP. It was pretty bad, the thing reaching out for me and all, but I knew it was just—"

The captain was staring at him in terror, all the ruddiness seeping yellowly out of his face. "My God," Fuller whispered."Dear God, you mean you dreamed that too?" He stood up. The cot creaked behind him and his dog tags clinked together on his bare chest. To his ears, at least, there seemed to be another sound; one from outside.

"God*damn* it!" Fuller shouted. His M16 lay under his cot, across the double V of the head and center legs. He snatched it out and snapped back the operating rod. The bolt clacked home, chambering a round. With the rifle in his hands and not another word for the sergeant, the captain stepped through the tent flaps. The radio operator glanced through the back of the tent to see what the commotion was about. Sergeant Peacock shrugged and shook his head. Outside the tent they could hear the CO's voice shouting angrily, "All right, who the hell is—"

The voice fluted horribly into a scream, high-pitched and terrified. "My God!" the radioman blurted and jumped back to his seat in front of the equipment. Sergeant Peacock scooped up his holstered pistol and the machete beside it, his right hand brushing the light switch and plunging the tent into darkness. In the track behind him the radios winked evilly as the big noncom dived out into the night.

There was nothing to be seen. The scream had cut off as quickly as it had begun. There was an angry hiss from one of the encircling tracks as somebody sent up a parachute flare. Its chill glare showed nothing more than the black overcast had as it drifted down smokily, moving southward on the sluggish wind. There was a clatter of equipment all around the circle now, men nervously activating weapons and kicking diesels into life. "There!" somebody shouted from the southern curve of the laager. The flare, yellow now, had in its dying moments caught something lying at the edge of the jungle.

"Cover me," Peacock shouted. Pistol in hand, he ran toward the afterimage of the object. Something hard skittered underfoot, not enough to throw him. It was an M16. He did not pause to pick it up. He pounded heavily between two tracks, out into the narrow strip between laager and jungle torn by the vehicles maneuvering there earlier in the day. He was very close to what the flare had illuminated. "Gimme some light!" the sergeant roared, heedless of the fact that it would show him up to any lurking sniper.

A five-cell flashlight beamed instantly from the nearest track. The light wobbled, then steadied when it found its target. The flat beam lay in a long oval across the thing glimpsed in the flare.

"Sarge, is that the captain?" someone shouted from the track. The radio operator must have told them who had screamed.

"No, not quite," the field first replied in a strange voice. He was looking farther out into the jungle, at the shadows leaping behind the light. "It's only his leg. No, I'm wrong—I think the rest of him's here after all. Jesus, I do hope his family knows an undertaker who likes jigsaw puzzles."

Lieutenant Worthington turned back to an angry soldier, scratching the brown hair that lay close to his scalp. On the card table in front of him were laid three sections of relief map, joined and covered by a layer of clear acetate.

"Look, Casely," the officer said with ebbing patience, "I know you're shook; we're all shook. And on top of that, I've got to keep this troop running until they get a replacement for Fuller out here. But I'm not going to send the troop back south to blow up a goddamn idol just because you have bad dreams about it. Besides, look here— "he thrust the map toward the TC, stubby finger pointing a long rectangle shaded in red crayon on it—"the location is off limits since six this morning until Sunday midnight. Somebody else is operating in there, I guess, and they don't want us shooting at each other."

The redhead's hands clenched. "I'm telling you," he grated, his voice tight, "it's coming for us. First Jody, then the captain—hell, what makes you think it's going to quit when it gets Peacock and me? All of you were there."

"Captain Fuller was eaten by a tiger," the lieutenant snapped. "Now why don't you cut the crap and get back to your track?"

"Goddamn funny tiger that doesn't leave footprints—"

"So it jumped! Are you going to get out of here, or are you going back to Quan Loi under guard?" Worthington started to rise out of his lawn chair to lend his words emphasis.

For an instant it seemed the enlisted man would hit him; then Casely turned and stalked off without saluting. Well, salutes weren't common in the field anyway, the lieutenant told himself as he went back to his job of sorting out the mess the captain had left for him.

Under the tarp by the supply track, Sergeant Peacock sat at another card table sipping juice from the five-gallon container there. He looked up as Casely approached. First platoon had gotten back late from a convoy run, and a few of the men were still eating their supper nearby.

"Can't you do something about him, Sarge?" the TC begged. His body, under its tan, had an unhealthy hue that the field first noted without comment. The younger man was about to crack.

"Well, I guess he's right," the Negro said without emphasis. "I know what you're thinking, it was a bad dream—"

"The same dream twice in a row!" Casely broke in. "And you had it too." He drew a cup of juice from the container, and the action seemed to steady him. "Jesus Christ, you can't tell me that's just a coincidence, not with the things that happened right when we were dreaming!"

The big noncom shrugged. "So maybe we smelled something," he agreed, "and it made us think about that stinkhole we opened up the other day. It could do that, you know. Maybe some tiger was using the place for a cave and caught the smell from it. The dream don't mean anything, that's all I'm saying. If there's a tiger roaming around, we'll shoot it the next time."

The redhead took a sip of his juice and sloshed it around in his mouth. He grinned wryly. "Sarge," he said, "I almost think you believe that. Even though you know damn well that the only chance for you and me and maybe the rest of the outfit is to blow up that idol before it gets us too. Stands to reason that if we see it dreaming with only one arm and if we blow the rest of it to smithereens, it won't be able to come for us at all."

The sergeant chuckled. "Well, you better hope you're wrong, son, 'cause they aren't going to let us go back and blow that thing up. Be a fine thing if the arvins ambushed us or we ran into a sheaf of our own one-five-fives, wouldn't it?"

"Goddamn it, how do you stay so calm?" the younger man exploded.

Sergeant Peacock looked him up and down before answering, "Well, I tell you, son, when I was about your age in Korea, my platoon was holding a ridge that the gooks wanted real bad. They came at us with bayonets; you know those old Russian ones, seventeen inches in the blade? There was one coming right for me and I swear he was the biggest gook I ever saw, bigger than me even. I had a carbine with a thirty-round box, and I shot that son of a bitch right through the chest. I mean I shot him thirty goddamn times. And he kept coming.

"I couldn't believe it. There was blood all over the front of his uniform, and he just kept coming. I put the last shot into him from closer than I am to you, and then he stuck his goddamn bayonet all the way through my guts before he died. I said to myself, Mrs. Peacock, your favorite son isn't coming back 'cause the gooks got zombies fighting for them. But I was wrong both times. They fixed me up in

Japan and had me back with the rest of the unit before the ceasefire. And that gook wasn't magic either; he was just tougher than anybody else in the world. Since then I just haven't let anything scare me—especially not magic, even when I could see it. That all went out of me when the bayonet slipped in."

Casely shook his head in resignation. "I hope to God you can say that tomorrow morning," he muttered. "And I hope to God that I'm around to hear you." He walked off in the direction of his track.

Bailey and Jones sat in front of the cupola, playing cribbage and keeping a desultory watch on the surrounding jungle. Bailey was driving now that Jody was gone; that meant that only one of the machine guns in back would be manned in a firefight. Christ, why should he worry about that? Casely asked himself savagely. "Hey, snake," the others greeted him. The TC nodded. He climbed into the cupola and sighted along the barrel of the cal fifty. It didn't give him the comfortable feeling it sometimes did.

"Say, Red," Jones said, keeping his eyes on his cards, "you been looking kinda rocky. Just for tonight, Pete and I thought we'd cover for you and let you get some sleep."

"No, thanks a lot, man, but no."

"Aw, come on, Red," Bailey put in. "You're so beat you're gonna fall right off the track if you don't get some sleep. Hell, we can't have that happening to a short-timer with only twenty-seven days left, can we?"

"Twenty-eight," Casely corrected automatically. God, that close to going home and this had to happen! It would have been bad enough to get zapped by the dinks now, but, hell, you figure on that. . . .

"What do you say, man?" Bailey prompted.

"Sorry, I really do appreciate it. But I'm not going to sleep tonight. I know what you're thinking, but I'm right. If it gets me, it's going to get me awake. That's how it is."

Below the TC's line of sight, Jones caught Bailey's eyes. The driver frowned and gave a shrug. "Fifteen-two, fifteen-four, and a pair for six," he counted morosely.

The sky was beautiful. Cloud streaks in the west broke the brilliant sunset into three orange blades stabbing across the heavens to bleed on a wrack of cumuli. The reflecting wedges, miles high, stood like three keystones of an arch, more stunning than any sunrise could have been. Swiftly they shrunk upward, deepened, disappeared. The same clouds that had made the display possible blocked off the moon and stars utterly. It was going to be another pitch-black night.

Jones stepped around to the cargo hatch and pulled three beers out of the cooler. He handed them up to the TC to open with the church key hanging from the side of the cupola. No pop-tops in Nam. Christ, little enough ice, Casely thought as he sipped his warm Pabst. What a hell of a place to die in!

Footsteps crunched on the gravelly soil. Casely's heart jumped as he turned around to find the source of the sounds. Tiger, monster, whatever, the thing could be on you before you saw it in this darkness.

"How's it going?" Sergeant Peacock's familiar voice asked.

The TC relaxed, almost able to laugh at his fright. "Not bad till you scared the crap out of me just now."

"You keep cool," the sergeant admonished. He didn't

attempt to climb onto the back deck; instead, he stood beside the ACAV, his head a little below the level of its sides. Casely climbed out of the cupola and squatted down beside it to see the big Negro better.

"You could have gone back on the supply bird tonight," Peacock said, his voice low but audible to Jones and Bailey inside the track now as well as to the TC.

Casely didn't care. He could live anything down, if he had more than a night or two to live. In normal tones he replied, "Didn't figure that was going to do much good, Sarge. We're at least ten klicks away from where we found that thing, right?" The field first nodded.

"Well, stands to reason that if it can follow us anyways at all, it could just as easy follow me back to Quan Loi. At least here I got a chance." His left hand reached out and patted the heavy barrel of the cal fifty, sticking more than three feet out from the cupola gunshield. "Oh, I know," the redhead went on, "the captain had a gun, and Jody was right here when it got him—but Christ, back at Quan Loi or Di An there wouldn't be a goddamn thing between me and it."

The sergeant chuckled without much humor. Casely thought he could see the outline of a machete, buckled onto the pistol belt under the massive bulge of the black's stomach. The only other time the TC could remember Peacock actually wearing the big knife was the evening they got word that the firebase was being hit by everything from one-oh-sevens on down and that the NDPs could expect their share any moment. "Hey, you want a beer?" he questioned. "It's warm, but—oh *Christ!*"

The younger man leaped back into his cupola. "What's

the matter?" the sergeant demanded. Then his nostrils wrinkled.

"Flares!" the noncom shouted at the top of his lungs. "Everybody shoot up flares!"

"What the hell?" Jones blurted in confusion as he and Bailey stuck their heads up out of the cargo hatch. The bolt of the cal fifty in the cupola clanged loudly as Casely snatched back the charging handle. Across the laager somebody had heard the sergeant's bellow and obeyed enthusiastically with a pair of white star clusters. They shot up like Roman candles, drawing weird shadows with their short multiple glare and silhouetting Sergeant Peacock himself as he pounded across the dirt toward the command track. A horrible stench lay over everything.

The flares burned out. The sergeant disappeared, black into the deeper blackness. Lieutenant Worthington lurched into sight at the flap of the command tent, his rifle in his hand. Then the sergeant bellowed, a terrible mixture of hatred and surprise that almost drowned out the hiss of another flare going up. In the cupola of three-six, Casely cursed with effort as he swung the squealing armor around and pointed the big machine gun in across the NDP.

"Red, what in God's name are you doing?" Jones shrieked. The flare popped and began floating down on its parachute. Sergeant Peacock was between three-six and the command track. His bloated shadow writhed across the soil; neither of his feet was touching the ground. Casely pressed down the butterfly trigger with both thumbs. The shattering muzzle blast pocked the sides of the command tent as the red tracers snicked out past it. The stream of fire was whipping almost straight across the laager, a long raking burst endangering everybody in the troop as it lashed the air just over Sergeant Peacock's head. The field first was struggling titanically with nothing at all; his right hand slashed the glinting machete blade again and again across the air in front of him while his left seemed clamped on the invisible something that held and supported him.

The southern sky brightened, flickered. Not another flare, Jones realized, not thunder either as the sound shuddered toward him. Arclight, a strike on the area they had started to laager in two nights back.

All around the NDP, men were shouting in confusion. The lieutenant had started running toward the field first, then collapsed gagging as he took a deep breath. Diesels rumbled, but no one else had started shooting. The barrel of Casely's machine gun was cherry red. You could watch tracers start to tumble in screaming arcs as soon as they left the burnt-out barrel, but the TC continued hosing the air. Sergeant Peacock gave a choked cry; his machete snapped, then dropped from his hand. At the same instant, the cal fifty came to the end of its belt of ammunition and stuttered into silence. The TC's despairing curses were barely audible over the rising thunder of bomb blasts raking the jungle south of them.

There was an incongruous pop from the air beside Sergeant Peacock. The field first dropped to the ground, unconscious but alive. With a smile of incredulous hope etched on his face by the last glow of the flare, Casely staggered out of his cupola. His eyes were fixed on the rippling glare in the south, and he didn't seem to notice when Jones plucked his sleeve.

"God bless the Air Force," the TC was whispering. "God bless the Air Force."

SOMETHING HAD
TO BE DONE

❧❦

There's a mistake in this story which a fan who'd been a unit clerk called to my attention. I haven't corrected it for this appearance, but I want to point it out.

A character is described as wearing "a Silver Star (medal) with V for Valor." The clerk explained that the Silver Star was by definition an award for valor; there was no additional V endorsement as there might be with the (lower-status) Bronze Star or Army Commendation Medal.

I made the mistake because I based the description on a real soldier whom I knew with 2nd Squadron and whom I'd been told had been awarded a Silver Star with V for his courage at Fort Defiance. Obviously I was told wrong. My bet now is that the guy got a Bronze Star with V because he was a Spec 4 and, quite frankly, medals were more a matter of rank than of merit in Viet Nam. (I know of a lieutenant colonel who got a Silver Star for being so detested by his men that they shot down his helicopter when he flew over them on a road march. The loss was attributed to enemy action, of course.)

But that brings up the question of truth, which is one I wrestle with a lot. I wrote these stories very close to the period of their setting, and they're as true as I could make them—but what the people on the ground "knew" isn't necessarily the truth.

For example, there was a widely hated form of 90-mm ammunition, a shrapnel round called Green Ball (from the nose color) or Dial-A-Dink (from the fact that you rotated the fuse to detonate the round at a chosen distance from the gun; ideally just short of the dink, the Vietnamese, you were trying to kill). It was a complex and not particularly reliable round. We got a lot of it, and it was always the first thing tank commanders burned up during Mad Minutes when they were firing as many rounds as possible into the darkness for sixty seconds.

The 90-mm gun of our M48 tanks had a T-shaped muzzle brake. I was told that Green Ball had a tendency to blow off the front half of the brake, and it was certainly true that many of the tanks had damaged muzzle brakes.

Actually, the damage (I now know) had nothing to do with the type of ammunition. It was simply a result of guns firing thousands of rounds in jungle anti-guerrilla operations, when they'd been designed to fire hundreds of rounds (at most) during armored battles in Europe. Because we disliked Green Ball, we blamed the failures on the ammunition.

So you can't depend on my fiction to tell you the truth . . . but as for how it felt and what we thought, that's real and I stand by it today. Writing short stories and writing novels is two different things— as different as writing prose fiction and scripting for television. There are people who do both superbly well (Arthur C. Clarke above all), but the ability to do one doesn't say much about the likelihood that the same person will be able to do the other. The marketplace today is geared to novels. That's fine, and it's by writing novels that I earn my living.

But I came up through short stories, which necessitated me developing skill in writing tight prose. "Something Had to Be Done" is the best I've ever done at packing a story effectively in a brief compass. I'm very proud of it.

☩ ☩ ☩

"He was out in the hall just a minute ago, sir," the pinched-faced WAC said, looking up from her typewriter in irritation. "You can't mistake his face."

Capt. Richmond shrugged and walked out of the busy office. Blinking in the dim marble were a dozen confused civilians, bussed in for their pre-induction physicals. No one else was in the hallway. The thick-waisted officer frowned, then thought to open the door of the men's room. "Sergeant Morzek?" he called.

Glass clinked within one of the closed stalls and a deep voice with a catch in it grumbled, "Yeah, be right with you." Richmond thought he smelled gin.

"You the other ghoul?" the voice questioned as the stall swung open. Any retort Richmond might have made withered when his eyes took in the cadaverous figure in ill-tailored greens. Platoon sergeant's chevrons on the sleeves, and below them a longer row of service stripes than the captain remembered having seen before. God, this walking corpse might have served in World War II! Most of the ribbons ranked above the sergeant's breast pockets were unfamiliar, but Richmond caught the little V for valor winking in the center of a silver star. Even in these medal-happy days in Southeast Asia they didn't toss many of those around.

The sergeant's cheeks were hollow, his fingers grotesquely thin where they rested on top of the door or clutched the handles of his zippered AWOL bag. Where no moles squatted, his skin was as white as a convict's; but the moles were almost everywhere, hands and face, dozens and scores of them, crowding together in welted obscenity.

The sergeant laughed starkly. "Pretty, aren't I? The docs tell me I got too much sun over there and it gave me runaway warts. Hell, four years is enough time for it to."

"Umm," Richmond grunted in embarrassment, edging back into the hall to have something to do. "Well, the car's in back . . . if you're ready, we can see the Lunkowskis."

"Yeah, Christ," the sergeant said, "that's what I came for, to see the Lunkowskis." He shifted his bag as he followed the captain and it clinked again. Always before, the other man on the notification team had been a stateside officer like Richmond himself. He had heard that a few low-casualty outfits made a habit of letting whoever knew the dead man best accompany the body home, but this was his first actual experience with the practice. He hoped it would be his last.

Threading the green Ford through the heavy traffic of the city center, Richmond said, "I take it Private First Class Lunkowski was one of your men?"

"Yeah, Stevie-boy was in my platoon for about three weeks," Morzek agreed with a chuckle. "Lost six men in that time and he was the last. Six out of twenty-nine, not very damn good, was it?"

"You were under heavy attack?"

"Hell, no, mostly the dinks were letting us alone for a change. We were out in the middle of War Zone C, you know, most Christ-bitten stretch of country you ever saw. No dinks, no trees—they'd all been defoliated. Not a damn thing but dust and each other's company."

"Well, what did happen?" Richmond prompted impatiently. Traffic had thinned somewhat among the blocks of old buildings and he began to look for house numbers.

"Oh, mostly they just died," Morzek said. He yawned alcoholically. "Stevie, now, he got blown to hell by a grenade."

Richmond had learned when he was first assigned to notification duty not to dwell on the ways his . . . missions had died. The possibilities varied from unpleasant to ghastly. He studiously avoided saying anything more to the sergeant beside him until he found the number he wanted. "One-sixteen. This must be the Lunkowskis."

Morzek got out on the curb side, looking more skeletal than before in the dappled sunlight. He still held his AWOL bag.

"You can leave that in the car," Richmond suggested. "I'll lock up."

"Naw, I'll take it in," the sergeant said as he waited for Richmond to walk around the car. "You know, this is every damn thing I brought from Nam? They didn't bother to open it at Travis, just asked me what I had in it. 'A quart of gin,' I told 'em, 'but I won't have it long,' and they waved me through to make my connections. One advantage to this kind of trip."

A bell chimed far within the house when Richmond pressed the button. It was cooler than he had expected on the pine-shaded porch. Miserable as these high, dark old houses were to heat, the design made a world of sense in the summer.

A light came on inside. The stained-glass window left of the door darkened and a latch snicked open. "Please to come in," invited a soft-voiced figure hidden by the dark oak panel. Morzek grinned inappropriately and led the way into the hall, brightly lighted by an electric chandelier.

"Mr. Lunkowski?" Richmond began to the wispy-little man who had admitted them. "We are—"

"But yes, you are here to tell us when Stefan shall come back, are you not?" Lunkowski broke in. "Come into the sitting room, please, Anna and my daughter Rose are there."

"Ah, Mr. Lunkowski," Richmond tried to explain as he followed, all too conscious of the sardonic grin on Morzek's face, "you have been informed by telegram that Pfc. Lunkowski was—"

"Was killed, yes," said the younger of the two red-haired women as she got up from the sofa. "But his body will come back to us soon, will he not? The man on the telephone said . . . ?"

She was gorgeous, Richmond thought, cool and assured, half-smiling as her hair cascaded over her left shoulder like a thick copper conduit. Disconcerted as he was by the whole situation, it was a moment before he realized that Sgt. Morzek was saying, "Oh, the coffin's probably at the airport now, but there's nothing in it but a hundred and fifty pounds of gravel. Did the telegram tell you what happened to Stevie?"

"Sergeant!" Richmond shouted. "You drunken—"

"Oh, calm down, Captain," Morzek interrupted bleakly. "The Lunkowskis, they understand. They want to hear the whole story, don't they?"

"Yes." There was a touch too much sibilance in the word as it crawled from the older woman, Stefan Lunkowski's mother. Her hair was too grizzled now to have more than a touch of red in it, enough to rust the tight ringlets clinging to her skull like a helmet of mail. Without quite appreciating its importance, Richmond noticed that Mr. Lunkowski was standing in front of the room's only door.

With perfect nonchalance, Sgt. Morzek sat down on an overstuffed chair, laying his bag across his knees.

"Well," he said, "there was quite a report on that one. We told them how Stevie was trying to booby-trap a white phosphorous grenade—fix it to go off as soon as some dink pulled the pin instead of four seconds later. And he goofed."

Mrs. Lunkowski's breath whistled out very softly. She said nothing. Morzek waited for further reaction before he smiled horribly and added, "He burned. A couple pounds of Willie Pete going blooie, well . . . it keeps burning all the way through you. Like I said, the coffin's full of gravel."

"My god, Morzek," the captain whispered. It was not the sergeant's savage grin that froze him but the icy-eyed silence of the three Lunkowskis.

"The grenade, that was real," Morzek concluded. "The rest of the report was a lie."

Rose Lunkowski reseated herself gracefully on a chair in front of the heavily draped windows. "Why don't you start at the beginning, Sergeant?" she said with a thin smile that did not show her teeth. "There is much we would like to know before you are gone."

"Sure," Morzek agreed, tracing a mottled forefinger across the pigmented callosities on his face. "Not much to tell. The night after Stevie got assigned to my platoon, the dinks hit us. No big thing. Had one fellow dusted off with brass in his ankle from his machine gun blowing up, that was all. But a burst of AK fire knocked Stevie off his tank right at the start."

"What's all this about?" Richmond complained. "If he was killed by rifle fire, why say a grenade—"

"Silence!" The command crackled like heel plates on concrete.

Sgt. Morzek nodded. "Why, thank you, Mr. Lunkowski. You see, the captain there doesn't know the bullets didn't hurt Stevie. He told us his flak jacket had stopped them. It couldn't have and it didn't. I saw it that night, before he burned it—five holes to stick your fingers through, right over the breast pocket. But Stevie was fine, not a mark on him. Well, Christ, maybe he'd had a bandolier of ammo under the jacket. I had other things to think about."

Morzek paused to glance around his audience. "All this talk, I could sure use a drink. I killed my bottle back at the Federal Building."

"You won't be long," the girl hissed in reply.

Morzek grinned. "They broke up the squadron, then," he rasped on, "gave each platoon a sector of War Zone C to cover to stir up the dinks. There's more life on the moon than there was on the stretch we patrolled. Third night out, one of the gunners died. They flew him back to Saigon for an autopsy but damned if I know what they found. Galloping malaria, we figured.

"Three nights later another guy died. Dawson on three-six . . . Christ, the names don't matter. Some time after midnight his track commander woke up, heard him moaning. We got him back to Quan Loi to a hospital, but he never came out of it. The lieutenant thought he got wasp stung on the neck—here, you know?" Morzek touched two fingers to his jugular. "Like he was allergic. Well, it happens."

"But what about Stefan?" Mrs. Lunkowski asked. "The others do not matter."

"Yes, finish it quickly, Sergeant," the younger woman said, and this time Richmond did catch the flash of her teeth.

"We had a third death," Morzek said agreeably, stroking the zipper of his AWOL bag back and forth. "We were all jumpy by then. I doubled the guard, two men awake on every track. Three nights later, and nobody in the platoon remembered anything from twenty-four hundred hours till Riggs's partner blinked at ten of one and found him dead.

"In the morning, one of the boys came to me. He'd seen Stevie slip over to Riggs, he said; but he was zonked out on grass and didn't think it really had happened until he woke up in the morning and saw Riggs under a poncho. By then, he was scared enough to tell the whole story. Well, we were all jumpy."

"You killed Stefan." It was not a question but a flat statement.

"Oh, hell, Lunkowski," Morzek said absently, "what does it matter who rolled the grenade into his bunk? The story got around and . . . something had to be done."

"Knowing what you know, you came here?" Mrs. Lunkowski murmured liquidly. "You must be mad."

"Naw, I'm not crazy, I'm just sick." The sergeant brushed his left hand over his forehead. "Malignant melanoma, the docs told me. Twenty-six years in the goddam army and in another week or two I'd be *warted* to death.

"Captain," he added, turning his cancerous face toward Richmond, "you better leave through the window."

"Neither of you will leave!" snarled Rose Lunkowski as she stepped toward the men.

Morzek lifted a fat gray cylinder from his bag. "Know what this is, honey?" he asked conversationally.

Richmond screamed and leaped for the window. Rose ignored him, slashing her hand out for the phosphorous grenade. Drapery wrapping the captain's body shielded him from glass and splintered window frame as he pitched out into the yard.

He was still screaming there when the blast of white fire bulged the walls of the house.

THE WAITING BULLET

❦❧

A lot of things happened to me in 1971. The most important was that I got back to the World on January 14 (returned from Viet Nam, that is); but a few weeks after that an army buddy introduced me to Karl Wagner, and I renewed my acquaintance with Manly Wade Wellman, whom I'd met shortly before heading for Nam. Friendship with those two writers caused me to pay more attention to my own writing than might otherwise have been the case, but their range of interests also broadened mine.

When Manly moved to North Carolina, he met the musician and folklorist Bascom Lamar Lunsford. Lunsford introduced Manly to Madison County in the Smoky Mountains. John, the wandering balladeer of Manly's most famous series, was born on Drowning Creek in the Sandhills (where Manly was living when he wrote that first story), but his adventures all take place in a recognizable version of Madison.

In 1971 an independent company bought the

rights to film Who Fears the Devil?, *the collection of John stories. (The result was released, to the extent that it was released at all, under a variety of titles. My tape is titled* The Legend of Hillbilly John. *Six of the seven weeks of filming took place in Arkansas, but the first week in October 1971, was shot in Madison County. The Wellmans, the Drakes, and Karl Wagner went up to watch.*

As a result of Nam, I had a very good camera (a Nikon F) with which I took a great number of pictures on the trip. Almost none of them are of any merit whatever. Instead of shooting people at the close range suitable for my 52mm lens, I have dozens of pictures of (say) Hedge Capers, the male lead, walking across a footbridge a hundred yards away. I got one good image of Sharon Henesy, the female lead, and a couple decent ones of Hedge Capers between takes.

My memory turned out to be a lot more valuable, however: I saw and heard a lot of things that stuck with me to this day. "The Waiting Bullet" came out of those memories.

I sold four stories to Arkham House, but August Derleth's death in 1971 ended that market. Trying desperately to sell to the few other SF/fantasy markets which existed then, I used Viet Nam/Cambodia as a setting (with some success), and I wrote "The Waiting Bullet" (probably in early 1972) as a folklore-based fantasy set in Madison County.

I wasn't satisfied with the result and filed the

*story in a drawer without polishing it into final
form. I did that with about two-thirds of the stories
I wrote at the time (and with all my attempts at
novels). That would have been the end of it had not
Stu Schiff in 1997 asked me for a story for the final
issue of* Whispers *magazine.*

I discuss elsewhere the importance of Whispers
*to me and to the horror field in the '70s and '80s. I
wanted to do a story for Stu, but I was very busy
writing novels under contract.*

*Then I thought of "The Waiting Bullet." Stu had
begun* Whispers *when the Army transferred him to
Ft. Bragg in Fayetteville, some sixty miles south of
where Manly, Karl and I lived in Chapel Hill. The
four of us discussed writers and artists; we helped
with one another's work and created our own. We
were all individuals, but our close association made
us individually greater that we would have been
without the support of the others.*

*I revised "The Waiting Bullet" and sent it to
Stuart. Rereading it recalls to me a time that fantasy
writing was bright and new again after decades of
eclipse.*

*The early '70s were bad in my head and bad in
many ways in my life as well. (America didn't
welcome her Nam vets back with open arms.) That
said, the period made me a professional writer.*

*"The Waiting Bullet" with its attention to
closely observed detail is part of the scaffolding on
which my future writing career was built.*

✠ ✠ ✠

The air was as crisp and clear as mountain air was supposed to be, but the water in the pine-shaded spring was shudderously cold. Ribaud swore as he plunged his arm in up to the elbow, sure there was a better way to spend Sunday morning than clearing debris out of the water system of the cabin he was renting. He had to clean the filter if he wanted coffee, though.

God knew he did not need the coffee to wake him up now.

He straightened and tossed a handful of wet pine-straw downslope toward the cabin. The sky was bright, but the sun had not yet risen above the rim of the hollow. White mist hung in the air.

Ribaud's shoulders felt tight in the denim jacket; he shrugged, trying to loosen them.

That did not help. His flesh tingled all over. He had read something recently about running water . . . .

Or perhaps it was just that he had spent too much time alone since he left graduate school to work on his novel.

Ribaud frowned, a little angry with himself for feeling uneasy. The filter was clear now, so it was time to make coffee. He started back toward the cabin.

Somebody walked out of the front door.

The stranger was only a hundred yards away. He looked so much at ease that for a disoriented instant, Ribaud thought the mistake must be his own, that the cabin below was not the one he had been renting for the past month.

The stranger was heavyset and of medium height. He wore a flannel shirt with broad red and white checks, and he had not bothered to tuck the tail into his dark slacks before stepping out of the house. He stretched nonchalantly and took a deep lungful of air.

Ribaud was certain that he had never seen the man before.

A vagrant breeze rustled the pines. The stranger glanced absently up the hillside, then sauntered around the side of the cabin toward the woodpile.

Ribaud blinked, unable to believe what he was seeing. "Hey, buddy!" he called, his voice shaky with indecision. "Hey there!"

The stranger paid no attention. As he turned the corner, Ribaud saw that the back of his head was bald and unpleasantly ridged with dull white scar tissue.

Was the fellow a nut of some kind? The mountains must have them, too . . . . Was this somebody who had lost his hair and his mind in an accident, but whom the locals saw no reason to commit since he had not murdered anybody yet?

While Ribaud hesitated, the stranger reappeared around the corner with an armload of firewood. The billets were chopped to length, not sawn. There were only sawn logs in Ribaud's woodpile.

The stranger's lips were pursed. Ribaud thought he could hear someone whistling "White Silver Sands" off-key. Three steps from the door, the stranger whirled around with a look of ghastly disbelief on his face. Logs spilled to the ground in bouncing confusion. He lunged for the portal, but in midair he stumbled and slammed against the side of the cabin.

The stranger's right hand scrabbled across the rough boards, feeling for a purchase. Slowly, painfully, he turned his face toward the spring. Only the ebbing strength of his right arm held his torso upright. A shattered artery had soaked the front of his shirt bright carmine.

The man's eyes glazed as his right arm buckled. His body slumped full length in a tangle of firewood.

Wind sighed in the pines.

Ribaud ran toward the cabin, his mind lumpy with what he had just watched. When he was only a step or two away from the hideously flaccid corpse, it vanished with a ripple in the air.

The cabin remained as Ribaud had left it. The door was closed, and the firewood had vanished with the stranger who dropped it.

Ribaud stopped. He began to tremble. There were no tracks in the dirt but his own, and no sign of blood.

He looked back up the hill. The sun had risen to the lower branches of the pines around the spring. The breeze stirred the needles gently, to no purpose. No other living thing was visible.

Still trembling, Ribaud entered the house. Water was rushing from the tap he had left on. The single room was just as it had been half an hour before, when Ribaud began to walk up the hill.

Lying beside the typewriter was the slim book Ribaud had glanced through the night before, *Ghost and Ghoul*, by an archaeologist named Lethbridge. The pages rustled as Ribaud thumbed through to find the line he remembered from an account of a ghost seen near a mill: *There often seems to be some kind of pressure built up, possibly by running water, at the point from which the ghost was seen.*

Ribaud had seen a ghost, or . . .

Or he could not think of a better explanation. He was sure there must *be* a better explanation, but he did not know where to go for it.

Mountain society is notoriously closed. Besides, Ribaud had come here to escape his acquaintances, not to make new ones. He knew almost none of the local people better than to nod to in the street on one of his infrequent visits to the county seat.

Various possibilities went through Ribaud's mind as he sat before his typewriter, in the cabin's only chair. At last the sparing drink he poured himself from the pint bottle decided him.

He had gotten the bonded whiskey the week before, under the counter of a little cross-roads grocery and gas station a few miles up the road. That the owner, Parry, had sold the liquor to him—the county was dry—showed that he had accepted Ribaud to some extent.

There was no one better for Ribaud to ask about what he had seen.

Recapping the bottle, Ribaud took the keys to his Mustang off the nail by the door and strode outside. He looked to see if there was a splash of blood on the weathered boards of the sidewall.

There was not.

The snake-track highway which ran alongside a tributary of the French Broad River forked three miles from Ribaud's cabin. One branch led down to the county seat; the other ran south toward Asheville. Between the forks stood a low rectangular building. The clumsily painted sign over the door in one of the short walls proclaimed Parry's.

There were two gas pumps in front. Parry's Ford was the only vehicle in the parking strip along the Asheville road, but a car on blocks peeked from behind the store. A sapling grew through the engine compartment.

"Morning!" Ribaud called as he unlatched the door.

There were shelves on both long walls of the store's interior, and another row of displays down the axis divided the floor into two narrow aisles.

Parry sat at the front behind his cash register. He was a fat, clean-shaven man of forty-five or so who spent most of his time in the store now that his sons were grown.

"Morning," he replied, his eyes fixed frankly on Ribaud's face. He touched the closed cabinet behind his swivel chair. "That pint not hold you?"

Ribaud glanced around. He and the owner were alone in the store. "I might pick up another at that," he said. "But what I really had in mind was some information."

Parry said nothing.

"What I wanted to know," Ribaud went on, "was if you knew a fellow maybe five-foot eight or thereabout, heavy set. I'd judge his age about thirty-five or so. He's got black hair, thick and curly in front, but the back of his head's all scarred."

The storekeeper's face was no longer friendly, even in a disinterested way. His tones were clipped as he said, "I might know somewhat of that. Whereabouts did you hear of this feller?"

Ribaud licked his lips, a little taken aback by the obvious hostility. He looked around the empty store again before saying, "Well, I . . ."

His mind stumbled over the phrasing. "I thought I

saw him around my cabin this morning. I was just curious, you see."

"I'll thank you to take your jokes back out onto the highway," Parry snapped. "I don't know whose idea this was but you can tell them not to try it on me again."

"For God's sake!" Ribaud blurted. "Nobody told me a thing. I was up at the spring clearing my water filter half a hour ago, and I saw this fellow come out of my cabin. He didn't take anything—I just want to know who he is."

Parry squinted. There was still suspicion in his look but he said, "This feller, what was he wearing?"

"A flannel shirt and jeans—or some kind of dark blue trousers," Ribaud answered promptly. "No hat, and I didn't pay any attention to his shoes."

"Well, that's the way he looked the last time I saw him too," Parry said. "With the hair that way, it couldn't be anybody but Jack Cutshall noways. He got burnt on Saipan when a gas dump blew up."

"Umm," Ribaud murmured, uncertain about what to say next.

Parry leaned back in his chair and added, "Yeah, it's going on twenty years now that we buried Jack. I reckon somebody's funnin' with you, son."

The door jangled open to admit two youths in jeans and T-shirts. Ribaud stood silent while they gathered up bread, soft drinks, and a carton of cigarettes; paid; and thundered away in a new-looking pickup truck.

With the store quiet again, he said to Parry, "Don't I remember the real estate agent saying the cabin I'm in belongs to a Cutshall?"

"Un-huh," the storekeeper agreed, "That'd be Myra,

old Jack's daughter. She lives down to Asheville. Did when Jack got killed, too, her mother'd had about enough of Jack and she'd left him. Marion —Jack's wife she was—she died herself some two, three years back, I'm told."

"What, ah . . ." Ribaud said. "What happened to Cutshall?"

Parry rubbed his neck and looked around the store while he made up his mind. At last he said, "Well, I don't see it can do any harm to say now. There's been talk, you know, but I guess if you're gonna be a son of a bitch all your life like Sam Barnard has, you get used to people talking about you."

Ribaud took a handful of change out of his pocket and walked over to the soft drink machine. "Have something?" he asked the storekeeper.

"A Coke, mebbe," Parry answered. While Ribaud fed the machine, Parry went on, "Well, the thing to remember is both Jack and Sam were meaner'n snakes. They were blockading together for a while—makin' white liquor. Had their still set up right on the Tennessee line so they could carry it either way if ever the state law come up one side or the other.

"They was doing all right but Jack, he never had a civil tongue. I don't know he was playing with a full deck ever since his hair got blowed off. Left him deaf as a post, that did, too. Never wore his hearing aid, just talked all the more. Jack was a marine, you see, and he was always and forever saying that the army never had a man in it with the guts to make a marine."

Ribaud handed him a bottle. The storekeeper drank deeply, then wiped his mouth with the back of his hand.

"He knew damn well," Parry continued, "that Sam Barnard had been in the army and he didn't take kindly to that sort of talk. One thing led to another, and before long, the two of them'd split up. The rest of us set around makin' bets on which one was gonna kill the other."

"You mean you knew there was going to be a murder before it even happened?" Ribaud said in disbelief. "Didn't somebody do something?"

"Son, around here, you always know about a murder ahead of time," Parry replied calmly. He drained the rest of his soda in a great swallow. "That don't mean it's healthy to mix in another man's quarrel."

He belched.

"Well, anyhow," the storekeeper continued, "Sam got in first. He's a cold-codded bastid, but nobody ever said he couldn't shoot. Jack lived down the road the same place you're in yourself, now. One Sunday morning—"

Parry paused. Two dump trucks passed outside, shaking the frame building and filling it with their roar.

"One Sunday," he resumed, "Dace Rowan come tearin' in here yelling he'd heard two shots when he was going by the Cutshall place and how 'bout a few of us riding back up there with him. He was a deppity shurrif, you see, but he wasn't in too big a hurry to go busting into Sam's doings alone. There'd already been words passed between them two over the whiskey business."

"My God," Ribaud muttered. He refused the cigarette Parry offered him and waited, half-sitting on the check-out counter while the storekeeper smoked a few puffs.

"There was three or four of us in the store," Parry continued, "so I just locked up and we all went over in

Dace's car to take a look. Sure 'nough, there was Jack layin' out in front of his cabin, dead as dead, and a hole you could stick your fist into through the center of his chest."

Ribaud's eyes narrowed. His tongue trembled over describing what he had seen this morning. Instead, he asked, "Barnard was convicted, then?"

"No, can't say he was," the storekeeper admitted with a frown. "Tell the truth, they never tried him, even. No evidence, you see. Course, everybody knew Sam'd done it, but the s'licitor says that wan't proof and he didn't have a damn thing more to go on."

He shrugged. "So that's where it ended, some talk and Sam leavin' the county for a few years. He's back now, but I don't guess he was missed."

"But they had bullets to match, didn't they?" Ribaud protested, dredging up notions of police procedure from mystery novels. "Had, ah, Barnard gotten rid of the gun or something?"

Parry laughed with the amused tolerance of a mountaineer for a man who had never fired a gun in his life. "You see, son," he explained, "Sam had himself a .222, 'bout the first one in the county. It don't have a big bullet, but it pushes it along pretty *god*dam fast. If it hits something solid, why, thet bullet *blows* up."

He pursed his lips. "Leastways, that's what the bullet what hit Jack done. Bruk his spine and nigh tore his breastbone outa him. I don't guess there was a scrap of thet bullet left bigger 'n a pinhead. They sent what they could find to Raleigh, but hell, them folk back there couldn't even say what kinda gun had shot it. Course, we *knew* that."

"Oh," Ribaud said. It was as if he had been told that ice sinks in water.

"Matter of fact," the storekeeper continued, "there was people what said Sam never did it neither."

He opened the front door and tossed his cigarette butt out onto the gravel drive. "Mostly Sam's kin, a course, but they had some others with 'em. Said Dace had heard two shots plain. Jack's gun was still in the cabin, so the other shot wan't him—and there wan't no way Sam Barnard was gonna miss a man clean at a hundert yards."

"A hundred yards?" Ribaud echoed weakly.

"Yeah, we figger whoever done it was up in that clump of pine by the spring —"

"I know the one you mean." Ribaud's mouth was beginning to feel sticky. He wished he had not just drunk the Coke. He was pretty sure Parry would not let him drink anything stronger in the store while he was open for business.

"We didn't find much up there when we looked," Parry went on. "Some needles mussed, but pinestraw don't take tracks. Sam musta hiked over the mountain, leavin' his car on one of the back roads. Nobody chanced on the car not that it would've proved much if they had. I don't know what Sam did with the other shot neither, but I guess we all of us miss once or twice in our lives."

"Umm," said Ribaud. He drew a five-dollar bill from his wallet. "Well. Look, maybe I will take another pint if you have one handy."

Parry glanced out the door, then slipped a pint of Bourbon Supreme from the cabinet behind him and quickly sheathed it in two paper bags. Ribaud took the bottle and pocketed his two quarters change. Nodding to Parry, he left the store.

Ribaud took a quick swig of the liquor before starting his car, and another drink when he parked the Mustang beside his cabin.

Everything in the cabin was just as he had left it.

On Thursday Ribaud dropped into Parry's again. He caught sight of his face in the glass of the door. He was looking drawn.

A lanky, gray-haired man wearing a stained suede jacket stood at the back of the store, mulling over the display of fishing rods. Parry nodded hello as Ribaud walked in, but he shook his head when the writer pointed his thumb at the Coke machine. Ribaud got himself an orange soda and began toying with the nail-clipper/key-chains on display beside the cash register.

A dump truck rumbled by the store, backfiring as the driver changed down.

"Naw, I'll let you keep what you got there till you come down on the price," called the man looking at fishing tackle. "Reckon I could get the same rig five dollar cheaper in Asheville."

"So go to Asheville, Sam," the storekeeper replied without concern.

"Reckon I may," the other man said with a snort.

He turned around and walked toward the front of the store. He was about Ribaud's height and looked to be in his mid-50s. The checked shirt beneath his jacket had, like his jeans, been too long since the last washing.

The man's face was merely sour for a moment; then

his eyes, as gray as concrete, focused on Ribaud. The man halted. All the hard lines went out of his visage, leaving behind a slackness all the more shocking for being unexpected on a face that harsh.

"What in hell bit you, Sam?" Parry asked callously. The only exit from the store was through the front, where Ribaud stood in the aisle beside Parry.

"Who are you?" Sam asked in a savage whisper.

Color rushed back into his face. His right hand eased toward his sagging jacket pocket.

The cash register clanged as Parry hit the "No Sale" key. "None of that!" the fat man snapped in a tone of authority. "Have you gone crazy, Sam Barnard?"

The lanky man cursed and darted for the door. Ribaud jumped aside to let him pass.

When the door slammed shut, Parry gave a sigh of relief. He replaced the worn revolver he had taken from the cash drawer.

Ribaud tried to set down his soft drink bottle. It banged on the edge of the counter and spilled across the Formica.

"Jesus God!" the storekeeper breathed. He reached down for an old undershirt to serve as a wiping rag. "What have you been saying to Sam Barnard? I've seen him with federal marshals after him and never lookin' that petered out!"

"I never saw him before," Ribaud croaked. He clasped his hands tight together, but the sickly trembling inside would not stop. He felt something walking over his grave.

An engine roared in the parking strip. An old Buick

shot away from the store. Barnard was hunched over its wheel like a frightened harpy.

"Well, he seen *you* before, son," Parry stated needlessly. He looked sharply at the writer. "Say," he continued, "you wouldn't a been talking to anybody about what you asked me Sunday, would you?"

"Not a soul," Ribaud insisted. "Hell, I don't know—"

The brakes of a dump truck squealed. The high-pitched sound continued for what seemed to be minutes, long after the beginning of the hideous rending crash of the track's front bumper crushing the Buick which had slid into its path in Barnard's haste to leave.

The truck stopped just short of the steel guardrail. The Buick continued on, bouncing and clanging for a hundred and fifty feet into the bed of the stream beneath.

Parry shook his head. He draped the rag on the edge of the wastebasket to dry.

"Well," he said, "I was wrong. I always figgered Sam Barnard'd die with somebody's bullet in him."

On Sunday Ribaud found himself awake before dawn. For an hour or so he lay in bed, trying to get back to sleep. At last he got up and made coffee.

It was chilly in the cabin, even after Ribaud had built up the fire in the stove.

After half an hour of indecision, Ribaud abandoned the still-blank piece of paper in his typewriter. He got into his car and drove to the store.

Parry's Ford was parked in the lot. Parry, as expected, was seated comfortably beside the doorway. His face took on a guarded expression when he saw Ribaud.

"How's it going, Parry?" the writer asked.

"Not so bad up here." The storekeeper scratched his head, then added, "You know, son, there's been some talk about you. How you start asking questions about Sam Barnard and then he lights out lookin' as close to scared as anybody ever seed him. Like you might be some kinda law. Eh?"

"I'm not," Ribaud said.

He tried to laugh, but the sound did not come out the way he would have wished. He had seen Parry's gun, and he did not want to learn whether the storekeeper would use it to keep from being arrested on liquor law violations.

"Besides," Ribaud went on, "I wasn't asking about Barnard, I was asking about my cabin. Maybe whoever was fooling around there called on Barnard, too."

"Maybe," the storekeeper agreed, his voice even. "You know, you're the first to stay up there since Jack died. Marion wouldn't rent it out, and Myra didn't try till this year, I reckon."

Ribaud shrugged. "There was something I wanted to ask you about that," he said, getting to the business that had brought him to the store this morning. "You say that Cutshall was shot one Sunday?"

"That's right."

"Ah . . . what time of day would that have been?"

"'Bout half-past nine in the morning," Parry said. He frowned and corrected himself, glancing out the window toward the deserted highway. "Mebbe a little before; half-past is when Dace come in. I was tinkerin' with my radia, and I wan't gettin' a blessed thing but a sermon from Asheville."

Ribaud looked at his watch. It was not quite nine, about the time he'd started up to the pond the previous Sunday. "Well, I'll be seeing you," he said, reaching for the door."

"Don't you want something?" Parry asked suspiciously.

"Ah . . . Ribaud said. "Ah, yeah. Give me another pint if you would. I finished the last one."

Parry's face hardened, but after a moment's hesitation he unlatched the cupboard.

It was a quarter past nine when Ribaud pulled up beside his cabin, skidding a little on the wet grass. As soon as he got out of the car, the feeling of pressure grew on him. He climbed toward the spring, paralleling the dew-gleaming length of copper water pipe.

A bird flew ahead of him. Nothing else moved.

The cabin squatted innocently below Ribaud. The front door was open. He was almost sure that he had latched it when he left.

He could not see the car where he had just parked it.

Jack Cutshall walked out of the cabin and stretched. The psychic pressure was insupportable.

"Run!" Ribaud screamed. "*Run!*"

He heard the double echo of his voice from the cabin wall and the far side of the hollow. Cutshall, stone deaf and twenty years dead, walked around the cabin to get firewood.

Ribaud ran down the hill. His foot slipped. He fell bruisingly against the rocky soil, but he jumped to his feet again.

Cutshall reappeared with an armload of firewood. He

took a step toward the cabin door and vanished from Ribaud's sight.

Ribaud slid to a halt. The door was closed; his Mustang was beside the cabin. Tingling pressure made the writer shudder.

Cutshall should have been right in front of him. Instead, everything looked as it had when Ribaud left the cabin to go to the store.

Cutshall should have been right in front of him . . . .

"Run!" Ribaud shouted again.

He turned and stared up the hilltop. He had only time to note the changed outline, the pines far smaller than the ones around the spring in his day but still shadowing all but a glint of sky reflected from a telescopic sight.

Ribaud's mouth opened to scream.

One hundred yards and twenty years away, a rifle shot slapped echoes from the hollow. Ribaud did not hear it. His skull exploded. His body was already dropping back into its own time.

The murderer cursed and jacked another shell into the chamber. Below him, Jack Cutshall broke into a run, but he would not live to tell why Sam Barnard's first bullet had missed him.

✢ ✢ ✢

Author's Note

In the Fall of 1971, I visited the mountains of North Carolina with Manly Wade Wellman and stayed with local friends of his for a few days after Manly returned to Chapel Hill. "The Waiting Bullet" grew out of the scenery and the stories I absorbed during that trip.

I wrote the first draft of the story shortly after I came home. I wrote it for Manly, really, an old-fashioned ghost story set among the places and people I'd encountered in his company. Though I read the draft to him, I didn't go on to polish the story into final form at that time.

Manly is gone now; and 1971 is gone also, in the mountains as surely as everywhere else. So, for my friend and for a time that are now both memories, I dug out that old draft and finished it as I would have done at the time if I'd been able to.

Honor to them both.

Dave Drake
Chapel Hill, NC

THE ELF HOUSE

Bill Fawcett, a friend and a book packager, put together for Baen Books what was supposed to be an original anthology of novellas by Dave Weber, Eric Flint, and me. (It was a little more complex than that to begin with, and a lot more complex before the book eventually came out.) For that volume I wrote a Hammer novella which became part of an episodic Hammer novel.

Bill then sold a fantasy equivalent and asked me to write a short story in the Isles universe. Each volume of my Isles fantasy series has four individual viewpoint strands which combine for the climax. If Bill had been able to use a novella, I might've written a sequence which I'd spread out over five or six chapters when it appeared in the next Isles novel. A short story didn't fit that novel format, so I simply wrote "The Elf House" from scratch with no expectation—then or now—of ever reusing it as part of an Isles novel.

I wrote the story to be self-standing. If it had any value at all beyond doing a favor to a friend, it *needed to be accessible to readers who had no previous familiarity with the Isles series. That meant limiting it to a single character.*

I picked Cashel because he's friendly, cheerful, and very direct. Basically, I like him. (I identify with Cashel's sister Ilna, who's angry, harsh, and generally depressed, but that's another matter entirely.)

I knew the concept of the "The Elf House" wasn't original to me, but until I'd finished the rough draft I couldn't have told you from whom I'd stolen it. In reading it through for the first time, the source was obvious: "Kazam Collects," an early work by Cyril Kornbluth.

If I needed proof of how much better a writer I could be than I am, all I'd have to do is reread any of a dozen or more pieces which Kornbluth dashed off before he was twenty. Because I don't need that proof, I reread Kornbluth simply for the pleasure of discovering new flashes of brilliance with each reading. I suggest that all of you read him also.

✣ ✣ ✣

Cashel didn't need to carry his quarterstaff in the corridors of the Vicar's palace—what'd been the Count of Haft's place till Prince Garric arrived the week before—but he was more comfortable holding the smooth, familiar hickory than he'd be otherwise. He didn't dislike big buildings, but he disliked being in them; and this palace had a nasty feel all its own.

Besides, the staff had been a friend in places where Cashel had no other friends. He wouldn't feel right about leaving it alone in the huge suite assigned to him while he went off to dinner with Garric in the roof garden. If the servants, officials, and the amazing number of other people crowding the palace stared at him, well, a man as big as Cashel or-Kenset was used to being stared at whether he carried a quarterstaff or not.

For a wonder there wasn't anybody around at the moment. Cashel sauntered down the hall looking at the cherub mural painted just above shoulder level. In the dim light through the transoms of the rooms to either side, there was something new to catch every time he passed.

Cashel started to grin at the little fellow with his wings spread as he struggled to lead a goat who didn't want to go. The sound of a girl crying jerked his head around.

He'd been holding the quarterstaff straight up and down in one hand. Now, without him thinking about it his left hand slipped into position a span below the right and he slanted the staff before him. "Ma'am?" he said, ready to deal with whatever was making a woman cry.

The girl wore servant's clothing, a cap and a simple gray tunic set off by a sash of bleached wool. She knelt a little way down a corridor which joined the main one from the right. Cashel didn't remember there being anything but a blank wall there, but he guessed he'd always missed it because he'd been intent on the mural opposite.

She gave another vain push at the inward-opening door in front of her, then looked up at Cashel with eyes glittering with tears. "Oh, sir!" she said. "I dropped the key and it slipped under the door. The steward will beat me if I don't get it back!"

"I don't guess he will," Cashel said. The notion that somebody'd beat a little slip of a girl surprised him into speaking in a growl. He didn't know her, but he didn't think men ought to hit any girls. He was real sure no man was going to try that twice in front of Cashel or-Kenset.

He cleared his throat and went on in a normal voice, "But anyhow, let's see if I can't get your key."

The door stood a finger's breadth ajar. Cashel pressed with the fingertips of his right hand without budging it further. It was stuck, that was all; rusty hinges, he figured, since the panel didn't bind to the lintel or transom. Through the crack at the edge he could see a glint of gold in what was otherwise darkness; the key was there, all right. It must've bounced wrong off the stone floor.

Cashel leaned his quarterstaff against the wall beside him and placed his hands one above the other on the latch side of the panel. The girl looked up at him intently. She seemed older, all of a sudden, and there was no sign of her frightened despair of a moment ago. He made sure his feet were set, then put his weight against the wood.

More people lived in the palace than did in all Barca's Hamlet where Cashel'd grown up. Even though there wasn't any traffic in the main corridor, sounds constantly echoed through the hallways and made the floor quiver. All that stopped; Cashel pressed against the panel in dead silence. Maybe it was the effort, because the door still didn't want to give—

And then it did, though with creaking unwillingness. It opened another finger's breadth, twice that. . . .

The girl stuck her arm in, calling something that Cashel could barely hear through the roar of blood in his ears. "I can't quite . . ." she said, so he kept pushing and the door gave some more, enough that she squeezed her torso into the room beyond.

Cashel shoved harder yet. He could feel the wood fighting him like the staff of a bent bow, ready to snap back if he let up the pressure. "I've got it!" the girl said, only her legs from the knees down out in the hallway where Cashel could see them. "I've—"

And then she shrieked, "Milord, I'm falling!" shrilly. Her legs slid out of sight, following the rest of her. She was wearing sandals with straps of green-dyed cut-work.

Cashel didn't understand what was happening, but as the girl slipped inward he slammed his shoulder hard against the panel instead of just shoving with his hands. He hadn't done that before because he didn't want to smash the door, but now he didn't care.

The door didn't break, neither the thick fir panel nor the squealing hinges that fought him all the way, and he swung it open at right angles. The room within was small and dingy. There was no furniture, and part of the rotten wainscoting had fallen onto the floor.

The girl had the key in one hand and reached toward Cashel with the other. She looked like she was sliding backwards, but she was already farther away than the far wall of the room.

Cashel grabbed the staff with his left hand and stretched it out to the girl. She couldn't reach it and screamed again. Her voice was growing fainter; he could see her body shrink as the distance increased.

"Duzi!" Cashel bellowed. He strode into the room, holding the quarterstaff out in both hands. The girl grabbed it, but Cashel's feet slipped like he was standing on an icy hillside.

The door slammed behind him. The only light was a dim, yellow-brown glow that silhouetted the girl's body and he and she plunged down an unseen slope.

Cashel felt himself spinning as he dropped, but his body wasn't touching anything. The girl held the other end of his staff; he couldn't see her expression, but she didn't bawl in fear or make any sound at all that he noticed.

They skidded onto a gritty hillside and stopped. Cashel looked over his shoulder. All he saw was gray sky and a rising slope. There wasn't any sign of the room where they'd come from. He looked all around and didn't see anything he liked better.

The bare hills ranged in color from yellow-white to the red of rusty iron. For the most part the rock had weathered into gravel, but there were outcrops where the stone must've been harder. The general landscape wasn't pretty, but the outcrops were worse. Whenever Cashel looked hard at one, he started to see a large, angry face.

He got up, brushing crumbled rock from the back of his tunic. He hadn't come down hard, for all that they'd seemed to be rushing headlong through emptiness. He glanced at the girl, already on her feet. She smiled and said, "My name is Mona, Lord Cashel. Do you know where we are?"

"Just Cashel, please, mistress," he said with a grimace. "I'm not lord anything."

He cleared his throat, looking around again. The landscape wasn't any more appealing on a careful survey than it'd been when he first landed in it. "And I don't know anything about this place, except I wish we were someplace else."

"It's where the house elf lives," Mona said. She was looking at the landscape also, turning her head slowly. "Used to live, I mean. There can't be anything alive here except the dwelling itself."

She held her arms across her bosom; her expression was coldly disapproving. From Mona's features she was younger than Cashel's nineteen years, but her eyes were a lot older than that.

Cashel followed the line of her gaze up a series of streaked, ragged slopes. On top of a butte was what at first he'd taken for white stone weathered into a spire. When he squinted and let it sink in angle by angle, he realized he was seeing a manmade tower with battlements on top. A slant of windows curved around the shaft the way they'd do to light a circular staircase.

"You mean that castle?" Cashel said, nodding toward the structure instead of pointing. "That there's people living there?"

"There's no people here and no elves either," the girl said as she stared toward the tower. "Only us. And I don't mean the building, Cashel. This whole world was the dwelling for the house elf."

Cashel cleared his throat. He took out the pad of raw wool he carried in his belt wallet and wiped the smooth hickory surface of his quarterstaff as he thought.

"Mona," he said while keeping his eyes fixed on his task. "The only house elves I've heard of are the little fellows who live under the hearth and, well, make things go right. The Luck of the House, some people call them."

He cleared his throat again. "Not that I've ever seen one. Or known anybody who did."

"How could anybody live under a hearth?" Mona asked, with a pretty smile that took the sting out of words that could've been pretty cutting if said the wrong way. "But they could live between the cracks of the real world, in a place that grew for them. A place like this was."

She looked around, no longer smiling. "When the elf died," she said, "the dwelling should've fallen apart like a web when the spider dies. This dwelling took a life of its own instead. A sort of life."

The sky was getting darker. It was solidly overcast, as heavy and oppressive as a block of gray stone. Cashel could feel a storm in the air. Duzi, the little god of shepherds, knew how many times he'd been caught by the weather while he was minding sheep; but he didn't have sheep to worry about this time, so he could go somewhere else.

"Ah, Mona?" he said. "I think we'd best get under cover while we can. Unless you've got a better idea, let's head for the castle up there."

"Yes," she said. "We'll do that. Though the storm will catch us anyway."

They had about a half-mile to go. The route was uphill on average, but Cashel could see there were several ridges and gullies between them and the castle. Experience had taught him that the terrain was always worse than it seemed at a distance, but he didn't foresee anything they couldn't cross even if he had to carry the girl part of the way.

He looked at Mona again. She wasn't the frail little girl that she'd seemed when he first saw her in the palace corridor. She stepped with determination across the rough terrain, avoiding head-sized chunks of rock but seemingly unperturbed by the coarse gravel. Maybe the soles of her sandals were sturdier than they seemed. Cashel himself was wearing thick boots. He didn't like the feel of footgear, especially in warm weather, but the stone floors of the palace and cobblestone streets of the city beyond were too much for the calluses he'd developed going barefoot on the mud and meadows where he grew up.

Lightning flashed somewhere above the clouds, giving them texture if not shape for an instant. Cashel held his staff crosswise, ready to brace himself with an iron butt-cap if the gravel slid or a rock turned under his foot. You couldn't trust your footing here. . . .

"I'm surprised there's nothing growing here," Cashel said. The girl was a couple steps in front of him, choosing each step and keeping in perfect balance. "This isn't good soil—" his boot toe gouged into the slope "—but with rain, there ought to be something."

"Nothing can live here," Mona said bitterly. She reached down and brushed at the loose grit. "Look."

The underlying rock was mostly dark brown and cream, with streaks of maroon and other colors. Cashel frowned as he let his eyes grapple with the pattern.

"It's a tree trunk," he said at last. "It's a stone statue of a tree trunk."

"It was a tree trunk," the girl said. "The house has turned it to stone to reabsorb it. Lesser vegetation is—"

She swept her left hand in a short arc, palm down.

"—already gone. Stone and dust. The house has only a half-life; it hates the real thing."

She smiled wryly at Cashel."Forgive me if I get carried

away," she said. "There's nothing evil about what's happening here, any more than there is with cancer or a wolf tree. But it's a perversion and can't be allowed."

Cashel nodded. "We'd best be getting on," he said, nodding toward the tower ahead of them. The hill was particularly steep right here; he could only see the crowning battlements from where he stood. "Though you were right about us not beating the storm."

They resumed, climbing steeply now. The girl dabbed a hand down frequently while Cashel used the butt of his staff to steady him where he didn't trust the grip of his feet.

He knew what a wolf tree was. If a forest grew wild, there'd always be a few trees, oaks more often than not, that through a combination of luck in soil and the weather spread over ground that could've supported a dozen ordinary trees. Their limbs shaded out lesser growth, and their trunks grew gnarled and rotted at the heart, useless for anything but firewood.

Forests didn't grow wild, of course: wood was too valuable a resource for that. If a tree started taking more than its share, the woodlot's owner hired a husky young man like Cashel to cut it down.

A steep-sided gully barred their way, not broad but deeper than twice Cashel's height. He figured he could get over it, but the girl'd have to climb down and then—

Mona jumped over the gully from a standing start, looking like nothing so much as a squirrel hopping the gap between trees. She glanced over her shoulder. "I'll wait for you here, Master Cashel," she said with a trace of laughter in her tone.

Cashel grunted. He checked the ground, then backed

two steps and came on again in a rush. He butted his quarterstaff firmly at the edge of the gully and used the great strength of his shoulders to loft him over. He landed beside her, flexing his knees to take his weight.

"You're graceful despite your size," the girl said as she resumed her way toward the tower.

"Who are you, Mistress Mona?" Cashel asked. "What are you?"

"I'm a servant," she said. "We're all servants of one kind or another, aren't we? You used to serve sheep, for example."

"I didn't serve sheep," Cashel said, shocked at the thought. "I—"

He broke off. A shepherd did a lot of things, but when you boiled them all down they amounted to making sure his sheep were safe and comfortable. Put like that it sure enough sounded like being a servant.

"Well, maybe that's so," he admitted, saying the words instead of just holding his tongue and pretending he hadn't been wrong to begin with. The rain hit, violent slashes from straight ahead. Each gust drove at Cashel's face like he was standing in the sluice of the mill back home in Barca's Hamlet. He didn't see how Mona could stand against it but she did, lowering her head and striding on.

The lightning was nearly constant, dancing in the clouds as the air shuddered with thunder. Runoff gouged fresh rivulets which gushed down the slopes as streams of thin mud.

The gully they'd crossed must be a raging freshet now. It'd be a bad time to lose your footing and slide into a torrent.

The storm stopped as abruptly as it'd begun. It paused,

at any rate; the rain no longer fell, but the sky stayed the same dark mat. Mona had a little peaked cap as part of her livery. It'd blown away, and her simple tunic stuck to her torso, sopping wet and three shades darker than its original light gray. Cashel figured he looked like a drowned rat himself.

He grinned and slicked the water off his staff between his thumbs and forefingers, sliding first his right hand to the ferrule and then cleaning the other half with his left. A drowned ox, maybe. On his worst day, nobody was going to confuse Cashel or-Kenset with a rat.

They'd reached the base of the great outcrop on which the tower stood. The cliff was pretty steep, but there was a path slanting up to the left. It looked badly worn . . . well, no. It looked more like the rock had been melted somehow. Anyway, they'd be able to get up it even if the rain started again.

"Wait!" the girl said, staring intently at the cliff to the side of the pathway. Her index finger traced a bump in the rock. It was about the size of a ripe cantaloupe and had a pearly luster instead of the dull, chalky surface holding it.

Now that Mona'd pointed out the first one, Cashel saw that there were more balls, as many as he could count on the fingers of one hand, in the rock beside it. They looked as much like frog's eggs as anything Cashel could think of; though much bigger, of course.

"The seeds of new dwellings," the girl said softly. She took her hand away from the stone. "Each seed should grow into a home for a young elf who'd make the people of a house in the waking world a little happier. This place is absorbing them too."

She turned her head toward Cashel. "I was wrong, I think," she said. Her voice didn't sound angry, but it rang as hard as a sword edge. "What's happening here is evil."

"Let's go on," said Cashel, but Mona had started up the path before he got the words out.

The wind rose again before they'd climbed halfway. It whirled around the outcrop, buffeting Cashel head-on no matter which direction he was facing as he walked along the curving path. Rain began to fall, a few drops at a time but big ones that stung like hard-thrown pebbles.

Mona's tunic was sleeveless and only knee-length. Even so Cashel was afraid that it'd give the storm's violence enough purchase to snatch her from the path and throw her onto the broken landscape below. Her balance remained perfect and her steps stayed steady despite the gusts.

The top of the outcrop was as flat as a table. The tower stood in the center with no more margin than Cashel could span by stretching his arms out to either side. He wondered if the spire itself was artificial, a pedestal built at the same time the tower was; though if what Mona said was true, this whole world had been made—or grown, which he supposed was the same thing.

The entrance was partway around the tower from where the path reached the top. Mona started for it with Cashel right behind. Now that they were close, Cashel saw that the windows in the tower were blocked up—filled with stone rather than just shuttered. What he'd seen were the outlines where the sashes used to be.

The rain resumed in torrents, now mixed with hail the size of quails' eggs. Cashel threw his left arm up to shield his eyes. He'd have bruises when this was over, that was for sure. Balls of ice shattered against the stone, cracking like a fire of pine boughs. Sharp bits bounced from the ground, pricking Cashel's ankles and lower legs.

The tower's doorway was recessed. Mona bent toward it, doing something with the panel. Cashel hunched behind her, trying to shelter her from the hailstones that slipped past the overhang.

The rattling hail drowned the thunder, but its deeper notes still vibrated through Cashel's boots. Lightning was a constant rippling presence overhead. The tower's walls were alabaster; Cashel ran his fingertips over them, trying to find joints between the courses. If there were any, they were too fine for his touch or eyesight, either one, to identify them.

"Mona, maybe I can break it down," Cashel said, speaking louder with each word of the short sentence. The hail made more noise than he appreciated until he tried to talk over it.

A crust flaked off the wall when Cashel rubbed it. Though the tower stood in open air, the stone was rotting like a statue buried in the acid soil of a forest.

"I've got it!" said the girl, and as she spoke the tower opened; she stepped inside.

Cashel was close on her heels, bumping the door as he entered. It was made of the same white stone as the rest of the building, pivoting on pins carved from one block with the panel. As soon as Cashel was past, it banged shut with a ringing sound more like a xylophone than that of stone on stone.

The storm's noise ended abruptly when the door closed. They were in an anteroom.

"There's light!" Cashel said in surprise, and there was: a soft, shadowless glow from the stone itself. The room was unfurnished, but on the walls were carved patterns as rich and fanciful as the engravings on a nobleman's gold dinner service.

Only a few patches remained to show what the original decoration had looked like, though. The scaly rot disfiguring the tower's exterior had claimed most of the inner surfaces, too.

Mona stepped through the inner doorway. Cashel followed, keeping his elbows close to his sides. The passage was so narrow that if he'd tried to swagger through arms-akimbo, he'd have bumped the jambs.

A slender woman stood in the center of the hall, her right hand out in greeting. "Oh!" Cashel said, straightening in surprise. The tower was so silent that he'd convinced himself it was empty

"Her name was Giglia," Mona said, walking toward the other woman. "She was the luck of the palace ever since the Count of Haft built it. There was never a house elf who could match what Giglia did with glass. She made the palace windows gleam like a thousand rainbows every sunrise."

Cashel touched his tongue to his lower lip. His staff was slantways before him, not so much a threat as a barrier between him and the silent Giglia. "Why doesn't she move?" he asked.

"Because she's dead, Cashel," Mona said. "She grew old and died; as things should do. Without death there can be no renewal."

She reached toward the dead woman; their faces were

as like as those of twins. When her fingers touched the other's cheek, Giglia disintegrated into dust motes. Her right arm fell to the floor intact, then erupted as a geyser of fine dust swirling in the air.

There was a dry, sweetish smell. Cashel threw his arm over his nose to breathe through the waterlogged sleeve of his tunic, though he didn't suppose it mattered. "Mona?" he said. "How can we get out of here? Back to the palace, I mean? Or somewhere!"

Instead of answering, the girl walked toward the door on the other side of the central room. Her feet stirred Giglia's remains into umber whorls. Grimacing, Cashel followed.

The room beyond was darker than the others. Against the far wall was a throne inexpertly hacked out of stone; on it sat a statue as brutal and primitive as the throne itself. It was male, but it had tusks and a crude ape's face. In its right hand was a stone club the length of Cashel's arm.

"Is this a chapel?" Cashel said. "Is that the god they worship here?"

The tower shuddered. Cashel heard the sharp *crack! crack! crack!* of stone breaking. The statue trembled side to side on its throne.

Cashel turned; the outer door had slammed behind them, but maybe he could smash it open again. "Earthquake!" he cried. "We've got to get out!"

"It's not an earthquake," Mona said impassively; she didn't move. "And we can't get out while this remains. The dwelling must have a master to exist, so it's created a master in its own image."

The statue stood up. It looked even bigger standing

than it'd seemed while seated; Cashel didn't think he could reach to the top of its head flat-footed. Not that he was likely to need to do that.

It started forward, raising its club. "Mona, get out of the way!" Cashel said in a growl.

He lifted the quarterstaff before him and began backing toward the door to the central room. The light was better there, and there was more space besides. He and his staff covered a lot of territory when the fight started.

Rock groaned against itself. The statue's face shifted as its mouth moved. "I will destroy you . . ." the stone said in a rumble almost too low for human ears.

Cashel knew where the doorway was behind him. He feinted at the statue's head, then stepped back quickly and surely. He kept his staff vertical to clear the narrow opening. Mona was somewhere nearby, a presence without form because all Cashel's attention was on the statue. He hoped the girl'd stay clear, but he couldn't worry about that right now.

The statue clumped through the doorway after him, barely clearing the jambs. It looked even uglier than it had in the relative shadow of the further room. "You cannot escape me . . ." it grated in a voice of emotionless menace.

Cashel spun his staff in a short sun-wise arc, crashing his left ferrule into the lumpish fist which gripped the stone club. There was a crack and flash of blue wizardlight; the creature growled like an approaching avalanche.

Cashel wasn't looking for escape. He'd come to fight.

The statue rushed him, swinging the stone club in an overhead blow. Cashel rammed his staff forward like a spear. The blunt butt-cap slammed into the thing's throat with another blue flash.

The creature's head jerked back. The mighty arc of its club touched nothing but air till it smashed itself on the floor, cratering the alabaster. The grip flew out of the stone hand.

Cashel backed, gasping in deep breaths. He'd struck swiftly and as hard as he could, and the quivers of wizardlight meant he was using more than the strength of his great muscles. He was uncomfortable about that other business—he was a shepherd, not a wizard—but when he was facing a creature like this he was glad of any help he could get.

The thing held its hands up in front of its face. Its fingers were thin scorings in stone mitts; only the thumbs were separate. Its blunt features were those of a bestial doll a child had molded from clay.

The creature's mouth opened. It screamed like millstones rubbing.

"Watch—" Mona cried, but Cashel didn't need to be told what to do in a fight. The creature leaped toward him like a missile from a huge catapult. Cashel stepped back and sideways, thrusting his quarterstaff low. He slipped the thick hickory pole between the stone ankles; it flexed but held. The creature plunged head-first into the wall with a crash that rocked the tower.

The alabaster fractured in scalloped flakes, leaving a crater at the point of impact. The creature dropped flat on the floor. It braced its stone arms beneath it, starting to rise.

Cashel, holding the staff like a battering ram, struck

the back of its head, bouncing it into the wall again. Light as blue as the heart of a sapphire flared at the double *crack!* of iron on stone and stone on stone.

Cashel stepped back, bending slightly and sucking air through his open mouth. The creature's arms moved feebly, like an infant trying to swim. The ferrule Cashel had just struck with glowed orange, cooling to dull red. He switched ends, then brought the staff back with both arms.

The creature got its hands under it and lifted its head slightly. Cashel lunged forward, driving the staff down with the whole weight of his body. The butt hammered the creature at the same point as before. The statue's head exploded in a flash and thunderclap. The massive body began to crumble the way a sand castle dissolves in the surf.

Cashel felt himself wavering. He planted the quarterstaff against the floor and used it to brace him as he let himself kneel. His breath was a rasping thunder, and his blood hammered in his ears.

The only part of the creature still remaining was the outstretched right arm. When it suddenly collapsed to a spill of sand, Cashel caught a brief reminder of the dry, sweet odor in which Giglia had vanished. Then nothing remained but air harsh with the faint brimstone reek of nearby lightning.

Cashel stayed like that for—well, for a time. He figured he could move if he had to, but since he didn't he was just going to rest till he felt like doing something else.

Though he'd kept his eyes open, he didn't have much awareness of his surroundings. There wasn't a lot to see, after all; just the trail of coarse grit that'd been a statue there on the floor in front of him. It looked like what he'd seen on the hills he'd climbed to reach the tower. . . .

"Are you ready to go home, Cashel?" Mona said.

Cashel's world clicked back into hard focus again. He turned his head and smiled at the girl, feeling a little embarrassed. How long had she been standing there, waiting for him to come to himself?

"I'm all right," he said, wondering how true that was. He stood, lifting himself partly by the strength of his arms on the quarterstaff. He swayed a little, but no worse than you always did when you'd been bent over and got up suddenly.

He grinned wider and said, "I'm fine," meaning it this time. "But how do we get back home, Mona?"

As Cashel spoke, he took a closer look at the walls. His eyes narrowed. "Mona?" he said. "Things don't look right. The stone looks thin. It wasn't like that before."

"This world is decaying," the girl said, "and not before time. We have to get you out of here, though. Come."

She stepped through the doorway to the room where the statue had waited; the gold key was out in her hand again. Cashel followed, as he'd been doing ever since he met the girl—except when there was the fighting.

He grinned again. That was all right. Mona was better at leading than Cashel ever wanted to be, and she'd kept out of the way when he went to work.

Mona looked back at him. "I'm sorry I had to trick you," she said. "Your help was very important."

Cashel shrugged. "You didn't have to trick me, Mona," he said. "You could just have asked. But that's all right."

The throne had fallen into a pile of sand and pebbles

like the thing that'd sat on it. On the wall behind was another door. Mona stuck the key into the door—there hadn't been a keyhole that Cashel could see, but he was sure about what she'd just done—and pulled the panel open.

"Go on through, Cashel," she said, smiling like the sun rising. "Thank you. We all thank you."

Cashel hesitated. "You're coming too, aren't you, Mona?" he said. Light and color without shape swirled in the door opening.

Her smile became pensive. She raised the key in the hand that didn't hold the door open. "I have to free the seeds we found," she said. "Otherwise they'll rot instead of growing as they should."

"But what happens to you?" Cashel said.

"Go on back to your own world, Cashel," Mona said, her voice hard without harshness. "There must be renewal."

Cashel cleared his throat. He didn't have anything to say, though, so he nodded and walked toward the opening. As his leading foot entered the blur of color, Mona said, "Your house will always be a happy one, dear friend."

For a moment Cashel stepped through nothingness so silent that he heard his heart beating; then his boot heel clacked on stone. He was standing in the familiar hallway down which he'd been going to dinner.

"Oh!" cried a servant, dropping the pair of silver ewers he'd been carrying to refill from the well in the courtyard at the end of the passage. They rang on the floor, sounding sweet or hollow by turns as they rolled.

Cashel squatted, holding his staff upright in one hand

as he caught the nearer pitcher. It might have a few new dings in it, but he didn't guess the servant would get in real trouble.

"Oh, your lordship, I'm so sorry!" the fellow babbled. He took the ewer from Cashel's hand but he was trembling so bad he looked like he might drop it again. "I didn't see you!"

Cashel glanced at the door he'd come out of . . . and found there wasn't one, just a blank wall between the entrances to a pair of large suites. He stood up. "Sorry," he said apologetically. "I didn't mean to startle you."

Cashel headed on in the direction he'd been going when he'd first heard the girl—well, first heard Mona—crying. He'd never really liked this palace. It was a dingy place, badly run-down before Garric arrived and replaced the Count of Haft with a vicar.

Nothing Cashel could see was different about it now, but the corridor seemed a little cheerier than it used to be. He smiled. He'd have started whistling if he could carry a tune.

THE HUNTING GROUND

I read (and always have read) both science fiction and fantasy. Mr. Derleth insisted that SF was merely a subset of fantasy, but even if that's true (and I'm not sure it is) the statement doesn't accurately describe most people's perceptions. Still, because I move between fantasy and SF as a reader, it's been easy for me to write both.

Nor do I see any reason that a horror story can't be SF. Many years ago Ramsey Campbell asked me for my choice of the ten top horror stories. One of those I picked instantly was "The Cold Equations" by Tom Godwin, a pure SF story which I find horrifying in ways that one more nut with a meat cleaver can never be.

"The Cold Equations" proves my point in another fashion also. It's well known that John Campbell published the story in Astounding, *the* quintessentially hard-SF magazine. It's less well known that Godwin borrowed the plot from an EC horror comic. The boundaries between horror and SF are easily permeable.

Ramsey Campbell asked me for a story for Superhorror, *an original horror anthology he was putting together. The only criterion was that the story be a good one. (One of the best in the collection was "The Viaduct" by Brian Lumley, a slice of autobiography with no fantasy element whatever.)*

I chose to write a story that was SF in form, although it could have been done just as easily as a fantasy. Payment was to be two cents per word, but instead I traded the piece for the pencil rough draft of the novel Ramsey had just finished: his first, The Doll Who Ate His Mother.

It's neither the science nor the could-be fantasy that makes "The Hunting Ground" a horror story; it's the character's situation. There's less fiction in that than I might wish.

I came back from Nam with no physical damage and an absolute refusal to admit that there might be other problems. We—my wife and I— rented rooms in an old house that had been split into three apartments for students and other people without a lot of money.

One of the nicest aspects of the house was the attached vacant lot. A large tree had been cut down a year or two past; the stump remained beside the driveway. I sat cross-legged on that stump, reading or writing, any time it wasn't raining. For whatever reason, it was what my soul needed.

You'll find that stump in "The Hunting Ground." You'll also find an accurate description of a neighborhood of Durham, NC, just north of Duke's East Campus. And you'll find a part of me; but I emphasize, only a small part.

✢ ✢ ✢

The patrol car's tires hissed on the warm asphalt as it pulled to the curb beside Lorne. "What you up to, snake?" asked the square-bodied policeman. The car's rumbling idle and the whirr of its air conditioner through the open window filled the evening.

Lorne smiled and nodded the lighted tip of his cigarette. "Sitting on a stump in my yard, watching cops park on the wrong side of the street. What're you up to, Ben?"

Instead of answering, the policeman looked hard at his friend. They were both in their late twenties; the man in the car stocky and dark with a close-cropped mustache; Lorne slender, his hair sand-colored and falling across his neck brace. "Hurting, snake?" Ben asked softly.

"Shit, four years is enough to get used to anything," the thinner man said. Though Lorne's eyes were on the chime tower of the abandoned Baptist church a block down Rankin Street, his mind was lost in the far past. "You know, some nights I sit out here for a while instead of going to bed."

Three cars in quick succession threw waves of light and sound against the rows of aging houses. One blinked its high beams at the patrol car briefly, blindingly. "Bastard," Ben grumbled without real anger. "Well, back to the war against crime." His smile quirked. "Better than the last war they had us fighting, hey?"

Lorne finished his cigarette with a long drag. "Hell, I don't know, sarge. How many jobs give you a full pension after two years?"

"See you, snake."

"See you, sarge."

The big cruiser snarled as Ben pulled back into the traffic lane and turned at the first corner. The city was on a system of neighborhood police patrols, an attempt to avoid the anonymous patrolling that turned each car into a miniature search and destroy mission. The first night he sat on the stump beside his apartment, Lorne had sworn in surprise to see that the face peering from the curious patrol car was that of Ben Gresham, his squad leader during the ten months and nineteen days he had carried an M60 in War Zone C.

And that was the only past remaining to Lorne.

The back door of Jenkins's house banged shut on its spring. A few moments later heavy boots began scratching up the gravel of the common drive. Lorne's seat was an oak stump, three feet in diameter. Instead of trying to turn his head, he shifted his whole body around on the wood. Jenkins, a plumpish, half-bald man in his late sixties, lifted a pair of canned Budweisers. "Must get thirsty out here, warm as it is."

"It's always thirsty enough to drink good beer," Lorne smiled. "I'll share my stump with you."

They sipped for a time without speaking. Mrs. Purefoy, Jenkins's widowed sister and a matronly Baptist, kept house for him. Lorne gathered that while she did not forbid her brother to drink an occasional beer, neither did she provide an encouragingly social atmosphere.

"I've seen you out here at 3 a.m.," the older man said. "What'll you do when the weather turns cold?"

"Freeze my butt for a while," Lorne answered. He

gestured his beer toward his dark apartment on the second floor of a house much like Jenkins's. "Sit up there with the light on. Hell, there's lots of VA hospitals, I've *been* in lots of them. If North Carolina isn't warm enough, maybe they'd find me one in Florida." He took another swallow and said, "I just sleep better in the daytime, is all. Too many ghosts around at night."

Jenkins turned quickly to make sure of the smile on the younger man's face. It flashed at his motion. "Not quite that sort of ghost," Lorne explained. "The ones I bring with me . . . ." And he kept his smile despite the sizzle of faces in the white fire sudden in his mind. The noise of popping, boiling flesh faded and he went on, "There was something weird going on last night, though—" he glanced at his big Japanese wristwatch—"well, damn early this morning."

"A Halloween ghost with a white sheet?" Jenkins suggested.

"Umm, no, down at the church," said Lorne, fumbling his cigarettes out. Jenkins shrugged refusal and the dart of butane flame ignited only one. "The tower there was—I don't know, I looked at it and it seemed to be vibrating. No sound, though, and then a big red flash without any sound either. I thought sure it'd caught fire, but it was just a flash and everything was back to normal. Funny. You know how you hold your fingers over a flashlight and it comes through, kind of? Well, the flash was like that, only through a stone wall."

"I never saw anything like that," Jenkins agreed. "Old church doesn't seem the worse for it, though. It'll be ready to fall down itself before the courts get all settled about who owns it, you know."

"Umm?"

"Fellowship Baptist built a new church half a mile north of here, more parking, and anyhow, it was going to cost more to repair that old firetrap than it would to build a new one." Jenkins grinned. "Mable hasn't missed a Sunday in forty years, so I heard all about it.

"The city bought the old lot for a boys' club or some such fool thing—I want to spit every time I think of my property taxes, I do—but it turns out the Rankins, that's who the street's named after, too, they'd given the land way back before the Kaiser's War. Damn if some of them weren't still around to sue to get the lot back if it wasn't going to be a church anymore. So that was last year, and it's like to be a few more before anybody puts money into tearing the old place down."

"From the way it's boarded up and padlocked, I figured it must have been a reflection I saw," Lorne admitted. "But it looked funny enough," he added sheepishly, "that I took a walk down there last night."

Jenkins shrugged and stood up. He had the fisherman's trick of dropping the pull tab into his beer before drinking any. Now it rattled in the bottom. "Well," he said, picking up Lorne's can as well, "it's bed time for me, I suppose. You better get yourself off soon or the bugs'll carry you away."

"Thanks for the beer and the company," Lorne said. "One of these nights I'll bring down an ice chest and we'll really tie one on."

Lorne's ears followed the old man back, his boots a friendly, even sound in the warm April darkness. A touch of breeze caught the wisteria hedge across the street and spread its sweetness, diluted, over Lorne. He ground out his cigarette and sat quietly, letting the vines breathe on him.

Jenkins's garbage can scrunched open and one of the empties echoed into it. The other did not fall. "What the hell?" Lorne wondered aloud. But there was something about the night, despite its urban innocence, that brought up memories from past years more strongly than ever before.

In a little while Lorne began walking. He was still walking when dawn washed the fiery pictures from his mind and he returned to his apartment to find three police cars parked in the street.

The two other tenants stored their cars in the side yard of the apartment house. Lorne had stepped between them when he heard a woman scream, "That's him! Don't let him get away!"

Lorne turned. White-haired Mrs. Purefoy and a pair of uniformed policemen faced him from the porch of Jenkins's house. The younger man had his revolver half-drawn. A third uniformed man, Ben, stepped quickly around from the back of the house. "I'm not going anywhere but to bed," Lorne said, spreading his empty hands. He began walking toward the others. "Look, what's the matter?"

The oldest, heaviest of the policemen took the porch steps in a leap and approached Lorne at a barely restrained trot. He had major's pips on his shoulder straps. "Where have you been, snake?" Ben asked, but the major was between them instantly, growling, "I'll handle this, Gresham. Mr. Charles Lorne?"

"Yes," Lorne whispered. His body flashed hot, as though the fat policeman were a fire, a towering sheet of orange rippling with the speckles of tracers cooking off. . . .

". . . and at any time during the questioning you may withdraw your consent and thereafter remain silent. Do you understand, Mr. Lorne?"

"Yes."

"Did you see Mr. Jenkins tonight?"

"Uh-huh. He came out—when did you leave me, Ben? 10:30?" Lorne paused to light another cigarette. His flame wavered like the blade of a kris. "We each drank a beer, shot the bull. That's all. What happened?"

"Where did you last see Mr. Jenkins?"

Lorne gestured. "I was on the stump. He walked around the back of the house—his house. I guess I could see him. Anyway, I heard him throw the cans in the trash and . . . that's all."

"Both cans?" Ben broke in despite his commander's scowl.

"No, you're right—just one. And I didn't hear the door close. It's got a spring that slams it like a one-oh-five going off, usually. Look, what happened?"

There was a pause. Ben tugged at a corner of his mustache. Low sunlight sprayed Lorne through the trees. Standing, he looked taller than his six feet, a knobbly staff of a man in wheat jeans and a green-dyed T-shirt. The shirt had begun to disintegrate in the years since it was issued to him on the way to the war zone. The brace was baby-flesh pink. It made him look incongruously bullnecked, alien.

"He could have changed clothes," suggested the young

patrolman. He had holstered his weapon but continued to toy with the butt.

"He didn't," Ben snapped, the signs of his temper obvious to Lorne if not to the other policemen. "He's wearing now what he had on when I left him."

"We'll take him around back," the major suddenly decided. In convoy, Ben and the other, nervous, patrolman to either side of Lorne, and the major bringing up the rear, they crossed into Jenkins's yard following the steep downslope. Mrs. Purefoy stared from the porch. Beneath her a hydrangea bush graded its blooms red on the left, blue on the right, with the carefully tended acidity of the soil. It was a mirror for her face, ruddy toward the sun and gray with fear in shadow.

"What's the problem?" Lorne wondered aloud as he viewed the back of the house. The trash can was open but upright, its lid lying on the smooth lawn beside it. Nearby was one of the Budweiser empties. The other lay alone on the bottom of the trash can. There was no sign of Jenkins himself.

Ben's square hand indicated an arc of spatters six to eight feet high, black against the white siding. "They promised us a lab team but hell, it's blood, snake. You and me've seen enough to recognize it. Mrs. Purefoy got up at four, didn't find her brother. I saw this when I checked and . . . ." He let his voice trail off.

"No body?" Lorne asked. He had lighted a fresh cigarette. The gushing flames surrounded him.

"No."

"And Jenkins weighs what? 220?" He laughed, a sound as thin as his wrists. "You'd play hell proving a man with a broken neck ran off with him, wouldn't you?"

"Broke? Sure, we'll believe that!" gibed the nervous patrolman.

"You'll believe *me,* meatball!" Ben snarled. "He broke it and he carried me out of a fucking burning Shithook while our ammo cooked off. And by God—"

"Easy, sarge," Lorne said quietly. "If anybody needs shooting, I'll borrow a gun and do it myself."

The major flashed his scowl from one man to the other. His sudden uncertainty was as obvious as the flag pin in his lapel: Lorne was now a veteran, not an aging hippy.

"I'm an outpatient at the VA hospital," Lorne said, seeing his chance to damp the fire. "Something's fucking up some nerves and they're trying to do something about it there. Wish to hell they'd do it soon."

"Gresham," the major said, motioning Ben aside for a low-voiced exchange. The third policeman had gone red when Ben snapped at him. Now he was white, realizing his mortality for the first time in his twenty-two years.

Lorne grinned at him. "Hang loose, turtle. Neither Ben or me ever killed anybody who didn't need it worse than you do."

The boy began to tremble.

"Mr. Lorne," the major said, his tone judicious but not hostile, "we'll be getting in touch with you later. And if you recall anything, anything at all that may have bearing on Mr. Jenkins's disappearance, call us at once."

Lorne's hands nodded agreement. Ben winked as the lab van arrived, then turned away with the others.

Lorne's pain was less than usual, but his dreams awakened him in a sweat each time he dropped off to sleep.

When at last he switched on the radio, the headline news was that three people besides Jenkins had disappeared during the night, all of them within five blocks of Lorne's apartment.

The air was very close, muffling the brilliance of the stars. It was Friday night and the roar of southbound traffic sounded from Donovan Avenue a block to the east. The three northbound lanes of Jones Street, the next one west of Rankin, were not yet as clotted with cars as they would be later at night, but headlights there were a nervous darting through the houses and trees whenever Lorne turned on his stump to look. Rankin Street lay quietly between, lighted at alternate blocks by blue globes of mercury vapor. It was narrow, so that cars could not pass those parked along the curb without slowing, easing; a placid island surrounded by modern pressures.

But no one had disappeared to the east of Donovan or the west of Jones.

Lorne stubbed out his cigarette in the punky wood of the stump. It was riddled with termites and sometimes he pictured them, scrabbling through the darkness. He hated insects, hated especially the grubs and hidden things, the corpse-white termites . . . but he sat on the stump above them. A perversely objective part of Lorne's mind knew that if he could have sat in the heart of a furnace like the companions of Daniel, he would have done so.

From the blocky shade of the porch next door came the creak of springs: Mrs. Purefoy, shifting her weight on the cushions of the old wing-back chair. In the early evening Lorne had caught her face staring at a parlor window, her muscles flat as wax. As the deeper darkness blurred and pooled, she had slipped out into its cover. Lorne felt her burning eyes, knowing that she would never forgive him for her brother's disappearance, not if it were proven that Jenkins had left by his own decision. Lorne had always been a sinner to her; innocence would not change that.

Another cigarette. Someone else was watching. A passing car threw Lorne's angled shadow forward and across Jenkins's house. Lorne's guts clenched and his fingers crushed the unlit cigarette. *Light. Twelve men in a rice paddy when the captured flare bursts above them. The pop-pop-pop of a gun far off, and the splashes columning around Lt. Burnes—*

"Christ!" Lorne shouted, standing with an immediacy that laced pain through his body. Something was terribly wrong in the night. The lights brought back memories, but they quenched the real threat that hid in the darkness. Lorne knew what he was feeling, *knew* that any instant a brown face would peer out of a spider hole behind an AK-47 or a mine would rip steel pellets down the trail . . . .

He stopped, forcing himself to sit down again. If it was his time, there was nothing he could do for it. A fresh cigarette fitted between his lips automatically and the needle-bright lighter focused his eyes.

And the watcher was gone.

Something had poised to kill Lorne, and had then passed on without striking. It was as unnatural as if a wall collapsing on him had separated in midair to leave him unharmed. Lorne's arms were trembling, his cigarette tip an orange blur. When Ben's cruiser pulled in beside him,

Lorne was at first unable to answer the other man's, "Hey, snake."

"Jesus, sarge," Lorne whispered, smoke spurting from his mouth and nostrils. "There's somebody out here and he's a *bad* fucker."

Carrier noise blatted before the car radio rapped a series of numbers and street names. Ben knuckled his mustache until he was sure his own cruiser was not mentioned. "Yeah, he's a bad one. Another one gone tonight, a little girl from three blocks down. Went to the store to trade six empties and a dime on a coke. Christ, I saw her two hours ago, snake. The bottles we found, the kid we didn't . . . . Seen any little girls?"

There was an upright shadow in front of Ben's radio: a riot gun, clipped to the dashboard. "Haven't seen anything but cars, sarge. Lots of police cars."

"They've got an extra ten men on," Ben agreed with a nod. "We went over the old Baptist church a few minutes ago. Great TAC Squad work. Nothing. Damn locks were rusted shut."

"Think the Baptists've taken up with baby sacrifice?" Lorne chuckled.

"Shit, there's five bodies somewhere. If the bastard's loading them in the back of a truck, you'd think he'd spread his pickups over a bit more of an area, wouldn't you?"

"Look, baby, anybody who packed Jenkins around on his back—I sure don't want to meet him."

"Don't guess Jenkins did either," Ben grunted. "Or the others."

"PD to D-5," the radio interrupted.

Ben keyed his microphone. "Go ahead."

"10-25 Lt. Cooper at Rankin and Duke."

"10-4, 10-76," Ben replied, starting to return the mike to its holder.

"D-5, acknowledge," the receiver ordered testily.

"Goddamn fucker!" Ben snarled, banging the instrument down. "Sends just about half the fucking time!"

"Keep a low profile, sarge," Lorne murmured, but even had he screamed, his words would have been lost in the boom of exhaust as Ben cramped the car around in the street, the left wheels bumping over the far curb. Then the accelerator flattened and the big car shot toward the rendezvous.

In Viet Nam, Lorne had kept his death wish under control during shelling by digging in and keeping his head down. Now he stood and went inside to his room. After a time, he slept. If his dreams were bright and tortured, then they always were. . . .

"Sure, you knew Jackson," Ben explained, the *poom-poom-poom* of his engine a live thing in the night. "He's the blond shit who . . . didn't believe you'd broken your neck. Yesterday morning."

"Small loss, then," Lorne grinned. "But you watch your own ass, hear? If there's nobody out but cops, there's going to be more cops than just Jackson disappearing."

"Cops and damned fools," Ben grumbled. "When I didn't see you out here on my first pass, I thought maybe you'd gotten sense enough to stay inside."

"I was going to. Decided . . . oh, hell. What's the box score now?"

"Seven gone. Seven for sure," the patrolman corrected

himself. "One got grabbed in the time he took to walk from his girl's front porch back to his car. That bastard's lucky, but he's crazy as hell if he thinks he'll stay that lucky."

"He's crazy as hell," Lorne agreed. A spring whispered from Jenkins's porch and Lorne bobbed the tip of his cigarette at the noise. "She's not doing so good either. All last night she was staring at me, and now she's at it again."

"Christ," Ben muttered. "Yeah, Major Hooseman talked to her this morning. You're about the baddest man ever, leading po' George into smoking and drinking and late hours before you killed him."

"Never did get him to smoke," Lorne said, lighting Ben's cigarette and another for himself. "Say, did Jackson smoke?"

"Huh? No." Ben frowned, staring at the closed passenger-side windows and their reflections of his instruments. "Yeah, come to think, he did. But never in uniform, he had some sort of thing about that."

"He sheered off last night when I lit a cigarette," Lorne said. "No, not Jackson—the other one. I just wondered . . . ."

"You saw him?" Ben's voice was suddenly sharp, the hunter scenting prey.

Lorne shook his head. "I just felt him. But he was there, baby."

"Just like before they shot us down," the policeman said quietly. "You squeezing my arm and shouting over the damn engines 'They're waiting for us, they're waiting for us!' And not a fucking thing I could do—I didn't order the assault and the captain sure wasn't going to call it off because my machine gunner said to. But you were right, snake."

"The flames . . ." Lorne whispered, his eyes unfocused.

"And you're a dumb bastard to have done it, but you carried me out of them. It never helped us a bit that you knew when the shit was about to hit the fan. But you're a damn good man to have along when it does."

Lorne's muscles trembled with memory. Then he stood and laughed into the night. "You know, sarge, in twenty-seven years I've only found one job I was any good at. I didn't much like that one, and anyhow—the world doesn't seem to need killers."

"They'll always need us, snake," Ben said quietly. "Some times they won't admit it." Then, "Well, I think I'll waste some more gas."

"Sarge—" The word hung in the empty darkness. There was engine noise and the tires hissing in the near distance and—nothing else. "Sarge, Mrs. Purefoy was on her porch a minute ago and she didn't go inside. But she's not there now."

Ben's five-cell flashlight slid its narrow beam across the porch: the glider, the wing-back chair. On the far railing, a row of potted violets with a gap for the one now spilled on the boards as if by someone vaulting the rail but dragging one heel . . . .

"Didn't hear it fall," the policeman muttered, clacking open the car door. The dome light spilled a startling yellow pool across the two men. As it did so, white motion trembled half a block down Rankin Street.

"Fucker!" Ben said. "He couldn't jump across the street, he threw something so it flashed." Ben was back in the car.

Lorne squinted, furious at being blinded at the critical

instant. "Sarge, I'll swear to God he headed for the church." Lorne strode stiffly around the front of the vehicle and got in on the passenger side.

"Mother *fuck!*" the stocky policeman snarled, dropping the microphone that had three times failed to get him a response. He reached for the shift lever, looked suddenly at Lorne as the slender man unclipped the shotgun. "Where d'ye think *you're* going?"

"With you."

Ben slipped the transmission into Drive and hung a shrieking U-turn in the empty street. "The first one's birdshot, the next four are double-ought buck," he said flatly.

Lorne jacked the slide twice, chambering the first round and then shucking it out the ejector. It gleamed palely in the instrument light. "Don't think we're going after birds," he explained.

Ben twisted across the street and bounced over the driveway cut. The car slammed to a halt in the small lot behind and shielded by the bulk of the old church. It was a high, narrow building with two levels of boarded windows the length of the east and west sides; the square tower stood at the south end. At some time after its construction, the church had been faced with artificial stone. It was dingy, a gray mass in the night with a darkness about it that the night alone did not explain.

Ben slid out of the car. His flash touched the small door to the right of the tower. "Nothing wrong with the padlock," Lorne said. It was a formidable one, set in a patinaed hasp to close the church against vandals and derelicts.

"They were all locked tight yesterday, too," the patrolman said. "He could still be getting in one of those windows. We'll see." He turned to the trunk of the car and opened it, holding his flashlight in the crook of his arm so his right hand could be free for his drawn revolver.

Lorne's quick eyes scanned the wall above them. He bent back at the waist instead of tilting his head alone. "Got the key?" he asked.

The stocky man chuckled, raising a pair of folding shovels, army surplus entrenching tools. "Keep that cornsheller ready," he directed, holstering his own weapon. He locked the blade of one shovel at 90° to the shaft and set it on top of the padlock. The other, still folded, cracked loudly against the head of the first and popped the lock open neatly. "Field expedients, snake," Ben laughed. "If we don't find anything, we can just shut the place up again and nobody'll know the difference."

He tossed the shovels aside and swung open the door. The air that puffed out had the expected mustiness of a long-closed structure with a sweetish overtone that neither man could have identified. Lorne glanced around the outside once more, then followed the patrolman within. The flames in his mind were very close.

"Looks about like it did last night," Ben said.

"And last year, I'd guess." The wavering oval of the flashlight picked over the floor. The hardwood was warping, pocked at frequent intervals by holes.

"They unbolted the old pews when they moved," Ben explained. "Took the stained glass, too, since the place was going to be torn down."

The nave was a single narrow room running from the

chancel in the north to the tower which had held the organ pipes and, above, the chimes. The main entrance was by a side aisle, through double doors in the middle of the west wall. The interior looked a gutted ruin.

"You checked the whole building?" Lorne asked. The pulpit had been ripped away. The chancel rail remained though half-splintered, apparently to pass the organ and altar. Fragments of wood, crumpled boxes, and glass littered the big room.

"The main part. We didn't have the key to the tower and the major didn't want to bust in." Ben took another step into the nave and kicked at a stack of old bulletins.

White heat, white fire—"Ben, did you check the ceiling when you were here last night?"

"Huh?" The narrow Gothic vault was blackness forty feet above the ground. Ben's flashlight knifed upward across painted plaster to the ribbed and paneled ceiling that sloped to the main beam. And—"Jesus!"

A large cocoon was tight against the roof peak. It shimmered palely azure, but the powerful light thrust through to the human outline within. Long shadows quivered on the wood, magnifying the trembling of the policeman's wrist as the beam moved from the cocoon to another beside it, to the third—

"Seven of the fuckers!" Ben cried, taking another step and slashing the light to the near end of the room where the south wall closed the inverted V of the ceiling. Above the door to the tower was the baize screen of the pipe loft. The cloth fluttered behind Mrs. Purefoy, who stood stiffly upright twenty feet in the air. Her face was locked in horror, framed by her tousled white hair. Both arms were slightly extended but were stone-rigid within the lace-fringed sleeves of her dress.

"She—" Lorne began, but as he spoke and Ben's hand fell to the butt of his revolver, Mrs. Purefoy began to fall, tilting a little in a rustle of skirts. Beneath the crumpled edge of the baize curtain, spiked on the beam of Ben's flashlight, gleamed the head and foreclaws of what had been clutching the woman.

The eyes glared like six-inch opals, fierce and hot in a dead-white exoskeleton.

The foreclaws clicked sideways. As though they had cocked a spring, the whole flat torso shot down at Ben.

An inch long and scuttling under a rock, it might have passed for a scorpion, but this lunging monster was six feet long without counting the length of the tail arced back across its body. Flashing legs, flashing body armor, and the fluid-jeweled sting that winked as Lorne's finger twitched in its killer's reflex—

Lorne's body screamed at the recoil of the heavy charge. The creature spun as if kicked in midair, smashing into the floor a yard from Ben instead of on top of the policeman. The revolver blasted, a huge yellow bottle-shape flaring from the muzzle. The bullet ripped away a window shutter because a six-inch pincer had locked Ben's wrist. The creature reared onto the back two pairs of its eight jointed legs. Lorne stepped sideways for a clear shot, the slide of his weapon slick-snacking another round into the chamber. On the creature's white belly was a smeared asterisk—the load of buckshot had ricocheted off, leaving a trail like wax on glass.

Ben clubbed his flashlight. It cracked harmlessly

between the glowing eyes and sprang from his hand. The other claw flashed to Ben's face and trapped it, not crushingly but hard enough to immobilize and start blood-trails down both cheeks. The blades of the pincer ran from nose to hairline on each side.

Lorne thrust his shotgun over Ben's right shoulder and fired point-blank. The creature rocked back, jerking a scream from the policeman as the claws tightened. The lead struck the huge left eye and splashed away, dulling the opal shine. The flashlight still glaring from the floor behind the creature silhouetted its sectioned tail as it arched above the policeman's head. The armed tip plunged into the base of his neck. Ben stiffened.

Lorne shouted and emptied his shotgun. The second dense red bloom caught like a strobe light the dotted line of blood droplets joining Ben's neck to the withdrawn injector. A claw seized Lorne's waist in the rolling echo of the shotgun blasts. His gunbutt cracked on the creature's armor, steel sparking as it slid off. The extending pincer brushed the shotgun aside and clamped over Lorne's face, half-shielding from him the sight of the rising sting.

Then it smashed on Lorne's neck brace, and darkness exploded over him in a flare of coruscant pain.

The oozing ruin of Mrs. Purefoy's face stared at Lorne through its remaining eye when he awoke. Everything swam in blue darkness except for one bright blur. He blinked and the blur suddenly resolved into a streetlight glaring up through a shattered board. Lorne's lungs burned and his stiffness seemed more than even unconsciousness and the pain skidding through his nerve paths could explain. He moved his arm and something clung to its surface; the world quivered.

Lorne was hanging from the roof of the church in a thin, transparent sheath. Mrs. Purefoy was a yard away, multiple wrappings shrouding her corpse more completely. With a strength not far from panic, Lorne forced his right fist into the bubble around him. The material, extruded in broad swathes by the creature rather than as a loom of threads, sagged but did not tear. The clear azure turned milky under stress and sucked in around Lorne's wrist.

He withdrew his hand. The membrane passed some oxygen but not enough for an active man. Lorne's hands patted the outside of his pockets finding, as he had expected, nothing with a sharp edge. He had not recently bitten off his thumbnails. Thrusting against the fire in his chest, he brought his left hand in front of his body. With a fold of the cocoon between each thumb and index finger, he thrust his hands apart. A rip started in the white opacity beneath his right thumb. Air, clean and cool, jetted in.

"Oh, Jesus," Lorne muttered, even the pain in his body forgotten as he widened the tear upwards to his face. The cocoon was bobbing on a short lead, rotating as the rip changed its balance. Lorne could see that he had become ninth in the line of hanging bodies, saved from their paralysis by the chance of his neck brace. Ben, his face blurred by the membrane holding him next to Lorne, had been less fortunate.

Ten yards from where Lorne hung and twenty feet below the roof beam, the baize curtain of the pipe loft twitched. Lorne froze in fearful immobility.

The creature had been able to leap the width of a street

carrying the weight of an adult; its strength must be as awesome as was the rigidity of its armor. Whether or not it could drive its sting through Lorne's brace, it could assuredly rip him to collops if it realized he was awake.

The curtain moved again, the narrow ivory tip of a pincer lifting it slightly. The creature was watching Lorne.

Ben carried three armor-piercing rounds in his .357 Magnum for punching through car doors. Lorne tried to remember whether the revolver had remained in Ben's hand as he fell. There was no image of that in Lorne's mind, only the torchlike muzzle blasts of his own shotgun. Slim as it was, his only hope was that the jacketed bullets would penetrate the creature's exoskeleton though the soft buckshot had not.

Lorne twisted his upper torso out of the hole for a closer look at Ben, making his own cocoon rock angrily. The baize lifted further. The streetlight lay across it in a pale band. Why didn't the creature scuttle out to finish the business?

Brief motion waked a flash of scintillant color from the pipe loft. The curtain flapped closed as if a volley of shots had ripped through it. Lorne recognized the reflex: the panic of a spider when a stick thrusts through its web. Not an object, though; the light itself, weak as it was, had slapped the creature back.

Ben's bright flashlight had not stopped it when necessity drove, but the monster must have felt pain at human levels of illumination. Its eyes were adapted to starlight or the glow of a sun immeasurably fainter than that of Earth. "Where did you come from, you bastard?" Lorne whispered.

Light. It gave him an idea and he fumbled out his

butane lighter, adjusting it to a maximum flame. The sheathes were relatively thin over the victims' faces to aid transpiration. At the waist, though, where a bulge showed Ben's arm locked to his torso, the membrane was thick enough to be opaque in the dim light. Lorne bent dangerously over, cursing the stiffness of his neck brace. Holding the inch-high jet close, he tried to peer through Ben's cocoon. Unexpectedly the fabric gave a little and Lorne bobbed forward, bringing the flame in contact with the material sheathing Ben.

The membrane sputtered, kissing Lorne's hand painfully. He jerked back and the lighter flicked away. It dropped, cold and silent until it cracked on the floor forty feet below. Despite the pattern of light over it, the curtain to the loft was shifting again. Lorne cursed in terror.

A line of green fire sizzled up the side of Ben's cocoon from the point at which the flame had touched it. The material across his face flared. The policeman gave no sign of feeling his skin curl away. The revolver in his hand winked green.

Lorne screamed. His own flexible prison lurched and sagged like heated polyethylene. Ben was wrapped in a cancerous hell that roared and heaved against the roofbeams as a live thing. Green tongues licked yellow-orange flames from the dry wood as well. Lorne's cocoon and that to the other side of Ben were deforming in the furnace heat. Another lurch and Lorne had slipped twenty feet, still gripped around the waist in a sack of blue membrane. He was gyrating like a top.

The loft curtain had twitched higher each time it spun past his vision.

The bottom of Ben's cocoon burned away and he plunged past Lorne, face upward and still afire. Bone crunched as he hit. The body rebounded a few inches to fall again on its face. The roar of the flames muffled Lorne's wail of rage. His own elongated capsule began to flow. Flames grasped at Lorne's support. Before they could touch the sheathing, the membrane pulled a last few inches and snapped like an overstretched rubber band. The impact of the floor smashed Lorne's jaw against his neck brace, grinding each tortured vertebra against the next. He did not lose consciousness, but the shock paralyzed him momentarily as thoroughly as the creature's sting could have done.

Bathed in green light and the orange of the blazing roof panels, the scorpion-thing thrust its thorax into the nave. It walking legs gripped the flat surface, dimpling the plaster. The creature turned upward toward the fire, three more cocoons alight and their hungry flames lapping across the beams. Then, partly colored by the illumination, its legs shifted and the opal eyes trained on Lorne. The light must be torture to it, muffling in indecision its responses, but it was about to act.

A small form wrapped in a flaming shroud dropped to thump the floor beside Lorne. His arms would move again. He used them to strip the remaining sheathing from his legs. It clung as the heat of the burning corpse began to melt the material. Something writhed from a crackling tumor on the child's neck. The thing was finger-long and seemed to paw the air with a score of tiny legs; its opalescent eyes proved its parentage. The creature brought more than paralysis to its victims: it was a gravid female.

Green flame touched the larva. It burst in a pustulant smear.

The adult went mad. Its legs shot it almost the length of the nave to rebound from a sidewall in a cloud of plaster. The creature's horizontally flattened tail ruddered it instinctively short of the fire as it leapt upward to the roof peak. It clung there in pale horror against the wood, eyes on the advancing flames. Three more bodies fell, splashing like ginkgo fruits.

Lorne staggered upright. The fire hammered down at him without bringing pain. His body had no feeling whatever. Ben's hair had burned. His neck and scalp were black where skin remained, red where it had cracked open to the muscle beneath. The marbled background showed clearly the tiny, pallid hatchling trying to twist across it.

Lorne's toe brushed the larva onto the floor. His boot heel struck it, struck again and twisted. Purulent ichor spurted between the leather and the boards. Lorne knelt. In one motion he swung Ben across his shoulders and stood, just as he had after their helicopter had nosed into the trees and exploded. Logic had been burned out of Lorne's mind, leaving only a memory of friendship. He did not look up. As his mechanical steps took him and his burden through the door they had entered, a shadow wavered across them. The creature had sprung back into the loft.

Lorne stumbled to his knees in the parking lot. The church had been rotten and dry. Orange flames fluffed through the roof in several places, thrusting corkscrews of sparks into the night sky. Twelve feet of roof slates thundered into the nave. Flame spewed up like a secondary explosion. There were sirens in the night.

Without warning, the east facade of the tower collapsed into the parking lot. Head-sized chunks of Tennessee-stone smashed at the patrol car, one of them missing Lorne by inches. He looked up, blank-eyed, his hands lightly touching the corpse of his friend. Of its own volition, the right hand traced down Ben's shoulder to the raw flesh of his elbow. The tower stairs spiraled out of the dust and rubble, laid bare to the steel framework when the wall fell. On the sagging floor of the pipe loft rested a machine like no other thing on Earth, and the creature was inside it. Tubes of silvery metal rose cradle-form from a base of similar metal. The interstices were not filled with anything material, but the atmosphere seemed to shiver, blurring the creature's outline.

And Lorne's hand was unwrapping Ben's stiff fingers from the grips of his revolver.

Lorne stood again, his left hand locking his right on the butt of the big magnum. He was familiar with the weapon: it was the one Ben had carried in Nam, the same tool he had used for five of his thirteen kills. It would kill again tonight.

Even in the soaring holocaust the sharp crack of Lorne's shot was audible. Lorne's forearms rocked up as a unit with the recoiling handgun. The creature lurched sideways to touch the shimmering construct around it. A red surface discharge rippled across the exoskeleton from the point of contact. Lorne fired again. He could see the armor dull at his point of aim in the center of the thorax.

Again the creature jumped. Neither bullet had penetrated, but the splashing lead of the second cut an upright from the machine. The creature spun, extending previously unglimpsed tendrils from the region of its mouth parts. They flickered over a control plate in the base. Machinery chimed in response.

The shivering quickened. The machine itself and the thing it enclosed seemed to fade. Lorne thumb-cocked the magnum, lowered the red vertical of the front sight until it was even with the rear notch; the creature was a white blur beyond them. The gun bucked back hard when he squeezed; the muzzle blast was sharper, flatter, than before. The first of the armor-piercing bullets hit the creature between the paired tendrils. The exoskeleton surrounding them shattered like safety glass struck by a brick.

The creature straightened in silent agony, rising onto its hind legs with its tail lying rigidly against its back. Its ovipositor was fully extended, thumb-thick and six inches long.

"Was it fun to kill them, bug?" Lorne screamed. "Was it as much fun as this is?" His fourth shot slammed, dimpling a belly plate which then burst outward in an ugly gush of fluids. The creature's members clamped tightly about its spasming thorax. The tail lashed the uprights in red spurts. The machine was fading and the torn paneling of the loft was beginning to show through the dying creature's body.

There was one shot left in the cylinder and Lorne steadied his sights on the control plate. He had already begun taking up the last pressure when he stopped and lowered the muzzle. No, let it go home, whatever place or time that might be. Let its fellows see that Earth was not their hunting ground alone. And if they came back anyway—*if they only would!*

There was a flash as penetrating as the first microsecond of a nuclear blast. The implosion dragged Lorne off his feet and sucked in the flames so suddenly that all sound seemed frozen. Then both sidewalls collapsed into the nave and the ruins of the tower twisted down on top of them. In the last instant, the pipe loft was empty of all but memory.

A fire truck picked its way through the rubble in the parking lot. Its headlights flooded across the figure of a sandy-haired man wearing scorched clothing and a neck brace. He was kneeling beside a body, and the tears were bright on his face.

THE AUTOMATIC
RIFLEMAN

※ ☲ ※

Fritz Leiber is credited with developing the horror story with an urban setting. His Fafhrd and Gray Mouser series is more a parallel development to Robert E. Howard's work than it's a copy (compare Le Fanu's Carmilla *with Stoker's* Dracula *for another case of "similar" not meaning "the same"). And for horror in an SF milieu, it'd be hard to better, say, "A Bad Day for Sales" or "A Pail of Air."*

I stole this idea from Leiber's urban fantasy "The Automatic Pistol."

Well, it's not quite that simple. Vergil was regularly accused of stealing from Homer, to which he would reply, "Why don't you try it yourself? If you did, you'd understand that it's easier to filch Hercules's club than it is to steal a verse from Homer." But "The Automatic Rifleman" wouldn't exist in the form it does were it not for Leiber's literally seminal story.

If you like my work, go out and read everything

Fritz Leiber wrote before, say, 1960. I don't know of a writer with a more varied and brilliant take on every subject he touched.

The story itself is a wish-fulfillment fantasy like a great deal of other horror fiction, some of it very good. The story posits the notion that things are in their present state because some external force is working to make them bad; in other words, the world's problems are not the result of mankind's own actions.

I wish I could really believe that was true.

✢ ✢ ✢

Coster was waiting for them in the darkened room, hidden by the greater shadow of the couch. His face was as lean and hard-edged as the automatic rifle he held pointed at the door. "Where's the goddam light?" Penske muttered. He found the switch, threw it, and froze with his hand halfway down to the knife in his boot.

Davidson bumped into Penske from behind and cursed, her lips twisting into the sneer she kept ready when she was around the short man. "Move your—" she began before she saw why Penske had stopped. Then, without hesitation, she cried, "George, look out!"

"Too late," said Coster with a bailiff's smirk and the least motion of the rifle muzzle to bring it to the attention of George Kerr. The black man in suit and tie loomed behind his two companions. His eyes were open and apparently guileless, shuttering a mind that had already realized that the flimsy apartment walls would be no obstacle to rifle bullets. "But we're all friends here," Coster went on, his grin broadening.

"Then I suggest we all come in and discuss matters," said Kerr in a cultured voice, showing his bad front tooth as he spoke. His fingers touched Davidson's right elbow and halted the stealthy motion of her hand toward her open purse.

"Sure," said Coster, nodding, "but stay bunched in that corner, if you will." His head and not the rifle twitched a direction. "Until you're convinced of my good intentions, you'll be tempted to—put yourselves in danger. We don't want that."

"Who the hell are you?" Penske demanded, shuffling sideways as directed. An angry flush turned his face almost as dark as that of Kerr beside him.

"My name's Coster," the rifleman said. "Agfield told me where I'd find you."

Davidson whirled angrily toward Kerr. "I told you not to trust that bastard!" she said. "Somebody ought to take one of his basketballs and stuff it—"

"Dee, that's enough," the big man said, his eyes still on the rifleman. He had closed the hall door softly behind him. Nothing in his manner called attention to the pistol holstered in the small of his back.

"He said you could use a rifleman for what you had in mind," Coster amplified. "We're what you need."

"We?" asked Penske tautly. The muscles beneath his leather jacket were as rigid as the bones to which they were anchored, for he recognized even better than the others the menace of the weapon which covered them.

"Me," said Coster, "and him." His left forefinger tapped the gunbarrel where it projected from its wooden shroud. His right hand stayed firm on the rifle's angled handgrip, finger ready on the trigger.

Calmly, Kerr said, "Agfield doesn't know what we have in mind." His right hand was now loose at his side, no longer restraining Davidson.

"Sure he does," said the rifleman, flashing his tight-lipped grin again. "Kawanishi, the Japanese Prime Minister. And I'm here to make sure you get him."

For a moment, no one even breathed. Coster leaned forward, his right elbow still gripping the gunstock to his ribs. He said earnestly, "Look, if I were the police, would I be talking to you? The whole World Proletarian Caucus is right here, right in front of . . . us. And if it was trials, convictions, they were after—the evidence is *on* you, or at least outside in your car. You blew away a teller in La Prensa, and you've still got the gun, don't you? And the one that killed that little girl in Mason City?"

Davidson mumbled a curse and looked hot-eyed at Penske.

"But we're friends," Coster repeated. Very deliberately, he rotated the automatic rifle so that its muzzle brake pointed at the ceiling. The rubber butt rested on his thigh.

"Friends," said Kerr. "Then we should get comfortable." He took off his suit coat and turned, as deliberate as Coster, to drape it over the back of a chair. The grip of the big Colt was a square black silhouette against his light shirt.

Everyone eased a little. Coster laid the rifle across his knees, one hand still caressing the receiver of the weapon. Davidson and Penske both lit cigarettes, the latter by flicking the head of a kitchen match with his thumbnail. He tossed the wooden sliver toward a wastebasket. It missed, but he ignored it as it continued to smoulder on the cheap carpet.

Kerr took one of the straight chairs from the kitchen-dinette and sat backwards on it, facing in toward the living room and Coster. The pistol did not gouge at him that way. "Penske, why don't you bring things in from the van," he said.

The short man glowered, but his expression suddenly cleared and he walked to the door. "I'll knock when I want you to open," he said as he left the room.

Davidson moved over beside Kerr, her fingertips brushing the point of his shoulder. "You sound very confident about your ability to use that gun," the big man said with a gesture toward the oddly shaped rifle. "But I don't know that I'd care to make plans based on something . . . suppositious."

Coster's tongue clicked in amusement. "Do you want references? Somebody who saw us put away Kennedy? Or King?"

Davidson snorted a puff of smoke. "You don't look like a fool," Kerr said.

"I'm not—not any longer," the rifleman replied. He shook his head as if to clear something from his hair. He went on, "What we've done doesn't matter. You won't believe me, and it doesn't matter. But if you have some place for a demonstration, we'll—demonstrate."

Kerr nodded. "That would be best," he said neutrally.

Coster suddenly turned and lowered the rifle again toward the door. "Speaking of fools," he said, "your Mr. Penske—"

There was no knock. The door slammed back. "All right you—" Penske shouted before he realized that the fat muzzle of the automatic rifle was centered on his breastbone. The swarthy man held a carbine waist high, his left hand locked on the curving 30-round magazine.

Obviously furious but with no more sound than his chair made clattering on the floor, Kerr strode toward the disconcerted Penske. With his left hand the black gripped the carbine and tugged the smaller man back within the room. Then his right hand slapped Penske's head against the wall. He stepped away, holding the carbine muzzle-down. "And if you'd used it, you damned fool?"the big man demanded. "If you'd brought the police down on us here, what chance would our plans have had then? *What chance?*"

"You didn't have to hit me," Penske said, not quite meeting Kerr's eyes.

Contemptuously, the black unloaded the carbine, tossing the magazine onto a stuffed chair and ejecting the round in the chamber. It winked against the carpet. "Get the things out of the van," he said.

Kerr had rented the furnished apartment a month before, but that was as far as preparations had gone. The can-opener beside the sink was broken and Penske, grumbling, had to hack their dinners open with his heavy-bladed dagger.

"If you were a real Green Beret, you could bite the lids off," Davidson gibed.

"Shut the hell up!" the short man snarled. He caught Coster eying him as the rifleman spread baked beans one-handed on a slice of bread. "I'da' made it, no goddam doubt," Penske said defensively. "Only they had us doing sprints up and down the company street with sand in our packs. Some wise-ass clerk thinks it's funny to laugh at me. I knocked his teeth out, and the bastard's goddam lucky they hadn't issued us ammo. But the goddam government don't want anybody that'll really fight, so they busted me out."

"Makes a good story," Davidson said. "I think they caught him with his—"

"Dee!" Kerr said.

Penske's eyes unglazed and he slowly lowered his knife back onto the can of spaghetti. He hammered the hilt down with his palm, splashing the red sauce onto the table.

Despite their hostility, Davidson and Penske settled down to a desultory game of cribbage after dinner.

Kerr sat in the living room across from the rifleman. "I don't play games that you have to score," the big black said. "When I win, the whole world will know it. When I win, there won't be any polite Orientals pumping mercury into the sea because poisoning children is cheaper than not. There won't be any blue-shirted gestapo beating in their brothers' heads because the bankers say to. There won't be any more nuclear powerplants pouring out their deadliness for a quarter-million years."

The rifleman smiled. He held a jelly glass he had filled with whiskey and had not diluted. "There won't be any three-year-olds orphaned in La Prensa because their daddy was too slow emptying his money drawer."

"What are you here for?" Kerr demanded.

Coster's free hand played with his rifle. "Now? To kill a Japanese politician in America discussing import quotas." He swigged his drink.

Kerr leaned forward. "To show the rich that there is justice for the people?" he pressed.

"Human society's a funny thing," said the rifleman, staring at the reflection of the overhead light in his whiskey. "Very complex. But if it gets enough little thrusts, all in the same direction . . . lots of people hate lots of other people anyway. Someday enough people are going to hate enough other people that one of them is going to push the button. Then it all stops."

Kerr's lips tightened. "Bad as things are, I don't believe they've come to that pass yet. Nobody would gain by that."

"Right. Nobody would gain."

Penske and Davidson were arguing about the count. The dinette was blurry with cigarette smoke. Kerr stared for a moment at the ex-soldier, then said to Coster, "There'll be bodyguards, you know. Secret Service men."

"Bodyguards," Coster snorted. "Like Huey Long had? It was one of his guards who killed him, you know, a bullet ricocheting in the marble hallway. And when King Alexander was killed in Marseilles, the gunman ran right through a line of mounted gendarmes."

"I suppose you shot him, too?" Kerr said acidly. "Like Kennedy?"

Coster looked at the heavier man with an odd expression. "I wasn't there," he said. "That was in 1934. The man who did it used a pistol, yes, but there was an automatic rifle backing him up. If it had been needed." He finished his drink with a long swallow and said, "A push here, a push there. . . ."

Kerr stood abruptly. "It's been a long day for us," he said. "Now that I've stopped seeing pavement, I'll go to bed. You can carry your things into the smaller bedroom, Coster. Penske fits the couch better, I think."

Coster nodded. "I don't have much," he said, toeing a canvas AWOL bag.

In the dinette, Davidson threw in her hand without a word. She followed Kerr into the larger bedroom, slamming the door behind them.

The rifleman walked over to the table, his weapon muzzle-down in his left hand. He poured a drink and raised it in an ironic salute. "Cheers," he said to the brooding Penske. He drank and walked into the remaining bedroom without bothering to take his bag.

Penske drove with Davidson on the front seat beside him. Her short hair was dark except at the roots where it was growing in blond. Kerr and Coster looked at each other from side benches in the windowless back of the van.

Over his shoulder Penske said, "Ah, George . . . the guy who owns the farm, Jesse, I met him when I was at Bragg, see? Could be he won't be around and he's not gonna care what we're shooting, choppers, grenades, whatever. Only maybe you better stay in the back, you know? It'd be better if Jesse didn't, you know . . . ."

"Jesse doesn't like his black brothers, is that it?" Kerr said easily. His face worked and he added, "Don't have much use fer a nigger 'cept to kick his black butt, that is."

"Well, George . . ." the short man mumbled. "We just needed a place to range in the guns. . . ."

"That's all right, it's no fault of yours," Kerr said. "Or your friends'."

He looked over at the rifleman. "You see what they do, splitting natural allies so that they'd rather tear each other's throats out than both tear at their oppressors. Turning humans into beasts."

"Humans are beasts, of course," Coster said without emphasis. "Whether or not Darwin was right, he was convincing on that score. I think that's why the concept of werebeasts is so much less terrifying today than it was in the fifteenth century. We're all basically convinced that man-beasts are normal reality. Hieronymus Bosch and his constructs of part flesh, part metal . . . that I don't think we've outgrown. Yet."

"Is that all injustice means to you?" Davidson asked sharply. "That we're all beasts, so what? Did you just get out of your flying saucer or something?"

Coster looked at her, his fingers toying with the selector switch below his rifle's gunsight. "Viewpoint, I suppose," he said. "But no, I'm human. Funny, I used to wonder what aliens . . . creatures from space, that is . . . would look like. I thought they might look just like you and me." He began to laugh brittlely.

No one in the van spoke again during the remainder of the drive.

After nearly an hour on the road, Penske pulled off on a farm track. A gate stopped the van immediately. The swarthy man jumped down, unhooked the chain, and tugged the sagging frame out of the way. As he got back in and slipped the van into gear, he explained, "Jesse said he'd loop it for me, not run it through the bars."

Penske pulled up just beyond the arc of the gate. He said to Davidson, "Go hook it shut. We don't want any a' the cows to get loose."

Davidson's eyes narrowed. "You opened it, you can shut it. Who the hell—"

"Look, bitch!" Penske said, his right hand curled by reflex into a fist, "You'll shake a leg or you'll—"

"Penske!" Kerr shouted, thrusting his torso over the seat and forcing the driver back without contact. "What do you think we are, exploiters ourselves who treat women like furniture? Want to try that with me too, is that what you think?"

"George, I . . ." Penske began. He shook his head fiercely to hide the tears of frustration. Then he unlatched the door, almost falling out backwards in the process. He closed the gate. It was almost a minute before the short man got back into the van and drove on. There were three more gates in the long track between the highway and the pasture swale in which they finally halted. Penske opened and closed each gate himself without saying anything more.

In wet weather the swale drained into a creek more than three hundred yards from the van. The bank beyond the watercourse was steep but generally grassy. There was a bare patch in line with the axis of the swale. Bits of cardboard and metal there brightened the bullet-gouged bank. Other target material lay in riddled clumps at various distances along the way. There was some scattered cartridge brass, mostly .22 caliber—centerfire empties had been picked up for reloading.

"The boys around here use it a lot," Penske said in satisfaction as he took cases out of the back of the van.

"The boys," Davidson snorted. "The Klan's more like it."

Penske looked at her without speaking or moving. He

had just begun to load a magazine into a carbine. He looked back downrange after a moment.

Davidson swallowed, then bit at a knuckle. "I'll set some targets up," she said.

"That'll take rigging," Penske said without turning around. "You get the rest a' the guns loaded. Coster'n me'll rig the targets."

"Sure," she said, and she slid a box of miscellaneous empty containers over to the automatic rifleman.

Coster gripped the box with his left hand and his jutting hip bone. His other hand held the rifle at its balance. "All right," he said, "where do you want them?"

"I doubt you'll have to fight off the field mice," Kerr observed from the van. "You can leave the gun here and save the trouble of carrying it."

"No trouble," Coster said. He began walking down the swale.

Penske, carrying an armload of clothesline and plastic milk jugs, trotted along beside the rifleman. "You put a few a' those at one hundred and two hundred," he said. "Save a lot for the bank across the creek, though, 'cause that's where it's really gonna be at. We'll see if you can handle that thing'r not."

The smaller man stopped some fifty yards from the van. He dropped his load and pointed. A fence post and a metal engineer stake stood on opposite rims of the swale. "I'm gonna rig a moving target," he said. "You set up the bottles."

Both men worked quickly. By the time Coster had returned to the line of the posts, the shorter man joined him, unreeling clothesline behind him. "Aw right," Penske said, wringing his hands with enthusiasm as they strode back to the firing line. "Aw right, now we just see how goddam good you are."

Coster said nothing.

On a blanket beside the van, Davidson had laid out half a dozen varied long arms. Kerr was still in the vehicle, either in deference to Penske's request or from a disinclination to be anywhere else. Penske had forgotten his shirt downrange. Sweat streaks trembled along valleys separating ridges of chest muscle. He picked up what looked like an ordinary autoloading rifle and checked its magazine before cradling the weapon in his left arm.

"We let the lady shoot, hey?" Penske said to Coster with a high-lipped grin. "Then you'n me try it."

The automatic rifleman shrugged.

Davidson passed Penske's reference with only a scowl. She picked up an M1 carbine and pointed it in the general direction of the nearest bottles. Her grip on the trim little weapon was fierce enough to whiten the skin across the tendons of her hands. She held the gunstock a good quarter-inch from her shoulder. The first shot was loud and metallic, startling even to those who were prepared for it.

"You don't wanna let it scare you," Penske said, reaching for the carbine.

"Go shove your head up your ass!" Davidson flared, snatching the weapon away with a clear willingness to empty it into the swarthy man. She whirled back to the targets and fired a long, savage volley as fast as she could jerk her trigger finger. When she paused, the muzzle had recoiled up to a 30° angle. None of the men spoke when she glared around fiercely. Squinting along the barrel,

Davidson resumed fire more deliberately until the banana magazine was empty. Her brass spun off in flat arcs to the right. Once a puff of dirt halfway to the targets marked a shot. Davidson flung the carbine back onto the blanket and stalked into the van.

Penske started to say something but thought better of it. He grinned at Coster and raised his own rifle. Instead of a shot, there was a ripping five-round burst, the rifle emptying its own magazine as Penske held the trigger back. Dirt spouted around the bottles, though the last three shots had been slung skyward by the recoiling muzzle.

"Thought you had the only automatic rifle here, huh?" the short man crowed. "Converted this myself, same as one a' the M1s and the .22 there. Not so special now, are you?"

"You only hit one bottle," Coster said. His left hand curled around the grip on the rifle's forearm.

"Only one?" Penske cried in a fury. "A man's a lot bigger target'n a goddam bottle!"

Metal clicked as Coster's forefinger slid forward the safety catch in his rifle's trigger guard. Speech crumbled into the shattering muzzle blasts of the automatic rifle.

Coster ignored the nearest targets. The bottles at 200, then 300, yards disintegrated in pluming earth. The weapon fired in short bursts of two and three rounds, the muzzle recovering momentarily between blasts to snuffle another target. When the bolt locked back on an empty magazine, there was nothing but dust and glass shards at either aiming point.

Coster's fingers relaxed on the handgrips. He extracted the magazine and began thumbing cartridges into it from a box on the ground. He looked sidelong at Penske.

"We'll try the moving one, wise guy," the shorter man said.

Behind them, Kerr had gotten out of the van. "What kind of gun is that?" he asked.

"M14E2," Penske replied. "The squad automatic version of the standard M14. Has pistolgrips and a straight-line stock. Made goddam few of 'em, too, before they switched from the fourteen to the sixteen." He looked at Coster. "Hey, ain't that so?"

Coster shrugged and locked home his magazine. Heat waves danced from the tip of the barrel where metal was exposed to the air.

"Well, don't you even goddam know?" Penske demanded. "How'd you get that rifle, anyway?"

The rifleman looked at him. "You'd better hope you never learn," he said. "Now, are we going to shoot guns or talk about them?"

"We'll shoot," the smaller man said fiercely. "We'll goddam shoot." He pointed to the gallon milk jug suspended beside the engineer stake. "One line's through the handle, the other's tied to it," he said. "When I pull this one—" he gestured with the loop of wire-core clothes line in his left-hand—" the jug runs to the other post. Don't sweat, I poured it full a' dirt so it'll show if you hit it. If you hit it."

"Then pull," Coster said, and braced himself. His knuckles were as white as Davidson's had been. His head, hunched low, looked more like that of a man trying to hide than one aiming.

Penske chuckled. "Won't hit nothing but air if you're that scared a' your weapon," he said. He tugged two-handed at the line bent around the fencepost. The jug spurted sideways and the first three bullets ripped it. Sandy loam sprayed from the torn plastic in all directions. The impacts spun the jug around its support line and the second burst caught it at the tip of its arc. Dirt flew again and both lines parted. The gun muzzle tracked the flying container, spiked it in the air, and then followed it down the swale, the bullets themselves kicking their target into a semblance of life.

Flying brass had driven Kerr back from where he stood to Coster's right. Now he massaged his left fist with his right palm, watching the rifleman reload methodically.

"That enough?" Coster asked. Kerr nodded.

Penske had silently begun to gather up the paraphernalia they had brought. Suddenly he stopped, staring at the empty cartridge box he held in his hand. "You reloaded from this," he said, waving the box in Coster's face. "Last time."

"So?" said the rifleman. "You want me to pay you for them?"

"You stupid bastard!"the shorter man blazed. "This was .30-'06 for my Remington there. It won't *fit* a goddam M14. You need .308!"

"Then I didn't use your ammunition after all," Coster said, backing a step. "I brought my own in my kit, you know." His foot tapped the AWOL bag gently.

"Let's see that goddam rifle," said Penske, lunging forward, and the safety clicked off with the muzzle only six inches from the bridge of his nose.

"Don't," said Coster very quietly.

Sullenly, the ex-soldier backed away. "Somebody gimme a hand with this crap," he said, thrusting weapons back into their cases.

"We aren't rivals, you know," Coster said without lowering the M14. "I wasn't Oswald's rival either. If you want a man dead and he dies, what else matters?"

"Just shut the hell up, will you?" Davidson burst out unexpectedly.

The three men looked around in surprise. Davidson's fists were clenched at waist-height, her elbows splayed. After a moment Coster said, "All right." He dropped the muzzle of his rifle and began handing guns back into the van.

A mercury-vapor streetlight threw a line of saw teeth through the Venetian blinds to the wall above the couch. Penske lay there, fully clothed, watching the whorls which his cigarette smoke etched across the pattern. The apartment was still.

Penske took a last drag on his cigarette. Its yellow-orange glow was momentarily brighter than the blue of the streetlight. He ground the butt out in the dish with the others and the crumpled pack from which they had come. Then Penske swung his feet over the side of the couch and stood, his right hand silently drawing his knife from its sheath in the same motion. He glided across the worn carpet to the door of Coster's room.

For a moment the swarthy man waited with his ear pressed against the panel. There was no sound within. The door did not have a working latch; its hinges were nearly silent. Penske pulled the door open just enough to slip through into the pitch-dark bedroom. His whole body followed the knife as if he were a serpent and the blade was his questing tongue.

There was a metallic click from the bed, tiny and lethal as a cobra.

"The light switch is on the right," Coster said quietly. "Better flip it on. Carefully."

Penske's hand found the switch. The room was narrow. The bed lay along its axis, the foot of it pointing to the door. The M14 pointed down that same axis. Coster's index finger was within the trigger guard. The safety catch had clicked as it slid forward. The shorter man stared at the muzzle brake of the automatic rifle. He remembered the way bullets had shredded the earth-filled jug that morning. Now his blood and tissue and splinters of his bones would spray the inside of the door panel.

"Put your knife away," Coster said.

The shorter man only blinked.

"We're not here to kill you, Penske," said the automatic rifleman. His voice was calm, almost wheedling. "Put your knife away and close my door behind you. It'll all look different tomorrow. Kawanishi will be dead, and you'll have as much of the credit for it as you want."

Penske swallowed and began to back through the doorway. The gun muzzle waggled disapproval. "First the knife," Coster said.

The shorter man hunched over, his eyes on the rifle except for quick dips down to the strait boot sheath. He jabbed the point into the flesh above his ankle the first time he tried. At last he succeeded.

"Fine," said the rifleman. "You can go now."

Penske's face contorted with rage. "You bastard, you gotta sleep sometime!" he said.

Coster smiled like a skull. "Do we?"

The swarthy man slammed the door, turned, and jumped back before he realized that the figure hulking on the arm of the couch was Kerr. "What're you doing up?" Penske demanded in a husky whisper.

Kerr shrugged. "Let's go out on the landing," he said. "Dee's asleep." But it was toward the rectangle of light around Coster's door that he nodded.

The second-floor apartment was served by an outside staircase. Its landing formed a small railed balcony, open to crisp air and the stars of early morning. Kerr waved Penske outside, then followed and swung the door closed behind them. The big man was barefoot, but he wore slacks and a shirt. The latter was unbloused to conceal his pistol.

Penske clenched his joined hands. "He can't shoot," he said in a low voice. "Not worth a damn."

"You could have fooled me, then," said Kerr. "What I saw this morning was pretty convincing."

"I tell you he's afraid of it!" Penske burst out. "The recoil, the noise even—he flinched every time Dee shot, and when he was shooting himself—I swear to *God* he kept his eyes shut!"

Kerr's fingers played at flaking paint from the bars of the railing. His complexion was richened to a true black in the wash of the streetlight. "It looked like that to me, too," he admitted, "but he hit everything he shot at. He couldn't have done that if—if you were right."

"Unless that goddam rifle was alive," said Penske under his breath. He gripped the railing with both hands. His eyes were focused on the cars parked in the lot beneath them.

"Don't be a fool," Kerr snapped.

"George, I've *seen* people who can shoot," Penske said urgently. "That bastard's not one of 'em. Besides, *nobody's* that goddam good to shoot like he did offhand. Nobody human. He got it somewhere, and he trained it up to look like an M14 and shoot for him. Christ, he don't even know the difference from one kinda ammo and another. But it don't matter 'cause he's trained this—thing—and it's just like a guard dog." The little man paused, breathing deeply. "Or a witch cat," he added.

Kerr's index finger began to massage the gum above his bad tooth. "That's nonsense," he muttered around his hand. He did not look at Penske.

The smaller man touched Kerr's wrist. "It *fits*, George," he said. "It's the only goddam thing that does. The whole truth an' nothing but."

Kerr pursed his lips and said, "If we suppose that . . . what you say . . . could be true, does that change anything?"

"It changes—" Penske blurted, but he stopped when Kerr raised his hand. The question had been rhetorical.

"We accepted him as a man with a sophisticated weapon," the big man continued as if he had not been interrupted. "That's no less true now than it was. And our need for his weapon is no less real."

Penske blinked. "Maybe you know what you're doing. But I don't like it."

Kerr patted him on the shoulder. "After tomorrow it won't matter," he said. "After this morning, that is. Let's both get some sleep."

Coster's door was dark when the two men reentered the silent apartment. Everything was peaceful. Penske wondered briefly at what would have happened if instead they had returned determined to kill the automatic rifleman. He took his mind off that thought as he would have taken his hand off a scorpion.

The three men in the back of the van were each expressionless in a different way. Davidson swung to the curb in front of the office building. The street was marked "No Parking" but there was little traffic this early on a Saturday morning. Kerr nodded minusculy. Penske, carrying a Dewar's carton, scrambled out the back door. Coster followed with a long, flat box stenciled "Ajax Shelving—Light—Adjustable—Efficient." His right hand reached through a hole in the side of the box, but a casual onlooker would not have noticed that.

The entranceway door was locked. After a moment's fumbling with the key Kerr had procured, Penske pulled it open. Behind them, the assassins heard the van pull away. It would wait in the lot of a nearby office building until time to pick them up.

The hallways were empty and bright under their banks of fluorescents. Coster stepped toward the elevators but Penske motioned him aside. "We take the fire stairs," he said. "Get in a elevator'n you got no control. We can't afford that."

The stairs were narrow and sterile, gray concrete steps in a dingy yellow well.

Penske slipped once as he took two hurrying steps at a time, barking his shins and falling with a clatter on the box he carried. He got up cursing and continued to leap steps, but now he held the liquor carton in his right hand and gripped the square iron rail with his left. At the third floor landing, the little man pulled open the door and peered suspiciously down the hall.

"Clear," he said, stepping through. He let the door swing closed as Coster grabbed for it. Penske was opening an office with another key when the rifleman joined him. Then they were inside, the hall door closed and the fluorescents in the ceiling flickering into life.

Coster threw down the shelving box and caressed the M14 with both hands. Penske squatted on the carpet as he reassembled the stock and action of his carbine. He sneered, "You shoulda took that down 'steada hauling a goddam box that size around. Or don't you know how?"

"I don't take him down," said Coster. "You handle your end, I'll handle mine."

Penske strutted into the inner office. From the letterheads on the desks, the suite was connected in some fashion or other to the university. The swarthy man pushed a swivel chair aside and raised the Venetian blinds. "There," he said, waving. "There's where the bastards'll be."

Coster's slight smile did not change as he ducked a little to follow Penske's gesture. The rifleman had not visited the ambush site before. The window looked out on a parking lot, almost empty now, and the back street which formed a one-way pair with the street in front of the building. Beyond the lot and the street was a chainlink fence surrounding the building that sprawled across the whole block. The gates were open, but there was a guardhouse with a sign which read "Carr Industries— Knitwear Division."

The name had amused Kerr.

In the paved yard between the gates and the two-story mill were already gathered a score of newsmen and perhaps an equal number of plain-clothes security personnel. Many of the latter carried attaché cases and binoculars. They looked bored and uncomfortably warm in their suits.

The phone beside Penske rang. He jumped, waggling his carbine. Coster grinned and lifted the instrument out of its cradle. He offered it to the shorter man. Penske glowered. "Yeah, everything's goddam fine," he said. "Just don't screw up yourself." He laid the receiver down on the desk instead of hanging up. At the other end of the open line was Kerr in a sidewalk phone booth. The sound of the shots through the telephone was the signal to start the van toward the pickup point.

Coster swung open the lowest window into the room. He pushed the desk further aside and knelt with the rifle muzzle a yard back from the frame. The relative gloom of the office shielded them from the security men who were dutifully sweeping windows and rooftops with their binoculars. Coster grinned in satisfaction. He lowered the automatic rifle and began scanning the crowd left-handed through the glasses Penske had brought.

"Gonna spray the whole load a'the bastards?" Penske asked. "Supposed to be some big mother from the State Department, too."

"Nobody dies but Kawanishi," said Coster. He did not take his eyes from the binoculars. "We'd lose the effect, otherwise."

Penske grunted. Coster grimaced at him and explained, "If Martin Luther King had been gunned down

with thirty whites, there would have been doubt as to just
. . . what we had in mind. It would have been an accident,
not an attack—and maybe no cities had burned. American
officials can die at, say, a Memorial Day parade. Here, only
the Japanese. Only a slant-eyed Nip." He turned back to
the crowd.

The swarthy man stared at the side of Coster's head.
His right hand began a stealthy, not wholly conscious,
movement to his boot. As his fingers touched the knife,
there was a sharp snap. Penske jumped as he had when the
phone rang. The rifle lay across Coster's lap, its muzzle
pointing at Penske. The safety had just clicked off.

The rifleman set the binoculars down between them.
"Don't even think of that," he said.

Penske's lips were dry, but he nodded.

There was a bustle around the mill entrance.
Uniformed officers had joined the plain-clothes team and
were forming a double cordon against the gathering
sightseers. Down the cordon and in through the gate drove
a city police car with its bar lights flashing, followed by a
trio of limousines. The first of the black cars disgorged its
load of civilians, both Westerners and Japanese. "Small
fry," mumbled Coster beneath the binoculars.

A security man from the third, open-topped, limousine
ran to the rear door of the second big car and opened it. A
tall, gray-haired man in a dark suit got out. He nodded and
reached a hand back to help his companion.

"Yes . . ." Coster breathed. He dropped the glasses and
fitted his left hand to the forward grip of the automatic
rifle. A stocky man, shorter than the first, straightened and
waved to the cameras. Then he hurtled forward, face-first

onto a patch of concrete already darkened by the spray of his blood.

The *BAM! BAM!* of the two-round burst struck the office like hammer blows. A Daumier print on the wall jarred loose and fell. Coster scrambled back to the outer office. Penske waited a moment, his eardrums still jagged from the punishing muzzle blasts. Three security men were thrusting the Undersecretary of State back into the armored limousine like a sacked quarterback. Cut-down Uzis had come out of the attaché cases, but they were useless without targets. A cluster of security men was shouting into walkie-talkies while trying to shield Kawanishi's body. They were useless too. Kawanishi was beyond human help, his spine shattered by two bullets.

Penske broke for the door, leaving his carbine and the binoculars where they lay. He could replace them in the van. They were too dangerous to be seen carrying now. The stairwell door was still bouncing when the shorter man reached it. Coster was taking the steps two and three at a time, his right hand hugging the rifle to him through the hole in the carton. Penske, unburdened, was only a step behind when the rifleman turned at the second-floor landing, lost his footing on the painted concrete, and slid headlong down the next flight of steps. The crack of his right knee on the first step was louder than contact alone could explain.

Penske paused, staring down at the rifleman. Coster's face was a sallow green. "Give me a hand," he wheezed, trying unsuccessfully to rise.

"You'll never make it with a broken kneecap," the swarthy man said, more to himself than to the fallen man.

"Goddamn you!" Coster shouted. He had flung the shielding carton away from the automatic rifle. He aimed the weapon at Penske's midriff. "Help me!"

The safety clicked on. Both men heard the sound. Coster went a shade still paler and tried to force the slotted bar forward with his index finger. It would not move.

"Sure, I'll help you," Penske said softly. He slipped his dagger from its sheath and stepped forward.

The van was waiting at the curb with its rear door ajar. Penske leaped in, thrusting the carton before him. He shouted, "Drive!"

"Wait!" Kerr snapped to Davidson. "Where's Coster?"

Penske had the automatic rifle out on his lap now. He was feeling a little dizzy. "He fell and I had to leave him," he said. "Don't worry—he won't talk."

Without further orders, Davidson swung the van out into traffic. Occasional pedestrians were looking around for the source of the sirens they heard, but no one gave the escape vehicle a second glance.

Kerr's eyes narrowed as he watched the smaller man's fingers play with the action of the automatic rifle. After a moment he said, "Well, maybe it's for the best."

Penske did not reply. His mind was filling with images of men staggering and falling, each scene a separate shard differing in costume and background. Together the images turned smoothly like gear teeth engaging, each a part of a construct as yet incomplete.

"You know, I don't think I ever got a chance to look at that," Kerr remarked conversationally. He reached out to take the weapon.

"No!" said Penske, and the automatic rifle swung to cover the black's chest.

For an instant Kerr thought of drawing his pistol, but the thought passed and the pressure on the trigger of the automatic rifle passed also. "Okay," the big man said, "so long as you shoot what you're told to shoot with it."

Penske was no longer listening. The pattern was now complete. It stretched from a cold world whose remaining energies were all harnessed in a great design, to an Earth without native life forms. Winds whipped sand and nerve gas around badlands carven in past millennia, and the poisoned seas surged against blue-glowing shorelines. But over those landscapes coursed metal creatures who glittered and shifted their forms and raised triumphant cities to the skies.

And in Penske's mind something clicked. A voice said in no human language, "Yes, this replacement will be quite satisfactory. . . ."

BLOOD DEBT

I got interested in witchcraft when I was in high
school (or maybe even earlier), as an outgrowth of
my interest in traditional fantasy. When I became
an undergraduate at Iowa the university library
gave me more to read on the subject, but the real
outpouring of material came in the later '60s when
"The Occult" became hugely popular. There's a lot
of crossover between the Occult and the more recent
New Age, but the earlier version seems to me to have
had more sharp edges.

I focused on scholarly sources like Margaret
Alice Murray and Montague Summers, writers who
purported to collect original documents and
theorize from them. I say "purported" because I
now know that both authorities were phony.

Murray was a real scholar, but she falsified her
cites to show that medieval witchcraft had an
organized structure which the facts do not support.
Summers was far, far worse. His erudition was as
false as his claim of a religious vocation, and his
retailing of the worst medieval bits of misogyny (for

example, the absurd derivation of femina, female, from fe mina, "lesser in faith") wears quickly even on me (who can't claim to be a feminist).

I never believed in the effectiveness of witchcraft. If my reading misled me, it was by causing me to accept that numbers of ordinary people in the Middle Ages practiced witchcraft in an organized fashion. That was no more harmful to a fiction writer (which is what I was trying to be) than believing in a reality behind the Airship Flap of 1897, now known to be a hoax, hurt "Travellers," one of my best novellas.

The thing is, though I don't believe in witchcraft at a gut level, I'm intellectually convinced that there's something real out there. Occasionally I ran into a writer—Elliott O'Donnell in his fiction (rather than his non-fiction) was a prime example— whom I thought and think really understood things that I'd prefer not to know about.

The fact that gangsters in Sierra Leone believed that bullets would bounce off their magically armored bodies didn't prevent the SAS from stacking up corpses like cordwood when they went in to rescue British hostages. Likewise, my personal disbelief in witchcraft won't help me if I'm attacked by someone who can manipulate occult powers. The effectiveness of the weapon doesn't depend on the belief system of the target. That's the background from which I wrote "Blood Debt." On rereading it, I'd say that the story accurately reflects my combination of scholarship and skepticism, leavened by the tiniest measure of fear.

✣ ✣ ✣

T he shadow of the house next door razored down Rigsbee's in the winter dawn. First the red light tinged the wrought-iron rail of the widow's walk. Spidery star-shapes writhed in the glow, the uprights molded as blunt arrowheads and the slanted pairs of limbs linked with fanciful hands. Below, the dark green shingles of the mansard roof sharpened but did not brighten when the light touched them. Only the small-paned French window winked back at the sun.

The left half was off the catch and swung as the air stirred around it. The dawn paled as it glided more swiftly down the white sidewalls of the second story, walking the crazy angles of the trellis and the ancient ivy clambering up into the gutters. There were already lights on in the kitchen on the ground floor. The tall, blonde woman put a last plate on the breakfast tray, then pushed the stairwell door open with her heel. She moved with precision, as she had for forty years. Life, ignoring her hopes and trampling her certainties, had been unable to change that; but crow's feet now softened the hard lines of her face.

Her shoes rapped steadily up the back stairs, pausing at the triangular landing where her dress flashed through the slit window before swinging up the flight. The old house had high-ceilinged rooms and she liked the feel of them, though of course heating was a great expense to Mr. Judson. She made out the checks herself, who should know better.

A bolt snicked back and the door to the second floor opened before she had to knock. Judson Rigsbee was wrapped in a velvet robe—the green one, this morning— and smiling at her. "Good morning, Mrs. Trader; I hope you slept well." He did not smile often, and even with her it was a slightly uncomfortable expression, that of a stranger who is afraid to embarrass by seeming overwarm.

Mrs. Trader set the breakfast things neatly on the table inside the door—toast, poached eggs, coffee, the big glass of orange juice. Mr. Judson didn't care for orange juice but she insisted, it was good for him. The man would waste away to nothing if she didn't bully him—no chance Anita would stir a finger for her uncle.

"Thank you, I did indeed," the tall woman said aloud. "Now that Harvey and Stella are back together, I haven't been having those headaches at all, Mr. Judson."

"Well, I'm certainly glad," he said diffidently. He edged back slightly from the housekeeper's determined confidences, a pudgy-seeming man of fifty with no hardness showing except in his eyes.

"I'm certain I don't understand men," Mrs. Trader plowed on as she poured the coffee, "not even my own boy. They were as sweet a couple as you could find, he and Stella. For five years, and I'll say it even though I didn't want the marriage myself, they were too young. And then with the little one due any day, there Harvey goes off with never a word to Stella or even to me. But he was there in the waiting room when Kimberly was born, and Stella took him back though I wouldn't have blamed her if she hadn't. . . . But it *was* a weight off my mind."

"Thank you, Mrs. Trader."

"Thank you, sir." She gathered up the part-loaded tray and stepped crisply up the remaining double flight of polished hardwood. Mr. Judson was looking peaked and she did wish he would eat bacon in the morning, but on that score he was more determined than she. "Orange juice or bacon, Mrs. Trader, but not both. Male, both of them, and together they would overbalance me hopelessly." Terrible things, queasy stomachs, and the green robe did nothing for his complexion. A pretty thing it was by itself with all the astrology symbols in silver on the hem, but not proper dress for a sickly man in the morning.

She rapped smartly on the door to the third story, squarely in the middle of the great red-lacquer eye Anita had painted there. "If Uncle Jud won't let me bolt my door, I at least have to know who's coming, don't I?" the girl had sneered. Mr. Judson never talked very much about his sister, but Mrs. Trader could guess that she had been the wild one of the family. Who could be surprised that the daughter took after the mother when the poor child had not so much as a father's name to bear?

A second knock brought no response. The baleful eye waited, unblinking. Well, this was the first time it had happened, but Mrs. Trader was not slow to act. Mr. Judson insisted the house be run to a schedule so as not to disturb his work. Anita should have learned that in the months she had stayed here. If she hadn't, well. . . . Mrs. Trader swung open the door.

The room within, its walls skewed a little to the shape of the roof, was far different from Rigsbee's own austere sitting room below. The dormers were blacked out by locked shutters; a volcano lamp lighted the rug and brocade chairs, but it had overheated during the night. Its paraffin and oil were in ugly stasis within the red glass base. Mrs. Trader switched it off as she strode past into the middle room.

A pentagram had been freshly chalked on the floor; the candles at its points still stood at half their original lengths, snuffed before they burned out, and the air was heavy with incense. "Anita, it's eight-thirty," Mrs. Trader called. Aping her uncle, she thought as she glanced around the room distastefully. Though in fairness to the girl, that couldn't be true. Mrs. Trader had seen the paraphernalia arrive with the rest of Anita's baggage. Runs in the family, then.

The girl failed to come to the bedroom door either. Mrs. Trader sniffed and unlatched it herself without knocking again.

The window slammed shut in the sudden air current. It left a damp chill in the room. The walls were a brilliant, metallic yellow that matched the spread, now rumpled at the foot of Anita's bed. Anita, too, was rumpled. The coils of hair that lay silken over the sheets beneath her were no blacker than her protruding tongue. The breakfast tray slipped, smearing the golden carpet with strawberry preserve and coffee.

Mrs. Trader turned stiffly and walked toward the stairs. A candle holder smashed unnoticed beneath her foot as she strode through the middle room. "Mis—" she started, but her voice cracked and she had to lick her lips before trying again. "Mr. Judson!"

Rigsbee opened the door just in time to catch the rigid woman as she stumbled on the last step and fell toward him. The unexpected impact drove them back into his sitting room. For once, Mrs. Trader would not meet her employer's eyes as she blurted, "Dead, Mr. Judson, she's dead and murdered. Oh dear God! In her own bed!"

Rigsbee rotated the blonde woman's weight into the

room, then disengaged her arms to dart up the stairs. She wept in one of the straight-backed chairs until he returned; and her tears were real, but they were shed for the thing and not the girl herself.

Rigsbee was very quiet when he came back a few minutes later. His slippers rasped a little on the steps, that was all. The skin of his face was almost the color of his neutrally short gray hair. "Look at me, Elinor," he said softly. His fingers, gentle but inexorable, guided her jaw around when she was slow to obey. He was a little man in a comic robe, but his eyes were molten zinc. "You will go home now and forget all that you saw upstairs. When you return tomorrow, you will never have known Anita, there will never have been anyone living on the third floor. Do you understand?"

"Yes." The voice from Mrs. Trader's lips was not her own, but it ruled her.

Alone in the center of his three rooms, Rigsbee changed into white. The symbols worked into the robe's borders were of thread the same shade, differing only in texture from the base cloth.

"Well?" a voice inquired from a corner.

Rigsbee shrugged. His bald spot was more apparent whenever he was depressed. "She was my niece. She was the last of my blood."

"You know what she was," the voice rasped. "She was a slut, a whore—"

"Some things are necessary . . . ."

"Not to her. She was never that deep in—"

"She was my blood!" Rigsbee's voice racketed through

the dim room and shook it to silence. He turned toward the outer wall, clasping his hands to keep them from trembling. The windows on that side were blocked by the bookshelves running the length of the long wall. Spines of blue, green, and dull red library tape marched across the polished walnut with no markings beyond a few digits in white ink. He touched one of them.

Each thin volume was a typescript of Rigsbee's own production, bound by him between sheets of gray card. No one had helped during the typing or compilation. Partly Rigsbee's purpose had been to give the volumes the slight added virtue resulting from that close contact with him. More important, however, was another consideration: each typescript was treble-columned with groups of letters and numbers in no order that would have made sense to one not adept. Rigsbee had not intentionally encoded the results of his years of searching, but the form of notation he had come to use was far more specialized than Latin and Arabic symbols could accommodate in their normal values. One trivial error of pagination, one transposition among millions of letters, unnoticed and unnoticeable, would mean instant disaster in the dark moment when the data were used again.

A very few of the cased books were not of Rigsbee's own composition. His hand moved to one of them: squat, age-blackened; its pigskin binding cracking away from the cords. He knew by heart every word of the cryptic Latin text, but he had never before seriously contemplated using it. The pages opened stiffly, parting with difficulty under his fingertips.

"You would go that far?" the voice behind him asked mournfully.

Rigsbee closed the book before answering, "Punishment that stopped with the body would not—would not for me—be enough. The finality of that act, whoever did it, can't be answered by a gas chamber or a motor accident. I'm sorry, Vera; but I have no choice."

And, "No," he said sharply, wheeling with a strand of diamond in his voice before his listener could reply, "don't tell me that I'll have to give up all this, this. . . ." Rigsbee's voice broke but his hand slashed an arc across the room. The books, the retorts joined by crystalline worms of tubing; the charts rolled in one corner beneath the ancient astrolabe. "That's already gone, it's dead. If I ignored what has happened . . . Vera, I wouldn't be the same man, the man who . . . did the things I have done."

His face was carved from gray steel. If he felt any hesitation, none of it trembled in his throat when he said, "You'll help me, Vera."

"So close," the voice whispered. "In this short time—and you will understand how short it was, some day before you are as old as I—you came closer to unity than I have done in all these ages. And now, nothing."

"Vera. You'll help me?"

"Even to make the responses to you would bring me closer to the Blackness than a thousand cycles of the Fire would erase. Dos Lintros tried to walk that line after he wrote the book you hold. Where is he now, since they came for him?"

"I know," Rigsbee admitted softly.

"You know? You think you know!" the voice shrieked. "But you will know, Judson, for eternity you will know if you. . . .

"But it's no good to tell you that, is it?" the voice went on. "You will do this thing, I see. And you are wiser than I can ever hope to be; but because of what I am, I *know* things that you only accept. Not even you, Judson, can imagine what you are about to do to yourself. To your soul."

Rigsbee shrugged, ran a hand through his thinning hair while his eyes stared unseeing at the numbered spines of his volumes. "I'm sorry, Vera—"

"Goodbye." Her word was as soft and as dull as the first handful of dirt on a coffin. Rigsbee shuffled to the corner, let his hand brush down the wire cage. The albino starling within croaked, darted its head forward to spike the ball of his thumb.

"Goodbye, Vera," Rigsbee muttered, and he turned away again.

The back door groaned. The lock had worked smoothly, but the hinges were frozen with the grit of long disuse. The girl glanced up the outer wall before entering. It was too dark to tell the ivy from the trellis it climbed.

"Nice place," she said as she followed Rigsbee up the stairs. Her knee-length coat was of a plastic imitation cowhide, now torn at two of the seams. The belt was missing and she held the front closed with one thin, white hand. "You been here long?"

"Most of my life," Rigsbee said as he unlocked the door to the second story. Despite the dimness of the stairwell, he inserted his key without fumbling.

Again the girl hung back, hipshot, in the doorway. She was a dark brunette; long snarls of hair bobbled against her coat as she suddenly giggled. "Aren't the neighbors gonna wonder if they saw me come in?" She laughed again, stepping over the threshold with an exaggerated stateliness. Shrugging away the coat, she tossed it onto one of the straight chairs and stood in tank top and jeans. Most of the bright embroidery had worn away. Her bare toes, poking through handmade sandals, were an unhealthy blue beneath their coating of grime.

"This way," Rigsbee directed briefly, swinging the stair door shut and motioning the girl inward toward his study.

"'Cause if you don't care," she went on, speaking over her shoulder as she slowly obeyed Rigsbee, "this doesn't have to be a onenight stand, you know."

Rigsbee's glance took in her too-thin face, her too-white skin. "That won't be necessary," he said flatly. "It's in the next room."

"It wouldn't be so much," the girl said with unshakable coquetry. "I mean, not another of these—very often." Both hands lifted the thin top up over the waistband of the jeans. A hundred dollar bill, folded vertically into eighths, was poked into the jeans on her midline. "I couldn't put it in the top," she said with another giggle. Raising the thin cloth higher, the girl pirouetted back toward Rigsbee. The motion flung out her breasts, bare beneath the hiked blouse. They were not large but seemed surprisingly full for a body so thin; the areoles were almost black against the dingy pallor of her flesh.

Rigsbee stepped past her, his neutral expression unchanged. He swung the room's other door soundlessly toward him. White light flooded out. "Go in," he ordered, holding the portal open. Its inner face was covered with a thin, hard fabric that seemed less reflectant than self-luminous. Despite the strangeness of it, the girl obeyed this time without hesitation. Her motion slowed; then, three steps inside the final room, she stopped completely.

The whole chamber and its only furnishing, a circular couch, were covered in the slick fabric. The high ceilings of the old house had allowed Rigsbee to dome the material smoothly in the center of the room without making the edges uncomfortably low. The light was not harsh but was shadowless and omnipresent, the interior of a cold, white star. Rigsbee entered behind the girl, closing the door on the last rectangle of reality left to the room. In his right hand swung the bird cage from his study. The starling hopped uneasily on its perch.

The girl let her blouse fall; her head rotated, taking in featurelessness. "Hey, this is unreal," she whispered. A hesitant step brought her to the couch. It was firm to the touch, warmer than blood. "You really go all out, don't you?" she said. For the first time, there was a trace of something genuine in her voice.

Rigsbee slid off his shoes and stepped onto the couch. The cage hung from the center of the dome on a hook that had been invisible until then.

"It's time now. You can take your clothes off," he said. He loosed the gold-shot sash he wore over his street clothes as a belt.

The girl pulled the top over her head, freeing it with a sharp tug when it caught in a loop of hair. With the same motion, she flipped the garment carelessly toward the wall. Seating herself on the edge of the couch, she hooked one long, slim-jointed toe over the backstrap of the other sandal, then paused. The surgical coldness of the light bit at her. "I—" she began. She hugged her breasts close without sexual intent. "Look," she said, "you want me to take a shower? I mean, they shut the water off . . . ."

"I hired you as you are," Rigsbee answered bleakly. "Afterwards you may bathe or not, as you please. Get off the rest of your clothes."

The girl obeyed without enthusiasm. Both sandals struck the wall. They should have clattered but did not. She thrust the folded bill into a side pocket before sliding the ragged jeans down her thighs. "Look," she repeated, her eyes on Rigsbee's short, soft body so as not to have to see her own so clearly, "have we got to have the lights so bright?"

For the first time that night, Rigsbee smiled. "Yes," he said, the tight rictus of irony still on his face as he reached for the girl, "but they'll dim later."

As she began the ancient mechanisms of her trade, the girl wondered again how a room with no visible light source could be so brilliant. Then, without paling, the lucence began to slip from white to violet in waves as mindless as the sea's.

The room was yellow-green, a throbbing chartreuse that washed the fine gray hairs of Rigsbee's chest into a new-sewn field. "Again," he said quietly.

"Again, honey?" The girl ran her calloused palm over his belly with something like affection as she snuggled closer. "Say, you're not bad. But this time—" She repositioned herself with a silken movement on the glowing couch.

"Yes," Rigsbee muttered in a gelatinous voice as he bent. The girl's high-thrusting legs flickered shadows across her prominent rib-cage. And the light in the room glissaded to orange.

✦ ✦ ✦

Garnet light the color of congealing blood oozed across them. Rigsbee rose to his feet awkwardly. The girl squirmed on the couch, stretched. "Now what, honey?"

"Nothing." Rigsbee's eyes were focused beyond the throbbing walls of the room. "Now you can leave."

Plucked eyebrows arched in surprise. "What's the matter? Wasn't I good?"

His tone itself a manner of ignoring the girl, Rigsbee went on, "The thing I had to do required that I be . . . sexless, that will suffice, to contact those who can aid me. With a female associate with whom I could have merged my spirit, I could have become a neuter entity. That was . . ."

He looked at the starling. It felt the impact of his eyes, the thin ruby whites around pupils which were still metal gray. The bird squawked, hopped to the far end of its perch.

". . . impossible under the circumstances," Rigsbee continued. "Where the body goes, the spirit must follow, then. It became necessary that I drain a part of my nature, the masculine portion. For that, I needed you. Nothing more."

"My God," the girl said, rising from her back to her elbows. "You mean you didn't even want to fuck?"

"You?" Rigsbee asked wearily.

"God, that's dirty!" the girl hissed. Grimy hands levered her shanks back across the couch to the edge.

Rigsbee laughed, a humorless cackle of sound that echoed in the room. "Yes. It is," he agreed, the skin stretched bone-tight across his face. "Far fouler than you can dream. I made the contact that I . . . desired."

He lifted down the bird cage. "Shall we see what they say?"

The starling chopped at Rigsbee's hand as he slipped it through the cage door. His pudgy fingers were swifter than the bird; thumb and forefinger closed about its neck and hooked it from the cage.

"What—" the girl blurted. Her muscles tensed as she tried to remember which swatch of burning fabric hid the exit.

Rigsbee was not speaking aloud, but the agonized tremors creeping across his flesh showed his concentration. The bird seemed forgotten, clasped in both his hands. The fingers on its throat kept the starling from crying, but it had enough freedom to snap its pinions. The feathers clattered together like boards slapping.

Rigsbee shifted his grip, then wrenched his fists in opposite directions. The girl's scream covered the faint pop as the starling's neck parted. The bird's tiny heart thumped out two powerful jets, the last choking off as the veins feeding it emptied.

The adept's eyes stared at the floor. Half-unwillingly, the girl leaned over to see what was there. Instead of lying in a ragged pool with satellite splotches, the blood was crawling of its own volition into connected words. The letters were spidery but perfect, and they stood out ironically black against the sanguine background:

CANES EXPECTANT

"My hounds await," Rigsbee whispered. He began to laugh. His mouth was open, lips unmoving, and the empty syllables tumbled out in a terrible cacophony.

"Stop!" the girl screamed, and she clapped her hands

over her ears. Rigsbee took no notice of her shuddering frame. He raised both hands in the air, choked off his laughter as if by main force, and shouted a word, inhuman and ghastly with power. For the girl, for all the world but Rigsbee and one other, time froze in that instant.

The red robes slipped over his head easily. They had no designs worked into them, and they billowed loosely, sashless. The bloody light permeating the chamber coalesced as Rigsbee moved, flowing into the semblance of an ape's skull hanging in the air before him. It leered, then glided silently through the door which opened for it. Rigsbee followed, his scuffling slippers making the only sounds in the static house.

Down the stairs into the street. The skull's pace was a deliberate walk, the certain leisure of the squad escorting the tumbril. Other movement joined Rigsbee; gentle rustlings from the ivy, a tremulous scraping of metal on masonry. Only a petrified night scene showed in the wash of scarlet light preceding him. Streetlights no longer poured their mercury blue in pools on the asphalt. A car was caught rigid in the middle of a turn, the tip of its driver's cigar dead and black. A dog skipped for the curb— one foot in the street and the other three in the air so that its brindled body hung at an impossible angle. House after high, old house, built close to the sidewalks with walled courts in back for privacy. Rigsbee followed his guide without turning his head to look for the things tittering just beyond his zone of vision.

Newer houses, smaller but set back further. Rigsbee's monocentric mind had no idea how far he had walked. The skull halted at last, rotated tremblingly toward a brickveneer residence. Rigsbee remained where he was, a hundred feet back in the middle of the street. His guide eased forward. The reflectors of the old Buick in the carport winked back in carmine brotherhood.

The inside of the house showed as red light approached, flooded through the front window. A woman had pulled the drapes back in the instant before stasis. Now she stared unseeing at the glass, her hair rinsed black and the cover of the baby in her arms striped red on red.

Shockingly loud in a universe that had only scufflings and scratching, a man's voice slashed out of the house, "Did you finally come, Rigsbee? I've been waiting for you."

A moment's pause. The front door banged back, the screen squealed open. The man on the narrow porch was tall, his hair a brighter yellow than his mother's in any normal light. Now it was a crown of dull carbuncle burning over his anguished face.

"Where are you, Rigsbee?" Trader called, taking a step out onto the gravel sidewalk, a step nearer the skull motionless in the air. "I know you're behind this. Your witch of a niece told me what you are.

"Do you want me to say it? I killed her! You can send me to any Hell you please, but I killed Anita and I'm glad of it. I rid the world of her!"

"She was my daughter, Harvey." Unlike Trader's harsh, desperate tones, Rigsbee's words were almost inaudible. His robes hung motionless, a frozen torrent of blood.

Trader took three steps down the gravel. The ape skull blocked his path without moving. A curse twisted Trader's powerful face and he spat at the thing. It burst soundlessly into a ball of glowing vapor that slowly dissipated in the still air. The murky red light continued to flow about the two men after its apparent source was gone.

"I wouldn't have anything to do with her," the younger man said tautly. "I told her Stella was plenty for me, even with the baby coming. But she couldn't take that, not your Anita, and she'd have me anyway. Up the ivy and in her window, Rigsbee, every night. And I couldn't go home in the mornings, then, and face Stella."

Rigsbee closed his eyes, rubbed them as if he were tired. Trader continued to advance, narrowing the distance between them. The globe of light shrank with every step he took. Beyond it, gravel skittered impatiently.

"I broke away when Kim was born," the tall man went on, his words as brittle as a coping saw on glass. He stretched his arms out in instinctive supplication. "She was . . . you can't imagine, Rigsbee! Hadn't she had enough? She'd proved she could take me away once, why did she have to—"

For the first time, Rigsbee stared straight into the other's tortured eyes. His tone softer than a fledgling's down, the adept said, "Harvey, when you strangled Anita, you made this certain. You and I are as much a part of nature as the sun and stars are, and our courses are as fixed. You chose then the course for both of us, and there is no changing now.

"Goodbye, Harvey." And Rigsbee raised his hand.

The world brightened stunningly as if the sun had risen scarlet. Harvey lurched back in shock, seeing what came scrabbling toward him. He tried to run.

A slender hand of wrought iron snatched his ankle. The railing from Rigsbee's house now scampered on the lawn, fifty separated manikins. Harvey screamed as his ankle crunched under the black fingers. Fifty faceless, pointed heads tossed in delight. They clanked as they minced toward their frenzied quarry, trembling as each new howl cut the air.

Trader disappeared behind the living fence. The human noises ceased a moment later when something round and bloody pitched into the air.

The light began to fade. Before long there was only a dull glow surrounding Rigsbee. Then the full moon came out and traffic moved again.

Dawn rained on the city. Rigsbee's empty house brightened slowly in the wan gray. A spatter of droplets whipped the shingles, followed by a pale drizzle that flowed over the eaves and splashed to the ground in sheets. The spidery pentacles of the railing blackened under the impacts of the rain, and the gutters ran red.

MEN LIKE US

In 1979 I had the start of a writing career going. I'd sold a fantasy novel (The Dragon Lord) and an SF short-story collection (Hammer's Slammers), plus quite a lot of short fiction about equally divided between fantasy and SF. In all, I had around 200,000 words in print when I stopped to think about it.

Which I mostly didn't. I was a full-time attorney and I had no intention of changing that—though I did before another year was out. (My life appears to conform to the evolutionary model of punctuated equilibrium.)

I'd sold stories to Jim Baen when he was editor of Galaxy magazine. When he became the SF editor of Ace Books he bought Hammer's Slammers and also started a paperback magazine, Destinies, which paid excellent rates. Over the years (and through various title changes), Destinies published a lot of my best short fiction.

I wrote "Men Like Us," which I thought was the best thing I'd written to date, and sent it to Jim. Jim thought it was the best thing I'd written also, and *instantly rejected it on the grounds that it supported a political philosophy with which he violently disagreed.*

Well, that was fair: it was his magazine, after all. I sent the story to Omni, *the slick-paper SF/fact magazine, where Ben Bova (who'd taken a number of my stories as editor of* Analog) *bought and published it. My wife and I used the $800 to vacation in New Orleans, where I got to know John Brunner (who had Ballantine Books hire me as his tech editor on the historical novel he was writing for them) and fired silenced submachine guns in the swamps across Lake Pontchartrain.*

"Men Like Us" was the only story I sold to Omni *and just about the only one that I sent there. My head wasn't normally in places that fit* Omni's *editorial policies, whereas Jim Baen and I usually meshed very well (partly because we'd knocked so many pieces off one another over the years). This one time, though . . .*

The story itself owes something to a novella by Poul Anderson, "UN-Man." In his early days, Poul's fiction could often be described as proselytizing for world government. Poul had an abrupt shift in philosophy during the 1950s, so that his later work frequently shows a libertarian bent. (In almost all cases, the story values remain strong; I'm talking about fiction with philosophical underpinnings, not propaganda screeds.)

Poul's later work has sparked a number of stories from me; "UN-Man," however, was early . . .

which may have something to do with the reactions both of Omni *and of Jim Baen to my story.*

I was born only weeks after the first atomic bomb, and I grew up through the depths of the Cold War when nuclear war seemed more probable than not. I still think "Men Like Us" is one of the best short stories I've written; and it's the one that always scares me when I reread it.

✣ ✣ ✣

There was a toad crucified against them at the head of the pass. Decades of cooking in the blue haze from the east had left it withered but incorruptible. It remained, even now that the haze was only a memory. The three travelers squatted down before the talisman and stared back at it.

"The village can't be far from here," Smith said at last. "I'll go down tomorrow."

Ssu-ma shrugged and argued, "Why waste time? We can all go down together."

"Time we've got," said Kozinski, playing absently with his ribs as he eyed the toad. "A lot of the stories we've been told come from ignorance, from fear. There may be no more truth to this one than to many of the others. We have a duty, but we have a duty as well not to disrupt needlessly. We'll wait for you and watch."

Smith chuckled wryly. "What sort of men would there be in the world," he said, "if it weren't for men like us?"

All three of them laughed, but no one bothered to finish their old joke.

The trail was steep and narrow. The stream was now

bubbling twenty feet below, but in springtime it would fill its sharp gorge with a torrent as cold as the snows that spawned it. Coming down the valley, Smith had a good view of Moseby when he had eased around the last facet of rock above the town. It sprawled in the angle of the creek and the river into which the creek plunged. In a niche across the creek from the houses was a broad stone building, lighted by slit windows at second-story level. Its only entrance was an armored door. The building could have been a prison or a fortress were it not for the power lines running from it, mostly to the smelter at the riverside. A plume of vapor overhung its slate roof.

One of the pair of guards at the door of the powerplant was morosely surveying the opposite side of the gorge for want of anything better to do. He was the first to notice Smith. His jaw dropped. The traveler waved to him. The guard blurted something to his companion and threw a switch beside the door.

What happened then frightened Smith as he thought nothing in the world could frighten him again: an air-raid siren on the roof of the powerplant sounded, rising into a wail that shook echoes from the gorge. Men and women darted into the streets, some of them armed; but Smith did not see the people, these people, and he did not fear anything they could do to him.

Then the traveler's mind was back in the present, a smile on his face and nothing in his hands but an oak staff worn by the miles of earth and rock it had butted against. He continued down into the village, past the fences and latrines of the nearest of the houses. Men with crossbows met him there, but they did not touch him, only motioned the traveler onward. The rest of the townsfolk gathered in an open area in the center of the town. It separated the detached houses on the east side from the row of flimsier structures built along the river. The latter obviously served as barracks, taverns, and brothels for bargees and smelter workers. The row buildings had no windows facing east, and even their latrines must have been dug on the river side. A few people joined the crowd from them and from the smelter itself, but only a few.

"That's close enough," said the foremost of those awaiting the traveler. The local was a big man with a pink scalp. It shone through the long wisps of white hair which he brushed carefully back over it. His jacket and trousers were of wool dyed blue so that it nearly matched the shirt of ancient polyester he wore over it. "Where have you come from?"

"Just about everywhere, one time or another," Smith answered with an engaging grin. "Dubuque, originally, but that was a long time ago."

"Don't play games with the Chief," hissed a somewhat younger man with a cruel face and a similar uniform. "You came over the mountains; and *nobody* comes from the Hot Lands."

Chief of Police, Smith marveled as he connected the title and the shirts now worn as regalia. Aloud he said, "When's the last time anybody from here walked over the mountains? Ever?"

Bearded faces went hard. The traveler continued, "A hundred years ago, two hundred, it was too hot for you to go anywhere that side of the hills . . . but not now. Now—maybe I'll never sire children of my own, but I never needed that, I needed to see the world. And I have done that, friends."

"Strip him," the Chief said flatly.

Smith did not wait for the grim-looking men to force him. He shrugged off his pack and handed it to the nearest of the guards armed with crossbows and hand-forged swords. He said, "Gently with it, friend. There's some of it that's fragile, and I need it to trade for room and board the next while." He began to unhook his leather vest.

Six of the men besides the Chief wore the remnants of police uniforms over their jackets. They were all older, not lean warriors like the crossbowmen—but they carried firearms. Five of them had M16 rifles. The anodized finish of the receivers had been polished down to the aluminum by ages of diligent ignorance. The sixth man had a disposable rocket launcher, certain proof that the villagers here had at some time looted an army base—or a guard room.

"Just a boy from the Midwest," Smith continued pleasantly, pulling out the tails of his woolen shirt. "I wanted to see New York City, can you believe that? But we'll none of us live forever, will we?"

He laid the shirt, folded from habit, on his vest and began unlacing his boots of caribou leather. "There's a crater there now, and the waves still glow blue if there's even an overcast to dim the sun. Your skin prickles."

The traveler grinned. "You won't go there, and I won't go there again; but I've seen it, where the observation deck of the World Trade Towers was the closest mortal man got to heaven with his feet on man's earth . . . ."

"We've heard the stories," the Chief grunted. He

carried a stainless-steel revolver in a holster of more recent vintage.

"Trousers?" Smith asked, cocking an eyebrow at the women in dull-colored dresses.

The Chief nodded curtly. "When a man comes from the Hot Lands, he has no secrets from us," he said. "Any of us."

"Well, I might do the same in your case," the traveler agreed, tugging loose the laces closing the woolen trousers, "but I can tell you there's little enough truth to the rumors of what walks the wastelands." He pulled the garment down and stepped out of it.

Smith's body was wiry, the muscles tight and thickly covered by hair. If he was unusual at all, it was in that he had been circumcised, no longer a common operation in a world that had better uses for a surgeon's time. Then a woman noticed Smith's left palm, never hidden but somehow never clearly seen until that moment. She screamed and pointed. Others leveled their weapons, buzzing as a hive does when a bear nears it.

Very carefully, his face as blank as the leather of his pack, Smith held his left hand toward the crowd and spread his fingers. Ridges of gnarled flesh stood out as if they had been paraffin refrozen a moment after being liquefied. "Yes, I burned it," the traveler said evenly, "getting too close to something the—something the Blast was too close to. And it'll never heal, no . . . but it hasn't gotten worse, either, and that was years ago. It's not the sort of world where I could complain to have lost so little, hey?"

"Put it down," the Chief said abruptly. Then, to the guard who was searching the pack, "Weapons?"

"Only this," the guard said, holding up a sling and a dozen dense pebbles fitted to its leather pocket.

"There's a little folding knife in my pants pocket," Smith volunteered. "I use it to skin the rabbits I take."

"Then put your clothes on," the Chief ordered, and the crowd's breath eased. "You can stay at the inn, since you've truck enough to pay for it—" he nodded toward the careful pile the guard had made of Smith's trading goods— "and perhaps you can find girls on Front Street to service you as well. There's none of that east of the Assembly here, I warn you. Before you do anything else, though, you talk to me and the boys in private at the Station."

The traveler nodded and began dressing without embarrassment.

The Police and their guards escorted Smith silently, acting as if they were still uncertain of his status. Their destination was a two-story building of native stone. It had probably been the Town Hall before the Blast. It was now the Chief's residence as well as the headquarters of the government. Despite that, the building was far less comfortable than many of the newer structures which had been designed to be heated by stoves and lighted by lamps and windows. In an office whose plywood paneling had been carefully preserved—despite its shoddy gloominess— the governing oligarchs of the town questioned Smith.

They were probing and businesslike. Smith answered honestly and as fully as he could. Weapons caches? Looted by survivors or rotted in the intervening centuries. Food depots? A myth, seeded by memories of supermarkets and brought to flower in the decades of famine and cold which slew ten times as many folk as the Blast had slain directly. Scrap metal for the furnaces? By the millions of tons, but there would be no way to transport if across the mountains . . . and besides, metals were often hot even at this remove from the Blast.

"All right," said the Chief at last, shutting the handbook of waxed boards on which he had been making notes. The room had become chilly about the time they had to light the sooty naphtha lamp. "If we think of more during the night, we can ask in the morning." His eyes narrowed. "How long are you expecting to stay?"

Smith shrugged. "A few days. I just like to . . . wander. I really don't have any desire to do anything else. "He raised his pack by the straps and added, "Can one of you direct me to your inn?"

Carter, the youngest of the six Policemen, stood. He was a blocky man with black hair and a pepper and salt beard. He had conducted much of the questioning himself. "I'll take him," he said. Unlike his colleagues, he carried a heavy fighting knife in addition to his automatic rifle. He held the door for Smith.

The night sky was patchy. When the sliver moon was clear, there was more light outside than the bud of naphtha gave within. The pall of steam above the powerplant bulged and waned like the mantle of an octopus. Tiny azure sparks traced the power lines across the bridge and down into the smelter.

Smith thumbed at the plant. "They made light from electricity, you know? Before the Blast. You ever try that?"

His guide looked at him sharply. "Not like they did. Things glow, but they burn up when we can't keep all the air away from 'em. But you'd be smarter not to ask questions, boy. And maybe you'd be smarter to leave here a little sooner than you planned. Not to be unfriendly, but if you talk to us, you'll talk to others. And we don't much care for talk about Moseby. It has a way of spreading where it shouldn't."

The Policeman turned through an open gate and up a graveled pathway. Rosy light leaked around the shutters of a large building on the edge of the Assembly. Sound and warm air bloomed into the night when he opened the door. In the mild weather, the anteroom door was open within.

"Carter!" shouted a big man at the bar of the taproom. "Just in time to buy us a round!" Then he saw Smith and blinked, and the dozen or so men of the company grew quieter than the hiss of the fire.

"Friends, I don't bite," said Smith with a smile, "but I do drink and I will sleep. If I can come to an agreement with our host here, that is . . ." he added, beaming toward the barman.

"Modell's the name," said the tall, knob-jointed local. Neither he nor the traveler offered to shake hands, but he returned the other's smile with a briefer, professional one of his own. "Let's see what you have to trade."

The men at the bar made room as Smith ranged his small stock on the mahogany. First the traveler set out an LP record, still sealed in plastic. Modell's lips moved silently as his finger hovered a millimeter above the title. "What's a 'Cher,'" he finally asked.

"The lady's name," said Smith. "She pronounced it 'share.'" Knowing grunts from the men around him chorused the explanation. "You've electricity here, I see. Perhaps there's a phonograph?"

"Naw, and the power's not trained enough yet anyhow," said Modell regretfully. His eyes were full of the jacket photograph. "It heats the smelters, is all, and—"

"Modell, you're supposed to be trading, not running your mouth," interrupted the Policeman. "Get on with it."

"Well, if not the record, then—" Smith said.

"I might make you an offer on the picture," one of the locals broke in.

"I won't separate them, I'm afraid," Smith rejoined, "and I won't have the record where it can't be used properly. These may be more useful, though I can't guarantee them after the time they've been sitting and he laid a red and green box of .30-30 cartridges on the wood.

"The Chief keeps all the guns in Moseby besides these," spoke Carter, patting the plastic stock of his M16. "It'll stay that way. And there's a righteous plenty of ammunition for them already."

"Fine, fine," said Smith, unperturbed, reaching again into his pack. He removed a plastic box which whirred until a tiny green hand reached out of the mechanism to shut itself off. It frightened the onlookers as much as Smith's own radiation scars had. The traveler thoughtfully hid the toy again in his pack before taking out his final item, a GI compass.

"It always shows North, unless you're too close to iron," Smith said as he demonstrated. "You can turn the base to any number of degrees and take a sighting through the slot there . . . but I'll want more than a night's lodging for it."

"Our tokens're good up and down the river," one of the

locals suggested, ringing a small brass disk on the bar. It had been struck with a complex pattern of lightning bolts on one side and the number "50" on the other. "You can redeem 'em for iron ingots at dockside," he explained, thumbing toward the river. "'Course, they discount 'em the farther away you get."

"I don't follow rivers a great deal," the traveler lied with a smile. "Let's say that I get room and board—and all I care to drink—for a week . . ."

The chaffering was good-natured and brief, concluding with three days' room and board, or—and here Smith nodded toward the stern-faced Carter—so much shorter a time as he actually stayed in the village. In addition, Smith would have all the provisions he requested for his journey and a round for the house now. When Modell took the traveler's hand, extended to seal the bargain, the whole room cheered. The demands for mugs of the sharp, potent beer drew the innkeeper when he would far rather have pored over his pre-Blast acquisition—marvelous, though of little enough use to him.

Dealing over, Smith carried his mug to one of the stools before the fire. Sausages, dried vegetables, and a pair of lanterns hung from the roof joists. Deer and elk antlers were pegged to the pine paneling all around the room, and above the mantelpiece glowered the skull of a rat larger than a German shepherd.

"I wonder that a man has the courage to walk alone out there," suggested a heavy-set local who tamped his pipe with the ball of his thumb, "what with the muties and all."

Smith chuckled, swigged his beer, and gestured with the mug at the rat skull. "Like that, you mean? But that's old. The giant rats were nasty enough, I have no doubt; but they weren't any stronger than the wolves, and they were a good deal stupider. Maybe you'd find a colony now and again in ruins downwind of a Strike . . . but they'll not venture far into the light, and the ones that're left—not many—are nothing that a sling stone or arrow can't cure if needs be. "He paused and smiled. "Besides, their meat's sweet enough. I'm told."

Despite the ruddy fire, the other faces in the circle went pale. Smith's eyes registered the reaction while his mouth continued to smile. "Now, travelers tell stories, you know," he said, "and there's an art to listening to them. There's little enough to joke about on the trail, so I have to do it here."

His face went serious for a moment and he added, "But I'll tell you this and swear to the truth of it: when I was near what may have been Cleveland, I thought I'd caught a mouse rummaging in my pack. And when I fetched it out, it was no bigger than a mouse, and its legs were folded under it so it could hop and scurry the way a mouse can. But its head . . . there was a horn just there—" the traveler touched the tip of his nose— "and another littler one just behind it. I figure some zoo keeper before the Blast would have called me a liar if I'd told him what his rhinos would breed to, don't you think?"

He drank deep. The company buzzed at the wonder and the easy fellowship of the man who had seen it.

"Scottie meant the half-men, didn't you, Scottie?" said a bulky man whose moustache and the beard fringing his mouth were dark with beer. He mimed an extra head with his clenched fist. "Monsters like that in the Hot Lands."

Smith's head bobbed sagely against the chorus of grim assent from the other men. "Sure, I know what you mean," he said. "Two-headed men? Girls with an extra pair of legs coming out of their bellies?"

Sounds of horror and agreement.

"You see," the traveler went on, "the Blast changed things . . . but you know as I do that it didn't change them to be easier for men. There've always been children born as . . . monsters, if you will. Maybe more born nowadays than there were before the Blast; but they *were* born, and I've seen books that were old at the Blast that talk of them. And they don't live now, my friends. Life everywhere is too hard, and those poor innocents remind folk of the Blast; and who would remember that?"

He looked around the room. The eyes that met his dropped swiftly. "There's been some born here in Moseby, haven't there?" Smith asked, his words thrusting like knifeblades and no doubt to them. "Where are they now?"

The man they had called Scottie bit through the reed stem of his pipe. He spluttered and the front legs of his stool clacked on the puncheon floor.

"Say, now, I'm not here to pry," Smith continued swiftly. "What you do is your own business. For my own part, I'd appreciate another mug of this excellent beer."

Chairs scraped in agreement as all the men stood, stretched, and moved to the bar. Modell drew beer smoothly, chalking drinks on the board on the back wall— everyone but Smith was a local. The innkeeper even broached a new cask without noticeable delay. Several of the company went out the rear door and returned, lacing their trousers. There was a brief pause as everyone settled back around the fire. Then Scottie swallowed, scowled, and said belligerently, "All right, what about the Changlings?"

"Pardon?" The traveler's eyes were friendly above the rim of his mug, but there was no comprehension in them.

"Oh, come on!" the local said, flushing in embarrassment. "You know about the Changlings, everybody does. The Blast made them. They were men before, but now they glow blue and change their shapes and walk around like skeletons, all bones!" Scottie lowered his eyes and slurped his beer in the silence. At last he repeated, "Everybody knows."

Gently, as if the suggestion did not appear as absurd to him as it suddenly did to everyone else in the room, Smith said, "I've seen some of the Strike Zones. . . . I guess I've said that. There's nothing there, friend. The destruction is total, everything. It isn't likely that anything was created by the Blast."

"The Blast changed things, we can all agree there," said Carter unexpectedly. Eyes turned toward the Policeman seated at one corner of the hearth. "Random change," Carter continued to muse aloud. "That generally'll mean destruction, yes. But there was a lot of power in the bombs, and a lot of bombs. So much power that . . . who knows what they could have done?"

Smith looked at the Policeman, raising his eyebrows. He nodded again. "Power, yes. But the *chance* that the changes, cell by cell, atom by atom, would be . . . not destructive. . . . That's a billion to one against, Mr. Carter."

"Well, the books say there were billions of men in the world before the Blast," the Policeman said, spreading the fingers of his left hand, palm upward.

The traveler's scarred left hand mirrored the Policeman's. "It's a wide world," he said, "as you must know and I surely do." He drank, smiled again, and said, "You're familiar with bombs it would seem, friend. I've heard talk in my travels that there was a stockpile of bombs in the mountains around here. Do you know that story?"

Carter looked at Smith with an expression that was terrible in its stillness. "Modell," he said in the silence, "it's time to throw another log on the fire." He paused; the innkeeper scurried to do as directed. "And it's time," the Policeman continued, "to talk of other things than the Blast. What sort of game do you find in the Hot Lands, for instance?"

"Well, I snare more than I knock on the head with my sling," Smith began easily, and the room relaxed a little.

They talked and drank late into the night. Smith told of gnarly woods and following miles of trails worn no higher than a hog's shoulder. The locals replied with tales of their farms in the river bottoms, managed for them by hirelings, and the wealth they drew from shares in the smelter's profits. Few of them actually did any of the heavy, dangerous work of steel production themselves. Moseby was a feudal state, but its basis was the powerplant rather than land.

When Carter finally left, only Scottie and another local remaining in company with Smith and Modell, the talk grew looser. Finally Scottie wheezed, "They drift in here to Moseby, up the river and down—you're the first across the mountains, boy, I'll tell the world. We put 'em to work in the fields or the smelter, or they crew the barges for us.

But they're not Moseby, they're not of the Assembly. It's *us* who've got the power, under the Chief and the Police, that is. *We* keep the Light and the—"

Modell touched the line of Scottie's jaw, silencing him. Scottie's surprise bloomed into awakened fright. "You've had enough tonight, old man," the innkeeper said. "Pook, you, too. Time for you both to get home, and for me to get to bed."

"And me," Smith agreed—Modell had already brought out blankets and opened a side bench into a cot. "Though first I'll take a leak and, say, a walk to settle my head. If you leave the door on the latch?"

Modell nodded dourly. "You've been listening to that fool Howes and his talk of the girls across the Assembly. Him with a wife and six children, too! Well, don't try to bring one back here with you. They should know better, but if one didn't, it'd be the worse for both of you." The innkeeper blew out one of the lamps and moved toward the other.

Smith urinated in the open ditch behind the building, letting his eyes readjust to the moonglow. Then he began to walk along the sewer with a deceptive purposelessness. In the shadow of the house nearest the creek he paused, eying the nodding guards across the gorge. The traveler took off his boots. He ducked into the ditch and used its cover to crawl down onto the creek bank.

The rock was steep, but it was limestone and weathered into irregularity enough for Smith's practiced digits to grip. Smoothly but without haste, the traveler slipped along below the line of sight of the guards at the powerplant. When he reached the bridge trestles he paused again, breathing carefully. His hands examined the nearest of the handsawn oak timbers, tracing it from where it butted into the rock to where it crossed another beam halfway to the stringers. Smith swung onto the trestle and began to negotiate the gorge like an ant in a clump of heavy grass.

Any sounds the traveler might have made were hidden by the creek. Its clatterings beneath echoed in a backdrop one could not easily talk over. That itself was a danger for Smith when he reached the far end of the bridge and would have listened to the guards' conversation before going on. Carefully, because a crook in the gorge threw most of the spray onto the rocks on this side, Smith edged left toward the west corner of the building. The wall there was built almost to the rim of the gorge. Smith's clothing matched the color of the wet stone so that his outline was at least blurred for a potential watcher from the village; but lack of alertness on the guards' part was his real defense.

Smith raised his head. Both guards were nodding in their chairs, crossbows leaning against the doorposts beside them. The traveler swung lithely up. A step later he was hugging the greater concealment of the powerplant's west wall. The stone hummed.

The building was as massive a construction as anything Smith had seen created after the Blast. The walls were drystone, using the natural layering of limestone and their two-foot thickness to attain an adequate seal without mortar. Their weathered seams made it easy for one of Smith's strength and condition to mount the fifteen feet of blank wall to the lighted slits just below the roof. The interior was much as the traveler had expected it to be, much as he had seen it before here and there across the face of the world.

Six huge electric motors were ranked below him. They were being used as generators, driven by a complex pattern of shafts and broad leather belts. Only one of them was turning at the moment. When the smelters were working at full capacity and called in turn for the maximum output of the plant, the room would be a bedlam of machines and their attendants. Now a man and a woman, scarcely less somnolent than the guards outside, were sufficient. The light of the naphtha lanterns illuminating the chamber may have exaggerated the attendants' pallor, but they certainly saw less of the sun than the villagers across the stream did. It was hard to believe that control of this apparatus was left to slaves; yet it was even more unlikely that free men who knew what they were doing would be willing to enter the chamber below.

In the center of the north wall, built against the living rock of the mountainside, was the reactor.

Its genesis was evident, for the black hulls of ten fusion bombs were ranged along the partition wall to the east. Smith, his head framed in the narrow window, licked his lips when he saw the bombs. They would no longer be weapons; the plutonium of their fission cores would have decayed beyond the capacity to form critical mass when compacted. But those cores, taken from their cocoons of lithium hydride and the inner baths of deuterium, could still fuel a reactor.

The latter was an ugly mass of stone blocks, overshadowed by a mantis-like derrick. Steam from the reactor drove the pistons of a crude engine. Unlike the pre-

Blast electric motors, the steam engine had been manufactured for its present purpose. Inefficient, it leaked vapor through seams and rope gaskets—but the power to create steam from water was practically inexhaustible on the scale required here.

Manufacturing skill and not theoretical knowledge had frequently been the brake on human progress: da Vinci could design a workable aircraft, but no one for four hundred years could build an engine to drive it. Nuclear power technology was so simple, given the refined fuel and expendable humans to work it, that an age which could not manufacture smokeless powder could nonetheless build a fission plant. All it would have taken was a weapons stockpile and a technician or two from Oak Ridge, vacationing in the mountains at the time of the Blast.

It was what Smith had come to learn.

There was a new sound in the night. A score or more of men were thudding across the bridge to the powerplant. Smith ducked his head beneath the sill of the window. As he did so, the siren on the roof hooted ferally. Knowing that there was no escape downward if he had been seen, the traveler slipped sideways and began to clamber up between a pair of the windows. As his fingers touched the edge of the slates, a voice from below shouted, "There he is!"

Smith gathered himself to swing onto the gently sloped roof; something tapped his knuckles. He looked up. The muzzle of Carter's M16 stared back at him. The Policeman smiled over the sights. "I saw something block one of the plant windows," the local man said. "Thought it might be worth waking the guards for. Now, 'friend', you just climb down easy to where the people are waiting, or me and the boys here won't wait for the ceremony."

The pair of guards flanking Carter had faces as tense as their cocked crossbows. Smith shook his head ruefully and descended into the waiting manacles.

The siren gave three long cries as the guards marched Smith back across the bridge. Citizens, warned by the initial signal, began walking out of their houses; the men armed, the women bleak as gray steel. They drifted toward the shrouded platform across the long axis of the Assembly from the bridge. None of the citizens seemed to want to be the first to reach the common destination. They dawdled in pairs and trios, turning aside as Smith and his captors passed through them.

The Chief and the remaining Policemen had hurried up the steps to what was clearly a covered altar by the time Smith reached it. Cords fluttered as the canvas roof was gathered within the screen of hoardings built on a base of stone blocks. Something mechanical purred and paused. Sparks hissed about the powerline strung to the platform along a line of low posts on the western edge of the Assembly.

"On up," Carter said, smiling. He tweaked Smith's manacles toward the steps. The guards were taking position at the base of the altar, facing out toward the Assembly. Despite the siren calls, there was no sign of life or movement from the smelter and its associated buildings. Their blank walls were no more than a physical reminder of the grip the freeholders of Moseby held on the minds and lives of those who would work in their village. The business tonight was no business of a bargee or a factory hand.

Smith mounted the steps. Two Policemen received him, holding their rifles by the pistolgrips as if they were still functional weapons. Well, perhaps they were.

There were other improbable things in this place . . . .

The moonlight was shadowed by the flimsy walls. It gave only hints of the enclosed area: the Policemen in their ragged uniforms; two large, vertical cylinders, the one mounted somewhat higher than the other; and, at the front of the platform, a wooden block the height of a man's knee.

"There," muttered one of the Policemen, guiding the traveler's neck onto the block. No force was necessary; Smith was as docile as a babe at its mother's breast. Carter took a quick lashing from Smith's right wrist to a staple set for the purpose in the flooring. "If it wasn't that you know too much," the Policeman said conversationally, "we'd let you spend the rest of your life inside the plant. But somebody's who's travelled as you have, seen what you have . . . we don't want to be like Samson, chaining you in the temple so you can bring it down on us, hey?"

"Tie him and we'll get this over with," the Chief growled.

Carter unlocked the manacles and bound Smith's left wrist to another staple. "It was a good idea when they chopped muties here every week," he said. "It's a good idea now. The ceremony reminds us all that it's us against the world and all of us together. I'll take the axe if you like."

Smith, facing the wooden panels, could not see the exchange. The air licked his neck and cheek as something passed from hand to hand between the two men. "Drop the walls," the Chief ordered. "And turn on the Light."

The pins locking together the corners of the hoardings slipped out. The panels arced down simultaneously in a rush of air and a collective sigh from the Assembly. The purring of an electric motor awoke under the platform, rising and becoming sibilant in the absence of competing sound. A taut drive-belt moaned; then the moan was buried in a sudden crackle and white light played like terror across the upturned faces.

Smith twisted his head. The Policemen stood in a line across the width of the platform. Carter, in the middle, gripped the haft of a fire axe. Its head was still darkened by flecks of red paint. He grinned at the traveler. Behind the rulers of the village glared another burst of lightning between the static generator's heads: the polished casings of a pair of fusion bombs. No objects could have been more fittingly symbolic of Moseby's power. The van de Graff generator provided a crude but effective way of converting electricity to light. Its DC motor pulled a belt from which electrons were combed into one bomb casing.

The static discharges to the grounded casing were all the more spectacular for being intermittent.

"You still have a chance to save yourselves if you let me go," said Smith, shouting over the ripping arcs. "There is no punishment too terrible for men who would use atomic power again, but you still have time to flee!"

Carter's smile broadened, his teeth flickering in light reflected onto his face. He roared, "We dedicate this victim to the power that preserves us all!" and he raised his axe.

"You fool," the traveler said quietly. He did not try to slide back from the block, even as he watched a multiple discharge strobe the edge of the descending axe. The hungry steel caught him squarely, shearing like a shard of ice through his flesh. His vertebrae popped louder in his ears than the hollow report of the blade against the wood. The axe head quivered, separating all but a finger's breadth of the traveler's neck. He blinked at Carter.

The Policeman rocked his blade free. Static discharges sizzled behind him at three-second intervals. Smith felt a line of warmth as his Blast-changed flesh knit together again as the steel withdrew.

Still kneeling, the Changling turned toward the crowd. "People!" he shouted. "Whatever it costs men today, men tomorrow must know that nuclear power is death! Nuclear power made this world what it is. Nuclear power is the one evil that cannot be tolerated, never again! For Man's sake, for the world's—"

Screaming, Carter slammed the axe down on the traveler's temple. The blade bit to the helve. Smith reached up with his right hand, tearing the staple from the flooring. He gripped the wood and it splintered as he drew the axe from where it was lodged in his bone. The Changling stood, his head flowing together like wax in a mold. His left wrist reformed as the rawhide lashing cut through it.

Sparks like shards of sunlight clawed through the high windows of the powerplant. That gush of light died. The siren began to wind, higher and higher. The motor of the van de Graff generator was speeding also, the current that drove it no longer controlled. The arcs were a constant white sheet between the bomb casings. Someone—two figures—crossed the bridge from the powerplant. The blue glow from the building backlighted them.

"Flee!" Smith cried, lifting to the crowd the scarred hand he had thrown up two centuries before to the flare of a hundred-megaton bomb. "Flee this abomination before it devours you—as it surely will, as it did the world before this world!"

Carter screamed again and struck with his riflebutt, hurling the Changling off the platform. Smith picked himself up. The guards backed away from him, their eyes wide, their cocked bows advanced as talismans and not threats.

The two figures on the bridge threw back their cloaks. The lapping arcs played across the half of Kozinski's face and torso that was naked bone. The bare organs pulsed within, and his one eye darted like a black jewel. The Blast had sometimes preserved and had sometimes destroyed; this once it had done both in near equality.

Ssu-ma would have stood out without the artificial lightning. She had the same trim, beautiful figure as the girl she had been the night she stared into the sky above Lop Nor and saw dawn blaze three hours early. Now that figure shone blue, brighter even than the spreading fire that ate through the wall of the powerplant behind her.

The crowd was scattering toward homes and toward the river. No one approached the platform except the two Changlings walking toward their fellow.

The Chief drew up his revolver and snapped it three times, four, and at the fifth attempt an orange flash and the thump of a shot in the open air. Five of the Policemen were triggering their automatic weapons and tugging at the

cocking pieces to spill misfired rounds on the platform. But
the old guns could still fire. Shots slapped and tore at the
night in short bursts that pattered over the flesh of the
Changlings like raindrops on thick dust. And still they
came, walking toward Smith and the platform.

Incredibly, the antitank rocket ignited when the sixth
Policeman tugged its lanyard. In ignorance he was holding
the tube against his shoulder like a conventional weapon.
The back-blast burned away the man's arm and chest in a
ghastly simulacrum of Kozinski's mutilation. The rocket
corkscrewed but chance slammed it into Ssu-ma's chest.
The red blast momentarily covered the Changling's own
fell glow. Her body splattered like the pulp of a grapefruit
struck by a maul. Simultaneously, the front wall of the
powerplant tore apart, snuffing the arcs dancing madly
between the bomb casings.

Then, evident in the sudden darkness, the bits of Ssu-
ma's glowing protoplasm began to draw together like
droplets of mercury sliding in the bowl of a spoon. Her
head had not been damaged. The waiting eyes smiled up at
the platform.

Only Carter still stood before the casings. He had
thrust the muzzle of his M16 into his mouth and was trying
to fire the weapon with his outstretched finger. The round
under the hammer misfired.

The powerplant exploded again, a gout of lava that
loosened the hillside beneath it and sprayed the village.
Wood and cloth began to burn in a pale imitation of what
was happening across the creek. In slagging down, the
reactor was fusing the rock and the hulls of the remaining
bombs. Plutonium flowed white-hot with its own internal

reactions, but it was spread too thin to self-trigger another Blast. The creek roared and boiled away as the rain of rock and metal spewed into it. The vapor that had been a plume over the powerplant was now a shroud to wrap the burning village.

"I hadn't called you yet," Smith said, shouting over the tumult as he clasped Kozinski's hand with his own left hand. He extended his right to the smiling Ssu-ma.

"We heard the siren," the Ruthenian said, his voice strange for coming from a mouth that was half bone . . . the half that had been turned away from the Strike which vaporized his infantry company, he had once explained.

"We could all tell they weren't burning coal, couldn't we?" Ssu-ma added.

The three travelers began groping through the night, through the smoke and the screaming. "I don't think we've ever checked whether the Oconee plant was still operable," Smith said. "It'd be a good time to see."

Kozinski shrugged. "We ought to get back to England some time. It's been too long since we were there."

"No, there's time for that," Smith argued. "Nobody there is going to build a fission plant as long as there's one man left to tell what we did when we found the one at Harewell."

A pair of burning buildings lighted their path, sweeping the air clear with an angry updraft. Kozinski squinted, then reached out his hand to halt Ssu-ma. "Your birthmark," he said, pointing to the star-shaped blotch beneath the girl's left breast. "It used to be on the right side."

She shrugged. "The rocket just now, I suppose."

Kozinski frowned. "Don't you see? If we can change at all, we can die someday."

"Sure," Smith agreed with a nod. "I've got some white hairs on my temples. My hair was solid brown the . . . when I went to New York."

"We'll live as long as the world needs us," Ssu-ma said quietly, touching each of the men and guiding them onward toward the trail back through the mountains. The steam and the night wrapped them, muffled them. Through it her words came: "After all, what sort of men would there be in the world if it weren't for men like us?"

And all three of them spoke the final line of the joke, their voices bright with remembered humor: "Men like us!"

A WORKING BIBLIOGRAPHY OF DAVID DRAKE'S WRITING

❧ ❦

by Karen Zimmerman, May 2012

David Drake sold his first story in 1966 and continues to write novels, short fiction, essays and other miscellaneous pieces. Although he is sometimes referred to as the "King of Military Science Fiction," his fiction spans multiple genres. He claims to have written just about every subgenre except SF romance. This is a *working* bibliography, not a *complete* bibliography. This list does not include foreign imprints, and offers only a sampling of electronic text versions. The list continues to be updated at David's official web site: http://david-drake.com. His web site also contains other pieces of his writing unavailable elsewhere, including his translations of Ovid, not included in this bibliography.

❧ BOOKS ❦

Active Measures. 1985, with J. Morris. Riverdale, NY: Baen. (Novel)

All the Way to the Gallows. 1996, Riverdale, NY: Baen. (Collection)
    2004, Baenebooks.com.

The Anvil. 1993, with S. M. Stirling. Riverdale, NY: Baen. *The General Series* (Collaboration)
    2003, In **Conqueror.** Riverdale, NY: Baen.

Arc Riders. 1995, with J. Morris. New York, NY: Warner Books. *Arc Riders Series* (Novel)
    2009, Amazon.com Kindle eBook.
    2009, Barnesandnoble.com Nook Book.

Arc Riders: The Fourth Rome. 1996, with J. Morris. New York, NY: Warner Books. *Arc Riders Series* (Novel)
    2009, Amazon.com Kindle eBook.
    2009, Barnesandnoble.com Nook Book.

Armageddon. 1998, D. Drake, B. S. Mosiman and M. H. Greenberg, eds. Riverdale, NY: Baen. (Edited Anthology)

At Any Price. 1985, Riverdale, NY: Baen. *Hammer's Slammers Series* (Novel)
    1998, In **The Butcher's Bill**. Riverdale, NY: Baen.
    2006, In **The Complete Hammer's Slammers, v. 2.** San Francisco, CA: Night Shade Books.
    2006, In **The Complete Hammer's Slammers, v. 2.** New York, NY: SFBC.
    2010, In **The Complete Hammer's Slammers, v. 2.** Riverdale, NY: Baen.
    2011, Audible.com.

Balefires. 2007, Limited edition. (Includes "Complete Bibliography of David Drake's Writing," by Karen Zimmerman) San Francisco, CA: Night Shade Books. (Collection)

>2007, San Francisco, CA: Night Shade Books.
>
>2007, Baenebooks.com.
>
>2009, San Francisco, CA: Night Shade Books.
>
>2012, In ***Night & Demons***, Riverdale, NY: Baen Books. (with updated Bibliography)

Battlestation Book One. 1992, D. Drake and B. Fawcett, eds. New York, NY: Ace. *Battlestation Series* (Edited Anthology)

Battlestation Book Two: Vanguard. 1993, D. Drake and B. Fawcett, eds. New York, NY: Ace. *Battlestation Series* (Edited Anthology)

Battlestations. 2011, D. Drake and B. Fawcett, eds. Gaithersburg, MD: Prime Books. *Battlestation Series* (Edited Anthology) Includes ***Battlestation Books One and Two***.

>2011, Amazon.com Kindle eBook.
>
>2011, Barnesandnoble.com Nook Book.

Belisarius I: Thunder at Dawn. 2008, with E. Flint. Riverdale, NY: Baen. $24.00. *Belisarius Series* (Collaboration) Includes ***An Oblique Approach*** and ***In the Heart of Darkness.***

>2009, Baenebooks.com.

Belisarius II: Storm at Noontide. 2009, with E. Flint. Riverdale, NY: Baen. *Belisarius Series* (Collaboration) Includes ***Destiny's Shield*** and ***Fortune's Stroke.***
2009, with E. Flint. Riverdale, NY: Baen.
2009, Baenebooks.com.

Belisarius III: The Flames of Sunset. 2009, with E. Flint. Riverdale, NY: Baen. *Belisarius Series* (Collaboration) Includes ***The Tide of Victory*** and ***The Dance of Time.***
2009, Baenebooks.com.

Beyond the Borders. 1996, by R. E. Howard. D. Drake, ed. Riverdale, NY: Baen. (Edited Collection)

Birds of Prey. 1984, Riverdale, NY: Baen. (Novel)
1985, New York, NY: Tor.
1991, New York, NY: Tor.
1999, Riverdale, NY: Baen.
2011, New York, NY: Tor.

Bluebloods. 1990, Riverdale, NY: Baen. *Starhunters Series* (Edited anthology)

Bran Mak Morn. 1995, by R. E. Howard. D. Drake, ed. Riverdale, NY: Baen. (Edited Collection)

Break Through. 1989, with B. Fawcett. New York, NY: Ace. *The Fleet Series.* (Edited anthology)
2002, New York, NY: Ace.

Bridgehead. 1986, New York, NY: Tor. (Novel)
1990, New York, NY: Tor.
2006, New York, NY: Tor.

The Butcher's Bill. 1998, Riverdale, NY: Baen. *Hammer's Slammers Series* (Collection)

Caught in the Crossfire. 1998, Riverdale, NY: Baen. *Hammer's Slammers Series* (Collection)

A Century of Horror, 1970-1979: The Greatest Stories of the Decade. 1996, New York, NY: MJF Books.

The Chosen. 1996, with S. M. Stirling. Riverdale, NY: Baen. *The General Series* (Collaboration)
    1998, Baenebooks.com.

Cluster Command. 1989, with W. C. Dietz. Riverdale, NY: Baen. *The Crisis of Empire Series* (Collaboration)

Codex. 2003, Chapel Hill: Sidecar Preservation Society. A limited edition of 175 copies, some of which were bound in boards.
    2012, In ***Night & Demons.*** Riverdale, NY: Baen.

The Complete Hammer's Slammers's, Volume 1. 2006, San Francisco, CA: Night Shade Books. *Hammer's Slammers Series* (Collection)
    2006, San Francisco, CA: Night Shade Books.
        Limited edition.
    2006, New York, NY: SFBC.
    2009, Riverdale, NY: Baen.
    2009, Baenebooks.com.

The Complete Hammer's Slammers's, Volume 2. 2007, San Francisco, CA: Night Shade Books. *Hammer's Slammers Series* (Collection)

2007, San Francisco, CA: Night Shade Books.
  Limited edition.
2007, New York, NY: SFBC.
2010, Riverdale, NY: Baen.
2010, Baenebooks.com.

The Complete Hammer's Slammers's, Volume 3. 2007, San Francisco, CA: Night Shade Books. *Hammer's Slammers Series* (Collection)
  2007, San Francisco, CA: Night Shade Books.
    Limited edition.
  2010, Riverdale, NY: Baen.
  2010, Baenebooks.com.

Conqueror. 2003, with S.M. Stirling. Riverdale, NY: Baen. *The General Series.* (Collaboration) Includes ***The Anvil***, ***The Steel***, and ***The Sword***.
  2003, Baenebooks.com.

Cormac Mac Art. 1995, by R. E. Howard. D. Drake, ed. Riverdale, NY: Baen. (Edited Collection)

Counter Attack. 1988, with B. Fawcett. New York, NY: Ace. *The Fleet Series.* (Edited Anthology)
  1989, New York, NY: Ace.
  1996, New York, NY: Ace.
  2002, New York, NY: Ace.
  2012, Amazon.com Kindle eBook.
  2012, Barnesandnoble.com Nook Book.

Counting the Cost. 1987, Riverdale, NY: Baen. *Hammer's Slammers Series* (Novel)

> *Caught in the Crossfire*. 1998, Riverdale, NY: Baen.
> *Hammer's Slammers Series*
> *The Complete Hammer's Slammers, v.2*. 2007,
> San Francisco, CA: Night Shade Books.
> *The Complete Hammer's Slammers, v.2*. 2007,
> New York, NY: SFBC.
> *The Complete Hammer's Slammers, v.2*. 2010,
> Riverdale, NY: Baen.
> 2011, Audible.com. *Hammer's Slammers Series*.

Crisis. 1991, with B. Fawcett. New York, NY: Ace. *The Fleet Series* (Edited Anthology)
> 2004, New York, NY: Ace.

Cross the Stars. 1984, New York, NY: Tor. Connected to *Hammer's Slammers Series*. (Novel)
> 1994, New York, NY: Tor.
> 1999, Riverdale, NY: Baen.
> 1999, Baenebooks.com.
> 2012. In **Voyage Across the Stars**. Riverdale,
> NY: Baen.

Crown of Empire. 1994, with C. Q. Yarbro. Riverdale, NY: Baen. *The Crisis of Empire Series* (Collaboration)

Cthulhu: The Mythos and Kindred Horrors. 1987, by R. E. Howard. D. Drake, ed. Riverdale, NY: Baen. (Edited Collection)

Dagger. 1988, New York, NY: Ace Books. *Thieves' World Series* (Novel)
> 1988, New York, NY: SFBC.

The Dance of Time. 2006, with E. Flint. Riverdale, NY: Baen. *Belisarius Series* (Collaboration)
>   2006, Riverdale, NY: Baen.
>   2006, Baenebooks.com.
>   2009, In ***Belisarius III: The Flames of Sunset***. Riverdale, NY: Baen.

Destiny's Shield. 1999, with E. Flint. Riverdale, NY: Baen. *Belisarius Series* (Collaboration)
>   2000, Baenebooks.com.

Dogs of War. 2002, with M. H. Greenberg. New York, NY: Warner Aspect. (Edited Anthology)
>   2008, Amazon.com Kindle eBook.
>   2008, Barnesandnoble.com Nook Book.

The Dragon Lord. 1979, New York, NY: Berkley. (This edition varies from the following paperback editions.) (Novel)
>   1982, New York, NY: Tor.
>   1989, New York, NY: Tor.
>   1994, New York, NY: Tor.
>   1998, Riverdale, NY: Baen.

Enemy of My Enemy. 1995, with B. Ohlander. Riverdale, NY: Baen. *Terra Nova Series* (Collaboration)

Eons of the Night. 1996, by R. E. Howard. D. Drake, ed. Riverdale, NY: Baen. (Edited Collection)

Eternal City. 1990, with M. H. Greenberg and C. G. Waugh. Riverdale, NY: Baen. (Edited Anthology)

Explorers in Hell. 1989, with J. Morris. Riverdale, NY: Baen. *Heroes in Hell Series*. (Novel)

Far Side of the Stars. 2003, Riverdale, NY: Baen. *RCN Series* (Novel)
    2003, Baenebooks.com.
    2004, Riverdale, NY: Baen.
    2005, New York, NY: SFBC.)
    2008, Audible.com.

Fireships. 1996, New York, NY: Ace. *The Reaches Series*. (Novel)
    1997, New York, NY: Ace.
    2004. In ***The Reaches.*** Riverdale, NY: Baen.

The Fleet. 1988, with B. Fawcett. New York, NY: Ace. *The Fleet Series* (Edited Anthology)
    1996, New York, NY: Ace.
    2002, New York, NY: Ace.
    2011, Amazon.com Kindle eBook.
    2011, Barnesandnoble.com Nook Book.

Foreign Legions. 2001, Riverdale, NY: Baen. (Edited Anthology)
    2001, Baenebooks.com.
    2002, Riverdale, NY: Baen. (Edited Anthology)

The Forge. 1991, with S. M. Stirling. Riverdale, NY: Baen. *The General Series* (Collaboration)
    2003, Riverdale, NY: Baen.

The Forlorn Hope. 1984, New York, NY: Tor. (Novel)
    1988, New York, NY: Tor.
    1991, New York, NY: Tor.
    2006, New York, NY: Tor.

Fortress. 1987, New York, NY: Tor. *Tom Kelly Series* (Novel)
    1988, New York, NY: Tor.
    1999, New York, NY: Tor.
    2011. In ***Loose Cannon.*** Riverdale, NY: Baen.
    2012. In ***Loose Cannon.*** Riverdale, NY: Baen.

The Fortress of Glass. 2006, New York, NY: Tor. *Isles Series; Crown of the Isles.* (Novel)
    2006, Baenebooks.com.
    2007, New York, NY: Tor.
    2007, Amazon.com Kindle eBook.
    2007, Barnesandnoble.com Nook Book.

Fortune's Stroke. 2000, with E. Flint. Riverdale, NY: Baen. *Belisarius Series* (Novel)
    2000, Baenebooks.com.
    2001, Riverdale, NY: Baen.

From the Heart of Darkness. 1983, New York, NY: Tor. (Collection)

Goddess of the Ice Realm. 2003, New York, NY: Tor. *Isles Series* (Novel)
    2003, New York, NY: Audio Renaissance.
        4 sound cassettes.
    2003, New York, NY: Audio Renaissance.
        5 sound cassettes.

2003, Audible.com.

2004, New York, NY: Tor.

2010, Amazon.com Kindle eBook.

2010, Barnesandnoble.com Nook Book.

The Gods Return. 2008, New York, NY: Tor. *Isles Series; Crown of the Isles* (Novel)

2008, Baenebooks.com.

2009, New York, NY: Tor.

2010, Amazon.com Kindle eBook.

2010, Barnesandnoble.com Nook Book.

Grimmer Than Hell. 2003, Riverdale, NY: Baen. (Collection)

2002, Baenebooks.com.

2004, Riverdale, NY: Baen.

The Hammer. 1992, with S. M. Stirling. Riverdale, NY: Baen. *The General Series* (Collaboration)

Hammer's Slammers. 1979, New York, NY: Ace. *Hammer's Slammers Series* (Collection)

1987, Riverdale, NY: Baen. (Expanded content from original.)

1989, Riverdale, NY: Baen. (Expanded content from original.)

Heads to the Storm. 1989, with S. Miesel. Riverdale, NY: Baen. (Edited anthology)

An Honorable Defense. 1988, with T. T. Thomas. Riverdale, NY: Baen. *The Crisis of Empire Series* (Collaboration)

The Hunter Returns. 1991, with J. Kjelgaard. Riverdale, NY: Baen. (Edited Collection)

Igniting the Reaches. 1994, New York, NY: Ace. *The Reaches Series* (Novel)
   1995, New York, NY: Ace.
   2004. In **The Reaches.** Riverdale, NY: Baen.

In the Heart of Darkness. 1998, with E. Flint. Riverdale, NY: Baen. *Belisarius Series* (Collaboration)
   1998, Baenebooks.com.
   2004, Riverdale, NY: Baen.

In the Stormy Red Sky. 2009, Riverdale, NY: Baen. *RCN Series* (Novel)
   2009, Baenebooks.com.
   2009, Audible.com.
   2010, Riverdale, NY: Baen.

Into the Hinterlands. 2011, with J. Lambshead. Riverdale, NY: Baen. *The Citizen Series* (Collaboration)
   2011, Baenebooks.com.

Into the Maelstrom. tba, with J. Lambshead. Riverdale, NY: Baen. *The Citizen Series* (Collaboration)

The Jungle. 1991, New York, NY: Tor. Includes **Clash By Night**, by H. Kuttner (Novel)
   1992, New York, NY: Tor.
   2002, In **The Seas of Venus.** Riverdale, NY: Baen.
   2004, In **The Seas of Venus.** Riverdale, NY: Baen.

Justice. 1992, New York, NY: Ace. *Northworld Series* (Novel) "Northworld: Justice (Extract)" *Amazing*, March 1992.

    1999, In *Northworld Trilogy*. Riverdale, NY: Baen.

Kill Ratio. 1987, with J. Morris. New York, NY: Ace. (Novel)

Killer. 1985, with K. E. Wagner. Riverdale, NY: Baen. (Novel)

    1990, New York, NY: Tor.
    2002, Riverdale, NY: Baen.
       This edition differs from earlier editions.
    2002, Baenebooks.com.

Kull. 1995, by R. E. Howard. D. Drake, ed. Riverdale, NY: Baen. (Edited Collection)

Lacey and His Friends. 1986, Riverdale, NY: Baen. (Collection)

The Legions of Fire. 2010, New York, NY: Tor. *The Books of the Elements* (Novel)

    2010, "Legions of Fire (Excerpt)",
      Bull Spec, Autumn 2010.
    2010, Amazon.com Kindle eBook.
    2011, Barnesandnoble.com Nook Book.
    2011, New York, NY: Tor.

Lest Darkness Fall/To Bring the Light. 1996, with L. S. de Camp, Riverdale, NY: Baen. (Edited collection)

    2011, Amazon.com Kindle eBook.

Loose Cannon. 2011, Riverdale, NY: Baen. *Tom Kelly Series* (Collection) Includes **Skyripper** and **Fortress**.

    2011, Baenebooks.com.

    2012, Riverdale, NY: Baen.

Lord of the Isles. 1997, New York, NY: Tor. *Isles Series* (Novel)

    1997, New York, NY: SFBC.

    1997, Grand Haven, MI: Brilliance Corp.
        Library edition. 12 sound cassettes.

    1997, Grand Haven, MI: Brilliance Corp.
        Unabridged edition. 6 sound cassettes.

    1997, Grand Haven, MI: Brilliance Corp.
        Abridged edition. 2 sound cassettes.

    1998, New York, NY: Tor.

    2002, New York, NY: Tor.

    2005, Baenebooks.com.

    2006, New York, NY: Tor.

    2006, Amazon.com Kindle eBook.

    2006, Barnesandnoble.com Nook Book.

Lt. Leary, Commanding. 2000, Riverdale, NY: Baen. *RCN Series* (Novel)

    2000, Baenebooks.com.

    2000, New York, NY: SFBC.

    2001, Riverdale, NY: Baen.

    2008, Audible.com.

Master of the Cauldron. 2004, New York, NY: Tor. *Isles Series* (Novel)

    2004, Baenebooks.com.

    2006, New York, NY: Tor.

2006, Amazon.com Kindle eBook.
2006, Barnesandnoble.com Nook Book.

Men Hunting Things. 1988, Riverdale, NY: Baen.
Starhunters Series. (Edited anthology)

Military Dimension. 1991, Riverdale, NY: Baen.
(Collection)

Military Dimension: Mark II. 1995, Riverdale, NY:
Baen. (Collection)
    1995, Baenebooks.com.
The Mirror of Worlds. 2007, New York, NY: Tor. *Isles
Series; Crown of the Isles* (Novel)
    2008, New York, NY: Tor.
    2008, Baenebooks.com.
    2010, Amazon.com Kindle eBook.
    2010, Barnesandnoble.com Nook Book.

Mistress of the Catacombs. 2001, New York, NY: Tor.
Isles Series (Novel)
    2001, New York, NY: SFBC.
    2002, New York, NY: Tor.
    2006, Baenebooks.com.
    2007, Amazon.com Kindle eBook.
    2007, Barnesandnoble.com Nook Book.

More Than Honor. 1998, D. Weber, ed. Riverdale, NY:
Baen. *Worlds of Honor Series* (Collection)
    1998, Baenebooks.com.
    1998, Audible.com.
    2012, Amazon.com Kindle eBook.

Mountain Magic. 2004, with H. Kuttner, E. Flint and R. E. Spoor. Riverdale, NY: Baen. (Collection) Includes *Old Nathan.*
   2004, Baenebooks.com.

Northworld. 1990. New York, NY: Ace. *Northworld Series* (Novel)
   1999, In *Northworld Trilogy*. Riverdale, NY: Baen.

Northworld Trilogy. 1999, Riverdale, NY: Baen. *Northworld Series* (Collection) Includes *Northworld, Vengeance,* and *Justice.*
   2007, Baenebooks.com.

An Oblique Approach. 1998, with E. Flint. Riverdale, NY: Baen. *Belisarius Series* (Collaboration)
   1998, Baenebooks.com.
   2008, In *Belisarius I: Thunder at Dawn.*
      Riverdale, NY: Baen.
Old Nathan. 1991, Riverdale, NY: Baen. (Collection)
   1991, Baenebooks.com.
   2004, In *Mountain Magic.* Riverdale, NY: Baen.

Other Times Than Peace. 2006, Riverdale, NY: Baen. (Collection)
   2006, Baenebooks.com.
   2008, Riverdale, NY: Baen.

Out of the Waters. 2011, New York, NY: Tor. *The Books of the Element.* (Novel)
   2011, Amazon.com Kindle eBook.

2011, Barnesandnoble.com Nook Book.
2012, New York, NY: Tor.

Patriots. 1996, New York, NY: Tor. (Novel)
1997, New York, NY: Tor.
2009, Riverdale, NY: Baen.
2009, Baenebooks.com.

Paying the Piper. 2002, Riverdale, NY: Baen. *Hammer's Slammers Series* (Episodic Novel)
2002, Baenebooks.com.
2003, Riverdale, NY: Baen.
2007, In *The Complete Hammer's Slammers, v. 3*.
    San Francisco, CA: Night Shade Books.
2010, In *The Complete Hammer's Slammers, v. 3.*
    Riverdale, NY: Baen.
2011, Audible.com.

Queen of Demons. 1998, New York, NY: Tor. *Isles Series* (Novel)
1998, Grand Haven, MI: Brilliance Corp.
    Library edition. 14 sound cassettes.
1998, Grand Haven, MI: Brilliance Corp.
    Unabridged edition. 7 sound cassettes.
1998, Grand Haven, MI: Brilliance Corp.
    Abridged edition. 2 sound cassettes.
1999, New York, NY: SFBC.
1999, New York, NY: Tor.
2002, New York, NY: Tor.
2006, Baenebooks.com.
2010, Amazon.com Kindle eBook.
2010, Barnesandnoble.com Nook Book.

Ranks of Bronze. 1986, Riverdale, NY: Baen. (Novel)
    1986, "Ranks of Bronze (Extract)" ***Far Frontiers,***
        Vol. V, J.E. Pournelle, J. Baen, and E. Mitchell, eds.
    2001, Baenebooks.com.

The Reaches. 2004, Riverdale, NY: Baen. *The Reaches Series* (Collection) Includes ***Igniting the Reaches, Through the Breach,*** and ***Fireships.***
    2004, Baenebooks.com.
    2004, New York, NY: SFBC.

Redliners. 1996, Riverdale, NY: Baen. (Novel)
    1997, Riverdale, NY: Baen.
    1997, Baenebooks.com.

The Reformer. 1999, with S. M. Stirling. Riverdale, NY: Baen. *The General Series* (Collaboration)
    2000, Riverdale, NY: Baen.
    2000, Baenebooks.com.

The Road of Danger. 2012, Riverdale, NY: Baen. *RCN Series* (Novel)
    2012, Baenebooks.com.
    2012, Audible.com

Rolling Hot. 1989, Riverdale, NY: Baen. *Hammer's Slammers Series* (Novel)
    1990, Riverdale, NY: Baen.
    1997, In ***The Tank Lords***. Riverdale, NY: Baen.
    2006, In ***The Complete Hammer's Slammers, v. 2.***
        San Francisco, CA: Night Shade Books.

2006, In *The Complete Hammer's Slammers, v. 2.*
New York, NY: SFBC.
2010, In *The Complete Hammer's Slammers, v. 2.*
Riverdale, NY: Baen.
2011, Audible.com.

The Sea Hag. 1988, Riverdale, NY: Baen. *The World of Crystal Walls Series* (Novel)
1988, Baenebooks.com.

Seas of Venus. 2002, Riverdale, NY: Baen. (Collection) Includes *The Jungle, Surface Action* and *The Real Jungle*: Belize 2001.
2002, Baenebooks.com.
2004, Riverdale, NY: Baen.

A Separate Star: A Science Fiction Tribute to Rudyard Kipling.
1989, with S. Miesel. Riverdale, NY: Baen. (Edited Anthology)

Servant of the Dragon. 1999, New York, NY: Tor. *Isles Series* (Novel)
1999, New York, NY: SFBC.
1999, Grand Haven, MI: Brilliance Corp.
Library edition. 14 cassettes.
1999, Grand Haven, MI: Brilliance Corp.
Unabridged edition. 7 cassettes.
1999, Grand Haven, MI: Brilliance Corp.
Abridged edition. 2 cassettes.
2000, New York, NY: Tor.

2002, New York, NY: Tor.

2004, New York, NY: Tor.

2006, Baenebooks.com.

2010, Amazon.com Kindle eBook.

2010, Barnesandnoble.com Nook Book.

The Sharp End. 1993, Riverdale, NY: Baen. *Hammer's Slammers Series.* (Novel)

1993, Baenebooks.com.

1993, "The Sharp End (Extract)" Amazing, October 1993.

1994, Riverdale, NY: Baen.

2007, In **The Complete Hammer's Slammers, v. 3.** San Francisco, CA: Night Shade Books.

2010, In **The Complete Hammer's Slammers, v. 3.** Riverdale, NY: Baen.

2011, Audible.com.

Skyripper. 1983, New York, NY: Tor. *Tom Kelly Series* (Novel)

1992, New York, NY: Tor.

2011, In **Loose Cannon.** Riverdale, NY: Baen.

2012, In **Loose Cannon.** Riverdale, NY: Baen.

Solomon Kane. 1995, by R. E. Howard. D. Drake, ed. Riverdale, NY: Baen. (Edited Collection)

Some Golden Harbor. 2006, Riverdale, NY: Baen. *RCN Series* (Novel)

2006, Baenebooks.com.

2006, New York, NY: SFBC.

2008, Audible.com.
2008, Riverdale, NY: Baen.

Space Dreadnoughts. 1990, with M. H. Greenberg and C. G. Waugh. New York, NY: Ace. (Edited anthology)

Space Gladiators. 1989, with C. G. Waugh and M. H. Greenberg. New York, NY: Ace. (Edited Anthology)

Space Infantry. 1989, with C. G. Waugh and M. H. Greenberg. New York, NY: Ace. (Edited Anthology)

The Square Deal. 1992, New York, NY: Tor. *Car Warriors* (Novel)
    1993, New York, NY: Tor.

Starliner. 1992, Riverdale, NY: Baen. (Novel)
    1992, Baenebooks.com.
    1993, Riverdale, NY: Baen. (Novel)

The Steel. 1993, with S. M. Stirling. Riverdale, NY: Baen. *The General Series* (Collaboration)
    2003, In **Conqueror.** Riverdale, NY: Baen.

Surface Action. 1990, New York, NY: Ace. (Novel)
    2002, In **Seas of Venus.** Riverdale, NY: Baen.
    2004, In **Seas of Venus.** Riverdale, NY: Baen.

The Sword. 1995, with S. M. Stirling. Riverdale, NY: Baen. *The General Series* (Collaboration)
    2003, In **Conqueror.** Riverdale, NY: Baen.

Sworn Allies. 1990, with B. Fawcett. New York, NY: Ace. *The Fleet Series* (Edited Anthology)
  2004, New York, NY: Ace.

The Tank Lords. 1997, Riverdale, NY: Baen. *Hammer's Slammers Series* (Collection)
  1999, Baenebooks.com.

Target. 1989, with J. Morris. New York, NY: Ace. (Novel)

Team Yankee (Comic Series). 1989, with H. Coyle, R. Whigham, and G. Forton. Chicago, IL: First Comics. 6 issues in series.
  (Graphic Novel). 1989, with H. Coyle, R. Whigham,
       and G. Forton. New York, NY: Berkley Trade.

Things Hunting Men. 1988, Riverdale, NY: Baen. *Starhunters Series* (Edited anthology)

Through the Breach. 1995, New York, NY: Ace. *The Reaches Series* (Novel)
  1996, New York, NY: Ace.
  2004, In **The Reaches.** Riverdale, NY: Baen.

The Tide of Victory. 2001, with E. Flint. Riverdale, NY: Baen. *Belisarius Series* (Collaboration)
  2001, Riverdale, NY: Baen.
  2001, Baenebooks.com.
  2009, In **Belisarius III: The Flames of Sunset.**
       Riverdale, NY: Baen.

Time Safari. 1982, New York, NY: Tor. (Collection)
    1989, Riverdale, NY: Baen.

Total War. 1990, with B. Fawcett. New York, NY: Ace.
The Fleet Series (Edited Anthology)
    2004, New York, NY: Ace.

Trails in Darkness. 1996, by R. E. Howard. D. Drake, ed. (Edited Collection)

Transgalactic. 2006, by A. E. Vogt. E. Flint and D. Drake, eds. Riverdale, NY: Baen. (Edited collection)
    2006, Baenebooks.com.

Tyrannosaur. 1993, New York, NY: Tor. (Novel) Part I and II were published in somewhat different form in **Time Safari.**

The Tyrant. 2002, with E. Flint. Riverdale, NY: Baen. *The General Series* (Collaboration)
    2002, Baenebooks.com.
    2003, Riverdale, NY: Baen.

The Undesired Princess & The Enchanted Bunny. 1990, with L. S. de Camp, Riverdale, NY: Baen. (Edited Collection)
Vanguard. See **Battlestation Book 2.**

Vengeance. 1991, New York, NY: Ace. *Northworld Series* (Novel)
    1999, In **Northworld Trilogy**. Riverdale, NY: Baen.

Vettius and His Friends. 1989, Riverdale, NY: Baen. (Collection)

The Voyage. 1994, New York, NY: Tor. Connected to *Hammer's Slammers Series* (Novel)
    1995, New York, NY: Tor.
    2012, In ***Voyage Across the Stars.*** Riverdale,
        NY: Baen.

Voyage Across the Stars. 2012, Riverdale, NY: Baen. Connected to *Hammer's Slammers Series* (Collection) Includes ***Cross the Stars*** and ***The Voyage.***
    2012, Baenebooks.com.
The War Machine. 1989, with R. M. Allen. Riverdale, NY: Baen. *The Crisis of Empire Series* (Collaboration)

Warlord. 2003, with S. M. Stirling. Riverdale, NY: Baen. *The General Series* (Collaboration) Includes ***The Forge*** and ***The Hammer.***
    2003, Baenebooks.com.

The Warmasters. 2002, B. Fawcett, ed. Riverdale, NY: Baen. (Collection)
    2002, Baenebooks.com.

The Warrior. 1991, Riverdale, NY: Baen. *Hammer's Slammers Series* (Novel)
    1991, "The Warrior (Extract)" ***Power,*** S. M. Stirling, Ed. Riverdale, NY: Baen.
    1998, In ***Caught in the Crossfire.***
        Riverdale, NY: Baen.

2007, In ***The Complete Hammer's Slammers, v. 2.***
San Francisco, CA: Night Shade Books.

2007, In ***The Complete Hammer's Slammers, v. 2.***
New York, NY: SFBC.

2010, In ***The Complete Hammer's Slammers, v. 2.***
Riverdale, NY: Baen.

2011, Audible.com.

The Way to Glory. 2005, Riverdale, NY: Baen. *RCN Series* (Novel)

2005, Baenebooks.com.

2005, New York, NY: SFBC.

2007, Riverdale, NY: Baen.

2008, Audible. com.

What Distant Deeps. 2010, Riverdale, NY: Baen. *RCN Series* (Novel)

2010, Baenebooks.com.

2010, Audible.com.

2011, Riverdale, NY: Baen.

When the Tide Rises. 2008, Norwalk, CT: Easton Press. Signed first edition, bound in leather. *RCN Series* (Novel)

2008, Baenebooks.com.

2008, Riverdale, NY: Baen.

2008, Audible.com

2009, Riverdale, NY: Baen.

Window of Opportunity: A Blueprint for the Future. 1984, with N. Gingrich and M. Gingrich. Riverdale, NY: T. Doherty Associates in association with Baen Enterprises. (Nonfiction)

With the Lightnings. 1998, Riverdale, NY: Baen. *RCN Series* (Novel)
> 1999, Riverdale, NY: Baen.
> 2000, Riverdale, NY: Baen.
> 2000, Baenebooks.com.
> 2008, Audible.com

The World Turned Upside Down. 2005, with E. Flint and J. Baen, eds. Riverdale, NY: Baen. (Edited Anthology)
> 2005, Baenebooks.com.
> 2005, New York, NY: SFBC.
> 2006, Riverdale, NY: Baen.

⊰SHORT FICTION⊱

"Airborne All the Way!" *Tapestries: An Anthology*, K. Ice, ed. 1995, New York, NY: HarperPrism.
> *All the Way to the Gallows*, 1996, Riverdale, NY: Baen.
> *This Is My Funniest 2: Leading Science Fiction Writers Present Their Funniest Stories Ever*, M. Resnick, ed. 2007, Dallas, TX: Benbella Books.

"Arclight" *F&SF*, April 1973.
> *The Military Dimension*, 1991, Riverdale, NY: Baen.
> *The Military Dimension: Mark II*, 1995, Riverdale, NY: Baen.
> *Balefires*, 2007, San Francisco: Night Shade Books.
> *Balefires*, 2009, San Francisco: Night Shade Books.
> *Night & Demons*, 2012, Riverdale, NY: Baen.

"As Our Strength Lessens" *Bolos: Honor of the Regiment*,
B. Fawcett, ed. 1993, Riverdale, NY: Baen.
> *The Military Dimension: Mark II*, 1995,
>> Riverdale, NY: Baen.
> *The Best of the Bolos: Their Finest Hour*,
> Created by Keith Laumer, Selected by Hank Davis.
> 2010, Riverdale, NY: Baen.

"The Automatic Rifleman" *Destinies*, Fall 1980.
> *From the Heart of Darkness*, 1983, New York, NY: Tor.
> *Balefires*, 2007, San Francisco: Night Shade Books.
> *Balefires*, 2009, San Francisco: Night Shade Books.
> *Night & Demons,* 2012, Riverdale, NY: Baen.

"Awakening" *Nameless Places*, G. W. Page, ed. 1975,
Sauk City, WI: Arkham House.
> *100 Twisted Little Tales of Torment*, S. Dziemianowicz,
>> R. Weinberg and M. H. Greenberg, eds. 1998,
>> New York, NY: Barnes & Noble.
> *Balefires*, 2007, San Francisco: Night Shade Books.
> *Balefires*, 2009, San Francisco: Night Shade Books.
> *Night & Demons,* 2012, Riverdale, NY: Baen.

"Backdrop to Chaos" *Hammer's Slammers*, 1979, New
York, NY: Ace.
> *Hammer's Slammers*, 1987, Riverdale, NY: Baen.
> *Hammer's Slammers*, 1989, Riverdale, NY: Baen.
> *The Tank Lords.* 1997, Riverdale, NY: Baen.
> *The Complete Hammer's Slammers, v.1*, 2006,
>> San Francisco, CA: Night Shade Books.
> *The Complete Hammer's Slammers, v.1*, 2006,
>> New York, NY: SFBC.

The Complete Hammer's Slammers, v.1, 2009,
      Riverdale, NY: Baen.

"Band of Brothers" *The Far Stars War*, B. Fawcett, ed.
1990, New York, NY: Penguin/ROC.
      The Military Dimension, 1991, Riverdale, NY: Baen.
      The Military Dimension: Mark II, 1995,
            Riverdale, NY: Baen.
      The Far Stars War. 2012,
            BarnesandNoble.com Nook Book.
      The Far Stars War. 2012,
            Amazon.com Kindle eBook.

"Bargain" *Masters in Hell*, J. Morris, ed. 1987,
Riverdale, NY: Baen.

"The Barrow Troll" *Whispers*, December 1975.
      Savage Heroes: Tales of Sorcery and Black Magic,
            M. Parry, ed. 1977, London: W. H. Allen.
      Whispers, S. D. Schiff, ed. 1977, Garden City, NY:
            Doubleday.
      The World Fantasy Awards, Volume Two, S. D. Schiff
            and F. Leiber, eds. 1980, Garden City,
            NY: Doubleday.
      From the Heart of Darkness. 1983, New York NY: Tor.
      Vettius and His Friends. 1989, Riverdale, NY: Baen.
      Heads to the Storm, D. Drake and S. Miesel, eds. 1989,
            Riverdale, NY: Baen.
      The Best of Whispers, S. D. Schiff, ed. 1994,
            Baltimore, MD: Borderlands Press.
      Balefires, 2007, San Francisco: Night Shade Books.

Balefires, 2009, San Francisco: Night Shade Books.
The Sword & Sorcery Anthology,
> D. G. Hartwell and J. Weisman, eds.,
> 2012, San Francisco, CA: Tachyon.

Night & Demons, 2012, Riverdale, NY: Baen.

"Best of Luck" *The Year's Best Horror Stories: Series VI*,
G. W. Page, ed. 1978, New York, NY: DAW.
> *From the Heart of Darkness*, 1983, New York, NY: Tor.
> *The Military Dimension*, 1991, Riverdale, NY: Baen.
> *The Military Dimension: Mark II*, 1995,
> Riverdale, NY: Baen.
> *100 Twisted Little Tales of Torment*, S. Dziemianowicz,
> R. Weinberg and M. H. Greenberg, eds. 1998,
> New York, NY: Barnes & Noble.

Balefires, 2007, San Francisco: Night Shade Books.
Balefires, 2009, San Francisco: Night Shade Books.
Night & Demons, 2012, Riverdale, NY: Baen.

"Black Iron" *Nameless Places*, G. W. Page, ed. 1975,
Sauk City, WI: Arkham House.
> *Vettius and His Friends*, 1989, Riverdale, NY: Baen.
> *Balefires*, 2007, San Francisco: Night Shade Books.
> *Balefires*, 2009, San Francisco: Night Shade Books.

Night & Demons, 2012, Riverdale, NY: Baen.

"Blood Debt" *The 4th Mayflower Book of Black Magic
Stories*, M. Parry, ed. 1976, St. Albans: Mayflower.
> *Balefires*, 2007, San Francisco: Night Shade Books.
> *Balefires*, 2009, San Francisco: Night Shade Books.
> *Night & Demons*, 2012, Riverdale, NY: Baen.

"The Bond" *Far Frontiers Vol. III*, J. E. Pournelle and J. Baen, eds. 1985, Riverdale, NY: Baen.
  All the Way to the Gallows, 1996, Riverdale, NY: Baen.

"The Bonding Authority" *Hammer's Slammers*. 1979, New York, NY: Ace.
  Hammer's Slammers, 1987, Riverdale, NY: Baen.
  Hammer's Slammers, 1989, Riverdale, NY: Baen.
  The Tank Lords. 1997, Riverdale, NY: Baen.
  The Complete Hammer's Slammers, v.1, 2006,
      San Francisco, CA: Night Shade Books.
  The Complete Hammer's Slammers, v.1, 2006,
      New York, NY: SFBC.
  The Complete Hammer's Slammers, v.1,. 2009,
      Riverdale, NY: Baen.

"Boundary Layer" *Time Safari*, 1982, New York, NY: Tor.
  Tyrannosaur, 1993, Riverdale, NY: Baen.
      (A somewhat different version from
      Time Safari, 1982.)

"The Box" *Old Nathan*, 1991, Riverdale, NY: Baen.
  Mountain Magic, 2004, Riverdale, NY: Baen.

"The Bull" *Whispers*, October 1987.
  Old Nathan, 1991, Riverdale, NY: Baen.
  Mountain Magic, 2004, Riverdale, NY: Baen.

"The Bullhead" *Old Nathan*, 1991, Riverdale, NY: Baen.
  Cats in Space, B. Fawcett, ed. 1992,
      New York, NY: Baen.

All the Way to the Gallows. 1996, Riverdale, NY: Baen.
Mountain Magic. 2004, Riverdale, NY: Baen.

"But Loyal to His Own" *Galaxy*, October 1975.
    Hammer's Slammers, 1979, New York, NY:
        Ace Science Fiction Books.
    Hammer's Slammers, 1987, Riverdale, NY: Baen.
    Hammer's Slammers, 1989, Riverdale, NY: Baen.
    Mercenaries of Tomorrow, P. Anderson, M. H.
Greenberg
        and C. G. Waugh, eds. 1985, New York, NY:
Lorevan.
    The Butcher's Bill. 1998, Riverdale, NY: Baen.
    The Complete Hammer's Slammers, v.1, 2006,
        San Francisco, CA: Night Shade Books.
    The Complete Hammer's Slammers, v.1, 2006,
        New York, NY: SFBC.
    The Complete Hammer's Slammers, v.1, 2009,
        Riverdale, NY: Baen.

"The Butcher's Bill" *Galaxy*, November 1974.
    Combat SF, G. R. Dickson, ed. 1975,
        Garden City, NY: Doubleday.
    Hammer's Slammers, 1979, New York, NY: Ace.
    Hammer's Slammers, 1987, Riverdale, NY: Baen.
    Hammer's Slammers, 1989, Riverdale, NY: Baen.
    Combat SF, G. R. Dickson, ed. 1981,
        New York, NY: Ace.
    The Butcher's Bill, 1998, Riverdale, NY: Baen.
    The Complete Hammer's Slammers, v.1, 2006,
        San Francisco, CA: Night Shade Books.

The Complete Hammer's Slammers, v.1, 2006,
New York, NY: SFBC.
The Complete Hammer's Slammers, v.1, 2009,
Riverdale, NY: Baen.

"Calibration Run" *Time Safari*, 1982, New York, NY: Tor.
Men Hunting Things, D. Drake, ed. 1988,
Riverdale, NY: Baen.

"Cannibal Plants from Heck" *Alien Pregnant by Elvis*,
E. M. Friesner and M. H. Greenberg, eds. 1994, New
York, NY: DAW.
All the Way to the Gallows. 1996,
Riverdale, NY: Baen.
Dangerous Vegetables,
K. Laumer, M. H. Greenberg and C. G.
Waugh, eds. 1998, Riverdale, NY: Baen.

"Caught in the Crossfire" *Chrysalis 2*, R. Torgeson, ed.
1978, New York, NY: Kensington/Zebra.
Hammer's Slammers. 1979, New York, NY: Ace.
Hammer's Slammers. 1987, Riverdale, NY: Baen.
Hammer's Slammers. 1989, Riverdale, NY: Baen.
Caught in the Crossfire, 1998, Riverdale, NY: Baen.
The Complete Hammer's Slammers, v.1, 2006,
San Francisco, CA: Night Shade Books.
The Complete Hammer's Slammers, v.1,. 2006,
New York, NY: SFBC.
The Complete Hammer's Slammers, v.1, 2009,
Riverdale, NY: Baen.
The Mammoth Book of SF Wars, 2012, I. Watson and I.
Whates, eds. London: Constable & Robinson.

"'Cause I Served My Time in Hell" *Rebels in Hell*, J. Morris, ed. 1986, Riverdale, NY: Baen.

"Children of the Forest" *F&SF*, November 1976. *The Year's Best Horror Stories: Series V*, G. W. Page, ed. 1977, New York, NY: DAW Books.
> *From the Heart of Darkness*, 1983, New York, NY: Tor.
> *Balefires*, 2007, San Francisco: Night Shade Books.
> *Balefires*, 2009, San Francisco: Night Shade Books.
> *Night & Demons*, 2012, Riverdale, NY: Baen.

"Choosing Sides" *The Warmasters*, D. Weber, D. Drake, and E. Flint. 2002, Riverdale, NY: Baen.
> *Paying the Piper*, 2002, Riverdale, NY: Baen.
> *The Complete Hammer's Slammers, v.3.*, 2007, San Francisco, CA: Night Shade Books.
> *The Complete Hammer's Slammers, v.3.*, 2010, Riverdale, NY: Baen.

"The Church of the Lord's Universe" *Hammer's Slammers*, 1979, New York, NY: Ace.
> *Hammer's Slammers*, 1987, Riverdale, NY: Baen.
> *Hammer's Slammers*, 1989, Riverdale, NY: Baen.
> *The Tank Lords*. 1997, Riverdale, NY: Baen.
> *The Complete Hammer's Slammers, v.1*, 2006, San Francisco, CA: Night Shade Books.
> *The Complete Hammer's Slammers, v.1*, 2006, New York, NY: SFBC.
> *The Complete Hammer's Slammers, v.1*, 2009, Riverdale, NY: Baen.

"Code-Name Feirefitz" *Men of War*, J. E. Pournelle, ed. 1984, New York, NY: Tor.

At Any Price, 1985, Riverdale, NY: Baen.
Space Infantry, D. Drake, C. G. Waugh and M. H.
    Greenberg, eds. 1989, New York, NY: Ace.
The Tank Lords. 1997, Riverdale, NY: Baen.
The Complete Hammer's Slammers, v.1, 2006,
    San Francisco, CA: Night Shade Books.
The Complete Hammer's Slammers, v.1, 2006,
    New York, NY: SFBC.
The Complete Hammer's Slammers, v.1, 2009,
    Riverdale, NY: Baen.

"Codex" *Night & Demons*, 2012, Riverdale, NY: Baen.
(First published 2003, Chapel Hill: Sidecar Preservation
Society. A limited edition of 175 copies, some of which
were bound in boards.)

"Coming Up Against It" *Grimmer Than Hell*, 2003,
Riverdale, NY: Baen.
    Grimmer Than Hell, 2004, Riverdale, NY: Baen.

"Contact!" *Analog*, October 1974.
    Body Armor: 2000, J. W. Haldeman, M. H. Greenberg
        and C. G. Waugh, eds. 1986, New York, NY: Ace.
    Encounters, I. Asimov, M. H. Greenberg
        and C. G. Waugh, eds. 1988, London: Headline.
    The Military Dimension, 1991, Riverdale, NY: Baen.
    The Military Dimension: Mark II, 1995,
        Riverdale, NY: Baen.

"Cultural Conflict" *Destinies*, January 1979.
    Hammer's Slammers, 1979, New York, NY: Ace.
    Hammer's Slammers, 1987, Riverdale, NY: Baen.

Hammer's Slammers, 1989, Riverdale, NY: Baen.
The Butcher's Bill, 1998, Riverdale, NY: Baen.
The Complete Hammer's Slammers, v.1, 2006,
   San Francisco, CA: Night Shade Books.
The Complete Hammer's Slammers, v.1, 2006,
   New York, NY: SFBC.
The Complete Hammer's Slammers, v.1, 2009,
   Riverdale, NY: Baen.

"The Dancer in the Flames" *Whispers*, August 1982.
From the Heart of Darkness, 1983, New York, NY:
Tor.
Whispers IV, S. D. Schiff, ed. 1983,
   Garden City, NY: Doubleday.
The Military Dimension, 1991, Riverdale, NY: Baen.
The Military Dimension: Mark II, 1995,
   Riverdale, NY: Baen.
100 Fiendish Little Frightmares, S. Dziemianowicz,
   R. Weinberg and M. H. Greenberg, eds. 1997,
   New York, NY: Barnes and Noble.
Balefires, 2007, San Francisco: Night Shade Books.
Balefires, 2009, San Francisco: Night Shade Books.
Night & Demons, 2012, Riverdale, NY: Baen.

"The Darkness" *Jim Baen's Universe (Online)*, June
2006, 1:1.
The Complete Hammer's Slammers, v.3, 2007,
   San Francisco, CA: Night Shade Books.
The Best of Jim Baen's Universe (Book 1), E. Flint, ed.,
   2008, Riverdale, NY: Baen.
The Complete Hammer's Slammers, v.3, 2010,
   Riverdale, NY: Baen.

"The Day of Glory" *Elemental: The Tsunami Relief Anthology*, S. Saville and A. Kontis, eds. 2006, New York, NY: Tor.
> *Other Times Than Peace*, 2006, Riverdale, NY: Baen.
> *The Complete Hammer's Slammers, v.2*, 2007, San Francisco, CA: Night Shade Books.
> *The Complete Hammer's Slammers, v.2*, 2007, New York, NY: SFBC.
> *The Complete Hammer's Slammers, v.2*, 2010, Riverdale, NY: Baen.

"A Death in Peacetime" *Oceans of the Mind*, 2005, Issue 15.
> *Other Times Than Peace*, 2006, Riverdale, NY: Baen.
> *The Complete Hammer's Slammers, v.1*, 2006, San Francisco, CA: Night Shade Books.
> *The Complete Hammer's Slammers, v.1*, 2006, New York, NY: SFBC.
> *The Complete Hammer's Slammers, v.1*, 2009, Riverdale, NY: Baen.

"Denkirch" *Travellers by Night*, A. Derleth, ed. 1967, Sauk City, WI: Arkham House.
> *Balefires*, 2007, San Francisco: Night Shade Books.
> *Balefires*, 2009, San Francisco: Night Shade Books.
> *Night & Demons*, 2012, Riverdale, NY: Baen.

"Dragon, the Book" *Catfantastic V*, A. Norton and M. H. Greenberg, eds. 1999, New York, NY: DAW.
> *Night & Demons,* 2012, Riverdale, NY: Baen.

"Dragon's Teeth" *Midnight Sun*, 1975 (#2).

Swords Against Darkness #1, A. J. Offutt, ed. 1977,
New York, NY: Kensington/Zebra.
Dragon Tales, I. Asimov, M. H. Greenberg
and C. G. Waugh, eds. 1982, New York, NY:
Ballantine Books.
From the Heart of Darkness, 1983, New York, NY: Tor.
Robert Adams' Book of Soldiers,
R. Adams, P. C. Adams and M. H. Greenberg,
eds. 1988, New York, NY: New American Library.
Vettius and His Friends, 1989, Riverdale, NY: Baen.
A Dragon-Lover's Treasury of the Fantastic,
M. Weis, ed. 1994, New York, NY: Warner Books.
Dragons: The Greatest Stories, M. H. Greenberg,
ed. 1997, New York, NY: MJF Books.

"Dreams in Amber" *Whispers V*, S. D. Schiff, ed. 1985,
Garden City, NY: Doubleday.
Vettius and His Friends. 1989, Riverdale, NY: Baen.
Other Times Than Peace. 2006, Riverdale, NY: Baen.

"The Elf House: An Isles Story" *Masters of Fantasy*, B.
Fawcett and B. Thomsen, eds. 2004, Riverdale, NY: Baen.
Balefires, 2007, San Francisco: Night Shade Books.
Balefires, 2009, San Francisco: Night Shade Books.
Night & Demons, 2012, Riverdale, NY: Baen.

"Elfin Pipes of Northworld" *The New York Review of
Science Fiction*, 1990, 3:4(28).
The Year's Best Horror Stories: XIX,
K. E. Wagner, ed. 1991, New York, NY: DAW.

"The Enchanted Bunny" *The Undesired Princess & The Enchanted Bunny*, 1990, Riverdale, NY: Baen.
>   *All the Way to the Gallows*. 1996,
>>   Riverdale, NY: Baen.

"The End" *Sworn Allies*, D. Drake and B. Fawcett, eds. 1990, New York, NY: Ace.
>   *The Military Dimension: Mark II*, 1995,
>>   Riverdale, NY: Baen.
>   *Grimmer Than Hell*, 2003, Riverdale, NY: Baen.
>   *Grimmer Than Hell*, 2004, Riverdale, NY: Baen.

"The End of the Hunt" *New Destinies, Vol. VIII*, J. Baen, ed. 1989, Riverdale, NY: Baen.
>   *The Year's Best Horror Stories: XVIII*,
>>   K. E. Wagner, ed. 1990, New York, NY: DAW.

"Exile" *Prophets in Hell*, J. Morris, ed. 1989, Riverdale, NY: Baen.

"Facing the Enemy" *Battlestation: Book One*, D. Drake and B. Fawcett, eds. 1992, New York, NY: Ace.
>   *Grimmer Than Hell*, 2003, Riverdale, NY: Baen.
>   *Grimmer Than Hell*, 2004, Riverdale, NY: Baen.
>   *Battlestations*, D. Drake and B. Fawcett, eds. 2011,
>>   Gaithersburg, MD: Prime Books.

"Failure Mode" *Battlestation: Vanguard*. 1993, New York, NY: Ace Books.
>   *Grimmer Than Hell*, 2003, Riverdale, NY: Baen.
>   *Grimmer Than Hell*, 2004, Riverdale, NY: Baen.
>   *Battlestations*, D. Drake and B. Fawcett, eds. 2011,
>>   Gaithersburg, MD: Prime Books.

"The False Prophet" *Vettius and His Friends*, 1989, Riverdale, NY: Baen.

> *Other Times Than Peace*, 2006, Riverdale, NY: Baen.
> *Balefires*, 2007, San Francisco: Night Shade Books.
> *Balefires*, 2009, San Francisco: Night Shade Books.
> *Night & Demons,* 2012, Riverdale, NY: Baen.

"Firefight" *Frights*, K. McCauley, ed. 1976, New York, NY: St. Martin's Press.

> *From the Heart of Darkness*, 1983, New York, NY: Tor.
> *The Military Dimension*, 1991, Riverdale, NY: Baen.
> *The Military Dimension: Mark II*, 1995, Riverdale, NY: Baen.
> *Balefires*, 2007, San Francisco: Night Shade Books.
> *Balefires*, 2009, San Francisco: Night Shade Books.
> *Night & Demons,* 2012, Riverdale, NY: Baen.

"The Fool" *Whispers VI*, S. D. Schiff, ed. 1987, Garden City, NY: Doubleday.

> *Old Nathan*, 1991, Riverdale, NY: Baen.
> *The American Fantasy Tradition*, B.M. Thomsen and M.H. Greenberg, eds. 2002, NewYork, NY: Tor.
> *Mountain Magic*, 2004, Riverdale, NY: Baen.

"From the Dark Waters" *Waves of Terror: Weird Stories About the Sea*, M. Parry, ed. 1976, London: Gollancz.

> *Giants*, I. Asimov, M. H. Greenberg and C. G. Waugh, eds. 1985, New York, NY: New American Library/Signet.
> *Vettius and His Friends*. 1989, Riverdale, NY: Baen.

"Goddess" *Tales from the Vulgar Unicorn*, R. Asprin, ed. 1980, New York, NY: Ace.
> *Sanctuary*, R. Asprin, ed. 1982, New York, NY: SFBC.
> *Thieves' World: First Blood*, R. Asprin and L. Abbey, eds. 2003, New York, NY: Tor.

"The Gold" *Old Nathan*, 1991, Riverdale, NY: Baen.
> *Mountain Magic*. 2004, Riverdale, NY: Baen.

"A Grand Tour" *More Than Honor*, D. Weber, ed. 1998, Riverdale, NY: Baen.
> *Other Times Than Peace*. 2006, Riverdale, NY: Baen.
> (This is a different version of the story.)

"The Great Beer Shortage" *Far Frontiers Vol. VI*, J. E. Pournelle, J. Baen and E. Mitchell, eds. 1986, Riverdale, NY: Baen. (Dave is listed as co-author but had no part in the writing of the story.)
> *The Burning Eye (War World 1)*, J. E. Pournelle, ed. 1988, Riverdale, NY: Baen.

"The Guardroom" *Afterwar*, J. Morris, ed. 1985, Riverdale, NY: Baen.
> *The Military Dimension*, 1991, Riverdale, NY: Baen.
> *The Military Dimension: Mark II*, 1995, Riverdale, NY: Baen.

"The Hand of Providence" *Heroes in Hell*, J. Morris, ed. 1986, Riverdale, NY: Baen.

"Hangman" *Hammer's Slammers*, 1979, New York, NY: Ace.

Hammer's Slammers, 1987, Riverdale, NY: Baen.

Hammer's Slammers, 1989, Riverdale, NY: Baen.

Supertanks, J. W. Haldeman, M. H. Greenberg and
     C. G. Waugh, eds. 1987, New York, NY: Ace.

Battlefields Beyond Tomorrow, C. G. Waugh
     and M. H. Greenberg, eds. 1987, New York, NY:
     Bonanza Books/Crown.

The Butcher's Bill, 1998, Riverdale, NY: Baen.

*The Best Military Science Fiction of the 20th
Century*,
     H. Turtledove and M. H. Greenberg, eds. 2001,
     New York, NY: Ballantine Del Ray.

The Complete Hammer's Slammers, v.1, 2006,
     San Francisco, CA: Night Shade Books.

The Complete Hammer's Slammers, v.1, 2006,
     New York, NY: SFBC.

The Complete Hammer's Slammers, v.1, 2009,
     Riverdale, NY: Baen.

"Hog" *Southern Fantasy*, R. Lindahn and V. L. Lindahn,
eds. 1987, Nashville, TN: World Fantasy Convention.

"The Hunting Ground" *Superhorror*, R. Campbell, ed.
1976, London: W. H. Allen.

From the Heart of Darkness, 1983, New York, NY: Tor.

Things Hunting Men, D. Drake, ed. 1988,
     Riverdale, NY: Baen.

Other Times Than Peace, 2006, Riverdale, NY: Baen.

Balefires, 2007, San Francisco: Night Shade Books.

Balefires, 2009, San Francisco: Night Shade Books.

Night & Demons, 2012, Riverdale, NY: Baen

"The Immovable Object" *Caught in the Crossfire*. 1998, Riverdale, NY: Baen.
> *The Complete Hammer's Slammers, v.1*, 2006,
> > San Francisco, CA: Night Shade Books.
> *The Complete Hammer's Slammers, v.1*, 2006,
> > New York, NY: SFBC.
> *The Complete Hammer's Slammers, v.1*, 2009,
> > Riverdale, NY: Baen.

"Inheritor" *Aftermath*, R. Asprin and L. Abbey, eds. 1987, New York, NY: Ace.
> *The Price of Victory*, R. Asprin and L. Abbey, eds. 1990,
> > New York, NY: SFBC.

"The Interrogation Team" *At Any Price*, 1985, Riverdale, NY: Baen.
> *There Will Be War, v.5*, J. E. Pournelle, ed. 1985,
> > New York, NY: Tor.
> *Caught in the Crossfire*, 1998, Riverdale, NY: Baen.
> *Other Times Than Peace*, 2006, Riverdale, NY: Baen.
> *The Complete Hammer's Slammers, v.1*, 2006,
> > San Francisco, CA: Night Shade Books.
> *The Complete Hammer's Slammers, v.1*, 2006,
> > New York, NY: SFBC.
> *The Complete Hammer's Slammers, v.1*, 2009,
> > Riverdale, NY: Baen.

"The Irresistible Force" *The Butcher's Bill*, 1998, Riverdale, NY: Baen.
> *The Complete Hammer's Slammers, v.1*, 2006,
> > San Francisco, CA: Night Shade Books.

The Complete Hammer's Slammers, v.1,
    2006, New York, NY: SFBC.
The Complete Hammer's Slammers, v.1, 2009,
    Riverdale, NY: Baen.

"Killer" with K. E. Wagner. *Midnight Sun #1,* 1974.
    Vettius and His Friends, 1989, Riverdale, NY: Baen.
    Space Gladiators, D. Drake, C. G. Waugh and M. H.
        Greenberg, eds. 1989, New York, NY: Ace
Books.
    Exorcisms and Ecstasies, 1997, Minneapolis, MN:
        Fedogan & Bremer.

"King Crocodile" *Whispers III,* S. D. Schiff, ed. 1981,
Garden City, NY: Doubleday.
    Vettius and His Friends, 1989, Riverdale, NY: Baen.

"King Tyrant Lizard" *Tyrannosaur,* 1993, New York,
NY: Tor.

"Lambs to the Slaughter" *Foreign Legions,* D. Drake,
ed. 2001, Riverdale, NY: Baen.
    Other Times Than Peace, 2006, Riverdale, NY: Baen.

"A Land of Romance" *The Enchanter Completed: A
Tribute Anthology for L. Sprague de Camp,* H. Turtledove,
ed. 2005, Riverdale, NY: Baen.
    Balefires, 2007, San Francisco: Night Shade Books.
    Balefires, 2009, San Francisco: Night Shade Books.
    Night & Demons, 2012, Riverdale, NY: Baen.

"The Land Toward Sunset" *Cormac Mac Art,* Robert E. Howard. 1995, Riverdale, NY: Baen.
　Night & Demons, 2012, Riverdale, NY: Baen.

"The Last Battalion" *Analog,* September 1977.
　Space Dreadnoughts, D. Drake, M. H. Greenberg
　　and C. G. Waugh, eds. 1990, New York, NY:
Ace.
　The Military Dimension. 1991, Riverdale, NY: Baen.
　The Military Dimension: Mark II. 1995, Riverdale,
NY: Baen.

"Learning Curve" *Angels in Hell*, J. Morris, ed. 1987, Riverdale, NY: Baen.

"Liberty Port" *Free Lancers*, E. Mitchell, ed. 1987, Riverdale, NY: Baen.
　The Butcher's Bill. 1998, Riverdale, NY: Baen.
　Dogs of War. 2002, New York, NY: Warner Aspect.
　The Complete Hammer's Slammers, v.1, 2006,
　　San Francisco, CA: Night Shade Books.
　The Complete Hammer's Slammers, v.1, 2006,
　　New York, NY: SFBC.
　The Complete Hammer's Slammers, v.1, 2009,
　　Riverdale, NY: Baen.

"Lord of the Depths" *Dark Things*, A. Derleth, ed. 1971, Sauk City, WI: Arkham House.
　Balefires, 2007, San Francisco: Night Shade Books.
　Balefires, 2009, San Francisco: Night Shade Books.
　Night & Demons, 2012, Riverdale, NY: Baen.

"The Mantichore" *Swords Against Darkness* #3, A. J. Offutt, ed. 1978, New York, NY: Kensington/Zebra.
    Vettius and His Friends, 1989, Riverdale, NY: Baen.

"The Master of Demons" *Dark Horizons, Issue 11*, Winter/Spring 1975.
    Balefires, 2007, San Francisco: Night Shade Books.
    Balefires, 2009, San Francisco: Night Shade Books.
    Night & Demons, 2012, Riverdale, NY: Baen.

"Men Like Us" *Omni*, May 1980.
    The Omni Book of Science Fiction, #3, E. Datlow, ed. 1980, New York, NY: Zebra.
    From the Heart of Darkness, 1983, New York, NY: Tor.
    Nuclear War, G. Benford and M. H. Greenberg, eds. 1988, New York, NY: Ace.
    Other Times Than Peace, 2006, Riverdale, NY: Baen.
    Balefires, 2007, San Francisco: Night Shade Books.
    Balefires, 2009, San Francisco: Night Shade Books.
    Night & Demons, 2012, Riverdale, NY: Baen.

"Mission Accomplished" *Crisis*, D. Drake and B. Fawcett, eds. 1991, New York, NY: Ace.
    Grimmer Than Hell, 2003, Riverdale, NY: Baen.
    Grimmer Than Hell, 2004, Riverdale, NY: Baen.

"Mom and the Kids" with L. Niven. *Sworn Allies*, D. Drake and B. Fawcett, eds. 1990, New York, NY: Ace.
    All the Way to the Gallows, 1996, Riverdale, NY: Baen.

"The Murder of Halley's Comet" with L. Niven. *Break Through*, D. Drake and B. Fawcett, eds. 1989, New York, NY: Ace.

    Other Times Than Peace, 2006, Riverdale, NY: Baen.

"Nation Without Walls" *Analog*, July 1977.

    Lacey and His Friends, 1986, Riverdale, NY: Baen.

    Grimmer Than Hell, 2003, Riverdale, NY: Baen.

    Grimmer Than Hell, 2004, Riverdale, NY: Baen.

"Neck or Nothing" *Paying the Piper*, 2002, Riverdale, NY: Baen.

    The Complete Hammer's Slammers, v.3, 2007, San Francisco, CA: Night Shade Books.

    The Complete Hammer's Slammers, v.3, 2010, Riverdale, NY: Baen.

"Nemesis Place" *Fantastic*, April 1978.

    The Year's Best Horror Stories: Series VII, G. W. Page, ed. 1979, New York, NY: DAW.

    Vettius and His Friends, 1989, Riverdale, NY: Baen.

    Horrorstory, vol. 3, K. E. Wagner, ed. 1992, Novato, CA: Underwood-Miller.

"Night March" *The Tank Lords*, 1997, Riverdale, NY: Baen.

    The Complete Hammer's Slammers, v.1, 2006, San Francisco, CA: Night Shade Books.

    The Complete Hammer's Slammers, v.1, 2006, New York, NY: SFBC.

    The Complete Hammer's Slammers, v.1, 2009, Riverdale, NY: Baen.

"The Noble Savages" *Blood and War*, G. R. Dickson, ed. 1993, Riverdale, NY: Baen.
> *All the Way to the Gallows*, 1996, Riverdale, NY: Baen.

"Out of Africa" *From the Heart of Darkness*, 1983, New York, NY: Tor.
> *The Year's Best Horror Stories XII*, K. E. Wagner, ed. 1984, New York, NY: DAW.
> *Horrorstory, vol. 4*, K. E. Wagner, ed. 1990, Novato, CA: Underwood-Miller.
> *100 Hair-Raising Little Horror Stories*, A. Sarrantonio and M. H. Greenberg, eds. 1993, New York, NY: Barnes and Noble.

"The Political Process" *Paying the Piper*, 2002, Riverdale, NY: Baen.
> *The Complete Hammer's Slammers, v.3*, 2007, San Francisco, CA: Night Shade Books.
> *The Complete Hammer's Slammers, v.3*, 2010, Riverdale, NY: Baen.

"Powerguns" *Hammer's Slammers*, 1979, New York, NY: Ace Science Fiction Books.
> *Hammer's Slammers*, 1987, Riverdale, NY: Baen.
> *Hammer's Slammers*, 1989, Riverdale, NY: Baen.
> *The Tank Lords*, 1997, Riverdale, NY: Baen.
> *The Complete Hammer's Slammers, v.1*, 2006, San Francisco, CA: Night Shade Books.
> *The Complete Hammer's Slammers, v.1*, 2006, New York, NY: SFBC.
> *The Complete Hammer's Slammers, v.1*, 2009, Riverdale, NY: Baen.

"The Predators" *Destinies*, October 1979.
   Lacey and His Friends, 1986, Riverdale, NY: Baen.
   Grimmer Than Hell, 2003, Riverdale, NY: Baen.
   Grimmer Than Hell, 2004, Riverdale, NY: Baen.

"Ranks of Bronze" *Galaxy*, August 1975.
   There Will Be War, J. E. Pournelle, ed. 1983,
      New York, NY: Tor.
   Vettius and His Friends, 1989, Riverdale, NY: Baen.
   The Eternal City, D. Drake, M. H. Greenberg and
      C. G. Waugh, eds. 1990, Riverdale, NY: Baen.
   Foreign Legions, D. Drake, ed. 2001,
      Riverdale, NY: Baen.
   The Space Opera Renaissance, D. Hartwell and
      K. Cramer, eds. 2006, New York, NY: Tor.
   Sense of Wonder: A Century of Science Fiction, 2011,
      L. R. Grossman, ed. Rockville, MD:
      Wildside Press.
   Sense of Wonder: A Century of Science Fiction, 2011,
      Amazon.com Kindle eBook.
   Sense of Wonder: A Century of Science Fiction, 2011,
      Barnesandnoble.com Nook Book.

"The Red Leer" *Whispers II*, S. D. Schiff, ed. 1979,
Garden City, NY: Doubleday.
   From the Heart of Darkness, 1983,
      New York, NY: Tor.
   Bluebloods, 1990, Riverdale, NY: Baen.
   Balefires, 2007, San Francisco: Night Shade Books.
   Balefires, 2009, San Francisco: Night Shade Books.
   Night & Demons, 2012, Riverdale, NY: Baen.

"Rescue Mission" *The Fleet*, 1988, New York, NY: Ace.
   The Military Dimension, 1991, Riverdale, NY: Baen.
   Commando Brigade 3000, M. H. Greenberg and
      C. G. Waugh, eds. 1994, New York, NY: Ace.
   The Military Dimension: Mark II, 1995,
      Riverdale, NY: Baen.
   Grimmer Than Hell, 2003, Riverdale, NY: Baen.
   Grimmer Than Hell, 2004, Riverdale, NY: Baen.

"Safe to Sea" *Space Fighters*, J. W. Haldeman, C. G. Waugh and M. H. Greenberg, eds. 1988, New York, NY: Ace.
   Other Times Than Peace, 2006, Riverdale, NY: Baen.

"The Shortest Way" *Whispers*, March 1974.
   First World Fantasy Awards, G. Wilson, ed. 1977,
      Garden City, NY: Doubleday.
   From the Heart of Darkness, 1983,
      New York, NY: Tor.
   Vettius and His Friends, 1989, Riverdale, NY: Baen.
   Balefires, 2007, San Francisco: Night Shade Books.
   Balefires, 2009, San Francisco: Night Shade Books.
   Night & Demons, 2012, Riverdale, NY: Baen.

"Smash and Grab" *Total War*, 1990, New York, NY: Ace.
   Grimmer Than Hell, 2003, Riverdale, NY: Baen.
   Grimmer Than Hell, 2004, Riverdale, NY: Baen.

"Smokie Joe" *More Devil's Kisses*, M. Parry, ed. 1977, London: Corgi.

Terrors, C. L. Grant, ed. 1982, New York,
 NY: Playboy Paperbacks.
From the Heart of Darkness, 1983, New York, NY: Tor.
Balefires, 2007, San Francisco: Night Shade Books.
Balefires, 2009, San Francisco: Night Shade Books.
Night & Demons, 2012, Riverdale, NY: Baen.

"Something Had to Be Done" *F&SF*, February 1975.
The Year's Best Horror Stories: Series IV, G. W. Page,
 ed. 1976, New York, NY: DAW.
From the Heart of Darkness, 1983, New York, NY: Tor.
100 Vicious Little Vampire Stories, R. Weinberg,
 S. Dziemianowicz and M. H. Greenberg,
 eds. 1995, New York, NY: Barnes and Noble.
The Military Dimension: Mark II, 1995, Riverdale,
NY: Baen.
A Century of Horror, 1970-1979, D. Drake and
 M. H. Greenberg, eds. 1996: MJF Books.
Vampires: The Greatest Stories, M. H. Greenberg,
 ed. 1997, New York, NY: MJF Books.
Balefires, 2007, San Francisco: Night Shade Books.
Balefires, 2009, San Francisco: Night Shade Books.
Night & Demons, 2012, Riverdale, NY: Baen.

"The Song of the Bone" *Whispers*, December 1973.
Balefires, 2007, San Francisco: Night Shade Books.
Balefires, 2009, San Francisco: Night Shade Books.
Night & Demons, 2012, Riverdale, NY: Baen.

"Springs Eternal" *Crusaders in Hell*, J. Morris, ed. 1987,
Riverdale, NY: Baen.

"Standing Down" *Hammer's Slammers*, 1979, New York, NY: Ace.

> *Hammer's Slammers*, 1987, Riverdale, NY: Baen.
> *Hammer's Slammers*, 1989, Riverdale, NY: Baen.
> *The Butcher's Bill*, 1998, Riverdale, NY: Baen.
> *The Complete Hammer's Slammers, v.1*, 2006, San Francisco, CA: Night Shade Books.
> *The Complete Hammer's Slammers, v.1*, 2006, New York, NY: SFBC.
> *The Complete Hammer's Slammers, v.1*, 2009, Riverdale, NY: Baen.

"Supertanks" *Hammer's Slammers*, 1979, New York, NY: Ace.

> *Hammer's Slammers*, 1987, Riverdale, NY: Baen.
> *Hammer's Slammers*, 1989, Riverdale, NY: Baen.
> *The Tank Lords*, 1997, Riverdale, NY: Baen.
> *The Complete Hammer's Slammers, v.1*, 2006, San Francisco, CA: Night Shade Books.
> *The Complete Hammer's Slammers, v.1*, 2006, New York, NY: SFBC.
> *The Complete Hammer's Slammers, v.1*, 2009, Riverdale, NY: Baen.

"Table of Organization and Equipment, Hammer's Regiment" *Hammer's Slammers*, 1979, New York, NY: Ace.

> *Hammer's Slammers*, 1987, Riverdale, NY: Baen.
> *Hammer's Slammers*, 1989, Riverdale, NY: Baen.
> *The Tank Lords*, 1997, Riverdale, NY: Baen.
> *The Complete Hammer's Slammers, v.1*, 2006, San Francisco, CA: Night Shade Books.

The Complete Hammer's Slammers, v.1, 2006,
New York, NY: SFBC.
The Complete Hammer's Slammers, v.1, 2009,
Riverdale, NY: Baen.

"The Tank Lords" *Far Frontiers*, vol. VI, Fall 1986
Hammer's Slammers, 1987, Riverdale, NY: Baen.
Hammer's Slammers, 1989, Riverdale, NY: Baen.
There Will Be War, v.7, J. E. Pournelle, ed. 1989,
New York, NY: Tor.
The Military Dimension, 1991, Riverdale, NY: Baen.
The Military Dimension: Mark II, 1995, Riverdale,
NY: Baen.
The Tank Lords, 1997, Riverdale, NY: Baen.
The Complete Hammer's Slammers, v.1, 2006,
San Francisco, CA: Night Shade Books.
The Complete Hammer's Slammers, v.1, 2006,
New York, NY: SFBC.
The Complete Hammer's Slammers, v.1, 2009,
Riverdale, NY: Baen.

"Team Effort" *Break Through*, D. Drake and B. Fawcett,
eds. 1989, New York, NY: Ace.
Grimmer Than Hell, 2003, Riverdale, NY: Baen.
Grimmer Than Hell, 2004, Riverdale, NY: Baen.

"Than Curse the Darkness" *New Tales of the Cthulhu
Mythos*, R. Campbell, ed. 1980, Sauk City, WI: Arkham
House.
From the Heart of Darkness, 1983, New York, NY: Tor.
Balefires, 2007, San Francisco: Night Shade Books.

Balefires, 2009, San Francisco: Night Shade Books.
The Book of Cthulhu, R. E. Lockhart, ed., 2011,
    San Francisco, CA: Night Shade Books.
Night & Demons, 2012, Riverdale, NY: Baen.

"Tigers of the Sea" by R. E. Howard and D. Drake.
Cormac Mac Art, Robert E. Howard. 1995, Riverdale, NY:
Baen. (A completion of R. E. Howard's unfinished story.)

"Time Safari" *Destinies*, 1981. v.3(no.2).
    Time Safari, 1982, New York, NY: Tor.
      (A somewhat different version
      from *Destinies*, 1981.)
    Baker's Dozen: 13 Short Science Fiction Novels, I.
      Asimov, M. H. Greenberg and C. G. Waugh,
      eds. 1985, New York, NY: Bonanza Books.
    Lacey and His Friends, 1986, Riverdale, NY: Baen.
    Loaded for Bear, M. H. Greenberg and C. G. Waugh,
      eds. 1990, New York, NY:
      Random House Value Publishing.
    Tyrannosaur, 1993, New York, NY: Tor.

"To Bring the Light" *Lest Darkness Fall/To Bring the
Light*, 1996, Riverdale, NY: Baen.
    2011, Amazon.com Kindle eBook.
    2011, Barnesandnoble.com Nook Book
    Lest Darkness Fall and Related Stories, L. S.
DeCamp,
      F. Pohl, S.M. Stirling and D. Drake. 2011,
      Rockville, MD: Phoenix Pick.

"The Tradesmen" *Drakas!*, S. M. Stirling, ed. 2000, Riverdale, NY: Baen.
> *Grimmer Than Hell*, 2003, Riverdale, NY: Baen.
> *Grimmer Than Hell*, 2004, Riverdale, NY: Baen.

"Travellers" *Destinies*, Winter 1981.
> *Lacey and His Friends*, 1986, Riverdale, NY: Baen.

"Under the Hammer" *Galaxy*, October 1974.
> *Hammer's Slammers*, 1979, New York, NY:
> Ace Science Fiction Books.
> *Hammer's Slammers*, 1987, Riverdale, NY: Baen.
> *Hammer's Slammers*, 1989, Riverdale, NY: Baen.
> *Machines That Kill*, F. Saberhagen and M. H.
> Greenberg, eds. 1984, New York, NY: Ace.
> *A Separate Star: A Science Fiction Tribute to
> Rudyard Kipling*, D. Drake and S. Miesel,
> eds. 1989, Riverdale, NY: Baen.
> *The Tank Lords*. 1997, Riverdale, NY: Baen.
> *The Complete Hammer's Slammers, v.1*, 2006,
> San Francisco, CA: Night Shade Books.
> *The Complete Hammer's Slammers, v.1*, 2006,
> New York, NY: SFBC.
> *The Complete Hammer's Slammers, v.1*, 2009,
> Riverdale, NY: Baen.
> *Citizens: Military Science Fiction by Military Veterans*,
> J. Ringo and B. M. Thomsen, eds. 2010,
> Riverdale, NY: Baen.

"Underground" *Destinies*, February 1980.
> *Lacey and His Friends*, 1986, Riverdale, NY: Baen.

Grimmer Than Hell, 2003, Riverdale, NY: Baen.
Grimmer Than Hell, 2004, Riverdale, NY: Baen.

"A Very Offensive Weapon" *Forever After*, R. Zelazny, ed. 1995, Riverdale, NY: Baen.
All the Way to the Gallows, 1996, Riverdale, NY: Baen.

"Votary" *The Face of Chaos*, R. Asprin and L. Abbey, eds. 1983, New York, NY: Ace.
Cross-Currents: Storm Season; Face of Chaos; Wings of Omen, R. Asprin and L. Abbey, eds. 1984, Garden City, NY: Doubleday.

"The Waiting Bullet" *Weirdbook 30 Combined with Whispers*, Spring, 1997.
Night & Demons, 2012, Riverdale, NY: Baen.

"The Way We Die" *The Military Dimension*, 1991, Riverdale, NY: Baen.
The Military Dimension: Mark II, 1995, Riverdale, NY: Baen.
"When the Devil Drives" *Counter Attack*, 1988, New York, NY: Ace Books.
Grimmer Than Hell, 2003, Riverdale, NY: Baen.
Grimmer Than Hell, 2004, Riverdale, NY: Baen.

"Wisdom" *War in Hell*, J. Morris, ed. 1988, Riverdale, NY: Baen.

"With the Sword He Must Be Slain" *Armageddon*, 1998, Riverdale, NY: Baen.

Grimmer Than Hell, 2003, Riverdale, NY: Baen.
Grimmer Than Hell, 2004, Riverdale, NY: Baen.

⊰ESSAYS, COMMENTS, BOOK INTRODUCTIONS, ⊱ AND MISCELLANEOUS MUSINGS

"Accidentally and By the Back Door" *The New York Review of Science Fiction*, 2004. 17:3(195): p. 17-18.
    The Complete Hammer's Slammers v.1, 2006,
        San Francisco CA: Night Shade Books.
    The Complete Hammer's Slammers v.1, 2006,
        New York, NY: SFBC.
    The Complete Hammer's Slammers v.1, 2009,
        Riverdale, NY: Baen.

"Afterword" *The Cold Equations & Other Stories*, by T. Godwin. E. Flint, ed. 2003, Riverdale, NY: Baen.

"Alien Landscape with Figures" *The New York Review of Science Fiction*, 2005. 17:11(203): p. 6.
    Warriors of the Steppes, by H. Lamb. H. A. Jones,
        ed. 2006, Lincoln, NE:
        University of Nebraska Press.
    Warriors of the Steppes, by H. Lamb. H. A. Jones,
        ed. 2006, Amazon Kindle eBook.

"Another Method" *Tor/Forge Newsletter (online),* July 2011.

"Appendix" *The Tank Lords,* 1997, Riverdale, NY: Baen.

"At Seventeen" *The New York Review of Science Fiction,* 1996. 8:12(96): p. 1.

"A Background Note" *Paying the Piper,* 2002, Riverdale, NY: Baen.

"Becoming a Professional Writer by Way of Southeast Asia" *The Butcher's Bill.* 1998, Riverdale, NY: Baen.
 The Complete Hammer's Slammers v.1, 2006,   San Francisco CA: Night Shade Books.
 The Complete Hammer's Slammers v.1, 2006,   New York, NY: SFBC.
 The Complete Hammer's Slammers v.1, 2009,   Riverdale, NY: Baen.

"Before Nineteen Eighty-Four: Thoughts on Orwell" *The New York Review of Science Fiction,* 2011. 23:5(269): p. 9.

"A Belated Thank-You" *The New York Review of Science Fiction,* 2009. 21:6(246): p. 21.

"A Brief Introduction to Karl Edward Wagner" *Weird Tales,* 1989. Fall 1989.

"Broken Things" *The New York Review of Science Fiction,* 2008. 20:6(234): p. 11.

"But Why on Earth Belisarius? (Introduction)" *Thunder at Dawn*, 2009, Riverdale, NY: Baen.

"Casualties of War: *Command Performance* by Walter M. Miller" *Command Performance*, by Walter M. Miller (The Galaxy Project), 2011, RosettaBooks. (eBook)
    2011, Amazon.com Kindle eBook.
    2011, Barnesandnoble.com Nook Book.

"The Classical Background" *The New York Review of Science Fiction*, 2011. 23:6(270): p. 22.

"The Classical Background: Letter of Comment" *The New York Review of Science Fiction*, 2011. 23:8(272): p. 23.

"*The Cold Equations*, by Tom Godwin" (with Barry Malzberg) *The New York Review of Science Fiction*, 2002. 14:7(163): p. 1, 4-5.

"Combat" *The American Warrior*, C. Morris and J. Morris, eds. 1992, Stamford, CT: Longmeadow Press.

"Coming Home by the Long Way (Introduction)" *Grimmer Than Hell*, 2003, Riverdale, NY: Baen.
    Grimmer Than Hell. 2004, Riverdale, NY: Baen.

"Costs and Benefits (Introduction)" *Dogs of War*, 2002, New York, N.Y.: Warner Aspect.

"The Creation of Rome (Introduction)" *The Eternal City*, D. Drake, M. H. Greenberg and C. G. Waugh, eds. 1990, Riverdale, NY: Baen.

"Cyberpunk and the New Wave: Ruptures and Continuities: Letter of Comment" *The New York Review of Science Fiction*, 2007. 20:1(229): p. 23.

"*Dark and Sinister Shades*: The Twilight Tales of Marjorie Bowen: Letter of Comment" *The New York Review of Science Fiction*, 2010. 23:2(266): p. 23.

"Dr. Syn Revisted" *The New York Review of Science Fiction*, 2010. 23:2(266): p. 11.

"The Earlier Version (Afterword)" *Assignment in Eternity*, by R. Heinlein, 2012, Riverdale, NY: Baen.

"Extraordinary Diplomats (Preface)" *Retief! The Graphic Album,* by D. Fujitake, J. Strnad and K. Laumer. 1990, Greencastle, PA: Apple Press.
 Retief!, K. Laumer; E. Flint, ed. 2002,
  Riverdale, NY: Baen.

"Faith, Hope, and Charity" *The New York Review of Science Fiction*, 2004. 16:11(191): p. 8-9.

"The Fifteen Years Afterword" *At Any Price*, 1985, Riverdale, NY: Baen.

"Five Firebases" *Thunder Run,* 2009. 24:3, p. 1, 4-5.
  an edited version as "Foreword" *Hammer's
   Slammers,* [Role-playing game] G. Hanrahan.
   2009. Swindon, UK: Mongoose Publishing.

"Forever Afterword" *Forever After*, R. Zelazny, ed. 1995, Riverdale, NY: Baen.

"Frank R. Paul's GoH Speech: Letter of Comment" *The New York Review of Science Fiction*, 2006. 19:2(218): p. 23.

"The Golden Age" *The New York Review of Science Fiction*, 2009. 21:10(250): p. 14.
    Nebula Awards Showcase, B. Fawcett, ed. 2010,
      New York: Roc.

"*The Hairless Ones Come:* L. Sprague de Camp" *The New York Review of Science Fiction*, 2005. 17:8(200): p. 18.

"Heroes (Introduction)" *Space Infantry*, D. Drake, C. G. Waugh and M. H. Greenberg, eds. 1989, New York: Ace.

"Hickmania" *Science Fiction Age*, 1993. November 1993.

"How They Got That Way: Afterword to *Counting the Cost.*" *Counting the Cost*, 1987, Riverdale, NY: Baen.
    The Complete Hammer's Slammers v.2, 2007,
      San Francisco CA: Night Shade Books.
    The Complete Hammer's Slammers v.2, 2007,
      New York, NY: SFBC.
    The Complete Hammer's Slammers v.2, 2010,
      Riverdale, NY: Baen.

"The Human Side (Introduction)" *Kull*, R. E. Howard, 1995, Riverdale, NY: Baen.

"In a Glass Brightly: *The Wind Between the Worlds* by Lester del Rey" *The Wind Between the Worlds,* Lester del Rey (The Galaxy Project), 2011, RosettaBooks. (eBook)
    2011, Amazon.com Kindle eBook.
    2011, Barnesandnoble.com Nook Book.

"An Interview with Tom Purdom: Letter of Comment" *The New York Review of Science Fiction,* 2006. 18:7(211): p. 23.

"Intolerance" *The New York Review of Science Fiction,* 1995. 7:10(82): p. 21.

"Introduction" *All the Way to the Gallows,* 1996, Riverdale, NY: Baen.

"Introduction" *Caught in the Crossfire,* 1998, Riverdale, NY: Baen.

"Introduction" *Cormac Mac Art,* R. E. Howard, 1995, Riverdale, NY: Baen.

"Introduction" *Cthulhu: The Mythos and Kindred Horrors,* D. Drake, ed. 1987, Riverdale, NY: Baen.

"Introduction" *Dogs of War,* 2002, New York: Warner Aspect.

"Introduction" *Dorsai Spirit,* G. R. Dickson. 2002, New York: Tor.

"Introduction" *Hammer's Anvils: Handbook* #2, J. Treadaway, 2006, Bournemouth, UK: Pireme.

"Introduction" *Hammer's Slammer's Handbook,* by J. Lambshead and J. Treadaway, 2004, Bournemouth, UK: Pireme.

"Introduction" *Heads to the Storm,* D. Drake and S. Miesel, eds. 1989, Riverdale, NY: Baen.

"Introduction" *The Mercenary,* J. Pournelle, 1988, New York: F. Watts
    Reprinted as "Mercenaries [Introduction]"
        Caught in the Crossfire, 1998,
        Riverdale, NY: Baen.

"Introduction" *Seas of Venus,* 2002, Riverdale, NY: Baen.

"Introduction" *A Separate Star: A Science Fiction Tribute to*
    Rudyard Kipling, D. Drake and S. Miesel,
        eds. 1989, Riverdale, NY: Baen.

"*The Iron Chancellor*: Professionalism at the Level of Genius" The Iron Chancellor, Robert Silverberg (The Galaxy Project), 2011, RosettaBooks. (eBook)
    2011, Amazon.com Kindle eBook.
    2011, Barnesandnoble.com Nook Book.

"Isaac Asimov: Letter of Comment" *The New York Review of Science Fiction*, 1999. 11:5(125): p. 23.

"It's a Lot Like War (Introduction)" *Men Hunting Things*, D. Drake, ed. 1988, Riverdale, NY: Baen.

"Jim Baen October 22, 1943 - June 28, 2006" [Jim Baen Obituary] *Jim Baen's Universe (online)*, 2006.
    The Complete Hammer's Slammers v.3. 2007,
        San Francisco CA: Night Shade Books.
    The Complete Hammer's Slammers v.3. 2010,
        Riverdale, NY: Baen.

"John Norman: Letter of Comment" *The New York Review of Science Fiction*, 1996. 9:4(100): p. 22.

"John W. Campbell: Letter of Comment" *The New York Review of Science Fiction*, 1998. 10:9(117): p. 23.

"A Kind of Humor" *Military Science Fiction on Tor.com (online)*, January 2012.

"L. Sprague de Camp: An Appreciation" *Locus*, 2000. 45:6(No.479).

"Let the Games Begin (Introduction)" *Space Gladiators*, D. Drake, C. G. Waugh and M. H. Greenberg, eds. 1989, New York: Ace Books.

"Manly in the Mountains (Foreword)" *John the Balladeer*, Manly Wade Wellman, 1988, Riverdale, NY: Baen.
    The Tome #6, 1990.

"Manly Wade Wellman and Alfred Bester" *The New York Review of Science Fiction*, 1996. 9:1(97): p. 9.

"Manly Wade Wellman and the Stone Age: The Hok Stories" *The New York Review of Science Fiction*, 2010. 22:10(262): p. 14.
> **"Manly and the Stone Age (Introduction)"**
> *Battle in the Dawn: The Complete Hok the Mighty*,
> by Manly Wade Wellman. 2011, Redmond,
> WA: Paizo Publishing.

"Manly's Stories" *The New York Review of Science Fiction*, 2002. 14:10(166): p. 15-16.
> *Sin's Doorway and Other Ominous Entrances*, M. W.
> Wellman, 2003, San Francisco:
> Night Shade Books.

"Mercenaries: An Introduction" *Caught in the Crossfire*. 1998, Riverdale, NY: Baen. (First published as "Introduction" in *The Mercenary*, J. Pournelle, 1988, New York: F. Watts.)

"The Motorcycle Way of Complex Plotting" *Tor/Forge Newsletter (online)*, May 2010.

"Musings on the Discovery of Pluto" *The New York Review of Science Fiction*, 2008. 20:5(233): p. 13.

"My Discovery of William B. Seabrook: Letter of Comment" *The New York Review of Science Fiction*, 2003. 16:3(183).

"My Friend Barry" *The New York Review of Science Fiction*, 2007. 19:6(222): p. 17.

"*The New King* (Shiel's Final Novel): An Appreciation" *Shiel in Diverse Hands*, A. R. Morse, ed. 1983, Cleveland OH: The Reynolds Morse Foundation.

"No Limit on Hippogrifs" (Poem), *The Arkham Collector,* Winter 1968.
    The Arkham Collector, vol. 1, 1971, Sauk City,
        WI: Arkham House.

"Non-Legal Writing" *The Senior Lawyer,* 1996. v.6 no. 2.

"A Note on Harry Bates" *The New York Review of Science Fiction*, 2007. 20:2(230): p.21.

"A Note on King Kong" *The New York Review of Science Fiction,* 2010. 22:8(260): p.15.

"A Note on Solomon Kane" *The New York Review of Science Fiction*, 1998. 11:2(122): p. 11.

"A Note on the Text" *Cormac Mac Art,* R. E. Howard, 1995, Riverdale, NY: Baen.

"Notes on *Neither Brute Nor Human*: Karl Edward Wagner" *The New York Review of Science Fiction*, 2004. 16:12(192): p. 20.

"On Cover Art" *The New York Review of Science Fiction*, 2008. 20:8(236): p. 20.

"The One That Got Away (Introduction)" *The Reaches*, 2004, Riverdale, NY: Baen.

"One War Later (Afterword)" *The Military Dimension: Mark II*, 1995, Riverdale, NY: Baen.

"Personal Commitment" *The American Warrior*, C. Morris and J. Morris, eds. 1992, Stamford, CT: Longmeadow Press.

"A Personal Note on Kurt Vonnegut" *The New York Review of Science Fiction*, 2007. 19:10(226): p.21.

"Pig Picking" *Serve It Forth — Cooking With Anne McCaffrey* A. McCaffrey and J. G. Betancourt, eds. 1996: Warner Aspect.

"Poul Anderson's *The High Crusade*: An Appreciation by David Drake" *Tor.com (Online)*, September 2010.

"Preface" *The Compleat Compleat Enchanter*, by L. S. de Camp and F. Pratt. 1989, Riverdale, NY: Baen.

"A Quick Look at Battle Fleets (Introduction)" *Space Dreadnoughts*, D. Drake, M. H. Greenberg and C. G. Waugh, eds. 1990, New York: Ace.

"A Range of Treatments (Introduction)" *Other Times Than Peace*, 2006, Riverdale, NY: Baen.

"Read This (Or Something Like It)" *The New York Review of Science Fiction*, 2002. 16:11(167): p. 7.

"The Real Jungle: Belize 2001" *Seas of Venus*, 2002, Riverdale, NY: Baen.

"The Road to Science Fiction: Letter of Comment" *The New York Review of Science Fiction*, 1999. 14:9(129): p. 23.

"The Roads to the RCN Series" *The Road of Danger*, 2012, Riverdale, NY: Baen.

"Sea Stories (Introduction)" *Seas of Venus*, 2002, Riverdale, NY: Baen.

"A Short Appreciation of Jim Rigney (Robert Jordan)" *The New York Review of Science Fiction*, 2008. 20:9(237): p.18.

"The Sixty-Five Million Years Afterword (Afterword)" *Time Safari*, 1982, New York, NY: Tor.

"Skeletons at the Feast (Introduction)" *Phantom Regiments*, R. Adams, P. C. Adams and M. H. Greenberg, eds. 1990, Riverdale, NY: Baen.

"Soldiers' Stories (Introduction)" *A Separate Star: A Science Fiction Tribute to Rudyard Kipling*, D. Drake and S. Miesel, eds. 1989, Riverdale, NY: Baen.

"Source Materials, By Way of Introduction" *Vettius and His Friends*, 1989, Riverdale, NY: Baen.

"Starting a Long Way From Here" *Voyage Across the Stars*, 2012, Riverdale, NY: Baen.

"Stolen Thunder" *The New York Review of Science Fiction*, 1998. 10:3(113): p. 16.

"Storytellers: A Guided Ramble into Sword and Sorcery Fiction" *The Sword & Sorcery Anthology*, D. G. Hartwell and J. Weisman, eds. 2012, San Francisco, CA: Tachyon.

"Surreal Splendor: Three Novels by Mark S. Geston" *The New York Review of Science Fiction*, 2009. 21:5(245): p. 11.
  The Books of the Wars, M. Geston. 2009, Riverdale, NY: Baen.

"Thomas Lanier Williams, Protofan" *The New York Review of Science Fiction*, 1995. 7, no.8(80): p. 21.

"Three or Six Passages to India (Introduction)" *Storm at Noontide*, E. Flint and D. Drake. 2009, Riverdale, NY: Baen.

"Tom Godwin: *The Cold Equations:* **Letter of Comment"** *The New York Review of Science Fiction*, 1995. 7:6(78): p. 23.

"Trout in the Milk: A Cautionary Tale" *The New York Review of Science Fiction*, 1999. 11:8(128): p. 13.

"The Truth Insofar as I Know It" *Exorcisms and Ecstasies*, 1997,
> Minneapolis: Fedogan & Bremer.
> *Karl Edward Wagner*, ed. by Stephen Jones, 2011,
> Lakewood CO: Centipede Press.

"An Uncharacteristic Polemic in Difficult Times: Letter of Comment" *The New York Review of Science Fiction*, 2009. 22:2(254): p. 22

"We Happy Few (Afterword)" *The Tank Lords*, 1997, Riverdale, NY: Baen.
> *The Complete Hammer's Slammers v.2.* 2007,
> San Francisco, CA: Night Shade Books.
> *The Complete Hammer's Slammers v.2.* 2007,
> New York, NY: SFBC.
> *The Complete Hammer's Slammers v.2.* 2010,
> Riverdale, NY: Baen.

"Welcome to the War Zone (Introduction)" *The Military Dimension*, 1991, Riverdale, NY: Baen.
> *The Military Dimension: Mark II*, 1995,
> Riverdale, NY: Baen.

"Well It Happened This Way (Introduction)" *Foreign Legions*, D. Drake, ed. 2001, Riverdale, NY: Baen.

"What's for Sale" *The New York Review of Science Fiction*, 2006. 18:11(215): p. 10-11.
> *The Complete Hammer's Slammers v.2*, 2007,
>> San Francisco, CA: Night Shade Books.
> *The Complete Hammer's Slammers v.2*, 2007,
>> New York, NY: SFBC.
> *The Complete Hammer's Slammers v.2*, 2010,
>> Riverdale, NY: Baen.

"Where I Get My Ideas" (Afterword) *Cross the Stars*, 1984, New York, NY: Tor.

"Why I'm Here" *The New York Review of Science Fiction*, 2007. 19:6(222): p. 20.
"Writer's Pay in the Pulps: An Exchange" *The New York Review of Science Fiction*, 2006. 19:1(217): p. 15.

"Writer's Pay in the Pulps: The Conversation Continues" *The New York Review of Science Fiction*, 2006. 19:4(220): p. 12.

"*The Year of the Sex Olympics* by Nigel Kneale" *Horror: Another 100 Best Books*, S. Jones, K. Newman and P. Straub, eds. 2005, New York, NY: Carroll & Graf.

IF YOU LIKE...
YOU SHOULD TRY...

DAVID DRAKE
David Weber

DAVID WEBER
John Ringo

JOHN RINGO
Michael Z. Williamson
Tom Kratman

ANNE MCCAFFREY
Mercedes Lackey
Liaden Universe® by Sharon Lee & Steve Miller

MERCEDES LACKEY
Wen Spencer, Andre Norton
Andre Norton
James H. Schmitz

LARRY NIVEN
Tony Daniel
James P. Hogan
Travis S. Taylor

ROBERT A. HEINLEIN
Jerry Pournelle
Lois McMaster Bujold
Michael Z. Williamson

HEINLEIN'S "JUVENILES"
Rats, Bats & Vats series by Eric Flint & Dave Freer

HORATIO HORNBLOWER OR
PATRICK O'BRIAN
David Weber's Honor Harrington series
David Drake's RCN series

HARRY POTTER
Mercedes Lackey's Urban Fantasy series

THE LORD OF THE RINGS
Elizabeth Moon's *The Deed of Paksenarrion*

H.P. LOVECRAFT
Larry Correia's Monster Hunter series
P.C. Hodgell's Kencyrath series
Princess of Wands by John Ringo

GEORGETTE HEYER
Lois McMaster Bujold
Catherine Asaro
Liaden Universe® by Sharon Lee & Steve Miller

GREEK MYTHOLOGY
Pyramid Scheme by Eric Flint & Dave Freer
Forge of the Titans by Steve White
Blood of the Heroes by Steve White

NORSE MYTHOLOGY
Northworld Trilogy by David Drake

URBAN FANTASY
Darkship Thieves by Sarah A. Hoyt
Gentleman Takes a Chance by Sarah A. Hoyt
Carousel Tides by Sharon Lee
The Wild Side ed. by Mark L. Van Name

SCA/HISTORICAL REENACTMENT
John Ringo's "After the Fall" series

FILM NOIR
Larry Correia's The Grimnoir Chronicles

CATS
Sarah A. Hoyt's *Darkship Thieves*
Larry Niven's Man-Kzin Wars series

PUNS
Rick Cook
Spider Robinson
Wm. Mark Simmons

VAMPIRES & WEREWOLVES
Larry Correia
Wm. Mark Simmons

NONFICTION
Hank Reinhardt
Tax Payer's Tea Party
by Sharon Cooper & Chuck Asay
The Science Behind The Secret by Travis Taylor
Alien Invasion by Travis Taylor & Bob Boan